D1127869

EVERYMAN'S LIBRARY

EVERYMAN,
I WILL GO WITH THEE,
AND BE THY GUIDE,
IN THY MOST NEED
TO GO BY THY SIDE

FRANZ KAFKA

COLLECTED STORIES

TRANSLATED BY WILLA AND EDWIN MUIR

EDITED AND INTRODUCED BY GABRIEL JOSIPOVICI

EVERYMAN'S LIBRARY
Alfred A. Knopf New York London Toronto
145

THIS IS A BORZOI BOOK
PUBLISHED BY ALFRED A. KNOPF

This selection first published by Everyman's Library, 1993

Typography by Peter B. Willberg
Tenth printing (US)

 Published in the United States by Alfred A. Knopf,
a division of Random House, Inc., New York, and in Canada by
Random House of Canada Limited, Toronto. Distributed by Random
House, Inc., New York. Published in the United Kingdom by
Everyman's Library, Northburgh House, 10 Northburgh Street,
London EC1V 0AT, and distributed by Random House (UK) Ltd.

US website: www.randomhouse/everymans

ISBN: 978-0-679-42303-4 (US)
1-85715-145-3 & 978-1-85715-145-9 (UK)

A CIP catalogue reference for this book is available from the
British Library

Library of Congress Cataloging-in-Publication Data
Kafka, Franz, 1883–1924.
[Short stories. English]
The collected stories / Franz Kafka.
p. cm.—(Everyman's library)
ISBN 978-0-679-42303-4
I. Title.
PT2621.A26A2 1993 93-1858
833′.912—dc20 CIP

Book design by Barbara de Wilde and Carol Devine Carson

Printed and bound in Germany by GGP Media GmbH, Pössne

FRANZ KAFKA
COLLECTED STORIES

CONTENTS

Introduction xiii
A Note on the Text xxxviii
Select Bibliography xli
Chronology xlii

Stories Published in Kafka's Lifetime

MEDITATION (1913) 3
Children on a Country Road 5
Unmasking a Confidence Trickster 8
The Sudden Walk 10
Resolutions 11
Excursion into the Mountains 12
Bachelor's Ill Luck 12
The Tradesman 13
Absent-minded Window-gazing 15
The Way Home 15
Passers-by 16
On the Tram 16
Clothes 17
Rejection 18
Reflections for Gentlemen-jockeys 18
The Street Window 19
The Wish to be a Red Indian 20
The Trees 20
Unhappiness 20

THE JUDGMENT (1913) 25

THE STOKER (1913) 41

THE METAMORPHOSIS (1915) 73

IN THE PENAL COLONY (1919) 129

A COUNTRY DOCTOR (1919) 161

CONTENTS

The New Advocate 163
A Country Doctor 164
Up in the Gallery 170
An Old Manuscript 171
Before the Law 173
Jackals and Arabs 175
A Visit to a Mine 179
The Next Village 182
An Imperial Message 182
The Cares of a Family Man 183
Eleven Sons 185
A Fratricide 190
A Dream 192
A Report to an Academy 195

The Bucket Rider (1921) 205

A HUNGER ARTIST (1924) 209
First Sorrow 211
A Little Woman 214
A Hunger Artist 222
Josephine the Singer, or the Mouse Folk 233

Stories Unpublished in Kafka's Lifetime

Description of a Struggle 253
Wedding Preparations in the Country 298
The Student 323
The Angel 324
The Village Schoolmaster [The Giant Mole] .. 327
Blumfeld, an Elderly Bachelor 342
The Hunter Gracchus 366
The Proclamation 371
The Bridge 372
The Great Wall of China 374
The Knock at the Manor Gate 387
An Ancient Sword 389
New Lamps 390
My Neighbor 392
A Crossbreed [A Sport] 393

CONTENTS

A Splendid Beast 395
The Watchman 396
A Common Confusion 396
The Truth About Sancho Panza 397
The Silence of the Sirens 398
Prometheus 399
The City Coat of Arms 400
Poseidon 401
Fellowship 403
At Night 404
The Problem of Our Laws 404
The Conscription of Troops 406
The Test 409
The Vulture 410
The Helmsman 411
The Top 412
Hands 412
A Little Fable 414
Isabella 414
Home-coming 415
A Chinese Puzzle 416
The Departure 417
Advocates 417
Investigations of a Dog 420
The Married Couple 460
Give It Up! 465
On Parables 466
The Burrow 467

INTRODUCTION

'I have eleven sons,' begins the story called 'Eleven Sons', and the entire piece consists of a description of the sons:

> The first is outwardly very plain, but serious and clever; yet, although I love him as I love all my children, I do not rate him very highly. His mental processes seem to me to be too simple. He looks neither to right nor to left, nor into the far distance; he runs around all the time, or rather revolves, within his own little circle of thoughts.
>
> The second is handsome, slim, well made; one draws one's breath with delight to watch him with a fencing foil. He is clever too, but has experience of the world as well; he has seen much, and therefore even our native country seems to yield more secrets to him than to the stay-at-home. Yet I am sure that this advantage is not only and not even essentially due to his travels, it is rather an attribute of his own inimitable nature, which is acknowledged for instance by everyone who has ever tried to copy him in, let us say, the fancy high dive he does into the water, somersaulting several times over, yet with almost violent self-control ... [D]espite all this (I ought really to feel blessed with such a son) my attachment to him is not untroubled. His left eye is a little smaller than his right and blinks a good deal; only a small fault, certainly, and one which even lends more audacity to his face than it would otherwise have ... Of course, it is not the physical blemish that worries me, but a small irregularity of the spirit that somehow corresponds to it, a kind of stray poison in the blood, a kind of inability to develop to the full the potentialities of his nature which I alone can see. On the other hand, this is just what makes him again my own true son, for this fault of his is a fault of our whole family and in him it is only too apparent.
>
> My third son ...

In a letter to Max Brod Kafka wrote: 'The eleven sons are quite simply eleven stories I am working on this very moment.' Inevitably, of course, critics have tried to relate each son to a specific story known to us. But this is misguided. Not because Kafka was having Brod on – it would be unlike him to do a thing like that – but because it implies that once we have matched the sons to the stories we have dealt with *this* story. Yet even if we knew – if Kafka had left us a list, say – which stories he was referring to with each description, that would only be the start rather than the end of our enquiry.

It is of course quite common for writers to talk about their books as their children, even to single one out as a favourite child, and we all know more or less what they mean. What is disconcerting about Kafka, here and everywhere else, is his literalism and his detail. It is already difficult enough to determine how to respond to these descriptions if we take them at face value – difficult because this ostensibly calm and scrupulous father-narrator seems to see so much more and more deeply than any of us is likely to be able to do even where those closest to us are concerned; and because the physical, mental and moral qualities of the sons seem to be so bafflingly intertwined. ('He looks neither to right nor to left, nor into the far distance; he runs around all the time, or rather revolves, within his own little circle of thoughts.') But our bafflement increases a hundredfold if we try to think of these sons as stories. Can stories really be imagined in this way? What can it mean to say that a story executes a fancy high dive so perfectly that it cannot be imitated, yet has a weakness in its left eye which seems to correspond to a deeper, a moral blemish, 'a kind of inability to develop the full potentialities of [its] nature'? What led Kafka to think of his fiction in this way, and what does it tell us about the fiction itself?

*

Throughout his life Kafka commented, in his diary and in letters to friends, on his own work and on that of writers he happened to be reading. These remarks suggest that though Kafka, unlike Proust, Eliot and Virginia Woolf, wrote no critical essays, he was anything but a naive untutored genius. Like them he had obviously thought long and hard about his craft, and his comments on literature, like theirs, carry an authority denied most critics because it clearly matters so profoundly.

We have also got so used to thinking of him as a morbid and even masochistic individual that it is worth stressing that many of his observations are as punchy and self-confident as

Eliot's. Thus on 8 October 1917 he noted in his diary that 'The Stoker' (which he had written in the great creative outburst of September–October 1912 and which later became the first chapter of his unfinished novel, *Amerika*) was 'a sheer imitation of Dickens'. He goes on, however, forsaking syntax in his eagerness to get his thoughts down on paper:

> Dickens's opulence and great, careless prodigality, but in consequence passages of awful insipidity in which he wearily works over effects he has already achieved. Gives one a barbaric impression because the whole does not make sense, a barbarism that I, it is true, thanks to my weakness and wiser for my epigonism, have been able to avoid. There is a heartlessness behind his sentimentally overflowing style. These rude characterisations which are artificially stamped on everyone and without which Dickens would not be able to get on with his story even for a moment.

And he adds that Robert Walser (and this may surprise those who have tried to compare Kafka and Walser) 'resembles [Dickens] in his use of vague, abstract metaphors'.

This kind of balanced, even self-confident judgment, should make us wary of taking Kafka's frequent self-criticism as nothing but self-torment, based on his perennially poor view of himself. May it not be that Kafka knows better? Of course, like every writer, he has a tendency to think of his own work as worse than it in fact is – but what does 'than it in fact is' mean in this sentence? We may rate his work very highly, but perhaps our standards are simply not high enough.

'Great antipathy to "Metamorphosis",' he writes in his diary on 19 January 1914. 'Unreadable ending. Imperfect almost to its very marrow.' 'Just now read the beginning [of 'Blumfeld, an Elderly Bachelor'],' he notes on 9 February 1915. 'It is ugly and gives me a headache. In spite of all its truth it is wicked, pedantic, mechanical, a fish barely breathing on a sandbank.' A few days before (18 January) he had started his diary in typical vein: 'Headache, slept badly. Incapable of sustained, concentrated work.' But then: 'In spite of that began a new story; I was afraid I should spoil the old ones. Four or five stories now stand on their hindlegs in front of me like the horses in front of Schumann, the circus ringmaster, at the beginning of the performance.'

How are we to take this? These horses can perform amazing, quite unhorsy feats, such as standing on their hind legs in front of their master, Kafka, ready to obey him. On the other hand they clearly have less natural life in them than their brethren who run on the open plain. Perhaps, though, it is the best that can be expected of story-horses: at least they are alive, not mechanical monsters or fish expiring on the bank.

But what leads Kafka to describe stories in this way?

First of all we have to realize that words themselves are alive for Kafka to an uncanny degree. In only the second sentence of the diary he jots down a phrase he has overheard and comments on it: ' "If he should forever ahsk me." The *ah*, released from the sentence, flew off like a ball on the meadow.' Words for him are always flying free of the sentences that contain them, or lying in wait to trip up the speaker, as when he describes himself dictating a report and,

> towards the end, where a climax was intended, I got stuck and could do nothing but look at K., the typist, who, in her usual way, became especially lively, moved her chair about, coughed, tapped on the table ... Finally I have the word 'stigmatize' and the appropriate sentence, but still hold it all in my mouth with disgust and a sense of shame as though it were raw meat, cut out of me ...

(3 October 1911)

Words not only lie in wait to trip you up, they can warp even so natural a thing as filial love. On 24 October 1911 he notes that perhaps he has not always loved his mother as she deserved 'only because the German language prevented it'. The word *Mutter*, he goes on,

> is peculiarly German for the Jew, it unconsciously contains, together with the Christian splendour Christian coldness also, the Jewish woman who is called 'Mutter' therefore becomes not only comic but strange. Mama would be a better name if only one didn't imagine 'Mutter' behind it.

At the same time the mere names of people he was attached to were capable of unleashing extraordinary torrents of feeling and prose, as in this passage from a letter to Milena:

Milena (what a rich heavy name, almost too full to be lifted, and in the beginning I didn't like it much, it seemed to me a Greek or Roman gone astray in Bohemia, violated by Czech, cheated of its accent, and yet in colour and form it is marvellously a woman, a woman whom one carries in one's arms out of the world, out of the fire, I don't know which, and she presses herself willingly and trustingly into your arms, only the strong accent on the 'i' is bad, doesn't the name keep leaping away from you? Or is it perhaps only the lucky leap which you yourself make with your burden?)

What must be noted about all these remarks is that they have nothing of the virtuoso quality Nabokov displays in his evocation of Lolita's name at the start of *Lolita*. What is disturbing about them is that we are never quite sure – as with the eleven sons – how much is being read *into* a word or name and how much is *being drawn* out of it. As always with Kafka, surface and depth, the literal and the metaphorical, mingle alarmingly.

Words threaten to make the sentences in which they appear fly apart; they conceal and reveal, acting as conduits to the depths of character and of life itself or as obstacles on the way to such depths. What is at issue is never the beauty of the word but something far more mysterious and difficult to articulate. What he is after in his writing, he notes in January 1911, is 'a description in which every word would be linked to my life, which I would draw to my heart and which would transport me out of itself'. But that, unfortunately, is an ideal which is for most of the time beyond his reach. 'Wrote badly,' he confides to his diary on 20 October 1911, 'without really arriving at that freedom of true description which releases one's foot from the experienced.' On 5 November he records his bitterness and sense of isolation as Max Brod read out to a group of friends 'my little motor-car story':

The disordered sentences of this story with holes into which one could stick both hands; one sentence sounds high, one sentence sounds low, as the case may be, one sentence rubs against another like the tongue against a hollow or false tooth; one sentence comes marching up with so rough a start that the entire story falls into sulky amazement.

He dreams then of being able one day to write something 'large and whole, well shaped from beginning to end', feeling that the story would then be able to detach itself from him 'and it would be possible for me calmly and with open eyes, as a blood relation of a healthy story, to hear it read'. As things stand though, he ends sadly, 'every little piece of the story runs around homeless and drives me away from it in the opposite direction'.

Unfortunately we don't know what the 'little motor-car story' was, but there are quite a few examples in the diaries of fragments of narrative followed by Kafka's caustic comments on them. 'Only the billowing overcoat remains,' he writes on 12 March 1912, 'everything else is made up.' But what does 'made up' mean here? Is not the whole fragment 'made up' by Kafka?

Two days earlier he had tried out a slightly longer story:

> He seduced a girl in a small place in the Iser mountains where he spent a summer to restore his delicate lungs. After a brief effort to persuade her, incomprehensibly, the way lung cases sometimes act, he threw the girl – his landlord's daughter, who liked to walk with him in the evening after work – down in the grass on the river bank and took her as she lay there unconscious with fright. Later he had to carry water from the river in his cupped hands and pour it over the girl's face to restore her. 'Julie, but Julie', he said countless times, bending over her. He was ready to accept complete responsibility for his offence and was only making an effort to make himself realize how serious his situation was. Without thinking about it he could not have realized it. The simple girl who lay before him, now breathing regularly again, her eyes still closed because of fear and embarrassment, could make no difficulty for him; with the tip of his toe, he, the great, strong person, could push the girl aside. She was weak and plain, could what had happened to her have any significance that would last even until tomorrow? Would not anyone who compared the two of them have come to this conclusion? The river stretched calmly between the meadows and fields to the distant hills. There was still sunshine only on the slope of the opposite shore. The last clouds were drifting out of that clear evening sky.

Here too his comment follows immediately:

> Nothing, nothing. This is the way I raise up ghosts before me. I was involved, even if only superficially, only in the passage, 'Later he had . . . ', mostly in the 'pour'. For a moment I thought I saw something real in the description of the landscape.

This is very revealing. Here is Kafka trying to write a conventional 'realist' narrative, and his heart isn't in it. The act does not involve him, only its aftermath. But note that the sentence and especially the word he picks out, 'pour' (*schütten*) is no more beautiful or interesting in itself than the words 'threw' (*warf*) and 'took' (*nahm*). It is just that it seems to touch on a truth the rest of the story lacks. I myself would have added the word 'embarrassment' ('her eyes still closed because of fear and embarrassment'), and I would agree that there was just a glimpse of 'something real' in the closing description of the landscape, calm and unaffected by the human drama which has just occurred within it.

And yet there are other moods when he can write: 'The firmness ... which the most insignificant writing brings about in me is beyond doubt and wonderful' (27 November 1913). It is even the case that, at times, he feels that his writing gives him a quite magical power: 'When I arbitrarily write down a single sentence, for instance, "He looked out of the window", it already has perfection' (19 February 1911). Those early stories or gropings towards novels, the 'Description of a Struggle' and 'Wedding Preparations in the Country', on which he pinned all his hopes in his early twenties, are clearly written in an effort to maintain just this mood. Here what happens is governed not by the conventions of fin-de-siècle story-telling but simply by the feelings of the protagonist: 'Because I love pinewoods I went through woods of this kind, and since I like gazing silently up at the stars, the stars appeared slowly in the sky.' Here mosquitoes can fly through the belly of a fat man and the moon ceases to be a moon when given another name. As for the narrator, since the world immediately submits itself to his whims, it is difficult for him to retain any sense of himself as a person. At moments he is an all-powerful human being, at the next he is only an avalanche rolling down a mountainside.

Writing of this kind may initially feel promising, but it soon palls. If I have simply to write something down to summon it into being, if everything depends entirely on my mood as I write, then what is the point of writing anything at all? No wonder these early efforts got nowhere and were eventually abandoned by Kafka.

There is another theme running through Kafka's early letters and diaries, a theme which Kafka at the time does not seem to know how to explain or exploit, but which is going to play a major part in his mature fiction. In a letter to Brod of 28 August 1904 he writes:

It is so easy to be cheerful at the beginning of summer. One has a lively heart, a reasonably brisk gait, and can face the future with a certain hope. One expects something out of the Arabian Nights, while disclaiming any such hope with a comic bow and bumbling speech ... And when people ask us about the life we intend to live, we form the habit, in spring, of answering with an expansive wave of the hand, which goes limp after a while, as if to say that it was ridiculously unnecessary to conjure up sure things.

This is the world of Kafka's febrile line drawings, which show ludicrously tall or squat people stretching, twisting, leaning towards or away from one another, in what would be grotesque if it was an attempt at realism but which instead conveys perfectly how we sometimes feel, both constrained in our bodies and lunging free, both playing a game and close to desperation. The early diaries are full of detailed descriptions of *gesturing*, which seems to be a sign of frustration when it is he himself who is doing the gesturing, but is clearly also as much a part of his extreme sensitivity to others as his response to words. These gestures are in fact the visual and physical equivalent of those words which suddenly take on a life of their own and burst free of the sentence in which normal, well-behaved words should quietly lie.

In a late diary entry (24 January 1922) Kafka, looking back at his life, mysteriously but quite specifically linked his writing with such gesturing:

Childish games (though I was well aware that they were so) marked the beginning of my intellectual decline. I deliberately cultivated a facial tic, for instance, or would walk across the Graben with arms crossed behind my head. A repulsively childish but successful game. (My writing began in the same way ...)

By this stage in his life Kafka had begun to think of writing not as a form of salvation but, on the contrary, as 'wages earned in the service of evil', as he put it in a terrible letter to Brod. But whether one accepts his judgment or not, it does not affect the clear link he makes here between writing and gesticulating. Just as excessive gestures were a way of escaping, even if only momentarily, the confines of his body and the behaviour required by society, so it was with his writing. The obverse of both is the image of the body turned to stone, the head sinking on to the chest, which recurs so often in the diary in moments of depression.

However, in order to grasp precisely what are the links between writing and gesturing we have to turn to a diary entry for 30 September 1911. There Kafka, after commenting on two well-known artists with whom he has obviously come into contact that day, Kubin the painter and Tucholsky the writer, focuses on a third figure:

> Szafranski, a disciple of Bernhardt's, grimaces while he observes and draws in a way that resembles what is drawn. Reminds me that I too have a pronounced talent for metamorphosing myself, which no one notices. How often I must have imitated Max. Yesterday evening, on the way home, if I had observed myself from the outside I should have taken myself for Tucholsky.

But this talent for entering into and becoming another is not an actor's gift. 'My urge to imitate has nothing of the actor in it,' he writes on 30 December. A good actor, he goes on, homes in on the essential details of the person he is impersonating, while the sign of the poor actor is precisely that he is overwhelmed by peripheral detail. Yet it is just such peripheral detail – 'the way certain people manipulate walking-sticks, the way they hold their hands, the movements of their fingers' – that he himself finds he can imitate with such ease.

And that fascination with peripheral detail, that ability to enter into the detail and live it, so to speak, is what immediately strikes us about even his earliest and most hesitant writing. The very first sentence of the diary, for example, runs: 'The onlookers go rigid when the train goes past' (the German avoids the repetition of 'go' and takes up only eight words: 'Die Zuschauer erstarren, wenn der Zug vorbeifährt.') Is this the jotting down of something seen that day or the start of a story? As usual with Kafka we cannot tell, and, indeed, the writing forces us to abandon such apparently well-founded distinctions. Though seemingly just a note to remind himself of an incident he has witnessed, the sentence actually catches and conveys an event. The diarist has not just looked hard, he has empathized instinctively not with this or that person on the station platform but with the entire episode of onlookers-at-a-station-platform-as-a-train-goes-past.

Nevertheless, it was to be some time before Kafka discovered what to do with this gift of his for empathy and metamorphosis. In 1912, when Brod urged him to put together a volume of short pieces for publication, he knew only that he must avoid the realism of the rape fragment and the expressionism of the long unfinished stories. Better to choose modest and even rather muted pieces which felt 'true' all the way through than fill a volume with excessive noise and falsehood. Thus, like Eliot's early 'Preludes' and 'Rhapsody on a Windy Night', or the quieter pieces Schoenberg and Webern were producing at roughly the same time, the 'stories' which make up Kafka's first published collection, *Meditation* (*Betrachtung*), are moving and disturbing precisely because they refuse to engage in narrative and yet are clearly more than simple descriptions. 'Absent-minded Window-gazing', for example, begins:

> What are we to do with these spring days that are now fast coming on? Early this morning the sky was gray, but if you go to the window now you are surprised and lean your cheek against the latch of the casement.

A drama is being enacted here, but it is secret, muffled, hardly aware of itself, as in Joyce's 'Eveline'. Elsewhere he retrieves a fragment from the diary entry for 5 January 1912 about suddenly deciding to go out for a walk and in another piece tells how, to lift himself from his miserable mood, 'I force myself out of my chair, stride around the table, exercise my head and neck, make my eyes sparkle, tighten the muscles around them.' In 'The Wish to be a Red Indian' the whole piece consists of a single sentence, poised between mundane reality and impossible desire:

> If one were only an Indian, instantly alert, and on a racing horse, leaning against the wind, kept on quivering jerkily over the quivering

ground, until one shed one's spurs, for there needed no spurs, threw away the reins, for there needed no reins, and hardly saw that the land before one was smoothly shorn heath when horse's neck and head would be already gone.

Yet, interesting and original as these pieces are, they could clearly not satisfy someone who felt, like Kafka, that a thousand worlds were waiting to burst out of his head. If he was to let them out he would have, sooner or later, to solve the problem of how to write narrative without falling into the traps of either expressionism and realism, of a dependence on subjective whim which was self-defeating and a dependence on the themes and styles of his contemporaries which only struck him as unbearably hollow and false.

*

I have been talking so far as though Kafka were alone with his demons, though I did give a glimpse of him with Brod and his other friends as the 'little motor-car story' was read aloud. Much more important, of course, was the attitude of his family. Kafka has left us plenty of evidence about what his father thought of his work, but the main actor in what is perhaps the key episode in his development as a writer was not his father but an unnamed uncle. Kafka recounts it in his diary on 19 January 1911:

Once I projected a novel in which two brothers fought each other, one of whom went to America while the other remained in a European prison. I only now and then began to write a few lines, for it tired me at once. So once I wrote down something about my prison on a Sunday afternoon when we were visiting my grandparents and had eaten an especially soft kind of bread, spread with butter, that was customary there. It is of course possible that I did it mostly out of vanity, and by shifting the paper about on the tablecloth, tapping with my pencil, looking around under the lamp, wanted to tempt someone to take what I had written from me, look at it, and admire me. It was chiefly the corridor of the prison that was described in the few lines, above all its silence and coldness ... Perhaps I had a momentary feeling of the worthlessness of my description, but before that afternoon I had never paid much attention to such feelings when among relatives to whom I was accustomed (my timidity was so great that the accustomed was enough to make me half-way happy), I sat at the round table in the familiar room and could not forget that I was young and called to great things out of this present tranquillity. An uncle who liked to make fun of people finally took the page that I was holding only weakly, looked at it briefly, handed it back to me, even without laughing, and only said to the others who were following him with their eyes, 'The usual stuff', to me he said nothing. To be sure, I remained seated and bent as before over the now useless page of mine, but with one thrust I had been banished from society, the judgment of my uncle repeated itself in me with what amounted almost to real significance and even within the feeling of belonging to a family I got an insight into the cold space of our world which I had to warm with a fire that first I wanted to seek out.

This stands, with the equivalent episode of Monsieur de Norpois' rejection of the young Marcel's literary efforts, as one of the key moments in modern literature. It is not an episode Chaucer, Milton or Goethe would have made much sense of, I suspect, for in their day it would have been pretty obvious if a young man was gifted or not, and 'the usual stuff' would have been less of a put-down than 'odd stuff'. In our world though – and in this respect Proust and Kafka inhabit our world – matters are different: few can spot what is truly original when it first appears, and the burden on the artist is for that reason much greater: should he trust his instinct, which has so often let him down, or the judgment of others, which seems so massively authoritative and yet is so often at odds with his own?

Of course what makes this moment so important in both Kafka and Proust is not only that they had the ability to describe it for us, but that they had the resources of character to react to it, not by simply dismissing the judgment out of hand, but by incorporating it into their work, thus at the same time accepting and reversing it.

Two and a half years after that terrible Sunday afternoon, on 24 May 1913, Kafka noted in his diary: 'In high spirits because I consider "The Stoker" so good. This evening I read it to my parents, there is no better critic than I when I read to my father, who listens with the most extreme reluctance. Many shallow passages followed by unfathomable depths.'

'The Stoker' is also a story about a young man going to America. But this time Kafka does not wait for someone to wrench the page from him and look at it. He has grown in confidence to such an extent that he actually reads it out loud to the sternest judge of all, his father. And though he notes that his father listened 'with the most extreme reluctance', he himself is not in the least put out by this. As he reads he sees clearly that there are 'many shallow passages' in the story, but that these are 'followed by unfathomable depths'.

What has happened to alter things in this way?

To put it simply, what has happened is the experience of the night of 22–23 September 1912. Under the date 23 September he transcribes the whole of a long short story and then comments:

> This story, 'The Judgment', I wrote at one sitting during the night of 22–23rd, from ten o'clock at night to six o'clock in the morning. I was hardly able to pull my legs out from under the desk, they had got so stiff from sitting. The fearful strain and joy, how the story developed before me, as if I were advancing over water. Several times during this night I heaved my own weight on my back. How everything can be said, how for everything, for the strangest fancies, there waits a great fire in which they perish and rise up again. How it turned blue outside the window. A wagon rolled by. Two men walked across the bridge ... The appearance of the undisturbed bed, as though it had just been brought in. The conviction verified that with my novel-writing I am in the shameful lowlands of writing. Only *in this way* can writing be done, only with such coherence, with such a complete opening out of the body and the soul.

All his life Kafka was to look back to this night as the fulfilment of his dream of writing. Never again was he to feel such total satisfaction: at last he was doing what he had long obscurely felt he had been put on earth to do.

'The Judgment' opens with Georg Bendemann sitting at an open window from which, as from Kafka's window, a bridge can be seen, daydreaming and writing a letter to a friend in far-off Russia. 'Absent-minded Window-gazing' had stopped there. Kafka had perhaps sensed that the scene was a kind of metaphor not just for modern life but also for the work of the writer, dreaming at his desk. Now, by bringing writing and window-gazing into the same orbit he discovers the way to move forward. Just as Kafka's story of the two brothers had been dismissed in a single sentence under the judgment of his uncle, so now both letter and daydreams are banished by Georg's father. The aged, enfeebled man suddenly rears up in bed where Georg had solicitously – as he no doubt put it to himself – tried to cover him up, and issues a judgment on the writer and dreamer: 'An innocent child, yes, that you were, truly, but still more truly have you been a devilish human being! – And therefore take note: I sentence you now to death by drowning.'

The terrible sentence is a strange kind of release for both Georg and the narrative: 'Georg felt himself urged from the room, the crash with which his father fell on the bed behind him was still in his ears as he fled ... Out of the front door he rushed, across the roadway, driven towards the water.' The force which drives him on makes all hesitation, all dreaming on his part, a thing of the past. He swings himself over the side of the bridge, 'like the distinguished gymnast he had once been in his youth, to his parents' pride', and then lets himself drop. 'At this moment an unending stream of traffic was just going over the bridge.'

The indifferent landscape of the fragment about the rape has turned into an image of the world going on its way as Georg's individual life of desire, frustration and compromise comes to an end. In the earlier fragment the narrator had been guilty but seemed unwilling to recognize his guilt; here he is guilty of no single evil act yet accepts his father's judgment, and so brings his own life and the story to its end. But it is as though the acceptance of that judgment has allowed a new kind of writing to be born.

Two days later 'The Stoker' was written. Karl Rossmann, as the rich long first sentence tells us, has been packed off to America by his parents for having got a serving girl with child, and the ship he is on has now entered New York Harbour. But if America stands – as it has for so many immigrants and writers – for freedom, for the chance to forge one's own life, one's own narrative, in the wide open spaces and the bustling cities, then the story promptly turns its back on it. Realizing suddenly that he has left his umbrella 'down below', Karl turns back and, descending into the bowels of the ship, finds, in those constraining corridors and boiler-rooms, the space where Kafka's narrative can function. From now on Kafka too will turn his back on the temptations of the free-floating novel (whether realist or expressionist) and concentrate on the stokers.

Yet free-floating narrative will always exert its pull (Kafka does after all go on trying to write an 'American' novel), and it is precisely in the tension between the temptation and its refusal, between the letter-writing by the open window and the self-immolation demanded by the tyrannical father, that Kafka will discover the ever renewable springs of his narrative powers.

Just as the narrative of 'The Judgment' emerges in all its power and inevitability out of a redirection of energy that had earlier been spent half combating and half agreeing with the judgments of his family, so the arbitrary bodily movement described in the early letters and taken up in *Meditation*, the arm-jerking and head-twisting and all the rest of it, here gives way to Georg's rediscovery of his earlier gymnastic ability, once the pride of his parents, now the means of his self-destruction. Two months after writing 'The Judgment' and 'The Stoker' Kafka completed the greatest of his early works, 'The Metamorphosis'. As he wakes from uneasy sleep Gregor Samsa finds himself transformed into a gigantic insect and thus having to come to terms with a body he cannot imagine and yet which is indubitably his (or should we say 'indubitably him'?). Forced to lie on his back, he can only glimpse his domelike brown belly, while 'his numerous legs, which were pitifully thin compared to the rest of his bulk, waved helplessly before his eyes'. This is no erstwhile gymnast; on the contrary, it is someone who has for too long tried to live without listening to his body, which now exacts its terrible revenge.

The long dense story which follows charts with dreadful precision the way in which Gregor is gradually forced to learn about what Donne, in a very different context, called 'my new found land'. And, as with Georg Bendemann, understanding arrives for Gregor, and a kind of peace, only with the recognition that he must accede to the wishes of his family, even –

perhaps especially – if those wishes concern his own disappearance. And, like the early rape fragment and 'The Judgment', this story ends with the world going on its way regardless of the passion of the protagonist. Here, though, this archetypal story of the body has to end with a celebration of the body as, having taken a tram out into the country, the parents gaze fondly at their sole remaining child, the sister Gregor had so wanted to help, 'And it was like a confirmation of their new dreams and excellent intentions that at the end of their journey their daughter sprang to her feet first and stretched her young body.'

In 'Reading Kafka' Maurice Blanchot has argued persuasively that that last sentence is in a sense the most terrible in the entire story. At the same time every reader has recognized, however obscurely, that our reactions to this, as to all Kafka's mature stories, are profoundly ambivalent. We experience horror at what happens to Gregor but at the same time a kind of joy at the fact that the story exists and allows us to read it. And if the reaction of the parents and sister mime out in the fiction our own inability to give meaning to Gregor's ordeal and death, then that too is a part of the meaning of the whole. And if Gregor finds himself constrained more and more by his horrible body, till death comes as a merciful release, then for Kafka the writing of the story was itself a merciful release from the frustration of years, even if he later had doubts about its ending, and a renewal of that sense that 'everything can be said . . . for everything, for the strangest fancies, there waits a great fire in which they perish and rise up again'. For now at last the excess of gesture, the arbitrary jerking of arms and legs, has been made the subject not of observation but of narrative; now at last his 'profound talent for metamorphosing myself, which no one notices', has found an outlet. Other writers have had the ability to empathize with a wide range of human beings; Kafka has now discovered in himself the unique gift of empathy with everything in the world, even a gigantic insect. It is a gift of which he will make full use in the years that follow.

But before that happens there is one story in the vein of 'The Judgment' that still needs to be written, though that does not happen till almost two years later, in October 1914. 'In the Penal Colony' is the most repulsive story Kafka ever wrote, for while there is a kind of serenity in the way in which both Georg and Gregor meet their deaths, and a deep sympathy with their bewilderment and despair, this story is glacial throughout. The peculiar horror of the two earlier stories lies in the combination of classic purity in the unfolding of the narrative and the almost unbearable subject-matter; that of 'In the Penal Colony' lies in the sense that not only is the subject-matter foul but the story itself, replicating the narrative, seems to have become a sort of malfunctioning machine:

> The explorer ... felt greatly troubled; the machine was obviously going to pieces; its silent working was a delusion ... The Harrow was not writing, it was only jabbing, and the Bed was not turning the body over but only bringing it up quivering against the needles.

Though in death the officer's look is 'calm and convinced', this is the result not of understanding but of madness, for there is no visible sign of 'the promised redemption', while 'through the forehead went the point of the great iron spike'.

The reason for this may lie in the fact that though Kafka was always to look back to his breakthrough as a wonder, a form of grace, he was also perhaps beginning to feel uneasy with the form it had taken. The narratives he had suddenly found it in himself to write and which had, for the first time, given him the kind of satisfaction he had always hoped for from his writing, may have struck him as too extreme, too full of anguish and pathos. It is as though he feels that the ambition of these early stories is too Utopian, too Romantic. 'In the Penal Colony' dramatizes the painful discovery that Truth cannot be written, not even on the body.

Other factors were perhaps also involved in the change of direction that now began to manifest itself, chief among them the growing realization of the ambivalence of his desire for marriage, and the coming of the war. Perhaps, he must have begun to think, it was not his job or his bachelorhood or his ill-health which were preventing the full outburst of his talents, but something else, something which had to do with what man is and what art can achieve. And if he suffered as a consequence, what was his suffering compared to what those at the front were experiencing?

Be that as it may, the work he did in the years 1914–17, much of which is included in the 1919 volume, *A Country Doctor*, shows a marked and significant shift of emphasis.

*

Kafka put together this volume of fourteen stories with the care of a Yeats or a Wallace Stevens planning a book of poems. 'The Bucket Rider', for example, which he had thought of including, he dropped at the last moment, presumably because it did not fit in with the rest of the volume. As it now stands the first and last stories call out to each other across the intervening gap, and each story (including 'Eleven Sons') adds a new twist to the central theme.

'We have a new advocate, Dr. Bucephalus,' the first story begins. 'There is little in his appearance to remind you that he was once Alexander of Macedon's battle charger. Of course, if you know his story, you are aware of something.' But even the usher at the law courts, who presumably does not know his story, though he is, it is true, 'a man with the professional appraisal of the regular small better at a racecourse', finds himself 'running an admiring eye over the advocate as he mounted the marble steps with a high action that made them ring beneath his feet'.

However, this high-stepping urge is now kept well under control, for '[n]owadays ... there is no Alexander the Great'. Of course, even in his day 'the gates of India were beyond reach, yet the King's sword pointed the way to them'. Today, however, no one even points the way – for in which direction would he point? Many, it is true, still carry swords, 'but only to brandish them, and the eye that tries to follow them is confused'. So, 'perhaps it is really best to do as Bucephalus has done and absorb oneself in law books. In the quiet lamplight, his flanks unhampered by the thighs of a rider, free and far from the clamor of battle, he reads and turns the pages of our ancient tomes.'

A loss has been incurred, yet the last little paragraph is neither pathetic nor anguished, but merely resigned: 'Perhaps it is really best to do as Bucephalus has done.' His flanks are at least unhampered by the thighs of any rider – yet we recall the high action of his legs as he strides up the staircase of the law courts and feel the waste: a rider pressing into those flanks would at least have given him a goal, a sense of direction. Instead, he consoles himself by poring over ancient law books, though whether he does this out of a sense of duty or desire or merely to pass the time, the story does not say.

Resignation and its cost is also the theme of the last story in the collection, 'A Report to an Academy'. In what is probably the funniest story this great comic writer ever produced, an ape addresses a distinguished gathering, recounting how he dragged himself by sheer will-power out of his simian condition and up to his present position. The reason he has done this, he explains, is not from any innate desire on the part of apes to achieve the level of men, but rather that, having been captured and stuck in a tiny cage, he understood that his only chance of escape lay in imitating the men he could see walking about unconstrained before him.

He cannot, he explains, really comply with the wishes of the academy and speak about his life as an ape; that closed behind him when he was captured and was lost to sight for ever when he decided to transform himself. He can only recount the stages of his transformation: 'I could never have achieved what I have done had I been stubbornly set on clinging to my origins, to the remembrances of my youth,' he explains, unconsciously echoing the tone of countless self-made men, Kafka's father among them. 'In revenge, however, my memory of the past has closed the door against me more and more.' As he grew increasingly at ease in the world of men, 'the strong wind that blew after me out of my past began to slacken; today it is a gentle puff of air that plays around my heels'. 'To put it plainly,' he tells the gentlemen of the academy, 'your life as apes ... insofar as something of that kind lies behind you, cannot be farther removed from you than mine is from me.' And yet, 'everyone on earth feels a tickling at the heels; the small chimpanzee and the great Achilles alike'.

He has transformed himself, he explains, because he had

no option. Not in order to find freedom, that is too large a word, associated perhaps with his early life in the forests of Africa, but simply in order to find a way out of his horrible predicament. It is solely for that reason that he has learned to imitate the ways of men – smoking, spitting, drinking, talking. As a result of this single-minded effort he is now able to command the best hotel suites and address such august assemblies as this. And '[w]hen I come home late at night from banquets, from scientific receptions, from social gatherings, there sits waiting for me a half-trained little chimpanzee and I take comfort from her as apes do'. And yet, '[b]y day I cannot bear to see her; for she has the insane look of the bewildered half-broken animal in her eye; no one else sees it, but I do, and I cannot bear it'.

So, like Bucephalus, he has managed to accommodate to new conditions without nostalgia and without recrimination. It is a decent enough life, even, perhaps, in the eyes of some (the animal in the zoo, the soldier at the front) an enviable one, but it entails a hardening of oneself, a willed denial of the breeze licking about one's heels, of the look in the eyes of the half-broken animal.

Nevertheless, this new-found balance testified to a second great creative period in Kafka's life. This is the period of the parables, the aphorisms, the re-telling of the myths of Poseidon and Prometheus, the meditations on Ulysses and the sirens and on Don Quixote and Sancho Panza, and of the innumerable perfect, tiny, yet ultimately mysterious stories that are as much a part of Kafka's legacy as the terrible stories of 1912–14. This is the period of the great flowering of his gift for impersonation, and no writer has ever managed to empathize with such a diversity not just of living creatures but even of bridges, and balls in wooden games. ('If the ball was unemployed, it spent most of the time strolling to and fro, its hands clasped behind its back, on the plateau, avoiding the paths . . . It had a rather straddling gait and maintained that it was not made for those narrow paths.')

No story of those years shows more clearly how far Kafka has travelled from his earlier concerns and practices than the one called 'The Cares of a Family Man'. It tells of Odradek, not exactly an object and not quite a creature, with a name which is not precisely Slav and not exactly German:

> At first glance it looks like a flat star-shaped spool for thread, and indeed it does seem to have thread wound upon it; to be sure, they are only old, broken-off bits of thread, knotted and tangled together, of the most varied sorts and colors. But it is not only a spool, for a small wooden crossbar sticks out of the middle of the star, and another small rod is joined to that at a right angle. By means of this latter rod on one side and one of the points of the star on the other, the whole thing can stand upright as if on two legs.

It is not that Odradek once had some sort of intelligible shape and is now only 'a broken-down remnant'; it has always been like that and though 'the whole thing looks senseless enough', it is, in its own way, 'perfectly finished'. In any case close scrutiny is impossible, for Odradek will never let himself be caught. He lurks in stairs and garrets and disappears for months on end, but always returns to 'our house'. When you ask him his name he squeaks 'Odradek', and when you ask where he lives he squeaks 'no fixed abode' and laughs – 'but it is only the kind of laughter that has no lungs behind it. It sounds rather like the rustling of fallen leaves.'

Not surprisingly he gets on the nerves of the narrator, that *Hausvater* or 'family man'. What is going to happen to Odradek? he wonders. Can he possibly die? But only that which is living can die, and 'that does not apply to Odradek'. Is he then always going to be rolling down the stairs 'before the feet of my children and my children's children'? And though he does no harm as far as one can see, 'the idea that he is likely to survive me I find almost painful'.

Kafka has come a long way from that early reading by Max Brod of the 'little motor-car story', when he confided to his diary that despite his desire for 'something large and whole and well-shaped from beginning to end', 'every little piece of my story runs around homeless and drives me away from it'. Odradek is completely himself/itself, yet is neither large nor whole nor well-made, and revels in the fact that he/it has 'no fixed abode'.

So long as Kafka imagined that art would help him enter a more meaningful realm than the one he inhabited in his daily life, so long as he imagined that the test of the quality of his art lay in the unbroken nature of the work he put into it, then it was inevitable that he would turn on himself and his surroundings in bitterness and frustration: he was lazy, he was weak, he was unhealthy, his family was suffocating him, his bachelorhood was crippling him, the office was destroying him, marriage would be the end of him. But now it is as though he comes to accept the romantic folly of such dreams and such despair. An art that respects the truth, he now comes to see, can only express its own and our human limitations, show that we become immortal only to the extent that we cease to be human and alive only to the extent that we renounce dreams of wholeness and of belonging.

Odradek is nobody's son and nobody's father. He does not know the cares of a *Hausvater* and is not graspable in his essence, only in his movement and his otherness. Odradek does not mean anything: he moves, gets in the way, disturbs. And accepting that writing stories is bringing Odradeks into being gives Kafka back the sense that there need be no end to the writing of stories and that the freedom from human cares lies precisely in such writing. As for us, we should cease to ask of them what they *mean* and ask instead how they *move* – both how they move in their own space and how they move *us*.

Here, for example, is a little piece that Max Brod did not even consider worthy of inclusion in any collection of Kafka's stories. Yet if it was all we had of Kafka it would immediately strike us as unique and irreplaceable. Though it is barely six lines long it is not a fragment in the sense that the rape piece was a fragment. It is only a fragment in the way an aphorism is a fragment, that is, as a questioning of the very notion of wholeness:

> I ran past the first watchman. Then I was horrified, ran back again and said to the watchman: 'I ran through here while you were looking the other way.' The watchman gazed ahead of him and said nothing. 'I suppose I really oughtn't to have done it,' I said. The watchman still said nothing. 'Does your silence indicate permission to pass?'

The German is considerably denser than the English. 'Ran past' misses the sense of 'overran' in *überlief*; 'then' hardly does justice to *Nachträglich*, which means 'retrospectively' or 'retroactively'; and 'you' of course fails to convey the fact the German uses the familiar *du*, with its suggestion that the Watchman is both a figure of authority and one to whom the speaker is very close. But even in English this is a piece of writing which demands to be read at least twice; indeed, as so often in Kafka, the narrative mimics the way we are forced to read it.

A story which told how I ran past the first watchman, hid myself from the second, overcame the third, and finally entered the castle or finally escaped from it, might be exciting to read, but, once read, it would lose all interest for us. Its fire would burn only so long as the end had not been reached, and we would feel, in reading it, as we do in our lives, that everything had gone by too fast, that the experience was somehow thin – but we would not have any idea how to slow things down, how to thicken and deepen the experience. Kafka has managed to do that. But he has done it by dramatizing the fact that we always *run past* and so are always *looking back*. Thinness of experience is what we are condemned to. (We would, of course, destroy the story, make it merely thin again, if we were to substitute for it some generalizing comment, such as 'to hesitate is to be lost', or 'human self-awareness will not allow us to act naturally'.)

This little story is almost totally free of the anguish and pain characteristic of 'The Judgment' and the stories that followed it. It opens a space and lives in it, a space which we too can enter and in which we too can live, though without Kafka we would never have been able to do so. Just as Ulysses escaped the silence of the Sirens by a mixture of luck, innocence and cunning, so it is with Kafka and these stories of his middle period: he sails unscathed across the sea of narrative and takes his readers with him.

*

But it was not to last. For Kafka this rich creative period was only a moment on a fateful journey, only a point on the circumference of his dreams and desires. In 1917 he was found to be suffering from tuberculosis and broke off finally with

Felice. The precarious balance of these years was disturbed by the intrusion of his body and the stench of mortality. In his last stories the pain of 'The Judgment' and 'Metamorphosis' returns, but displaced, so to speak, no longer at the heart of the narrative but at the periphery. I am not sure if it is not the more painful for that.

'A Hunger Artist', the story whose proofs Kafka was correcting as he lay dying in Kierling Sanatorium in the spring of 1924, is the fullest expression of the change. 'I always wanted you to admire my fasting,' says the Hunger Artist. 'We do admire it,' says the overseer. 'But you shouldn't,' says the Artist. 'Well then we don't,' says the overseer. 'But why shouldn't we admire it?' 'Because I have to fast, I can't help it.' 'What a fellow you are,' says the overseer, 'and why can't you help it?' 'Because I couldn't find the food I liked. If I had found it, believe me, I should have made no fuss and stuffed myself like you or anyone else.'

Like Bucephalus and the ape the Hunger Artist has simply done what had to be done. In his case, however, it is not enough, for fasting, unlike the reading of old books or lectures to academies, kills.

> 'Well, clear this out now!' said the overseer, and they buried the hunger artist, straw and all. Into the cage they put a young panther. Even the most insensitive felt it refreshing to see this wild creature leaping around the cage that had so long been dreary.

But even this is perhaps still too close to pathos for Kafka. 'Josephine the Singer, or the Mouse Folk', probably the last story he wrote, takes matters one step further. Josephine's art, of which she has been so proud, is perhaps not even art, her singing no different from the cheeping of all the other mice when properly listened to. Her people will not miss her when she is gone, and, 'since we are no historians,' says the narrator, she will soon be forgotten, 'like all her brothers'.

Many years before, Kafka's uncle had taken the manuscript from his hands and declared to the assembled family that it contained only 'the usual stuff'. In this story Kafka sends a final answer to that uncle. For it recognizes the human desire for song, for art, that will give meaning to our world and bring the singer recognition. But it accepts at the same time that such desires are, from another perspective, absurd, childish, and unwarranted.

We are far, in this story, from the young Kafka's mixture of self-confidence ('I . . . could not forget that I was called to great things . . .') and self-doubt ('with one thrust I had been banished from society'). We are rather in the hands of a master who must have taken pride and pleasure in what he could do and yet who could also recognize its complete insignificance, and who had the skill and the imagination to convey this double perspective without self-pity and without denying the total validity of either.

The paradox is that, because he gives us food we need, Kafka himself will not be forgotten as long as there are books to read and human beings to read them. He lives for us in his fragmentary and living children more than he ever lived for himself in the bosom of his family, the Kafkas, and his city, Prague.

Gabriel Josipovici

A NOTE ON THE TEXT

Contrary to current belief, Kafka was as concerned as any author to see his works in print, and as careful as any poet about the order in which the stories in any particular collection should be printed. However, like Eliot, he was extremely fastidious and only published a very small number of works in his lifetime. In 1912, largely at Brod's urging, and with considerable misgivings, he put together a volume of early pieces, which was published the following year under the title *Betrachtung*, translated by Willa and Edwin Muir as *Meditation*. 1913 also saw the publication of his two great early stories, 'The Judgment' and 'The Stoker', followed in 1915 by his longest and greatest early work, 'Die Verwandlung', translated by the Muirs as 'The Metamorphosis'. In 1919 two more slim volumes came out, 'In the Penal Colony', which he had written in October 1914, and *A Country Doctor*, a collection of fourteen stories written between 1914 and 1917. He had originally intended to include 'The Bucket Rider', but eventually decided that it did not fit into the volume, and it was published separately in the 'Prager Presse' in December 1921. In the last two years of his life Kafka was planning a further volume, consisting of four stories, and this appeared shortly after his death, in 1924, as *Ein Hungerkünstler*, translated by the Muirs as *A Hunger Artist*. Everything else, including the three novels, *Amerika*, *The Trial* and *The Castle*, remained in manuscript, to be eventually published by Brod in a variety of formats.

The most readily available edition of the Collected Stories, edited by Nahum Glatzer (Penguin originally but now Minerva, 1992) divides the stories into two sections, 'longer' and 'shorter'. This seems needlessly arbitrary, and in the present volume I have preferred to follow the procedure of the Fischer Verlag edition of the stories, *Sämtliche Erzählungen*, edited by Paul Raabe and first published in 1970. Raabe essentially divides the stories into those published in Kafka's lifetime and those which remained unpublished. This has a number of advantages. It allows the reader of *Meditation*, *A*

Country Doctor and *A Hunger Artist*, to see these collections as wholes, made up of more than their parts; and it makes clear which stories carry titles given them by Kafka and which by later editors. One or two of the unpublished stories, it is true, such as 'The Great Wall of China', were given titles by Kafka, but even these do not, obviously, carry the authority of the titles of the published stories where, as in 'The Cares of a Family Man' ('Die Sorge des Hausvaters'), discussed in the Introduction, the title forms an important part of the meaning.

Like Raabe, but unlike Glatzer, I have included 'The Stoker', which Kafka subsequently intended should form Chapter I of *Amerika*. As I suggest in the Introduction, this remained an important story in its own right for Kafka and helps us understand his development. I have also naturally left in place in *A Country Doctor* two short pieces, 'Before the Law' and 'An Imperial Message', which Kafka incorporated into *The Trial* and 'The Great Wall of China' respectively. Since 'The Great Wall of China' is included here, 'An Imperial Message' appears twice. However, I have taken the opposite decision for two fragments from the early 'Description of a Struggle'. Since Kafka published these in magazine form but did not see fit to include them in *Meditation* it seemed pedantic to print them twice in this volume. I have also refrained from including the play, 'The Guardian of the Tomb' or variants for some of the stories, as Glatzer did. We still await a full critical edition of Kafka's writings, though that is under way, and it will be for that to provide us with all the versions and variants. What is needed at the present time is a full and clearly organized volume of the stories.

But what do we mean by 'the stories'? Brod himself has admitted that the task before any editor of Kafka is in a way an impossible one, since it will always be a matter of personal decision as to which bits of the notebooks and diaries one chooses to regard as finished stories. I have added two stories to Glatzer's selection which have been translated and published by Malcolm Pasley in *Franz Kafka: Shorter Works*, vol. I, Secker and Warburg, London, 1973: 'The Proclamation' and 'New Lamps'; and eight stories which I have culled from the Diaries and Notebooks: 'The Student', 'The Angel', and 'An

Ancient Sword', from *The Diaries of Franz Kafka*, edited by Max Brod, translated by Joseph Kresh and by Martin Greenberg with the co-operation of Hannah Arendt, Peregrine Books, Harmondsworth, 1964, and 'A Splendid Beast', 'The Watchman', 'Hands', 'Isabella' and 'A Chinese Puzzle', from *Wedding Preparations in the Country*, translated by Eithne Wilkins and Ernst Kaiser, Secker and Warburg, 1954. These are not the only stories I could have chosen, they merely reflect my own sense that they are as good as many of the pieces in the Glatzer volume and that they should be included in a volume of *Collected Stories*. The titles of these stories are, of course, my own.

It is often impossible to date accurately the stories Kafka did not choose to publish in his lifetime, but I have arranged them in roughly chronological order. The reader can thus follow two separate trajectories through Kafka's writing life, from *Meditation* (1913) to *A Hunger Artist* (1924), and from 'Description of a Struggle' (1904–05) to 'The Burrow' (1923–24).

Gabriel Josipovici

About the editor: GABRIEL JOSIPOVICI is a novelist, playwright and critic, and part-time Professor of English at the University of Sussex. His many books include *The World and the Book* and *The Book of God: A Response to the Bible* and the novels *Contre-Jour*, *The Big Glass* and *In a Hotel Garden.*

SELECT BIBLIOGRAPHY

As with any writer, the best way in to Kafka's stories is through other works of his. His novels, diaries and letters are all available in English.

There is no outstanding biography but Ronald Hayman's *A Biography of Franz Kafka* (Weidenfeld, 1981) and Ernst Pawel's *The Nightmare of Reason: A Life of Franz Kafka* (Harvill, 1984) are both interesting and informative.

I have learnt most from the following books and articles:

Walter Benjamin, 'Franz Kafka on the Tenth Anniversary of His Death' and 'Max Brod's Book on Kafka', both in *Illuminations*, edited and introduced by Hannah Arendt and translated by Harry Zohn, Cape, 1970.

Maurice Blanchot, 'Reading Kafka', 'Kafka and Literature', and 'Kafka and the Demands of Literature', all in *The Sirens' Song: Selected Essays of Maurice Blanchot*, edited and introduced by Gabriel Josipovici and translated by Sacha Rabinovitch, Harvester, 1982.

Elias Canetti, *Kafka's Other Trial*, tr. C. Middleton, Calder, 1974 (reprinted as the Introduction to the Penguin edition of the *Letters to Felice*).

Gilles Deleuze and Felix Guatari, *Kafka: Towards a Minor Literature*, tr. Dana Polan, University of Minnesota Press, 1986.

Erich Heller, 'The World of Franz Kafka', in *The Disinherited Mind*, Penguin, 1951.

Milan Kundera, 'In Saint Garta's Shadow', *Times Literary Supplement*, May 24, 1981.

Marthe Robert, *Franz Kafka's Loneliness*, tr. Ralph Manheim, Faber, 1982.

I have dealt with aspects of Kafka's life and work in 'An Art for the Wilderness', in *The Lessons of Modernism*, Macmillan, 1977, and in 'A Bird Was in the Room', in *Text and Voice: Essays 1981–1991*, Carcanet, 1992.

CHRONOLOGY

DATE	AUTHOR'S LIFE	LITERARY CONTEXT
1883	Birth in Prague (3 July) of Franz Kafka, son of a prosperous Jewish businessman who will later insist on German schools and the German University. Franz Kafka is brought up as a non-orthodox, Western Jew.	Maupassant: *Une Vie.* Nietzsche: *Thus Spake Zarathustra* (to 1884). Death of Turgenev.
1884		Huysmans: *À Rebours.* Tolstoy's *What I Believe* is banned.
1885		Howells: *The Rise of Silas Lapham.* Maupassant: *Bel Ami.* Nietzsche: *Beyond Good and Evil.*
1886		Rimbaud: *Les Illuminations.* Hardy: *The Mayor of Casterbridge.* Tolstoy: *The Death of Ivan Ilych.* His play, *The Power of Darkness*, offends the Tsar and is banned. Henry James: *The Bostonians* and *The Princess Casamassima.*
1888		Mallarmé: *Poésies.* Strindberg: *Miss Julie.* Sudermann: *Frau Sorge.* Birth of Anna Akhmatova.
1889	Attends German elementary school until 1893. Birth of the first of his three sisters (two younger brothers die in infancy).	Ibsen: *Hedda Gabler.* Hauptmann: *Before Sunrise.* Strindberg: *The Creditors.* Birth of Jean Cocteau.
1890		Hamsun: *Hunger.* Wilde: *The Picture of Dorian Gray* and *The Critic as Artist.* Henry James: *The Tragic Muse.* William James: *The Principles of Psychology.*

HISTORICAL EVENTS

Death of Wagner, Marx, Manet. Birth of Mussolini, Webern. First Russian Marxist revolutionary organization, the Liberation of Labour, founded in Geneva by Georgi Plekhanov. Opening of National Theatre in Prague. First skyscraper built (10 stories) in Chicago.

Fall of Khartoum. Berlin conference on African affairs; Togo and the Cameroons become part of the German Empire. Death of Smetana.

Bulgarian Crisis (to 1886); Ferdinand of Saxe-Coburg becomes Prince of Bulgaria. Formation of the German East Africa protectorate. Karl Benz produces first car. Birth of Alban Berg.

German deputies in the Bohemian Diet leave in protest at the Czechs' not acknowledging restricted German-language areas in Bohemia (Germans return to Diet, 1890). Neutrality agreement between the Russian and German Empires (1887).

Death of German Emperor, Wilhelm I. Convention of Constantinople: Suez Canal declared open to ships of all nations. Mahler's first symphony.

Second International founded in Paris, and the establishment of 1st May as a workers' holiday (first celebrated in Austria-Hungary, 1890). Eiffel Tower built. Birth of Hitler.

Fall of Bismarck. Wilhelm II's personal rule begins. Death of Van Gogh and Heinrich Schliemann.

DATE	AUTHOR'S LIFE	LITERARY CONTEXT
1891		Wilde: *The Soul of Man under Socialism.* Howells: *A Modern Instance.* Shaw: *Quintessence of Ibsenism.* Birth of Bulgakov.
1892		Hamsun: *Mysteries.* Ibsen: *The Master Builder.* Hauptmann: *The Weavers.* Hofmannsthal: *The Death of Titian.*
1893	Attends German Staatgymnasium until 1901.	Fontane: *Frau Jenny Treibel.* Tolstoy: *The Kingdom of God is within You.* Sudermann: *Heimat.* Schnitzler: *Anatol.* Death of Maupassant.
1894		Hamsun: *Pan.* Bryusov publishes *The Russian Symbolists.* Heinrich Mann: *In a Family.*
1895		Hardy: *Jude the Obscure.* Fontane: *Effi Briest.* Wilde's trial and imprisonment; writes *An Ideal Husband* and *The Importance of Being Earnest.* Gorky: *Chelkash.* Birth of Ernst Jünger.
1896		Chekhov: *The Seagull.* Fontane: *Poggenpuhls.*
1897		Housman: *A Shropshire Lad.* Henry James: *What Maisie Knew.*
1898		Tolstoy: *What is Art?* Zola: *J'accuse.* Shaw: *Plays Pleasant and Unpleasant.* Wilde: *The Ballad of Reading Gaol.* Strindberg: *Inferno.* Thomas Mann: *Little Herr Friedemann.* Svevo: *As a Man Grows Older.* Birth of Erich Maria Remarque. Death of Fontane and Mallarmé.

HISTORICAL EVENTS

Decisive election victory for liberal Young Czech party. 20,000 Jews brutally evicted from Moscow. Work begins on Trans-Siberian railway.

Panama scandal in France. Anarchist outrages in Paris. Munich *Sezession* (German artists under Franz von Stuck rebel against salon system). Diesel patents internal combustion engine.

Independent Labour Party founded in England. Omladina show-trial of radical youth movements in Prague. Death of Marshal MacMahon. Dvořák's 'New World' Symphony. Munch: *The Scream.*

Dreyfus trial begins. German–Russian commercial treaty. Beginning of Armenian massacres in Turkey. *Yellow Book* launched. Debussy: *L'Après-midi d'un faune.*

Lenin leads the St Petersburg Union of Struggle for the Liberation of the Working Class. Arrested; banished to Siberia (1897–1900). Cézanne exhibition in Paris. Lumière brothers invent cinematograph. Marconi invents wireless telegraphy. X-rays discovered. Freud's *Studien über Hysterie* inaugurates psychoanalysis. Masaryk: *Czech Question*, *Our Present Crisis.* Mahler: *Till Eulenspiegel's Merry Pranks.*

Establishment of Nobel prizes. Theodore Herzl, founder of modern political Zionism, publishes *Der Judenstraat* putting forward the idea of a Jewish national home in Palestine. Henry Ford produces his first car.
Badeni Language Decrees give Czech the status of 'internal official language'; implementation hampered by Germans, leading to anti-German riots in Prague with an anti-Semitic element, and the withdrawal of the Decrees. First Zionist Congress in Basel. Graeco–Turkish War. Vienna *Sezession* founded by Klimt to further modern (*Jugendstil*, Symbolist) movement. Beginning of Klondike gold rush. Electron discovered. Death of Brahms.
First German Navy Law begins the arms race. Death of Bismarck. The Gautsch Language Decrees, a watered-down version of the Badeni decrees, are accepted: Czech could be 'official language' in mixed German–Czech communities. First Congress of Russian Social Democratic Workers' Party in Minsk. War between Spain and USA. British reconquer the Sudan. German fleet seizes Kiaochow; secures 99-year lease from China. Curie discovers radium. Moscow Arts Theatre founded.

FRANZ KAFKA

DATE	AUTHOR'S LIFE	LITERARY CONTEXT
1899		Yeats: *The Wind Among the Reeds.* Tolstoy: *Resurrection.* Chekhov: *The Lady with the Little Dog.* Gorky: *Foma Gordeev.* Birth of Borges.
1900		Conrad: *Lord Jim.* Freud: *Interpretation of Dreams.* Schnitzler: *La Ronde.* Dreiser: *Sister Carrie.* Death of Wilde and Nietzsche.
1901	Studies Law at the German Karl-Ferdinand University in Prague but is drawn to the literary circles of the city.	Chekhov: *Three Sisters.* Thomas Mann: *Buddenbrooks.* Strindberg: *Dance of Death.*
1902	Kafka very quickly defines his ideal style – cool, sober and very elegant: a language 'ohne Schnörkel und Schleier und Warzen'. Meets Max Brod.	Rilke: *The Book of Pictures.* Gide: *L'Immoraliste.* Sudermann: *The Joy of Living.* Henry James: *The Wings of the Dove.* Death of Zola.
1903		Thomas Mann: *Tristan, Tonio Kröger.* Moore: *Principia Ethica.* Shaw: *Man and Superman.*
1904	Begins 'Description of a Struggle'.	Henry James: *The Golden Bowl.* Conrad: *Nostromo.* Pirandello: *The Late Mattia Pascal.*
1905		Thomas Mann: *Fiorenza. The Blood of the Walsungs* is withdrawn. Rilke: *The Book of Hours.* Gumilev: *The Path of the Conquistadors.* Wharton: *The House of Mirth.* Birth of Sholokhov.
1906	Receives law degree. Embarks on his year of practical training in Prague Law Courts.	Gorky: *The Mother* (to 1907). Hofmannsthal: *Oedipus and the Sphinx.* Death of Ibsen.

CHRONOLOGY

HISTORICAL EVENTS

Renewal of *Ausgleich* of 1867 (established Dual Monarchy of Austria-Hungary) following agitation for its repeal and (in 1897) breakdown in constitutional government and government by imperial decree. In Prague, Polná or Hilsner Affair: a Jewish vagabond accused of ritual murder of Czech girl. Boer War (to 1902). Second Dreyfus trial and pardon. Karl Kraus founds the journal *Die Fackel* in Vienna. Schoenberg: *Verklärte Nacht.* Berlin *Sezession* formed by German *avant-garde* artists under Max Liebermann.

Beginning of severe recession in Austria-Hungary. Economy does not recover until 1906–07. Czech People's Party founded (programme composed by Masaryk). Bülow becomes Chancellor of Germany. Founding of British Labour Party. Boxer Rebellion in China (to 1901). Max Planck formulates quantum theory. Birth of German composer Kurt Weill.

Death of Queen Victoria. Accession of Edward VII. Roosevelt succeeds assassinated McKinley as president of USA. Marconi's first radio communication between USA and Europe. Beginning of Picasso 'Blue' period. Dvořák: *Russalka.*

Conflict between 'Bolsheviks' and 'Mensheviks' at 2nd Congress of Russian Social Democratic Workers' Party. Death of Gauguin. King Alexander of Serbia and Queen Draga murdered. Austria-Hungary and Russia conclude agreement about their respective rights in south-east Europe. In Britain, Emmeline Pankhurst founds Women's Social and Political Union. First flight by Wright brothers.

Entente Cordiale between Britain and France. Russo-Japanese War (to 1905). Work begins on Panama Canal. Janáček: *Jenůfa.*

First Russian Revolution. 'Red Sunday' in St Petersburg. Foundation of German Agrarian Party in Bohemia. Einstein's Special Theory of Relativity. Beginning of Fauvism. Die Brücke formed in Dresden by leading German Expressionists. Richard Strauss: *Salome.*

Constitution in Russia. First Duma meets and is speedily dissolved. Conference of Algeciras; French successfully resist German attempt to gain influence in Morocco (Austria-Hungary alone supports Germany). Young Czech movement reorganized under Karel Kramář.

DATE	AUTHOR'S LIFE	LITERARY CONTEXT
1907	Writes 'Wedding Preparations in the Country'. Takes temporary position with Assicurazioni Generali, Italian insurance company.	Blok: *The Terrible World.* Rilke: *New Poems.* Strindberg: *The Ghost Sonata.* Adams: *The Education of Henry Adams.* Conrad: *The Secret Agent.* William James: *Pragmatism.*
1908	Accepts position in Prague with Workers' Accident Insurance Company, the Arbeiter-Unfall-Versicherungs-Anstalt.	Forster: *A Room with a View.* Bennett: *The Old Wives' Tale.*
1909	Eight prose pieces published in *Hyperion.* Trip to Riva and Brescia (with Max and Otto Brod). Writes *Die Aeroplane in Brescia.*	Bely: *The Silver Dove.* Gide: *La Porte étroite.*
1910	Begins to write a diary in which he relentlessly analyses his inner life. Five prose pieces published in *Bohemia.* Trip to Paris (with Max and Otto Brod). Visit to Berlin.	Tsetsaeva: *Evening Album.* Rilke: *Sketches of Malte Laurids Brigge.* Forster: *Howards End.* Wells: *Mr Polly.* Döblin co-founds the Expressionist *Der Sturm.* Death of Tolstoy.
1911	Official trip to Friedland and Reichenberg. Trip (with Max Brod) to Switzerland, Italy and France, writing travelogues. Becomes interested in Yiddish theatre and literature.	Pound: *Canzoni.* Conrad: *Under Western Eyes.* Heinrich Mann's manifesto: *Spirit and Deed.* The Poets' Guild formed (founders of Russian Acmeism). Wharton: *Ethan Frome.*
1912	Meets a Jewish girl from Berlin, Felice Bauer, to whom he will be engaged twice. The short story 'Das Urteil' ('The Judgment') is written six weeks later. Visits Leipzig and Weimar. Works on a novel to be called *Der Verschollene,* to be published posthumously in 1927 as *Amerika.*	Thomas Mann: *Death in Venice.* Pound: *Ripostes.* Heinrich Mann begins *Man of Straw.* Dreiser: *The Financier.* Hofmannsthal: *Everyman.*

HISTORICAL EVENTS

Ausgleich again renewed. New financial and commercial arrangements made which last until the Great War. Monarchy embarks on the last stage of its foreign policy – greater influence in the Balkans coupled with closer union with Germany. Law of universal suffrage in Austria-Hungary; first elections under that law. Triple Entente of Britain, France and Russia. Failure of Hague Peace Conference to halt the arms race.

Austria annexes Bosnia and Herzegovina. By obstructive tactics, German minority (German speakers form only 30% of the electorate) succeed in paralysing regional parliament in Bohemia. Second Slav Congress in Prague. Cubism begins in Paris. First performance in Vienna of Schoenberg's *3 Pieces* (demonstrating atonality, or keyless music) arouses vehement hostility.
Zionists found Tel Aviv. Blériot flies English Channel. *La Nouvelle Revue Française* founded. Futurist movement founded by Italian poet Marinetti.

Post-Impressionist Exhibition in London. Death of Edward VII.

Assassination of Stolypin, Russian Minister of the Interior, by a Socialist Revolutionary terrorist. Italo–Turkish War (to 1912). Strikes in Britain: dockers, miners, weavers, railwaymen. George V announces transfer of capital of India from Calcutta to Delhi. Revolutions in China: Manchu dynasty overthrown. *Der Blaue Reiter* founded in Berlin. Bartók: *Bluebeard's Castle*; *Allegro barbaro*. Amundsen becomes first man to reach the South Pole.

Haldane (British Secretary for War) visits Berlin, but fails to secure reduction of naval build-up. German Social Democratic party poll more votes in general election than any other party. German Socialists declare themselves anti-war; assert international proletarian solidarity. Formation of Balkan League – Serbia, Bulgaria, Montenegro. Serious disorder in Croatia leads to policy of repression; elsewhere in the Austro-Hungarian Empire local diets suppressed and constitutional methods of government replaced by autocracy. Sinking of the *Titanic*. Schoenberg: *Pierrot Lunaire*.

FRANZ KAFKA

DATE	AUTHOR'S LIFE	LITERARY CONTEXT
1913	Publication of *Betrachtung* (*Meditation*), *The Judgment* and *Der Heizer* (*The Stoker*). Visits Felice in Berlin. Travels to Vienna and Italy. Meeting with Grete Bloch and beginning of correspondence. (She becomes the mother of his son who dies in 1921, and of whose existence Kafka is ignorant.)	Proust: *A la Recherche du temps perdu* (to 1927). Lawrence: *Sons and Lovers*. Trakl: *Poems*. Alain Fournier: *Le Grand Meaulnes*. Apollinaire: *Alcools*. Mandelstam: *Stone*. Gorky: *Childhood*. Cather: *O Pioneers!*
1914	Engaged to Felice. Breaks off his engagement. Visit to Germany. Starts working on *Der Prozess* (*The Trial*). Writes 'In der Strafkolonie' ('In the Penal Colony').	Joyce: *Dubliners*. Kaiser: *The Burghers of Calais*. Blok: *Carmen*. Akhmatova: *Rosary*.
1915	'Die Verwandlung' ('The Metamorphosis'), an acknowledged masterpiece of precision, lucidity and grotesque implication, is published. Reconciliation with Felice.	Ford: *The Good Soldier*. Lawrence: *The Rainbow*. Woolf: *The Voyage Out*. Mayakovsky: *A Cloud in Trousers*.
1916	Resumes writing after two years' silence: the fragment of 'A Country Doctor', 'The Hunter Gracchus' and other stories later included in *A Country Doctor*.	Joyce: *A Portrait of the Artist as a Young Man*. Death of Henry James.
1917	Tuberculosis of the lung is confirmed. Relationship with Felice ends. Writes stories, among others: 'A Report to an Academy', 'The Cares of a Family Man' and 'The Great Wall of China'. Learning Hebrew.	Yeats: *The Wild Swans at Coole*. Eliot: *Prufrock and other Observations*. Pasternak: *Above the Barriers*.
1918		Joyce: *Exiles*. Kraus: *The Last Days of Mankind* (to 1922). Thomas Mann: *Considerations of an Unpolitical Man*. Spengler: *The Decline of the West* (to 1923). Kaiser: *Gas* (to 1920). Blok: 'The Twelve'. Birth of Solzhenitsyn.

CHRONOLOGY

HISTORICAL EVENTS

Treaty of London ends First Balkan War. Second Balkan War (June–August). Treaty of Bucharest; partitioning of the Balkans. Woodrow Wilson president of USA (later a strong supporter of the dissolution of the Hapsburg monarchy). Bohr's discovery of atomic structure. First Charlie Chaplin film. Stravinsky: *The Rite of Spring.*

Heir to Austro-Hungarian throne, Archduke Franz-Ferdinand d'Este and his wife, Sophie, assassinated in Sarajevo (June). Austria-Hungary declares war on Serbia (July). World War I breaks out (August). Russia invades Galicia. President Wilson proclaims US neutrality. Political periodicals *L'Indépendence tchèque* and *La Nation tchèque* founded in Paris. Leading politically active Czechs begin to be arrested in Austria. Panama Canal opens. Vorticist movement founded.

Sinking of the *Lusitania.* Entrance of Italy into the war against Austria-Hungary. Serbia and Poland overrun by Austro-Hungarian and German troops. Gallipoli disaster. Malevich's Suprematist manifesto. Einstein's General Theory of Relativity.

Franz Joseph I dies; Charles I's accession to Austro-Hungarian throne. Russian troops again on Austrian soil. Murder of Austrian premier Stürgh; growing unpopularity of the war leads to strikes and rioting. Huge death tolls at the battles of Verdun and the Somme. Lloyd George becomes British Prime Minister. Easter Rising in Dublin. Political strike in Berlin. Rasputin assassinated. Tzara founds the Dada group in Zürich.

February and October Revolutions in Russia. In March, fall of the monarchy; Petrograd riots. US declares war on Germany, 6 April. Balfour Declaration, promising the Jews a home in Palestine. *Ausgleich* due for renewal but proves impossible to negotiate.

Wilson's Fourteen Points (January); point 10 includes notion of self-determination for the nationalities of Austria-Hungary. Russia accepts terms dictated at Brest-Litovsk (March). Pittsburgh Accord on the union of Czechs and Slovaks in a joint republic (May). Brazil declares war on Austria-Hungary (September). Declaration of Czecho-Slovak independence (October). German deputies from Bohemia and Moravia meet in Vienna under leadership of Lodgman von Allen, aiming to establish a German *Land* in Bohemia with its own parliament, as a province of German Austria. To forestall the build-up of a 'greater Germany', the Allies join with the

DATE	AUTHOR'S LIFE	LITERARY CONTEXT
1918 *cont*		
1919	Stays in various sanatoria. Briefly engaged to Julie Wohryzek who inspires him to write 'Brief an der Vater' ('Letter to his Father'). 'In the Penal Colony' and *A Country Doctor* are published.	Sherwood Anderson: *Winesburg, Ohio.* Dos Passos: *One Man's Initiation.* Cocteau: *Ode to Picasso.*
1920	Meets Milena Jesenska-Pollak, with whom he later corresponds.	Lawrence: *Women in Love.* Wharton: *The Age of Innocence.* Sinclair Lewis: *Main Street.* Pound: *Hugh Selwyn Mauberley.* Mayakovsky: *150,000,000.* Čapek: *RUR*.
1921	Goes back to work with the Workers' Accident Insurance Company. 'The Bucket Rider' published.	Death of Blok and Gumilev. Thomas Mann: *Goethe and Tolstoy.* Hašek: *The Good Soldier Švejk.* Pirandello: *Six Characters in Search of an Author.*
1922	Writes *Der Schloss* (*The Castle*), 'A Hunger Artist' and 'Investigations of a Dog'. Breaks off relations with Milena Jesenska-Pollak. Retires from the insurance company because of his ill-health and works until his death in a sanatorium near Vienna. 'A Hunger Artist' published.	Eliot: *The Waste Land.* Woolf: *Jacob's Room.* Joyce's *Ulysses* published in Paris. Brecht: *Baal, Drums in the Night.* Pasternak: *My Sister Life.* Toller: *The Machine Wreckers.* Mandelstam: *Tristia.* Borges: *Fervor de Buenos Aires.* Čapek: *The Absolute at Large.* Death of Proust.
1923	Meets Dora Dymant, daughter of an orthodox Polish rabbi, and lives with her for a time in Berlin. His illness drives him to Prague before he enters a sanatorium near Vienna. Writes 'The Burrow'.	Gorky: *My Universities.* Babel: *Red Cavalry* (to 1925). Rilke: *Duino Elegies, Sonnets to Orpheus.* Cather: *A Lost Lady.*

HISTORICAL EVENTS

Czechs to take action against the separatists. Conclusion of World War I: Armistice Day, 11 November. Abdication of Wilhelm II. Masaryk elected President of Czecho-Slovakia. In Great Britain the Suffrage Bill is passed, giving women over thirty the vote. Irish rebel Con Markiewitz elected first British woman MP. Russian Civil War. Nicholas II assassinated. Rutherford splits the atom.

Versailles Peace Conference. Weimar republic created in Germany; a 'Soviet Republic' established in Munich and quickly suppressed. Collapse of Austro-Hungarian Empire. Food shortages and demonstrations in Prague; some channelled into anti-Semitic pogroms. Social Democrats win election and ally with Agrarians to form a government. The 'Red Scare' in the US. First Atlantic flight. Death of Renoir. Foundation of the Bauhaus, teaching institution for the arts, by Walter Gropius. Marinetti's *Manifestos of Futurism*.

League of Nations meets for first time. Russians driven out of Warsaw. 'Little Entente' between Czechoslovakia, Rumania and Yugoslavia. Chauvinistic activities of right-wing Czech extremists lead to bloody clashes with German population. Jewish shops attacked. Social Democrats win convincing election victory (even winning 43.5% of the German vote); Marxist left-wing expelled. Ensuing General Strike crushed. Irish Civil War. Kapp *putsch* in Germany to effect Nationalist counter-revolution defeated by Berlin workers. Robert Wiene's *The Cabinet of Dr Caligari* – epitome of Expressionism in German cinema. Gandhi initiates campaign of civil disobedience in India.

Irish Free State (excluding six counties) founded. New Economic Plan in Russia. Communist Party of Czechoslovakia founded. Rise of Fascism in Italy. Janáček: *Katya Kabanova*.

Stalin becomes General Secretary of the Central Committee. USSR established. Fascist march on Rome; Mussolini becomes Italian Prime Minister. Creation of Czech Fascist Party. In Germany, political assassinations of Erzberger and Rathenau by right-wing extremists.

Czechoslovak Minister of Finance, Rašín, assassinated. National revolution in Turkey under Kemel Pasha. Munich *putsch* by Nazis fails. Hyperinflation in Germany.

DATE	AUTHOR'S LIFE	LITERARY CONTEXT
1924	Moves back to Prague. Writes 'Josephine the Singer'. He is nursed in his last months by Dora Dymant, in a nursing home at Kierling. Dies there and is buried in Prague. Collection, *A Hunger Artist*, published shortly after his death. He leaves a testamentary direction that his work has to be destroyed after his death, which is disregarded by his friend and executor Max Brod.	Mann: *The Magic Mountain* published. Pasternak: *The Childhood of Luvers*, *Themes and Variations*. Mayakovsky: *Vladimir Ilich Lenin*. Ford: *Some Do Not*. Forster: *A Passage to India*. O'Neill: *Desire under the Elms*. O'Casey: *Juno and the Paycock*.
1925	Publication by Max Brod of *Der Prozess* (*The Trial*).	Woolf: *Mrs Dalloway* and *The Common Reader*. Cather: *The Professor's House*. Scott Fitzgerald: *The Great Gatsby*. O'Neill: *The Fountain*. Dreiser: *An American Tragedy*. Stein: *The Making of Americans*.
1926	Publication by Max Brod of *Das Schloss* (*The Castle*).	Gide: *Si le Grain ne meurt*. Ford: *A Man Could Stand Up*. Death of Rilke.
1927	Publication by Max Brod of the unfinished *Amerika*.	Woolf: *To the Lighthouse*. Hesse: *Der Steppenwolf*. Brecht: *Man is Man*. Birth of Günter Grass.

HISTORICAL EVENTS

First Labour Government in Britain, under Ramsay MacDonald. In Italy, Fascists obtain almost two thirds of votes in election amidst widespread use of violence and intimidation. Murder of Mateotti, openly opposed to Mussolini. Death of Lenin. Breton: *Manifesto of Surrealism.*

Hindenburg becomes German Chancellor. 'Monkey Trial' (Scopes), Dayton, Tennessee. Eisenstein: *Battleship Potemkin.* Trotsky's *Literature and Revolution.* Berg: *Wozzeck.* G. B. Shaw awarded Nobel Prize.

General Strike in Britain. Germany admitted to membership of League of Nations.

Socialist riots in Vienna following acquittal of Nazis for political murder. Leon Trotsky expelled from Communist Party. World economic crisis. Lindbergh's solo Atlantic flight. Invention of cinema sound.

Stories published in Kafka's Lifetime

Meditation (1913)

Children on a Country Road

I HEARD the wagons rumbling past the garden fence, sometimes I even saw them through gently swaying gaps in the foliage. How the wood of their spokes and shafts creaked in the summer heat! Laborers were coming from the fields and laughing so that it was a scandal.

I was sitting on our little swing, just resting among the trees in my parents' garden.

On the other side of the fence the traffic never stopped. Children's running feet were past in a moment; harvest wagons with men and women perched on and around the sheaves darkened the flower beds; toward evening I saw a gentleman slowly promenading with a walking stick, and a couple of girls who met him arm in arm stepped aside into the grass as they greeted him.

Then birds flew up as if in showers, I followed them with my eyes and saw how high they soared in one breath, till I felt not that they were rising but that I was falling, and holding fast to the ropes began to swing a little out of sheer weakness. Soon I was swinging more strongly as the air blew colder and instead of soaring birds trembling stars appeared.

I was given my supper by candlelight. Often both my arms were on the wooden board and I was already weary as I bit into my bread and butter. The coarse-mesh window curtains bellied in the warm wind and many a time some passer-by outside would stay them with his hands as if he wanted to see me better and speak to me. Usually the candle soon went out and in the sooty candle smoke the assembled midges went on circling for a while. If anyone asked me a question from the window I would gaze at him as if at a distant mountain or into vacancy, nor did he particularly care whether he got an answer or not. But if one jumped over the window sill and announced that the others were already waiting, then I did get to my feet with a sigh.

'What are you sighing for? What's wrong? Has something dreadful happened that can never be made good? Shan't we ever recover from it? Is everything lost?'

Nothing was lost. We ran to the front of the house. 'Thank God, here you are at last!' – 'You're always late!' – 'Why just me?' – 'Especially you, why don't you stay at home if you don't want to come.' – 'No quarter!' – 'No quarter? What kind of way is that to talk?'

We ran our heads full tilt into the evening. There was no daytime and no nighttime. Now our waistcoat buttons would be clacking together like teeth, again we would be keeping a steady distance from each other as we ran, breathing fire like wild beasts in the tropics. Like cuirassiers in old wars, stamping and springing high, we drove each other down the short alley and with this impetus in our legs a farther stretch along the main road. Stray figures went into the ditch, hardly had they vanished down the dusky escarpment when they were standing like newcomers on the field path above and looking down.

'Come on down!' – 'Come on up first!' – 'So's you can push us down, no thanks, we're not such fools.' – 'You're afraid, you mean. Come on up, you cowards!' – 'Afraid? Of the likes of you? You're going to push us down, are you? That's a good one.'

We made the attempt and were pushed head over heels into the grass of the roadside ditch, tumbling of our own free will. Everything was equally warm to us, we felt neither warmth nor chill in the grass, only one got tired.

Turning on one's right side, with a hand under the ear, one could easily have fallen asleep there. But one wanted to get up again with chin uplifted, only to roll into a deeper ditch. Then with an arm thrust out crosswise and legs threshing to the side one thought to launch into the air again only to fall for certain into a still deeper ditch. And of this one never wanted to make an end.

How one might stretch oneself out, especially in the knees, properly to sleep in the last ditch, was something scarcely thought of, and one simply lay on one's back, like an invalid, inclined to weep a little. One blinked as now and then a youngster with elbows pressed to his sides sprang over one's head with dark-looming soles, in a leap from the escarpment to the roadway.

The moon was already some way up in the sky, in its light a mail coach drove past. A small wind began to blow everywhere, even in the ditch one could feel it, and nearby the forest began to rustle. Then one was no longer so anxious to be alone.

'Where are you?' – 'Come here!' – 'All together!' – 'What are you hiding for, drop your nonsense!' – 'Don't you know the mail's gone past already?' – 'Not already?' – 'Of course; it went past while you were sleeping.' – 'I wasn't sleeping. What an idea!' – 'Oh shut up, you're still half asleep.' – 'But I wasn't.' – 'Come on!'

We ran bunched more closely together, many of us linked hands, one's head could not be held high enough, for now the way was downhill. Someone whooped an Indian war cry, our legs galloped us as never before, the wind lifted our hips as we sprang. Nothing could have checked us; we were in such full stride that even in overtaking others we could fold our arms and look quietly around us.

At the bridge over the brook we came to a stop; those who had overrun it came back. The water below lapped against stones and roots as if it were not already late evening. There was no reason why one of us should not jump onto the parapet of the bridge.

From behind clumps of trees in the distance a railway train came past, all the carriages were lit up, the window-panes were certainly let down. One of us began to sing a popular catch, but we all felt like singing. We sang much faster than the train was going, we waved our arms because our voices were not enough, our voices rushed together in an avalanche of sound that did us good. When one joins in song with others it is like being drawn on by a fish hook.

So we sang, the forest behind us, for the ears of the distant travelers. The grownups were still awake in the village, the mothers were making down the beds for the night.

Our time was up. I kissed the one next to me, reached hands to the three nearest, and began to run home, none called me back. At the first crossroads where they could no longer see me I turned off and ran by the field paths into the forest again. I was making for that city in the south of which it was said in our village:

'There you'll find queer folk! Just think, they never sleep!'

'And why not?'

'Because they never get tired.'

'And why not?'

'Because they're fools.'

'Don't fools get tired?'

'How could fools get tired!'

Translated by Willa and Edwin Muir

Unmasking a Confidence Trickster

AT LAST, about ten o'clock at night, I came to the doorway of the fine house where I was invited to spend the evening, after the man beside me, whom I was barely acquainted with and who had once again thrust himself unasked upon me, had marched me for two long hours around the streets.

'Well!' I said, and clapped my hands to show that I really had to bid him goodbye. I had already made several less explicit attempts to get rid of him. I was tired out.

'Are you going straight in?' he asked. I heard a sound in his mouth that was like the snapping of teeth.

'Yes.'

I had been invited out, I told him when I met him. But it was to enter a house where I longed to be that I had been invited, not to stand here at the street door looking past the ears of the man before me. Nor to fall silent with him, as if we were doomed to stay for a long time on this spot. And yet the houses around us at once took a share in our silence, and the darkness over them, all the way up to the stars. And the steps of invisible passers-by, which one could not take the trouble to elucidate, and the wind persistently buffeting the other side of the street, and a gramophone singing behind the closed windows of some room – they all announced themselves in this silence, as if it were their own possession for the time past and to come.

And my companion subscribed to it in his own name and – with a smile – in mine too, stretched his right arm up along the wall and leaned his cheek upon it, shutting his eyes.

But I did not wait to see the end of that smile, for shame suddenly caught hold of me. It had needed that smile to let me know that the man was a confidence trickster, nothing else. And yet I had been months in the town and thought I knew all about confidence tricksters, how they came slinking out of side streets by night to meet us with outstretched hands like tavernkeepers, how they haunted the advertisement pillars we stood beside, sliding around them as if playing hide-and-seek and spying on us with at least one eye, how they suddenly appeared on the curb of the pavement at cross-streets when we were hesitating! I understood them so well, they were the first acquaintances I had made in the town's small taverns, and to them I owed my first inkling of a ruthless hardness which I was now so conscious of, everywhere on earth, that I was even beginning to feel it in myself. How persistently they blocked our way, even when we had long shaken ourselves free, even when, that is, they had nothing more to hope for! How they refused to give up, to admit defeat, but kept shooting glances at us that even from a distance were still compelling! And the means they employed were always the same: they planted themselves before us, looking as large as possible, tried to hinder us from going where we purposed, offered us instead a habitation in their own bosoms, and when at last all our balked feelings rose in revolt they welcomed that like an embrace into which they threw themselves face foremost.

And it had taken me such a long time in this man's

company to recognize the same old game. I rubbed my finger tips together to wipe away the disgrace.

My companion was still leaning there as before, still believing himself a successful trickster, and his self-complacency glowed pink on his free cheek.

'Caught in the act!' said I, tapping him lightly on the shoulder. Then I ran up the steps, and the disinterested devotion on the servants' faces in the hall delighted me like an unexpected treat. I looked at them all, one after another, while they took my greatcoat off and wiped my shoes clean.

With a deep breath of relief and straightening myself to my full height, I then entered the drawing room.

Translated by Willa and Edwin Muir

The Sudden Walk

WHEN it looks as if you had made up your mind finally to stay at home for the evening, when you have put on your house jacket and sat down after supper with a light on the table to the piece of work or the game that usually precedes your going to bed, when the weather outside is unpleasant so that staying indoors seems natural, and when you have already been sitting quietly at the table for so long that your departure must occasion surprise to everyone, when, besides, the stairs are in darkness and the front door locked, and in spite of all that you have started up in a sudden fit of restlessness, changed your jacket, abruptly dressed yourself for the street, explained that you must go out and with a few curt words of leave-taking actually gone out, banging the flat door more or less hastily according to the degree of displeasure you think you have left behind you, and when you find yourself once more in the street with limbs swinging extra freely in answer to the unexpected liberty you have procured for them, when as a result of this decisive action you feel concentrated within yourself all the potentialities of decisive action, when you recognize with more than usual significance that your strength is greater than your need to accomplish effortlessly the swiftest of changes and to cope with it, when in this frame of mind you go striding down the long streets – then for that evening you have completely got away from your family, which fades into insubstantiality, while you yourself, a firm, boldly drawn black figure, slapping yourself on the thigh, grow to your true stature.

All this is still heightened if at such a late hour in the evening you look up a friend to see how he is getting on.

Translated by Willa and Edwin Muir

Resolutions

TO LIFT YOURSELF out of a miserable mood, even if you have to do it by strength of will, should be easy. I force myself out of my chair, stride around the table, exercise my head and neck, make my eyes sparkle, tighten the muscles around them. Defy my own feelings, welcome A. enthusiastically supposing he comes to see me, amiably tolerate B. in my room, swallow all that is said at C.'s, whatever pain and trouble it may cost me, in long draughts.

Yet even if I manage that, one single slip, and a slip cannot be avoided, will stop the whole process, easy and painful alike, and I will have to shrink back into my own circle again.

So perhaps the best resource is to meet everything passively, to make yourself an inert mass, and, if you feel that you are being carried away, not to let yourself be lured into taking a single unnecessary step, to stare at others with the eyes of an animal, to feel no compunction, in short, with your own hand to throttle down whatever ghostly life remains in you, that is, to enlarge the final peace of the graveyard and let nothing survive save that.

A characteristic movement in such a condition is to run your little finger along your eyebrows.

Translated by Willa and Edwin Muir

Excursion into the Mountains

'I DON'T KNOW,' I cried without being heard, 'I do not know. If nobody comes, then nobody comes. I've done nobody any harm, nobody's done me any harm, but nobody will help me. A pack of nobodies. Yet that isn't all true. Only, that nobody helps me – a pack of nobodies would be rather fine, on the other hand. I'd love to go on an excursion – why not? – with a pack of nobodies. Into the mountains, of course, where else? How these nobodies jostle each other, all these lifted arms linked together, these numberless feet treading so close! Of course they are all in dress suits. We go so gaily, the wind blows through us and the gaps in our company. Our throats swell and are free in the mountains! It's a wonder that we don't burst into song.'

Translated by Willa and Edwin Muir

Bachelor's Ill Luck

IT SEEMS so dreadful to stay a bachelor, to become an old man struggling to keep one's dignity while begging for an invitation whenever one wants to spend an evening in company, to lie ill gazing for weeks into an empty room from the corner where one's bed is, always having to say good night at the front door, never to run up a stairway beside one's wife, to have only side doors in one's room leading into other people's living rooms, having to carry one's supper home in one's hand, having to admire other people's children and not even being allowed to go on saying: 'I have none myself,' modeling oneself in appearance and behavior on one or two bachelors remembered from one's youth.

That's how it will be, except that in reality, both today and later, one will stand there with a palpable body and a real head, a real forehead, that is, for smiting on with one's hand.

Translated by Willa and Edwin Muir

The Tradesman

IT IS POSSIBLE that some people are sorry for me, but I am not aware of it. My small business fills me with worries that make my forehead and temples ache inside yet without giving any prospect of relief, for my business is a small business.

I have to spend hours beforehand making things ready, jogging the caretaker's memory, warning him about mistakes he is likely to commit, and puzzling out in one season of the year what the next season's fashions are to be, not such as are followed by the people I know but those that will appeal to inaccessible peasants in the depths of the country.

My money is in the hands of strangers; the state of their affairs must be a mystery to me; the ill luck that might overwhelm them I cannot foresee; how could I possibly avert it! Perhaps they are running into extravagance and giving a banquet in some inn garden, some of them may be attending the banquet as a brief respite before their flight to America.

When at the close of a working day I turn the key on my business and suddenly see before me hours in which I shall be able to do nothing to satisfy its never-ending demands, then the excitement which I drove far away from me in the morning comes back like a returning tide, but cannot be contained in me and sweeps me aimlessly away with it.

And yet I can make no use of this impulse, I can only go home, for my face and hands are dirty and sweaty, my clothes are stained and dusty, my working cap is on my head, and my shoes are scratched with the nails of crates. I go home as if lifted on a wave, snapping the fingers of both hands, and caress the hair of any children I meet.

But the way is short. Soon I reach my house, open the door of the lift, and step in.

I see that now, of a sudden, I am alone. Others who have to climb stairways tire a little as they climb, have to wait with quick panting breath till someone opens the door of the flat, which gives them an excuse for being irritable and impatient, have to traverse the hallway where hats are hung up, and not until they go down a lobby past several glass doors and come into their own room are they alone.

But I am alone in the lift, immediately, and on my knees gaze into the narrow looking glass. As the lift begins to rise, I say:

'Quiet now, back with you, is it the shadow of the trees you want to make for, or behind the window curtains, or into the garden arbor?'

I say that behind my teeth, and the staircase flows down past the opaque glass panes like running water.

'Fly then; let your wings, which I have never seen, carry you into the village hollow or as far as Paris, if that's where you want to go.

'But enjoy yourselves there looking out of the window, see the processions converging out of three streets at once, not giving way to each other but marching through each other and leaving the open space free again as their last ranks draw off. Wave your handkerchiefs, be indignant, be moved, acclaim the beautiful lady who drives past.

'Cross over the stream on the wooden bridge, nod to the children bathing and gape at the Hurrah! rising from the thousand sailors on the distant battleship.

'Follow the trail of the inconspicuous little man, and when you have pushed him into a doorway, rob him, and then watch him, each with your hands in your pockets, as he sadly goes his way along the left-hand street.

'The police dispersed on galloping horses rein in their mounts and thrust you back. Let them, the empty streets will dishearten them, I know. What did I tell you, they are riding away already in couples, slowly around the corners, at full speed across the squares.'

Then I have to leave the lift, send it down again, and ring

the bell, and the maid opens the door while I say: Good evening.

Translated by Willa and Edwin Muir

Absent-minded Window-gazing

WHAT are we to do with these spring days that are now fast coming on? Early this morning the sky was gray, but if you go to the window now you are surprised and lean your cheek against the latch of the casement.

The sun is already setting, but down below you see it lighting up the face of the little girl who strolls along looking about her, and at the same time you see her eclipsed by the shadow of the man behind overtaking her.

And then the man has passed by and the little girl's face is quite bright.

Translated by Willa and Edwin Muir

The Way Home

SEE what a persuasive force the air has after a thunderstorm! My merits become evident and overpower me, though I don't put up any resistance, I grant you.

I stride along and my tempo is the tempo of all my side of the street, of the whole street, of the whole quarter. Mine is the responsibility, and rightly so, for all the raps on doors or on the flat of a table, for all toasts drunk, for lovers in their beds, in the scaffolding of new buildings, pressed to each other against the house walls in dark alleys, or on the divans of a brothel.

I weigh my past against my future, but find both of them admirable, cannot give either the preference, and find nothing to grumble at save the injustice of providence that has so clearly favored me.

Only as I come into my room I feel a little meditative,

without having met anything on the stairs worth meditating about. It doesn't help me much to open the window wide and hear music still playing in a garden.

Translated by Willa and Edwin Muir

Passers-by

WHEN you go walking by night up a street and a man, visible a long way off – for the street mounts uphill and there is a full moon – comes running toward you, well, you don't catch hold of him, not even if he is a feeble and ragged creature, not even if someone chases yelling at his heels, but you let him run on.

For it is night, and you can't help it if the street goes uphill before you in the moonlight, and besides, these two have maybe started that chase to amuse themselves, or perhaps they are both chasing a third, perhaps the first is an innocent man and the second wants to murder him and you would become an accessory, perhaps they don't know anything about each other and are merely running separately home to bed, perhaps they are night birds, perhaps the first man is armed.

And anyhow, haven't you a right to be tired, haven't you been drinking a lot of wine? You're thankful that the second man is now long out of sight.

Translated by Willa and Edwin Muir

On the Tram

I STAND on the end platform of the tram and am completely unsure of my footing in this world, in this town, in my family. Not even casually could I indicate any claims that I might rightly advance in any direction. I have not even any defense to offer for standing on this platform, holding on to this strap, letting myself be carried along by this tram, nor for the people who give way to the tram or walk quietly along or stand gazing into shopwindows. Nobody asks me to put up a defense, indeed, but that is irrelevant.

The tram approaches a stopping place and a girl takes up her position near the step, ready to alight. She is as distinct to me as if I had run my hands over her. She is dressed in black, the pleats of her skirt hang almost still, her blouse is tight and has a collar of white fine-meshed lace, her left hand is braced flat against the side of the tram, the umbrella in her right hand rests on the second top step. Her face is brown, her nose, slightly pinched at the sides, has a broad round tip. She has a lot of brown hair and stray little tendrils on the right temple. Her small ear is close-set, but since I am near her I can see the whole ridge of the whorl of her right ear and the shadow at the root of it.

At that point I asked myself: How is it that she is not amazed at herself, that she keeps her lips closed and makes no such remark?

Translated by Willa and Edwin Muir

Clothes

OFTEN when I see clothes with manifold pleats, frills, and appendages which fit so smoothly onto lovely bodies I think they won't keep that smoothness long, but will get creases that can't be ironed out, dust lying so thick in the embroidery that it can't be brushed away, and that no one would want to be so unhappy and so foolish as to wear the same valuable gown every day from early morning till night.

And yet I see girls who are lovely enough and display attractive muscles and small bones and smooth skin and masses of delicate hair, and nonetheless appear day in, day out, in this same natural fancy dress, always propping the same face on the same palms and letting it be reflected from the looking glass.

Only sometimes at night, on coming home late from a

party, it seems in the looking glass to be worn out, puffy, dusty, already seen by too many people, and hardly wearable any longer.

Translated by Willa and Edwin Muir

Rejection

WHEN I meet a pretty girl and beg her: 'Be so good as to come with me,' and she walks past without a word, this is what she means to say:

'You are no Duke with a famous name, no broad American with a Red Indian figure, level, brooding eyes and a skin tempered by the air of the prairies and the rivers that flow through them, you have never journeyed to the seven seas and voyaged on them wherever they may be, I don't know where. So why, pray, should a pretty girl like myself go with you?'

'You forget that no automobile swings you through the street in long thrusts; I see no gentlemen escorting you in a close half-circle, pressing on your skirts from behind and murmuring blessings on your head; your breasts are well laced into your bodice, but your thighs and hips make up for that restraint; you are wearing a taffeta dress with a pleated skirt such as delighted all of us last autumn, and yet you smile – inviting mortal danger – from time to time.'

'Yes, we're both in the right, and to keep us from being irrevocably aware of it, hadn't we better just go our separate ways home?'

Translated by Willa and Edwin Muir

Reflections for Gentlemen-jockeys

WHEN you think it over, winning a race is nothing to sigh for.

The fame of being hailed as the best rider in the country is too intoxicating a pleasure when the applause strikes up not to bring a reaction the morning after.

The envy of your opponents, cunning and fairly influential men, must trouble you in the narrow enclosure you now traverse after the flat racecourse, which soon lay empty before you save for some laggards of the previous round, small figures charging the horizon.

Many of your friends are rushing to gather their winnings and only cry 'Hurrah!' to you over their shoulders from distant pay boxes; your best friends laid no bet on your horse, since they feared that they would have to be angry with you if you lost, and now that your horse has come in first and they have won nothing, they turn away as you pass and prefer to look along the stands.

Your rivals behind you, firmly in the saddle, are trying to ignore the bad luck that has befallen them and the injustice they have somehow suffered; they are putting a brave new face on things, as if a different race were due to start, and this time a serious one after such child's play.

For many ladies the victor cuts a ridiculous figure because he is swelling with importance and yet cannot cope with the never-ending handshaking, saluting, bowing, and waving, while the defeated keep their mouths shut and casually pat the necks of their whinnying horses.

And finally from the now overcast sky rain actually begins to fall.

Translated by Willa and Edwin Muir

The Street Window

WHOEVER leads a solitary life and yet now and then wants to attach himself somewhere, whoever, according to changes in the time of day, the weather, the state of his business, and the like, suddenly wishes to see any arm at all to which he might cling – he will not be able to manage for long without a window looking on to the street. And if he is in the mood of not desiring anything and only goes to his window sill a tired man, with eyes turning from his public to heaven and back again, not wanting to look out and having thrown his head up a little, even then the horses below will draw him down into their train of wagons and tumult, and so at last into the human harmony.

Translated by Willa and Edwin Muir

The Wish to be a Red Indian

IF ONE WERE only an Indian, instantly alert, and on a racing horse, leaning against the wind, kept on quivering jerkily over the quivering ground, until one shed one's spurs, for there needed no spurs, threw away the reins, for there needed no reins, and hardly saw that the land before one was smoothly shorn heath when horse's neck and head would be already gone.

Translated by Willa and Edwin Muir

The Trees

FOR WE are like tree trunks in the snow. In appearance they lie sleekly and a little push should be enough to set them rolling. No, it can't be done, for they are firmly wedded to the ground. But see, even that is only appearance.

Translated by Willa and Edwin Muir

Unhappiness

WHEN it was becoming unbearable – once toward evening in November – and I ran along the narrow strip of carpet in my room as on a racetrack, shrank from the sight of the lit-up street, then turning to the interior of the room found a new goal in the depths of the looking glass and screamed aloud, to hear only my own scream which met no answer nor anything that could draw its force away, so that it rose up without check and could not stop even when it ceased being audible, the door in the wall opened toward me, how swiftly, because swiftness was needed and even the cart horses down below on the paving stones were rising in the air like horses driven wild in a battle, their throats bare to the enemy.

Like a small ghost a child blew in from the pitch-dark corridor, where the lamp was not yet lit, and stood a-tiptoe on a floor board that quivered imperceptibly. At once dazzled by the twilight in my room she made to cover her face quickly with her hands, but contented herself unexpectedly with a glance at the window, where the mounting vapor of the street lighting had at last settled under its cover of darkness behind the crossbars. With her right elbow she supported herself against the wall in the open doorway and let the draught from outside play along her ankles, her throat, and her temples.

I gave her a brief glance, then said 'Good day,' and took my jacket from the hood of the stove, since I didn't want to stand there half-undressed. For a little while I let my mouth hang open, so that my agitation could find a way out. I had a bad taste in my mouth, my eyelashes were fluttering on my cheeks, in short this visit, though I had expected it, was the one thing needful.

The child was still standing by the wall on the same spot, she had pressed her right hand against the plaster and was quite taken up with finding, her cheeks all pink, that the whitewashed walls had a rough surface and chafed her finger tips. I said: 'Are you really looking for me? Isn't there some mistake? Nothing easier than to make a mistake in this big building. I'm called So-and-so and I live on the third floor. Am I the person you want to find?'

'Hush, hush,' said the child over her shoulder, 'it's all right.'

'Then come farther into the room, I'd like to shut the door.'

'I've shut it this very minute. Don't bother. Just be easy in your mind.'

'It's no bother. But there's a lot of people living on this corridor, and I know them all, of course; most of them are coming back from work now; if they hear someone talking in a room, they simply think they have a right to open the door and see what's happening. They're just like that. They've turned their backs on their daily work and in their provisionally free evenings they're not going to be dictated to by anyone. Besides, you know that as well as I do. Let me shut the door.'

'Why, what's the matter with you? I don't mind if the whole house comes in. Anyhow, as I told you, I've already shut the door, do you think you're the only person who can shut doors? I've even turned the key in the lock.'

'That's all right then. I couldn't ask for more. You didn't need to turn the key, either. And now that you are here, make yourself comfortable. You are my guest. You can trust me entirely. Just make yourself at home and don't be afraid. I won't compel you either to stay or to go away. Do I have to tell you that? Do you know me so little?'

'No. You really didn't need to tell me that. What's more, you shouldn't have told me. I'm just a child; why stand on so much ceremony with me?'

'It's not so bad as that. A child, of course. But not so very small. You're quite big. If you were a young lady, you wouldn't dare to lock yourself so simply in a room with me.'

'We needn't worry about that. I just want to say: my knowing you so well isn't much protection to me, it only relieves you of the effort of keeping up pretenses before me. And yet you're paying me a compliment. Stop it, I beg you, do stop it. Anyhow, I don't know you everywhere and all the time, least of all in this darkness. It would be much better if you were to light up. No, perhaps not. At any rate I'll keep it in mind that you have been threatening me.'

'What? Am I supposed to have threatened you? But, look here. I'm so pleased that you've come at last. I say "at last" because it's already rather late. I can't understand why you've come so late. But it's possible that in the joy of seeing you I have been speaking at random and you took up my words in the wrong sense. I'll admit ten times over that I said something of the kind, I've made all kinds of threats, anything you like. Only no quarreling, for Heaven's sake! But how could you think of such a thing? How could you hurt me so? Why do you insist on spoiling this brief moment of your presence here? A stranger would be more obliging than you are.'

'That I can well believe; that's no great discovery. No stranger could come any nearer to you than I am already by nature. You know that, too, so why all this pathos? If you're only wanting to stage a comedy I'll go away immediately.'

'What? You have the impudence to tell me that? You make a little too bold. After all, it's my room you're in. It's my wall you're rubbing your fingers on like mad. My room, my wall! And besides, what you are saying is ridiculous as well as impudent. You say your nature forces you to speak to me like that. Is that so? Your nature forces you? That's kind of your nature. Your nature is mine, and if I feel friendly to you by nature, then you mustn't be anything else.'

'Is that friendly?'

'I'm speaking of earlier on.'

'Do you know how I'll be later on?'

'I don't know anything.'

And I went to the bed table and lit the candle on it. At that time I had neither gas nor electric light in my room. Then I sat for a while at the table till I got tired of it, put on my greatcoat, took my hat from the sofa, and blew out the candle. As I went out I tripped over the leg of a chair.

On the stairs I met one of the tenants from my floor.

'Going out again already, you rascal?' he asked, pausing with his legs firmly straddled over two steps.

'What can I do?' I said, 'I've just had a ghost in my room.'

'You say that exactly as if you had just found a hair in your soup.'

'You're making a joke of it. But let me tell you, a ghost is a ghost.'

'How true. But what if one doesn't believe in ghosts at all?'

'Well, do you think I believe in ghosts? But how can my not believing help me?'

'Quite simply. You don't need to feel afraid if a ghost actually turns up.'

'Oh, that's only a secondary fear. The real fear is a fear of what caused the apparition. And that fear doesn't go away. I have it fairly powerfully inside me now.' Out of sheer nervousness I began to hunt through all my pockets.

'But since you weren't afraid of the ghost itself, you could easily have asked it how it came to be there.'

'Obviously you've never spoken to a ghost. One never gets straight information from them. It's just a hither and thither. These ghosts seem to be more dubious about their existence than we are, and no wonder, considering how frail they are.'

'But I've heard that one can fatten them up.'

'How well informed you are. It's quite true. But is anyone likely to do it?'

'Why not? If it were a feminine ghost, for instance,' said he, swinging onto the top step.

'Aha,' said I, 'but even then it's not worth while.'

I thought of something else. My neighbor was already so far up that in order to see me he had to bend over the well of the staircase. 'All the same,' I called up, 'if you steal my ghost from me all is over between us, forever.'

'Oh, I was only joking,' he said and drew his head back.

'That's all right,' said I, and now I really could have gone quietly for a walk. But because I felt so forlorn I preferred to go upstairs again and so went to bed.

Translated by Willa and Edwin Muir

The Judgment (1913)

The Judgment

IT WAS a Sunday morning in the very height of spring. Georg Bendemann, a young merchant, was sitting in his own room on the first floor of one of a long row of small, ramshackle houses stretching beside the river which were scarcely distinguishable from each other in height and coloring. He had just finished a letter to an old friend of his who was now living abroad, had put it into its envelope in a slow and dreamy fashion, and with his elbows propped on the writing table was gazing out of the window at the river, the bridge, and the hills on the farther bank with their tender green.

He was thinking about his friend, who had actually run away to Russia some years before, being dissatisfied with his prospects at home. Now he was carrying on a business in St. Petersburg, which had flourished to begin with but had long been going downhill, as he always complained on his increasingly rare visits. So he was wearing himself out to no purpose in a foreign country, the unfamiliar full beard he wore did not quite conceal the face Georg had known so well since childhood, and his skin was growing so yellow as to indicate some latent disease. By his own account he had no regular connection with the colony of his fellow countrymen out there and almost no social intercourse with Russian families, so that he was resigning himself to becoming a permanent bachelor.

What could one write to such a man, who had obviously run off the rails, a man one could be sorry for but could not help. Should one advise him to come home, to transplant himself and take up his old friendships again – there was nothing to hinder him – and in general to rely on the help of his friends? But that was as good as telling him, and the more kindly the more offensively, that all his efforts hitherto had miscarried, that he should finally give up, come back home, and be gaped at by everyone as a returned prodigal, that only his friends knew what was what and that he himself was just a big child who should do what his successful and home-keeping friends prescribed. And was it certain, besides, that all the pain one would have to inflict on him would achieve its object? Perhaps it would not even be possible to get him to come home at all – he said himself that he was now out of touch with commerce in his native country – and then he would still be left an alien in a foreign land embittered by his friends' advice and more than ever estranged from them. But if he did follow their advice and then didn't fit in at home – not out of malice, of course, but through force of circumstances – couldn't get on with his friends or without them, felt humiliated, couldn't be said to have either friends or a country of his own any longer, wouldn't it have been better for him to stay abroad just as he was? Taking all this into account, how could one be sure that he would make a success of life at home?

For such reasons, supposing one wanted to keep up correspondence with him, one could not send him any real news such as could frankly be told to the most distant acquaintance. It was more than three years since his last visit, and for this he offered the lame excuse that the political situation in Russia was too uncertain, which apparently would not permit even the briefest absence of a small businessman while it allowed hundreds of thousands of Russians to travel peacefully abroad. But during these three years Georg's own position in life had changed a lot. Two years ago his mother had died, since when he and his father had shared the household together, and his friend had of course been informed of that and had expressed his sympathy in a letter phrased so dryly that the grief caused by such an event, one had to conclude, could not be realized in a distant country. Since that time, however, Georg had applied himself with greater determination to the business as well as to everything else.

Perhaps during his mother's lifetime his father's insistence on having everything his own way in the business had hindered him from developing any real activity of his own, perhaps since her death his father had become less aggressive, although he was still active in the business, perhaps it was mostly due to an accidental run of good fortune – which was very probable indeed – but at any rate during those two years the business had developed in a most unexpected way, the staff had had to be doubled, the turnover was five times as great; no doubt about it, further progress lay just ahead.

But Georg's friend had no inkling of this improvement. In earlier years, perhaps for the last time in that letter of condolence, he had tried to persuade Georg to emigrate to Russia and had enlarged upon the prospects of success for precisely Georg's branch of trade. The figures quoted were microscopic by comparison with the range of Georg's present operations. Yet he shrank from letting his friend know about his business success, and if he were to do it now retrospectively that certainly would look peculiar.

So Georg confined himself to giving his friend unimportant items of gossip such as rise at random in the memory when one is idly thinking things over on a quiet Sunday. All he desired was to leave undisturbed the idea of the home town which his friend must have built up to his own content during the long interval. And so it happened to Georg that three times in three fairly widely separated letters he had told his friend about the engagement of an unimportant man to an equally unimportant girl, until indeed, quite contrary to his intentions, his friend began to show some interest in this notable event.

Yet Georg preferred to write about things like these rather than to confess that he himself had got engaged a month ago to a Fräulein Frieda Brandenfeld, a girl from a well-to-do family. He often discussed this friend of his with his fiancée and the peculiar relationship that had developed between them in their correspondence. 'So he won't be coming to our wedding,' said she, 'and yet I have a right to get to know all your friends.' 'I don't want to trouble him,' answered Georg, 'don't misunderstand me, he would probably come, at least I think so, but he would feel that his hand had been forced and he would be hurt, perhaps he would envy me and certainly he'd be discontented and without being able to do anything about his discontent he'd have to go away again alone. Alone – do you know what that means?' 'Yes, but may he not hear about our wedding in some other fashion?' 'I can't prevent that, of course, but it's unlikely, considering the way he lives.' 'Since your friends are like that, Georg, you shouldn't ever have got engaged at all.' 'Well, we're both to blame for that; but I wouldn't have it any other way now.' And when, breathing quickly under his kisses, she still brought out: 'All the same, I do feel upset,' he thought it could not really involve him in trouble were he to send the news to his friend. 'That's the kind of man I am and he'll just have to take me as I am,' he said to himself, 'I can't cut myself to another pattern that might make a more suitable friend for him.'

And in fact he did inform his friend, in the long letter he had been writing that Sunday morning, about his engagement, with these words: 'I have saved my best news to the end. I have got engaged to a Fräulein Frieda Brandenfeld, a girl from a well-to-do family, who only came to live here a long time after you went away, so that you're hardly likely to know her. There will be time to tell you more about her later, for today let me just say that I am very happy and as between you and me the only difference in our relationship is that instead of a quite ordinary kind of friend you will now have in me a happy friend. Besides that, you will acquire in my fiancée, who sends her warm greetings and will soon write you herself, a genuine friend of the opposite sex, which is not without importance to a bachelor. I know that there are many reasons why you can't come to see us, but would not my wedding be precisely the right occasion for giving all obstacles the go-by? Still, however that may be, do just as seems good to you without regarding any interests but your own.'

With this letter in his hand Georg had been sitting a

long time at the writing table, his face turned toward the window. He had barely acknowledged, with an absent smile, a greeting waved to him from the street by a passing acquaintance.

At last he put the letter in his pocket and went out of his room across a small lobby into his father's room, which he had not entered for months. There was in fact no need for him to enter it, since he saw his father daily at business and they took their midday meal together at an eating house; in the evening, it was true, each did as he pleased, yet even then, unless Georg – as mostly happened – went out with friends or, more recently, visited his fiancée, they always sat for a while, each with his newspaper, in their common sitting room.

It surprised Georg how dark his father's room was even on this sunny morning. So it was overshadowed as much as that by the high wall on the other side of the narrow courtyard. His father was sitting by the window in a corner hung with various mementoes of Georg's dead mother, reading a newspaper which he held to one side before his eyes in an attempt to overcome a defect of vision. On the table stood the remains of his breakfast, not much of which seemed to have been eaten.

'Ah, Georg,' said his father, rising at once to meet him. His heavy dressing gown swung open as he walked and the skirts of it fluttered around him. – 'My father is still a giant of a man,' said Georg to himself.

'It's unbearably dark here,' he said aloud.

'Yes, it's dark enough,' answered his father.

'And you've shut the window, too?'

'I prefer it like that.'

'Well, it's quite warm outside,' said Georg, as if continuing his previous remark, and sat down.

His father cleared away the breakfast dishes and set them on a chest.

'I really only wanted to tell you,' went on Georg, who had been vacantly following the old man's movements, 'that

I am now sending the news of my engagement to St. Petersburg.' He drew the letter a little way from his pocket and let it drop back again.

'To St. Petersburg?' asked his father.

'To my friend there,' said Georg, trying to meet his father's eye. – In business hours he's quite different, he was thinking, how solidly he sits here with his arms crossed.

'Oh yes. To your friend,' said his father, with peculiar emphasis.

'Well, you know, Father, that I wanted not to tell him about my engagement at first. Out of consideration for him, that was the only reason. You know yourself he's a difficult man. I said to myself that someone else might tell him about my engagement, although he's such a solitary creature that that was hardly likely – I couldn't prevent that – but I wasn't ever going to tell him myself.'

'And now you've changed your mind?' asked his father, laying his enormous newspaper on the window sill and on top of it his spectacles, which he covered with one hand.

'Yes, I've been thinking it over. If he's a good friend of mine, I said to myself, my being happily engaged should make him happy too. And so I wouldn't put off telling him any longer. But before I posted the letter I wanted to let you know.'

'Georg,' said his father, lengthening his toothless mouth, 'listen to me! You've come to me about this business, to talk it over with me. No doubt that does you honor. But it's nothing, it's worse than nothing, if you don't tell me the whole truth. I don't want to stir up matters that shouldn't be mentioned here. Since the death of our dear mother certain things have been done that aren't right. Maybe the time will come for mentioning them, and maybe sooner than we think. There's many a thing in the business I'm not aware of, maybe it's not done behind my back – I'm not going to say that it's done behind my back – I'm not equal to things any longer, my memory's failing, I haven't an eye for so many things any longer. That's the course of nature in the first place, and in the second place the death of our dear mother hit me harder than it did you. – But since we're talking about it, about this letter, I beg you, Georg, don't deceive me. It's a trivial affair, it's hardly worth mentioning, so don't deceive me. Do you really have this friend in St. Petersburg?'

Georg rose in embarrassment. 'Never mind my friends. A thousand friends wouldn't make up to me for my father. Do you know what I think? You're not taking enough care of yourself. But old age must be taken care of. I can't do without you in the business, you know that very well, but if the business is going to undermine your health, I'm ready to close it down tomorrow forever. And that won't do. We'll have to make a change in your way of living. But a radical change. You sit here in the dark, and in the sitting room you would have plenty of light. You just take a bite of breakfast instead of properly keeping up your strength. You sit by a closed window, and the air would be so good for you. No, Father! I'll get the doctor to come, and we'll follow his orders. We'll change your room, you can move into the front room and I'll move in here. You won't notice the change, all your things will be moved with you. But there's time for all that later, I'll put you to bed now for a little, I'm sure you need to rest. Come, I'll help you to take off your things, you'll see I can do it. Or if you would rather go into the front room at once, you can lie down in my bed for the present. That would be the most sensible thing.'

Georg stood close beside his father, who had let his head with its unkempt white hair sink on his chest.

'Georg,' said his father in a low voice, without moving.

Georg knelt down at once beside his father, in the old man's weary face he saw the pupils, overlarge, fixedly looking at him from the corners of the eyes.

'You have no friend in St. Petersburg. You've always been a leg-puller and you haven't even shrunk from pulling my leg. How could you have a friend out there! I can't believe it.'

'Just think back a bit, Father,' said Georg, lifting his father from the chair and slipping off his dressing gown as he stood feebly enough, 'it'll soon be three years since my friend came to see us last. I remember that you used not to like him very much. At least twice I kept you from seeing him, although he was actually sitting with me in my room. I could quite well understand your dislike of him, my friend has his peculiarities. But then, later, you got on with him very well. I was proud because you listened to him and nodded and asked him questions. If you think back you're bound to remember. He used to tell us the most incredible stories of the Russian Revolution. For instance, when he was on a business trip to Kiev and ran into a riot, and saw a priest on a balcony who cut a broad cross in blood on the palm of his hand and held the hand up and appealed to the mob. You've told that story yourself once or twice since.'

Meanwhile Georg had succeeded in lowering his father down again and carefully taking off the woolen drawers he wore over his linen underpants and his socks. The not particularly clean appearance of his underwear made him reproach himself for having been neglectful. It should have certainly been his duty to see that his father had clean changes of underwear. He had not yet explicitly discussed with his bride-to-be what arrangements should be made for his father in the future, for they had both of them silently taken it for granted that the old man would go on living alone in the old house. But now he made a quick, firm decision to take him into his own future establishment. It almost looked, on closer inspection, as if the care he meant to lavish there on his father might come too late.

He carried his father to bed in his arms. It gave him a dreadful feeling to notice that while he took the few steps toward the bed the old man on his breast was playing with his watch chain. He could not lay him down on the bed for a moment, so firmly did he hang on to the watch chain.

But as soon as he was laid in bed, all seemed well. He

covered himself up and even drew the blankets farther than usual over his shoulders. He looked up at Georg with a not unfriendly eye.

'You begin to remember my friend, don't you?' asked Georg, giving him an encouraging nod.

'Am I well covered up now?' asked his father, as if he were not able to see whether his feet were properly tucked in or not.

'So you find it snug in bed already,' said Georg, and tucked the blankets more closely around him.

'Am I well covered up?' asked the father once more, seeming to be strangely intent upon the answer.

'Don't worry, you're well covered up.'

'No!' cried his father, cutting short the answer, threw the blankets off with a strength that sent them all flying in a moment and sprang erect in bed. Only one hand lightly touched the ceiling to steady him.

'You wanted to cover me up, I know, my young sprig, but I'm far from being covered up yet. And even if this is the last strength I have, it's enough for you, too much for you. Of course I know your friend. He would have been a son after my own heart. That's why you've been playing him false all these years. Why else? Do you think I haven't been sorry for him? And that's why you had to lock yourself up in your office – the Chief is busy, mustn't be disturbed – just so that you could write your lying little letters to Russia. But thank goodness a father doesn't need to be taught how to see through his son. And now that you thought you'd got him down, so far down that you could set your bottom on him and sit on him and he wouldn't move, then my fine son makes up his mind to get married!'

Georg stared at the bogey conjured up by his father. His friend in St. Petersburg, whom his father suddenly knew too well, touched his imagination as never before. Lost in the vastness of Russia he saw him. At the door of an empty, plundered warehouse he saw him. Among the wreckage of his showcases, the slashed remnants of his wares, the falling gas brackets, he was just standing up. Why did he have to go so far away!

'But attend to me!' cried his father, and Georg, almost distracted, ran toward the bed to take everything in, yet came to a stop halfway.

'Because she lifted up her skirts,' his father began to flute, 'because she lifted her skirts like this, the nasty creature,' and mimicking her he lifted his shirt so high that one could see the scar on his thigh from his war wound, 'because she lifted her skirts like this and this you made up to her, and in order to make free with her undisturbed you have disgraced your mother's memory, betrayed your friend, and stuck your father into bed so that he can't move. But he can move, or can't he?'

And he stood up quite unsupported and kicked his legs out. His insight made him radiant.

Georg shrank into a corner, as far away from his father as possible. A long time ago he had firmly made up his mind to watch closely every least movement so that he should not be surprised by any indirect attack, a pounce from behind or above. At this moment he recalled this long-forgotten resolve and forgot it again, like a man drawing a short thread through the eye of a needle.

'But your friend hasn't been betrayed after all!' cried his father, emphasizing the point with stabs of his forefinger. 'I've been representing him here on the spot.'

'You comedian!' Georg could not resist the retort, realized at once the harm done and, his eyes starting in his head, bit his tongue back, only too late, till the pain made his knees give.

'Yes, of course I've been playing a comedy! A comedy! That's a good expression! What other comfort was left to a poor old widower? Tell me – and while you're answering me be you still my living son – what else was left to me, in my back room, plagued by a disloyal staff, old to the marrow of my bones? And my son strutting through the world, finishing off deals that I had prepared for him, bursting with triumphant glee, and stalking away from his father with the closed face of a respectable businessman! Do you think I didn't love you, I, from whom you are sprung?'

Now he'll lean forward, thought Georg, what if he topples and smashes himself! These words went hissing through his mind.

His father leaned forward but did not topple. Since Georg did not come any nearer, as he had expected, he straightened himself again.

'Stay where you are, I don't need you! You think you have strength enough to come over here and that you're only hanging back of your own accord. Don't be too sure! I am still much the stronger of us two. All by myself I might have had to give way, but your mother has given me so much of her strength that I've established a fine connection with your friend and I have your customers here in my pocket!'

'He has pockets even in his shirt!' said Georg to himself, and believed that with this remark he could make him an impossible figure for all the world. Only for a moment did he think so, since he kept on forgetting everything.

'Just take your bride on your arm and try getting in my way! I'll sweep her from your very side, you don't know how!'

Georg made a grimace of disbelief. His father only nodded, confirming the truth of his words, toward Georg's corner.

'How you amused me today, coming to ask me if you should tell your friend about your engagement. He knows it already, you stupid boy, he knows it all! I've been writing to him, for you forgot to take my writing things away from me. That's why he hasn't been here for years, he knows everything a hundred times better than you do yourself, in his left hand he crumples your letters unopened while in his right hand he holds up my letters to read through!'

In his enthusiasm he waved his arm over his head. 'He knows everything a thousand times better!' he cried.

'Ten thousand times!' said Georg, to make fun of his

father, but in his very mouth the words turned into deadly earnest.

'For years I've been waiting for you to come with some such question! Do you think I concern myself with anything else? Do you think I read my newspapers? Look!' and he threw Georg a newspaper sheet which he had somehow taken to bed with him. An old newspaper, with a name entirely unknown to Georg.

'How long a time you've taken to grow up! Your mother had to die, she couldn't see the happy day, your friend is going to pieces in Russia, even three years ago he was yellow enough to be thrown away, and as for me, you see what condition I'm in. You have eyes in your head for that!'

'So you've been lying in wait for me!' cried Georg.

His father said pityingly, in an offhand manner: 'I suppose you wanted to say that sooner. But now it doesn't matter.' And in a louder voice: 'So now you know what else there was in the world besides yourself, till now you've known only about yourself! An innocent child, yes, that you were, truly, but still more truly have you been a devilish human being! – And therefore take note: I sentence you now to death by drowning!'

Georg felt himself urged from the room, the crash with which his father fell on the bed behind him was still in his ears as he fled. On the staircase, which he rushed down as if its steps were an inclined plane, he ran into his charwoman on her way up to do the morning cleaning of the room. 'Jesus!' she cried, and covered her face with her apron, but he was already gone. Out of the front door he rushed, across the roadway, driven toward the water. Already he was grasping at the railings as a starving man clutches food. He swung himself over, like the distinguished gymnast he had once been in his youth, to his parents' pride. With weakening grip he was still holding on when he spied between the railings a motor-bus coming which would easily cover the noise of his fall, called in a low voice: 'Dear parents,

I have always loved you, all the same,' and let himself drop.

At this moment an unending stream of traffic was just going over the bridge.

Translated by Willa and Edwin Muir

The Stoker (1913)

The Stoker

AS KARL ROSSMANN, a poor boy of sixteen who had been packed off to America by his parents because a servant girl had seduced him and got herself with child by him, stood on the liner slowly entering the harbor of New York, a sudden burst of sunshine seemed to illumine the Statue of Liberty, so that he saw it in a new light, although he had sighted it long before. The arm with the sword rose up as if newly stretched aloft, and round the figure blew the free winds of heaven.

'So high!' he said to himself, and was gradually edged to the very rail by the swelling throng of porters pushing past him, since he was not thinking at all of getting off the ship.

A young man with whom he had struck up a slight acquaintance on the voyage called out in passing: 'Not very anxious to go ashore, are you?' 'Oh, I'm quite ready,' said Karl with a laugh, and being both strong and in high spirits he heaved his box onto his shoulder. But as his eye followed his acquaintance, who was already moving on among the others, lightly swinging a walking-stick, he realized with dismay that he had forgotten his umbrella down below. He hastily begged his acquaintance, who did not seem particularly gratified, to oblige him by waiting beside the box for a minute, took another survey of the situation to get his bearings for the return journey, and hurried away. Below decks he found to his disappointment that a gangway which made a handy short-cut had been barred for the first time in his experience, probably in connexion with the disembarkation of so many passengers, and he had painfully to find his way down endlessly recurring stairs, through corridors with countless turnings, through an empty room with a deserted writing-table, until in the end, since he had taken this route no more than once or twice and always among a crowd of other people, he lost himself completely. In his bewilderment, meeting no one and hearing nothing but the ceaseless shuffling of thousands of feet above him, and in the distance, like faint breathing, the last throbbings of the engines, which had already been shut off, he began unthinkingly to hammer on a little door by which he had chanced to stop in his wanderings.

'It isn't locked,' a voice shouted from inside, and Karl opened the door with genuine relief. 'What are you hammering at the door for, like a madman?' asked a huge man, scarcely even glancing at Karl. Through an opening of some kind a feeble glimmer of daylight, all that was left after the top decks had used it up, fell into the wretched cubby-hole in which a bunk, a cupboard, a chair and the man were packed together, as if they had been stored there. 'I've lost my way,' said Karl. 'I never noticed it during the voyage, but this is a terribly big ship.' 'Yes, you're right there,' said the man with a certain pride, fiddling all the time with the lock of a little sea-chest, which he kept pressing with both hands in the hope of hearing the wards snap home. 'But come inside,' he went on, 'you don't want to stand out there!' 'I'm not disturbing you?' asked Karl. 'Why, how should you disturb me?' 'Are you a German?' Karl asked to reassure himself further, for he had heard a great deal about the perils which threatened newcomers to America, particularly from the Irish. 'That's what I am, yes,' said the man. Karl still hesitated. Then the man suddenly seized the door handle and pulling the door shut with a hasty movement swept Karl into the cabin.

'I can't stand being stared at from the passage,' he said, beginning to fiddle with his chest again, 'people keep passing and staring in, it's more than a man can bear.' 'But the passage is quite empty,' said Karl, who was standing squeezed uncomfortably against the end of the bunk. 'Yes, now,' said the man. 'But it's now we were speaking about,' thought Karl, 'it's hard work talking to this man.' 'Lie down on the bunk, you'll have more room there,' said the man. Karl scrambled in as well as he could, and laughed aloud at his first unsuccessful attempt to swing himself over. But scarcely was he in the bunk when he cried: 'Good Lord, I've quite forgotten my box!' 'Why, where is it?' 'Up on deck, a man I know is looking after it. What's his name again?' And he fished a visiting-card from a pocket which his mother had made in the lining of his coat for the voyage. 'Butterbaum, Franz Butterbaum.' 'Can't you do without your box?' 'Of course not.' 'Well, then, why did you leave it in a stranger's hands?' 'I forgot my umbrella down below and rushed off to get it; I didn't want to drag my box with me. Then on top of that I got lost.' 'You're all alone? Without anyone to look after you?' 'Yes, all alone.' 'Perhaps I should join up with this man,' the thought came into Karl's head, 'where am I likely to find a better friend?' 'And now you've lost the box as well. Not to mention the umbrella.' And the man sat down on the chair as if Karl's business had at last acquired some interest for him. 'But I think my box can't be lost yet.' 'You can think what you like,' said the man, vigorously scratching his dark, short, thick hair. 'But morals change every time you come to a new port. In Hamburg your Butterbaum might maybe have looked after your box; while here it's most likely that they've both disappeared.' 'But then I must go up and see about it at once,' said Karl, looking round for the way out. 'You just stay where you are,' said the man, giving him a push with one hand on the chest, quite roughly, so that he fell back on the bunk again. 'But why?' asked Karl in exasperation. 'Because there's no point in it,' said the man, 'I'm leaving too very soon, and we can go together. Either the box is stolen and then there's no help for it, or the man has left it standing where it was, and then we'll find it all the more easily when the ship is empty. And the same with your umbrella.' 'Do you know your way about the ship?' asked Karl suspiciously, and it seemed to him that the idea, otherwise plausible, that his things would be easier to find when the ship was empty must have a catch in it somewhere. 'Why, I'm a stoker,' said the man. 'You're a stoker!' cried Karl delightedly, as if this surpassed all his expectations, and he rose up on his elbow to look at the man more closely. 'Just outside the room where I slept with the Slovaks there was a little window through which we could see into the engine room.' 'Yes, that's where I've been working,' said the stoker. 'I have always had a passion for machinery,' said Karl, following his own train of thought, 'and I would have become an engineer in time, that's certain, if I hadn't had to go to America.' 'Why did you have to go?' 'Oh, that!' said Karl, dismissing the whole business with a wave of the hand. He looked with a smile at the stoker, as if begging his indulgence for not telling. 'There was some reason for it, I suppose,' said the stoker, and it was hard to tell whether in saying that he wanted to encourage or discourage Karl to tell. 'I could be a stoker now too,' said Karl, 'it's all one now to my father and mother what becomes of me.' 'My job's going to be free,' said the stoker, and to point his full consciousness of it, he stuck his hands into his trouser pockets and flung his legs in their baggy, leather-like trousers on the bunk to stretch them. Karl had to shift nearer to the wall. 'Are you leaving the ship?' 'Yes, we're paid off today.' 'But why? Don't you like it?' 'Oh, that's the way things are run; it doesn't always depend on whether a man likes it or not. But you're quite right, I don't like it. I don't suppose you're thinking seriously of being a stoker, but that's just the time when you're most likely to turn into one. So I advise you strongly against it. If you wanted to study engineering in Europe, why shouldn't you study it here? The American universities are ever so much better than the European ones.' 'That's possible,' said Karl, 'but I have hardly any money to study on. I've read of someone who worked all day in a shop and studied at night until he became a doctor, and a mayor, too, I think, but that needs a lot of perseverance, doesn't it? I'm afraid I haven't got that. Besides, I wasn't a particularly good scholar; it was no great wrench for me to leave school. And maybe the schools here are more difficult. I can hardly speak any English at all. Anyhow, people here have a prejudice against foreigners, I think.' 'So you've come up against that kind of thing too, have you? Well, that's all to the good. You're the man for me. See here, this is a German ship we're on, it belongs to the Hamburg-American Line; so why aren't the crew all Germans, I ask you? Why is the Chief Engineer a Roumanian? A man called Schubal. It's hard to believe it. A measly hound like that slave-driving us Germans on a German ship! You mustn't think' – here his voice failed him and he gesticulated with his hands – 'that I'm complaining for the sake of complaining. I know you have no influence and that you're a poor lad yourself. But it's too much!' And he brought his fist several times down on the table, never taking his eyes from it while he flourished it. 'I've signed on in ever so many ships' – and he reeled off twenty names one after the other as if they were one word, which quite confused Karl – 'and I've done good work in all of them, been praised, pleased every captain I ever had, actually stuck to the same cargo boat for several years, I did' – he rose to his feet as if that had been the greatest achievement of his life – 'and here on this tub, where everything's done by rule and you don't need any wits at all, here I'm no good, here I'm just in Schubal's way, here I'm a slacker who should be kicked out and doesn't begin to earn his pay. Can you understand that? I can't.' 'Don't you put up with it!' said Karl excitedly. He had almost lost the feeling that he was on the uncertain boards of a ship, beside the coast of an unknown continent, so much at home did he feel here in the stoker's bunk. 'Have you seen the Captain about it? Have you asked him to give you your rights?' 'Oh, get away with you, out you get, I don't want you here. You don't listen to what I say, and then you give me advice. How could I go to the Captain?' Wearily the stoker sat down again and hid his face in his hands.

'I can't give him any better advice,' Karl told himself. And it occurred to him that he would have done better to go and get his box instead of handing out advice that was merely regarded as stupid. When his father had given him the box for good he had said in jest: 'How long will you keep it?' and now that faithful box had perhaps been lost in earnest. His sole remaining consolation was that his father could hardly learn of his present situation, even if he were to inquire. All that the shipping company could say was that he had safely reached New York. But Karl felt sorry to think that he had hardly used the things in the box yet, although, to take an instance, he should long since have changed his shirt. So his economies had started at the wrong point, it seemed; now, at the very beginning of his career, when it was essential to show himself in clean clothes, he would have to appear in a dirty shirt. Otherwise the loss of the box would not have been so serious, for the suit which he was wearing was actually better than the one in the box, which in reality was merely an emergency suit that his mother had hastily mended just before he left. Then he remembered that in the box there was a piece of Veronese salami which his mother had packed as an extra tit-bit, only he had not been able to eat more than a scrap of it, for during the voyage he had been quite without any appetite, and the soup which was served in the steerage had been more than sufficient for him. But now he would have liked to have the salami at hand, so as to present it to the stoker. For such people were easily won over by the gift of some trifle or other; Karl had learned that from his father, who deposited cigars in the pockets of the subordinate officials with whom he did business, and so won them over. Yet all that Karl now possessed in the way of gifts was his money, and he did not want to touch that for the time being, in case he should have lost his box. Again his thoughts turned back to the box, and he simply could not understand why he should have watched it during the voyage so vigilantly that he had almost lost his sleep over it, only to let that same box be filched from him so easily now. He remembered the five nights during which he had kept a suspicious eye on a little Slovak whose bunk was two places away from him on the left, and who had designs, he was sure, on the box. This Slovak was merely waiting for Karl to be overcome by sleep and doze off for a minute, so that he might maneuver the box away with a long, pointed stick which he was always playing or practicing with during the day. By day the Slovak looked innocent enough, but hardly did night come on than he kept rising up from his bunk to cast melancholy glances at Karl's box. Karl had seen this quite clearly, for every now and then someone would light a little candle, although it was forbidden by the ship's regulations, and with the anxiety of the emigrant would peer into some incomprehensible prospectus of an emigration agency. If one of these candles was burning near him, Karl could doze off for a little, but if it was farther away or if the place was quite dark, he had to keep his eyes open. The strain of this task had quite exhausted him, and now perhaps it had all been in vain. Oh, that Butterbaum, if ever he met him again!

At that moment, in the distance, the unbroken silence was disturbed by a series of small, short taps, like the tapping of children's feet; they came nearer, growing louder, until they sounded like the tread of quietly marching men. Men in single file, as was natural in the narrow passage, and a clashing as of arms could be heard. Karl, who had been on the point of relaxing himself in a sleep free of all worries about boxes and Slovaks, started up and nudged the stoker to draw his attention, for the head of the procession seemed just to have reached the door. 'That's the ship's band,' said the stoker, 'they've been playing up above and have come back to pack up. All's clear now, and we can go. Come!' He took Karl by the hand, snatched at the last moment a framed picture of the Madonna from the wall above the bed, stuck it into his breast pocket, seized his chest, and with Karl hastily left the cubby-hole.

'I'm going to the office now to give them a piece of my mind. All the passengers are gone; I don't need to care what I do.' The stoker kept repeating this theme with variations, and as he walked on kicked out his foot sideways at a rat which crossed his way, but merely drove it more quickly into its hole, which it reached just in time. He was slow in all his movements, for though his legs were long they were massive as well.

They went through part of the kitchen, where some girls in dirty white aprons – which they splashed deliberately – were washing dishes in great tubs. The stoker hailed a girl called Lina, put his arm round her waist, and since she coquettishly resisted the embrace dragged her a part of the way with him. 'It's pay-day; aren't you coming along?' he asked. 'Why take the trouble; you can bring me the money here,' she replied, squirming under his arm and running away. 'Where did you pick up that good-looking boy?' she cried after him, but without waiting for an answer. They could hear the laughter of the other girls, who had all stopped their work.

But they went on and came to a door above which there was a little pediment, supported by tiny, gilded caryatides. For a ship's fitting it looked extravagantly sumptuous. Karl realized that he had never been in this part of the ship, which during the voyage had probably been reserved for passengers of the first and second class; but the doors that cut it off had now been thrown open to prepare for the cleaning down of the ship. Indeed, they had already met some men with brooms on their shoulders, who had greeted the stoker. Karl was amazed at the extent of the ship's organization; as a steerage passenger he had seen very little of it. Along the corridors ran wires of electric installations, and a little bell kept sounding every now and then.

The stoker knocked respectfully at the door, and when someone cried 'Come in!' urged Karl with a wave of the hand to enter boldly. Karl stepped in, but remained standing beside the door. The three windows of this room framed a view of the sea, and gazing at the cheerful motion of the waves his heart beat faster, as if he had not been looking at the sea without interruption for five long days. Great ships crossed each other's courses in either direction, yielding to the assault of the waves only as far as their ponderous weight permitted them. If one almost shut one's eyes, these ships seemed to be staggering under their own weight. From their masts flew long, narrow pennants which, though kept taut by the speed of their going, at the same time fluttered a little. Probably from some battleship there could be heard salvoes, fired in salute, and a warship of some kind passed at no great distance; the muzzles of its guns, gleaming with the reflection of sunlight on steel, seemed to be nursed along by the sure, smooth motion, although not on an even keel. Only a distant view of the smaller ships and boats could be had, at least from the door, as they darted about in swarms through the gaps between the great ships. And behind them all rose New York, and its skyscrapers stared at Karl with their hundred thousand eyes. Yes, in this room one realized where one was.

At a round table three gentlemen were sitting, one a ship's officer in the blue ship's uniform, the two others harbor officials in black American uniforms. On the table lay piles of various papers, which the officer first glanced over, pen in hand, and then handed to the two others, who read them, made excerpts, and filed them away in portfolios, except when they were not actually engaged in taking down some kind of protocol which one of them dictated to his colleagues, making clicking noises with his teeth all the time.

By the first window a little man was sitting at a desk with his back to the door; he was busy with some huge ledgers ranked on a stout book-shelf on a level with his head. Beside him stood an open safe which, at first glance at least, seemed empty.

The second window was vacant and gave the better view. But near the third two gentlemen were standing conversing in low tones. One of them was leaning against the window; he was wearing the ship's uniform and playing with the hilt of his sword. The man to whom he was speaking faced the window, and now and then a movement of his disclosed part of a row of decorations on the breast of his interlocutor. He was in civilian clothes and carried a thin bamboo cane which, as both his hands were resting on his hips, also stood out like a sword.

Karl did not have much time to see all this, for almost at once an attendant came up to them and asked the stoker, with a glance which seemed to indicate that he had no business here, what he wanted. The stoker replied as softly as he had been asked that he wished to speak to the Head Purser. The attendant made a gesture of refusal with his hand, but all the same tiptoed toward the man with the ledgers, avoiding the round table by a wide detour. The ledger official – this could clearly be seen – stiffened all over at the words of the attendant, but at last turned round toward this man who wished to speak to him and waved him away violently, repudiating the attendant too, to make quite certain. The attendant then sidled back to the stoker and said in the voice of one imparting a confidence: 'Clear out of here at once!'

At this reply the stoker turned his eyes on Karl, as if Karl were his heart, to whom he was silently bewailing his grief. Without stopping to think, Karl launched himself straight across the room, actually brushing against one of the officers' chairs, while the attendant chased after him, swooping with widespread arms as if to catch an insect; but Karl was the first to reach the Head Purser's desk; which he gripped firmly in case the attendant should try to drag him away.

The whole room naturally sprang to life at once. The ship's officer at the table leapt to his feet; the harbor officials looked on calmly but attentively; the two gentlemen by the window moved closer to each other; the attendant, who thought it was no longer his place to interfere, since his masters were now involved, stepped back. The stoker waited tensely by the door for the moment when his intervention should be required. And the Head Purser at last made a complete rightabout turn in his chair.

From his secret pocket, which he did not mind showing to these people, Karl hauled out his passport, which he opened and laid on the desk in lieu of further introduction. The Head Purser seemed to consider the passport irrelevant, for he flicked it aside with two fingers, whereupon Karl, as if that formality were satisfactorily settled, put it back in his pocket again.

'May I be allowed to say,' he then began, 'that in my opinion an injustice has been done to my friend the stoker? There's a certain man Schubal aboard who bullies him. He has a long record of satisfactory service on many ships, whose names he can give you, he is diligent, takes an interest in his work, and it's really hard to see why on this particular ship, where the work isn't so heavy as on cargo boats, for instance, he should get so little credit. It must be sheer slander that keeps him back and robs him of the recognition that should certainly be his. I have confined myself, as you can see, to generalities; he can lay his specific complaints before you himself.' In saying this Karl had addressed all the gentlemen present, because in fact they were all listening to him, and because it seemed much more likely that among so many at least one just man might be found, than that the one just man should be the Head Purser. Karl also guilefully concealed the fact that he had known the stoker for such a short time. But he would have made a much better speech had he not been distracted by the red face of the man with the bamboo cane, which was now in his line of vision for the first time.

'It's all true, every word of it,' said the stoker before anyone even asked him, indeed before anyone so much as looked at him. This over-eagerness on his part might have proved a great mistake if the man with the decorations who, it now dawned on Karl, was of course the Captain, had not clearly made up his mind to hear the case. For he stretched out his hand and called to the stoker: 'Come here!' in a voice as firm as a rock. Everything now depended on the stoker's behavior, for about the justice of his case Karl had no doubt whatever.

Luckily it appeared at this point that the stoker was a man of some worldly experience. With exemplary composure he drew out of his sea-chest, at the first attempt, a little bundle of papers and a notebook, walked over with them to the

Captain as if that were a matter of course, entirely ignoring the Head Purser, and spread out his evidence on the window-ledge. There was nothing for the Head Purser to do but also to come forward. 'The man is a notorious grumbler,' he said in explanation, 'he spends more time in the pay-room than in the engine-room. He has driven Schubal, who's a quiet fellow, to absolute desperation. Listen to me!' Here he turned to the stoker. 'You're a great deal too persistent in pushing yourself forward. How often have you been flung out of the pay-room already, and serve you right too, for your impudence in demanding things to which you have no right whatever? How often have you gone running from the pay-room to the Purser's office? How often has it been patiently explained to you that Schubal is your immediate superior, and that it's him you have to deal with, and him alone? And now you actually come here, when the Captain himself is present, to pester him with your impudence, and as if that weren't enough you bring a mouth-piece with you to reel off the absurd grievances you've drilled into him, a boy I've never even seen on the ship before!'

Karl forcibly restrained himself from springing forward. But the Captain had already intervened with the remark: 'Better hear what the man has to say for himself. Schubal's getting a good deal too big for his boots these days, but that doesn't mean I think you're right.' The last words were addressed to the stoker; it was only natural that the Captain should not take his part at once, yet everything seemed to be going the right way. The stoker began to state his case and controlled himself so far at the very beginning as to call Schubal 'Mr. Schubal'. Standing beside the Head Purser's vacant desk, Karl felt so pleased that in his delight he kept pressing the letter-scales down with his finger. Mr. Schubal was unfair! Mr. Schubal gave the preference to foreigners! Mr. Schubal ordered the stoker out of the engine-room and made him clean water-closets, which was not a stoker's job at all! At one point even the capability of Mr. Schubal was called in question, as being more apparent than real. At this point Karl fixed his eyes on the Captain and stared at him with earnest deference, as if they had been colleagues, to keep him from being influenced against the stoker by the man's awkward way of expressing himself. All the same, nothing definite emerged from the stoker's outpourings, and although the Captain still listened thoughtfully, his eyes expressing a resolution to hear the stoker this time to the end, the other gentlemen were growing impatient and the stoker's voice no longer dominated the room, which was a bad sign. The gentleman in civilian clothes was the first to show his impatience by bringing his bamboo stick into play and tapping, though only softly, on the floor. The others still looked up now and then; but the two harbor officials, who were clearly pressed for time, snatched up their papers again and began, though somewhat absently, to glance over them; the ship's officer turned to his desk, and the Head Purser, who now thought he had won the day, heaved a loud ironical sigh. From the general dispersion of interest the only one who seemed to be exempt was the attendant, who sympathized to some extent with this poor man confronting the great, and gravely nodded to Karl as though trying to explain something.

Meanwhile, outside the windows, the life of the harbor went on; a flat barge laden with a mountain of barrels, which must have been wonderfully well packed, since they did not roll off, went past, almost completely obscuring the daylight; little motor-boats, which Karl would have liked to examine thoroughly if he had had time, shot straight past in obedience to the slightest touch of the man standing erect at the wheel. Here and there curious objects bobbed independently out of the restless water, were immediately submerged again and sank before his astonished eyes; boats belonging to the ocean liners were rowed past by sweating sailors; they were filled with passengers sitting silent and expectant as if they had been stowed there, except that some of them could not refrain from turning their heads to gaze at the changing scene. A movement without end, a restlessness transmitted from the restless element to helpless human beings and their works!

But everything demanded haste, clarity, exact statement; and what was the stoker doing? Certainly he was talking himself into a sweat; his hands were trembling so much that he could no longer hold the papers he had laid on the window-ledge; from all points of the compass complaints about Schubal streamed into his head, each of which, it seemed to him, should have been sufficient to dispose of Schubal for good; but all he could produce for the Captain was a wretched farrago in which everything was lumped together. For a long time the man with the bamboo cane had been staring at the ceiling and whistling to himself; the harbor officials now detained the ship's officer at their table and showed no sign of ever letting him go again; the Head Purser was clearly restrained from letting fly only by the Captain's composure; the attendant stood at attention, waiting every moment for the Captain to give an order concerning the stoker.

At that Karl could no longer remain inactive. So he advanced slowly toward the group, running over in his mind the more rapidly all the ways in which he could most adroitly handle the affair. It was certainly high time; a little longer, and they might quite well both of them be kicked out of the office. The Captain might be a good man and might also, or so it seemed to Karl, have some particular reason at the moment to show that he was a just master; but after all he wasn't a mere instrument to be recklessly played on, and that was exactly how the stoker was treating him in the boundless indignation of his heart.

Accordingly Karl said to the stoker: 'You must put things more simply, more clearly; the Captain can't do justice to what you are telling him. How can he know all the mechanics and ship's boys by name, far less by their first names, so that when you mention So-and-so he can tell at once who is meant? Take your grievances in order, tell the most important ones first and the lesser ones afterwards; perhaps you'll find that it won't be necessary even to mention most of them.

You always explained them clearly enough to me!' If boxes could be stolen in America, one could surely tell a lie now and then as well, he thought in self-excuse.

But was his advice of any use? Might it not already be too late? The stoker certainly stopped speaking at once when he heard the familiar voice, but his eyes were so blinded with tears of wounded dignity, of dreadful memory, of extreme present grief, that he could hardly even recognize Karl. How could he at this stage – Karl silently realized this, facing the now silent stoker – how could he at this stage suddenly change his style of argument, when it seemed plain to him that he had already said all there was to say without evoking the slightest sympathy, and at the same time that he had said nothing at all, and could not expect these gentlemen to listen to the whole rigmarole over again? And at such a moment Karl, his sole supporter, had to break in with so-called good advice which merely made it clear that everything was lost, everything.

'If I had only spoken sooner, instead of looking out of the window,' Karl told himself, dropping his eyes before the stoker and letting his hands fall to his sides as a sign that all hope was ended.

But the stoker mistook the action, feeling, no doubt, that Karl was nursing some secret reproach against him, and, in the honest desire to disabuse him, crowned all his other offenses by starting to wrangle at this moment with Karl. At this very moment, when the men at the round table were completely exasperated by the senseless babble that disturbed their important labors, when the Head Purser was gradually beginning to find the Captain's patience incomprehensible and was just on the point of exploding, when the attendant, once more entirely translated to his masters' sphere, was measuring the stoker with savage eyes, and when, finally, the gentleman with the bamboo cane, whom even the Captain eyed now and then in a friendly manner, already quite bored by the stoker, indeed disgusted at him, had pulled out a little notebook and was obviously preoccupied with quite different thoughts, glancing first at the notebook and then at Karl.

'I know,' said Karl, who had difficulty in turning aside the torrent which the stoker now directed at him, but yet could summon up a friendly smile for him in spite of all dissension, 'that you're right, you're right, I have never doubted it.' In his fear of being struck by the stoker's gesticulating hands he would have liked to catch hold of them, and still better to force the man into a corner so as to whisper a few soothing, reassuring words to him which no one else could hear. But the stoker was past all bounds. Karl now began actually to take a sort of comfort in the thought that in case of need the stoker could overwhelm the seven men in the room with the very strength of his desperation. But on the desk, as he could see at a glance, there was a bell-arrangement with far too many buttons; the mere pressure of one hand on them would raise the whole ship and call up all the hostile men that filled its passage-ways.

But here, in spite of his air of bored detachment, the gentleman with the bamboo cane came over to Karl and asked, not very loudly yet clearly enough to be heard above the stoker's ravings: 'By the way, what's your name?' At that moment, as if someone behind the door had been waiting to hear this remark, there was a knock. The attendant looked across at the Captain; the Captain nodded. Thereupon the attendant went to the door and opened it. Outside was standing a middle-sized man in an old military coat, not looking at all like the kind of person who would attend to machinery – and yet he was Schubal. If Karl had not guessed this from the expression of satisfaction which lit up all eyes, even the Captain's, he must have recognized it with horror from the demeanor of the stoker, who clenched his fists at the end of his outstretched arms with a vehemence that made the clenching of them seem the most important thing about him, to which he was prepared to sacrifice everything else in life. All his strength was concentrated in his fists, including the very strength that held him upright.

And so here was the enemy, fresh and gay in his shore-going clothes, a ledger under his arm, probably containing a statement of the hours worked and the wages due to the stoker, and he was openly scanning the faces of everyone present, a frank admission that his first concern was to discover on which side they stood. All seven of them were already his friends, for even though the Captain had raised some objections to him earlier, or had pretended to do so because he felt sorry for the stoker, it was now apparent that he had not the slightest fault to find with Schubal. A man like the stoker could not be too severely repressed, and if Schubal were to be reproached for anything, it was for not having subdued the stoker's recalcitrance sufficiently, since the fellow had dared to face the Captain after all.

Yet it might still be assumed that the confrontation of Schubal and the stoker would achieve, even before a human tribunal, the result which would have been awarded by divine justice, since Schubal, even if he were good at making a show of virtue, might easily give himself away in the long run. A brief flare-up of his evil nature would suffice to reveal it to those gentlemen, and Karl would arrange for that. He already had a rough and ready knowledge of the shrewdness, the weaknesses, the temper of the various individuals in the room, and in this respect the time he had spent there had not been wasted. It was a pity that the stoker was not more competent; he seemed quite incapable of decisive action. If one were to thrust Schubal at him, he would probably split the man's hated skull with his fists. But it was beyond his power to take the couple of steps needed to bring Schubal within reach. Why had Karl not foreseen what so easily could have been foreseen: that Schubal would inevitably put in an appearance, if not of his own accord, then by order of the Captain? Why had he not outlined an exact plan of campaign with the stoker when they were on their way here, instead of simply walking in, hopelessly unprepared, as soon as they found a door, which was what they had done? Was the stoker even capable of saying a word by this time, of answering yes and no, as he must do if he were now to be cross-examined, although, to be sure, a cross-examination was almost too much to hope for? There he stood, his legs a-sprawl, his knees uncertain, his head thrown back, and the air flowed in and out of his open mouth as if the man had no lungs to control its motion.

But Karl himself felt more strong and clear-headed than perhaps he had ever been at home. If only his father and mother could see him now, fighting for justice in a strange land before men of authority, and, though not yet triumphant, dauntlessly resolved to win the final victory! Would they revise their opinion of him? Set him between them and praise him? Look into his eyes at last, at last, those eyes so filled with devotion to them? Ambiguous questions, and this the most unsuitable moment to ask them!

'I have come here because I believe this stoker is accusing me of dishonesty or something. A maid in the kitchen told me she saw him making in this direction. Captain, and all you other gentlemen, I am prepared to show papers to disprove any such accusation, and, if you like, to adduce the evidence of unprejudiced and incorruptible witnesses, who are waiting outside the door now.' Thus spake Schubal. It was, to be sure, a clear and manly statement, and from the altered expression of the listeners one might have thought they were hearing a human voice for the first time after a long interval. They certainly did not notice the holes that could be picked in that fine speech. Why, for instance, had the first relevant word that occurred to him been 'dishonesty'? Should he have been accused of that, perhaps instead of nationalistic prejudice? A maid in the kitchen had seen the stoker on his way to the office, and Schubal had immediately divined what that meant? Wasn't it his consciousness of guilt that had sharpened his apprehension? And he had immediately collected witnesses, had he, and then called them unprejudiced and incorruptible to boot? Imposture, nothing but imposture! And these gentlemen were not only taken in by it, but regarded it with approval? Why had he allowed so much time to elapse between the kitchen-maid's report and his arrival here? Simply in order to let the stoker weary the gentlemen, until they began to lose their powers of clear judgment, which Schubal feared most of all. Standing for a long time behind the door, as he must have done, had he deliberately refrained from knocking until he heard the casual question of the gentleman with the bamboo cane, which gave him grounds to hope that the stoker was already despatched?

Everything was clear enough now and Schubal's very behavior involuntarily corroborated it, but it would have to be proved to those gentlemen by other and still more palpable means. They must be shaken up. Now then, Karl, quick, make the best of every minute you have, before the witnesses come in and confuse everything!

At that very moment, however, the Captain waved Schubal away, and at once – seeing that his case seemed to be provisionally postponed – he stepped aside and was joined by the attendant, with whom he began a whispered conversation involving many side glances at the stoker and Karl, as well as the most impressive gestures. It was as if Schubal were rehearsing his next fine speech.

'Didn't you want to ask this youngster something, Mr Jacob?' the Captain said in the general silence to the gentleman with the bamboo cane.

'Why, yes,' replied the other, with a slight bow in acknowledgment of the Captain's courtesy. And he asked Karl again: 'What is your name?'

Karl, who thought that his main business would be best served by satisfying his stubborn questioner as quickly as possible, replied briefly, without, as was his custom, introducing himself by means of his passport, which he would have had to tug out of his pocket: 'Karl Rossmann.'

'But really!' said the gentleman who had been addressed as Jacob, recoiling with an almost incredulous smile. The Captain too, the Head Purser, the ship's officer, even the attendant, all showed an excessive astonishment on hearing Karl's name. Only the harbor officials and Schubal remained indifferent.

'But really!' repeated Mr. Jacob, walking a little stiffly up to Karl, 'then I'm your Uncle Jacob and you're my own dear nephew. I suspected it all the time!' he said to the Captain before embracing and kissing Karl, who dumbly submitted to everything.

'And what may your name be?' asked Karl when he felt himself released again, very courteously, but quite coolly, trying hard to estimate the consequences which this new development might have for the stoker. At the moment, there was nothing to indicate that Schubal could extract any advantage out of it.

'But don't you understand your good fortune, young man?' said the Captain, who thought that Mr. Jacob was wounded in his dignity by Karl's question, for he had retired to the window, obviously to conceal from the others the agitation on his face, which he also kept dabbing with a handkerchief. 'It is Senator Edward Jacob who has just declared himself to be your uncle. You have now a brilliant career in front of you, against all your previous expectations, I dare say. Try to realize this, as far as you can in the first shock of the moment, and pull yourself together!'

'I certainly have an Uncle Jacob in America,' said Karl, turning to the Captain, 'but if I understand rightly, Jacob is only the surname of this gentleman.'

'That is so,' said the Captain, encouragingly.

'Well, my Uncle Jacob, who is my mother's brother, had Jacob for a Christian name, but his surname must of course be the same as my mother's, whose maiden name was Bendelmayer.'

'Gentlemen!' cried the Senator, coming forward in response to Karl's explanation, quite cheerful now after his recuperative retreat to the window. Everyone except the harbor officials laughed a little, some as if really touched, others for no visible reason.

'Yet what I said wasn't so ridiculous as all that,' thought Karl.

'Gentlemen,' repeated the Senator, 'you are involved against my will and your own in a little family scene, and so I can't but give you an explanation, since, I fancy, no one but the Captain here' – this reference was followed by a reciprocal bow – 'is fully informed of the circumstances.'

'Now I must really attend to every word,' Karl told himself, and glancing over his shoulder he was delighted to see that life was beginning to return to the figure of the stoker.

'For the many years of my sojourn in America – though sojourn is hardly the right word to use of an American citizen, and I am an American citizen from my very heart – for all these many years, then, I have lived completely cut off from my relatives in Europe, for reasons which, in the first place, do not concern us here, and in the second, would really give me too much pain to relate. I actually dread the moment when I may be forced to explain them to my dear nephew, for some frank criticisms of his parents and their friends will be unavoidable, I'm afraid.'

'It is my uncle, no doubt about it,' Karl told himself, listening eagerly, 'he must have had his name changed.'

'Now, my dear nephew has simply been turned out – we may as well call a spade a spade – has simply been turned out by his parents, just as you turn a cat out of the house when it annoys you. I have no intention of extenuating what my nephew did to merit that punishment, yet his transgression was of a kind that merely needs to be named to find indulgence.'

'That's not too bad,' thought Karl, 'but I hope he won't tell the whole story. Anyhow, he can't know much about it. Who would tell him?'

'For he was,' Uncle Jacob went on, rocking himself a little on the bamboo cane which was braced in front of him, a gesture that actually succeeded in deprecating any unnecessary solemnity which otherwise must have characterized his statement, 'for he was seduced by a maidservant, Johanna

Brummer, a person of round about thirty-five. It is far from my wishes to offend my nephew by using the word "seduced", but it is difficult to find another and equally suitable word.'

Karl, who had moved up quite close to his uncle, turned round to read from the gentlemen's faces the impression the story had made. None of them laughed, all were listening patiently and seriously. After all, one did not laugh at the nephew of a Senator on the first possible opportunity. It was rather the stoker who now smiled at Karl, though very faintly, but that was satisfactory in the first place, as a sign of reviving life, and excusable in the second place, since in the stoker's bunk Karl had tried to make an impenetrable mystery of this very story which was now being made so public.

'Now this Brummer,' Uncle Jacob went on, 'had a child by my nephew, a healthy boy, who was given the baptismal name of Jacob, evidently in memory of my unworthy self, since my nephew's doubtless quite casual references to me had managed to make a deep impression on the woman. Fortunately, let me add. For the boy's parents, to avoid alimony or being personally involved in any scandal – I must insist that I know neither how the law stands in their district nor their general circumstances – to avoid the scandal, then, and the payment of alimony, they packed off their son, my dear nephew, to America, shamefully unprovided for, as you can see, and the poor lad, but for the signs and wonders which still happen in America if nowhere else, would have come to a wretched end in New York, being thrown entirely on his own resources, if this servant girl hadn't written a letter to me, which after long delays reached me the day before yesterday, giving me the whole story, along with a description of my nephew and, very wisely, the name of the ship as well. If I were setting out to entertain you, gentlemen, I could read a few passages to you from this letter' – he pulled out and flourished before them two huge, closely written sheets of letter-paper. 'You would certainly be interested, for the letter is written with somewhat simple but well-meant cunning and with much loving care for the father of the child. But I have no intention either of entertaining you for longer than my explanation needs, or of wounding at the very start the perhaps still sensitive feelings of my nephew, who if he likes can read the letter for his own instruction in the seclusion of the room already waiting for him.'

But Karl had no feelings for Johanna Brummer. Hemmed in by a vanishing past, she sat in her kitchen beside the kitchen dresser, resting her elbows on top of it. She looked at him whenever he came to the kitchen to fetch a glass of water for his father or do some errand for his mother. Sometimes, awkwardly sitting sideways at the dresser, she would write a letter, drawing her inspiration from Karl's face. Sometimes she would sit with her hand over her eyes, heeding nothing that was said to her. Sometimes she would kneel in her tiny room next the kitchen and pray to a wooden crucifix; then Karl would feel shy if he passed by and caught a glimpse of her through the crack of the slightly open door. Sometimes she would bustle about her kitchen and recoil, laughing like a witch, if Karl came near her. Sometimes she would shut the kitchen door after Karl entered, and keep hold of the door-handle until he had to beg to be let out. Sometimes she would bring him things which he did not want and press them silently into his hand. And once she called him 'Karl' and, while he was still dumbfounded at this unusual familiarity, led him into her room, sighing and grimacing, and locked the door. Then she flung her arms round his neck, almost choking him, and while urging him to take off her clothes, she really took off his and laid him on her bed, as if she would never give him up to anyone and would tend and cherish him to the end of time. 'Oh Karl, my Karl!' she cried; it was as if her eyes were devouring him, while his eyes saw nothing at all and he felt uncomfortable in all the warm bedclothes which she seemed to have piled up for him alone. Then she lay down by him and wanted some secret from him, but he could tell her none, and she showed anger, either in jest or in earnest, shook him, listened to his heart, offered her breast that he might listen to hers in turn, but could not bring him to do it, pressed her naked belly against his body, felt with her hand between his legs, so disgustingly that his head and neck started up from the pillows, then thrust her body several times against him – it was as if she were part of himself, and for that reason, perhaps, he was seized with a terrible feeling of yearning. With the tears running down his cheeks he reached his own bed at last, after many entreaties from her to come again. That was all that had happened, and yet his uncle had managed to make a great song out of it. And it seemed the cook had also been thinking about him and had informed his uncle of his arrival. That had been very good of her and he would make some return for it later, if he could.

'And now,' cried the Senator, 'I want you to tell me candidly whether I am your uncle or not?'

'You are my uncle,' said Karl, kissing his hand and receiving a kiss on the brow. 'I'm very glad to have found you, but you're mistaken if you think my father and mother never speak kindly of you. In any case, you've got some points quite wrong in your story; I mean that it didn't all happen like that in reality. But you can't really be expected to understand things at such a distance, and I fancy it won't do any great harm if these gentlemen are somewhat incorrectly informed about the details of an affair which can't have much interest for them.'

'Well spoken,' said the Senator, leading Karl up to the Captain, who was visibly sympathetic, and asking: 'Haven't I a splendid nephew?'

'I am delighted,' said the Captain, making a bow which showed his military training, 'to have met your nephew, Mr. Senator. My ship is highly honored in providing the scene for such a reunion. But the voyage in the steerage must have been very unpleasant, for we have, of course, all kinds of people traveling steerage. We do everything possible to make conditions tolerable, far more, for instance, than the

American lines do, but to turn such a passage into pleasure is more than we've been able to manage yet.'

'It did me no harm,' said Karl.

'It did him no harm!' repeated the Senator, laughing loudly.

'Except that I'm afraid I've lost my box –' and with that he remembered all that had happened and all that remained to be done, and he looked round him and saw the others still in the same places, silent with respect and surprise, their eyes fixed upon him. Only the harbor officials, insofar as their severe, self-satisfied faces were legible, betrayed some regret at having come at such an unpropitious time, and the watch which they had laid on the table before them was probably more important to them than everything that had happened in the room or might still happen there.

The first to express his sympathy, after the Captain, was curiously enough the stoker. 'I congratulate you heartily,' he said, and shook Karl's hand, making the gesture a token of something like gratitude. Yet when he turned to the Senator with the same words the Senator drew back, as if the stoker were exceeding his rights; and the stoker immediately retreated.

But the others now saw what should be done and at once pressed in a confused throng round Karl and the Senator. So it happened that Karl actually received Schubal's congratulations, accepted them and thanked him for them. The last to advance in the ensuing lull were the harbor officials, who said two words in English, which made a ludicrous impression.

The Senator now felt moved to extract the last ounce of enjoyment from the situation by refreshing his own and the others' minds with the less important details, and this was not merely tolerated but of course welcomed with interest by everyone. So he told them that he had entered in his notebook, for consultation in a possible emergency, his nephew's most distinctive characteristics as enumerated by the cook in her letter. Bored by the stoker's ravings, he had pulled out the notebook simply to distract himself, and had begun for his own amusement to compare the cook's descriptions, which were not so exact as a detective might wish, with Karl's appearance. 'And that's how to find a nephew!' he concluded proudly, as if he wanted to be congratulated all over again.

'What will happen to the stoker now?' asked Karl, ignoring his uncle's last remarks. In his new circumstances he thought he was entitled to say whatever came into his mind.

'The stoker will get what he deserves,' said the Senator, 'and what the Captain considers to be right. I think we have had enough and more than enough of the stoker, a view in which every gentleman here will certainly concur.'

'But that's not the point in a question of justice,' said Karl. He was standing between his uncle and the Captain, and, perhaps influenced by his position, thought that he was holding the balance between them.

And yet the stoker seemed to have abandoned hope. His hands were half stuck into the belt of his trousers, which together with a strip of checked shirt had come prominently into view during his excited tirade. That did not worry him in the least; he had displayed the misery of his heart, now they might as well see the rags that covered his body, and then they could thrust him out. He had decided that the attendant and Schubal, as the two least important men in the room, should do him that last kindness. Schubal would have peace then and no longer be driven to desperation, as the Head Purser had put it. The Captain could take on crowds of Roumanians; Roumanian would be spoken all over the ship; and then perhaps things would really be all right. There would be no stoker pestering the head office any more with his ravings, yet his last effort would be held in almost friendly memory, since, as the Senator expressly declared, it had been the direct cause of his recognizing his nephew. The nephew himself had several times tried to help him already and so had more than repaid him beforehand for his services in the recognition scene; it did not even occur to the stoker to ask anything else from him now. Besides, even if he were the nephew of a senator, he was far from being a captain yet, and it was from the mouth of the Captain that the stern verdict would fall. And thinking all this, the stoker did his best not to look at Karl, though unfortunately in that roomful of enemies there was no other resting-place for his eyes.

'Don't mistake the situation,' said the Senator to Karl, 'this may be a question of justice, but at the same time it's a question of discipline. On this ship both of these, and most especially the latter, are entirely within the discretion of the Captain.'

'That's right,' muttered the stoker. Those who heard him and understood smiled uneasily.

'But we have already obstructed the Captain far too long in his official duties, which must be piling up considerably now that he has reached New York, and it's high time we left the ship, instead of adding to our sins by interfering quite unnecessarily in this petty quarrel between two mechanics and so making it a matter of importance. I understand your attitude perfectly, my dear nephew, but that very fact justifies me in hurrying you away from here immediately.'

'I shall have a boat lowered for you at once,' said the Captain, without deprecating in the least the Senator's words, to Karl's great surprise, since his uncle could be said to have humbled himself. The Head Purser rushed hastily to his desk and telephoned the Captain's order to the bos'un. 'There's hardly any time left,' Karl told himself, 'but I can't do anything without offending everybody. I really can't desert my uncle now, just when he's found me. The Captain is certainly polite, but that's all. In matters of discipline his politeness fades out. And my uncle certainly meant what he said. I don't want to speak to Schubal; I'm sorry that I even shook hands with him. And the other people here are of no consequence.'

Thinking these things he slowly went over to the stoker, pulled the man's right hand out of his belt and held it gently in his.

'Why don't you say something?' he asked. 'Why do you put up with everything?'

The stoker merely knitted his brows, as if he were seeking some formula for what he had to say. While doing this he looked down at his own hand and Karl's.

'You've been unjustly treated, more than anyone else on this ship; I know that well enough.' And Karl drew his fingers backward and forward between the stoker's, while the stoker gazed round him with shining eyes, as if blessed by a great happiness that no one could grudge him.

'Now you must get ready to defend yourself, answer yes and no, or else these people won't have any idea of the truth. You must promise me to do what I tell you, for I'm afraid, and I've good reason for it, that I won't be able to help you anymore.' And then Karl burst out crying and kissed the stoker's hand, taking that seamed, almost nerveless hand and pressing it to his cheek like a treasure which he would soon have to give up. But now his uncle the Senator was at his side and very gently yet firmly led him away.

'The stoker seems to have bewitched you,' he said, exchanging an understanding look with the Captain over Karl's head. 'You felt lonely, then you found the stoker, and you're grateful to him now; that's all to your credit, I'm sure. But if only for my sake, don't push things too far, learn to understand your position.'

Outside the door a hubbub had arisen, shouts could be heard; it sounded even as if someone were being brutally banged against the door. A sailor entered in a somewhat disheveled state with a girl's apron tied round his waist. 'There's a mob outside,' he cried, thrusting out his elbows as if he were still pushing his way through a crowd. He came to himself with a start and made to salute the Captain, but at that moment he noticed the apron, tore it off, threw it on the floor and shouted: 'This is a bit too much; they've tied a girl's apron on me.' Then he clicked his heels together and saluted. Someone began to laugh, but the Captain said severely: 'This is a fine state of things. Who is outside?'

'It's my witnesses,' said Schubal, stepping forward. 'I humbly beg your pardon, sir, for their bad behavior. The men sometimes go a bit wild when they've finished a voyage.'

'Bring them in here at once!' the Captain ordered, then immediately turning to the Senator said, politely but hastily: 'Have the goodness now, Mr. Senator, to take your nephew and follow this man, who will conduct you to your boat. I need hardly say what a pleasure and an honor it has been to me to make your personal acquaintance. I only wish, Mr. Senator, that I may have an early opportunity to resume our interrupted talk about the state of the American fleet, and that it may be again interrupted in as pleasant a manner.'

'One nephew is quite enough for me, I assure you,' said Karl's uncle, laughing. 'And now accept my best thanks for your kindness and good-bye. Besides it isn't altogether impossible that we' – he put his arm warmly round Karl – 'might see quite a lot of you on our next voyage to Europe.'

'That would give me great pleasure,' said the Captain. The two gentlemen shook hands with each other, Karl barely touched the Captain's hand in silent haste, for the latter's attention was already engrossed by the fifteen men who were now being shepherded into the room by Schubal, somewhat chastened but still noisy enough. The sailor begged the Senator to let him lead the way and opened a path through the crowd for him and Karl, so that they passed with ease through ranks of bowing men. It seemed that these good-natured fellows regarded the quarrel between Schubal and the stoker as a joke, and not even the Captain's presence could make them take it seriously. Karl noticed among them the kitchen-maid Lina, who with a sly wink at him was now tying round her waist the apron which the sailor had flung away, for it was hers.

Still following the sailor, they left the office and turned into a small passage which brought them in a couple of steps to a little door, from which a short ladder led down to the boat that was waiting for them. Their conductor leapt down into the boat with a single bound, and the sailors in the boat rose and saluted. The Senator was just warning Karl to be careful how he came down, when Karl, as he stood on the top rung, burst into violent sobs. The Senator put his right hand under Karl's chin, drew him close to him and caressed him with his left hand. In this posture they slowly descended step by step and, still clinging together, entered the boat, where the Senator found a comfortable place for Karl, immediately facing him. At a sign from the Senator the sailors pushed off from the ship and at once began rowing at full speed. They were scarcely a few yards from the ship when Karl made the unexpected discovery that they were on the side of the ship toward which the windows of the office looked out. All three windows were filled with Schubal's witnesses, who saluted and waved in the most friendly way; Uncle Jacob actually waved back and one of the sailors showed his skill by flinging a kiss toward the ship without interrupting the regular rhythm of his rowing. It was now as if there were really no stoker at all. Karl took a more careful look at his uncle, whose knees were almost touching his own, and doubts came into his mind whether this man would ever be able to take the stoker's place. And his uncle evaded his eye and stared at the waves on which their boat was tossing.

The Metamorphosis (1915)

The Metamorphosis

I

AS GREGOR SAMSA awoke one morning from uneasy dreams he found himself transformed in his bed into a gigantic insect. He was lying on his hard, as it were armor-plated, back and when he lifted his head a little he could see his domelike brown belly divided into stiff arched segments on top of which the bed quilt could hardly keep in position and was about to slide off completely. His numerous legs, which were pitifully thin compared to the rest of his bulk, waved helplessly before his eyes.

What has happened to me? he thought. It was no dream. His room, a regular human bedroom, only rather too small, lay quiet between the four familiar walls. Above the table on which a collection of cloth samples was unpacked and spread out – Samsa was a commercial traveler – hung the picture which he had recently cut out of an illustrated magazine and put into a pretty gilt frame. It showed a lady, with a fur cap on and a fur stole, sitting upright and holding out to the spectator a huge fur muff into which the whole of her forearm had vanished!

Gregor's eyes turned next to the window, and the overcast sky – one could hear raindrops beating on the window gutter – made him quite melancholy. What about sleeping a little longer and forgetting all this nonsense, he thought, but it could not be done, for he was accustomed to sleep on his right side and in his present condition he could not turn himself over. However violently he forced himself toward his right side he always rolled onto his back again. He tried it at least a hundred times, shutting his eyes to keep from seeing his struggling legs, and only desisted when he began to feel in his side a faint dull ache he had never experienced before.

Oh God, he thought, what an exhausting job I've picked on! Traveling about day in, day out. It's much more irritating work than doing the actual business in the office, and on top of that there's the trouble of constant traveling, of worrying about train connections, the bed and irregular meals, casual acquaintances that are always new and never become intimate friends. The devil take it all! He felt a slight itching up on his belly; slowly pushed himself on his back nearer to the top of the bed so that he could lift his head more easily; identified the itching place which was surrounded by many small white spots the nature of which he could not understand and made to touch it with a leg, but drew the leg back immediately, for the contact made a cold shiver run through him.

He slid down again into his former position. This getting up early, he thought, makes one quite stupid. A man needs his sleep. Other commercials live like harem women. For instance, when I come back to the hotel of a morning to write up the orders I've got, these others are only sitting down to breakfast. Let me just try that with my chief; I'd be sacked on the spot. Anyhow, that might be quite a good thing for me, who can tell? If I didn't have to hold my hand because of my parents I'd have given notice long ago, I'd have gone to the chief and told him exactly what I think of him. That would knock him endways from his desk! It's a queer way of doing, too, this sitting on high at a desk and talking down to employees, especially when they have to come quite near because the chief is hard of hearing. Well, there's still hope; once I've saved enough money to pay back my parents' debts to him – that should take another five or six years – I'll do it without fail. I'll cut myself completely loose then. For the moment, though, I'd better get up, since my train goes at five.

He looked at the alarm clock ticking on the chest. Heavenly Father! he thought. It was half-past six o'clock and the hands were quietly moving on, it was even past the half-hour, it was getting on toward a quarter to seven. Had the alarm clock not gone off? From the bed one could see that it had been properly set for four o'clock; of course it must have gone off. Yes, but was it possible to sleep quietly through that ear-splitting noise? Well, he had not slept quietly, yet apparently all the more soundly for that. But what was he to do now? The next train went at seven o'clock; to catch that he would need to hurry like mad and his samples weren't even packed up, and he himself wasn't feeling particularly fresh and active. And even if he did catch the train he wouldn't avoid a row with the chief, since the firm's porter would have been waiting for the five o'clock train and would have long since reported his failure to turn up. The porter was a creature of the chief's, spineless and stupid. Well, supposing he were to say he was sick? But that would be most unpleasant and would look suspicious, since during his five years' employment he had not been ill once. The chief himself would be sure to come with the sick-insurance doctor, would reproach his parents with their son's laziness, and would cut all excuses short by referring to the insurance doctor, who of course regarded all mankind as perfectly healthy malingerers. And would he be so far wrong on this occasion? Gregor really felt quite well, apart from a drowsiness that was utterly superfluous after such a long sleep, and he was even unusually hungry.

As all this was running through his mind at top speed without his being able to decide to leave his bed – the alarm clock had just struck a quarter to seven – there came a cautious tap at the door behind the head of his bed. 'Gregor,' said a voice – it was his mother's – 'it's a quarter to seven. Hadn't you a train to catch?' That gentle voice! Gregor had a shock as he heard his own voice answering hers, unmistakably his own voice, it was true, but with a persistent horrible twittering squeak behind it like an undertone, which left the words in their clear shape only for the first moment and then rose up reverberating around them to destroy their sense, so that one could not be sure one had heard them rightly. Gregor wanted to answer at length and explain everything, but in the circumstances he confined himself to saying: 'Yes, yes, thank you, Mother, I'm getting up now.' The wooden door between them must have kept the change in his voice from being noticeable outside, for his mother contented herself with this statement and shuffled away. Yet this brief exchange of words had made the other members of the family aware that Gregor was still in the house, as they had not expected, and at one of the side doors his father was already knocking, gently, yet with his fist. 'Gregor, Gregor,' he called, 'what's the matter with you?' And after a little while he called again in a deeper voice: 'Gregor! Gregor!' At the other side door his sister was saying in a low, plaintive tone: 'Gregor? Aren't you well? Are you needing anything?' He answered them both at once: 'I'm just ready,' and did his best to make his voice sound as normal as possible by enunciating the words very clearly and leaving long pauses between them. So his father went back to his breakfast, but his sister whispered: 'Gregor, open the door, do.' However, he was not thinking of opening the door, and felt thankful for the prudent habit he had acquired in traveling of locking all doors during the night, even at home.

His immediate intention was to get up quietly without being disturbed, to put on his clothes and above all eat his breakfast, and only then consider what else was to be done, since in bed, he was well aware, his meditations would come to no sensible conclusion. He remembered that often enough in bed he had felt small aches and pains, probably caused by awkward postures, which had proved purely imaginary once he got up, and he looked forward eagerly to seeing this morning's delusions gradually fall away. That the change in his voice was nothing but the precursor of a severe chill, a standing ailment of commercial travelers, he had not the least possible doubt.

To get rid of the quilt was quite easy; he had only to inflate himself a little and it fell off by itself. But the next move was difficult, especially because he was so uncommonly broad. He would have needed arms and hands to hoist himself up; instead he had only the numerous little legs which never stopped waving in all directions and which he could not control in the least. When he tried to bend one of them it was the first to stretch itself straight; and did he succeed at last in making it do what he wanted, all the other legs meanwhile waved the more wildly in a high degree of unpleasant agitation. 'But what's the use of lying idle in bed,' said Gregor to himself.

He thought that he might get out of bed with the lower part of his body first, but this lower part, which he had not yet seen and of which he could form no clear conception, proved too difficult to move; it shifted so slowly; and when finally, almost wild with annoyance, he gathered his forces together and thrust out recklessly, he had miscalculated the direction and bumped heavily against the lower end of the bed, and the stinging pain he felt informed him that precisely this lower part of his body was at the moment probably the most sensitive.

So he tried to get the top part of himself out first, and cautiously moved his head toward the edge of the bed. That proved easy enough, and despite its breadth and mass the bulk of his body at last slowly followed the movement of his head. Still, when he finally got his head free over the edge of the bed he felt too scared to go on advancing, for after all if he let himself fall in this way it would take a miracle to keep his head from being injured. And at all costs he must not lose consciousness now, precisely now; he would rather stay in bed.

But when after a repetition of the same efforts he lay in his former position again, sighing, and watched his little legs struggling against each other more wildly than ever, if that were possible, and saw no way of bringing any order into this arbitrary confusion, he told himself again that it was impossible to stay in bed and that the most sensible course was to risk everything for the smallest hope of getting away from it. At the same time he did not forget to remind himself occasionally that cool reflection, the coolest possible, was much better than desperate resolves. In such moments he focused his eyes as sharply as possible on the window, but, unfortunately, the prospect of the morning fog, which muffled even the other side of the narrow street, brought him little encouragement and comfort. 'Seven o'clock already,' he said to himself when the alarm clock chimed again, 'seven o'clock already and still such a thick fog.' And for a little while he lay quiet, breathing lightly, as if perhaps expecting such complete repose to restore all things to their real and normal condition.

But then he said to himself: 'Before it strikes a quarter past seven I must be quite out of this bed, without fail. Anyhow, by that time someone will have come from the office to ask for me, since it opens before seven.' And he set himself to rocking his whole body at once in a regular rhythm, with the idea of swinging it out of the bed. If he tipped himself out in that way he could keep his head from injury by lifting it at an acute angle when he fell. His back seemed to be hard and was not likely to suffer from a fall on the carpet. His biggest worry was the loud crash he would not be able to help making, which would probably cause anxiety, if not terror, behind all the doors. Still, he must take the risk.

When he was already half out of the bed – the new method was more a game than an effort, for he needed only to hitch himself across by rocking to and fro – it struck him how simple it would be if he could get help. Two strong people – he thought of his father and the servant girl – would be amply sufficient; they would only have to thrust their arms under his convex back, lever him out of the bed, bend down with their burden, and then be patient enough to let him turn himself right over onto the floor, where it was to be hoped his legs would then find their proper function. Well, ignoring the fact that the doors were all locked, ought he really to call for help? In spite of his misery he could not suppress a smile at the very idea of it.

He had got so far that he could barely keep his equilibrium

when he rocked himself strongly, and he would have to nerve himself very soon for the final decision since in five minutes' time it would be quarter past seven – when the front doorbell rang. 'That's someone from the office,' he said to himself, and grew almost rigid, while his little legs only jigged about all the faster. For a moment everything stayed quiet. 'They're not going to open the door,' said Gregor to himself, catching at some kind of irrational hope. But then of course the servant girl went as usual to the door with her heavy tread and opened it. Gregor needed only to hear the first good morning of the visitor to know immediately who it was – the chief clerk himself. What a fate, to be condemned to work for a firm where the smallest omission at once gave rise to the gravest suspicion! Were all employees in a body nothing but scoundrels, was there not among them one single loyal devoted man who, had he wasted only an hour or so of the firm's time in a morning, was so tormented by conscience as to be driven out of his mind and actually incapable of leaving his bed? Wouldn't it really have been sufficient to send an apprentice to inquire – if any inquiry were necessary at all – did the chief clerk himself have to come and thus indicate to the entire family, an innocent family, that this suspicious circumstance could be investigated by no one less versed in affairs than himself? And more through the agitation caused by these reflections than through any act of will Gregor swung himself out of bed with all his strength. There was a loud thump, but it was not really a crash. His fall was broken to some extent by the carpet, his back, too, was less stiff than he thought, and so there was merely a dull thud, not so very startling. Only he had not lifted his head carefully enough and had hit it; he turned it and rubbed it on the carpet in pain and irritation.

'That was something falling down in there,' said the chief clerk in the next room to the left. Gregor tried to suppose to himself that something like what had happened to him today might someday happen to the chief clerk; one really could not deny that it was possible. But as if in brusque reply to this supposition the chief clerk took a couple of firm steps in the next-door room and his patent leather boots creaked. From the right-hand room his sister was whispering to inform him of the situation: 'Gregor, the chief clerk's here.' 'I know,' muttered Gregor to himself; but he didn't dare to make his voice loud enough for his sister to hear it.

'Gregor,' said his father now from the left-hand room, 'the chief clerk has come and wants to know why you didn't catch the early train. We don't know what to say to him. Besides, he wants to talk to you in person. So open the door, please. He will be good enough to excuse the untidiness of your room.' 'Good morning, Mr. Samsa,' the chief clerk was calling amiably meanwhile. 'He's not well,' said his mother to the visitor, while his father was still speaking through the door, 'he's not well, sir, believe me. What else would make him miss a train! The boy thinks about nothing but his work. It makes me almost cross the way he never goes out in the evenings; he's been here the last eight days and has stayed at home every single evening. He just sits there quietly at the table reading a newspaper or looking through railway timetables. The only amusement he gets is doing fretwork. For instance, he spent two or three evenings cutting out a little picture frame; you would be surprised to see how pretty it is; it's hanging in his room; you'll see it in a minute when Gregor opens the door. I must say I'm glad you've come, sir; we should never have got him to unlock the door by ourselves; he's so obstinate; and I'm sure he's unwell, though he wouldn't have it to be so this morning.' 'I'm just coming,' said Gregor slowly and carefully, not moving an inch for fear of losing one word of the conversation. 'I can't think of any other explanation, madame,' said the chief clerk, 'I hope it's nothing serious. Although on the other hand I must say that we men of business – fortunately or unfortunately – very often simply have to ignore any slight indisposition, since business must be attended to.' 'Well, can the chief clerk come in now?' asked Gregor's father impatiently, again knocking on the door. 'No,' said Gregor. In the left-hand room a painful silence followed this refusal, in the right-hand room his sister began to sob.

Why didn't his sister join the others? She was probably newly out of bed and hadn't even begun to put on her clothes yet. Well, why was she crying? Because he wouldn't get up and let the chief clerk in, because he was in danger of losing his job, and because the chief would begin dunning his parents again for the old debts? Surely these were things one didn't need to worry about for the present. Gregor was still at home and not in the least thinking of deserting the family. At the moment, true, he was lying on the carpet and no one who knew the condition he was in could seriously expect him to admit the chief clerk. But for such a small discourtesy, which could plausibly be explained away somehow later on, Gregor could hardly be dismissed on the spot. And it seemed to Gregor that it would be much more sensible to leave him in peace for the present than to trouble him with tears and entreaties. Still, of course, their uncertainty bewildered them all and excused their behavior.

'Mr. Samsa,' the chief clerk called now in a louder voice, 'what's the matter with you? Here you are, barricading yourself in your room, giving only "yes" and "no" for answers, causing your parents a lot of unnecessary trouble and neglecting – I mention this only in passing – neglecting your business duties in an incredible fashion. I am speaking here in the name of your parents and of your chief, and I beg you quite seriously to give me an immediate and precise explanation. You amaze me, you amaze me. I thought you were a quiet, dependable person, and now all at once you seem bent on making a disgraceful exhibition of yourself. The chief did hint to me early this morning a possible explanation for your disappearance – with reference to the cash payments that were entrusted to you recently – but I almost pledged my solemn word of honor that this could not be so. But now that I see how incredibly obstinate you are, I no longer have the slightest desire to take your part at all. And your position in the firm is not so unassailable. I came with the intention of telling you all this in private, but since you are wasting my time so needlessly I don't see why your parents shouldn't hear it too. For some time past your work has been most unsatisfactory; this is not the season of the year for doing no business at all, that does not exist, Mr. Samsa, must not exist.'

'But, sir,' cried Gregor, beside himself and in his agitation forgetting everything else, 'I'm just going to open the door this very minute. A slight illness, an attack of giddiness, has kept me from getting up. I'm still lying in bed. But I feel all right again. I'm getting out of bed now. Just give me a moment or two longer! I'm not quite so well as I thought. But I'm all right, really. How a thing like that can suddenly strike one down! Only last night I was quite well, my parents can tell you, or rather I did have a slight presentiment. I must have showed some sign of it. Why didn't I report it at the office! But one always thinks that an indisposition can be got over without staying in the house. Oh sir, do spare my parents! All that you're reproaching me with now has no foundation; no one has ever said a word to me about it. Perhaps you haven't looked at the last orders I sent in. Anyhow, I can still catch the eight o'clock train, I'm much the better for my few hours' rest. Don't let me detain you here, sir; I'll be attending to business very soon, and do be good enough to tell the chief so and to make my excuses to him!'

And while all this was tumbling out pell-mell and Gregor hardly knew what he was saying, he had reached the chest quite easily, perhaps because of the practice he had had in bed, and was now trying to lever himself upright by means of it. He meant actually to open the door, actually to show himself and speak to the chief clerk; he was eager to find out what the others, after all their insistence, would say at the sight of him. If they were horrified then the responsibility was no longer his and he could stay quiet. But if they took it calmly, then he had no reason either to be upset, and could really get to the station for the eight o'clock train if he hurried. At first he slipped down a few times from the polished surface of the chest, but at length with a last heave he stood upright; he paid no more attention to the pains in the lower part of his body, however they smarted. Then he let himself fall against the back of a nearby chair, and clung with his little legs to the edges of it. That brought him into control of himself again and he stopped speaking, for now he could listen to what the chief clerk was saying.

'Did you understand a word of it?' the chief clerk was asking; 'surely he can't be trying to make fools of us?' 'Oh dear,' cried his mother, in tears, 'perhaps he's terribly ill and we're tormenting him. Grete! Grete!' she called out then. 'Yes Mother?' called his sister from the other side. They were calling to each other across Gregor's room. 'You must go this minute for the doctor. Gregor is ill. Go for the doctor, quick. Did you hear how he was speaking?' 'That was no human voice,' said the chief clerk in a voice noticeably low beside the shrillness of the mother's. 'Anna! Anna!' his father was calling through the hall to the kitchen, clapping his hands, 'get a locksmith at once!' And the two girls were already running through the hall with a swish of skirts – how could his sister have got dressed so quickly? – and were tearing the front door open. There was no sound of its closing again; they had evidently left it open, as one does in houses where some great misfortune has happened.

But Gregor was now much calmer. The words he uttered were no longer understandable, apparently, although they seemed clear enough to him, even clearer than before, perhaps because his ear had grown accustomed to the sound of them. Yet at any rate people now believed that something was wrong with him, and were ready to help him. The positive certainty with which these first measures had been taken comforted him. He felt himself drawn once more into the human circle and hoped for great and remarkable results from both the doctor and the locksmith, without really distinguishing precisely between them. To make his voice as clear as possible for the decisive conversation that was now imminent he coughed a little, as quietly as he could, of course, since this noise too might not sound like a human cough for all he was able to judge. In the next room meanwhile there was complete silence. Perhaps his parents were sitting at the table with the chief clerk, whispering, perhaps they were all leaning against the door and listening.

Slowly Gregor pushed the chair toward the door, then let go of it, caught hold of the door for support – the soles at the end of his little legs were somewhat sticky – and rested against it for a moment after his efforts. Then he set himself to turning the key in the lock with his mouth. It seemed, unhappily, that he hadn't really any teeth – what could he grip the key with? – but on the other hand his jaws were certainly very strong; with their help he did manage to set the key in motion, heedless of the fact that he was undoubtedly damaging them somewhere, since a brown fluid issued from his mouth, flowed over the key, and dripped on the floor. 'Just listen to that,' said the chief clerk next door; 'he's turning the key.' That was a great encouragement to Gregor; but they should all have shouted encouragement to him, his father and mother too: 'Go on, Gregor,' they should have called out, 'keep going, hold on to that key!' And in the belief that they were all following his efforts intently, he clenched his jaws recklessly on the key with all the force at his command. As the turning of the key progressed he circled around the lock, holding on now only with his mouth, pushing on the key, as required, or pulling it down again with all the weight of his body. The louder click of the finally yielding lock literally quickened Gregor. With a deep breath of relief he said to himself: 'So I didn't need the locksmith,' and laid his head on the handle to open the door wide.

Since he had to pull the door toward him, he was still invisible when it was really wide open. He had to edge himself slowly around the near half of the double door, and to do it very carefully if he was not to fall plump upon his back just on the threshold. He was still carrying out this difficult maneuver, with no time to observe anything else, when he heard the chief clerk utter a loud 'Oh!' – it sounded like a gust of wind – and now he could see the man, standing as he was nearest to the door, clapping one hand before his open mouth and slowly backing away as if driven by some invisible steady pressure. His mother – in spite of the chief clerk's being there her hair was still undone and sticking up in all directions – first clasped her hands and looked at his father, then took two steps toward Gregor and fell on the floor among her outspread skirts, her face quite hidden on her breast. His father knotted his fist with a fierce expression on his face as if he meant to knock Gregor back into his room, then looked uncertainly around the living room, covered his eyes with his hands, and wept till his great chest heaved.

Gregor did not go now into the living room, but leaned against the inside of the firmly shut wing of the door, so that only half his body was visible and his head above it bending sideways to look at the others. The light had meanwhile strengthened; on the other side of the street one could see clearly a section of the endlessly long, dark gray building opposite – it was a hospital – abruptly punctuated by its row of regular windows; the rain was still falling, but only in large singly discernible and literally singly splashing drops. The breakfast dishes were set out on the table lavishly, for breakfast was the most important meal of the day to Gregor's father, who lingered it out for hours over various newspapers. Right opposite Gregor on the wall hung a photograph of himself in military service, as a lieutenant, hand on sword, a carefree smile on his face, inviting one to respect his uniform and military bearing. The door leading to the hall was open, and one could see that the front door stood open too, showing the landing beyond and the beginning of the stairs going down.

'Well,' said Gregor, knowing perfectly that he was the only one who had retained any composure, 'I'll put my clothes on at once, pack up my samples, and start off. Will you only let me go? You see, sir, I'm not obstinate, and I'm willing to work; traveling is a hard life, but I couldn't live without it. Where are you going, sir? To the office? Yes? Will you give a true account of all this? One can be temporarily incapacitated, but that's just the moment for remembering former services and bearing in mind that later on, when the incapacity has been got over, one will certainly work with all the more industry and concentration. I'm loyally bound to serve the chief, you know that very well. Besides, I have to provide for my parents and my sister. I'm in great difficulties, but I'll get out of them again. Don't make things any worse for me than they are. Stand up for me in the firm. Travelers are not popular there, I know. People think they earn sacks of money and just have a good time. A prejudice there's no particular reason for revising. But you, sir, have a more comprehensive view of affairs than the rest of the staff, yes, let me tell you in confidence, a more comprehensive view than the chief himself, who, being the owner, lets his judgment easily be swayed against one of his employees. And you know very well that the traveler, who is never seen in the office almost the whole year around, can so easily fall a victim to gossip and ill luck and unfounded complaints, which he mostly knows nothing about, except when he comes back exhausted from his rounds, and only then suffers in person from their evil consequences, which he can no longer trace back to the original causes. Sir, sir, don't go away without a word to me to show that you think me in the right at least to some extent!'

But at Gregor's very first words the chief clerk had already backed away and only stared at him with parted lips over one twitching shoulder. And while Gregor was speaking he did not stand still one moment but stole away toward the door, without taking his eyes off Gregor, yet only an inch at a time, as if obeying some secret injunction to leave the room. He was already at the hall, and the suddenness with which he took his last step out of the living room would have made one believe he had burned the sole of his foot. Once in the hall he stretched his right arm before him toward the staircase, as if some supernatural power were waiting there to deliver him.

Gregor perceived that the chief clerk must on no account be allowed to go away in this frame of mind if his position in the firm were not to be endangered to the utmost. His parents did not understand this so well; they had convinced themselves in the course of years that Gregor was settled for life in this firm, and besides they were so preoccupied with their immediate troubles that all foresight had forsaken them. Yet Gregor had this foresight. The chief clerk must be detained, soothed, persuaded, and finally won over; the whole future of Gregor and his family depended on it! If only his sister had been there! She was intelligent; she had begun to cry while Gregor was still lying quietly on his back. And no doubt the chief clerk, so partial to ladies, would have been guided by her; she would have shut the door of the flat and in the hall talked him out of his horror. But she was not there, and Gregor would have to handle the situation himself. And without remembering that he was still unaware what powers of movement he possessed, without even remembering that his words in all possibility, indeed in all likelihood, would again be unintelligible, he let go the wing of the door, pushed himself through the opening, started to walk toward the chief clerk, who was already ridiculously clinging with both hands to the railing on the landing; but immediately, as he was feeling for a support, he fell down with a little cry upon all his numerous legs. Hardly was he down when he experienced for the first time this morning a sense of physical comfort; his legs had firm ground under them; they were completely obedient, as he noted with joy; they even strove to carry him forward in whatever direction he chose; and he was inclined to believe that a final relief from all his sufferings was at hand. But in the same moment as he found himself on the floor, rocking with suppressed eagerness to move, not far from his mother, indeed just in front of her, she, who had seemed so completely crushed, sprang all at once to her feet, her arms and fingers outspread, cried: 'Help, for God's sake, help!' bent her head down as if to see Gregor better, yet on the contrary kept backing senselessly away;

had quite forgotten that the laden table stood behind her; sat upon it hastily, as if in absence of mind, when she bumped into it; and seemed altogether unaware that the big coffeepot beside her was upset and pouring coffee in a flood over the carpet.

'Mother, Mother,' said Gregor in a low voice, and looked up at her. The chief clerk, for the moment, had quite slipped from his mind; instead, he could not resist snapping his jaws together at the sight of the streaming coffee. That made his mother scream again, she fled from the table and fell into the arms of his father, who hastened to catch her. But Gregor had now no time to spare for his parents; the chief clerk was already on the stair; with his chin on the banisters he was taking one last backward look. Gregor made a spring, to be as sure as possible of overtaking him; the chief clerk must have divined his intention, for he leaped down several steps and vanished; he was still yelling 'Ugh!' and it echoed through the whole staircase.

Unfortunately, the flight of the chief clerk seemed completely to upset Gregor's father, who had remained relatively calm until now, for instead of running after the man himself, or at least not hindering Gregor in his pursuit, he seized in his right hand the walking stick that the chief clerk had left behind on a chair, together with a hat and greatcoat, snatched in his left hand a large newspaper from the table, and began stamping his feet and flourishing the stick and the newspaper to drive Gregor back into his room. No entreaty of Gregor's availed, indeed no entreaty was even understood, however humbly he bent his head his father only stamped on the floor the more loudly. Behind his father his mother had torn open a window, despite the cold weather, and was leaning far out of it with her face in her hands. A strong draught set in from the street to the staircase, the window curtains blew in, the newspapers on the table fluttered, stray pages whisked over the floor. Pitilessly Gregor's father drove him back, hissing and crying 'Shoo!' like a savage. But Gregor was quite unpracticed in walking backwards, it really was a slow business. If he only had a chance to turn around he could get back to his room at once, but he was afraid of exasperating his father by the slowness of such a rotation and at any moment the stick in his father's hand might hit him a fatal blow on the back or on the head. In the end, however, nothing else was left for him to do since to his horror he observed that in moving backwards he could not even control the direction he took; and so, keeping an anxious eye on his father all the time over his shoulder, he began to turn around as quickly as he could, which was in reality very slowly. Perhaps his father noted his good intentions, for he did not interfere except every now and then to help him in the maneuver from a distance with the point of the stick. If only he would have stopped making that unbearable hissing noise! It made Gregor quite lose his head. He had turned almost completely around when the hissing noise so distracted him that he even turned a little the wrong way again. But when at last his head was fortunately right in front of the doorway, it appeared that his body was too broad simply to get through the opening. His father, of course, in his present mood was far from thinking of such a thing as opening the other half of the door, to let Gregor have enough space. He had merely the fixed idea of driving Gregor back into his room as quickly as possible. He would never have suffered Gregor to make the circumstantial preparations for standing up on end and perhaps slipping his way through the door. Maybe he was now making more noise than ever to urge Gregor forward, as if no obstacle impeded him; to Gregor, anyhow, the noise in his rear sounded no longer like the voice of one single father; this was really no joke, and Gregor thrust himself – come what might – into the doorway. One side of his body rose up, he was tilted at an angle in the doorway, his flank was quite bruised, horrid blotches stained the white door, soon he was stuck fast and, left to himself, could not have moved at all, his legs on one side fluttered trembling in the air, those on the other were crushed painfully to the floor – when from behind his father gave him a strong push which was literally a deliverance and he flew far into the room, bleeding freely. The door was slammed behind him with the stick, and then at last there was silence.

II

Not until it was twilight did Gregor awake out of a deep sleep, more like a swoon than a sleep. He would certainly have waked up of his own accord not much later, for he felt himself sufficiently rested and well slept, but it seemed to him as if a fleeting step and a cautious shutting of the door leading into the hall had aroused him. The electric lights in the street cast a pale sheen here and there on the ceiling and the upper surfaces of the furniture, but down below, where he lay, it was dark. Slowly, awkwardly trying out his feelers, which he now first learned to appreciate, he pushed his way to the door to see what had been happening there. His left side felt like one single long, unpleasantly tense scar, and he had actually to limp on his two rows of legs. One little leg, moreover, had been severely damaged in the course of that morning's events – it was almost a miracle that only one had been damaged – and trailed uselessly behind him.

He had reached the door before he discovered what had really drawn him to it: the smell of food. For there stood a basin filled with fresh milk in which floated little sops of white bread. He could almost have laughed with joy, since he was now still hungrier than in the morning, and he dipped his head almost over the eyes straight into the milk. But soon in disappointment he withdrew it again; not only did he find it difficult to feed because of his tender left side – and he could only feed with the palpitating collaboration of his whole body – he did not like the milk either, although milk had been his favorite drink and that was certainly why his sister had set it there for him, indeed it was almost with repulsion that he turned away from the basin and crawled back to the middle of the room.

He could see through the crack of the door that the gas

was turned on in the living room, but while usually at this time his father made a habit of reading the afternoon newspaper in a loud voice to his mother and occasionally to his sister as well, not a sound was now to be heard. Well, perhaps his father had recently given up this habit of reading aloud, which his sister had mentioned so often in conversation and in her letters. But there was the same silence all around, although the flat was certainly not empty of occupants. 'What a quiet life our family has been leading,' said Gregor to himself, and as he sat there motionless staring into the darkness he felt great pride in the fact that he had been able to provide such a life for his parents and sister in such a fine flat. But what if all the quiet, the comfort, the contentment were now to end in horror? To keep himself from being lost in such thoughts Gregor took refuge in movement and crawled up and down the room.

Once during the long evening one of the side doors was opened a little and quickly shut again, later the other side door too; someone had apparently wanted to come in and then thought better of it. Gregor now stationed himself immediately before the living-room door, determined to persuade any hesitating visitor to come in or at least to discover who it might be; but the door was not opened again and he waited in vain. In the early morning, when the doors were locked, they had all wanted to come in, now that he had opened one door and the other had apparently been opened during the day, no one came in and even the keys were on the other side of the doors.

It was late at night before the gas went out in the living room, and Gregor could easily tell that his parents and his sister had all stayed awake until then, for he could clearly hear the three of them stealing away on tiptoe. No one was likely to visit him, not until the morning, that was certain; so he had plenty of time to meditate at his leisure on how he was to arrange his life afresh. But the lofty, empty room in which he had to lie flat on the floor filled him with an apprehension he could not account for, since it had been his very own room for the past five years – and with a half-unconscious action, not without a slight feeling of shame, he scuttled under the sofa, where he felt comfortable at once, although his back was a little cramped and he could not lift his head up, and his only regret was that his body was too broad to get the whole of it under the sofa.

He stayed there all night, spending the time partly in a light slumber, from which his hunger kept waking him up with a start, and partly in worrying and sketching vague hopes, which all led to the same conclusion, that he must lie low for the present and, by exercising patience and the utmost consideration, help the family to bear the inconvenience he was bound to cause them in his present condition.

Very early in the morning, it was still almost night, Gregor had the chance to test the strength of his new resolutions, for his sister, nearly fully dressed, opened the door from the hall and peered in. She did not see him at once, yet when she caught sight of him under the sofa – well, he had to be somewhere, he couldn't have flown away, could he? – she was so startled that without being able to help it she slammed the door shut again. But as if regretting her behavior she opened the door again immediately and came in on tiptoe, as if she were visiting an invalid or even a stranger. Gregor had pushed his head forward to the very edge of the sofa and watched her. Would she notice that he had left the milk standing, and not for lack of hunger, and would she bring in some other kind of food more to his taste? If she did not do it of her own accord, he would rather starve than draw her attention to the fact, although he felt a wild impulse to dart out from under the sofa, throw himself at her feet, and beg her for something to eat. But his sister at once noticed, with surprise, that the basin was still full, except for a little milk that had been spilled all around it, she lifted it immediately, not with her bare hands, true, but with a cloth and carried it away. Gregor was wildly curious to know what she would bring instead, and made various speculations about it. Yet what she actually did next, in the goodness of her heart, he could never have guessed at. To find out what he liked she brought him a whole selection of food, all set out on an old newspaper. There were old, half-decayed vegetables, bones from last night's supper covered with a white sauce that had thickened; some raisins and almonds; a piece of cheese that Gregor would have called uneatable two days ago; a dry roll of bread, a buttered roll, and a roll both buttered and salted. Besides all that, she set down again the same basin, into which she had poured some water, and which was apparently to be reserved for his exclusive use. And with fine tact, knowing that Gregor would not eat in her presence, she withdrew quickly and even turned the key, to let him understand that he could take his ease as much as he liked. Gregor's legs all whizzed toward the food. His wounds must have healed completely, moreover, for he felt no disability, which amazed him and made him reflect how more than a month ago he had cut one finger a little with a knife and had still suffered pain from the wound only the day before yesterday. Am I less sensitive now? he thought, and sucked greedily at the cheese, which above all the other edibles attracted him at once and strongly. One after another and with tears of satisfaction in his eyes he quickly devoured the cheese, the vegetables, and the sauce; the fresh food, on the other hand, had no charms for him, he could not even stand the smell of it and actually dragged away to some little distance the things he could eat. He had long finished his meal and was only lying lazily on the same spot when his sister turned the key slowly as a sign for him to retreat. That roused him at once, although he was nearly asleep, and he hurried under the sofa again. But it took considerable self-control for him to stay under the sofa, even for the short time his sister was in the room, since the large meal had swollen his body somewhat and he was so cramped he could hardly breathe. Slight attacks of breathlessness afflicted him and his eyes were standing a little out of his head as he watched his unsuspecting sister sweeping together with a broom not only the remains of what he had eaten but even the things he had not touched, as if these were now of no use to anyone, and hastily shoveling it all into a bucket, which she covered with a wooden lid and carried away. Hardly had she turned her back when Gregor came from under the sofa and stretched and puffed himself out.

In this manner Gregor was fed, once in the early morning while his parents and the servant girl were still asleep, and a second time after they had all had their midday dinner, for then his parents took a short nap and the servant girl could be sent out on some errand or other by his sister. Not that they would have wanted him to starve, of course, but perhaps they could not have borne to know more about his feeding than from hearsay, perhaps too his sister wanted to spare them such little anxieties wherever possible, since they had quite enough to bear as it was.

Under what pretext the doctor and the locksmith had been got rid of on that first morning Gregor could not discover, for since what he said was not understood by the others it never struck any of them, not even his sister, that he could understand what they said, and so whenever his sister came into his room he had to content himself with hearing her utter only a sigh now and then and an occasional appeal to the saints. Later on, when she had got a little used to the situation – of course she could never get completely used to it – she sometimes threw out a remark which was kindly meant or could be so interpreted. 'Well, he liked his dinner today,' she would say when Gregor had made a good clearance of his food; and when he had not eaten, which gradually happened more and more often, she would say almost sadly: 'Everything's been left standing again.'

But although Gregor could get no news directly, he overheard a lot from the neighboring rooms, and as soon as voices were audible, he would run to the door of the room concerned and press his whole body against it. In the first few days especially there was no conversation that did not refer to him somehow, even if only indirectly. For two whole days there were family consultations at every mealtime about what should be done; but also between meals the same subject was discussed, for there were always at least two members of the family at home, since no one wanted to be alone in the flat and to leave it quite empty was unthinkable. And on the very first of these days the household cook – it was not quite clear what and how much she knew of the situation – went down on her knees to his mother and begged leave to go, and when she departed, a quarter of an hour later, gave thanks for her dismissal with tears in her eyes as if for the greatest benefit that could have been conferred on her, and without any prompting swore a solemn oath that she would never say a single word to anyone about what had happened.

Now Gregor's sister had to cook too, helping her mother; true, the cooking did not amount to much, for they ate scarcely anything. Gregor was always hearing one of the family vainly urging another to eat and getting no answer but: 'Thanks, I've had all I want,' or something similar. Perhaps they drank nothing either. Time and again his sister kept asking his father if he wouldn't like some beer and offered kindly to go and fetch it herself, and when he made no answer suggested that she could ask the concierge to fetch it, so that he need feel no sense of obligation, but then a round 'No' came from his father and no more was said about it.

In the course of that very first day Gregor's father explained the family's financial position and prospects to both his mother and his sister. Now and then he rose from the table to get some voucher or memorandum out of the small safe he had rescued from the collapse of his business five years earlier. One could hear him opening the complicated lock and rustling papers out and shutting it again. This statement made by his father was the first cheerful information Gregor had heard since his imprisonment. He had been of the opinion that nothing at all was left over from his father's business, at least his father had never said anything to the contrary, and of course he had not asked him directly. At that time Gregor's sole desire was to do his utmost to help the family to forget as soon as possible the catastrophe that had overwhelmed the business and thrown them all into a state of complete despair. And so he had set to work with unusual ardor and almost overnight had become a commercial traveler instead of a little clerk, with of course much greater chances of earning money, and his success was immediately translated into good round coin which he could lay on the table for his amazed and happy family. These had been fine times, and they had never recurred, at least not with the same sense of glory, although later on Gregor had earned so much money that he was able to meet the expenses of the whole household and did so. They had simply got used to it, both the family and Gregor; the money was gratefully accepted and gladly given, but there was no special uprush of warm feeling. With his sister alone had he remained intimate, and it was a secret plan of his that she, who loved music, unlike himself, and could play movingly on the violin, should be sent next year to study at the Conservatorium, despite the great expense that would entail, which must be made up in some other way. During his brief visits home the Conservatorium was often mentioned in the talks he had with his sister, but always merely as a beautiful dream which could never come true, and his parents discouraged even these innocent references to it; yet Gregor had made up his mind firmly about it and meant to announce the fact with due solemnity on Christmas Day.

Such were the thoughts, completely futile in his present condition, that went through his head as he stood clinging upright to the door and listening. Sometimes out of sheer weariness he had to give up listening and let his head fall negligently against the door, but he always had to pull himself together again at once, for even the slight sound his head made was audible next door and brought all conversation to a stop. 'What can he be doing now?' his father would say after a while, obviously turning toward the door, and only then would the interrupted conversation gradually be set going again.

Gregor was now informed as amply as he could wish – for his father tended to repeat himself in his explanations, partly because it was a long time since he had handled such matters and partly because his mother could not always grasp things at once – that a certain amount of investments, a very small amount it was true, had survived the wreck of their fortunes and had even increased a little because the dividends had not been touched meanwhile. And besides that, the money Gregor brought home every month – he had kept only a few dollars for himself – had never been quite used up and now amounted to a small capital sum. Behind the door Gregor nodded his head eagerly, rejoiced at this evidence of unexpected thrift and foresight. True, he could really have paid off some more of his father's debts to the chief with this extra money, and so brought much nearer the day on which he could quit his job, but doubtless it was better the way his father had arranged it.

Yet this capital was by no means sufficient to let the family live on the interest of it; for one year, perhaps, or at the most two, they could live on the principal, that was all. It was simply a sum that ought not to be touched and should be kept for a rainy day; money for living expenses would have to be earned. Now his father was still hale enough but an old man, and he had done no work for the past five years and could not be expected to do much; during these five years, the first years of leisure in his laborious though unsuccessful life, he had grown rather fat and become sluggish. And Gregor's old mother, how was she to earn a living with her asthma, which troubled her even when she walked through the flat and kept her lying on a sofa every other day panting for breath beside an open window? And was his sister to earn her bread, she who was still a child of seventeen and whose life hitherto had been so pleasant, consisting as it did in dressing herself nicely, sleeping long, helping in the housekeeping, going out to a few modest entertainments, and above all playing the violin? At first whenever the need for earning money was mentioned Gregor let go his hold on the door and threw himself down on the cool leather sofa beside it, he felt so hot with shame and grief.

Often he just lay there the long nights through without sleeping at all, scrabbling for hours on the leather. Or he nerved himself to the great effort of pushing an armchair to the window, then crawled up over the window sill and, braced against the chair, leaned against the windowpanes, obviously in some recollection of the sense of freedom that looking out of a window always used to give him. For in reality day by day things that were even a little way off were growing dimmer to his sight; the hospital across the street, which he used to execrate for being all too often before his eyes, was now quite beyond his range of vision, and if he had not known that he lived in Charlotte Street, a quiet street but still a city street, he might have believed that his window gave on a desert waste where gray sky and gray land blended indistinguishably into each other. His quick-witted sister only needed to observe twice that the armchair stood by the window; after that whenever she had tidied the room she always pushed the chair back to the same place at the window and even left the inner casements open.

If he could have spoken to her and thanked her for all she had to do for him, he could have borne her ministrations better; as it was, they oppressed him. She certainly tried to make as light as possible of whatever was disagreeable in her task, and as time went on she succeeded, of course, more and more, but time brought more enlightenment to Gregor too. The very way she came in distressed him. Hardly was she in the room when she rushed to the window, without even taking time to shut the door, careful as she was usually to shield the sight of Gregor's room from the others, and as if she were almost suffocating tore the casements open with hasty fingers, standing then in the open draught for a while even in the bitterest cold and drawing deep breaths. This noisy scurry of hers upset Gregor twice a day; he would crouch trembling under the sofa all the time, knowing quite well that she would certainly have spared him such a disturbance had she found it at all possible to stay in his presence without opening the window.

On one occasion, about a month after Gregor's metamorphosis, when there was surely no reason for her to be still startled at his appearance, she came a little earlier than usual and found him gazing out of the window, quite motionless, and thus well placed to look like a bogey. Gregor would not have been surprised had she not come in at all, for she could not immediately open the window while he was there, but not only did she retreat, she jumped back as if in alarm and banged the door shut; a stranger might well have thought that he had been lying in wait for her there meaning to bite her. Of course he hid himself under the sofa at once, but he had to wait until midday before she came again, and she seemed more ill at ease than usual. This made him realize how repulsive the sight of him still was to her, and that it was bound to go on being repulsive, and what an effort it must cost her not to run away even from the sight of the small portion of his body that stuck out from under the sofa. In order to spare her that, therefore, one day he carried a sheet on his back to the sofa – it cost him four hours' labor – and arranged it there in such a way as to hide him completely, so that even if she were to bend down she could not see him. Had she considered the sheet unnecessary, she would certainly have stripped it off the sofa again, for it was clear enough that this curtaining and confining of himself was not likely to conduce to Gregor's comfort, but she left it where it was, and Gregor even fancied that he caught a thankful glance from her eye when he lifted the sheet carefully a very little with his head to see how she was taking the new arrangement.

For the first fortnight his parents could not bring themselves to the point of entering his room, and he often heard them expressing their appreciation of his sister's activities, whereas formerly they had frequently scolded her for being as they thought a somewhat useless daughter. But now, both of them often waited outside the door, his father and his mother, while his sister tidied his room, and as soon as she came out she had to tell them exactly how things were in the room, what Gregor had eaten, how he had conducted himself this time, and whether there was not perhaps some slight improvement in his condition. His mother, moreover, began relatively soon to want to visit him, but his father and sister dissuaded her at first with arguments which Gregor listened to very attentively and altogether approved. Later, however, she had to be held back by main force, and when she cried out: 'Do let me in to Gregor, he is my unfortunate son! Can't you understand that I must go to him?' Gregor thought that it might be well to have her come in, not every day, of course, but perhaps once a week; she understood things, after all, much better than his sister, who was only a child despite the efforts she was making and had perhaps taken on so difficult a task merely out of childish thoughtlessness.

Gregor's desire to see his mother was soon fulfilled. During the daytime he did not want to show himself at the window, out of consideration for his parents, but he could not crawl very far around the few square yards of floor space he had, nor could he bear lying quietly at rest all during the night, while he was fast losing any interest he had ever taken in food, so that for mere recreation he had formed the habit of crawling crisscross over the walls and ceiling. He especially enjoyed hanging suspended from the ceiling; it was much better than lying on the floor; one could breathe more freely; one's body swung and rocked lightly; and in the almost blissful absorption induced by this suspension it could happen to his own surprise that he let go and fell plump on the floor. Yet he now had his body much better under control than formerly, and even such a big fall did him no harm. His sister at once remarked the new distraction Gregor had found for himself – he left traces behind him of the sticky stuff on his soles wherever he crawled – and she got the idea in her head of giving him as wide a field as possible to crawl in and of removing the pieces of furniture that hindered him, above all the chest of drawers and the writing desk. But that was more than she could manage all by herself; she did not dare ask her father to help her; and as for the servant girl, a young creature of sixteen who had had the courage to stay on after the cook's departure, she could not be asked to help, for she had begged as a special favor that she might keep the kitchen door locked and open it only on a definite summons; so there was nothing left but to apply to her mother at an hour when her father was out. And the old lady did come, with exclamations of joyful eagerness, which, however, died away at the door of Gregor's room. Gregor's sister, of course, went in first, to see that everything was in order before letting his mother enter. In great haste Gregor pulled the sheet lower and rucked it more in folds so that it really looked as if it had been thrown accidentally over the sofa. And this time he did not peer out from under it; he renounced the pleasure of seeing his mother on this occasion and was only glad that she had come at all. 'Come in, he's out of sight,' said his sister, obviously leading her mother in by the hand. Gregor could now hear the two women struggling to shift the heavy old chest from its place, and his sister claiming the greater part of the labor for herself, without listening to the admonitions of her mother, who feared she might overstrain herself. It took a long time. After at least a quarter of an hour's tugging his mother objected that the chest had better be left where it was, for in the first place it was too heavy and could never be got out before his father came home, and standing in the middle of the room like that it would only hamper Gregor's movements, while in the second place it was not at all certain that removing the furniture would be doing a service to Gregor. She was inclined to think to the contrary; the sight of the naked walls made her own heart heavy, and why shouldn't Gregor have the same feeling, considering that he had been used to his furniture for so long and might feel forlorn without it. 'And doesn't it look,' she concluded in a low voice – in fact she had been almost whispering all the time as if to avoid letting Gregor, whose exact whereabouts she did not know, hear even the tones of her voice, for she was convinced that he could not understand her words – 'doesn't it look as if we were showing him, by taking away his furniture, that we have given up hope of his ever getting better and are just leaving him coldly to himself? I think it would be best to keep his room exactly as it has always been, so that when he comes back to us he will find everything unchanged and be able all the more easily to forget what has happened in between.'

On hearing these words from his mother Gregor realized that the lack of all direct human speech for the past two months together with the monotony of family life must have confused his mind, otherwise he could not account for the fact that he had quite earnestly looked forward to having his room emptied of furnishing. Did he really want his warm room, so comfortably fitted with old family furniture, to be turned into a naked den in which he would certainly be able to crawl unhampered in all directions but at the price of shedding simultaneously all recollection of his human background? He had indeed been so near the brink of forgetfulness that only the voice of his mother, which he had not heard for so long, had drawn him back from it. Nothing should be taken out of his room; everything must stay as it was; he could not dispense with the good influence of the furniture on his state of mind; and even if the furniture did hamper him in his senseless crawling around and around, that was no drawback but a great advantage.

Unfortunately his sister was of the contrary opinion; she had grown accustomed, and not without reason, to consider herself an expert in Gregor's affairs as against her parents, and so her mother's advice was now enough to make her determined on the removal not only of the chest and the writing desk, which had been her first intention, but of all the furniture except the indispensable sofa. This determination was not, of course, merely the outcome of childish recalcitrance and of the self-confidence she had recently developed so unexpectedly and at such cost; she had in fact perceived that Gregor needed a lot of space to crawl about in, while on the other hand he never used the furniture at all, so far as could be seen. Another factor might also have been the enthusiastic temperament of an adolescent girl, which seeks to indulge itself on every opportunity and which now tempted Grete to exaggerate the horror of her brother's circumstances in order that she might do all the more for him. In a room where Gregor lorded it all alone over empty walls no one save herself was likely ever to set foot.

And so she was not to be moved from her resolve by her mother, who seemed moreover to be ill at ease in Gregor's room and therefore unsure of herself, was soon reduced to silence, and helped her daughter as best she could to push the chest outside. Now, Gregor could do without the chest, if need be, but the writing desk he must retain. As soon as the two women had got the chest out of his room, groaning as they pushed it, Gregor stuck his head out from under the sofa to see how he might intervene as kindly and cautiously as possible. But as bad luck would have it, his mother was the first to return, leaving Grete clasping the chest in the room next door where she was trying to shift it all by herself, without of course moving it from the spot. His mother however was not accustomed to the sight of him, it might sicken her and so in alarm Gregor backed quickly to the other end of the sofa, yet could not prevent the sheet from swaying a little in front. That was enough to put her on the alert. She paused, stood still for a moment, and then went back to Grete.

Although Gregor kept reassuring himself that nothing out of the way was happening, but only a few bits of furniture were being changed around, he soon had to admit that all this trotting to and fro of the two women, their little ejaculations, and the scraping of furniture along the floor affected him like a vast disturbance coming from all sides at once, and however much he tucked in his head and legs and cowered to the very floor he was bound to confess that he would not be able to stand it for long. They were clearing his room out; taking away everything he loved; the chest in which he kept his fret saw and other tools was already dragged off; they were now loosening the writing desk which had almost sunk into the floor, the desk at which he had done all his homework when he was at the commercial academy, at the grammar school before that, and, yes, even at the primary school – he had no more time to waste in weighing the good intentions of the two women, whose existence he had by now almost forgotten, for they were so exhausted that they were laboring in silence and nothing could be heard but the heavy scuffling of their feet.

And so he rushed out – the women were just leaning against the writing desk in the next room to give themselves a breather – and four times changed his direction, since he really did not know what to rescue first, then on the wall opposite, which was already otherwise cleared, he was struck by the picture of the lady muffled in so much fur and quickly crawled up to it and pressed himself to the glass, which was a good surface to hold on to and comforted his hot belly. This picture at least, which was entirely hidden beneath him, was going to be removed by nobody. He turned his head toward the door of the living room so as to observe the women when they came back.

They had not allowed themselves much of a rest and were already coming; Grete had twined her arm around her mother and was almost supporting her. 'Well, what shall we take now?' said Grete, looking around. Her eyes met Gregor's from the wall. She kept her composure, presumably because of her mother, bent her head down to her mother, to keep her from looking up, and said, although in a fluttering, unpremeditated voice: 'Come, hadn't we better go back to the living room for a moment?' Her intentions were clear enough to Gregor, she wanted to bestow her mother in safety and then chase him down from the wall. Well, just let her try it! He clung to his picture and would not give it up. He would rather fly in Grete's face.

But Grete's words had succeeded in disquieting her mother,

who took a step to one side, caught sight of the huge brown mass on the flowered wallpaper, and before she was really conscious that what she saw was Gregor, screamed in a loud, hoarse voice: 'Oh God, oh God!' fell with outspread arms over the sofa as if giving up, and did not move. 'Gregor!' cried his sister, shaking her fist and glaring at him. This was the first time she had directly addressed him since his metamorphosis. She ran into the next room for some aromatic essence with which to rouse her mother from her fainting fit. Gregor wanted to help too – there was still time to rescue the picture – but he was stuck fast to the glass and had to tear himself loose; he then ran after his sister into the next room as if he could advise her, as he used to do; but then had to stand helplessly behind her; she meanwhile searched among various small bottles and when she turned around started in alarm at the sight of him; one bottle fell on the floor and broke; a splinter of glass cut Gregor's face and some kind of corrosive medicine splashed him; without pausing a moment longer Grete gathered up all the bottles she could carry and ran to her mother with them; she banged the door shut with her foot. Gregor was now cut off from his mother, who was perhaps nearly dying because of him; he dared not open the door for fear of frightening away his sister, who had to stay with her mother; there was nothing he could do but wait; and harassed by self-reproach and worry he began now to crawl to and fro, over everything, walls, furniture, and ceiling, and finally in his despair, when the whole room seemed to be reeling around him, fell down onto the middle of the big table.

A little while elapsed, Gregor was still lying there feebly and all around was quiet, perhaps that was a good omen. Then the doorbell rang. The servant girl was of course locked in her kitchen, and Grete would have to open the door. It was his father. 'What's been happening?' were his first words; Grete's face must have told him everything. Grete answered in a muffled voice, apparently hiding her head on his breast: 'Mother has been fainting, but she's better now. Gregor's broken loose.' 'Just what I expected,' said his father, 'just what I've been telling you, but you women would never listen.' It was clear to Gregor that his father had taken the worst interpretation of Grete's all too brief statement and was assuming that Gregor had been guilty of some violent act. Therefore Gregor must now try to propitiate his father, since he had neither time nor means for an explanation. And so he fled to the door of his own room and crouched against it, to let his father see as soon as he came in from the hall that his son had the good intention of getting back into his room immediately and that it was not necessary to drive him there, but that if only the door were opened he would disappear at once.

Yet his father was not in the mood to perceive such fine distinctions. 'Ah!' he cried as soon as he appeared, in a tone that sounded at once angry and exultant. Gregor drew his head back from the door and lifted it to look at his father. Truly, this was not the father he had imagined to himself; admittedly he had been too absorbed of late in his new recreation of crawling over the ceiling to take the same interest as before in what was happening elsewhere in the flat, and he ought really to be prepared for some changes. And yet, and yet, could that be his father? The man who used to lie wearily sunk in bed whenever Gregor set out on a business journey; who welcomed him back of an evening lying in a long chair in a dressing gown; who could not really rise to his feet but only lifted his arms in greeting, and on the rare occasions when he did go out with his family, on one or two Sundays a year and on highest holidays, walked between Gregor and his mother, who were slow walkers anyhow, even more slowly than they did, muffled in his old greatcoat, shuffling laboriously forward with the help of his crook-handled stick which he set down most cautiously at every step and, whenever he wanted to say anything, nearly always came to a full stop and gathered his escort around him? Now he was standing there in fine shape; dressed in a smart blue uniform with gold buttons, such as bank messengers wear; his strong double chin bulged over the stiff high collar of his jacket; from under his bushy eyebrows his black eyes darted fresh and penetrating glances; his onetime tangled white hair had been combed flat on either side of a shining and carefully exact parting. He pitched his cap, which bore a gold monogram, probably the badge of some bank, in a wide sweep across the whole room onto a sofa and with the tail-ends of his jacket thrown back, his hands in his trouser pockets, advanced with a grim visage toward Gregor. Likely enough he did not himself know what he meant to do; at any rate he lifted his feet uncommonly high, and Gregor was dumbfounded at the enormous size of his shoe soles. But Gregor could not risk standing up to him, aware as he had been from the very first day of his new life that his father believed only the severest measures suitable for dealing with him. And so he ran before his father, stopping when he stopped and scuttling forward again when his father made any kind of move. In this way they circled the room several times without anything decisive happening, indeed the whole operation did not even look like a pursuit because it was carried out so slowly. And so Gregor did not leave the floor, for he feared that his father might take as a piece of peculiar wickedness any excursion of his over the walls or the ceiling. All the same, he could not stay this course much longer, for while his father took one step he had to carry out a whole series of movements. He was already beginning to feel breathless, just as in his former life his lungs had not been very dependable. As he was staggering along, trying to concentrate his energy on running, hardly keeping his eyes open; in his dazed state never even thinking of any other escape than simply going forward; and having almost forgotten that the walls were free to him, which in this room were well provided with finely carved pieces of furniture full of knobs and crevices – suddenly something lightly flung landed close behind him and rolled before him. It was an apple; a second apple followed immediately; Gregor came to a stop in alarm; there was no point in running on, for his father was determined to bombard him. He had filled his pockets with fruit from the dish on the sideboard and was now shying apple after apple, without taking particularly good aim for the moment. The small red apples rolled about the floor as if magnetized and cannoned into each other. An apple thrown without much force grazed Gregor's back and glanced off harmlessly. But another following immediately landed right on his back and sank in; Gregor wanted to drag himself forward, as if this startling, incredible pain could be left behind him; but he felt as if nailed to the spot and flattened himself out in a complete derangement of all his senses. With his last conscious look he saw the door of his room being torn open and his mother rushing out ahead of his screaming sister, in her underbodice, for her daughter had loosened her clothing to let her breathe more freely and recover from her swoon, he saw his mother rushing toward his father, leaving one after another behind her on the floor her loosened petticoats, stumbling over her petticoats straight to his father and embracing him, in complete union with him – but here Gregor's sight began to fail – with her hands clasped around his father's neck as she begged for her son's life.

III

The serious injury done to Gregor, which disabled him for more than a month – the apple went on sticking in his body as a visible reminder, since no one ventured to remove it – seemed to have made even his father recollect that Gregor was a member of the family, despite his present unfortunate and repulsive shape, and ought not to be treated as an enemy, that, on the contrary, family duty required the suppression of disgust and the exercise of patience, nothing but patience.

And although his injury had impaired, probably forever, his powers of movement, and for the time being it took him long, long minutes to creep across his room like an old invalid – there was no question now of crawling up the wall – yet in his own opinion he was sufficiently compensated for this worsening of his condition by the fact that toward evening the living-room door, which he used to watch intently for an hour or two beforehand, was always thrown open, so that lying in the darkness of his room, invisible to the family, he could see them all at the lamp-lit table and listen to their talk, by general consent as it were, very different from his earlier eavesdropping.

True, their intercourse lacked the lively character of former times, which he had always called to mind with a certain wistfulness in the small hotel bedrooms where he had been wont to throw himself down, tired out, on damp bedding. They were now mostly very silent. Soon after supper his father would fall asleep in his armchair; his mother and sister would admonish each other to be silent; his mother, bending low over the lamp, stitched at fine sewing for an underwear firm; his sister, who had taken a job as a salesgirl, was learning shorthand and French in the evenings on the chance of bettering herself. Sometimes his father woke up, and as if quite unaware that he had been sleeping said to his mother: 'What a lot of sewing you're doing today!' and at once fell asleep again, while the two women exchanged a tired smile.

With a kind of mulishness his father persisted in keeping his uniform on even in the house; his dressing gown hung uselessly on its peg and he slept fully dressed where he sat, as if he were ready for service at any moment and even here only at the beck and call of his superior. As a result, his uniform, which was not brand-new to start with, began to look dirty, despite all the loving care of the mother and sister to keep it clean, and Gregor often spent whole evenings gazing at the many greasy spots on the garment, gleaming with gold buttons always in a high state of polish, in which the old man sat sleeping in extreme discomfort and yet quite peacefully.

As soon as the clock struck ten his mother tried to rouse his father with gentle words and to persuade him after that to get into bed, for sitting there he could not have a proper sleep and that was what he needed most, since he had to go on duty at six. But with the mulishness that had obsessed him since he became a bank messenger he always insisted on staying longer at the table, although he regularly fell asleep again and in the end only with the greatest trouble could be got out of his armchair and into his bed. However insistently Gregor's mother and sister kept urging him with gentle reminders, he would go on slowly shaking his head for a quarter of an hour, keeping his eyes shut, and refuse to get to his feet. The mother plucked at his sleeve, whispering endearments in his ear, the sister left her lessons to come to her mother's help, but Gregor's father was not to be caught. He would only sink down deeper in his chair. Not until the two women hoisted him up by the armpits did he open his eyes and look at them both, one after the other, usually with the remark: 'This is a life. This is the peace and quiet of my old age.' And leaning on the two of them he would heave himself up, with difficulty, as if he were a great burden to himself, suffer them to lead him as far as the door and then wave them off and go on alone, while the mother abandoned her needlework and the sister her pen in order to run after him and help him farther.

Who could find time, in this overworked and tired-out family, to bother about Gregor more than was absolutely needful? The household was reduced more and more; the servant girl was turned off; a gigantic bony charwoman with white hair flying around her head came in morning and evening to do the rough work; everything else was done by Gregor's mother, as well as great piles of sewing. Even various family ornaments, which his mother and sister used to wear with pride at parties and celebrations, had to be sold, as Gregor discovered of an evening from hearing them all discuss the prices obtained. But what they lamented most was the fact that they could not leave the flat which was much too big for their present circumstances, because they could not think of any way to shift Gregor. Yet Gregor saw well enough that consideration for him was not the main difficulty preventing the removal, for they could have easily shifted him in some suitable box with a few air holes in it; what really kept them from moving into another flat was rather their own complete hopelessness and the belief that they had been singled out for a misfortune such as had never happened to any of their relations or acquaintances. They fulfilled to the uttermost all that the world demands of poor people, the father fetched breakfast for the small clerks in the bank, the mother devoted her energy to making underwear for strangers, the sister trotted to and fro behind the counter at the behest of customers, but more than this they had not the strength to do. And the wound in Gregor's back began to nag at him afresh when his mother and sister, after getting his father into bed, came back again, left their work lying, drew close to each other, and sat cheek by cheek; when his mother, pointing toward his room, said: 'Shut that door now, Grete,' and he was left again in darkness, while next door the women mingled their tears or perhaps sat dry-eyed staring at the table.

Gregor hardly slept at all by night or by day. He was often haunted by the idea that next time the door opened he would take the family's affairs in hand again just as he used to do; once more, after this long interval, there appeared in his thoughts the figures of the chief and the chief clerk, the commercial travelers and the apprentices, the porter who was so dull-witted, two or three friends in other firms, a chambermaid in one of the rural hotels, a sweet and fleeting memory, a cashier in a milliner's shop, whom he had wooed earnestly but too slowly – they all appeared, together with strangers or people he had quite forgotten, but instead of helping him and his family they were one and all unapproachable and he was glad when they vanished. At other times he would not be in the mood to bother about his family, he was only filled with rage at the way they were neglecting him, and although he had no clear idea of what he might care to eat he would make plans for getting into the larder to take the food that was after all his due, even if he were not hungry. His sister no longer took thought to bring him what might especially please him, but in the morning and at noon before she went to business hurriedly pushed into his room with her foot any food that was available, and in the evening cleared it out again with one sweep of the broom, heedless of whether it had been merely tasted, or – as most frequently happened – left untouched. The cleaning of his room, which she now did always in the evenings, could not have been more hastily done. Streaks of dirt stretched along the walls, here and there lay balls of dust and filth. At first Gregor used to station himself in some particularly filthy corner when his sister arrived, in order to reproach her with it, so to speak. But he could have sat there for weeks without getting her to make any improvement; she could see the dirt as well as he did, but she had simply made up her mind to leave it alone. And yet, with a touchiness that was new to her, which seemed anyhow to have infected the whole family, she jealously guarded her claim to be the sole caretaker of Gregor's room. His mother once subjected his room to a thorough cleaning, which was achieved only by means of several buckets of water – all this dampness of course upset Gregor too and he lay widespread, sulky, and motionless on the sofa – but she was well punished for it. Hardly had his sister noticed the changed aspect of his room that evening than she rushed in high dudgeon into the living room and, despite the imploringly raised hands of her mother, burst into a storm of weeping, while her parents – her father had of course been startled out of his chair – looked on at first in helpless amazement; then they too began to go into action; the father reproached the mother on his right for not having left the cleaning of Gregor's room to his sister; shrieked at the sister on his left that never again was she to be allowed to clean Gregor's room; while the mother tried to pull the father into his bedroom, since he was beyond himself with agitation; the sister, shaken with sobs, then beat upon the table with her small fists; and Gregor hissed loudly with rage because not one of them thought of shutting the door to spare him such a spectacle and so much noise.

Still, even if the sister, exhausted by her daily work, had grown tired of looking after Gregor as she did formerly, there was no need for his mother's intervention or for Gregor's being neglected at all. The charwoman was there. This old widow, whose strong bony frame had enabled her to survive the worst a long life could offer, by no means recoiled from Gregor. Without being in the least curious she had once by chance opened the door of his room and at the sight of Gregor, who, taken by surprise, began to rush to and fro although no one was chasing him, merely stood there with her arms folded. From that time she never failed to open his door a little for a moment, morning and evening, to have a look at him. At first she even used to call him to her, with words which apparently she took to be friendly, such as: 'Come along, then, you old dung beetle!' or 'Look at the old dung beetle, then!' To such allocutions Gregor made no answer, but stayed motionless where he was, as if the door had never been opened. Instead of being allowed to disturb him so senselessly whenever the whim took her, she should rather have been ordered to clean out his room daily, that charwoman! Once, early in the morning – heavy rain was lashing on the windowpanes, perhaps a sign that spring was on the way – Gregor was so exasperated when she began addressing him again that he ran at her, as if to attack her, although slowly and feebly enough. But the charwoman instead of showing fright merely lifted high a chair that happened to be beside the door, and as she stood there with her mouth wide open it was clear that she meant to shut it only when she brought the chair down on Gregor's back. 'So you're not coming any nearer?' she asked, as Gregor turned again, and quietly put the chair back into the corner.

Gregor was now eating hardly anything. Only when he happened to pass the food laid out for him did he take a bit of something in his mouth as a pastime, kept it there for an hour at a time, and usually spat it out again. At first he thought it was chagrin over the state of his room that prevented him from eating, yet he soon got used to the various changes in his room. It had become a habit in the family to push into his room things there was no room for elsewhere, and there were plenty of these now, since one of the rooms had been let to three lodgers. These serious gentlemen – all three of them with full beards, as Gregor once observed through a crack in the door – had a passion for order, not only in their own room but, since they were now members of the household, in all its arrangements, especially in the kitchen. Superfluous, not to say dirty, objects they could not bear. Besides, they had brought with them most of the furnishings they needed. For this reason many things could be dispensed with that it was no use trying to sell but that should not be thrown away either. All of them found their way into Gregor's room. The ash can likewise and the kitchen garbage can. Anything that was not needed for the moment was simply flung into Gregor's room by the charwoman, who did everything in a hurry; fortunately Gregor usually saw only the object, whatever it was, and the hand that held it. Perhaps she intended to take the things away again as time and opportunity offered, or to collect them until she could throw them all out in a heap, but in fact they just lay wherever she happened to throw them, except when Gregor pushed his way through the junk heap and shifted it somewhat, at first out of necessity, because he had not room enough to crawl, but later with increasing enjoyment, although after such excursions, being sad and weary to death, he would lie motionless for hours. And since the lodgers often ate their supper at home in the common living room, the living-room door stayed shut many an evening, yet Gregor reconciled himself quite easily to the shutting of the door, for often enough on evenings when it was opened he had disregarded it entirely and lain in the darkest corner of his room, quite unnoticed by the family. But on one occasion the charwoman left the door open a little and it stayed ajar even when the lodgers came in for supper and the lamp was lit. They set themselves at the top end of the table where formerly Gregor and his father and mother had eaten their meals, unfolded their napkins, and took knife and fork in hand. At once his mother appeared in the other doorway with a dish of meat and close behind her his sister with a dish of potatoes piled high. The food steamed with a thick vapor. The lodgers bent over the food set before them as if to scrutinize it before eating, in fact the man in the middle, who seemed to pass for an authority with the other two, cut a piece of meat as it lay on the dish, obviously to discover if it were tender or should be sent back to the kitchen. He showed satisfaction, and Gregor's mother and sister, who had been watching anxiously, breathed freely and began to smile.

The family itself took its meals in the kitchen. Nonetheless, Gregor's father came into the living room before going into the kitchen and with one prolonged bow, cap in hand, made a round of the table. The lodgers all stood up and murmured something in their beards. When they were alone again they ate their food in almost complete silence. It seemed remarkable to Gregor that among the various noises coming from the table he could always distinguish the sound of their masticating teeth, as if this were a sign to Gregor that one needed teeth in order to eat, and that with toothless jaws even of the finest make one could do nothing. 'I'm hungry enough,' said Gregor sadly to himself, 'but not for that kind of food. How these lodgers are stuffing themselves, and here am I dying of starvation!'

On that very evening – during the whole of his time there Gregor could not remember ever having heard the violin – the sound of violin-playing came from the kitchen. The lodgers had already finished their supper, the one in the middle had brought out a newspaper and given the other two a page apiece, and now they were leaning back at ease reading and smoking. When the violin began to play they pricked up their ears, got to their feet, and went on tiptoe to the hall door where they stood huddled together. Their movements must have been heard in the kitchen, for Gregor's father called out: 'Is the violin-playing disturbing you, gentlemen? It can be stopped at once.' 'On the contrary,' said the middle lodger, 'could not Fräulein Samsa come and play in this room, beside us, where it is much more convenient and comfortable?' 'Oh certainly,' cried Gregor's father, as if he were the violin-player. The lodgers came back into the living room and waited. Presently Gregor's father arrived with the music stand, his mother carrying the music and his sister with the violin. His sister quietly made everything ready to start playing; his parents, who had never let rooms before and so had an exaggerated idea of the courtesy due to lodgers, did not venture to sit down on their own chairs; his father leaned against the door, the right hand thrust between two buttons of his livery coat, which was formally buttoned up; but his mother was offered a chair by one of the lodgers and, since she left the chair just where he had happened to put it, sat down in a corner to one side.

Gregor's sister began to play; the father and mother, from either side, intently watched the movements of her hands. Gregor, attracted by the playing, ventured to move forward a little until his head was actually inside the living room. He felt hardly any surprise at his growing lack of consideration for the others; there had been a time when he prided himself on being considerate. And yet just on this occasion he had more reason than ever to hide himself, since, owing to the amount of dust that lay thick in his room and rose into the air at the slightest movement, he too was covered with dust; fluff and hair and remnants of food trailed with him, caught on his back and along his sides; his indifference to everything was much too great for him to turn on his back and scrape himself clean on the carpet, as once he had done several times a day. And in spite of his condition, no shame deterred him from advancing a little over the spotless floor of the living room.

To be sure, no one was aware of him. The family was entirely absorbed in the violin-playing; the lodgers, however, who first of all had stationed themselves, hands in pockets, much too close behind the music stand so that they could all have read the music, which must have bothered his sister, had soon retreated to the window, half whispering with downbent heads, and stayed there while his father turned an anxious eye on them. Indeed, they were making it more than obvious that they had been disappointed in their expectation of hearing good or enjoyable violin-playing, that they had had more than enough of the performance and only out of courtesy suffered a continued disturbance of their peace. From the way they all kept blowing the smoke of their cigars high in the air through nose and mouth one could divine their irritation. And yet Gregor's sister was playing so beautifully. Her face leaned sideways, intently and sadly her eyes followed the notes of music. Gregor crawled a little farther forward and lowered his head to the ground so that it might be possible for his eyes to meet hers. Was he an animal, that music had such an effect upon him? He felt as if the way were opening before him to the unknown nourishment he craved. He was determined to push forward till he reached his sister, to pull at her skirt and so let her know that she was to come into his room with her violin, for no one here appreciated her playing as he would appreciate it. He would never let her out of his room, at least, not so long as he lived; his frightful appearance would become, for the first time, useful to him; he would watch all the doors of his room at once and spit at intruders; but his sister should need no constraint, she should stay with him of her own free will; she should sit beside him on the sofa, bend down her ear to him, and hear him confide that he had had the firm intention of sending her to the Conservatorium, and that, but for his mishap, last Christmas – surely Christmas was long past? – he would have announced it to everybody without allowing a single objection. After this confession his sister would be so touched that she would burst into tears, and Gregor would then raise himself to her shoulder and kiss her on the neck, which, now that she went to business, she kept free of any ribbon or collar.

'Mr. Samsa!' cried the middle lodger to Gregor's father,

and pointed, without wasting any more words, at Gregor, now working himself slowly forward. The violin fell silent, the middle lodger first smiled to his friends with a shake of the head and then looked at Gregor again. Instead of driving Gregor out, his father seemed to think it more needful to begin by soothing down the lodgers, although they were not at all agitated and apparently found Gregor more entertaining than the violin-playing. He hurried toward them and, spreading out his arms, tried to urge them back into their own room and at the same time to block their view of Gregor. They now began to be really a little angry, one could not tell whether because of the old man's behavior or because it had just dawned on them that all unwittingly they had such a neighbor as Gregor next door. They demanded explanations of his father, they waved their arms like him, tugged uneasily at their beards, and only with reluctance backed toward their room. Meanwhile Gregor's sister, who stood there as if lost when her playing was so abruptly broken off, came to life again, pulled herself together all at once after standing for a while holding violin and bow in nervelessly hanging hands and staring at her music, pushed her violin into the lap of her mother, who was still sitting in her chair fighting asthmatically for breath, and ran into the lodgers' room to which they were now being shepherded by her father rather more quickly than before. One could see the pillows and blankets on the beds flying under her accustomed fingers and being laid in order. Before the lodgers had actually reached their room she had finished making the beds and slipped out.

The old man seemed once more to be so possessed by his mulish self-assertiveness that he was forgetting all the respect he should show to his lodgers. He kept driving them on and driving them on until in the very door of the bedroom the middle lodger stamped his foot loudly on the floor and so brought him to a halt. 'I beg to announce,' said the lodger, lifting one hand and looking also at Gregor's mother and sister, 'that because of the disgusting conditions prevailing in this household and family' – here he spat on the floor with emphatic brevity – 'I give you notice on the spot. Naturally I won't pay you a penny for the days I have lived here, on the contrary I shall consider bringing an action for damages against you, based on claims – believe me – that will be easily susceptible of proof.' He ceased and stared straight in front of him, as if he expected something. In fact his two friends at once rushed into the breach with these words: 'And we too give notice on the spot.' On that he seized the door handle and shut the door with a slam.

Gregor's father, groping with his hands, staggered forward and fell into his chair; it looked as if he were stretching himself there for his ordinary evening nap, but the marked jerkings of his head, which were as if uncontrollable, showed that he was far from asleep. Gregor had simply stayed quietly all the time on the spot where the lodgers had espied him. Disappointment at the failure of his plan, perhaps also the weakness arising from extreme hunger, made it impossible for him to move. He feared, with a fair degree of certainty, that at any moment the general tension would discharge itself in a combined attack upon him, and he lay waiting. He did not react even to the noise made by the violin as it fell off his mother's lap from under her trembling fingers and gave out a resonant note.

'My dear parents,' said his sister, slapping her hand on the table by way of introduction, 'things can't go on like this. Perhaps you don't realize that, but I do. I won't utter my brother's name in the presence of this creature, and so all I say is: we must try to get rid of it. We've tried to look after it and to put up with it as far as is humanly possible, and I don't think anyone could reproach us in the slightest.'

'She is more than right,' said Gregor's father to himself. His mother, who was still choking for lack of breath, began to cough hollowly into her hand with a wild look in her eyes.

His sister rushed over to her and held her forehead. His father's thoughts seemed to have lost their vagueness at Grete's words, he sat more upright, fingering his service cap that lay among the plates still lying on the table from the lodgers' supper, and from time to time looked at the still form of Gregor.

'We must try to get rid of it,' his sister now said explicitly to her father, since her mother was coughing too much to hear a word, 'it will be the death of both of you, I can see that coming. When one has to work as hard as we do, all of us, one can't stand this continual torment at home on top of it. At least I can't stand it any longer.' And she burst into such a passion of sobbing that her tears dropped on her mother's face, where she wiped them off mechanically.

'My dear,' said the old man sympathetically, and with evident understanding, 'but what can we do?'

Gregor's sister merely shrugged her shoulders to indicate the feeling of helplessness that had now overmastered her during her weeping fit, in contrast to her former confidence.

'If he could understand us,' said her father, half questioningly; Grete, still sobbing, vehemently waved a hand to show how unthinkable that was.

'If he could understand us,' repeated the old man, shutting his eyes to consider his daughter's conviction that understanding was impossible, 'then perhaps we might come to some agreement with him. But as it is —'

'He must go,' cried Gregor's sister, 'that's the only solution, Father. You must just try to get rid of the idea that this is Gregor. The fact that we've believed it for so long is the root of all our trouble. But how can it be Gregor? If this were Gregor, he would have realized long ago that human beings can't live with such a creature, and he'd have gone away on his own accord. Then we wouldn't have any brother, but we'd be able to go on living and keep his memory in honor. As it is, this creature persecutes us, drives away our lodgers, obviously wants the whole apartment to himself, and would have us all sleep in the gutter. Just look, Father,' she shrieked all at once, 'he's at it again!' And in an access of panic that was quite incomprehensible to Gregor she even quitted her mother, literally thrusting the chair from her as if she would rather sacrifice her mother than stay so near to Gregor, and rushed behind her father, who also rose up, being simply upset by her agitation, and half spread his arms out as if to protect her.

Yet Gregor had not the slightest intention of frightening anyone, far less his sister. He had only begun to turn around in order to crawl back to his room, but it was certainly a startling operation to watch, since because of his disabled condition he could not execute the difficult turning movements except by lifting his head and then bracing it against the floor over and over again. He paused and looked around. His good intentions seemed to have been recognized; the alarm had only been momentary. Now they were all watching him in melancholy silence. His mother lay in her chair, her legs stiffly outstretched and pressed together, her eyes almost closing for sheer weariness; his father and his sister were sitting beside each other, his sister's arm around the old man's neck.

Perhaps I can go on turning around now, thought Gregor, and began his labors again. He could not stop himself from panting with the effort, and had to pause now and then to take breath. Nor did anyone harass him, he was left entirely to himself. When he had completed the turn-around he began at once to crawl straight back. He was amazed at the distance separating him from his room and could not understand how in his weak state he had managed to accomplish the same journey so recently, almost without remarking it. Intent on crawling as fast as possible, he barely noticed that not a single word, not an ejaculation from his family, interfered with his progress. Only when he was already in the doorway did he turn his head around, not completely, for his neck muscles were getting stiff, but enough to see that nothing had changed behind him except that his sister had risen to her feet. His last glance fell on his mother, who was not quite overcome by sleep.

Hardly was he well inside his room when the door was

hastily pushed shut, bolted, and locked. The sudden noise in his rear startled him so much that his little legs gave beneath him. It was his sister who had shown such haste. She had been standing ready waiting and had made a light spring forward, Gregor had not even heard her coming, and she cried 'At last!' to her parents as she turned the key in the lock.

'And what now?' said Gregor to himself, looking around in the darkness. Soon he made the discovery that he was now unable to stir a limb. This did not surprise him, rather it seemed unnatural that he should ever actually have been able to move on these feeble little legs. Otherwise he felt relatively comfortable. True, his whole body was aching, but it seemed that the pain was gradually growing less and would finally pass away. The rotting apple in his back and the inflamed area around it, all covered with soft dust, already hardly troubled him. He thought of his family with tenderness and love. The decision that he must disappear was one that he held to even more strongly than his sister, if that were possible. In this state of vacant and peaceful meditation he remained until the tower clock struck three in the morning. The first broadening of light in the world outside the window entered his consciousness once more. Then his head sank to the floor of its own accord and from his nostrils came the last faint flicker of his breath.

When the charwoman arrived early in the morning – what between her strength and her impatience she slammed all the doors so loudly, never mind how often she had been begged not to do so, that no one in the whole apartment could enjoy any quiet sleep after her arrival – she noticed nothing unusual as she took her customary peep into Gregor's room. She thought he was lying motionless on purpose, pretending to be in the sulks; she credited him with every kind of intelligence. Since she happened to have the long-handled broom in her hand she tried to tickle him up with it from the doorway. When that too produced no reaction she felt provoked and poked at him a little harder, and only when she had pushed him along the floor without meeting any resistance was her attention aroused. It did not take her long to establish the truth of the matter, and her eyes widened, she let out a whistle, yet did not waste much time over it but tore open the door of the Samsas' bedroom and yelled into the darkness at the top of her voice: 'Just look at this, it's dead; it's lying here dead and done for!'

Mr. and Mrs. Samsa started up in their double bed and before they realized the nature of the charwoman's announcement had some difficulty in overcoming the shock of it. But then they got out of bed quickly, one on either side, Mr. Samsa throwing a blanket over his shoulders, Mrs. Samsa in nothing but her nightgown; in this array they entered Gregor's room. Meanwhile the door of the living room opened, too, where Grete had been sleeping since the advent of the lodgers; she was completely dressed as if she had not been to bed, which seemed to be confirmed also by the paleness of her face. 'Dead?' said Mrs. Samsa, looking questioningly at the charwoman, although she would have investigated for herself, and the fact was obvious enough without investigation. 'I should say so,' said the charwoman, proving her words by pushing Gregor's corpse a long way to one side with her broomstick. Mrs. Samsa made a movement as if to stop her, but checked it. 'Well,' said Mr. Samsa, 'now thanks be to God.' He crossed himself, and the three women followed his example. Grete, whose eyes never left the corpse, said: 'Just see how thin he was. It's such a long time since he's eaten anything. The food came out again just as it went in.' Indeed, Gregor's body was completely flat and dry, as could only now be seen when it was no longer supported by the legs and nothing prevented one from looking closely at it.

'Come in beside us, Grete, for a little while,' said Mrs. Samsa with a tremulous smile, and Grete, not without looking back at the corpse, followed her parents into their bedroom. The charwoman shut the door and opened the window wide. Although it was so early in the morning a certain softness was perceptible in the fresh air. After all, it was already the end of March.

The three lodgers emerged from their room and were surprised to see no breakfast; they had been forgotten. 'Where's our breakfast?' said the middle lodger peevishly to the charwoman. But she put her finger to her lips and hastily, without a word, indicated by gestures that they should go into Gregor's room. They did so and stood, their hands in the pockets of their somewhat shabby coats, around Gregor's corpse in the room where it was now fully light.

At that the door of the Samsas' bedroom opened and Mr. Samsa appeared in his uniform, his wife on one arm, his daughter on the other. They all looked a little as if they had been crying; from time to time Grete hid her face on her father's arm.

'Leave my house at once!' said Mr. Samsa, and pointed to the door without disengaging himself from the women. 'What do you mean by that?' said the middle lodger, taken somewhat aback, with a feeble smile. The two others put their hands behind them and kept rubbing them together, as if in gleeful expectation of a fine set-to in which they were bound to come off the winners. 'I mean just what I say,' answered Mr. Samsa, and advanced in a straight line with his two companions toward the lodger. He stood his ground at first quietly, looking at the floor as if his thoughts were taking a new pattern in his head. 'Then let us go, by all means,' he said, and looked up at Mr. Samsa as if in a sudden access of humility he were expecting some renewed sanction for this decision. Mr. Samsa merely nodded briefly once or twice with meaning eyes. Upon that the lodger really did go with long strides into the hall, his two friends had been listening and had quite stopped rubbing their hands for some moments and now went scuttling after him as if afraid that Mr. Samsa might get into the hall before them and cut them off from their leader. In the hall they all three took their hats from the rack, their sticks from the umbrella stand, bowed in silence, and quitted the apartment. With a suspiciousness that proved quite unfounded Mr. Samsa and the two women followed them out to the landing; leaning over the banister they watched the three figures slowly but surely going down the long stairs, vanishing from sight at a certain turn of the staircase on every floor and coming into view again after a moment or so; the more they dwindled, the more the Samsa family's interest in them dwindled, and when a butcher's boy met them and passed them on the stairs coming up proudly with a tray on his head, Mr. Samsa and the two women soon left the landing and as if a burden had been lifted from them went back into their apartment.

They decided to spend this day in resting and going for a stroll; they had not only deserved such a respite from work, but absolutely needed it. And so they sat down at the table and wrote three notes of excuse, Mr. Samsa to his board of management, Mrs. Samsa to her employer, and Grete to the head of her firm. While they were writing, the charwoman came in to say that she was going now, since her morning's work was finished. At first they only nodded without looking up, but as she kept hovering there they eyed her irritably. 'Well?' said Mr. Samsa. The charwoman stood grinning in the doorway as if she had good news to impart to the family but meant not to say a word unless properly questioned. The small ostrich feather standing upright on her hat, which had annoyed Mr. Samsa ever since she was engaged, was waving gaily in all directions. 'Well, what is it then?' asked Mrs. Samsa, who obtained more respect from the charwoman than the others. 'Oh,' said the charwoman, giggling so amiably that she could not at once continue, 'just this, you don't need to bother about how to get rid of the thing next door. It's been seen to already.' Mrs. Samsa and Grete bent over their letters again, as if preoccupied; Mr. Samsa, who perceived that she was eager to begin describing it all in detail, stopped her with a decisive hand. But since she was not allowed to tell her story, she remembered the great hurry she was in, obviously deeply huffed: 'Bye, everybody,' she said, whirling off violently, and departed with a frightful slamming of doors.

'She'll be given notice tonight,' said Mr. Samsa, but neither from his wife nor his daughter did he get any answer, for the charwoman seemed to have shattered again the composure they had barely achieved. They rose, went to the window and stayed there, clasping each other tight. Mr. Samsa turned in his chair to look at them and quietly observed them for a little. Then he called out: 'Come along, now, do. Let bygones be bygones. And you might have some consideration for me.' The two of them complied at once, hastened to him, caressed him, and quickly finished their letters.

Then they all three left the apartment together, which was more than they had done for months, and went by tram into the open country outside the town. The tram, in which they were the only passengers, was filled with warm sunshine. Leaning comfortably back in their seats they canvassed their prospects for the future, and it appeared on closer inspection that these were not at all bad, for the jobs they had got, which so far they had never really discussed with each other, were all three admirable and likely to lead to better things later on. The greatest immediate improvement in their condition would of course arise from moving to another house; they wanted to take a smaller and cheaper but also better situated and more easily run apartment than the one they had, which Gregor had selected. While they were thus conversing, it struck both Mr. and Mrs. Samsa, almost at the same moment, as they became aware of their daughter's increasing vivacity, that in spite of all the sorrow of recent times, which had made her cheeks pale, she had bloomed into a pretty girl with a good figure. They grew quieter and half unconsciously exchanged glances of complete agreement, having come to the conclusion that it would soon be time to find a good husband for her. And it was like a confirmation of their new dreams and excellent intentions that at the end of their journey their daughter sprang to her feet first and stretched her young body.

Translated by Willa and Edwin Muir

In the Penal Colony (1919)

In the Penal Colony

'IT's a remarkable piece of apparatus,' said the officer to the explorer and surveyed with a certain air of admiration the apparatus which was after all quite familiar to him. The explorer seemed to have accepted merely out of politeness the Commandant's invitation to witness the execution of a soldier condemned to death for disobedience and insulting behavior to a superior. Nor did the colony itself betray much interest in this execution. At least, in the small sandy valley, a deep hollow surrounded on all sides by naked crags, there was no one present save the officer, the explorer, the condemned man, who was a stupid-looking, wide-mouthed creature with bewildered hair and face, and the soldier who held the heavy chain controlling the small chains locked on the prisoner's ankles, wrists, and neck, chains that were themselves attached to each other by communicating links. In any case, the condemned man looked so like a submissive dog that one might have thought he could be left to run free on the surrounding hills and would only need to be whistled for when the execution was due to begin.

The explorer did not much care about the apparatus and walked up and down behind the prisoner with almost visible indifference while the officer made the last adjustments, now creeping beneath the structure, which was bedded deep in the earth, now climbing a ladder to inspect its upper parts. These were tasks that might well have been left to a mechanic, but the officer performed them with great zeal, whether because he was a devoted admirer of the apparatus or because of other reasons the work could be entrusted to no one else. 'Ready now!' he called at last and climbed down from the ladder. He looked uncommonly limp, breathed with his mouth wide open, and had tucked two fine ladies' handkerchiefs under the collar of his uniform. 'These uniforms are too heavy for the tropics, surely,' said the explorer, instead of making some inquiry about the apparatus, as the officer had expected. 'Of course,' said the officer, washing his oily and greasy hands in a bucket of water that stood ready, 'but they mean home to us; we don't want to forget about home. Now just have a look at this machine,' he added at once, simultaneously drying his hands on a towel and indicating the apparatus. 'Up till now a few things still had to be set by hand, but from this moment it works all by itself.' The explorer nodded and followed him. The officer, anxious to secure himself against all contingencies, said: 'Things sometimes go wrong, of course; I hope that nothing goes wrong today, but we have to allow for the possibility. The machinery should go on working continuously for twelve hours. But if anything does go wrong it will only be some small matter that can be set right at once.'

'Won't you take a seat?' he asked finally, drawing a cane chair out from among a heap of them and offering it to the explorer, who could not refuse it. He was now sitting at the edge of a pit, into which he glanced for a fleeting moment. It was not very deep. On one side of the pit the excavated soil had been piled up in a rampart, on the other side of it stood the apparatus. 'I don't know,' said the officer, 'if the Commandant has already explained this apparatus to you.' The explorer waved one hand vaguely; the officer asked for nothing better, since now he could explain the apparatus himself. 'This apparatus,' he said, taking hold of a crank handle and leaning against it, 'was invented by our former Commandant. I assisted at the very earliest experiments and had a share in all the work until its completion. But the credit of inventing it belongs to him alone. Have you ever heard of our former Commandant? No? Well, it isn't saying too much if I tell you that the organization of the whole penal colony is his work. We who were his friends knew even before he died that the organization of the colony was so perfect that his successor, even with a thousand new schemes in his head, would find it impossible to alter anything, at least for many years to come. And our prophecy has come true; the new Commandant has had to acknowledge its truth. A pity you never met the old Commandant! – But,' the officer interrupted himself, 'I am rambling on, and here stands his apparatus before us. It consists, as you see, of three parts. In the course of time each of these parts has acquired a kind of popular nickname. The lower one is called the "Bed," the upper one the "Designer," and this one here in the middle that moves up and down is called the "Harrow." ' 'The Harrow?' asked the explorer. He had not been listening very attentively, the glare of the sun in the shadeless valley was altogether too strong, it was difficult to collect one's thoughts. All the more did he admire the officer, who in spite of his tight-fitting full-dress uniform coat, amply befrogged and weighed down by epaulettes, was pursuing his subject with such enthusiasm and, besides talking, was still tightening a screw here and there with a spanner. As for the soldier, he seemed to be in much the same condition as the explorer. He had wound the prisoner's chain around both his wrists, propped himself on his rifle, let his head hang, and was paying no attention to anything. That did not surprise the explorer, for the officer was speaking French, and certainly neither the soldier nor the prisoner understood a word of French. It was all the more remarkable, therefore, that the prisoner was nonetheless making an effort to follow the officer's explanations. With a kind of drowsy persistence he directed his gaze wherever the officer pointed a finger, and at the interruption of the explorer's question he, too, as well as the officer, looked around.

'Yes, the Harrow,' said the officer, 'a good name for it. The needles are set in like the teeth of a harrow and the whole thing works something like a harrow, although its action is limited to one place and contrived with much more artistic skill. Anyhow, you'll soon understand it. On the Bed here the condemned man is laid – I'm going to describe the apparatus first before I set it in motion. Then you'll be able to follow the proceedings better. Besides, one of the cogwheels in the Designer is badly worn; it creaks a lot when it's working; you can hardly hear yourself speak; spare parts, unfortunately, are difficult to get here. – Well, here is the Bed, as I told you. It is completely covered with a layer of cotton wool; you'll find out why later. On this cotton wool the condemned man is laid, face down, quite naked, of course; here are straps for the hands, here for the feet, and here for the neck, to bind him fast. Here at the head of the Bed, where the man, as I said, first lays down his face, is this little gag of felt, which can be easily regulated to go straight into his mouth. It is meant to keep him from screaming and biting his tongue. Of course the man is forced to take the felt into his mouth, for otherwise his neck would be broken by the strap.' 'Is that cotton wool?' asked the explorer, bending forward. 'Yes, certainly,' said the officer, with a smile, 'feel it for yourself.' He took the explorer's hand and guided it over the Bed. 'It's specially prepared cotton wool, that's why it looks so different; I'll tell you presently what it's for.' The explorer already felt a dawning interest in the apparatus; he sheltered his eyes from the sun with one hand and gazed up at the structure. It was a huge affair. The Bed and the Designer were of the same size and looked like two dark wooden chests. The Designer hung about two meters above the Bed; each of them was bound at the corners with four rods of brass that almost flashed out rays in the sunlight. Between the chests shuttled the Harrow on a ribbon of steel.

The officer had scarcely noticed the explorer's previous indifference, but he was now well aware of his dawning interest; so he stopped explaining in order to leave a space of time for quiet observation. The condemned man imitated the explorer; since he could not use a hand to shelter his eyes he gazed upwards without shade.

'Well, the man lies down,' said the explorer, leaning back in his chair and crossing his legs.

'Yes,' said the officer, pushing his cap back a little and passing one hand over his heated face, 'now listen! Both the Bed and the Designer have an electric battery each; the Bed needs one for itself, the Designer for the Harrow. As soon as the man is strapped down, the Bed is set in motion. It quivers in minute, very rapid vibrations, both from side to side and up and down. You will have seen similar apparatus in hospitals; but in our Bed the movements are all precisely calculated; you see, they have to correspond very exactly to the movements of the Harrow. And the Harrow is the instrument for the actual execution of the sentence.'

'And how does the sentence run?' asked the explorer.

'You don't know that either?' said the officer in amazement, and bit his lips. 'Forgive me if my explanations seem rather incoherent. I do beg your pardon. You see, the Commandant always used to do the explaining; but the new Commandant shirks this duty; yet that such an important visitor' – the explorer tried to deprecate the honor with both hands, the officer, however, insisted – 'that such an important visitor should not even be told about the kind of sentence we pass is a new development, which —' He was just on the point of using strong language but checked himself and said only: 'I was not informed, it is not my fault. In any case, I am certainly the best person to explain our procedure, since I have here' – he patted his breast pocket – 'the relevant drawings made by our former Commandant.'

'The Commandant's own drawings?' asked the explorer. 'Did he combine everything in himself, then? Was he soldier, judge, mechanic, chemist, and draughtsman?'

'Indeed he was,' said the officer, nodding assent, with a remote, glassy look. Then he inspected his hands critically; they did not seem clean enough to him for touching the drawings; so he went over to the bucket and washed them again. Then he drew out a small leather wallet and said: 'Our sentence does not sound severe. Whatever commandment the prisoner has disobeyed is written upon his body by the Harrow. This prisoner, for instance' – the officer indicated the man – 'will have written on his body: HONOR THY SUPERIORS!'

The explorer glanced at the man; he stood, as the officer

pointed him out, with bent head, apparently listening with all his ears in an effort to catch what was being said. Yet the movement of his blubber lips, closely pressed together, showed clearly that he could not understand a word. Many questions were troubling the explorer, but at the sight of the prisoner he asked only: 'Does he know his sentence?' 'No,' said the officer, eager to go on with his exposition, but the explorer interrupted him: 'He doesn't know the sentence that has been passed on him?' 'No,' said the officer again, pausing a moment as if to let the explorer elaborate his question, and then said: 'There would be no point in telling him. He'll learn it on his body.' The explorer intended to make no answer, but he felt the prisoner's gaze turned on him; it seemed to ask if he approved such goings-on. So he bent forward again, having already leaned back in his chair, and put another question: 'But surely he knows that he has been sentenced?' 'Nor that either,' said the officer, smiling at the explorer as if expecting him to make further surprising remarks. 'No,' said the explorer, wiping his forehead, 'then he can't know either whether his defense was effective?' 'He has had no chance of putting up a defense,' said the officer, turning his eyes away as if speaking to himself and so sparing the explorer the shame of hearing self-evident matters explained. 'But he must have had some chance of defending himself,' said the explorer, and rose from his seat.

The officer realized that he was in danger of having his exposition of the apparatus held up for a long time; so he went up to the explorer, took him by the arm, waved a hand toward the condemned man, who was standing very straight now that he had so obviously become the center of attention – the soldier had also given the chain a jerk – and said: 'This is how the matter stands. I have been appointed judge in this penal colony. Despite my youth. For I was the former Commandant's assistant in all penal matters and know more about the apparatus than anyone. My guiding principle is this: Guilt is never to be doubted. Other courts cannot follow that principle, for they consist of several opinions and have higher courts to scrutinize them. That is not the case here, or at least, it was not the case in the former Commandant's time. The new man has certainly shown some inclination to interfere with my judgments, but so far I have succeeded in fending him off and will go on succeeding. You wanted to have the case explained; it is quite simple, like all of them. A captain reported to me this morning that this man, who had been assigned to him as a servant and sleeps before his door, had been asleep on duty. It is his duty, you see, to get up every time the hour strikes and salute the captain's door. Not an exacting duty, and very necessary, since he has to be a sentry as well as a servant, and must be alert in both functions. Last night the captain wanted to see if the man was doing his duty. He opened the door as the clock struck two and there was his man curled up asleep. He took his riding whip and lashed him across the face. Instead of getting up and begging pardon, the man caught hold of his master's legs, shook him, and cried: "Throw that whip away or I'll eat you alive." – That's the evidence. The captain came to me an hour ago, I wrote down his statement and appended the sentence to it. Then I had the man put in chains. That was all quite simple. If I had first called the man before me and interrogated him, things would have got into a confused tangle. He would have told lies, and had I exposed these lies he would have backed them up with more lies, and so on and so forth. As it is, I've got him and I won't let him go. – Is that quite clear now? But we're wasting time, the execution should be beginning and I haven't finished explaining the apparatus yet.' He pressed the explorer back into his chair, went up again to the apparatus, and began: 'As you see, the shape of the Harrow corresponds to the human form; here is the harrow for the torso, here are the harrows for the legs. For the head there is only this one small spike. Is that quite clear?' He bent amiably forward toward the explorer, eager to provide the most comprehensive explanations.

The explorer considered the Harrow with a frown. The explanation of the judicial procedure had not satisfied him.

He had to remind himself that this was in any case a penal colony where extraordinary measures were needed and that military discipline must be enforced to the last. He also felt that some hope might be set on the new Commandant, who was apparently of a mind to bring in, although gradually, a new kind of procedure which the officer's narrow mind was incapable of understanding. This train of thought prompted his next question: 'Will the Commandant attend the execution?' 'It is not certain,' said the officer, wincing at the direct question, and his friendly expression darkened. 'That is just why we have to lose no time. Much as I dislike it, I shall have to cut my explanations short. But of course tomorrow, when the apparatus has been cleaned – its one drawback is that it gets so messy – I can recapitulate all the details. For the present, then, only the essentials. – When the man lies down on the Bed and it begins to vibrate, the Harrow is lowered onto his body. It regulates itself automatically so that the needles barely touch his skin; once contact is made the steel ribbon stiffens immediately into a rigid band. And then the performance begins. An ignorant onlooker would see no difference between one punishment and another. The Harrow appears to do its work with uniform regularity. As it quivers, its points pierce the skin of the body which is itself quivering from the vibration of the Bed. So that the actual progress of the sentence can be watched, the Harrow is made of glass. Getting the needles fixed in the glass was a technical problem, but after many experiments we overcame the difficulty. No trouble was too great for us to take, you see. And now anyone can look through the glass and watch the inscription taking form on the body. Wouldn't you care to come a little nearer and have a look at the needles?'

The explorer got up slowly, walked across, and bent over the Harrow. 'You see,' said the officer, 'there are two kinds of needles arranged in multiple patterns. Each long needle has a short one beside it. The long needle does the writing, and the short needle sprays a jet of water to wash away the blood and keep the inscription clear. Blood and water together are then conducted here through small runnels into this main runnel and down a waste pipe into the pit.' With his finger the officer traced the exact course taken by the blood and water. To make the picture as vivid as possible he held both hands below the outlet of the waste pipe as if to catch the outflow, and when he did this the explorer drew back his head and feeling behind him with one hand sought to return to his chair. To his horror he found that the condemned man too had obeyed the officer's invitation to examine the Harrow at close quarters and had followed him. He had pulled forward the sleepy soldier with the chain and was bending over the glass. One could see that his uncertain eyes were trying to perceive what the two gentlemen had been looking at, but since he had not understood the explanation he could not make head or tail of it. He was peering this way and that way. He kept running his eyes along the glass. The explorer wanted to drive him away, since what he was doing was probably culpable. But the officer firmly restrained the explorer with one hand and with the other took a clod of earth from the rampart and threw it at the soldier. He opened his eyes with a jerk, saw what the condemned man had dared to do, let his rifle fall, dug his heels into the ground, dragged his prisoner back so that he stumbled and fell immediately, and then stood looking down at him, watching him struggling and rattling in his chains. 'Set him on his feet!' yelled the officer, for he noticed that the explorer's attention was being too much distracted by the prisoner. In fact he was even leaning right across the Harrow, without taking any notice of it, intent only on finding out what was happening to the prisoner. 'Be careful with him!' cried the officer again. He ran around the apparatus, himself caught the condemned man under the shoulders, and with the soldier's help got him up on his feet, which kept slithering from under him.

'Now I know all about it,' said the explorer as the officer came back to him. 'All except the most important thing,' he answered, seizing the explorer's arm and pointing upwards:

'In the Designer are all the cogwheels that control the movements of the Harrow, and this machinery is regulated according to the inscription demanded by the sentence. I am still using the guiding plans drawn by the former Commandant. Here they are' – he extracted some sheets from the leather wallet – 'but I'm sorry I can't let you handle them, they are my most precious possessions. Just take a seat and I'll hold them in front of you like this, then you'll be able to see everything quite well.' He spread out the first sheet of paper. The explorer would have liked to say something appreciative, but all he could see was a labyrinth of lines crossing and recrossing each other, which covered the paper so thickly that it was difficult to discern the blank spaces between them. 'Read it,' said the officer. 'I can't,' said the explorer. 'Yet it's clear enough,' said the officer. 'It's very ingenious,' said the explorer evasively, 'but I can't make it out.' 'Yes,' said the officer with a laugh, putting the paper away again, 'it's no calligraphy for school children. It needs to be studied closely. I'm quite sure that in the end you would understand it too. Of course the script can't be a simple one; it's not supposed to kill a man straight off, but only after an interval of, on an average, twelve hours; the turning point is reckoned to come at the sixth hour. So there have to be lots and lots of flourishes around the actual script; the script itself runs around the body only in a narrow girdle; the rest of the body is reserved for the embellishments. Can you appreciate now the work accomplished by the Harrow and the whole apparatus? – Just watch it!' He ran up the ladder, turned a wheel, called down: 'Look out, keep to one side!' and everything started working. If the wheel had not creaked, it would have been marvelous. The officer, as if surprised by the noise of the wheel, shook his fist at it, then spread out his arms in excuse to the explorer, and climbed down rapidly to peer at the working of the machine from below. Something perceptible to no one save himself was still not in order; he clambered up again, did something with both hands in the interior of the Designer, then slid down one of the rods, instead of using the ladder, so as to get down quicker, and with the full force of his lungs, to make himself heard at all in the noise, yelled in the explorer's ear: 'Can you follow it? The Harrow is beginning to write; when it finishes the first draft of the inscription on the man's back, the layer of cotton wool begins to roll and slowly turns the body over, to give the Harrow fresh space for writing. Meanwhile the raw part that has been written on lies on the cotton wool, which is specially prepared to staunch the bleeding and so makes all ready for a new deepening of the script. Then these teeth at the edge of the Harrow, as the body turns further around, tear the cotton wool away from the wounds, throw it into the pit, and there is more work for the Harrow. So it keeps on writing deeper and deeper for the whole twelve hours. The first six hours the condemned man stays alive almost as before, he suffers only pain. After two hours the felt gag is taken away, for he has no longer strength to scream. Here, into this electrically heated basin at the head of the Bed, some warm rice pap is poured, from which the man, if he feels like it, can take as much as his tongue can lap. Not one of them ever misses the chance. I can remember none, and my experience is extensive. Only about the sixth hour does the man lose all desire to eat. I usually kneel down here at that moment and observe what happens. The man rarely swallows his last mouthful, he only rolls it around his mouth and spits it out into the pit. I have to duck just then or he would spit it in my face. But how quiet he grows at just about the sixth hour! Enlightenment comes to the most dull-witted. It begins around the eyes. From there it radiates. A moment that might tempt one to get under the Harrow oneself. Nothing more happens than that the man begins to understand the inscription, he purses his mouth as if he were listening. You have seen how difficult it is to decipher the script with one's eyes; but our man deciphers it with his wounds. To be sure, that is a hard task; he needs six hours to accomplish it. By that time the Harrow has pierced him quite through and casts him into the pit, where he pitches down upon the blood and water and the cotton wool. Then the judgment has been fulfilled, and we, the soldier and I, bury him.'

The explorer had inclined his ear to the officer and with his hands in his jacket pockets watched the machine at work. The condemned man watched it too, but uncomprehendingly. He bent forward a little and was intent on the moving needles when the soldier, at a sign from the officer, slashed through his shirt and trousers from behind with a knife, so that they fell off; he tried to catch at his falling clothes to cover his nakedness, but the soldier lifted him into the air and shook the last remnants from him. The officer stopped the machine, and in the sudden silence the condemned man was laid under the Harrow. The chains were loosened and the straps fastened on instead; in the first moment that seemed almost a relief to the prisoner. And now the Harrow was adjusted a little lower, since he was a thin man. When the needle points touched him a shudder ran over his skin; while the soldier was busy strapping his right hand, he flung out his left hand blindly; but it happened to be in the direction toward where the explorer was standing. The officer kept watching the explorer sideways, as if seeking to read from his face the impression made on him by the execution, which had been at least cursorily explained to him.

The wrist strap broke; probably the soldier had drawn it too tight. The officer had to intervene, the soldier held up the broken piece of strap to show him. So the officer went over to him and said, his face still turned toward the explorer: 'This is a very complex machine, it can't be helped that things are breaking or giving way here and there; but one must not thereby allow oneself to be diverted in one's general judgment. In any case, this strap is easily made good; I shall simply use a chain; the delicacy of the vibrations for the right arm will of course be a little impaired.' And while he fastened the chains, he added: 'The resources for maintaining the machine are now very much reduced. Under the former Commandant I had free access to a sum of money set aside entirely for this purpose. There was a store, too, in which spare parts were kept for repairs of all kinds. I confess I have been almost prodigal with them, I mean in the past, not now as the new Commandant pretends, always looking for an excuse to attack our old way of doing things. Now he has taken charge of the machine money himself, and if I send for a new strap they ask for the broken old strap as evidence, and the new strap takes ten days to appear and then is of shoddy material and not much good. But how I am supposed to work the machine without a strap, that's something nobody bothers about.'

The explorer thought to himself: It's always a ticklish matter to intervene decisively in other people's affairs. He was neither a member of the penal colony nor a citizen of the state to which it belonged. Were he to denounce this execution or actually try to stop it, they could say to him: You are a foreigner, mind your own business. He could make no answer to that, unless he were to add that he was amazed at himself in this connection, for he traveled only as an observer, with no intention at all of altering other people's methods of administering justice. Yet here he found himself strongly tempted. The injustice of the procedure and the inhumanity of the execution were undeniable. No one could suppose that he had any selfish interest in the matter, for the condemned man was a complete stranger, not a fellow countryman or even at all sympathetic to him. The explorer himself had recommendations from high quarters, had been received here with great courtesy, and the very fact that he had been invited to attend the execution seemed to suggest that his views would be welcome. And this was all the more likely since the Commandant, as he had heard only too plainly, was no upholder of the procedure and maintained an attitude almost of hostility to the officer.

At that moment the explorer heard the officer cry out in rage. He had just, with considerable difficulty, forced the felt gag into the condemned man's mouth when the man in an irresistible access of nausea shut his eyes and vomited.

Hastily the officer snatched him away from the gag and tried to hold his head over the pit; but it was too late, the vomit was running all over the machine. 'It's all the fault of that Commandant!' cried the officer, senselessly shaking the brass rods in front, 'the machine is befouled like a pigsty.' With trembling hands he indicated to the explorer what had happened. 'Have I not tried for hours at a time to get the Commandant to understand that the prisoner must fast for a whole day before the execution. But our new, mild doctrine thinks otherwise. The Commandant's ladies stuff the man with sugar candy before he's led off. He has lived on stinking fish his whole life long and now he has to eat sugar candy! But it could still be possible, I should have nothing to say against it, but why won't they get me a new felt gag, which I have been begging for the last three months. How should a man not feel sick when he takes a felt gag into his mouth which more than a hundred men have already slobbered and gnawed in their dying moments?'

The condemned man had laid his head down and looked peaceful, the soldier was busy trying to clean the machine with the prisoner's shirt. The officer advanced toward the explorer who in some vague presentiment fell back a pace, but the officer seized him by the hand, and drew him to one side. 'I should like to exchange a few words with you in confidence,' he said, 'may I?' 'Of course,' said the explorer, and listened with downcast eyes.

'This procedure and method of execution, which you are now having the opportunity to admire, has at the moment no longer any open adherents in our colony. I am its sole advocate, and at the same time the sole advocate of the old Commandant's tradition. I can no longer reckon on any further extension of the method, it takes all my energy to maintain it as it is. During the old Commandant's lifetime the colony was full of his adherents; his strength of conviction I still have in some measure, but not an atom of his power; consequently the adherents have skulked out of sight, there are still many of them but none of them will admit it. If you were to go into the teahouse today, on execution day, and listen to what is being said, you would perhaps hear only ambiguous remarks. These would all be made by adherents, but under the present Commandant and his present doctrines they are of no use to me. And now I ask you: because of this Commandant and the women who influence him, is such a piece of work, the work of a lifetime' – he pointed to the machine – 'to perish? Ought one to let that happen? Even if one has only come as a stranger to our island for a few days? But there's no time to lose, an attack of some kind is impending on my function as judge; conferences are already being held in the Commandant's office from which I am excluded; even your coming here today seems to me a significant move; they are cowards and use you as a screen, you, a stranger. – How different an execution was in the old days! A whole day before the ceremony the valley was packed with people; they all came only to look on; early in the morning the Commandant appeared with his ladies; fanfares roused the whole camp; I reported that everything was in readiness; the assembled company – no high official dared to absent himself – arranged itself around the machine; this pile of cane chairs is a miserable survival from that epoch. The machine was freshly cleaned and glittering, I got new spare parts for almost every execution. Before hundreds of spectators – all of them standing on tiptoe as far as the heights there – the condemned man was laid under the Harrow by the Commandant himself. What is left today for a common soldier to do was then my task, the task of the presiding judge, and was an honor for me. And then the execution began! No discordant noise spoiled the working of the machine. Many did not care to watch it but lay with closed eyes in the sand; they all knew: Now Justice is being done. In the silence one heard nothing but the condemned man's sighs, half-muffled by the felt gag. Nowadays the machine can no longer wring from anyone a sigh louder than the felt gag can stifle; but in those days the writing needles let drop an acid fluid, which we're no longer permitted to use. Well, and then came the sixth hour! It was impossible to grant all the requests to be allowed to watch it from nearby. The Commandant in his wisdom ordained that the children should have the preference; I, of course, because of my office had the privilege of always being at hand; often enough I would be squatting there with a small child in either arm. How we all absorbed the look of transfiguration on the face of the sufferer, how we bathed our cheeks in the radiance of that justice, achieved at last and fading so quickly! What times these were, my comrade!' The officer had obviously forgotten whom he was addressing; he had embraced the explorer and laid his head on his shoulder. The explorer was deeply embarrassed, impatiently he stared over the officer's head. The soldier had finished his cleaning job and was now pouring rice pap from a pot into the basin. As soon as the condemned man, who seemed to have recovered entirely, noticed this action he began to reach for the rice with his tongue. The soldier kept pushing him away, since the rice pap was certainly meant for a later hour, yet it was just as unfitting that the soldier himself should thrust his dirty hands into the basin and eat out of it before the other's avid face.

The officer quickly pulled himself together. 'I didn't want to upset you,' he said, 'I know it is impossible to make those days credible now. Anyhow, the machine is still working and it is still effective in itself. It is effective in itself even though it stands alone in this valley. And the corpse still falls at the last into the pit with an incomprehensibly gentle wafting motion, even though there are no hundreds of people swarming around like flies as formerly. In those days we had to put a strong fence around the pit, it has long since been torn down.'

The explorer wanted to withdraw his face from the officer and looked around him at random. The officer thought he was surveying the valley's desolation; so he seized him by the hands, turned him around to meet his eyes, and asked: 'Do you realize the shame of it?'

But the explorer said nothing. The officer left him alone

for a little; with legs apart, hands on hips, he stood very still, gazing at the ground. Then he smiled encouragingly at the explorer and said: 'I was quite near you yesterday when the Commandant gave you the invitation. I heard him giving it. I know the Commandant. I divined at once what he was after. Although he is powerful enough to take measures against me, he doesn't dare to do it yet, but he certainly means to use your verdict against me, the verdict of an illustrious foreigner. He has calculated it carefully: this is your second day on the island, you did not know the old Commandant and his ways, you are conditioned by European ways of thought, perhaps you object on principle to capital punishment in general and to such mechanical instruments of death in particular, besides you will see that the execution has no support from the public, a shabby ceremony – carried out with a machine already somewhat old and worn – now, taking all that into consideration, would it not be likely (so thinks the Commandant) that you might disapprove of my methods? And if you disapprove, you wouldn't conceal the fact (I'm still speaking from the Commandant's point of view), for you are a man to feel confidence in your own well-tried conclusions. True, you have seen and learned to appreciate the peculiarities of many peoples, and so you would not be likely to take a strong line against our proceedings, as you might do in your own country. But the Commandant has no need of that. A casual, even an unguarded remark will be enough. It doesn't even need to represent what you really think, so long as it can be used speciously to serve his purpose. He will try to prompt you with sly questions, of that I am certain. And his ladies will sit around you and prick up their ears; you might be saying something like this: "In our country we have a different criminal procedure," or "In our country the prisoner is interrogated before he is sentenced," or "We haven't used torture since the Middle Ages." All these statements are as true as they seem natural to you, harmless remarks that pass no judgment on my methods. But how would the Commandant react to them? I can see him, our good Commandant, pushing his chair away immediately and rushing onto the balcony, I can see his ladies streaming out after him, I can hear his voice – the ladies call it a voice of thunder – well, and this is what he says: "A famous Western investigator, sent out to study criminal procedure in all the countries of the world, has just said that our old tradition of administering justice is inhumane. Such a verdict from such a personality makes it impossible for me to countenance these methods any longer. Therefore from this very day I ordain . . ." and so on. You may want to interpose that you never said any such thing, that you never called my methods inhumane, on the contrary your profound experience leads you to believe they are most humane and most in consonance with human dignity, and you admire the machine greatly – but it will be too late; you won't even get onto the balcony, crowded as it will be with ladies; you may try to draw attention to yourself; you may want to scream out; but a lady's hand will close your lips – and I and the work of the old Commandant will be done for.'

The explorer had to suppress a smile; so easy, then, was the task he had felt to be so difficult. He said evasively: 'You overestimate my influence; the Commandant has read my letters of recommendation, he knows that I am no expert in criminal procedure. If I were to give an opinion, it would be as a private individual, an opinion no more influential than that of any ordinary person, and in any case much less influential than that of the Commandant, who, I am given to understand, has very extensive powers in this penal colony. If his attitude to your procedure is as definitely hostile as you believe, then I fear the end of your tradition is at hand, even without any humble assistance from me.'

Had it dawned on the officer at last? No, he still did not understand. He shook his head emphatically, glanced briefly around at the condemned man and the soldier, who both flinched away from the rice, came close up to the explorer, and without looking at his face but fixing his eye on some spot on his coat said in a lower voice than before: 'You don't know the Commandant; you feel yourself – forgive the expression – a kind of outsider so far as all of us are concerned; yet, believe me, your influence cannot be rated too highly. I was simply delighted when I heard that you were to attend the execution all by yourself. The Commandant arranged it to aim a blow at me, but I shall turn it to my advantage. Without being distracted by lying whispers and contemptuous glances – which could not have been avoided had a crowd of people attended the execution – you have heard my explanations, seen the machine, and are now in course of watching the execution. You have doubtless already formed your own judgment; if you still have some small uncertainties the sight of the execution will resolve them. And now I make this request to you: help me against the Commandant!'

The explorer would not let him go on. 'How could I do that,' he cried, 'it's quite impossible. I can neither help nor hinder you.'

'Yes, you can,' the officer said. The explorer saw with a certain apprehension that the officer had clenched his fists. 'Yes, you can,' repeated the officer, still more insistently. 'I have a plan that is bound to succeed. You believe your influence is insufficient. I know that it is sufficient. But even granted that you are right, is it not necessary, for the sake of preserving this tradition, to try even what might prove insufficient? Listen to my plan, then. The first thing necessary for you to carry it out is to be as reticent as possible today regarding your verdict on these proceedings. Unless you are asked a direct question you must say nothing at all; but what you do say must be brief and general; let it be remarked that you would prefer not to discuss the matter, that you are out of patience with it, that if you are to let yourself go you would use strong language. I don't ask you to tell any lies; by no means; you should only give curt answers, such as: "Yes, I saw the execution," or "Yes, I had it explained to me." Just that, nothing more. There are grounds enough for any impatience you betray, although not such as will occur to the Commandant. Of course, he will mistake your meaning and interpret it to please himself. That's what my plan depends on. Tomorrow in the Commandant's office there is to be a large conference of all the high administrative officials, the Commandant presiding. Of course the Commandant is the kind of man to have turned these conferences into public spectacles. He has had a gallery built that is always packed with spectators. I am compelled to take part in the conferences, but they make me sick with disgust. Now, whatever happens, you will certainly be invited to this conference; if you behave today as I suggest, the invitation will become an urgent request. But if for some mysterious reason you're not invited, you'll have to ask for an invitation; there's no doubt of your getting it then. So tomorrow you're sitting in the Commandant's box with the ladies. He keeps looking up to make sure you're there. After various trivial and ridiculous matters, brought in merely to impress the audience – mostly harbor works, nothing but harbor works! – our judicial procedure comes up for discussion too. If the Commandant doesn't introduce it, or not soon enough, I'll see that it's mentioned. I'll stand up and report that today's execution has taken place. Quite briefly, only a statement. Such a statement is not usual, but I shall make it. The Commandant thanks me, as always, with an amiable smile, and then he can't restrain himself, he seizes the excellent opportunity. "It has just been reported," he will say, or words to that effect, "that an execution has taken place. I should like merely to add that this execution was witnessed by the famous explorer who has, as you all know, honored our colony so greatly by his visit to us. His presence at today's session of our conference also contributes to the importance of this occasion. Should we not now ask the famous explorer to give us his verdict on our traditional mode of execution and the procedure that leads up to it?" Of course there is loud applause, general agreement, I am more insistent than anyone. The Commandant bows to you and says:

"Then in the name of the assembled company, I put the question to you." And now you advance to the front of the box. Lay your hands where everyone can see them, or the ladies will catch them and press your fingers. – And then at last you can speak out. I don't know how I'm going to endure the tension of waiting for that moment. Don't put any restraint on yourself when you make your speech, publish the truth aloud, lean over the front of the box, shout, yes indeed, shout your verdict, your unshakable conviction, at the Commandant. Yet perhaps you wouldn't care to do that, it's not in keeping with your character, in your country perhaps people do these things differently, well, that's all right too, that will be quite as effective, don't even stand up, just say a few words, even in a whisper, so that only the officials beneath you will hear them, that will be quite enough, you don't even need to mention the lack of public support for the execution, the creaking wheel, the broken strap, the filthy gag of felt, no, I'll take all that upon me, and, believe me, if my indictment doesn't drive him out of the conference hall, it will force him to his knees to make the acknowledgment: Old Commandant, I humble myself before you. – That is my plan; will you help me to carry it out? But of course you are willing, what is more, you must.' And the officer seized the explorer by both arms and gazed, breathing heavily, into his face. He had shouted the last sentence so loudly that even the soldier and the condemned man were startled into attending; they had not understood a word but they stopped eating and looked over at the explorer, chewing their previous mouthfuls.

From the very beginning the explorer had no doubt about what answer he must give; in his lifetime he had experienced too much to have any uncertainty here; he was fundamentally honorable and unafraid. And yet now, facing the soldier and the condemned man, he did hesitate, for as long as it took to draw one breath. At last, however, he said, as he had to: 'No.' The officer blinked several times but did not turn his eyes away. 'Would you like me to explain?' asked the explorer. The officer nodded wordlessly. 'I do not approve of your procedure,' said the explorer then, 'even before you took me into your confidence – of course I shall never in any circumstances betray your confidence – I was already wondering whether it would be my duty to intervene and whether my intervention would have the slightest chance of success. I realized to whom I ought to turn: to the Commandant, of course. You have made that fact even clearer, but without having strengthened my resolution, on the contrary, your sincere conviction has touched me, even though it cannot influence my judgment.'

The officer remained mute, turned to the machine, caught hold of a brass rod, and then, leaning back a little, gazed at the Designer as if to assure himself that all was in order. The soldier and the condemned man seemed to have come to some understanding; the condemned man was making signs to the soldier, difficult though his movements were because of the tight straps; the soldier was bending down to him; the condemned man whispered something and the soldier nodded.

The explorer followed the officer and said: 'You don't know yet what I mean to do. I shall tell the Commandant what I think of the procedure, certainly, but not at a public conference, only in private; nor shall I stay here long enough to attend any conference; I am going away early tomorrow morning, or at least embarking on my ship.'

It did not look as if the officer had been listening. 'So you did not find the procedure convincing,' he said to himself and smiled, as an old man smiles at childish nonsense and yet pursues his own meditations behind the smile.

'Then the time has come,' he said at last, and suddenly looked at the explorer with bright eyes that held some challenge, some appeal for cooperation. 'The time for what?' asked the explorer uneasily, but got no answer.

'You are free,' said the officer to the condemned man in the native tongue. The man did not believe it at first. 'Yes, you are set free,' said the officer. For the first time the condemned man's face woke to real animation. Was it true? Was it only a caprice of the officer's that might change again? Had the foreign explorer begged him off? What was it? One could read these questions on his face. But not for long. Whatever it might be, he wanted to be really free if he might, and he began to struggle so far as the Harrow permitted him.

'You'll burst my straps,' cried the officer, 'lie still! We'll soon loosen them.' And signing the soldier to help him, he set about doing so. The condemned man laughed wordlessly to himself, now he turned his face left toward the officer, now right toward the soldier, nor did he forget the explorer.

'Draw him out,' ordered the officer. Because of the Harrow this had to be done with some care. The condemned man had already torn himself a little in the back through his impatience.

From now on, however, the officer paid hardly any attention to him. He went up to the explorer, pulled out the small leather wallet again, turned over the papers in it, found the one he wanted, and showed it to the explorer. 'Read it,' he said. 'I can't,' said the explorer, 'I told you before that I can't make out these scripts.' 'Try taking a close look at it,' said the officer and came quite near to the explorer so that they might read it together. But when even that proved useless, he outlined the script with his little finger, holding it high above the paper as if the surface dared not be sullied by touch, in order to help the explorer to follow the script in that way. The explorer did make an effort, meaning to please the officer in this respect at least, but he was quite unable to follow. Now the officer began to spell it, letter by letter, and then read out the words. ' "BE JUST!" is what is written there,' he said, 'surely you can read it now.' The explorer bent so close to the paper that the officer feared he might touch it and drew it farther away; the explorer made no remark, yet it was clear that he still could not decipher it. ' "BE JUST!" is what is written there,' said the officer once more. 'Maybe,' said the explorer, 'I am prepared to believe you.' 'Well, then,' said the officer, at least partly satisfied, and climbed up the ladder with the paper; very carefully he laid it inside the Designer and seemed to be changing the disposition of all the cogwheels; it was a troublesome piece of work and must have involved wheels that were extremely small, for sometimes the officer's head vanished altogether from sight inside the Designer, so precisely did he have to regulate the machinery.

The explorer, down below, watched the labor uninterruptedly, his neck grew stiff and his eyes smarted from the glare of sunshine over the sky. The soldier and the condemned man were now busy together. The man's shirt and trousers, which were already lying in the pit, were fished out by the point of the soldier's bayonet. The shirt was abominably dirty and its owner washed it in the bucket of water. When he put on the shirt and trousers both he and the soldier could not help guffawing, for the garments were of course slit up behind. Perhaps the condemned man felt it incumbent on him to amuse the soldier, he turned around and around in his slashed garments before the soldier, who squatted on the ground beating his knees with mirth. All the same, they presently controlled their mirth out of respect for the gentlemen.

When the officer had at length finished his task aloft, he surveyed the machinery in all its details once more, with a smile, but this time shut the lid of the Designer, which had stayed open till now, climbed down, looked into the pit and then at the condemned man, noting with satisfaction that the clothing had been taken out, then went over to wash his hands in the water bucket, perceived too late that it was disgustingly dirty, was unhappy because he could not wash his hands, in the end thrust them into the sand – this alternative did not please him, but he had to put up with it – then stood upright and began to unbutton his uniform jacket. As he did this, the two ladies' handkerchiefs he had tucked under his collar fell into his hands. 'Here are your handkerchiefs,' he said, and threw them to the condemned man. And to the explorer he said in explanation: 'A gift from the ladies.'

In spite of the obvious haste with which he was discarding first his uniform jacket and then all his clothing, he handled each garment with loving care, he even ran his fingers caressingly over the silver lace on the jacket and shook a tassel into place. This loving care was certainly out of keeping with the fact that as soon as he had a garment off he flung it at once with a kind of unwilling jerk into the pit. The last thing left to him was his short sword with the sword belt. He drew it out of the scabbard, broke it, then gathered all together, the bits of the sword, the scabbard, and the belt, and flung them so violently down that they clattered into the pit.

Now he stood naked there. The explorer bit his lips and said nothing. He knew very well what was going to happen, but he had no right to obstruct the officer in anything. If the judicial procedure which the officer cherished were really so near its end – possibly as a result of his own intervention, as to which he felt himself pledged – then the officer was doing the right thing; in his place the explorer would not have acted otherwise.

The soldier and the condemned man did not understand at first what was happening, at first they were not even looking on. The condemned man was gleeful at having got the handkerchiefs back, but he was not allowed to enjoy them for long, since the soldier snatched them with a sudden, unexpected grab. Now the condemned man in turn was trying to twitch them from under the belt where the soldier had tucked them, but the soldier was on his guard. So they were wrestling, half in jest. Only when the officer stood quite naked was their attention caught. The condemned man especially seemed struck with the notion that some great change was impending. What had happened to him was now going to happen to the officer. Perhaps even to the very end. Apparently the foreign explorer had given the order for it. So this was revenge. Although he himself had not suffered to the end, he was to be revenged to the end. A broad, silent grin now appeared on his face and stayed there all the rest of the time.

The officer, however, had turned to the machine. It had been clear enough previously that he understood the machine well, but now it was almost staggering to see how he managed it and how it obeyed him. His hand had only to approach the Harrow for it to rise and sink several times till it was adjusted to the right position for receiving him; he touched only the edge of the Bed and already it was vibrating; the felt gag came to meet his mouth, one could see that the officer was really reluctant to take it but he shrank from it only a moment, soon he submitted and received it. Everything was ready, only the straps hung down at the sides, yet they were obviously unnecessary, the officer did not need to be fastened down. Then the condemned man noticed the loose straps, in his opinion the execution was incomplete unless the straps were buckled, he gestured eagerly to the soldier and they ran together to strap the officer down. The latter had already stretched out one foot to push the lever that started the Designer; he saw the two men coming up; so he drew his foot back and let himself be buckled in. But now he could not reach the lever; neither the soldier nor the condemned man would be able to find it, and the explorer was determined not to lift a finger. It was not necessary; as soon as the straps were fastened the machine began to work; the Bed vibrated, the needles flickered above the skin, the Harrow rose and fell. The explorer had been staring at it quite a while before he remembered that a wheel in the Designer should have been creaking; but everything was quiet, not even the slightest hum could be heard.

Because it was working so silently the machine simply escaped one's attention. The explorer observed the soldier and the condemned man. The latter was the more animated of the two, everything in the machine interested him, now he was bending down and now stretching up on tiptoe, his forefinger was extended all the time pointing out details to the soldier. This annoyed the explorer. He was resolved to stay till the end, but he could not bear the sight of these two. 'Go back home,' he said. The soldier would have been willing enough, but the condemned man took the order as a punishment. With clasped hands he implored to be allowed to stay, and when the explorer shook his head and would not relent, he even went down on his knees. The explorer saw that it was no use merely giving orders, he was on the point of going over and driving them away. At that moment he heard a noise above him in the Designer. He looked up. Was that cogwheel going to make trouble after all? But it was something quite different. Slowly the lid of the Designer rose up and then clicked wide open. The teeth of a cogwheel showed themselves and rose higher, soon the whole wheel was visible, it was as if some enormous force were squeezing the Designer so that there was no longer room for the wheel, the wheel moved up till it came to the very edge of the Designer, fell down, rolled along the sand a little on its rim, and then lay flat. But a second wheel was already rising after it, followed by many others, large and small and indistinguishably minute, the same thing happened to all of them, at every moment one imagined the Designer must now really be empty, but another complex of numerous wheels was already rising into sight, falling down, trundling along the sand, and lying flat. This phenomenon made the condemned man completely forget the explorer's command, the cogwheels fascinated him, he was always trying to catch one and at the same time urging the soldier to help, but always drew back his hand in alarm, for another wheel always came hopping along which, at least on its first advance, scared him off.

The explorer, on the other hand, felt greatly troubled; the machine was obviously going to pieces; its silent working was a delusion; he had a feeling that he must now stand by the officer, since the officer was no longer able to look after himself. But while the tumbling cogwheels absorbed his whole attention he had forgotten to keep an eye on the rest of the machine; now that the last cogwheel had left the Designer, however, he bent over the Harrow and had a new and still more unpleasant surprise. The Harrow was not writing, it was only jabbing, and the Bed was not turning the body over but only bringing it up quivering against the needles. The explorer wanted to do something, if possible, to bring the whole machine to a standstill, for this was no exquisite torture such as the officer desired, this was plain murder. He stretched out his hands. But at that moment the Harrow rose with the body spitted on it and moved to the side, as it usually did only when the twelfth hour had come. Blood was flowing in a hundred streams, not mingled with water, the water jets too had failed to function. And now the last action failed to fulfill itself, the body did not drop off the long needles, streaming with blood it went on hanging over the pit without falling into it. The Harrow tried to move back to its old position, but as if it had itself noticed that it had not yet got rid of its burden it stuck after all where it was, over the pit. 'Come and help!' cried the explorer to the other two, and himself seized the officer's feet. He wanted to push against the feet while the others seized the head from the opposite side and so the officer might be slowly eased off the needles. But the other two could not make up their minds to come; the condemned man actually turned away; the explorer had to go over to them and force them into position at the officer's head. And here, almost against his will, he had to look at the face of the corpse. It was as it had been in life; no sign was visible of the promised redemption; what the others had found in the machine the officer had not found; the lips were firmly pressed together, the eyes were open, with the same expression as in life, the look was calm and convinced, through the forehead went the point of the great iron spike.

As the explorer, with the soldier and the condemned man behind him, reached the first houses of the colony, the soldier pointed to one of them and said: 'There is the teahouse.'

In the ground floor of the house was a deep, low, cavernous space, its walls and ceiling blackened with smoke. It was open to the road all along its length. Although this teahouse was very little different from the other houses of the colony, which were all very dilapidated, even up to the Commandant's palatial headquarters, it made on the explorer the impression of a historic tradition of some kind, and he felt the power of past days. He went near to it, followed by his companions, right up between the empty tables that stood in the street before it, and breathed the cool, heavy air that came from the interior. 'The old man's buried here,' said the soldier, 'the priest wouldn't let him lie in the churchyard. Nobody knew where to bury him for a while, but in the end they buried him here. The officer never told you about that, for sure, because of course that's what he was most ashamed of. He even tried several times to dig the old man up by night, but he was always chased away.' 'Where is the grave?' asked the explorer, who found it impossible to believe the soldier. At once both of them, the soldier and the condemned man, ran before him pointing with outstretched hands in the direction where the grave should be. They led the explorer right up to the back wall, where guests were sitting at a few tables. They were apparently dock laborers, strong men with short, glistening, full black beards. None had a jacket, their shirts were torn, they were poor, humble creatures. As the explorer drew near, some of them got up, pressed close to the wall, and stared at him. 'It's a foreigner,' ran the whisper around him, 'he wants to see the grave.' They pushed one of the tables aside, and under it there was really a gravestone. It was a simple stone, low enough to be covered by a table. There was an inscription on it in very small letters, the explorer had to kneel down to read it. This was what it said: 'Here rests the old Commandant. His adherents, who now must be nameless, have dug this grave and set up this stone. There is a prophecy that after a certain number of years the Commandant will rise again and lead his adherents from this house to recover the colony. Have faith and wait!' When the explorer had read this and risen to his feet he saw all the bystanders around him smiling, as if they too had read the inscription, had found it ridiculous, and were expecting him to agree with them. The explorer ignored this, distributed a few coins among them, waiting till the table was pushed over the grave again, quitted the teahouse, and made for the harbor.

The soldier and the condemned man had found some acquaintances in the teahouse, who detained them. But they must have soon shaken them off, for the explorer was only halfway down the long flight of steps leading to the boats when they came rushing after him. Probably they wanted to force him at the last minute to take them with him. While he was bargaining below with a ferryman to row him to the steamer, the two of them came headlong down the steps, in silence, for they did not dare to shout. But by the time they reached the foot of the steps the explorer was already in the boat, and the ferryman was just casting off from the shore. They could have jumped into the boat, but the explorer lifted a heavy knotted rope from the floor boards, threatened them with it, and so kept them from attempting the leap.

Translated by Willa and Edwin Muir

A Country Doctor (1919)

The New Advocate

WE HAVE a new advocate, Dr. Bucephalus. There is little in his appearance to remind you that he was once Alexander of Macedon's battle charger. Of course, if you know his story, you are aware of something. But even a simple usher whom I saw the other day on the front steps of the Law Courts, a man with the professional appraisal of the regular small bettor at a racecourse, was running an admiring eye over the advocate as he mounted the marble steps with a high action that made them ring beneath his feet.

In general the Bar approves the admission of Bucephalus. With astonishing insight people tell themselves that, modern society being what it is, Bucephalus is in a difficult position, and therefore, considering also his importance in the history of the world, he deserves at least a friendly reception. Nowadays – it cannot be denied – there is no Alexander the Great. There are plenty of men who know how to murder people; the skill needed to reach over a banqueting table and pink a friend with a lance is not lacking; and for many Macedonia is too confining, so that they curse Philip, the father – but no one, no one at all, can blaze a trail to India. Even in his day the gates of India were beyond reach, yet the King's sword pointed the way to them. Today the gates have receded to remoter and loftier places; no one points the way; many carry swords, but only to brandish them, and the eye that tries to follow them is confused.

So perhaps it is really best to do as Bucephalus has done and absorb oneself in law books. In the quiet lamplight, his flanks unhampered by the thighs of a rider, free and far from the clamor of battle, he reads and turns the pages of our ancient tomes.

Translated by Willa and Edwin Muir

A Country Doctor

I WAS in great perplexity; I had to start on an urgent journey; a seriously ill patient was waiting for me in a village ten miles off; a thick blizzard of snow filled all the wide spaces between him and me; I had a gig, a light gig with big wheels, exactly right for our country roads; muffled in furs, my bag of instruments in my hand, I was in the courtyard all ready for the journey; but there was no horse to be had, no horse. My own horse had died in the night, worn out by the fatigues of this icy winter; my servant girl was now running around the village trying to borrow a horse; but it was hopeless, I knew it, and I stood there forlornly, with the snow gathering more and more thickly upon me, more and more unable to move. In the gateway the girl appeared, alone, and waved the lantern; of course, who would lend a horse at this time for such a journey? I strode through the courtyard once more; I could see no way out; in my confused distress I kicked at the dilapidated door of the yearlong uninhabited pigsty. It flew open and flapped to and fro on its hinges. A steam and smell as of horses came out from it. A dim stable lantern was swinging inside from a rope. A man, crouching on his hams in that low space, showed an open blue-eyed face. 'Shall I yoke up?' he asked, crawling out on all fours. I did not know what to say and merely stooped down to see what else was in the sty. The servant girl was standing beside me. 'You never know what you're going to find in your own house,' she said, and we both laughed. 'Hey there, Brother, hey there, Sister!' called the groom, and two horses, enormous creatures with powerful flanks, one after the other, their legs tucked close to their bodies, each well-shaped head lowered like a camel's, by sheer strength of buttocking squeezed out through the door hole which they filled entirely. But at once they were standing up, their legs long and their bodies steaming thickly. 'Give him a hand,' I said, and the willing girl hurried to help the groom with the harnessing. Yet hardly was she beside him when the groom clipped hold of her and pushed his face against hers. She screamed and fled back to me; on her cheek stood out in red the marks of two rows of teeth. 'You brute,' I yelled in fury, 'do you want a whipping?' but in the same moment reflected that the man was a stranger; that I did not know where he came from, and that of his own free will he was helping me out when everyone else had failed me. As if he knew my thoughts he took no offense at my threat but, still busied with the horses, only turned around once toward me. 'Get in,' he said then, and indeed: everything was ready. A magnificent pair of horses, I observed, such as I had never sat behind, and I climbed in happily. 'But I'll drive, you don't know the way,' I said. 'Of course,' said he, 'I'm not coming with you anyway, I'm staying with Rose.' 'No,' shrieked Rose, fleeing into the house with a justified presentiment that her fate was inescapable; I heard the door chain rattle as she put it up; I heard the key turn in the lock; I could see, moreover, how she put out the lights in the entrance hall and in further flight all though the rooms to keep herself from being discovered. 'You're coming with me,' I said to the groom, 'or I won't go, urgent as my journey is. I'm not thinking of paying for it by handing the girl over to you.' 'Gee up!' he said; clapped his hands; the gig whirled off like a log in a freshet; I could just hear the door of my house splitting and bursting as the groom charged at it and then I was deafened and blinded by a storming rush that steadily buffeted all my senses. But this only for a moment, since, as if my patient's farmyard had opened out just before my courtyard gate, I was already there; the horses had come quietly to a standstill; the blizzard had stopped; moonlight all around; my patient's parents hurried out of the house, his sister behind them; I was almost lifted out of the gig; from their confused ejaculations I gathered not a word; in the sickroom the air was almost unbreathable; the neglected stove was smoking; I wanted to push open a window; but first I had to look at my patient.

Gaunt, without any fever, not cold, not warm, with vacant eyes, without a shirt, the youngster heaved himself up from under the feather bedding, threw his arms around my neck, and whispered in my ear: 'Doctor, let me die.' I glanced around the room; no one had heard it; the parents were leaning forward in silence waiting for my verdict; the sister had set a chair for my handbag; I opened the bag and hunted among my instruments; the boy kept clutching at me from his bed to remind me of his entreaty; I picked up a pair of tweezers, examined them in the candlelight, and laid them down again. 'Yes,' I thought blasphemously, 'in cases like this the gods are helpful, send the missing horse, add to it a second because of the urgency, and to crown everything bestow even a groom—' And only now did I remember Rose again; what was I to do, how could I rescue her, how could I pull her away from under that groom at ten miles' distance, with a team of horses I couldn't control. These horses, now, they had somehow slipped the reins loose, pushed the windows open from outside, I did not know how; each of them had stuck a head in at a window and, quite unmoved by the startled cries of the family, stood eyeing the patient. 'Better go back at once,' I thought, as if the horses were summoning me to the return journey, yet I permitted the patient's sister, who fancied that I was dazed by the heat, to take my fur coat from me. A glass of rum was poured out for me, the old man clapped me on the shoulder, a familiarity justified by this offer of his treasure. I shook my head; in the narrow confines of the old man's thoughts I felt ill; that was my only reason for refusing the drink. The mother stood by the bedside and cajoled me toward it; I yielded, and, while one of the horses whinnied loudly to the ceiling, laid my head to the boy's breast, which shivered under my wet beard. I confirmed what I already knew; the boy was quite sound, something a little wrong with his circulation, saturated with coffee by his solicitous mother, but sound and best turned out of bed with one shove. I am no world reformer and so I let him lie. I was the district doctor and did my duty to the uttermost, to the point where it became almost too much. I was badly paid and yet generous and helpful to the poor. I had still to see that Rose was all right, and then the boy might have his way and I wanted to die too. What was I doing there in that endless winter! My horse was dead, and not a single person in the village would lend me another. I had to get my team out of the pigsty; if they hadn't chanced to be horses I should have had to travel with swine. That was how it was. And I nodded to the family. They knew nothing about it, and, had they known, would not have believed it. To write prescriptions is easy, but to come to an understanding with people is hard. Well, this should be the end of my visit, I had once more been called out needlessly, I was used to that, the whole district made my life a torment with my night bell, but that I should have to sacrifice Rose this time as well, the pretty girl who had lived in my house for years almost without my noticing her – that sacrifice was too much to ask, and I had somehow to get it reasoned out in my head with the help of what craft I could muster, in order not to let fly at this family, which with the best will in the world could not restore Rose to me. But as I shut my bag and put an arm out for my fur coat, the family meanwhile standing together, the father sniffing at the glass of rum in his hand, the mother, apparently disappointed in me – why, what do people expect? – biting her lips with tears in her eyes, the sister fluttering a blood-soaked towel, I was somehow ready to admit conditionally that the boy might be ill after all. I went toward him, he welcomed me smiling as if I were bringing him the most nourishing invalid broth – ah, now both horses were whinnying together; the noise, I suppose, was ordained by heaven to assist my examination of the patient – and this time I discovered that the boy was indeed ill. In his right side, near the hip, was an open wound as big as the palm of my hand. Rose-red, in many variations of shade, dark in the hollows, lighter at the edges, softly granulated, with irregular clots of blood, open as a surface mine to the daylight. That was how it looked from a distance. But on a closer inspection there was another complication. I could not help a low whistle of surprise. Worms, as thick and as long as my little finger, themselves rose-red and blood-spotted as well, were wriggling from their fastness in the interior of the wound toward the light, with small white heads and many little legs. Poor boy, you were past helping. I had discovered your great wound; this blossom in your side was destroying you. The family was pleased; they saw me busying myself; the sister told the mother, the mother the father, the father told several guests who were coming in, through the moonlight at the open door, walking on tiptoe, keeping their balance with outstretched arms. 'Will you save me?' whispered the boy with a sob, quite blinded by the life within his wound. That is what people are like in my district. Always expecting the impossible from the doctor. They have lost their ancient beliefs; the parson sits at home and unravels his vestments, one after another; but the doctor is supposed to be omnipotent with his merciful surgeon's hand. Well, as it pleases them; I have not thrust my services on them; if they misuse me for sacred ends, I let that happen to me too; what better do I want, old country doctor that I am, bereft of my servant girl! And so they came, the family and the village elders, and stripped my clothes off me; a school choir with the teacher at the head of it stood before the house and sang these words to an utterly simple tune:

> Strip his clothes off, then he'll heal us,
> If he doesn't, kill him dead!
> Only a doctor, only a doctor.

Then my clothes were off and I looked at the people quietly, my fingers in my beard and my head cocked to one side. I was altogether composed and equal to the situation and remained so, although it was no help to me, since they now took me by the head and feet and carried me to the bed. They laid me down in it next to the wall, on the side of the wound. Then they all left the room; the door was shut; the singing stopped; clouds covered the moon; the bedding was warm around me; the horses' heads in the open windows wavered like shadows. 'Do you know,' said a voice in my ear, 'I have very little confidence in you. Why, you were only blown in here, you didn't come on your own feet. Instead of helping me, you're cramping me on my deathbed. What I'd like best is to scratch your eyes out.' 'Right,' I said, 'it is a shame. And yet I am a doctor. What am I to do? Believe me, it is not too easy for me either.' 'Am I supposed to be content with this apology? Oh, I must be, I can't help it. I always have to put up with things. A fine wound is all I brought into the world; that was my sole endowment.' 'My young friend,' said I, 'your mistake is: you have not a wide enough view. I have been in all the sickrooms, far and wide, and I tell you: your wound is not so bad. Done in a tight corner with two strokes of the ax. Many a one proffers his side and can hardly hear the ax in the forest, far less that it is coming nearer to him.' 'Is that really so, or are you deluding me in my fever?' 'It is really so, take the word of honor of an official doctor.' And he took it and lay still. But now it was time for me to think of escaping. The horses were still standing faithfully in their places. My clothes, my fur coat, my bag were quickly collected; I didn't want to waste time dressing; if the horses raced home as they had come, I should only be springing, as it were, out of this bed into my own. Obediently a horse backed away from the window; I threw my bundle into the gig; the fur coat missed its mark and was caught on a hook only by the sleeve. Good enough. I swung myself onto the horse. With the reins loosely trailing, one horse barely fastened to the other, the gig swaying behind, my fur coat last of all in the snow. 'Gee up!' I said, but there was no galloping; slowly, like old men, we crawled through the snowy wastes; a long time echoed behind us the new but faulty song of the children:

> O be joyful, all you patients,
> The doctor's laid in bed beside you!

Never shall I reach home at this rate; my flourishing practice is done for; my successor is robbing me, but in vain, for he cannot take my place; in my house the disgusting groom is raging; Rose is his victim; I do not want to think about it anymore. Naked, exposed to the frost of this most unhappy of ages, with an earthly vehicle, unearthly horses, old man that I am, I wander astray. My fur coat is hanging from the back of the gig, but I cannot reach it, and none of my limber pack of patients lifts a finger. Betrayed! Betrayed! A false alarm on the night bell once answered – it cannot be made good, not ever.

Translated by Willa and Edwin Muir

Up in the Gallery

IF SOME FRAIL, consumptive equestrienne in the circus were to be urged around and around on an undulating horse for months on end without respite by a ruthless, whip-flourishing ringmaster, before an insatiable public, whizzing along on her horse, throwing kisses, swaying from the waist, and if this performance were likely to continue in the infinite perspective of a drab future to the unceasing roar of the orchestra and hum of the ventilators, accompanied by ebbing and renewed swelling bursts of applause which are really steam hammers – then, perhaps, a young visitor to the gallery might race down the long stairs through all the circles, rush into the ring, and yell: Stop! against the fanfares of the orchestra still playing the appropriate music.

But since that is not so; a lovely lady, pink and white, floats in between the curtains, which proud lackeys open before her; the ringmaster, deferentially catching her eye, comes toward her breathing animal devotion; tenderly lifts her up on the dapple-gray, as if she were his own most precious granddaughter about to start on a dangerous journey; cannot make up his mind to give the signal with his whip, finally masters himself enough to crack the whip loudly; runs along beside the horse, open-mouthed; follows with a sharp eye the leaps taken by its rider; finds her artistic skill almost beyond belief; calls to her with English shouts of warning; angrily exhorts the grooms who hold the hoops to be most closely attentive; before the great somersault lifts up his arms and implores the orchestra to be silent; finally lifts the little one down from her trembling horse, kisses her on both cheeks, and finds that all the ovation she gets from the audience is barely sufficient; while she herself, supported by him, right up on the tips of her toes, in a cloud of dust, with outstretched arms and small head thrown back, invites the whole circus to share her triumph – since that is so, the visitor to the gallery lays his face on the rail before him and, sinking into the closing march as into a heavy dream, weeps without knowing it.

Translated by Willa and Edwin Muir

An Old Manuscript

IT LOOKS as if much had been neglected in our country's system of defense. We have not concerned ourselves with it until now and have gone about our daily work; but things that have been happening recently begin to trouble us.

I have a cobbler's workshop in the square that lies before the Emperor's palace. Scarcely have I taken my shutters down, at the first glimmer of dawn, when I see armed soldiers already posted in the mouth of every street opening on the square. But these soldiers are not ours, they are obviously nomads from the North. In some way that is incomprehensible to me they have pushed right into the capital, although it is a long way from the frontier. At any rate, here they are; it seems that every morning there are more of them.

As is their nature, they camp under the open sky, for they abominate dwelling houses. They busy themselves sharpening swords, whittling arrows, and practicing horsemanship. This peaceful square, which was always kept so scrupulously clean, they have made literally into a stable. We do try every now and then to run out of our shops and clear away at least the worst of the filth, but this happens less and less often, for the labor is in vain and brings us besides into danger of falling under the hoofs of the wild horses or of being crippled with lashes from the whips.

Speech with the nomads is impossible. They do not know our language, indeed they hardly have a language of their own. They communicate with each other much as jackdaws do. A screeching as of jackdaws is always in our ears. Our way of living and our institutions they neither understand nor care to understand. And so they are unwilling to make sense even out of our sign language. You can gesture at them till you dislocate your jaws and your wrists and still they will not have understood you and will never understand. They often make grimaces; then the whites of their eyes turn up and foam gathers on their lips, but they do not mean anything by that, not even a threat; they do it because it is their nature to do it. Whatever they need, they take. You cannot call it taking by force. They grab at something and you simply stand aside and leave them to it.

From my stock, too, they have taken many good articles. But I cannot complain when I see how the butcher, for instance, suffers across the street. As soon as he brings in any meat the nomads snatch it all from him and gobble it up. Even their horses devour flesh; often enough a horseman and his horse are lying side by side, both of them gnawing at the same joint, one at either end. The butcher is nervous and does not dare to stop his deliveries of meat. We understand that, however, and subscribe money to keep him going. If the nomads got no meat, who knows what they might think of doing; who knows anyhow what they may think of, even though they get meat every day.

Not long ago the butcher thought he might at least spare himself the trouble of slaughtering, and so one morning he brought along a live ox. But he will never dare to do that again. I lay for a whole hour flat on the floor at the back of my workshop with my head muffled in all the clothes and rugs and pillows I had simply to keep from hearing the bellowing of that ox, which the nomads were leaping on from all sides, tearing morsels out of its living flesh with their teeth. It had been quiet for a long time before I risked coming out; they were lying overcome around the remains of the carcass like drunkards around a wine cask.

This was the occasion when I fancied I actually saw the Emperor himself at a window of the palace; usually he never enters these outer rooms but spends all his time in the innermost garden; yet on this occasion he was standing, or so at least it seemed to me, at one of the windows, watching with bent head the goings-on before his residence.

'What is going to happen?' we all ask ourselves. 'How long can we endure this burden and torment? The Emperor's palace has drawn the nomads here but does not know how to drive them away again. The gate stays shut; the guards, who used to be always marching out and in with ceremony, keep close behind barred windows. It is left to us artisans and tradesmen to save our country; but we are not equal to such a task; nor have we ever claimed to be capable of it. This is a misunderstanding of some kind; and it will be the ruin of us.'

Translated by Willa and Edwin Muir

Before the Law

BEFORE THE LAW stands a doorkeeper. To this doorkeeper there comes a man from the country and prays for admittance to the Law. But the doorkeeper says that he cannot grant admittance at the moment. The man thinks it over and then asks if he will be allowed in later. 'It is possible,' says the doorkeeper, 'but not at the moment.' Since the gate stands open, as usual, and the doorkeeper steps to one side, the man stoops to peer through the gateway into the interior. Observing that, the doorkeeper laughs and says: 'If you are so drawn to it, just try to go in despite my veto. But take note:

I am powerful. And I am only the least of the doorkeepers. From hall to hall there is one doorkeeper after another, each more powerful than the last. The third doorkeeper is already so terrible that even I cannot bear to look at him.' These are difficulties the man from the country has not expected; the Law, he thinks, should surely be accessible at all times and to everyone, but as he now takes a closer look at the doorkeeper in his fur coat, with his big sharp nose and long, thin, black Tartar beard, he decides that it is better to wait until he gets permission to enter. The doorkeeper gives him a stool and lets him sit down at one side of the door. There he sits for days and years. He makes many attempts to be admitted, and wearies the doorkeeper by his importunity. The doorkeeper frequently has little interviews with him, asking him questions about his home and many other things, but the questions are put indifferently, as great lords put them, and always finish with the statement that he cannot be let in yet. The man, who has furnished himself with many things for his journey, sacrifices all he has, however valuable, to bribe the doorkeeper. The doorkeeper accepts everything, but always with the remark: 'I am only taking it to keep you from thinking you have omitted anything.' During these many years the man fixes his attention almost continuously on the doorkeeper. He forgets the other doorkeepers, and this first one seems to him the sole obstacle preventing access to the Law. He curses his bad luck, in his early years boldly and loudly; later, as he grows old, he only grumbles to himself. He becomes childish, and since in his yearlong contemplation of the doorkeeper he has come to know even the fleas in his fur collar, he begs the fleas as well to help him and to change the doorkeeper's mind. At length his eyesight begins to fail, and he does not know whether the world is really darker or whether his eyes are only deceiving him. Yet in his darkness he is now aware of a radiance that streams inextinguishably from the gateway of the Law. Now he has not very long to live. Before he dies, all his experiences in these long years gather themselves in his head to one point, a question he has not yet asked the doorkeeper. He waves him nearer, since he can no longer raise his stiffening body. The doorkeeper has to bend low toward him, for the difference in height between them has altered much to the man's disadvantage. 'What do you want to know now?' asks the doorkeeper; 'you are insatiable.' 'Everyone strives to reach the Law,' says the man, 'so how does it happen that for all these many years no one but myself has ever begged for admittance?' The doorkeeper recognizes that the man has reached his end, and, to let his failing senses catch the words, roars in his ear: 'No one else could ever be admitted here, since this gate was made only for you. I am now going to shut it.'

Translated by Willa and Edwin Muir

Jackals and Arabs

WE were camping in the oasis. My companions were asleep. The tall, white figure of an Arab passed by; he had been seeing to the camels and was on his way to his own sleeping place.

I threw myself on my back in the grass; I tried to fall asleep; I could not; a jackal howled in the distance; I sat up again. And what had been so far away was all at once quite near. Jackals were swarming around me, eyes gleaming dull gold and vanishing again, lithe bodies moving nimbly and rhythmically, as if at the crack of a whip.

One jackal came from behind me, nudging right under my arm, pressing against me, as if he needed my warmth, and then stood before me and spoke to me almost eye to eye.

'I am the oldest jackal far and wide. I am delighted to have met you here at last. I had almost given up hope, since we have been waiting endless years for you; my mother waited for you, and her mother, and all our foremothers right back to the first mother of all the jackals. It is true, believe me!'

'That is surprising,' said I, forgetting to kindle the pile of firewood which lay ready to smoke away jackals, 'that is very surprising for me to hear. It is by pure chance that I have come here from the far North, and I am making only a short tour of your country. What do you jackals want, then?'

As if emboldened by this perhaps too-friendly inquiry the ring of jackals closed in on me; all were panting and open-mouthed.

'We know,' began the eldest, 'that you have come from the North; that is just what we base our hopes on. You Northerners have the kind of intelligence that is not to be found among Arabs. Not a spark of intelligence, let me tell you, can be struck from their cold arrogance. They kill animals for food, and carrion they despise.'

'Not so loud,' said I, 'there are Arabs sleeping nearby.'

'You are indeed a stranger here,' said the jackal, 'or you would know that never in the history of the world has any jackal been afraid of an Arab. Why should we fear them? Is it not misfortune enough for us to be exiled among such creatures?'

'Maybe, maybe,' said I, 'matters so far outside my province I am not competent to judge; it seems to me a very old quarrel; I suppose it's in the blood, and perhaps will only end with it.'

'You are very clever,' said the old jackal; and they all began to pant more quickly; the air pumped out of their lungs although they were standing still; a rank smell which at times I had to set my teeth to endure streamed from their open jaws, 'you are very clever; what you have just said agrees with our old tradition. So we shall draw blood from them and the quarrel will be over.'

'Oh!' said I, more vehemently than I intended, 'they'll defend themselves; they'll shoot you down in dozens with their muskets.'

'You misunderstand us,' said he, 'a human failing which persists apparently even in the far North. We're not proposing to kill them. All the water in the Nile couldn't cleanse us of that. Why, the mere sight of their living flesh makes us turn tail and flee into cleaner air, into the desert, which for that very reason is our home.'

And all the jackals around, including many newcomers from farther away, dropped their muzzles between their forelegs and wiped them with their paws; it was as if they were trying to conceal a disgust so overpowering that I felt like leaping over their heads to get away.

'Then what are you proposing to do?' I asked, trying to rise to my feet; but I could not get up; two young beasts behind me had locked their teeth through my coat and shirt; I had to go on sitting. 'These are your trainbearers,' explained the old jackal, quite seriously, 'a mark of honor.' 'They must let go!' I cried, turning now to the old jackal, now to the youngsters. 'They will, of course,' said the old one, 'if that is your wish. But it will take a little time, for they have got their teeth well in, as is our custom, and must first loosen their jaws bit by bit. Meanwhile, give ear to our petition.' 'Your conduct hasn't exactly inclined me to grant it,' said I. 'Don't hold it against us that we are clumsy,' said he, and now for the first time had recourse to the natural plaintiveness of his voice, 'we are poor creatures, we have nothing but our teeth; whatever we want to do, good or bad, we can tackle it only with our teeth.' 'Well, what do you want?' I asked, not much mollified.

'Sir,' he cried, and all the jackals howled together; very remotely it seemed to resemble a melody. 'Sir, we want you to end this quarrel that divides the world. You are exactly the man whom our ancestors foretold as born to do it. We want to be troubled no more by Arabs; room to breathe; a skyline cleansed of them; no more bleating of sheep knifed by an Arab; every beast to die a natural death; no interference till we have drained the carcass empty and picked its bones clean. Cleanliness, nothing but cleanliness is what we want' – and now they were all lamenting and sobbing – 'how can you bear to live in such a world, O noble heart and kindly bowels? Filth is their white; filth is their black; their beards are a horror; the very sight of their eye sockets makes one want to spit; and when they lift an arm, the murk of hell yawns in the armpit. And so, sir, and so, dear sir, by means of your all-powerful hands slit their throats through with these scissors!' And in answer to a jerk of his head a jackal came trotting up with a small pair of sewing scissors, covered with ancient rust, dangling from an eyetooth.

'Well, here's the scissors at last, and high time to stop!' cried the Arab leader of our caravan who had crept upwind toward us and now cracked his great whip.

The jackals fled in haste, but at some little distance rallied in a close huddle, all the brutes so tightly packed and rigid that they looked as if penned in a small fold girt by flickering will-o'-the-wisps.

'So you've been treated to this entertainment too, sir,' said the Arab, laughing as gaily as the reserve of his race permitted. 'You know, then, what the brutes are after?' I asked. 'Of course,' said he, 'it's common knowledge; so long as Arabs exist, that pair of scissors goes wandering through the desert and will wander with us to the end of our days. Every European is offered it for the great work; every European is just the man that Fate has chosen for them. They have the most lunatic hopes, these beasts; they're just fools, utter fools. That's why we like them; they are our dogs; finer dogs than any of yours. Watch this, now, a camel died last night and I have had it brought here.'

Four men came up with the heavy carcass and threw it down before us. It had hardly touched the ground before the jackals lifted up their voices. As if irresistibly drawn by cords each of them began to waver forward, crawling on his belly. They had forgotten the Arabs, forgotten their hatred, the all-obliterating immediate presence of the stinking carrion bewitched them. One was already at the camel's throat, sinking his teeth straight into an artery. Like a vehement small pump endeavoring with as much determination as hopefulness to extinguish some raging fire, every muscle in his body twitched and labored at the task. In a trice they were all on top of the carcass, laboring in common, piled mountain-high.

And now the caravan leader lashed his cutting whip criss-cross over their backs. They lifted their heads; half swooning in ecstasy; saw the Arabs standing before them; felt the sting of the whip on their muzzles; leaped and ran backwards a stretch. But the camel's blood was already lying in pools, reeking to heaven, the carcass was torn wide open in many places. They could not resist it; they were back again; once more the leader lifted his whip; I stayed his arm.

'You are right, sir,' said he, 'we'll leave them to their business; besides, it's time to break camp. Well, you've seen them. Marvelous creatures, aren't they? And how they hate us!'

Translated by Willa and Edwin Muir

A Visit to a Mine

TODAY the chief engineers have been down to our part of the mine. The management has issued some instructions or other about boring new galleries, and so the engineers arrived to make the initial survey. How young these men are and yet how different from each other! They have all grown up in freedom and show clearly defined characters without self-consciousness even in their youth.

One, a lively man with black hair, has eyes that take in everything.

A second with a notebook makes jottings as he goes, looks around him, compares, notes down.

A third, his hands in his coat pockets, so that everything about him is taut, walks very upright; maintains his dignity; only the fact that he keeps biting his lips betrays his impatient, irrepressible youth.

A fourth showers explanations on the third, who does not ask for them; smaller than the other, trotting beside him like a temper, his index finger always in the air, he seems to be making a running commentary on everything he sees.

A fifth, perhaps the senior in rank, suffers no one to

accompany him; now he is in front, now behind; the group accommodates its pace to him; he is pallid and frail; responsibility has made his eyes hollow; he often presses his hand to his forehead in thought.

The sixth and seventh walk leaning forward a little, their heads close together, arm in arm, in confidential talk; if this were not unmistakably our coal mine and our working station in the deepest gallery, one could easily believe that these bony, clean-shaven, knobbly-nosed gentlemen were young clerics. One of them laughs mostly to himself with a catlike purring; the other, smiling too, leads the conversation and beats some kind of time to it with his free hand. How sure these two must be of their position; yes, what services must they have already rendered to our mine in spite of their youth, to be able here, on such an important survey, under the eyes of their chief, to devote themselves so unwaveringly to their own affairs, or at least to affairs that have nothing to do with the immediate task? Or might it be possible that, in spite of their laughter and apparent inattention, they are very well aware of whatever is needful? One scarcely ventures to pass a decisive judgment on gentlemen like these.

On the other hand, there is no doubt at all that the eighth man, for instance, is incomparably more intent on his work than these two, indeed more than all the other gentlemen. He has to touch everything and tap it with a little hammer which he keeps taking out of his pocket and putting back again. He often goes down on his knees in the dirt, despite his elegant attire, and taps the ground, then again taps the walls as he walks along or the roof over his head. Once he stretched himself out at full length and lay still; we were beginning to think something had gone wrong with him; then with a sudden recoil of his lithe body he sprang to his feet. He had only been making another investigation. We fancy that we know our mine and its rock formations, but what this engineer can be sounding all the time in such a manner lies beyond our comprehension.

A ninth man pushes a kind of perambulator in front of

him with the surveying instruments. Extremely expensive apparatus, deeply embedded in the softest cotton wool. The office porter ought really to be pushing this vehicle, but he is not trusted with it; an engineer has to do it, and one can see that he does it with good will. He is probably the youngest, perhaps he doesn't even understand all the apparatus yet, but he keeps his eye on the instruments all the time, which brings him often into danger of running his vehicle into the wall.

But there is another engineer walking alongside who prevents that from happening. Obviously he understands the apparatus thoroughly and seems to be really the man in charge of it. From time to time, without stopping the vehicle, he takes up a part of some instrument, peers through it, screws it open or shut, shakes it and taps it, holds it to his ear and listens; and finally, while the man pushing the instruments usually stands still, he lays the small thing, which one can scarcely discern at a distance, back into its packing with great care. This engineer is a little domineering, but only in the service of his instruments. Ten paces ahead of the perambulator we have to give way to it at a wordless sign of his finger, even where there is no room for us to make way.

Behind these two gentlemen stalks the office porter, with nothing to do. The gentlemen, as is to be expected from men of their great knowledge, have long dropped any arrogance they ever had, but the porter seems to have picked it all up and kept it. With one hand tucked behind him, the other in front fingering the gilt buttons or fine facecloth of his uniform, he keeps bowing to right and left as if we had saluted him and he were answering, or rather as if he assumed that we had saluted him, he being too high and mighty to see any salutes. Of course we do not salute him, yet one could almost believe, to look at him, that it is a great distinction to be a porter at the head office of the mine. Behind his back, to be sure, we burst out laughing, but as not even a thunderbolt could make him look around, he remains an unsolved riddle for us to respect.

Today we shall not do much work; the interruption has been too interesting; such a visit draws away with it all thoughts of work. It is too tempting to stand gazing after the gentlemen as they vanish into the darkness of the trial gallery. Besides, our shift will soon come to an end; we shall not be here to see them coming back.

Translated by Willa and Edwin Muir

The Next Village

MY grandfather used to say: 'Life is astoundingly short. To me, looking back over it, life seems so foreshortened that I scarcely understand, for instance, how a young man can decide to ride over to the next village without being afraid that – not to mention accidents – even the span of a normal happy life may fall far short of the time needed for such a journey.'

Translated by Willa and Edwin Muir

An Imperial Message

THE EMPEROR, so a parable runs, has sent a message to you, the humble subject, the insignificant shadow cowering in the remotest distance before the imperial sun; the Emperor from his deathbed has sent a message to you alone. He has commanded the messenger to kneel down by the bed, and has whispered the message to him; so much store did he lay on it that he ordered the messenger to whisper it back into his ear again. Then by a nod of the head he has confirmed that it is right. Yes, before the assembled spectators of his death – all the obstructing walls have been broken down, and on the spacious and loftily mounting open staircases stand in a ring the great princes of the Empire – before all these he has delivered his message. The messenger immediately sets out on his journey; a powerful, an indefatigable man; now pushing with his right arm, now with his left, he cleaves a way for himself through the throng; if he encounters resistance he points to his breast, where the symbol of the sun glitters; the way is made easier for him than it would be for any other man. But the multitudes are so vast; their numbers have no end. If he could reach the open fields how fast he would fly, and soon doubtless you would hear the welcome hammering of his fists on your door. But instead how vainly does he wear out his strength; still he is only making his way through the chambers of the innermost palace; never will he get to the end of them; and if he succeeded in that nothing would be gained; he must next fight his way down the stair; and if he succeeded in that nothing would be gained; the courts would still have to be crossed; and after the courts the second outer palace; and once more stairs and courts; and once more another palace; and so on for thousands of years; and if at last he should burst through the outermost gate – but never, never can that happen – the imperial capital would lie before him, the center of the world, crammed to bursting with its own sediment. Nobody could fight his way through here even with a message from a dead man. But you sit at your window when evening falls and dream it to yourself.

Translated by Willa and Edwin Muir

The Cares of a Family Man

SOME SAY the word Odradek is of Slavonic origin, and try to account for it on that basis. Others again believe it to be of German origin, only influenced by Slavonic. The uncertainty of both interpretations allows one to assume with justice that neither is accurate, especially as neither of them provides an intelligent meaning of the word.

No one, of course, would occupy himself with such studies if there were not a creature called Odradek. At first glance it looks like a flat star-shaped spool for thread, and indeed it does seem to have thread wound upon it; to be sure, they are only old, broken-off bits of thread, knotted and tangled together, of the most varied sorts and colors. But it is not only a spool, for a small wooden crossbar sticks out of the middle of the star, and another small rod is joined to that at a right angle. By means of this latter rod on one side and one of the points of the star on the other, the whole thing can stand upright as if on two legs.

One is tempted to believe that the creature once had some sort of intelligible shape and is now only a broken-down remnant. Yet this does not seem to be the case; at least there is no sign of it; nowhere is there an unfinished or unbroken surface to suggest anything of the kind; the whole thing looks senseless enough, but in its own way perfectly finished. In any case, closer scrutiny is impossible, since Odradek is extraordinarily nimble and can never be laid hold of.

He lurks by turns in the garret, the stairway, the lobbies, the entrance hall. Often for months on end he is not to be seen; then he has presumably moved into other houses; but he always comes faithfully back to our house again. Many a time when you go out of the door and he happens just to be leaning directly beneath you against the banisters you feel inclined to speak to him. Of course, you put no difficult questions to him, you treat him – he is so diminutive that you cannot help it – rather like a child. 'Well, what's your name?' you ask him. 'Odradek,' he says. 'And where do you live?' 'No fixed abode,' he says and laughs; but it is only the kind of laughter that has no lungs behind it. It sounds rather like the rustling of fallen leaves. And that is usually the end of the conversation. Even these answers are not always forthcoming; often he stays mute for a long time, as wooden as his appearance.

I ask myself, to no purpose, what is likely to happen to him? Can he possibly die? Anything that dies has had some kind of aim in life, some kind of activity, which has worn out; but that does not apply to Odradek. Am I to suppose, then, that he will always be rolling down the stairs, with ends of thread trailing after him, right before the feet of my children, and my children's children? He does no harm to anyone that one can see; but the idea that he is likely to survive me I find almost painful.

Translated by Willa and Edwin Muir

Eleven Sons

I HAVE eleven sons.

The first is outwardly very plain, but serious and clever; yet, although I love him as I love all my children, I do not rate him very highly. His mental processes seem to me to be too simple. He looks neither to right nor to left, nor into the far distance; he runs around all the time, or rather revolves, within his own little circle of thoughts.

The second is handsome, slim, well made; one draws one's breath with delight to watch him with a fencing foil. He is clever too, but has experience of the world as well; he has seen much, and therefore even our native country seems to yield more secrets to him than to the stay-at-home. Yet I am sure that this advantage is not only and not even essentially due to his travels, it is rather an attribute of his own inimitable nature, which is acknowledged for instance by everyone who has ever tried to copy him in, let us say, the fancy high dive he does into the water, somersaulting several times over, yet with almost violent self-control. To the very end of the springboard the emulator keeps up his courage and his desire to follow; but at that point, instead of leaping into the air, he sits down suddenly and lifts his arms in excuse. – And despite all this (I ought really to feel blessed with such a son) my attachment to him is not untroubled. His left eye is a little smaller than his right and blinks a good deal; only a small fault, certainly, and one which even lends more audacity to his face than it would otherwise have, nor, considering his unapproachable self-sufficiency, would anyone think of noticing and finding fault with this smaller eye and the way it blinks. Yet I, his father, do so. Of course, it is not the physical blemish that worries me, but a small irregularity of the spirit that somehow corresponds to it, a kind of stray poison in the blood, a kind of inability to develop to the full the potentialities of his nature which I alone can see. On the other hand, this is just what makes him again my own true son, for this fault of his is a fault of our whole family and in him it is only too apparent.

My third son is handsome too, but not in a way that I appreciate. He has the good looks of a singer: the curving lips; the dreaming eye; the kind of head that asks for drapery behind it to make it effective; the too-deeply arched chest; hands that are quick to fly up and much too quick to fall limp; legs that move delicately because they cannot support a weight. And besides: the tone of his voice is not round and full; it takes you in for a moment; the connoisseur pricks up his ears; but almost at once its breath gives out. – Although, in general, everything tempts me to bring this son of mine into the limelight, I prefer to keep him in the background; he himself is not insistent, yet not because he is aware of his shortcomings but out of innocence. Moreover, he does not feel at home in our age; as if he admitted belonging to our family, yet knew that he belonged also to another which he has lost forever, he is often melancholy and nothing can cheer him.

My fourth son is perhaps the most companionable of all. A true child of his age, he is understood by everyone, he stands on what is common ground to all men, and everyone feels inclined to give him a nod. Perhaps this universal appreciation is what makes his nature rather facile, his movements rather free, his judgments rather unconcerned. Many of his remarks are worth quoting over and over again, but by no means all of them, for by and large his extreme facility becomes irritating. He is like a man who makes a wonderful take-off from the ground, cleaves the air like a swallow, and after all comes down helplessly in a desert waste, a nothing. Such reflections gall me when I look at him.

My fifth son is kind and good; promised less than he

performed; used to be so insignificant that one literally felt alone in his presence; but has achieved a certain reputation. If I were asked how this came about, I could hardly tell you. Perhaps innocence makes its way easiest through the elemental chaos of this world, and innocent he certainly is. Perhaps too innocent. Friendly to everyone. Perhaps too friendly. I confess: I don't feel comfortable when I hear him praised. It seems to make praise rather too cheap to bestow it on anyone so obviously praiseworthy as this son of mine.

My sixth son seems, at first glance anyhow, the most thoughtful of all. He is given to hanging his head, and yet he is a great talker. So he is not easy to get at. If he is on the down grade, he falls into impenetrable melancholy; if he is in the ascendant, he maintains his advantage by sheer talk. Yet I grant him a certain self-forgetful passionate absorption; in the full light of day he often fights his way through a tangle of thoughts as if in a dream. Without being ill – his health on the contrary is very good – he sometimes staggers, especially in the twilight, but he needs no help, he never falls. Perhaps his physical growth is the cause of this phenomenon, he is much too tall for his age. That makes him look ugly in general, although he has remarkable beauty in detail, in hands and feet, for instance. His forehead, too, is ugly; both its skin and its bone formation are somehow arrested in their development.

The seventh son belongs to me perhaps more than all the others. The world would not know how to appreciate him; it does not understand his peculiar brand of wit. I do not overvalue him; I know he is of little enough importance; if the world had no other fault than that of not appreciating him, it would still be blameless. But within the family circle I should not care to be without this son of mine. He contributes a certain restlessness as well as a reverence for tradition, and combines them both, at least that is how I feel it, into an incontestable whole. True, he knows less than anyone what to do with this achievement; the wheel of the future will never be started rolling by him; but his disposition is so stimulating, so rich in hope; I wish that he had children and children's children. Unfortunately he does not seem inclined to fulfill my wish. With a self-satisfaction that I understand as much as I deplore, and which stands in magnificent contrast to the verdict of the world, he goes everywhere alone, pays no attention to girls, and yet will never lose his good humor.

My eighth son is my child of sorrow, and I do not really know why. He keeps me at a distance and yet I feel a close paternal tie binding me to him. Time has done much to lessen the pain; but once I used often to tremble at the mere thought of him. He goes his own way; he has broken off all communication with me; and certainly with his hard head, his small athletic body – only his legs were rather frail when he was a boy, but perhaps that has meanwhile righted itself – he will make a success of anything he chooses. Many a time I used to want to call him back, to ask him how things really were with him, why he cut himself off so completely from his father, and what his fundamental purpose was in life, but now he is so far away and so much time has passed that things had better stay as they are. I hear that he is the only one of my sons to grow a full beard; that cannot look well, of course, on a man so small as he is.

My ninth son is very elegant and has what women consider a definitely melting eye. So melting that there are occasions when he can cajole even me, although I know that a wet sponge is literally enough to wipe away all that unearthly brilliance. But the curious thing about the boy is that he makes no attempt to be seductive; he would be content to spend his life lying on the sofa and wasting his glances on the ceiling, or still better, keeping them to himself under his eyelids. When he is lying in this favorite position, he enjoys talking and talks quite well; concisely and pithily; but still only within narrow limits; once he oversteps these, which he cannot avoid doing since they are so narrow, what he says is quite empty. One would sign him to stop, if one had any hope that such slumbrous eyes were even aware of the gesture.

My tenth son is supposed to be an insincere character. I shall not entirely deny or confirm this supposition. Certainly anyone who sees him approaching with the pomposity of a man twice his age, in a frock coat always tightly buttoned, an old but meticulously brushed black hat, with an expressionless face, slightly jutting chin, protruding eyelids that mask the light behind them, two fingers very often at his lips – anyone seeing him thus is bound to think: what an utter hypocrite. But then, just listen to him talking! With understanding; thoughtfully; brusquely; cutting across questions with satirical vivacity; in complete accord with the universe, an accord that is surprising, natural and gay; an accord that of necessity straightens the neck and makes the body proud. Many who think themselves very clever and for this reason, as they fancied, felt a dislike for his outward appearance, have become strongly attached to him because of his conversation. There are other people, again, who are unaffected by his appearance but who find his conversation hypocritical. I, being his father, will not pronounce a verdict, but I must admit that the latter critics are at least to be taken more seriously than the former.

My eleventh son is delicate, probably the frailest of my sons; but deceptive in his weakness; for at times he can be strong and resolute, though even then there is somehow always an underlying weakness. Yet it is not a weakness to be ashamed of, merely something that appears as weakness only on this solid earth of ours. For instance, is not a readiness for flight a kind of weakness too, since it consists in a wavering, an unsteadiness, a fluttering? Something of that nature characterizes my son. These are not, of course, the characteristics to rejoice a father; they tend obviously to destroy a family. Sometimes he looks at me as if he would say: 'I shall take you with me, Father.' Then I think: 'You are the last person I would trust myself to.' And again his look seems to say: 'Then let me be at least the last.'

These are my eleven sons.

Translated by Willa and Edwin Muir

A Fratricide

THE EVIDENCE shows that this is how the murder was committed:

Schmar, the murderer, took up his post about nine o'clock one night in clear moonlight by the corner where Wese, his victim, had to turn from the street where his office was into the street he lived in.

The night air was shivering cold. Yet Schmar was wearing only a thin blue suit; the jacket was unbuttoned, too. He felt no cold; besides, he was moving about all the time. His weapon, half a bayonet and half a kitchen knife, he kept firmly in his grasp, quite naked. He looked at the knife against the light of the moon; the blade glittered; not enough for Schmar; he struck it against the bricks of the pavement till the sparks flew; regretted that, perhaps; and to repair the damage drew it like a violin bow across his boot sole while he bent forward, standing on one leg, and listened both to the whetting of the knife on his boot and for any sound out of the fateful side street.

Why did Pallas, the private citizen who was watching it all from his window nearby in the second storey, permit it to happen? Unriddle the mysteries of human nature! With his collar turned up, his dressing gown girt around his portly body, he stood looking down, shaking his head.

And five houses further along, on the opposite side of the street, Mrs. Wese, with a fox-fur coat over her nightgown, peered out to look for her husband who was lingering unusually late tonight.

At last there rang out the sound of the doorbell before Wese's office, too loud for a doorbell, right over the town and up to heaven, and Wese, the industrious nightworker, issued from the building, still invisible in that street, only heralded by the sound of the bell; at once the pavement registered his quiet footsteps.

Pallas bent far forward; he dared not miss anything. Mrs. Wese, reassured by the bell, shut her window with a clatter. But Schmar knelt down; since he had no other parts of his body bare, he pressed only his face and his hands against the pavement; where everything else was freezing, Schmar was glowing hot.

At the very corner dividing the two streets Wese paused, only his walking stick came around into the other street to support him. A sudden whim. The night sky invited him, with its dark blue and its gold. Unknowing, he gazed up at it, unknowing he lifted his hat and stroked his hair; nothing up there drew together in a pattern to interpret the immediate future for him; everything stayed in its senseless, inscrutable place. In itself it was a highly reasonable action that Wese should walk on, but he walked onto Schmar's knife.

'Wese!' shrieked Schmar, standing on tiptoe, his arm outstretched, the knife sharply lowered, 'Wese! You will never see Julia again!' And right into the throat and left into the throat and a third time deep into the belly stabbed Schmar's knife. Water rats, slit open, give out such a sound as came from Wese.

'Done,' said Schmar, and pitched the knife, now superfluous blood-stained ballast, against the nearest house front. 'The bliss of murder! The relief, the soaring ecstasy from the shedding of another's blood! Wese, old nightbird, friend, alehouse crony, you are oozing away into the dark earth below the street. Why aren't you simply a bladder of blood so that I could stamp on you and make you vanish into nothingness. Not all we want comes true, not all the dreams that blossomed have borne fruit, your solid remains lie here, already indifferent to every kick. What's the good of the dumb question you are asking?'

Pallas, choking on the poison in his body, stood at the double-leafed door of his house as it flew open. 'Schmar! Schmar! I saw it all, I missed nothing.' Pallas and Schmar scrutinized each other. The result of the scrutiny satisfied Pallas, Schmar came to no conclusion.

Mrs. Wese, with a crowd of people on either side, came rushing up, her face grown quite old with the shock. Her fur coat swung open, she collapsed on top of Wese, the nightgowned body belonged to Wese, the fur coat spreading over the couple like the smooth turf of a grave belonged to the crowd.

Schmar, fighting down with difficulty the last of his nausea, pressed his mouth against the shoulder of the policeman who, stepping lightly, led him away.

Translated by Willa and Edwin Muir

A Dream

JOSEF K. was dreaming.

It was a beautiful day and K. felt like going for a walk. But hardly had he taken a couple of steps when he was already at the cemetery. The paths there were very winding, ingeniously made, and unpractical, but he glided along one of them as if on a rushing stream with unshaken poise and balance. From a long way off his eye was caught by a freshly heaped grave mound which he wanted to pause beside. This grave mound exerted almost a fascination over him and he felt he could not reach it fast enough. But he often nearly lost sight of it, for his view was obscured by banners which veered and flapped against each other with great force; one could not see the standard-bearers, but there seemed to be a very joyous celebration going on.

While he was still peering into the distance, he suddenly saw the grave mound quite near his path, indeed he was almost leaving it behind him. He made a hasty spring onto the grass. But since the path went rushing on under his shifting foot, he tottered and fell on his knees just in front of the grave mound. Two men were standing behind the grave and were holding a gravestone between them in the air; scarcely had K. arrived when they thrust the stone into the earth and it stood as if cemented there. Out of some bushes there came at once a third man, whom K. recognized immediately as an artist. He was clad only in trousers and a badly buttoned shirt; on his head was a velvet cap; in his hand he held an ordinary pencil with which he was already drawing figures in the air as he approached.

With this pencil he now addressed himself to the top end of the gravestone; the stone was very tall, he did not have to bend down, though he had to bend forward, since the grave mound, on which he shrank from setting foot, came between him and the stone. So he stood on tiptoe and steadied himself with his left hand on the stone's flat surface. With an astonishing turn of skill he managed to produce golden letters from his ordinary pencil; he wrote: HERE LIES — Every letter was clear and beautifully made, deeply incised and of the purest gold. When he had inscribed these two words he looked at K. over his shoulder; K., who was very eager to know how the inscription would go, paid hardly any attention to the man but was intent only on the stone. And in fact the man turned again to continue writing, but he could not go on, something was hindering him, he let the pencil sink and once more turned toward K. This time K. looked back at him and noted that he was deeply embarrassed and yet unable to explain himself. All his earlier vivacity had vanished. That made K. feel embarrassed too; they exchanged helpless glances; there was some dreadful misunderstanding between them which neither could resolve. An untimely little bell now began to ring from the cemetery chapel, but the artist made a sign with uplifted hand and the bell stopped. In a little while it began again; this time quite softly and without any insistence, breaking off again at once; as if it were only testing its own tone. K. felt miserable because of the artist's predicament, he began to cry and sobbed for a long time into his cupped hands. The artist waited until K. had calmed down and then decided, since there was no help for it, just to go on with the inscription. The first small stroke that he made was a relief to K., but the artist obviously achieved it only with the greatest reluctance;

the work, too, was no longer beautifully finished, above all there seemed to be a lack of gold leaf, pale and uncertain the stroke straggled down, only it turned into a very big letter. It was a J, it was almost finished, and at that moment the artist stamped angrily on the grave mound with one foot so that the soil all around flew up in the air. At long last K. understood him; it was too late to start apologizing now; with all his fingers he dug into the earth which offered almost no resistance; everything seemed prepared beforehand; a thin crust of earth had been constructed only for the look of the thing; immediately beneath it a great hole opened out, with steep sides, into which K. sank, wafted onto his back by a gentle current. And while he was already being received into impenetrable depths, his head still straining upwards on his neck, his own name raced across the stone above him in great flourishes.

Enchanted by the sight, he woke up.

Translated by Willa and Edwin Muir

A Report to an Academy

HONORED MEMBERS of the Academy!

You have done me the honor of inviting me to give your Academy an account of the life I formerly led as an ape.

I regret that I cannot comply with your request to the extent you desire. It is now nearly five years since I was an ape, a short space of time, perhaps, according to the calendar, but an infinitely long time to gallop through at full speed, as I have done, more or less accompanied by excellent mentors, good advice, applause, and orchestral music, and yet essentially alone, since all my escorters, to keep the image, kept well off the course. I could never have achieved what I have done had I been stubbornly set on clinging to my origins, to the remembrances of my youth. In fact, to give up being stubborn was the supreme commandment I laid upon myself; free ape as I was, I submitted myself to that yoke. In revenge, however, my memory of the past has closed the door against me more and more. I could have returned at first, had human beings allowed it, through an archway as wide as the span of heaven over the earth, but as I spurred myself on in my forced career, the opening narrowed and shrank behind me; I felt more comfortable in the world of men and fitted it better; the strong wind that blew after me out of my past began to slacken; today it is only a gentle puff of air that plays around my heels; and the opening in the distance, through which it comes and through which I once came myself, has grown so small that, even if my strength and my will power sufficed to get me back to it, I should have to scrape the very skin from my body to crawl through. To put it plainly, much as I like expressing myself in images, to put it plainly: your life as apes, gentlemen, insofar as something of that kind lies behind you, cannot be farther removed from you than mine is from me. Yet everyone on earth feels a tickling at the heels; the small chimpanzee and the great Achilles alike.

But to a lesser extent I can perhaps meet your demand, and indeed I do so with the greatest pleasure. The first thing I learned was to give a handshake; a handshake betokens frankness; well, today, now that I stand at the very peak of my career, I hope to add frankness in words to the frankness of that first handshake. What I have to tell the Academy will contribute nothing essentially new, and will fall far behind what you have asked of me and what with the best will in the world I cannot communicate – nonetheless, it should indicate the line an erstwhile ape has had to follow in entering and establishing himself in the world of men. Yet I could not risk putting into words even such insignificant information as I am going to give you if I were not quite sure of myself and if my position on all the great variety stages of the civilized world had not become quite unassailable.

I belong to the Gold Coast. For the story of my capture I must depend on the evidence of others. A hunting expedition sent out by the firm of Hagenbeck – by the way, I have drunk many a bottle of good red wine since then with the leader of that expedition – had taken up its position in the bushes by the shore when I came down for a drink at evening among a troop of apes. They shot at us; I was the only one that was hit; I was hit in two places.

Once in the cheek; a slight wound; but it left a large, naked, red scar which earned me the name of Red Peter, a horrible name, utterly inappropriate, which only some ape could have thought of, as if the only difference between me and the performing ape Peter, who died not so long ago and had some small local reputation, were the red mark on my cheek. This by the way.

The second shot hit me below the hip. It was a severe wound, it is the cause of my limping a little to this day. I read an article recently by one of the ten thousand windbags who vent themselves concerning me in the newspapers, saying: my ape nature is not yet quite under control; the proof being that when visitors come to see me, I have a predilection for taking down my trousers to show them where the shot went in. The hand which wrote that should have its fingers shot away one by one. As for me, I can take my trousers down before anyone if I like; you would find nothing but a well-groomed fur and the scar made – let me be particular in the choice of a word for this particular purpose, to avoid misunderstanding – the scar made by a wanton shot. Everything is open and above board; there is nothing to conceal; when the plain truth is in question, great minds discard the niceties of refinement. But if the writer of the article were to take down his trousers before a visitor, that would be quite another story, and I will let it stand to his credit that he does not do it. In return, let him leave me alone with his delicacy!

After these two shots I came to myself – and this is where my own memories gradually begin – between decks in the Hagenbeck steamer, inside a cage. It was not a four-sided barred cage; it was only a three-sided cage nailed to a locker; the locker made the fourth side of it. The whole construction was too low for me to stand up in and too narrow to sit down in. So I had to squat with my knees bent and trembling all the time, and also, since probably for a time I wished to see no one, and to stay in the dark, my face was turned toward the locker while the bars of the cage cut into my flesh behind. Such a method of confining wild beasts is supposed to have its advantages during the first days of captivity, and out of my own experiences I cannot deny that from the human point of view this is really the case.

But that did not occur to me then. For the first time in my life I could see no way out; at least no direct way out; directly in front of me was the locker, board fitted close to board. True, there was a gap running right through the boards which I greeted with the blissful howl of ignorance when I first discovered it, but the hole was not even wide enough to stick one's tail through and not all the strength of an ape could enlarge it.

I am supposed to have made uncommonly little noise, as I was later informed, from which the conclusion was drawn that I would either soon die or if I managed to survive the first critical period would be very amenable to training. I did survive this period. Hopelessly sobbing, painfully hunting for fleas, apathetically licking a cocoanut, beating my skull against the locker, sticking out my tongue at anyone who came near me – that was how I filled in time at first in my new life. But over and above it all only the one feeling: no way out. Of course what I felt then as an ape I can represent now only in human terms, and therefore I misrepresent it, but although I cannot reach back to the truth of the old ape life, there is no doubt that it lies somewhere in the direction I have indicated.

Until then I had had so many ways out of everything, and now I had none. I was pinned down. Had I been nailed down, my right to free movement would not have been lessened. Why so? Scratch your flesh raw between your toes, but you won't find the answer. Press yourself against the bar behind you till it nearly cuts you in two, you won't find the answer. I had no way out but I had to devise one, for without it I could not live. All the time facing that locker – I should certainly have perished. Yet as far as Hagenbeck was concerned, the place for apes was in front of a locker – well then, I had to stop being an ape. A fine, clear train of thought, which I must have constructed somehow with my belly, since apes think with their bellies.

I fear that perhaps you do not quite understand what I mean by 'way out.' I use the expression in its fullest and most popular sense. I deliberately do not use the word 'freedom.' I do not mean the spacious feeling of freedom on all sides. As an ape, perhaps, I knew that, and I have met men who yearn for it. But for my part I desired such freedom neither then nor now. In passing: may I say that all too often men are betrayed by the word freedom. And as freedom is counted among the most sublime feelings, so the corresponding disillusionment can be also sublime. In variety theaters

I have often watched, before my turn came on, a couple of acrobats performing on trapezes high in the roof. They swung themselves, they rocked to and fro, they sprang into the air, they floated into each other's arms, one hung by the hair from the teeth of the other. 'And that too is human freedom,' I thought, 'self-controlled movement.' What a mockery of holy Mother Nature! Were the apes to see such a spectacle, no theater walls could stand the shock of their laughter.

No, freedom was not what I wanted. Only a way out; right or left, or in any direction; I made no other demand; even should the way out prove to be an illusion; the demand was a small one, the disappointment could be no bigger. To get out somewhere, to get out! Only not to stay motionless with raised arms, crushed against a wooden wall.

Today I can see it clearly; without the most profound inward calm I could never have found my way out. And indeed perhaps I owe all that I have become to the calm that settled within me after my first few days in the ship. And again for that calmness it was the ship's crew I had to thank.

They were good creatures, in spite of everything. I find it still pleasant to remember the sound of their heavy footfalls which used to echo through my half-dreaming head. They had a habit of doing everything as slowly as possible. If one of them wanted to rub his eyes, he lifted a hand as if it were a drooping weight. Their jests were coarse, but hearty. Their laughter had always a gruff bark in it that sounded dangerous but meant nothing. They always had something in their mouths to spit out and did not care where they spat it. They always grumbled that they got fleas from me; yet they were not seriously angry about it; they knew that my fur fostered fleas, and that fleas jump; it was a simple matter of fact to them. When they were off duty some of them often used to sit down in a semicircle around me; they hardly spoke but only grunted to each other; smoked their pipes, stretched out on lockers; smacked their knees as soon as I made the slightest movement; and now and then one of them would take a stick and tickle me where I liked being tickled. If I were to be invited today to take a cruise on that ship I should certainly refuse the invitation, but just as certainly the memories I could recall between its decks would not all be hateful.

The calmness I acquired among these people kept me above all from trying to escape. As I look back now, it seems to me I must have had at least an inkling that I had to find a way out or die, but that my way out could not be reached through flight. I cannot tell now whether escape was possible, but I believe it must have been; for an ape it must always be possible. With my teeth as they are today I have to be careful even in simply cracking nuts, but at that time I could certainly have managed by degrees to bite through the lock of my cage. I did not do it. What good would it have done me? As soon as I had poked out my head I should have been caught again and put in a worse cage; or I might have slipped among the other animals without being noticed, among the pythons, say, who were opposite me, and so breathed out my life in their embrace; or supposing I had actually succeeded in sneaking out as far as the deck and leaping overboard, I should have rocked for a little on the deep sea and then been drowned. Desperate remedies. I did not think it out in this human way, but under the influence of my surroundings I acted as if I had thought it out.

I did not think things out; but I observed everything quietly. I watched these men go to and fro, always the same faces, the same movements, often it seemed to me there was only the same man. So this man or these men walked about unimpeded. A lofty goal faintly dawned before me. No one promised me that if I became like them the bars of my cage would be taken away. Such promises for apparently impossible contingencies are not given. But if one achieves the impossible, the promises appear later retrospectively precisely where one had looked in vain for them before. Now, these men in themselves had no great attraction for me. Had I been devoted to the aforementioned idea of freedom, I should certainly have preferred the deep sea to the way out that suggested itself in the heavy faces of these men. At any rate, I watched them for a long time before I even thought of such things, indeed, it was only the mass weight of my observations that impelled me in the right direction.

It was so easy to imitate these people. I learned to spit in the very first days. We used to spit in each other's faces; the only difference was that I licked my face clean afterwards and they did not. I could soon smoke a pipe like an old hand; and if I also pressed my thumb into the bowl of the pipe, a roar of appreciation went up between-decks; only it took me a very long time to understand the difference between a full pipe and an empty one.

My worst trouble came from the schnapps bottle. The smell of it revolted me; I forced myself to it as best I could; but it took weeks for me to master my repulsion. This inward conflict, strangely enough, was taken more seriously by the crew than anything else about me. I cannot distinguish the men from each other in my recollection, but there was one of them who came again and again, alone or with friends, by day, by night, at all kinds of hours; he would post himself before me with the bottle and give me instructions. He could not understand me, he wanted to solve the enigma of my being. He would slowly uncork the bottle and then look at me to see if I had followed him; I admit that I always watched him with wildly eager, too eager attention; such a student of humankind no human teacher ever found on earth. After the bottle was uncorked he lifted it to his mouth; I followed it with my eyes right up to his jaws; he would nod, pleased with me, and set the bottle to his lips; I, enchanted with my gradual enlightenment, squealed and scratched myself comprehensively wherever scratching was called for; he rejoiced, tilted the bottle, and took a drink; I, impatient and desperate to emulate him, befouled myself in my cage, which again gave him great satisfaction; and then, holding the bottle at arm's length and bringing it up with a swing, he would empty it at one draught, leaning back at an exaggerated angle for my better instruction. I, exhausted by too much effort, could follow him no farther and hung limply to the bars, while he ended his theoretical exposition by rubbing his belly and grinning.

After theory came practice. Was I not already quite exhausted by my theoretical instruction? Indeed I was; utterly exhausted. That was part of my destiny. And yet I would take hold of the proffered bottle as well as I was able; uncork it, trembling; this successful action would gradually inspire me with new energy; I would lift the bottle, already following my original model almost exactly; put it to my lips and – and then throw it down in disgust, utter disgust, although it was empty and filled only with the smell of the spirit, throw it down on the floor in disgust. To the sorrow of my teacher, to the greater sorrow of myself; neither of us being really comforted by the fact that I did not forget, even though I had thrown away the bottle, to rub my belly most admirably and to grin.

Far too often my lesson ended in that way. And to the credit of my teacher, he was not angry; sometimes indeed he would hold his burning pipe against my fur, until it began to smolder in some place I could not easily reach, but then he would himself extinguish it with his own kind, enormous hand; he was not angry with me, he perceived that we were both fighting on the same side against the nature of apes and that I had the more difficult task.

What a triumph it was then both for him and for me, when one evening before a large circle of spectators – perhaps there was a celebration of some kind, a gramophone was playing, an officer was circulating among the crew – when on this evening, just as no one was looking, I took hold of a schnapps bottle that had been carelessly left standing before my cage, uncorked it in the best style, while the company began to watch me with mounting attention, set it to my lips without hesitation, with no grimace, like a professional drinker, with rolling eyes and full throat, actually and truly drank it empty; then threw the bottle away, not this time in despair but as an artistic performer; forgot, indeed, to rub my belly; but instead of that, because I could not help it, because my senses were reeling, called a brief and unmistakable 'Hallo!' breaking into human speech, and with this outburst broke into the human community, and felt its echo: 'Listen, he's talking!' like a caress over the whole of my sweat-drenched body.

I repeat: there was no attraction for me in imitating human beings; I imitated them because I needed a way out, and for no other reason. And even that triumph of mine did not achieve much. I lost my human voice again at once; it did not come back for months; my aversion for the schnapps bottle returned again with even greater force. But the line I was to follow had in any case been decided, once for all.

When I was handed over to my first trainer in Hamburg I soon realized that there were two alternatives before me: the Zoological Gardens or the variety stage. I did not hesitate. I said to myself: do your utmost to get onto the variety stage; the Zoological Gardens means only a new cage; once there, you are done for.

And so I learned things, gentlemen. Ah, one learns when one has to; one learns when one needs a way out; one learns at all costs. One stands over oneself with a whip; one flays oneself at the slightest opposition. My ape nature fled out of me, head over heels and away, so that my first teacher was almost himself turned into an ape by it, had soon to give up teaching and was taken away to a mental hospital. Fortunately he was soon let out again.

But I used up many teachers, indeed, several teachers at once. As I became more confident of my abilities, as the public took an interest in my progress and my future began to look bright, I engaged teachers for myself, established them in five communicating rooms, and took lessons from them all at once by dint of leaping from one room to the other.

That progress of mine! How the rays of knowledge penetrated from all sides into my awakening brain! I do not deny it: I found it exhilarating. But I must also confess: I did not overestimate it, not even then, much less now. With an effort which up till now has never been repeated I managed to reach the cultural level of an average European. In itself that might be nothing to speak of, but it is something insofar as it has helped me out of my cage and opened a special way out for me, the way of humanity. There is an excellent idiom: to fight one's way through the thick of things; that is what I have done, I have fought through the thick of things. There was nothing else for me to do, provided always that freedom was not to be my choice.

As I look back over my development and survey what I have achieved so far, I do not complain, but I am not complacent either. With my hands in my trouser pockets, my bottle of wine on the table, I half lie and half sit in my rocking chair and gaze out of the window: if a visitor arrives, I receive him with propriety. My manager sits in the anteroom; when I ring, he comes and listens to what I have to say. Nearly every evening I give a performance, and I have a success that could hardly be increased. When I come home late at night from banquets, from scientific receptions, from social gatherings, there sits waiting for me a half-trained little chimpanzee and I take comfort from her as apes do. By day I cannot bear to see her; for she has the insane look of the bewildered half-broken animal in her eye; no one else sees it, but I do, and I cannot bear it. On the whole, at any rate, I have achieved what I set out to achieve. But do not tell me that it was not worth the trouble. In any case, I am not appealing for any man's verdict, I am only imparting knowledge, I am only making a report. To you also, honored Members of the Academy, I have only made a report.

Translated by Willa and Edwin Muir

The Bucket Rider (1921)

COAL all spent; the bucket empty; the shovel useless; the stove breathing out cold; the room freezing; the trees outside the window rigid, covered with rime; the sky a silver shield against anyone who looks for help from it. I must have coal; I cannot freeze to death; behind me is the pitiless stove, before me the pitiless sky, so I must ride out between them and on my journey seek aid from the coaldealer. But he has already grown deaf to ordinary appeals; I must prove irrefutably to him that I have not a single grain of coal left, and that he means to me the very sun in the firmament. I must approach like a beggar, who, with the death rattle already in his throat, insists on dying on the doorstep, and to whom the cook accordingly decides to give the dregs of the coffee-pot; just so must the coaldealer, filled with rage, but acknowledging the command 'Thou shalt not kill,' fling a shovelful of coal into my bucket.

My mode of arrival must decide the matter; so I ride off on the bucket. Seated on the bucket, my hands on the handle, the simplest kind of bridle, I propel myself with difficulty down the stairs; but once downstairs my bucket ascends, superbly, superbly; camels humbly squatting on the ground do not rise with more dignity, shaking themselves under the sticks of their drivers. Through the hard-frozen streets we go at a regular canter; often I am upraised as high as the first storey of a house; never do I sink as low as the house doors. And at last I float at an extraordinary height above the vaulted cellar of the dealer, whom I see far below crouching over his table, where he is writing; he has opened the door to let out the excessive heat.

'Coaldealer!' I cry in a voice burned hollow by the frost and muffled in the cloud made by my breath, 'please, coaldealer, give me a little coal. My bucket is so light that I can ride on it. Be kind. When I can I'll pay you.'

The dealer puts his hand to his ear. 'Do I hear right?' he throws the question over his shoulder to his wife. 'Do I hear right? A customer.'

'I hear nothing,' says his wife, breathing in and out peacefully while she knits on, her back pleasantly warmed by the heat.

'Oh yes, you must hear,' I cry. 'It's me; an old customer; faithful and true; only without means at the moment.'

'Wife,' says the dealer, 'it's someone, it must be; my ears can't have deceived me so much as that; it must be an old, a very old customer, that can move me so deeply.'

'What ails you, man?' says his wife, ceasing from her work for a moment and pressing her knitting to her bosom. 'It's nobody, the street is empty, all our customers are provided for; we could close down the shop for several days and take a rest.'

'But I'm sitting up here on the bucket,' I cry, and numb, frozen tears dim my eyes, 'please look up here, just once; you'll see me directly; I beg you, just a shovelful; and if you give me more it'll make me so happy that I won't know what to do. All the other customers are provided for. Oh, if I could only hear the coal clattering into the bucket!'

'I'm coming,' says the coaldealer, and on his short legs he makes to climb the steps of the cellar, but his wife is already beside him, holds him back by the arm and says: 'You stay here; seeing you persist in your fancies I'll go myself. Think of the bad fit of coughing you had during the night. But for a piece of business, even if it's one you've only fancied in your head, you're prepared to forget your wife and child and sacrifice your lungs. I'll go.'

'Then be sure to tell him all the kinds of coal we have in stock! I'll shout out the prices after you.'

'Right,' says his wife, climbing up to the street. Naturally she sees me at once. 'Frau Coaldealer,' I cry, 'my humblest greetings; just one shovelful of coal; here in my bucket; I'll carry it home myself. One shovelful of the worst you have. I'll pay you in full for it, of course, but not just now, not just now.' What a knell-like sound the words 'not just now' have, and how bewilderingly they mingle with the evening chimes that fall from the church steeple nearby!

'Well, what does he want?' shouts the dealer. 'Nothing,' his wife shouts back, 'there's nothing here; I see nothing, I hear nothing; only six striking, and now we must shut up the shop. The cold is terrible; tomorrow we'll likely have lots to do again.'

She sees nothing and hears nothing; but all the same she loosens her apron strings and waves her apron to waft me away. She succeeds, unluckily. My bucket has all the virtues of a good steed except powers of resistance, which it has not; it is too light; a woman's apron can make it fly through the air.

'You bad woman!' I shout back, while she, turning into the shop, half-contemptuous, half-reassured, flourishes her fist in the air. 'You bad woman! I begged you for a shovelful of the worst coal and you would not give it me.' And with that I ascend into the regions of the ice mountains and am lost forever.

Translated by Willa and Edwin Muir

A Hunger Artist (1924)

First Sorrow

A TRAPEZE ARTIST – this art, practiced high in the vaulted domes of the great variety theaters, is admittedly one of the most difficult humanity can achieve – had so arranged his life that, as long as he kept working in the same building, he never came down from his trapeze by night or day, at first only from a desire to perfect his skill, but later because custom was too strong for him. All his needs, very modest needs at that, were supplied by relays of attendants who watched from below and sent up and hauled down again in specially constructed containers whatever he required. This way of living caused no particular inconvenience to the theatrical people, except that, when other turns were on the stage, his being still up aloft, which could not be dissembled, proved somewhat distracting, as also the fact that, although at such times he mostly kept very still, he drew a stray glance here and there from the public. Yet the management overlooked this, because he was an extraordinary and unique artist. And of course they recognized that this mode of life was no mere prank, and that only in this way could he really keep himself in constant practice and his art at the pitch of its perfection.

Besides, it was quite healthful up there, and when in the warmer seasons of the year the side windows all around the dome of the theater were thrown open and sun and fresh air came pouring irresistibly into the dusky vault, it was even beautiful. True, his social life was somewhat limited, only sometimes a fellow acrobat swarmed up the ladder to him, and then they both sat on the trapeze, leaning left and right against the supporting ropes, and chatted, or builders' workmen repairing the roof exchanged a few words with him through an open window, or the fireman, inspecting the emergency lighting in the top gallery, called over to him something that sounded respectful but could hardly be made out. Otherwise nothing disturbed his seclusion; occasionally, perhaps, some theater hand straying through the empty theater of an afternoon gazed thoughtfully up into the great height of the roof, almost beyond eyeshot, where the trapeze artist, unaware that he was being observed, practiced his art or rested.

The trapeze artist could have gone on living peacefully like that, had it not been for the inevitable journeys from place to place, which he found extremely trying. Of course his manager saw to it that his sufferings were not prolonged one moment more than necessary; for town travel, racing automobiles were used, which whirled him, by night if possible or in the earliest hours of the morning, through the empty streets at breakneck speed, too slow all the same for the trapeze artist's impatience; for railway journeys, a whole compartment was reserved, in which the trapeze artist, as a possible though wretched alternative to his usual way of living, could pass the time up on the luggage rack; in the next town on their circuit, long before he arrived, the trapeze was already slung up in the theater and all the doors leading to the stage were flung wide open, all corridors kept free – yet the manager never knew a happy moment until the trapeze artist set his foot on the rope ladder and in a twinkling, at long last, hung aloft on his trapeze.

Despite so many journeys having been successfully arranged by the manager, each new one embarrassed him again, for the journeys, apart from everything else, got on the nerves of the artist a great deal.

Once when they were again traveling together, the trapeze artist lying on the luggage rack dreaming, the manager leaning back in the opposite window seat reading a book, the trapeze artist addressed his companion in a low voice. The manager was immediately all attention. The trapeze artist, biting his lips, said that he must always in future have two trapezes for his performance instead of only one, two trapezes opposite each other. The manager at once agreed. But the trapeze artist, as if to show that the manager's consent counted for as little as his refusal, said that never again would he perform on only one trapeze, in no circumstances whatever. The very idea that it might happen at all seemed to make him shudder. The manager, watchfully feeling his way, once more emphasized his entire agreement, two trapezes were better than one, besides it would be an advantage to have a second bar, more variety could be introduced into the performance. At that the trapeze artist suddenly burst into tears. Deeply distressed, the manager sprang to his feet and asked what was the matter, then getting no answer climbed up on the seat and caressed him, cheek to cheek, so that his own face was bedabbled by the trapeze artist's tears. Yet it took much questioning and soothing endearment until the trapeze artist sobbed: 'Only the one bar in my hands – how can I go on living!' That made it somewhat easier for the manager to comfort him; he promised to wire from the very next station for a second trapeze to be installed in the first town on their circuit; reproached himself for having let the artist work so long on only one trapeze; and thanked and praised him warmly for having at last brought the mistake to his notice. And so he succeeded in reassuring the trapeze artist, little by little, and was able to go back to his corner. But he himself was far from reassured, with deep uneasiness he kept glancing secretly at the trapeze artist over the top of his book. Once such ideas began to torment him, would they ever quite leave him alone? Would they not rather increase in urgency? Would they not threaten his very existence? And indeed the manager believed he could see, during the apparently peaceful sleep which had succeeded the fit of tears, the first furrows of care engraving themselves upon the trapeze artist's smooth, childlike forehead.

Translated by Willa and Edwin Muir

A Little Woman

SHE IS a little woman; naturally quite slim, she is tightly laced as well; she is always in the same dress when I see her, it is made of grayish-yellow stuff something the color of wood and is trimmed discreetly with tassels or buttonlike hangings of the same color; she never wears a hat, her dull, fair hair is smooth and not untidy, but worn very loose. Although she is tightly laced she is quick and light in her movements, actually she rather overdoes the quickness, she loves to put her hands on her hips and abruptly turn the upper part of her body sideways with a suddenness that is surprising. The impression her hand makes on me I can convey only by saying that I have never seen a hand with the separate fingers so sharply differentiated from each other as hers; and yet her hand has no anatomical peculiarities, it is an entirely normal hand.

This little woman, then, is very ill-pleased with me, she always finds something objectionable in me, I am always doing the wrong thing to her, I annoy her at every step; if a life could be cut into the smallest of small pieces and every scrap of it could be separately assessed, every scrap of my life would certainly be an offense to her. I have often wondered why I am such an offense to her; it may be that everything about me outrages her sense of beauty, her feeling for justice, her habits, her traditions, her hopes, there are such completely incompatible natures, but why does that upset her so much? There is no connection between us that could force her to suffer because of me. All she has to do is to regard me as an utter stranger, which I am, and which I do not object to being, indeed I should welcome it, she only needs to forget my existence, which I have never thrust upon her attention, nor ever would, and obviously her torments would be at an end. I am not thinking of myself, I am quite leaving out of account the fact that I find her attitude of course rather trying, leaving it out of account because I recognize that my discomfort is nothing to the suffering she endures. All the same I am well aware that hers is no affectionate suffering; she is not concerned to make any real improvement in me, besides, whatever she finds objectionable in me is not of a nature to hinder my development. Yet she does not care about my development either, she cares only for her personal interest in the matter, which is to revenge herself for the torments I cause her now and to prevent any torments that threaten her from me in the future. I have already tried once to indicate the best way of putting a stop to this perpetual resentment of hers, but my very attempt wrought her up to such a pitch of fury that I shall never repeat it.

I feel too a certain responsibility laid upon me, if you like to put it that way, for strangers as we are to each other, the little woman and myself, and however true it is that the sole connection between us is the vexation I cause her, or rather the vexation she lets me cause her, I ought not to feel indifferent to the visible physical suffering which this induces in her. Every now and then, and more frequently of late, information is brought to me that she has risen of a morning pale, unslept, oppressed by headache, and almost unable to work; her family are worried about her, they wonder what can have caused her condition, and they have not yet found the answer. I am the only one who knows that it is her settled and daily renewed vexation with me. True, I am not so worried about her as her family; she is hardy and tough; anyone who is capable of such strong feeling is likely also to be capable of surviving its effects; I have even a suspicion that her sufferings – or some of them, at least – are only a pretense put up to bring public suspicion on me. She is too proud to admit openly what a torment my very existence is to her; to make any appeal to others against me she would consider beneath her dignity; it is only disgust, persistent and active disgust, that drives her to be preoccupied with me; to discuss in public this unclean affliction of hers would be too shameful. But to keep utterly silent about something that so persistently rankles would be also too much for her. So with feminine guile she steers a middle course; she keeps silent but betrays all the outward signs of a secret sorrow in order to draw public attention to the matter. Perhaps she even hopes that once public attention is fixed on me a general public rancor against me will rise up and use all its great powers to condemn me definitively much more effectively and quickly than her relatively feeble private rancor could do; she would then retire into the background, draw a breath of relief, and turn her back on me. Well, if that is what her hopes are really set on, she is deluding herself. Public opinion will not take over her role; public opinion would never find me so infinitely objectionable, even under its most powerful magnifying glass. I am not so altogether useless a creature as she thinks; I don't want to boast and especially not in this connection; but if I am not conspicuous for specially useful qualities, I am certainly not conspicuous for the lack of them; only to her, only to her almost bleached eyes, do I appear so, she won't be able to convince anyone else. So in this respect I can feel quite reassured, can I? No, not at all; for if it becomes generally known that my behavior is making her positively ill, which some observers, those who most industriously bring me information about her, for instance, are not far from perceiving, or at least look as if they perceived it, and the world should put questions to me, why am I tormenting the poor little woman with my incorrigibility, and do I mean to drive her to her death, and when am I going to show some sense and have enough decent human feeling to stop such goings-on – if the world were to ask me that, it would be difficult to find an answer. Should I admit frankly that I don't much believe in these symptoms of illness, and thus produce the unfavorable impression of being a man who blames others to avoid being blamed himself, and in such an ungallant manner? And how could I say quite openly that even if I did believe that she were really ill, I should not feel the slightest sympathy for her, since she is a complete stranger to me and any connection between us is her own invention and entirely one-sided. I don't say that people wouldn't believe me; they wouldn't be interested enough to get so far as belief; they would simply note the answer I gave concerning such a frail, sick woman, and that would be little in my favor. Any answer I made would inevitably come up against the world's incapacity to keep down the suspicion that there must be a love affair behind such a case as this, although it is as clear as daylight that such a relationship does not exist, and that if it did it would come from my side rather than hers, since I should be really capable of admiring the little woman for the decisive quickness of her judgment and her persistent vitality in leaping to conclusions, if these very qualities were not always turned as weapons against me. She, at any rate, shows not a trace of friendliness toward me; in that she is honest and true; therein lies my last hope; not even to help on her campaign would she so far forget herself as to let any such suspicion arise. But public opinion which is wholly insensitive in such matters would abide by its prejudices and always denounce me.

So the only thing left for me to do would be to change myself in time, before the world could intervene, just sufficiently to lessen the little woman's rancor, not to wean her from it altogether, which is unthinkable. And indeed I have often asked myself if I am so pleased with my present self as to be unwilling to change it, and whether I could not attempt some changes in myself, even though I should be doing so not because I found them needful but merely to propitiate the little woman. And I have honestly tried, taking some trouble and care, it even did me good, it was almost a diversion; some changes resulted which were visible a long way off, I did not need to draw her attention to them, she perceives all that kind of thing much sooner than I do, she can even perceive by my expression beforehand what I have in mind; but no success crowned my efforts. How could it possibly do so? Her objection to me, as I am now aware, is a fundamental one; nothing can remove it, not even the removal of myself; if she heard that I had committed suicide she would fall into transports of rage.

Now I cannot imagine that such a sharp-witted woman as she is does not understand as well as I do both the hopelessness of her own course of action and the helplessness of mine, my inability, with the best will in the world, to conform to her requirements. Of course she understands it, but being a fighter by nature she forgets it in the lust of battle, and my unfortunate disposition, which I cannot help since it is mine by nature, conditions me to whisper gentle admonitions to anyone who flies into a violent passion. In this way, naturally, we shall never come to terms. I shall keep on leaving the house in the gay mood of early morning only to meet that countenance of hers, lowering at the sight of me, the contemptuous curl of her lips, the measuring glance, aware beforehand of what it is going to find, that sweeps over me and however fleeting misses nothing, the sarcastic smile furrowing her girlish cheek, the complaining lift of the eyes to Heaven, the planting of the hands on the hips, to fortify herself, and then the access of rage that brings pallor with it and trembling.

Not long ago I took occasion, for the very first time as I realized with some astonishment, to mention the matter to a very good friend of mine, just in passing, casually, in a word or two, reducing it to even less than its just proportions, trivial as it is in essence when looked at objectively. It was curious that my friend all the same did not ignore it, indeed of his own accord he even made more of it than I had done, would not be sidetracked, and insisted on discussing it. But it was still more curious that in one important particular he underestimated it, for he advised me seriously to go away for a short time. No advice could be less understandable; the matter was simple enough, anyone who looked closely at it could see right through it, yet it was not so simple that my mere departure would set all of it right, or even the greater part of it. On the contrary, such a departure is just what I must avoid; if I am to follow a plan at all it must be that of keeping the affair within its present narrow limits which do not yet involve the outside world, that is to say, I must stay quietly where I am and not let it affect my behavior as far as can be seen, and that includes mentioning it to no one, but not at all because it is a kind of dangerous mystery, merely because it is a trivial, purely personal matter and as such to be taken lightly, and to be kept on that level. So my friend's remarks were not profitless after all, they taught me nothing new yet they strengthened my original resolution.

And on closer reflection it appears that the developments which the affair seems to have undergone in the course of time are not developments in the affair itself, but only in my attitude to it, insofar as that has become more composed on the one hand, more manly, penetrating nearer the heart of the matter, while on the other hand, under the influence of the continued nervous strain which I cannot overcome, however slight, it has increased in irritability.

I am less upset by the affair now that I think I perceive how unlikely it is to come to any decisive crisis, imminent as that sometimes seems to be; one is easily disposed, especially when one is young, to exaggerate the speed with which decisive moments arrive; whenever my small critic, grown faint at the very sight of me, sank sideways into a chair, holding on to the back of it with one hand and plucking at her bodice strings with the other, while tears of rage and despair rolled down her cheeks, I used to think that now the moment had come and I was just on the point of being summoned to answer for myself. Yet there was no decisive moment, no summons, women faint easily, the world has no time to notice all their doings. And what has really happened in all these years? Nothing except that such occasions have repeated themselves, sometimes more and sometimes less violently, and that their sum total has increased accordingly. And that people are hanging around in the offing and would like to interfere if they could find some way of doing it; but they can find none, so up till now they have had to rely on what they could smell out, and although that by itself is fully qualified to keep the owners of the noses busy it can't do anything more. Yet the situation was always like that, fundamentally, always provided with superfluous bystanders and nosy onlookers, who always justified their presence by some cunning excuse, for preference claiming to be relatives, always stretching their necks and sniffing trouble, but all they have achieved is to be still standing by. The only difference is that I have gradually come to recognize them and distinguish one face from another; once upon a time I believed that they had just gradually trickled in from outside, that the affair was having wider repercussions, which would themselves compel a crisis; today I think I know that these onlookers were always there from the beginning and have little or nothing to do with the imminence of a crisis. And the crisis itself, why should I dignify it by such a name? If it ever should happen – and certainly not tomorrow or the day after tomorrow, most likely never – that public opinion concerns itself with the affair, which, I must repeat, is beyond its competence, I certainly won't escape unharmed, but on the other hand people are bound to take into account that I am not unknown to the public, that I have lived for long in the full light of publicity, trustingly and trustworthily, and that this distressed little woman, this latecomer in my life, who, let me remark in passing, another man might have brushed off like a burr and privately trodden underfoot without a sound, that this woman at the very worst could add only an ugly little flourish to the diploma in which public opinion long ago certified me to be a respectable member of society. That is how things stand today, little likely to cause me any uneasiness.

The fact that in the course of years I have all the same become somewhat uneasy has nothing to do with the real significance of this affair; a man simply cannot endure being a continual target for someone's spite, even when he knows well enough that the spite is gratuitous; he grows uneasy, he begins, in a kind of physical way only, to expect final decisions, even when like a sensible man he does not much believe that they are forthcoming. Partly, too, it is a symptom of increasing age; youth sheds a bloom over everything; awkward characteristics are lost to sight in the endless upwelling of youthful energy; if as a youth a man has a somewhat wary eye it is not counted against him, it is not noticed at all, even by himself; but the things that survive in old age are residues, each is necessary, none is renewed, each is under scrutiny, and the wary eye of an aging man is clearly a wary eye and is not difficult to recognize. Only, as also in this case, it is not an actual degeneration of his condition.

So from whatever standpoint I consider this small affair, it appears, and this I will stick to, that if I keep my hand over it, even quite lightly, I shall quietly continue to live my own life for a long time to come, untroubled by the world, despite all the outbursts of the woman.

Translated by Willa and Edwin Muir

A Hunger Artist

DURING these last decades the interest in professional fasting has markedly diminished. It used to pay very well to stage such great performances under one's own management, but today that is quite impossible. We live in a different world now. At one time the whole town took a lively interest in the hunger artist; from day to day of his fast the excitement mounted; everybody wanted to see him at least once a day; there were people who bought season tickets for the last few days and sat from morning till night in front of his small barred cage; even in the nighttime there were visiting hours, when the whole effect was heightened by torch flares; on fine days the cage was set out in the open air, and then it was the children's special treat to see the hunger artist; for their elders he was often just a joke that happened to be in fashion, but the children stood openmouthed, holding each other's hands for greater security, marveling at him as he sat there pallid in black tights, with his ribs sticking out so prominently, not even on a seat but down among straw on the ground, sometimes giving a courteous nod, answering questions with a constrained smile, or perhaps stretching an arm through the bars so that one might feel how thin it was, and then again withdrawing deep into himself, paying no attention to anyone or anything, not even to the all-important striking of the clock that was the only piece of furniture in his cage, but merely staring into vacancy with half-shut eyes, now and then taking a sip from a tiny glass of water to moisten his lips.

Besides casual onlookers there were also relays of permanent watchers selected by the public, usually butchers, strangely enough, and it was their task to watch the hunger artist day and night, three of them at a time, in case he should have some secret recourse to nourishment. This was nothing but a formality, instituted to reassure the masses, for the initiates knew well enough that during his fast the artist would never in any circumstances, not even under forcible compulsion, swallow the smallest morsel of food; the honor of his profession forbade it. Not every watcher, of course, was capable of understanding this, there were often groups of night watchers who were very lax in carrying out their duties and deliberately huddled together in a retired corner to play cards with great absorption, obviously intending to give the hunger artist the chance of a little refreshment, which they supposed he could draw from some private hoard. Nothing annoyed the artist more than such watchers; they made him miserable; they made his fast seem unendurable; sometimes he mastered his feebleness sufficiently to sing during their watch for as long as he could keep going, to show them how unjust their suspicions were. But that was of little use; they only wondered at his cleverness in being able to fill his mouth even while singing. Much more to his taste were the watchers who sat close up to the bars, who were not content with the dim night lighting of the hall but focused him in the full glare of the electric pocket torch given them by the impresario. The harsh light did not trouble him at all, in any case he could never sleep properly, and he could always drowse a little, whatever the light, at any hour, even when the hall was thronged with noisy onlookers. He was quite happy at the prospect of spending a sleepless night with such watchers; he was ready to exchange jokes with them, to tell them stories out of his nomadic life, anything at all to keep them awake and demonstrate to them again that he had no eatables in his cage and that he was fasting as not one of them could fast. But his happiest moment was when the morning came and an enormous breakfast was brought them, at his expense, on which they flung themselves with the keen appetite of healthy men after a weary night of wakefulness. Of course there were people who argued that this breakfast was an unfair attempt to bribe the watchers, but that was going rather too far, and when they were invited to take on a night's vigil without a breakfast, merely for the sake of the cause, they made themselves scarce, although they stuck stubbornly to their suspicions.

Such suspicions, anyhow, were a necessary accompaniment to the profession of fasting. No one could possibly watch the hunger artist continuously, day and night, and so no one could produce first-hand evidence that the fast had really been rigorous and continuous; only the artist himself could know that, he was therefore bound to be the sole completely satisfied spectator of his own fast. Yet for other reasons he was never satisfied; it was not perhaps mere fasting that had brought him to such skeleton thinness that many people had regretfully to keep away from his exhibitions, because the sight of him was too much for them, perhaps it was dissatisfaction with himself that had worn him down. For he alone knew, what no other initiate knew, how easy it was to fast. It was the easiest thing in the world. He made no secret of this, yet people did not believe him, at the best they set him down as modest, most of them, however, thought he was out for publicity or else was some kind of cheat who found it easy to fast because he had discovered a way of making it easy, and then had the impudence to admit the fact, more or less. He had to put up with all that, and in the course of time had got used to it, but his inner dissatisfaction always rankled, and never yet, after any term of fasting – this must be granted to his credit – had he left the cage of his own free will. The longest period of fasting was fixed by his impresario at forty days, beyond that term he was not allowed to go, not even in great cities, and there was good reason for it, too. Experience had proved that for about forty days the interest of the public could be stimulated by a steadily increasing pressure of advertisement, but after that the town began to lose interest, sympathetic support began notably to fall off; there were of course local variations as between one town and another or one country and another, but as a general rule forty days marked the limit. So on the fortieth day the flower-bedecked cage was opened, enthusiastic spectators filled the hall, a military band played, two doctors entered the cage to measure the results of the fast, which were announced through a megaphone, and finally two young ladies appeared, blissful at having been selected for the honor, to help the hunger artist down the few steps leading to a small table on which was spread a carefully chosen invalid repast. And at this very moment the artist always turned stubborn. True, he would entrust his bony arms to the outstretched helping hands of the ladies bending over him, but stand up he would not. Why stop fasting at this particular moment, after forty days of it? He had held out for a long time, an illimitably long time; why stop now, when he was in his best fasting form, or rather, not yet quite in his best fasting form? Why should he be cheated of the fame he would get for fasting longer, for being not only the record hunger artist of all time, which presumably he was already, but for beating his own record by a performance beyond human imagination, since he felt that there were no limits to his capacity for fasting? His public pretended to admire him so much, why should it have so little patience with him; if he could endure fasting longer, why shouldn't the public endure it? Besides, he was tired, he was comfortable sitting in the straw, and now he was supposed to lift himself to his full height and go down to a meal the very thought of which gave him a nausea that only the presence of the ladies kept him from betraying, and even that with an effort. And he looked up into the eyes of the ladies who were apparently so friendly and in reality so cruel, and shook his head, which felt too heavy on its strengthless neck. But then there happened yet again what always happened. The impresario came forward, without a word – for the band made speech impossible – lifted his arms in the air above the artist, as if inviting Heaven to look down upon its creature here in the straw, this suffering martyr, which indeed he was, although in quite another sense; grasped him around the emaciated waist, with exaggerated caution, so that the frail condition he was in might be appreciated; and committed him to the care of the blenching ladies, not without secretly giving him a shaking so that his legs and body tottered and swayed. The artist now submitted completely; his head lolled on his breast as if it had landed there by chance; his body was hollowed out; his legs in a spasm of self-preservation clung close to each other at the knees, yet scraped on the ground as if it were not really solid ground, as if they were only trying to find solid ground; and the whole weight of his body, a featherweight after all, relapsed onto one of the ladies, who, looking around for help and panting a little – this post of honor was not at all what she had expected it to be – first stretched her neck as far as she could to keep her face at least free from contact with the artist, then finding this impossible, and her more fortunate companion not coming to her aid but merely holding extended in her own trembling hand the little bunch of knucklebones that was the artist's, to the great delight of the spectators burst into tears and had to be replaced by an attendant who had long been stationed in readiness. Then came the food, a little of which the impresario managed to get between the artist's lips, while he sat in a kind of half-fainting trance, to the accompaniment of cheerful patter designed to distract the public's attention from the artist's condition; after that, a toast was drunk to the public, supposedly prompted by a whisper from the artist in the impresario's ear; the band confirmed it with a mighty flourish, the spectators melted away, and no one had any cause to be dissatisfied with the proceedings, no one except the hunger artist himself, he only, as always.

So he lived for many years, with small regular intervals of recuperation, in visible glory, honored by the world, yet in spite of that troubled in spirit, and all the more troubled because no one would take his trouble seriously. What comfort could he possibly need? What more could he possibly wish for? And if some good-natured person, feeling sorry for him, tried to console him by pointing out that his melancholy was probably caused by fasting, it could happen, especially when he had been fasting for some time, that he reacted with an outburst of fury and to the general alarm began to shake the bars of his cage like a wild animal. Yet the impresario had a way of punishing these outbreaks which he rather enjoyed putting into operation. He would apologize publicly for the artist's behavior, which was only to be excused, he admitted, because of the irritability caused by fasting; a condition hardly to be understood by well-fed people; then by natural transition he went on to mention the artist's equally incomprehensible boast that he could fast for much longer than he was doing; he praised the high ambition, the good will, the great self-denial undoubtedly implicit in such a statement; and then quite simply countered it by bringing out photographs, which were also on sale to the public, showing the artist on the fortieth day of a fast lying in bed almost dead from exhaustion. This perversion of the truth, familiar to the artist though it was, always unnerved him afresh and proved too much for him. What was a consequence of the premature ending of his fast was here presented as the cause of it! To fight against this lack of understanding, against a whole world of non-understanding, was impossible. Time and again in good faith he stood by the bars listening to the impresario, but as soon as the photographs appeared he always let go and sank with a groan back into his straw, and the reassured public could once more come close and gaze at him.

A few years later when the witnesses of such scenes called them to mind, they often failed to understand themselves at all. For meanwhile the aforementioned change in public interest had set in; it seemed to happen almost overnight; there may have been profound causes for it, but who was going to bother about that; at any rate the pampered hunger artist suddenly found himself deserted one fine day by the amusement-seekers, who went streaming past him to other more-favored attractions. For the last time the impresario hurried him over half Europe to discover whether the old interest might still survive here and there; all in vain; everywhere, as if by secret agreement, a positive revulsion from professional fasting was in evidence. Of course it could not really have sprung up so suddenly as all that, and many premonitory symptoms which had not been sufficiently remarked or suppressed during the rush and glitter of success now came retrospectively to mind, but it was now too late to take any countermeasures. Fasting would surely come into fashion again at some future date, yet that was no comfort for those living in the present. What, then, was the hunger artist to do? He had been applauded by thousands in his time and could hardly come down to showing himself in a street booth at village fairs, and as for adopting another profession, he was not only too old for that but too fanatically devoted to fasting. So he took leave of the impresario, his partner in an unparalleled career, and hired himself to a large circus; in order to spare his own feelings he avoided reading the conditions of his contract.

A large circus with its enormous traffic in replacing and recruiting men, animals, and apparatus can always find a use for people at any time, even for a hunger artist, provided of course that he does not ask too much, and in this particular case anyhow it was not only the artist who was taken on but his famous and long-known name as well, indeed considering the peculiar nature of his performance, which was not impaired by advancing age, it could not be objected that here was an artist past his prime, no longer at the height of his professional skill, seeking a refuge in some quiet corner of a circus; on the contrary, the hunger artist averred that he could fast as well as ever, which was entirely credible, he even alleged that if he were allowed to fast as he liked, and this was at once promised him without more ado, he could astound the world by establishing a record never yet achieved, a statement that certainly provoked a smile among the other professionals, since it left out of account the change in public opinion, which the hunger artist in his zeal conveniently forgot.

He had not, however, actually lost his sense of the real situation and took it as a matter of course that he and his cage should be stationed, not in the middle of the ring as a main attraction, but outside, near the animal cages, on a site that was after all easily accessible. Large and gaily painted placards made a frame for the cage and announced what was to be seen inside it. When the public came thronging out in the intervals to see the animals, they could hardly avoid passing the hunger artist's cage and stopping there for a moment, perhaps they might even have stayed longer had not those pressing behind them in the narrow gangway, who did not understand why they should be held up on their way toward the excitements of the menagerie, made it impossible for anyone to stand gazing quietly for any length of time. And that was the reason why the hunger artist, who had of course been looking forward to these visiting hours as the main achievement of his life, began instead to shrink from them. At first he could hardly wait for the intervals; it was exhilarating to watch the crowds come streaming his way, until only too soon – not even the most obstinate self-deception, clung to almost consciously, could hold out against the fact – the conviction was borne in upon him that these people, most of them, to judge from their actions, again and again, without exception, were all on their way to the menagerie. And the first sight of them from the distance remained the best. For when they reached his cage he was at once deafened by the storm of shouting and abuse that arose from the two contending factions, which renewed themselves continuously, of those who wanted to stop and stare at him – he soon began to dislike them more than the others – not out of real interest but only out of obstinate self-assertiveness, and those who wanted to go straight on to the animals. When the first great rush was past, the stragglers came along, and these, whom nothing could have prevented from stopping to look at him as long as they had breath, raced past with long strides, hardly even glancing at him, in their haste to get to the menagerie in time. And all too rarely did it happen that he had a stroke of luck, when some father of a family fetched up before him with his children, pointed a finger at the hunger artist, and explained at length what the phenomenon meant, telling stories of earlier years when he himself had watched similar but much more thrilling performances, and the children, still rather uncomprehending, since neither inside nor outside school had they been sufficiently prepared for this lesson – what did they care about fasting? – yet showed by the brightness of their intent eyes that new and better times might be coming. Perhaps, said the hunger artist to himself many a time, things would be a little better if his cage were set not quite so near the menagerie. That made it too easy for people to make their choice, to say nothing of what he suffered from the stench of the menagerie, the animals' restlessness by night, the carrying past of raw lumps of flesh for the beasts of prey, the roaring at feeding times, which depressed him continually. But he did not dare to lodge a complaint with the management; after all, he had the animals to thank for the troops of people who passed his cage, among whom there might always be one here and there to take an interest in him, and who could tell where they might seclude him if he called attention to his existence and thereby to the fact that, strictly speaking, he was only an impediment on the way to the menagerie.

A small impediment, to be sure, one that grew steadily less. People grew familiar with the strange idea that they could be expected, in times like these, to take an interest in a hunger artist, and with this familiarity the verdict went out against him. He might fast as much as he could, and he did so; but nothing could save him now, people passed him by. Just try to explain to anyone the art of fasting! Anyone who has no feeling for it cannot be made to understand it. The fine placards grew dirty and illegible, they were torn down; the little notice board telling the number of fast days achieved, which at first was changed carefully every day, had long stayed at the same figure, for after the first few weeks even this small task seemed pointless to the staff; and so the artist simply fasted on and on, as he had once dreamed of doing, and it was no trouble to him, just as he had always foretold, but no one counted the days, no one, not even the artist himself, knew what records he was already breaking, and his heart grew heavy. And when once in a while some leisurely passer-by stopped, made merry over the old figure on the board, and spoke of swindling, that was in its way the stupidest lie ever invented by indifference and inborn malice, since it was not the hunger artist who was cheating, he was working honestly, but the world was cheating him of his reward.

Many more days went by, however, and that too came to an end. An overseer's eye fell on the cage one day and he asked the attendants why this perfectly good cage should be left standing there unused with dirty straw inside it; nobody knew, until one man, helped out by the notice board, remembered about the hunger artist. They poked into the straw with sticks and found him in it. 'Are you still fasting?' asked the overseer, 'when on earth do you mean to stop?' 'Forgive me, everybody,' whispered the hunger artist; only the overseer, who had his ear to the bars, understood him. 'Of course,' said the overseer, and tapped his forehead with a finger to let the attendants know what state the man was in, 'we forgive you.' 'I always wanted you to admire my fasting,' said the hunger artist. 'We do admire it,' said the overseer, affably. 'But you shouldn't admire it,' said the hunger artist. 'Well then we don't admire it,' said the overseer, 'but why shouldn't we admire it?' 'Because I have to fast, I can't help it,' said the hunger artist. 'What a fellow you are,' said the overseer, 'and why can't you help it?' 'Because,' said the hunger artist, lifting his head a little and speaking, with his lips pursed, as if for a kiss, right into the overseer's ear, so that no syllable might be lost, 'because I couldn't find the food I liked. If I had found it, believe me, I should have made no fuss and stuffed myself like you or anyone else.' These were his last words, but in his dimming eyes remained the firm though no longer proud persuasion that he was still continuing to fast.

'Well, clear this out now!' said the overseer, and they

buried the hunger artist, straw and all. Into the cage they put a young panther. Even the most insensitive felt it refreshing to see this wild creature leaping around the cage that had so long been dreary. The panther was all right. The food he liked was brought him without hesitation by the attendants; he seemed not even to miss his freedom; his noble body, furnished almost to the bursting point with all that it needed, seemed to carry freedom around with it too; somewhere in his jaws it seemed to lurk; and the joy of life streamed with such ardent passion from his throat that for the onlookers it was not easy to stand the shock of it. But they braced themselves, crowded around the cage, and did not want ever to move away.

Translated by Willa and Edwin Muir

Josephine the Singer, or the Mouse Folk

OUR SINGER is called Josephine. Anyone who has not heard her does not know the power of song. There is no one but is carried away by her singing, a tribute all the greater as we are not in general a music-loving race. Tranquil peace is the music we love best; our life is hard, we are no longer able, even on occasions when we have tried to shake off the cares of daily life, to rise to anything so high and remote from our usual routine as music. But we do not much lament that; we do not get even so far; a certain practical cunning, which admittedly we stand greatly in need of, we hold to be our greatest distinction, and with a smile born of such cunning we are wont to console ourselves for all shortcomings, even supposing – only it does not happen – that we were to yearn once in a way for the kind of bliss which music may provide. Josephine is the sole exception; she has a love for music and knows too how to transmit it; she is the only one; when she dies, music – who knows for how long – will vanish from our lives.

I have often thought about what this music of hers really means. For we are quite unmusical; how is it that we understand Josephine's singing or, since Josephine denies that, at least think we can understand it. The simplest answer would be that the beauty of her singing is so great that even the most insensitive cannot be deaf to it, but this answer is not satisfactory. If it were really so, her singing would have to give one an immediate and lasting feeling of being something out of the ordinary, a feeling that from her throat something is sounding which we have never heard before and which we are not even capable of hearing, something that Josephine alone and no one else can enable us to hear. But in my opinion that is just what does not happen, I do not feel this and have never observed that others feel anything of the kind. Among intimates we admit freely to one another that Josephine's singing, as singing, is nothing out of the ordinary.

Is it in fact singing at all? Although we are unmusical we have a tradition of singing; in the old days our people did sing; this is mentioned in legends and some songs have actually survived, which, it is true, no one can now sing. Thus we have an inkling of what singing is, and Josephine's art does not really correspond to it. So is it singing at all? Is it not perhaps just a piping? And piping is something we all know about, it is the real artistic accomplishment of our people, or rather no mere accomplishment but a characteristic expression of our life. We all pipe, but of course no one dreams of making out that our piping is an art, we pipe without thinking of it, indeed without noticing it, and there are even many among us who are quite unaware that piping is one of our characteristics. So if it were true that Josephine does not sing but only pipes and perhaps, as it seems to me at least, hardly rises above the level of our usual piping – yet, perhaps her strength is not even quite equal to our usual piping, whereas an ordinary farmhand can keep it up effortlessly all day long, besides doing his work – if that were all true, then indeed Josephine's alleged vocal skill might be disproved, but that would merely clear the ground for the real riddle which needs solving, the enormous influence she has.

After all, it is only a kind of piping that she produces. If you post yourself quite far away from her and listen, or, still better, put your judgment to the test, whenever she happens to be singing along with others, by trying to identify her voice, you will undoubtedly distinguish nothing but a quite ordinary piping tone, which at most differs a little from the others through being delicate or weak. Yet if you sit down before her, it is not merely a piping; to comprehend her art it is necessary not only to hear but to see her. Even if hers were only our usual workaday piping, there is first of all this peculiarity to consider, that here is someone making a ceremonial performance out of doing the usual thing. To crack a nut is truly no feat, so no one would ever dare to collect an audience in order to entertain it with nut-cracking. But if all the same one does do that and succeeds in entertaining the public, then it cannot be a matter of simple nut-cracking. Or it is a matter of nut-cracking, but it turns out that we have overlooked the art of cracking nuts because we were too skilled in it and that this newcomer to it first shows us its real nature, even finding it useful in making his effects to be rather less expert in nut-cracking than most of us.

Perhaps it is much the same with Josephine's singing; we admire in her what we do not at all admire in ourselves; in this respect, I may say, she is of one mind with us. I was once present when someone, as of course often happens, drew her attention to the folk piping everywhere going on, making only a modest reference to it, yet for Josephine that was more than enough. A smile so sarcastic and arrogant as she then assumed I have never seen; she, who in appearance is delicacy itself, conspicuously so even among our people who are prolific in such feminine types, seemed at that moment actually vulgar; she was at once aware of it herself, by the way, with her extreme sensibility, and controlled herself. At any rate she denies any connection between her art and ordinary piping. For those who are of the contrary opinion she has only contempt and probably unacknowledged hatred. This is not simple vanity, for the opposition, with which I too am half in sympathy, certainly admires her no less than the crowd does, but Josephine does not want mere admiration, she wants to be admired exactly in the way she prescribes, mere admiration leaves her cold. And when you take a seat before her, you understand her; opposition is possible only at a distance, when you sit before her, you know: this piping of hers is no piping.

Since piping is one of our thoughtless habits, one might think that people would pipe up in Josephine's audience too; her art makes us feel happy, and when we are happy we pipe; but her audience never pipes, it sits in mouselike stillness; as if we had become partakers in the peace we long for, from which our own piping at the very least holds us back, we make no sound. Is it her singing that enchants us or is it not rather the solemn stillness enclosing her frail little voice? Once it happened while Josephine was singing that some silly little thing in all innocence began to pipe up too. Now it was just the same as what we were hearing from Josephine; in front of us the piping sound that despite all rehearsal was still tentative and here in the audience the unselfconscious piping of a child; it would have been impossible to define the difference; but yet at once we hissed and whistled the interrupter down, although it would not really have been necessary, for in any case she would certainly have crawled away in fear and shame, whereas Josephine struck up her most triumphal notes and was quite beyond herself, spreading her arms wide and stretching her throat as high as it could reach.

That is what she is like always, every trifle, every casual incident, every nuisance, a creaking in the parquet, a grinding of teeth, a failure in the lighting incites her to heighten the effectiveness of her song; she believes anyhow that she is singing to deaf ears; there is no lack of enthusiasm and applause, but she has long learned not to expect real understanding, as she conceives it. So all disturbance is very welcome to her; whatever intervenes from outside to hinder the purity of her song, to be overcome with a slight effort, even with no effort at all, merely by confronting it, can help to awaken the masses, to teach them not perhaps understanding but awed respect.

And if small events do her such service, how much more do great ones. Our life is very uneasy, every day brings surprises, apprehensions, hopes, and terrors, so that it would be impossible for a single individual to bear it all did he not always have by day and night the support of his fellows; but even so it often becomes very difficult; frequently as many as a thousand shoulders are trembling under a burden that was really meant only for one pair. Then Josephine holds that her time has come. So there she stands, the delicate creature, shaken by vibrations especially below the breast-bone, so that one feels anxious for her, it is as if she has concentrated all her strength on her song, as if from everything in her that does not directly subserve her singing all strength has been withdrawn, almost all power of life, as if she were laid bare, abandoned, committed merely to the care of good angels, as if while she is so wholly withdrawn and living only in her song a cold breath blowing upon her might kill her. But just when she makes such an appearance, we who are supposed to be her opponents are in the habit of saying: 'She can't even pipe; she has to put such a terrible strain on herself to force out not a song – we can't call it song – but some approximation to our usual customary piping.' So it seems to us, but this impression although, as I said, inevitable is yet fleeting and transient. We too are soon sunk in the feeling of the mass, which, warmly pressed body to body, listens with indrawn breath.

And to gather around her this mass of our people who are almost always on the run and scurrying hither and thither for reasons that are often not very clear, Josephine mostly needs to do nothing else than take up her stand, head thrown back, mouth half-open, eyes turned upwards, in the position that indicates her intention to sing. She can do this where she likes, it need not be a place visible a long way off, any secluded corner pitched on in a moment's caprice will serve as well. The news that she is going to sing flies around at once and soon whole processions are on the way there. Now, sometimes, all the same, obstacles intervene, Josephine likes best to sing just when things are most upset, many worries and dangers force us then to take devious ways, with the best will in the world we cannot assemble ourselves as quickly as Josephine wants, and on occasion she stands there in ceremonial state for quite a time without a sufficient audience – then indeed she turns furious, then she stamps her feet, swearing in most unmaidenly fashion; she actually bites. But even such behavior does no harm to her reputation; instead of curbing a little her excessive demands, people exert themselves to meet them; messengers are sent out to summon fresh hearers; she is kept in ignorance of the fact that this is being done; on the roads all around sentries can be seen posted who wave on newcomers and urge them to hurry; this goes on until at last a tolerably large audience is gathered.

What drives the people to make such exertions for Josephine's sake? This is no easier to answer than the first question about Josephine's singing, with which it is closely connected. One could eliminate that and combine them both in the second question, if it were possible to assert that because of her singing our people are unconditionally devoted to Josephine. But this is simply not the case; unconditional devotion is hardly known among us; ours are people who love slyness beyond everything, without any malice, to be sure, and childish whispering and chatter, innocent, superficial chatter, to be sure, but people of such a kind cannot go in for unconditional devotion, and that Josephine herself certainly feels, that is what she is fighting against with all the force of her feeble throat.

In making such generalized pronouncements, of course, one should not go too far, our people are all the same devoted to Josephine, only not unconditionally. For instance, they would not be capable of laughing at Josephine. It can be admitted: in Josephine there is much to make one laugh; and laughter for its own sake is never far away from us; in spite of all the misery of our lives quiet laughter is always, so to speak, at our elbows; but we do not laugh at Josephine. Many a time I have had the impression that our people interpret their relationship to Josephine in this way, that she, this frail creature, needing protection and in some way remarkable, in her own opinion remarkable for her gift of song, is entrusted to their care and they must look after her; the reason for this is not clear to anyone, only the fact seems to be established. But what is entrusted to one's care one does not laugh at; to laugh would be a breach of duty; the utmost malice which the most malicious of us wreak on Josephine is to say now and then: 'The sight of Josephine is enough to make one stop laughing.'

So the people look after Josephine much as a father takes into his care a child whose little hand – one cannot tell whether in appeal or command – is stretched out to him. One might think that our people are not fitted to exercise such paternal duties, but in reality they discharge them, at least in this case, admirably; no single individual could do what in this respect the people as a whole are capable of doing. To be sure, the difference in strength between the people and the individual is so enormous that it is enough for the nursling to be drawn into the warmth of their nearness and he is sufficiently protected. To Josephine, certainly, one does not dare mention such ideas. 'Your protection isn't worth an old song,' she says then. Sure, sure, old song, we think. And besides her protest is no real contradiction, it is rather a thoroughly childish way of doing, and childish gratitude, while a father's way of doing is to pay no attention to it.

Yet there is something else behind it which is not so easy to explain by this relationship between the people and Josephine. Josephine, that is to say, thinks just the opposite, she believes it is she who protects the people. When we are in a bad way politically or economically, her singing is supposed to save us, nothing less than that, and if it does not drive away the evil, at least gives us the strength to bear it. She does not put it in these words or in any other, she says very little anyhow, she is silent among the chatterers, but it flashes from her eyes, on her closed lips – few among us can keep their lips closed, but she can – it is plainly legible. Whenever we get bad news – and on many days bad news comes thick and fast at once, lies and half-truths included – she rises up at once, whereas usually she sits listlessly on the ground, she rises up and stretches her neck and tries to see over the heads of her flock like a shepherd before a thunderstorm. It is certainly a habit of children, in their wild, impulsive fashion, to make such claims, but Josephine's are not quite so unfounded as children's. True, she does not save us and she gives us no strength; it is easy to stage oneself as a savior of our people, inured as they are to suffering, not sparing themselves, swift in decision, well acquainted with death, timorous only to the eye in the atmosphere of reckless daring which they constantly breathe, and as prolific besides as they are bold – it is easy, I say, to stage oneself after the event as the savior of our people, who have always somehow managed to save themselves, although at the cost of sacrifices which make historians – generally speaking we ignore historical research entirely – quite horror-struck. And yet it is true that just in emergencies we hearken better than at other times to Josephine's voice. The menaces that loom over us make us quieter, more humble, more submissive to Josephine's domination; we like to come together, we like to huddle close to each other, especially on an occasion set apart from the troubles preoccupying us; it is as if we were drinking in all haste – yes, haste is necessary, Josephine too often forgets that – from a cup of peace in common before the battle. It is not so much a performance of songs as an assembly of the people, and an assembly where except for the small piping voice in front there is complete stillness; the hour is much too grave for us to waste it in chatter.

A relationship of this kind, of course, would never content Josephine. Despite all the nervous uneasiness that fills Josephine because her position has never been quite defined, there is still much that she does not see, blinded by her self-conceit, and she can be brought fairly easily to overlook much more, a swarm of flatterers is always busy about her to this end, thus really doing a public service – and yet to be only an incidental, unnoticed performer in a corner of an assembly of the people, for that, although in itself it would be no small thing, she would certainly not make us the sacrifice of her singing.

Nor does she need to, for her art does not go unnoticed. Although we are at bottom preoccupied with quite other things and it is by no means only for the sake of her singing that stillness prevails and many a listener does not even look up but buries his face in his neighbor's fur, so that Josephine up in front seems to be exerting herself to no purpose, there is yet something – it cannot be denied – that irresistibly makes its way into us from Josephine's piping. This piping, which rises up where everyone else is pledged to silence, comes almost like a message from the whole people to each individual; Josephine's thin piping amidst grave decisions is almost like our people's precarious existence amidst the tumult of a hostile world. Josephine exerts herself, a mere nothing in voice, a mere nothing in execution, she asserts herself and gets across to us; it does us good to think of that. A really trained singer, if ever such a one should be found among us, we could certainly not endure at such a time and we should unanimously turn away from the senselessness of any such performance. May Josephine be spared from perceiving that the mere fact of our listening to her is proof that she is no singer. An intuition of it she must have, else why does she so passionately deny that we do listen, only she keeps on singing and piping her intuition away.

But there are other things she could take comfort from: we do really listen to her in a sense, probably much as one listens to a trained singer; she gets effects which a trained singer would try in vain to achieve among us and which are only produced precisely because her means are so inadequate. For this, doubtless, our way of life is mainly responsible.

Among our people there is no age of youth, scarcely the briefest childhood. Regularly, it is true, demands are put forward that the children should be granted a special freedom, a special protection, that their right to be a little carefree, to have a little senseless giddiness, a little play, that this right should be respected and the exercise of it encouraged; such demands are put forward and nearly everyone approves them, there is nothing one could approve more, but there is also nothing, in the reality of our daily life, that is less likely to be granted, one approves these demands, one makes attempts to meet them, but soon all the old ways are back again. Our life happens to be such that a child, as soon as it can run about a little and a little distinguish one thing from another, must look after itself just like an adult; the areas on which, for economic reasons, we have to live in dispersion are too wide, our enemies too numerous, the dangers lying everywhere in wait for us too incalculable – we cannot shelter our children from the struggle for existence, if we did so, it would bring them to an early grave. These depressing considerations are reinforced by another, which is not depressing: the fertility of our race. One generation – and each is numerous – treads on the heels of another, the children have no time to be children. Other races may foster their children carefully, schools may be erected for their little ones, out of these schools the children may come pouring daily, the future of the race, yet among them it is always the same children that come out day after day for a long time. We have no schools, but from our race come pouring at the briefest intervals the innumerable swarms of our children, merrily lisping or chirping so long as they cannot yet pipe, rolling or tumbling along by sheer impetus so long as they cannot yet run, clumsily carrying everything before them by mass weight so long as they cannot yet see, our children! And not the same children, as in those schools, no, always new children again and again, without end, without a break, hardly does a child appear than it is no more a child, while behind it new childish faces are already crowding so fast and so thick that they are indistinguishable, rosy with happiness. Truly, however delightful this may be and however much others may envy us for it, and rightly, we simply cannot give a real childhood to our children. And that has its consequences. A kind of unexpended, ineradicable childishness pervades our people; in direct opposition to what is best in us, our infallible practical common sense, we often behave with the utmost foolishness, with exactly the same foolishness as children, senselessly, wastefully, grandiosely, irresponsibly, and all that often for the sake of some trivial amusement. And although our enjoyment of it cannot of course be so wholehearted as a child's enjoyment, something of this survives in it without a doubt. From this childishness of our people Josephine too has profited since the beginning.

Yet our people are not only childish, we are also in a sense prematurely old. Childhood and old age come upon us not as upon others. We have no youth, we are all at once grown-up, and then we stay grown-up too long, a certain weariness and hopelessness spreading from that leaves a broad trail through our people's nature, tough and strong in hope that it is in general. Our lack of musical gifts has surely some connection with this; we are too old for music, its excitement, its rapture do not suit our heaviness, wearily we wave it away; we content ourselves with piping; a little piping here and there, that is enough for us. Who knows, there may be talents for music among us; but if there were, the character of our people would suppress them before they could unfold. Josephine on the other hand can pipe as much as she will, or sing or whatever she likes to call it, that does not disturb us, that suits us, that we can well put up with; any music there may be in it is reduced to the least possible trace; a certain tradition of music is preserved, yet without making the slightest demand upon us.

But our people, being what they are, get still more than this from Josephine. At her concerts, especially in times of stress, it is only the very young who are interested in her singing as singing, they alone gaze in astonishment as she purses her lips, expels the air between her pretty front teeth, half dies in sheer wonderment at the sounds she herself is producing and after such a swooning swells her performance to new and more incredible heights, whereas the real mass of the people – this is plain to see – are quite withdrawn into themselves. Here in the brief intervals between their struggles our people dream, it is as if the limbs of each were loosened, as if the harried individual once in a while could relax and stretch himself at ease in the great, warm bed of the community. And into these dreams Josephine's piping drops note by note; she calls it pearl-like, we call it staccato;

but at any rate here it is in its right place, as nowhere else, finding the moment wait for it as music scarcely ever does. Something of our poor brief childhood is in it, something of lost happiness that can never be found again, but also something of active daily life, of its small gaieties, unaccountable and yet springing up and not to be obliterated. And indeed this is all expressed not in full round tones but softly, in whispers, confidentially, sometimes a little hoarsely. Of course it is a kind of piping. Why not? Piping is our people's daily speech, only many a one pipes his whole life long and does not know it, where here piping is set free from the fetters of daily life and it sets us free too for a little while. We certainly should not want to do without these performances.

But from that point it is a long, long way to Josephine's claim that she gives us new strength and so on and so forth. For ordinary people, at least, not for her train of flatterers. 'What other explanation could there be?' – they say with quite shameless sauciness – 'how else could you explain the great audiences, especially when danger is most imminent, which have even often enough hindered proper precautions being taken in time to avert danger.' Now, this last statement is unfortunately true, but can hardly be counted as one of Josephine's titles to fame, especially considering that when such large gatherings have been unexpectedly flushed by the enemy and many of our people left lying for dead, Josephine, who was responsible for it all, and indeed perhaps attracted the enemy by her piping, has always occupied the safest place and was always the first to whisk away quietly and speedily under cover of her escort. Still, everyone really knows that, and yet people keep running to whatever place Josephine decides on next, at whatever time she rises up to sing. One could argue from this that Josephine stands almost beyond the law, that she can do what she pleases, at the risk of actually endangering the community, and will be forgiven for everything. If this were so, even Josephine's claims would be entirely comprehensible, yes, in this freedom to be allowed her, this extraordinary gift granted to her and to no one else in direct contravention of the laws, one could see an admission of the fact that the people do not understand Josephine, just as she alleges, that they marvel helplessly at her art, feel themselves unworthy of it, try to assuage the pity she rouses in them by making really desperate sacrifices for her and, to the same extent that her art is beyond their comprehension, consider her personality and her wishes to lie beyond their jurisdiction. Well, that is simply not true at all, perhaps as individuals the people may surrender too easily to Josephine, but as a whole they surrender unconditionally to no one, and not to her either.

For a long time back, perhaps since the very beginning of her artistic career, Josephine has been fighting for exemption from all daily work on account of her singing; she should be relieved of all responsibility for earning her daily bread and being involved in the general struggle for existence, which – apparently – should be transferred on her behalf to the people as a whole. A facile enthusiast – and there have been such – might argue from the mere unusualness of this demand, from the spiritual attitude needed to frame such a demand, that it has an inner justification. But our people draw other conclusions and quietly refuse it. Nor do they trouble much about disproving the assumptions on which it is based. Josephine argues, for instance, that the strain of working is bad for her voice, that the strain of working is of course nothing to the strain of singing, but it prevents her from being able to rest sufficiently after singing and to recuperate for more singing, she has to exhaust her strength completely and yet, in these circumstances, can never rise to the peak of her abilities. The people listen to her arguments and pay no attention. Our people, so easily moved, sometimes cannot be moved at all. Their refusal is sometimes so decided that even Josephine is taken aback, she appears to submit, does her proper share of work, sings as best she can, but all only for a time, then with renewed strength – for this purpose her strength seems inexhaustible – she takes up the fight again.

Now it is clear that what Josephine really wants is not what she puts into words. She is honorable, she is not work-shy, shirking in any case is quite unknown among us, if her petition were granted she would certainly live the same life as before, her work would not at all get in the way of her singing nor would her singing grow any better – what she wants is public, unambiguous, permanent recognition of her art, going far beyond any precedent so far known. But while almost everything else seems within her reach, this eludes her persistently. Perhaps she should have taken a different line of attack from the beginning, perhaps she herself sees that her approach was wrong, but now she cannot draw back, retreat would be self-betrayal, now she must stand or fall by her petition.

If she really had enemies, as she avers, they could get much amusement from watching this struggle, without having to lift a finger. But she has no enemies, and even though she is often criticized here and there, no one finds this struggle of hers amusing. Just because of the fact that the people show themselves here in their cold, judicial aspect, which is otherwise rarely seen among us. And however one may approve it in this case, the very idea that such an aspect might be turned upon oneself some day prevents amusement from breaking in. The important thing, both in the people's refusal and in Josephine's petition, is not the action itself, but the fact that the people are capable of presenting a stony, impenetrable front to one of their own, and that it is all the more impenetrable because in other respects they show an anxious paternal care, and more than paternal care, for this very member of the people.

Suppose that instead of the people one had an individual to deal with: one might imagine that this man had been giving in to Josephine all the time while nursing a wild desire to put an end to his submissiveness one fine day; that he had made superhuman sacrifices for Josephine in the firm belief that there was a natural limit to his capacity for sacrifice; yes, that he had sacrificed more than was needful merely to hasten the process, merely to spoil Josephine and encourage her to ask for more and more until she did indeed reach the limit with this last petition of hers; and that he then cut her off with a final refusal which was curt because long held in reserve. Now, this is certainly not how the matter stands, the people have no need of such guile, besides, their respect for Josephine is well tried and genuine, and Josephine's demands are after all so far-reaching that any simple child could have told her what the outcome would be; yet it may be that such considerations enter into Josephine's way of taking the matter and so add a certain bitterness to the pain of being refused.

But whatever her ideas on the subject, she does not let them deter her from pursuing the campaign. Recently she has even intensified her attack; hitherto she has used only words as her weapons but now she is beginning to have recourse to other means, which she thinks will prove more efficacious but which we think will run her into greater dangers.

Many believe that Josephine is becoming so insistent because she feels herself growing old and her voice falling off, and so she thinks it high time to wage the last battle for recognition. I do not believe it. Josephine would not be Josephine if that were true. For her there is no growing old and no falling off in her voice. If she makes demands it is not because of outward circumstances but because of an inner logic. She reaches for the highest garland not because it is momentarily hanging a little lower but because it is the highest; if she had any say in the matter she would have it still higher.

This contempt for external difficulties, to be sure, does not hinder her from using the most unworthy methods. Her rights seem beyond question to her; so what does it matter how she secures them; especially since in this world, as she sees it, honest methods are bound to fail. Perhaps that is why she has transferred the battle for her rights from the field of song to another which she cares little about. Her supporters have let it be known that, according to herself, she feels quite capable of singing in such a way that all levels of the populace, even to the remotest corners of the opposition, would find it a real delight, a real delight not by popular standards, for the people affirm that they have always delighted in her singing, but a delight by her own standards. However, she adds, since she cannot falsify the highest standards nor pander to the lowest, her singing will have to stay as it is. But when it comes to her campaign for exemption from work, we get a different story; it is of course also a campaign on behalf of her singing, yet she is not fighting directly with the priceless weapon of her song, so any instrument she uses is good enough. Thus, for instance, the rumor went around that Josephine meant to cut short her grace notes if her petition were not granted. I know nothing about grace notes, and have never noticed any in Josephine's singing. But Josephine is going to cut short her grace notes, not, for the present, to cut them out entirely, only to cut them short. Presumably she has carried out her threat, although I for one have observed no difference in her performance. The people as a whole listened in the usual way without making any pronouncement on the grace notes, nor did their response to her petition vary by a jot. It must be admitted that Josephine's way of thinking, like her figure, is often very charming. And so, for instance, after that performance, just as if her decision about the grace notes had been too severe or too sudden a move against the people, she announced that next time she would put in all the grace notes again. Yet after the next concert she changed her mind once more, there was to be definitely an end of these great arias with the grace notes, and until her petition was favorably regarded they would never recur. Well, the people let all these announcements, decisions and counterdecisions go in at one ear and out at the other, like a grown-up person deep in thought turning a deaf ear to a child's babble, fundamentally well disposed but not accessible.

Josephine, however, does not give in. The other day, for

instance, she claimed that she had hurt her foot at work, so that it was difficult for her to stand up to sing; but since she could not sing except standing up, her songs would now have to be cut short. Although she limps and leans on her supporters, no one believes that she is really hurt. Granted that her frail body is extra sensitive, she is yet one of us and we are a race of workers; if we were to start limping every time we got a scratch, the whole people would never be done limping. Yet though she lets herself be led about like a cripple, though she shows herself in this pathetic condition oftener than usual, the people all the same listen to her singing thankfully and appreciatively as before, but do not bother much about the shortening of her songs.

Since she cannot very well go on limping forever, she thinks of something else, she pleads that she is tired, not in the mood for singing, feeling faint. And so we get a theatrical performance as well as a concert. We see Josephine's supporters in the background begging and imploring her to sing. She would be glad to oblige, but she cannot. They comfort and caress her with flatteries, they almost carry her to the selected spot where she is supposed to sing. At last, bursting inexplicably into tears, she gives way, but when she stands up to sing, obviously at the end of her resources, weary, her arms not widespread as usual but hanging lifelessly down, so that one gets the impression that they are perhaps a little too short – just as she is about to strike up, there, she cannot do it after all, an unwilling shake of the head tells us so and she breaks down before our eyes. To be sure, she pulls herself together again and sings, I fancy, much as usual; perhaps, if one has an ear for the finer shades of expression, one can hear that she is singing with unusual feeling, which is, however, all to the good. And in the end she is actually less tired than before, with a firm tread, if one can use such a term for her tripping gait, she moves off, refusing all help from her supporters and measuring with cold eyes the crowd which respectfully makes way for her.

That happened a day or two ago; but the latest is that she

has disappeared, just at a time when she was supposed to sing. It is not only her supporters who are looking for her, many are devoting themselves to the search, but all in vain; Josephine has vanished, she will not sing; she will not even be cajoled into singing, this time she has deserted us entirely.

Curious, how mistaken she is in her calculations, the clever creature, so mistaken that one might fancy she has made no calculations at all but is only being driven on by her destiny, which in our world cannot be anything but a sad one. Of her own accord she abandons her singing, of her own accord she destroys the power she has gained over people's hearts. How could she ever have gained that power, since she knows so little about these hearts of ours? She hides herself and does not sing, but our people, quietly, without visible disappointment, a self-confident mass in perfect equilibrium, so constituted, even though appearances are misleading, that they can only bestow gifts and not receive them, even from Josephine, our people continue on their way.

Josephine's road, however, must go downhill. The time will soon come when her last notes sound and die into silence. She is a small episode in the eternal history of our people, and the people will get over the loss of her. Not that it will be easy for us; how can our gatherings take place in utter silence? Still, were they not silent even when Josephine was present? Was her actual piping notably louder and more alive than the memory of it will be? Was it even in her lifetime more than a simple memory? Was it not rather because Josephine's singing was already past losing in this way that our people in their wisdom prized it so highly?

So perhaps we shall not miss so very much after all, while Josephine, redeemed from the earthly sorrows which to her thinking lay in wait for all chosen spirits, will happily lose herself in the numberless throng of the heroes of our people, and soon, since we are no historians, will rise to the heights of redemption and be forgotten like all her brothers.

Translated by Willa and Edwin Muir

Stories unpublished in Kafka's Lifetime

Description of a Struggle

And people in their Sunday best
Stroll about, swaying over the gravel
Under this enormous sky
Which, from hills in the distance,
Stretches to distant hills.

I

AT ABOUT MIDNIGHT a few people rose, bowed, shook hands, said it had been a pleasant evening, and then passed through the wide doorway into the vestibule, to put on their coats. The hostess stood in the middle of the room and made graceful bowing movements, causing the dainty folds in her skirt to move up and down.

I sat at a tiny table – it had three curved, thin legs – sipping my third glass of benedictine, and while I drank I surveyed my little store of pastry which I myself had picked out and arranged in a pile.

Then I saw my new acquaintance, somewhat disheveled and out of shape, appear at the doorpost of an adjoining room; but I tried to look away for it was no concern of mine. He, however, came toward me and, smiling absent-mindedly at my occupation, said: 'Excuse me for disturbing you, but until this very moment I've been sitting alone with my girl in the room next door. Ever since half-past ten. Lord, what an evening! I know it isn't right for me to be telling you this, for we hardly know one another. We only met on the stairs this evening and exchanged a few words as guests of the same house. And now – but you must forgive me, please – my happiness just cannot be contained, I can't help it. And since I have no other acquaintance here whom I can trust—'

I looked at him sadly – the piece of fruitcake which I had in my mouth did not taste particularly good – and said into his rather flushed face: 'I'm glad of course that you consider me trustworthy, but displeased that you have confided in me. And you yourself, if you weren't in such a state, would know how improper it is to talk about an amorous girl to a man sitting alone drinking schnapps.'

When I said this, he sat down with a jolt, leaned back in his chair, and let his arms hang down. Then he pressed them back, his elbows pointed, and began talking in rather a loud voice: 'Only a little while ago we were alone in that room, Annie and I. And I kissed her, I kissed her – her mouth, her ears, her shoulders. Oh, my Lord and Savior!'

A few guests, suspecting ours to be a rather more animated conversation, approached us closer, yawning. Whereupon I stood up and said so that all could hear: 'All right then, if you insist, I'll go with you, but I repeat: it's ridiculous to climb up the Laurenziberg now, in winter and in the middle of the night. Besides, it's freezing, and as it has been snowing the roads out there are like skating rinks. Well, as you like—'

At first he gazed at me in astonishment and parted his wet lips; but then, noticing the guests who had approached quite close, he laughed, stood up, and said: 'I think the cold will do us good; our clothes are full of heat and smoke; what's more, I'm slightly tipsy without having drunk very much; yes, let's say goodbye and go.'

So we went to the hostess, and as he kissed her hand she said: 'I am glad to see you looking so happy today.'

Touched by the kindness of these words, he kissed her hand again; whereupon she smiled. I had to drag him away. In the vestibule stood a housemaid, whom we hadn't seen before. She helped us into our coats and then took a small lantern to light us down the stairs. Her neck was bare save for a black velvet ribbon around her throat; her loosely clothed body was stooped and kept stretching as she went down the stairs before us, holding the lantern low. Her cheeks were flushed, for she had drunk some wine, and in the weak lamplight which filled the whole stairwell, I could see her lips trembling.

At the foot of the stairs she put down the lantern, took a step toward my acquaintance, embraced him, kissed him, and remained in the embrace. Only when I pressed a coin into her hand did she drowsily detach her arms from him, slowly open the front door, and let us out into the night.

Over the deserted, evenly lit street stood a large moon in a slightly clouded, and therefore unusually extended, sky. On the frozen snow one had to take short steps.

Hardly were we outside when I evidently began to feel very gay. I raised my legs, let my joints crack, I shouted a name down the street as though a friend of mine had just vanished around the corner; leaping, I threw my hat in the air and caught it boastfully.

My acquaintance, however, walked on beside me, unconcerned. He held his head bent. He didn't even speak.

This surprised me, for I had calculated that he, once I had got him away from the party, would give vent to his joy. Now I too could calm down. No sooner had I given him an encouraging slap on the back than I suddenly no longer understood his mood, and withdrew my hand. Since I had no use for it, I stuck it in the pocket of my coat.

So we walked on in silence. Listening to the sound of our steps, I couldn't understand why I was incapable of keeping step with my acquaintance – especially since the air was clear and I could see his legs quite plainly. Here and there someone leaned out of a window and watched us.

On turning into the Ferdinandstrasse I realized that my acquaintance had begun to hum a melody from the *Dollar Princess*. It was low, but I could hear it distinctly. What did this mean? Was he trying to insult me? As for me, I was ready to do without not only this music, but the walk as well. Why wasn't he speaking to me, anyway? And if he didn't need me, why hadn't he left me in peace in the warm room with the benedictine and the pastry? It certainly wasn't I who had insisted on this walk. Besides, I could have gone for a walk on my own. I had merely been at a party, had saved an ungrateful young man from disgrace, and was now wandering about in the moonlight. That was all right, too. All day in the office, evenings at a party, at night in the streets, and nothing to excess. A way of life so natural that it borders on the excessive!

Yet my acquaintance was still behind me. Indeed, he even quickened his steps when he realized that he had fallen in the rear. No word was uttered, nor could it be said that we were running. But I wondered if it wouldn't be a good idea to turn down a side street; after all, I wasn't obliged to go on this walk with him. I could go home alone and no one could stop me. Then, secretly, I could watch my acquaintance pass the entrance to my street. Goodbye, dear acquaintance! On reaching my room I'll feel warm, I'll light the lamp in its iron stand on my table, and when I've done that I'll lie back in my armchair which stands on the torn Oriental carpet. Pleasant prospects! Why not? But then? No then. The lamp will shine in the warm room, shine on my chest as I lie in the armchair. Then I'll cool off and spend hours alone between the painted walls and the floor which, reflected in the gilt-framed mirror hanging on the rear wall, appears slanted.

My legs were growing tired and I had already decided to go home and lie down, when I began to wonder if, before going away, I ought to say good night to my acquaintance. But I was too timid to go away without a word and too weak to call to him out loud. So I stood still, leaned against the moonlit wall of a house, and waited.

My acquaintance came sailing along the pavement toward me as fast as though he expected me to catch him. He winked at me, suggesting some agreement which I had apparently forgotten.

'What's up?' I asked.

'Oh, nothing,' he said. 'I only wanted to ask your opinion about that housemaid who kissed me on the staircase. Who is the girl? Have you ever seen her before? No? Nor have I. Was she a housemaid at all? I had meant to ask you this before, while she was walking down the stairs in front of us.'

'I saw at once by her red hands that she's a housemaid, and not even the first housemaid, and when I gave her the money I felt her hard skin.'

'But that merely proves that she has been some time in service, which no doubt is the case.'

'You may be right about that. In that light one couldn't distinguish everything, but her face reminded me of the elder daughter of an officer I happen to know.'

'Not me,' he said.

'That won't stop me going home; it's late and I have to be in the office early. One sleeps badly there.' Whereupon I put out my hand to say goodbye to him.

'Whew, what a cold hand!' he cried. 'I wouldn't like to go home with a hand like that. You should have let yourself be kissed, too, my friend. That was an omission. Still, you can make up for it. But sleep? On a night like this? What an idea! Just think how many thoughts a blanket smothers while one lies alone in bed, and how many unhappy dreams it keeps warm.'

'I neither smother anything nor warm anything,' I said.

'Oh, go on!' he concluded, 'you're a humorist!'

At the same time he began walking again and I followed without realizing it, for I was busy thinking of what he had said.

From these words I imagined that my acquaintance suspected in me something which, although it wasn't there, made me nevertheless rise in his estimation by his suspecting it. So it was just as well I hadn't gone home. Who knows, this man – thinking of housemaid affairs while walking beside me, his mouth steaming with cold – might be capable of bestowing on me in the eyes of the world a value without my having to work for it. Let's pray the girls won't spoil him! By all means let them kiss and hug him, that's their duty and his right, but they mustn't carry him off. After all, when they kiss him they also kiss me a little – with the corners of their mouths, so to speak. But if they carry him off, then they steal him from me. And he must always remain with me, always. Who is to protect him, if not I? And he's so stupid. Someone says to him in February: Come up the Laurenziberg – and off he goes. And supposing he falls down now, or catches cold? Suppose some jealous man appears from the Postgasse and attacks him? What will happen to me? Am I to be just kicked out of the world? I'll believe that when I see it! No, he won't get rid of me.

Tomorrow he'll be talking to Fräulein Anna, about ordinary things at first, as is natural, but suddenly he won't be able to keep it from her any longer: Last night, Annie, after the party, you remember, I was with a man the like of whom you've certainly never seen. He looked – how can I describe him to you? – like a stick dangling in the air, he looked, with a black-haired skull on top. His body was clad in a lot of small, dull-yellow patches of cloth which covered him completely because they hung closely about him in the still air of last night. Well, Annie, does that spoil your appetite? It does? In that case it's my fault, then I told the whole thing badly. If only you'd seen him, walking timidly beside me, reading infatuation on my face (which wasn't very difficult), and going a long way ahead of me so as not to disturb me. I think, Annie, you'd have laughed a bit and been a bit afraid; but I was glad of his company. For where were you, Annie? You were in your bed, and your bed was far away – it might just as well have been in Africa. But sometimes I really felt as though the starry sky rose and fell with the gasping of his flat chest. You think I'm exaggerating? No, Annie. Upon my soul, no. Upon my soul which belongs to you, no.

And I didn't spare my acquaintance – we had just reached the first steps of the Franzensquai – the smallest fraction of the humiliation he must have felt at making such a speech. Save that my thoughts grew blurred at this moment, for the Moldau and the quarter of the town on the farther shore lay together in the dark. A number of lights burning there teased the eye.

We crossed the road in order to reach the railing along the river, and there we stood still. I found a tree to lean against. Because of the cold blowing up from the water, I put on my gloves, sighed for no good reason, as one is inclined to do at night beside a river, but then I wanted to walk on. My acquaintance, however, was staring into the water, and didn't budge. Then he moved closer to the railing; his legs were already against the iron bar, he propped his elbows up and laid his forehead in his hands. What next? After all, I was shivering and had to put up the collar of my coat. My acquaintance stretched himself – his back, shoulders, neck – and held the upper half of his body, which rested on his taut arms, bent over the railing.

'Oh well, memories,' said I. 'Yes, even remembering in itself is sad, yet how much more its object! Don't let yourself in for things like that, it's not for you and not for me. It only weakens one's present position without strengthening the former one – nothing is more obvious – quite apart from the fact that the former one doesn't need strengthening. Do you think I have no memories? Oh, ten for every one of yours. Now, for instance, I could remember sitting on a bench in L. It was in the evening, also near a river. In summer, of course. And on such evenings it's my habit to pull up my legs and put my arms around them. I had leaned my head against the wooden back of the bench, and from there I watched the cloudlike mountains on the other shore. A violin was playing softly in the hotel by the river. Now and again on both shores trains chuffed by amid shining smoke.'

Turning suddenly around, my acquaintance interrupted me; he almost looked as though he were surprised to see me still here. 'Oh, I could tell you much more,' I said, nothing else.

'Just imagine,' he began, 'and it always happens like this. Today, as I was going downstairs to take a short walk before the evening party, I couldn't help being surprised by the way my hands were dangling about in my cuffs, and they were doing it so gaily. Which promptly made me think: Just wait, something's going to happen today. And it did, too.' He said this while turning to go and looked at me smiling out of his big eyes.

So I had already got as far as that. He could tell me things like that and at the same time smile and look at me with big eyes. And I – I had to restrain myself from putting my arm around his shoulders and kissing him on the eyes as a reward for having absolutely no use for me. But the worst was that even that could no longer do any harm because it couldn't change anything, for now I had to go away, away at any price.

While I was still trying urgently to think of some means by which I could stay at least a little while longer with my acquaintance, it occurred to me that perhaps my long body displeased him by making him feel too small. And this thought – although it was late at night and we had hardly met a soul – tormented me so much that while walking I bent my back until my hands reached my knees. But in order to prevent my acquaintance from noticing my intentions I changed my position only very gradually, tried to divert his attention from myself, once even turning him toward the river, pointing out to him with outstretched hands the trees on the Schützeninsel and the way the bridge lamps were reflected in the river.

But wheeling suddenly around, he looked at me – I hadn't quite finished yet – and said: 'What's this? You're all crooked! What on earth are you up to?'

'Quite right. You're very observant,' said I, my head on the seam of his trousers, which was why I couldn't look up properly.

'Enough of that! Stand up straight! What nonsense!'

'No,' I said, my face close to the ground, 'I'll stay as I am.'

'You really can annoy a person, I must say. Such a waste of time! Come on, put an end to it.'

'The way you shout! In the quiet of the night!' I said.

'Oh well, just as you like,' he added, and after a while: 'It's a quarter to one.' He had evidently seen the time on the clock of the Mühlenturm.

I promptly stood up straight as though I'd been pulled up by the hair. For a while I kept my mouth open, to let my agitation escape. I understood: he was sending me away. There was no place for me near him, or if there were one, at least it could not be found. Why, by the way, was I so intent on staying with him? No, I ought to go away – and this at once – to my relatives and friends who were waiting for me. But if I didn't have any relatives and friends then I must fend for myself (what was the good of complaining!), but I must leave here no less quickly. For in his eyes nothing could redeem me any longer, neither my length, my appetite, nor my cold hand. But if I were of the opinion that I had to remain with him, it was a dangerous opinion.

'I wasn't in need of your information,' I said, which happened to be true.

'Thank God you're standing up straight again. All I said was that it's a quarter to one.'

'That's all right,' said I, and stuck two fingernails in the gaps between my chattering teeth. 'If I didn't need your information, how much less do I need an explanation. The fact is, I need nothing but your mercy. Please, take back what you said just now!'

'That it's a quarter to one? But with pleasure, especially since a quarter to one passed long ago.'

He lifted his right arm, flicked his hand, and listened to the castanetlike sound of his cuff links.

Obviously, this is the time for the murder. I'll stay with him and slowly he'll draw the dagger – the handle of which he is already holding in his pocket – along his coat, and then plunge it into me. It's unlikely that he'll be surprised at the simplicity of it all – yet maybe he will, who knows? I won't scream, I'll just stare at him as long as my eyes can stand it.

'Well?' he said.

In front of a distant coffeehouse with black windowpanes a policeman let himself glide over the pavement like a skater. His sword hampering him, he took it in his hand, and now he glided along for quite a while, finally ending up by almost describing a circle. At last he yodeled weakly and, melodies in his head, began once more to skate.

It wasn't until the arrival of this policeman – who, two hundred feet from an imminent murder, saw and heard only himself – that I began to feel a certain fear. I realized that whether I allowed myself to be stabbed or ran away, my end had come. Would it not be better, then, to run away and thus expose myself to a difficult and therefore more painful death? I could not immediately put my finger on the reasons in favor of this form of death, but I couldn't afford to spend my last remaining seconds looking for reasons. There would be time for that later provided I had the determination, and the determination I had.

I had to run away, it would be quite easy. At the turning to the left onto the Karlsbrücke I could jump to the right into the Karlsgasse. It was winding, there were dark doorways, and taverns still open; I didn't need to despair.

As we stepped from under the arch at the end of the quay onto the Kreuzherrenplatz, I ran into that street with my arms raised. But in front of a small door in the Seminarkirche I fell, for there was a step which I had not expected. It made a little noise, the next street lamp was sufficiently far away, I lay in the dark.

From a tavern opposite came a fat woman with a lantern to see what had happened in the street. The piano within continued playing, but fainter, with only one hand, because the pianist had turned toward the door which, until now ajar, had been opened wide by a man in a high-buttoned coat. He spat and then hugged the woman so hard she was obliged to raise the lantern in order to protect it.

'Nothing's happened!' he shouted into the room, whereupon they both turned, went inside, and the door was closed.

When I tried to get up I fell down again. 'Sheer ice,' I said, and felt a pain in my knee. Yet I was glad that the people in the tavern hadn't seen me and that I could go on lying here peacefully until dawn.

My acquaintance had apparently walked on as far as the

bridge without having noticed my disappearance, for it was some time before he joined me. I saw no signs of surprise as he bent down over me – lowering little more than his neck, exactly like a hyena – and stroked me with a soft hand. He passed it up and down my cheekbone and then laid his palm on my forehead. 'You've hurt yourself, eh? Well, it's icy and one must be careful – didn't you tell me so yourself? Does your head ache? No? Oh, the knee. H'm. That's bad.'

But it didn't occur to him to help me up. I supported my head with my right hand, my elbow on a cobblestone, and said: 'Here we are together again.' And as my fear was beginning to return, I pressed both hands against his shinbone in order to push him away. 'Do go away,' I said.

He had his hands in his pockets and looked up the empty street, then at the Seminarkirche, then up at the sky. At last, at the sound of a carriage in one of the nearby streets, he remembered me: 'Why don't you say something, my friend? Do you feel sick? Why don't you get up? Shall I look for a cab? If you like, I'll get you some wine from the tavern. In any case, you mustn't lie here in the cold. Besides, we wanted to go up the Laurenziberg.'

'Of course,' said I, and got up on my own, but with great pain. I began to sway, and had to look severely at the statue of Karl IV to be sure of my position. However, even this would not have helped me had I not remembered that I was loved by a girl with a black velvet ribbon around her neck, if not passionately, at least faithfully. And it really was kind of the moon to shine on me, too, and out of modesty I was about to place myself under the arch of the tower bridge when it occurred to me that the moon, of course, shone on everything. So I happily spread out my arms in order fully to enjoy the moon. And by making swimming movements with my weary arms it was easy for me to advance without pain or difficulty. To think that I had never tried this before! My head lay in the cool air and it was my right knee that flew best; I praised it by patting it. And I remembered that once upon a time I didn't altogether like an acquaintance, who was probably still walking below me, and the only thing that pleased me about the whole business was that my memory was good enough to remember even a thing like that. But I couldn't afford to do much thinking, for I had to go on swimming to prevent myself from sinking too low. However, to avoid being told later that anyone could swim on the pavement and that it wasn't worth mentioning, I raised myself above the railing by increasing my speed and swam in circles around the statue of every saint I encountered. At the fifth – I was holding myself just above the footpath by imperceptible flappings – my acquaintance gripped my hand. There I stood once more on the pavement and felt a pain in my knee.

'I've always admired,' said my acquaintance, clutching me with one hand and pointing with the other at the statue of St. Ludmila, 'I've always admired the hands of this angel here to the left. Just see how delicate they are! Real angel's hands! Have you ever seen anything like them? You haven't, but I have, for this evening I kissed hands—'

But for me there was now a third possibility of perishing. I didn't have to let myself be stabbed, I didn't have to run away, I could simply throw myself into the air. Let him go up his Laurenziberg, I won't interfere with him, not even by running away will I interfere with him.

And now I shouted: 'Out with your stories! I no longer want to hear scraps. Tell me everything, from beginning to end. I won't listen to less, I warn you. But I'm burning to hear the whole thing.' When he looked at me I stopped shouting so loud. 'And you can count on my discretion! Tell me everything that's on your mind. You've never had so discreet a listener as I.'

And rather low, close to his ear, I said: 'And you don't need to be afraid of me, that's quite unnecessary.'

I heard him laugh.

'Yes, yes,' I said. 'I believe that. I don't doubt it,' and so saying I pinched him in the calves – where they were exposed. But he didn't feel it. Whereupon I said to myself:

'Why walk with this man? You don't love him, nor do you hate him, because all he cares about is a girl and it's not even certain that she wears a white dress. So to you this man is indifferent – I repeat: indifferent. But he is also harmless, as has been proved. So walk on with him up the Laurenziberg, for you are already on your way, it's a beautiful night, but let him do the talking and enjoy yourself after your fashion, for this is the very best way (say it in a whisper) to protect yourself.'

II

DIVERSIONS *or* PROOF THAT IT'S IMPOSSIBLE TO LIVE

i A RIDE

And now – with a flourish, as though it were not the first time – I leapt onto the shoulders of my acquaintance, and by digging my fists into his back I urged him into a trot. But since he stumped forward rather reluctantly and sometimes even stopped, I kicked him in the belly several times with my boots, to make him more lively. It worked and we came fast enough into the interior of a vast but as yet unfinished landscape.

The road on which I was riding was stony and rose considerably, but just this I liked and I let it become still stonier and steeper. As soon as my acquaintance stumbled I pulled him up by the collar and the moment he sighed I boxed his head. In doing so I felt how healthy this ride in the good air was for me, and in order to make him wilder I let a strong wind blow against us in long gusts.

Now I even began to exaggerate my jumping movements on my acquaintance's broad shoulders, and gripping his neck tight with both hands I bent my head far back and contemplated the many and various clouds which, weaker than I, sailed clumsily with the wind. I laughed and trembled with courage. My coat spread out and gave me strength. I pressed my hands hard together and in doing so happened to make my acquaintance choke. Only when the sky became gradually hidden by the branches of the trees, which I let grow along the road, did I come to myself.

'I don't know,' I cried without a sound, 'I really don't know. If nobody comes, then nobody comes. I have done nobody any harm, nobody has done me any harm, but nobody will help me. A pack of nobodies. But it isn't quite like that. It's just that nobody helps me, otherwise a pack of nobodies would be nice, I would rather like (what do you think?) to go on an excursion with a pack of nobodies. Into the mountains, of course, where else? Just look at these nobodies pushing each other, all these arms stretched across or hooked into one another, these feet separated by tiny steps! Everyone in frock coats, needless to say. We walk along so happily, a fine wind is whistling through the gaps made by us and our limbs. In the mountains our throats become free. It's a wonder we don't break into song.'

Then my acquaintance collapsed, and when I examined him I discovered that he was badly wounded in the knee. Since he could no longer be of any use to me, I left him there on the stones without much regret and whistled down a few vultures which, obediently and with serious beaks, settled down on him in order to guard him.

ii A WALK

I walked on, unperturbed. But since, as a pedestrian, I dreaded the effort of climbing the mountainous road, I let it become gradually flatter, let it slope down into a valley in the distance. The stones vanished at my will and the wind disappeared.

I walked at a brisk pace and since I was on my way down I raised my head, stiffened my body, and crossed my arms behind my head. Because I love pinewoods I went through woods of this kind, and since I like gazing silently up at the stars, the stars appeared slowly in the sky, as is their wont. I saw only a few fleecy clouds which a wind, blowing just at their height, pulled through the air, to the astonishment of the pedestrian.

Opposite and at some distance from my road, probably separated from it by a river as well, I caused to rise an enormously high mountain whose plateau, overgrown with brushwood, bordered on the sky. I could see quite clearly the little ramifications of the highest branches and their movements. This sight, ordinary as it may be, made me so happy that I, as a small bird on a twig of those distant scrubby bushes, forgot to let the moon come up. It lay already behind the mountain, no doubt angry at the delay.

But now the cool light that precedes the rising of the moon spread over the mountain and suddenly the moon itself appeared from beyond one of the restless bushes. I on the other hand had meanwhile been gazing in another direction, and when I now looked ahead of me and suddenly saw it glowing in its almost full roundness, I stood still with troubled eyes, for my precipitous road seemed to lead straight into this terrifying moon.

After a while, however, I grew accustomed to it and watched with composure the difficulty it had in rising, until finally, having approached one another a considerable part of the way, I felt overcome by an intense drowsiness caused, I assumed, by the fatigue of the walk, to which I was unaccustomed. I wandered on for a while with closed eyes, keeping myself awake only by a loud and regular clapping of my hands.

But then, as the road threatened to slip away from under my feet and everything, as weary as I myself, began to vanish, I summoned my remaining strength and hastened to scale the slope to the right of the road in order to reach in time the high tangled pinewood where I planned to spend the night that probably lay ahead of us.

The haste was necessary. The stars were already fading and I noticed the moon sink feebly into the sky as though into troubled waters. The mountain already belonged to the darkness, the road crumbled away at the point where I had turned toward the slope, and from the interior of the forest I heard the approaching crashes of collapsing trees. Now I could have thrown myself down on the moss to sleep, but since I feared to sleep on the ground I crept – the trunk sliding quickly down the rings formed by my arms and legs – up a tree which was already reeling without wind. I lay down on a branch and, leaning my head against the trunk, went hastily to sleep while a squirrel of my whim sat stiff-tailed at the trembling end of the branch, and rocked itself.

My sleep was deep and dreamless. Neither the waning moon nor the rising sun awoke me. And even when I was about to wake up, I calmed myself by saying: 'You made a great effort yesterday, so spare your sleep,' and went to sleep again.

Although I did not dream, my sleep was not free from a continuous slight disturbance. All night long I heard someone talking beside me. The words themselves I could hardly hear – except isolated ones like 'bench . . . by the river,' 'cloudlike mountains,' 'trains . . . amidst shining smoke'; what I did hear was the special kind of emphasis placed on them; and I remember that even in my sleep I rubbed my hands with pleasure at not being obliged to recognize single words, since I was asleep.

'Your life was monotonous,' I said aloud in order to convince myself, 'it really was necessary for you to be taken somewhere else. You ought to be content, it's gay here. The sun's shining.'

Whereupon the sun shone and the rain clouds grew white and light and small in the blue sky. They sparkled and billowed out. I saw a river in the valley.

'Yes, your life was monotonous, you deserve this diversion,' I continued as though compelled, 'but was it not also perilous?' At that moment I heard someone sigh terribly near.

I tried to climb down quickly, but since the branch

trembled as much as my hand I fell rigid from the top. I did not fall heavily, nor did I feel any pain, but I felt so weak and unhappy that I buried my face in the ground: I could not bear the strain of seeing around me the things of the earth. I felt convinced that every movement and every thought was forced, and that one had to be on one's guard against them. Yet nothing seemed more natural than to lie here on the grass, my arms beside my body, my face hidden. And I tried to persuade myself that I ought to be pleased to be already in this natural position, for otherwise many painful contortions, such as steps or words, would be required to arrive at it.

The river was wide and its noisy little waves reflected the light. On the other shore lay meadows which farther on merged into bushes behind which, at a great distance, one could see bright avenues of fruit trees leading to green hills.

Pleased by this sight, I lay down and, stopping my ears against the dread sound of sobs, I thought: Here I could be content. For here it is secluded and beautiful. It won't take much courage to live here. One will have to struggle here as anywhere else, but at least one won't have to do it with graceful movements. That won't be necessary. For there are only mountains and a wide river and I have sense enough to regard them as inanimate. Yes, when I totter alone up the steep path through the meadows in the evening I will be no more forsaken than the mountains, except that I will feel it. But I think that this, too, will pass.

Thus I toyed with my future life and tried stubbornly to forget. And all the time I blinked at that sky which was of an unusually promising color. It was a long time since I'd seen it like this; I was moved and reminded of certain days when I thought I had seen it in the same way. I took my hands from my ears, spread out my arms, and let them fall in the grass.

I heard someone sob softly from afar. A wind sprang up and a great mass of leaves, which I had not seen before, rose rustling into the air. Unripe fruit thudded senselessly from the trees onto the ground. Ugly clouds rose from behind the mountain. The waves on the river creaked and receded from the wind.

I got up quickly. My heart hurt, for now it seemed impossible to escape from my suffering. I was already about to turn and leave this region and go back to my former way of life when the following idea occurred to me: 'How strange it is that even in our time distinguished people are transported across a river in this complicated way. There's no other explanation than that it is an old custom.' I shook my head, for I was surprised.

iii THE FAT MAN

a An Address to the Landscape

From the thicket on the opposite bank four naked men strode vehemently forth, carrying on their shoulders a wooden litter. On this litter sat, Oriental fashion, a monstrously fat man. Although carried through the thicket on an untrodden path, he did not push the thorny branches apart but simply let his motionless body thrust through them. His folds of fat were so carefully spread out that although they covered the whole litter and even hung down its side like the hem of a yellowish carpet, they did not hamper him. His hairless skull was small and gleamed yellow. His face bore the artless expression of a man who meditates and makes no effort to conceal it. From time to time he closed his eyes: on opening them again his chin became distorted.

'The landscape disturbs my thought,' he said in a low voice. 'It makes my reflections sway like suspension bridges in a furious current. It is beautiful and for this reason wants to be looked at.'

I close my eyes and say: You green mountain by the river, with your rocks rolling against the water, you are beautiful.

But it is not satisfied; it wants me to open my eyes to it.

Then I might say to it with my eyes closed: 'Mountain, I do not love you, for you remind me of the clouds, of the sunset, of the rising sky, and these are things that almost make me cry because one can never reach them while being carried on a small litter. But when showing me this, sly mountain, you block the distant view which gladdens me, for it reveals the attainable at a glance. That's why I do not love you, mountain by the water – no, I do not love you.'

But the mountain would be as indifferent to this speech as to my former one so long as I did not talk with my eyes open. This is the only way to please it.

And must we not keep it well disposed toward us in order to keep it up at all – this mountain which has such a capricious fondness for the pulp of our brains? It might cast on me its jagged shadow, it might silently thrust terrible bare walls in front of me and my bearers would stumble over the little pebbles on the road.

But it is not only the mountain that is so vain, so obtrusive and vindictive – everything else is, too. So I must go on repeating with wide-open eyes – oh, how they hurt!:

'Yes, mountain, you are beautiful and the forests on your western slope delight me. – With you, flower, I am also pleased, and your pink gladdens my soul. – You, grass of the meadows, are already high and strong and refreshing. – And you, exotic bushes, you prick so unexpectedly that our thoughts start leaping. – But with you, river, I am so delighted that I will let myself be carried through your supple water.'

After he had shouted this paean of praise ten times, accompanied by some humble shifting of his body, he let his head droop and said with closed eyes:

'But now – I implore you – mountain, flowers, grass, bush, and river, give me some room so that I may breathe.'

At that moment the surrounding mountains began to shift in hasty obedience, then withdrew behind a curtain of fog. Although the avenues stood firm for a while and guarded the width of the road, they soon merged into one another. In the sky in front of the sun lay a humid cloud with a delicately transparent edge in whose shade the country sank deeper and deeper while everything else lost its lovely outline.

The sound of the bearers' steps reached my side of the river and yet I could not distinguish any details in the dark square of their faces. I only saw them bending their heads sideways and arching their backs, for their burden was excessive. I was worried about them, for I realized that they were tired. So it was in suspense that I watched them step into the rushes, then walk through the wet sand, their strides still regular, until they finally sank into the muddy swamp where the two rear bearers bent even lower so as to keep the litter in its horizontal position. I pressed my hands together. By now they had to raise their feet high at every step until their bodies glistened with sweat in the cool air of this unsettled afternoon.

The fat man sat quiet, hands on his thighs; the long pointed tips of the reeds grazed him as they flipped up in the wake of the bearers in front.

The bearers' movements grew more irregular the nearer they came to the water. At times the litter swayed as though it were already on the waves. Small puddles in the rushes had to be jumped over or walked around, for they might possibly be deep.

At one moment wild ducks rose shrieking, mounting steeply into the rain cloud. It was then that I caught a glimpse of the fat man's face; it looked alarmed. I got up and in hectic leaps I zigzagged over the stony slope separating me from the water. I paid no heed to the danger, was concerned only with helping the fat man should his servants no longer be able to carry him. I ran so recklessly that I couldn't stop, and was forced to dash into the splashing water, coming to a halt only when the water reached my knees.

Meanwhile the servants, with considerable distortions of their bodies, had carried the litter into the river, and holding themselves above the unruly water with one hand, they propped up the litter with four hairy arms, their muscles standing out in relief.

The water lapped against their chins, then rose to their mouths; the bearers bent their heads back and the litter handles fell on their shoulders. The water was already playing around the bridges of their noses, and yet they did not give up, although they had hardly reached the middle of the river. Then a low wave swept over the heads of those in front and the four men drowned in silence, their desperate hands pulling the litter down with them. Water gushed after them.

And now the evening sun's slanting rays broke forth from behind the rims of the great cloud and illuminated the hills and mountains as far as the eye could see, while the river and the region beneath the cloud lay in an uncertain light.

The fat man turned slowly in the direction of the flowing water and was carried down the river like a yellow wooden idol which had become useless and so had been cast into the river. He sailed along on the reflection of the rain cloud. Elongated clouds pulled and small hunched ones pushed him, creating considerable commotion, the effect of which could even be noticed by the lapping of water against my knees and the stones on the shore.

I crept quickly up the slope so as to be able to accompany the fat man on his way, for I truly loved him. And perhaps I could learn something about the dangers of this apparently safe country. So I walked along a strip of sand to the narrowness of which one had to grow accustomed, hands in my pockets and my face turned at right angles to the river so that my chin rested almost on my shoulder.

Swallows sat on the stones by the shore.

The fat man said: 'Dear sir on the shore, don't try to rescue me. This is the water's and the wind's revenge; now I am lost. Yes, revenge it is, for how often have we attacked them, I and my friend the supplicant, amidst the singing of our swords, the flash of cymbals, the great splendor of trumpets, and the leaping blaze of drums!'

A tiny mosquito with stretched wings flew straight through his belly without losing its speed.

The fat man continued:

b Beginning of a Conversation with the Supplicant

There was a time when I went to a church day after day, for a girl I was in love with used to kneel there in prayer for half an hour every evening, which enabled me to watch her at my leisure.

Once when the girl failed to appear and in dismay I was watching the other people praying, my eye was caught by a young man who had flung his long emaciated figure on the ground. From time to time he clutched his skull with all his strength and, moaning loudly, beat it in the palms of his hands on the stone floor.

In the church there were only a few old women who kept turning their shawled heads sideways to glance at the praying man. This attention seemed to please him, for before each of his pious outbursts he let his eyes rove about to see how many people were watching him. Finding this unseemly, I decided to accost him on his way out of the church and ask him outright why he prayed in this manner. For since my arrival in this town clarity had become more important to me than anything else, even though at this moment I felt only annoyance at my girl's failure to appear.

Yet an hour passed before he stood up, brushed his trousers for such a long time that I felt like shouting: 'Enough, enough! We can all see that you have trousers on,' crossed himself carefully, and with the lumbering gait of a sailor walked to the font of holy water.

I placed myself between the font and the door, determined not to let him pass without an explanation. I screwed up my mouth, this being the best preparation for resolute speech, and supported myself by standing on my right leg while resting the left one on its toes, for this position as I have often experienced gives me a sense of stability.

Now it is possible that this young man had already caught sight of me while sprinkling his face with holy water; perhaps my stare had alarmed him even earlier, for he now quite unexpectedly rushed to the door and out. I involuntarily jumped to stop him. The glass door slammed. And when I passed through it a moment later I could not find him, for the narrow streets were numerous and the traffic considerable.

During the following days he failed to appear, but the girl came and again prayed in a corner of a side chapel. She wore a black dress with a transparent lace yoke – the crescent of her chemise could be seen through it – from the lower edge of which the silk hung down in a finely cut frill. And now that the girl had returned I was glad to forget about the young man, ignoring him even when he continued to appear regularly and to pray in his usual fashion.

Yet he always passed me by in sudden haste, his face averted. While praying, on the other hand, he kept glancing at me. It almost looked as though he were angry with me for not having accosted him earlier and was thinking that for my first attempt to talk to him I had actually taken upon me the duty to do so. One day as I was following the girl out as usual after a service, I ran into him in the semidarkness and thought I saw him smile.

The duty to talk to him, needless to say, did not exist, nor had I much desire to do so anymore. And even when I hurried up to the church one evening while the clock was striking seven and found, instead of the girl who of course had left long ago, only the young man exerting himself in front of the altar railings, I still hesitated.

At last I tiptoed to the door, slipped a coin to the blind beggar sitting there, and squeezed in beside him behind the open wing. And there for about half an hour I looked forward to the surprise I was planning to spring upon the supplicant. But this feeling did not last. Before long I was morosely watching spiders creeping over my clothes and finding it tiresome to have to bend forward every time someone came breathing loud out of the darkness of the church.

But finally he came. The ringing of the great bells which had started a little while ago did not agree with him, I realized. Each time before taking a step he had to touch the ground lightly with his foot.

I straightened myself, took a long stride forward, and grabbed him. 'Good evening,' said I, and with my hand on his coat collar I pushed him down the steps onto the lighted square.

When we had reached ground level he turned toward me while I was still holding on to him from behind, so that we stood breast to breast.

'If only you'd let go of me!' he said. 'I don't know what you suspect me of, but I'm innocent.' Then he repeated once more: 'Of course I don't know what you suspect me of.'

'There is no question here of suspicion or innocence. I ask you not to mention it again. We are strangers; our acquaintance is no older than the church steps are high. What would happen if we were immediately to start discussing our innocence?'

'Precisely what I think,' he said. 'As a matter of fact, you said "our innocence." Do you mean to suggest that if I had proved my innocence you would have to prove yours, too? Is that what you mean?'

'That or something else,' I said. 'I accosted you only because I wanted to ask you something, remember that!'

'I'd like to go home,' he said, and made an effort to turn.

'I quite believe it. Would I have accosted you otherwise? Don't get the idea that I accosted you on account of your beautiful eyes.'

'Aren't you being a little too sincere?'

'Must I repeat that there's no question of such things? What has it to do with sincerity or insincerity? I ask, you answer, and then goodbye. So far as I'm concerned you can even go home, and as fast as you like.'

'Would it not be better to meet some other time? At a more suitable hour? Say in a coffeehouse? Besides, your fiancée left only a few minutes ago, you can easily catch her up, she has waited so long for you.'

'No!' I shouted into the noise of the passing tram. 'You won't escape me. I like you more and more. You're a lucky catch. I congratulate myself.'

To which he said: 'Oh God, you have a sound heart, as they say, but a head of wood. You call me a lucky catch, how lucky you must be! For my bad luck is precariously balanced and when touched it falls onto the questioner. And so: Good night.'

'Fine,' said I, surprised him and seized his right hand. 'If you don't answer of your own accord, I'll force you. I'll follow you wherever you go, right or left, even up the stairs to your room, and in your room I'll sit down, wherever there's space. Go on then, keep staring at me, I can stand it. But how' – I stepped up close and because he was a head taller I spoke into his throat – 'how are you going to summon up the courage to stop me?'

Whereupon, stepping back, he kissed my hands in turn, and wetted them with his tears. 'One cannot deny you anything. Just as you knew I want to go home, I knew even earlier that I cannot deny you anything. All I ask is that we go over there into the side street.' I nodded and we went over. When a carriage separated us and I was left behind, he beckoned to me with both hands, to make me hurry.

But once there, not satisfied with the darkness of the street where the lamps were widely separated from one another and almost as high as the first floor, he led me into the low hallway of an old house and under a small lamp which hung dripping in front of the wooden stairs.

Spreading his handkerchief over the hollow in a worn step, he invited me to be seated: 'It's easier for you to ask questions sitting down. I'll remain standing, it's easier for me to answer. But don't torment me!'

I sat down because he took it all so seriously, but nevertheless felt I had to say: 'You've led me to this hole as though we are conspirators, whereas I am bound to you simply by curiosity, you to me by fear. Actually, all I want to ask is why you pray like that in church. The way you carry on there! Like an utter fool! How ridiculous it all is, how unpleasant for the onlookers, how intolerable for the devout!'

He had pressed his body against the wall, only his head moved slowly in space. 'You're wrong! The devout consider my behavior natural, the others consider it devout.'

'My annoyance proves you're mistaken.'

'Your annoyance – assuming it's real – only proves that you belong neither to the devout nor to the others.'

'You're right. I was exaggerating when I said your behavior annoyed me; no, it aroused my curiosity as I stated correctly at first. But you, to which group do you belong?'

'Oh, I just get fun out of people watching me, out of occasionally casting a shadow on the altar, so to speak.'

'Fun?' I asked, making a face.

'No, if you want to know. Don't be angry with me for expressing it wrongly. It's not fun, for me it's a need; a need to let myself be nailed down for a brief hour by those eyes, while the whole town around me—'

'The things you say!' I cried far too loud for the insignificant remark and the low hallway, but I was afraid of falling silent or of lowering my voice. 'Really, the things you say! Now I realize, by God, that I guessed from the very beginning the state you are in. Isn't it something like a fever, a seasickness on land, a kind of leprosy? Don't you feel it's this very feverishness that is preventing you from being properly satisfied with the real names of things, and that now, in your frantic haste, you're just pelting them with any old names? You can't do it fast enough. But hardly have you run away from them when you've forgotten the names you gave them. The poplar in the fields, which you've called the "Tower of Babel" because you didn't want to know it was a poplar, sways again without a name, so you have to call it "Noah in his cups." '

He interrupted me: 'I'm glad I haven't understood a word you've been saying.'

Irritated, I said quickly: 'Your being glad about it proves that you have understood it.'

'Didn't I say so before? One cannot deny you anything.'

I put my hands on a step above me, leaned back, and in this all but unassailable position, the wrestler's last resort, I asked: 'Excuse me, but to throw back at me an explanation which I gave you is insincere.'

At this he grew daring. To give his body unity he clasped his hands together and said with some reluctance: 'You ruled out quarrels about insincerity from the very beginning. And truly, I'm no longer concerned with anything but to give you a proper explanation for my way of praying. Do you know why I pray like that?'

He was putting me to the test. No, I didn't know, nor did I want to know. I hadn't even wanted to come here, I said to myself, but this creature had practically forced me to listen to him. So all I had to do was to shake my head and everything would be all right, but at the moment this was just what I couldn't do. The creature opposite me smiled. Then he crouched down on his knees and said with a sleepy expression: 'Now I can also tell you at last why I let you accost me. Out of curiosity, from hope. Your stare has been comforting me for a long time. And I hope to learn from you how things really are, why it is that around me things sink away like fallen snow, whereas for other people even a little liqueur glass stands on the table steady as a statue.'

As I remained silent and only an involuntary twitching passed over my face, he asked: 'So you don't believe this happens to other people? You really don't? Just listen, then. When as a child I opened my eyes after a brief afternoon nap, still not quite sure I was alive, I heard my mother up on the balcony asking in a natural tone of voice: "What are you doing, my dear? Goodness, isn't it hot?" From the garden a woman answered: "Me, I'm having my tea on the lawn." They spoke casually and not very distinctly, as though this woman had expected the question, my mother the answer.'

Feeling that this required an answer, I put my hand in the hip pocket of my trousers as though I were looking for something. Actually, I wasn't looking for anything, I just wished to change my appearance in order to show interest in the conversation. Finally I said I thought this a most remarkable incident and that I couldn't make head or tail of it. I also added that I didn't believe it was true and that it must have been invented for a special reason whose purpose wasn't clear to me just now. Then I closed my eyes so as to shut out the bad light.

'Well, isn't that encouraging! For once you agree with me, and you accosted me to tell me that out of sheer unselfishness. I lose one hope and acquire another.

'Why, after all, should I feel ashamed of not walking upright and taking normal steps, of not tapping the pavement with my stick, and not touching the clothes of the people who pass noisily by? Am I not rather entitled to complain bitterly at having to skip along the houses like a shadow without a clear outline, sometimes disappearing in the panes of the shopwindows?

'Oh, what dreadful days I have to live through! Why is everything so badly built that high houses collapse every now and again for no apparent reason? On these occasions I clamber over the rubble, asking everyone I meet: "How could this have happened? In our town – a new house – how many does that make today?— Just think of it!" And no one can give me an answer.

'Frequently people fall in the street and lie there dead. Whereupon all the shop people open their doors laden with wares, hurry busily out, cart the dead into a house, come out again all smiles, then the chatter begins: "Good morning – it's a dull day – I'm selling any amount of kerchiefs – ah yes, the war." I rush into the house, and after raising my hand several times timidly with my finger crooked, I finally knock on the janitor's little window: "Good morning," I say, "I understand a dead man was carried in here just now. Would you be kind enough to let me see him?" And when he shakes his head as though unable to make up his mind, I add: "Take care, I'm a member of the secret police and insist on seeing the dead man at once!" Now he is no longer undecided. "Out with you!" he shouts. "This riffraff is getting in the habit of snooping about here every day. There's no dead man here. Maybe next door." I raise my hat and go.

'But then, on having to cross a large square, I forget everything. If people must build such huge squares from sheer wantonness, why don't they build a balustrade across them as well? Today there's a southwest wind blowing. The spire of the Town Hall is moving in little circles. All the windowpanes are rattling, and the lampposts are bending like bamboos. The Virgin Mary's cloak is coiling around her pillar and the wind is tugging at it. Does no one notice this? The ladies and gentlemen who should be walking on the pavement are floating. When the wind falls they stand still, say a few words, and bow to one another, but when the wind rises again they are helpless, and all their feet leave the ground at the same time. Although obliged to hold on to their hats, their eyes twinkle gaily enough and no one has the slightest fault to find with the weather. I'm the only one who's afraid.'

To which I was able to say: 'That story you told me earlier about your mother and the woman in the garden I really don't find so remarkable. Not only have I heard and experienced many stories of this kind, I have even taken part in some. The whole thing is perfectly natural. Do you really mean to suggest that had I been on that balcony in the summer, I could not have asked the same question and given the same answer from the garden? Quite an ordinary occurrence!'

After I had said this, he seemed relieved at last. He told me I was well dressed and that he very much liked my tie. And what a fine complexion I had. And that confessions became most comprehensible when they were retracted.

c The Supplicant's Story

Then he sat down beside me, for I had grown timid and, bending my head to one side, had made room for him.

Nevertheless, it didn't escape my notice that he too was sitting there rather embarrassed, trying to keep some distance from me and speaking with difficulty:

'Oh, what dreadful days I have to live through! Last night I was at a party. I was just bowing to a young lady in the gaslight and saying: "I'm so glad winter's approaching" – I was just bowing with these words when to my annoyance I noticed that my right thigh had slipped out of joint. The kneecap had also become a little loose.

'So I sat down, and as I always try to keep control over my sentences, I said: "for winter's much less of an effort; it's easier to comport oneself, one doesn't have to take so much trouble with one's words. Don't you agree, Fräulein? I do hope I'm right about this." My right leg was now giving me a lot of trouble. At first it seemed to have fallen apart completely, and only gradually did I manage to get it more or less back into shape by manipulation and careful rearrangement.

'Then I heard the girl, who, out of sympathy, had also sat down, say in a low voice: "No, you don't impress me at all because—"

' "Just a moment," I said, pleased and full of expectation, "you mustn't waste so much as five minutes talking to me, dear Fräulein. Please eat something while you're talking, I implore you."

'And stretching out my arm I took a large bunch of grapes hanging heavily from a bowl held up by a bronze winged cupid, dangled it for a moment in the air, and then laid it on a small blue plate which I handed to the girl, not without a certain elegance, I trust.

' "You don't impress me at all," she said. "Everything you say is boring and incomprehensible, but that alone doesn't make it true. What I really think, sir – why do you always call me dear Fräulein? – is that you can't be bothered with the truth simply because it's too tiring."

'God, how good that made me feel! "Yes, Fräulein, Fräulein!" I almost shouted, "how right you are! Dear Fräulein, if you only knew what a wild joy it is to find oneself so well understood – and without having made any effort!"

'"There's no doubt, sir, that for you the truth is too tiring. Just look at yourself! The entire length of you is cut out of tissue paper, yellow tissue paper, like a silhouette, and when you walk one ought to hear you rustle. So one shouldn't get annoyed at your attitude or opinion, for you can't help bending to whatever draft happens to be in the room."

'"I don't understand that. True, several people are standing about here in this room. They lay their arms on the backs of chairs or they lean against the piano or they raise a glass tentatively to their mouths or they walk timidly into the next room, and having knocked their right shoulders against a cupboard in the dark, they stand breathing by the open window and think: There's Venus, the evening star. Yet here I am, among them. If there is a connection, I don't understand it. But I don't even know if there is a connection. – And you see, dear Fräulein, of all these people who behave so irresolutely, so absurdly as a result of their confusion, I alone seem worthy of hearing the truth about myself. And to make this truth more palatable you put it in a mocking way so that something concrete remains, like the outer walls of a house whose interior has been gutted. The eye is hardly obstructed; by day the clouds and sky can be seen through the great window holes, and by night the stars. But the clouds are often hewn out of gray stones, and the stars form unnatural constellations. – How would it be if in return I were to tell you that one day everyone wanting to live will look like me – cut out of tissue paper, like silhouettes, as you pointed out – and when they walk they will be heard to rustle? Not that they will be any different from what they are now, but that is what they will look like. Even you, dear Fräulein—"

'Then I noticed that the girl was no longer sitting beside me. She must have left soon after her last words, for now she was standing far away from me by a window, surrounded by three young men who were talking and laughing out of high white collars.

'So I happily drank a glass of wine and walked over to the pianist who, all alone and nodding to himself, happened to be playing something sad. I bent carefully down to his ear so as not to frighten him and whispered into the melody: "Be so kind, sir, as to let me play now, for I'm just beginning to feel happy."

'Since he paid no attention to me, I stood there for a while embarrassed, but then, overcoming my timidity, I went from one guest to another, saying casually: "Today I'm going to play the piano. Yes."

'Everyone seemed to know I couldn't play, but they smiled in a friendly way, pleased by the welcome interruption of their conversation. They paid proper attention to me only when I said to the pianist in a very loud voice: "Do me the favor, sir, of letting me play now. After all, I'm just beginning to feel happy. A triumph is at stake."

'Although the pianist stopped, he neither left his brown bench nor appeared to understand me. He sighed and covered his face with his long fingers.

'I felt a trifle sorry for him and was about to encourage him to continue playing when the hostess approached with a group of people.

' "That's a funny coincidence," they said and laughed aloud as though I were about to do something unnatural.

'The girl also joined them, looked at me contemptuously, and said: "Please, madame, do let him play. Perhaps he wants to make some contribution to the entertainment. He ought to be encouraged. Please let him."

'Everyone laughed, obviously thinking, as I did, that it was meant ironically. Only the pianist was silent. Holding his head low, he stroked the wood of the bench with the forefinger of his left hand, as though he were making designs in sand. I began to tremble, and to hide it, thrust my hands into my trouser pockets. Nor could I speak clearly any longer, for my whole face wanted to cry. Thus I had to choose the words in such a way that the thought of my wanting to cry would appear ludicrous to the listeners.

' "Madame," I said, "I must play now because—" As I had forgotten the reason I abruptly sat down at the piano. And then I remembered again. The pianist stood up and stepped tactfully over the bench, for I was blocking his way. "Please turn out the light, I can only play in the dark." I straightened myself.

'At that moment two gentlemen seized the bench and, whistling a song and rocking me to and fro, carried me far away from the piano to the dining table.

'Everyone watched with approval and the girl said: "You see, madame, he played quite well. I knew he would. And you were so worried."

'I understood and thanked her with a bow, which I carried out well.

'They poured me some lemonade and a girl with red lips held my glass while I drank. The hostess offered me a meringue on a silver salver and a girl in a pure white dress put the meringue in my mouth. Another girl, voluptuous and with a mass of fair hair, held a bunch of grapes over me, and all I had to do was pluck them off with my lips while she gazed into my receding eyes.

'Since everyone was treating me so well I was a little surprised that they were so unanimous in holding me back when I tried to return to the piano.

' "That's enough now," said the host, whom I had not noticed before. He went out and promptly returned with an enormous top hat and a copper-brown overcoat with a flowery design. "Here are your things."

'They weren't my things, of course, but I didn't want to put him to the trouble of looking again. The host helped me into the overcoat which fitted beautifully, clinging tightly to my thin body. Bending over slowly, a lady with a kind face buttoned the coat all the way down.

' "Goodbye," said the hostess, "and come back soon. You know you're always welcome." Whereupon everyone bowed as though they thought it necessary. I tried to do likewise, but my coat was too tight. So I took my hat and, no doubt awkwardly, walked out of the room.

'But as I passed through the front door with short steps I was assaulted from the sky by moon and stars and a great vaulted expanse, and from the Ringplatz by the Town Hall, the Virgin's pillar, the church.

'I walked calmly from the shadow into the moonlight, unbuttoned my overcoat, and warmed myself; then I put a stop to the humming of the night by raising my hands, and began to reflect as follows:

' "What is it that makes you all behave as though you were real? Are you trying to make me believe I'm unreal, standing here absurdly on the green pavement? You, sky, surely it's a long time since you've been real, and as for you, Ringplatz, you never have been real.

' "It's true, you're all still superior to me, but only when I leave you alone.

' "Thank God, moon, you are no longer moon, but perhaps it's negligent of me to go on calling you so-called moon, moon. Why do your spirits fall when I call you 'forgotten paper lantern of a strange color'? And why do you almost withdraw when I call you 'the Virgin's pillar'? As for you, pillar of the Virgin Mary, I hardly recognize your threatening attitude when I call you 'moon shedding yellow light.'

' "It really seems to me that thinking about you doesn't do you any good; you lose in courage and health.

' "God, how much more profitable it would be if the Thinker could learn from the Drunk!

' "Why has everything become so quiet? I think the wind has dropped. And the small houses which often used to roll across the square as though on little wheels are rooted to the spot – calm – calm – one can't even see the thin black line that used to separate them from the ground."

'And I started to run. I ran unimpeded three times around the great square, and as I didn't meet a drunk I ran on toward the Karlsgasse without slowing down and without any effort.

My shadow, often smaller than myself, ran beside me along the wall as though in a gorge between the wall and the street level.

'As I passed the fire station I heard a noise coming from the Kleiner Ring, and as I turned into it I saw a drunk standing by the iron railing of the fountain, his arms held out sideways and his feet in wooden shoes stamping the ground.

'Stopping to get my breath, I went up to him, raised my top hat, and introduced myself:

' "Good evening, gentle nobleman, I am twenty-three years of age, but as yet I have no name. But you, no doubt, hail from the great city of Paris – bearing extraordinary, well-nigh singable names. You are surrounded by the quite unnatural odor of the dissolute Court of France. No doubt your tinted eyes have beheld those great ladies standing on the high shining terrace, ironically twisting their narrow waists while the ends of their decorated trains, spread over the steps, are still lying on the sand in the garden. – And surely, men-servants in daringly cut gray tailcoats and white knee breeches climb tall poles, their legs hugging them but their torsos frequently bent back and to the side, for they have to raise enormous gray linen sheets off the ground with thick ropes and spread them in the air, because the great lady has expressed the wish for a misty morning.'

'When he belched I felt almost frightened. "Is it really true, sir," I said, "that you hail from our Paris, from that tempestuous Paris – ah, from that luxuriant hailstorm?"

'When he belched again, I said with embarrassment: "I know, a great honor is being bestowed upon me."

'And with nimble fingers I buttoned up my overcoat; then with ardor and yet timidly I said: "I know you do not consider me worthy of an answer, but if I did not ask you today my life would be spent in weeping. I ask you, much-bespangled sir, is it true what I have been told? Are there people in Paris who consist only of sumptuous dresses, and are there houses that are only portals, and is it true that on summer days the sky over the city is a fleeting blue embellished only by little white clouds glued onto it, all in the shape of hearts? And have they a highly popular panopticon there containing nothing but trees to which small plaques are fastened bearing the names of the most famous heroes, criminals, and lovers?

' "And then this other piece of news! This clearly fabricated news! These Paris streets, for instance, they suddenly branch off, don't they? They're turbulent, aren't they? Things are not always as they should be, how could they be, after all? Sometimes there's an accident, people gather together from the side streets with that urban stride that hardly touches the pavement; they are all filled with curiosity, but also with fear of disappointment; they breathe fast and stretch out their little heads. But when they touch one another they bow low and apologize: 'I'm awfully sorry – I didn't mean it – there's such a crowd; forgive me, I beg you – it was most clumsy of me, I admit. My name is – my name's Jerome Faroche, I'm a grocer in the rue de Cabotin – allow me to invite you to lunch tomorrow – my wife would also be delighted.'

' "So they go on talking while the street lies numb and the smoke from the chimneys falls between the houses. That's how it is. But it might happen that two carriages stop on a crowded boulevard of a distinguished neighborhood. Serious-looking menservants open the doors. Eight elegant Siberian wolfhounds come prancing out and jump barking across the boulevard. And it's said that they are young Parisian dandies in disguise."

'His eyes were almost shut. When I fell silent, he stuck both hands in his mouth and tore at his lower jaw. His clothes were covered with dirt. Perhaps he had been thrown out of some tavern and hadn't yet realized it.

'Perhaps it was that short quiet lull between night and day when our heads loll back unexpectedly, when everything stands still without our knowing it, since we are not looking at it, and then disappears; we remain alone, our bodies bent, then look around but no longer see anything, nor even feel any resistance in the air yet inwardly we cling to the memory that at a certain distance from us stand houses with roofs and with fortunately angular chimneys down which the darkness flows through garrets into various rooms. And it is fortunate that tomorrow will be a day on which, unlikely as it may seem, one will be able to see everything.

'Now the drunk jerked up his eyebrows so that a brightness appeared between them and his eyes, and he explained in fits and starts: "It's like this, you see – I'm sleepy, you see, so that's why I'm going to sleep. – You see, I've a brother-in-law on the Wenzelsplatz – that's where I'm going, for I live there, for that's where I have my bed – so I'll be off –. But I don't know his name, you see, or where he lives – seems I've forgotten – but never mind, for I don't even know if I have a brother-in-law at all. – But I'll be off now, you see –. Do you think I'll find him?"

'To which, without thinking, I said: "That's certain. But you're coming from abroad and your servants don't happen to be with you. Allow me to show you the way."

'He didn't answer. So I offered him my arm, to give him some support.'

d Continued Conversation Between the Fat Man and the Supplicant

For some time already I had been trying to cheer myself up. I rubbed my body and said to myself: 'It's time you spoke. You're becoming embarrassed. Do you feel oppressed? Just wait! You know these situations. Think it over at your leisure. Even the landscape will wait.

'It's the same as it was at the party last week. Someone is reading aloud from a manuscript. At his request I myself have copied one page. When I see my handwriting among the pages written by him, I take fright. It's without any stability. People are bending over it from three sides of the table. In tears, I swear it's not my handwriting.'

'But what is the connection with today? It's entirely up to you to start a sensible conversation. Everything's peaceful.

Just make an effort, my friend! – You surely can find an objection. – You can say: "I'm sleepy. I've a headache. Goodbye." Quick then, quick! Make yourself conspicuous! – What's that? Again obstacles and more obstacles? What does it remind you of? – I remember a high plateau which rose against the wide sky as a shield to the earth. I saw it from a mountain and prepared myself to wander through it. I began to sing.'

My lips were dry and disobedient as I said: 'Ought it not to be possible to live differently?'

'No,' he said, questioning, smiling.

'But why do you pray in church every evening?' I asked then, while everything between him and me, which until then I had been holding together as though in my sleep, collapsed.

'Oh, why should we talk about it? People who live alone have no responsibility in the evenings. One fears a number of things – that one's body could vanish, that human beings may really be what they appear to be at twilight, that one might not be allowed to walk without a stick, that it might be a good idea to go to church and pray at the top of one's voice in order to be looked at and acquire a body.'

Because he talked like that and then fell silent, I pulled my red handkerchief out of my pocket, bent my head, and wept.

He stood up, kissed me, and said: 'What are you crying for? You're tall, I like that; you have long hands which all but obey your will; why aren't you happy about it? Always wear dark cuffs, that's my advice. – No – I flatter you and yet you cry? I think you cope quite sensibly with the difficulty of living.'

'We build useless war machines, towers, walls, curtains of silk, and we could marvel at all this a great deal if we had the time. We tremble in the balance, we don't fall, we flutter, even though we may be uglier than bats. And on a beautiful day hardly anyone can prevent us from saying: "Oh God, today is a beautiful day," for we are already established on this earth and live by virtue of an agreement.

'For we are like tree trunks in the snow. They lie there

apparently flat on the ground and it looks as though one could push them away with a slight kick. But no, one can't, for they are firmly stuck to the ground. So you see even this is only apparent.'

The following thought prevented me from sobbing: 'It is night and no one will reproach me tomorrow for what I might say now, for it could have been said in my sleep.'

Then I said: 'Yes, that's it, but what were we talking about? We can't have been talking about the light in the sky because we are standing in the darkness of a hallway. No – we could have talked about it, nevertheless, for are we not free to say what we like in conversation? After all, we're not aiming at any definite purpose or at the truth, but simply at making jokes and having a good time. Even so, couldn't you tell me the story of the woman in the garden once more? How admirable, how clever this woman is! We must follow her example. How fond I am of her! So it's a good thing I met you and waylaid you as I did. It has given me great pleasure to talk to you. I've learned several things that, perhaps intentionally, were hitherto unknown to me. – I'm grateful.'

He looked pleased. And although contact with a human body is always repugnant to me, I couldn't help embracing him.

Then we stepped out of the hallway under the sky. My friend blew away a few bruised little clouds, allowing the uninterrupted surface of the stars to emerge. He walked with difficulty.

iv DROWNING OF THE FAT MAN

And now everything was seized by speed and fell into the distance. The water of the river was dragged toward a precipice, tried to resist, whirled about a little at the crumbling edge, but then crashed in foaming smoke.

The fat man could not go on talking, he was forced to turn and disappear in the loud roar of the waterfall.

I, who had experienced so many pleasant diversions, stood on the bank and watched. 'What are our lungs supposed to do?' I shouted. Shouted: 'If they breathe fast they suffocate themselves from inner poisons; if they breathe slowly they suffocate from unbreathable air, from outraged things. But if they try to search for their own rhythm they perish from the mere search.'

Meanwhile the banks of the river stretched beyond all bounds, and yet with the palm of my hand I touched the metal of a signpost which gleamed minutely in the far distance. This I really couldn't quite understand. After all I was small, almost smaller than usual, and a bush of white hips shaking itself very fast towered over me. This I saw, for a moment ago it had been close to me.

Nevertheless I was mistaken, for my arms were as huge as the clouds of a steady country rain, save that they were more hasty. I don't know why they were trying to crush my poor head. It was no larger than an ant's egg, but slightly damaged, and as a result no longer quite round. I made some beseeching, twisting movements with it, for the expression of my eyes could not have noticed, they were so small.

But my legs, my impossible legs lay over the wooded mountains and gave shade to the village-studded valleys. They grew and grew! They already reached into the space that no longer owned any landscape, for some time their length had gone beyond my field of vision.

But no, it isn't like that – after all, I'm small, small for the time being – I'm rolling – I'm rolling – I'm an avalanche in the mountains! Please, passers-by, be so kind as to tell me how tall I am – just measure these arms, these legs.

III

'Let me think,' said my acquaintance, who had accompanied me from the party and was walking quietly beside me on a path up the Laurenziberg. 'Just stand still a moment so that I can get it clear. – I have something to settle, you know.

It's all such a strain – the night is radiant, though rather cold, but this discontented wind, it sometimes even seems to change the position of those acacias.'

The moon made the gardener's house cast a shadow over the slightly humped path on which lay scanty patches of snow. When I saw the bench that stood beside the door, I pointed at it with a raised finger, and as I was not brave and expected reproaches I laid my left hand on my chest.

He sat down wearily, disregarding his beautiful clothes, and astonished me by pressing his elbows against his hips and laying his forehead on the tips of his overstretched fingers.

'Yes, now I want to say this. You know, I live a regular life. No fault can be found with it, everything I do is considered correct and generally approved. Misfortune, as it is known in the society I frequent, has not spared me, as my surroundings and I have realized with satisfaction, and even the general good fortune has not failed me and I myself have been able to talk about it in a small circle of friends. True, until now I had never been really in love. I regretted it occasionally, but used the phrase when I needed it. And now I must confess: Yes, I am in love and quite beside myself with excitement. I am an ardent lover, just what the girls dream of. But ought I not to have considered that just this former lack of mine gave an exceptional and gay, an especially gay, twist to my circumstances?'

'Calm yourself,' I said without interest, thinking only of myself. 'Your loved one is beautiful, as I couldn't help hearing.'

'Yes, she is beautiful. While sitting next to her, all I could think was: What an adventure – am I not daring! – there I go embarking on a sea voyage – drinking wine by the gallon. But when she laughs she doesn't show her teeth as one would expect; instead, all one sees is the dark, narrow, curved opening of the mouth. Now this looks sly and senile, even though she throws back her head while laughing.'

'I can't deny that,' I said, sighing. 'I've probably seen it, too, for it must be conspicuous. But it's not only that. It's the beauty of girls altogether. Often when I see dresses with manifold pleats, frills, and flounces smoothly clinging to beautiful bodies, it occurs to me that they will not remain like this for long, that they will get creases that cannot be ironed out, dust will gather in the trimmings too thick to be removed, and that no one will make herself so miserable and ridiculous as every day to put on the same precious dress in the morning and take it off at night. And yet I see girls who are beautiful enough, displaying all kinds of attractive muscles and little bones and smooth skin and masses of fine hair, and who appear every day in the same natural fancy dress, always laying the same face in the same palm and letting it be reflected in the mirror. Only sometimes at night, on returning late from a party, this face stares out at them from the mirror worn out, swollen, already seen by too many people, hardly worth wearing anymore.'

'I've asked you several times on our walk whether you found my girl beautiful, but you always turned away without answering. Tell me, are you up to some mischief? Why don't you comfort me?'

I dug my feet into the shadow and said kindly: 'You don't need to be comforted. After all, you're being loved.' To avoid catching cold I held over my mouth a handkerchief with a design of blue grapes.

Now he turned toward me and leaned his fat face against the low back of the bench: 'Actually I've still time, you know. I can still end this budding love affair at once, either by committing some misdeed, by unfaithfulness, or by going off to some distant land. For I've grave doubts about whether I should let myself in for all this excitement. Nothing is certain, no one can tell the direction or the duration for sure. If I go into a tavern with the intention of getting drunk, I know I'll be drunk that evening. But in this case! In a week's time we're planning to go on an excursion with some friends. Imagine the storm this will create in the heart for the next fortnight! Last night's kisses make me sleepy and prepare the way for savage dreams. I fight this by going for a walk at night, with the result that I'm in a permanent state of turmoil, my face goes hot and cold as though blown about by the wind, I have to keep fingering a pink ribbon in my pocket all the time, I'm filled with the gravest apprehensions about myself which I cannot follow up, and I can even stand your company, sir, whereas normally I would never spend so much time talking to you.'

I was feeling very cold and the sky was already turning a whitish color. 'I'm afraid no misdeed, no unfaithfulness or departure to some distant land will be of any avail. You'll have to kill yourself,' I said, adding a smile.

Opposite us on the other side of the avenue stood two bushes and down below these bushes was the town. There were still a few lights on.

'All right,' he cried, and hit the bench with his little tight fist which, however, he left lying there. 'But you go on living. You don't kill yourself. No one loves you. You don't achieve anything. You can't cope with the next moment. Yet you dare to talk to me like that, you brute. You're incapable of loving, only fear excites you. Just take a look at my chest.'

Whereupon he quickly opened his overcoat and waistcoat and his shirt. His chest was indeed broad and beautiful.

'Yes, such obstinate moods come over one sometimes,' I began to say. 'This summer I was in a village which lay by a river. I remember it well. I frequently sat on a bench by the shore in a twisted position. There was a hotel, and one often heard the sound of violins. Young healthy people sat in the garden at tables with beer and talked of hunting and adventures. And on the other shore were cloudlike mountains.'

Then, with a limp, distorted mouth, I got up, stepped onto the lawn behind the bench, broke a few snow-covered twigs, and whispered into my acquaintance's ear: 'I'm engaged, I confess it.'

My acquaintance wasn't surprised that I had got up. 'You're engaged?' He sat there really quite exhausted, supported only by the back of the bench. Then he took off his hat and I saw his hair which, scented and beautifully combed, set off the round head on a fleshy neck in a sharp curving line, as was the fashion that winter.

I was pleased to have answered him so cleverly. 'Just think,' I said to myself, 'how he moves in society with flexible neck and free-swinging arms. Keeping up an intelligent conversation, he can steer a lady right through a drawing room, and the fact that it's raining outside, that some timid man is standing about or some other wretched thing is happening, does not make him nervous. No, he goes on bowing with the same courtesy to the ladies. And there he sits now.'

My acquaintance mopped his brow with a batiste handkerchief. 'Please put your hand on my forehead,' he said. 'I beg you.' When I didn't do so at once, he folded his hands.

As though our sorrow had darkened everything, we sat high up on the mountain as in a small room, although a little earlier we had already noticed the light and the wind of the morning. We sat close together in spite of not liking one another at all, but we couldn't move far apart because the walls were firmly and definitely drawn. We could, however, behave absurdly and without human dignity, for we didn't have to be ashamed in the presence of the branches above us and the trees standing opposite us.

Then, without further ado, my acquaintance pulled a knife out of his pocket, opened it thoughtfully, and then, as though he were playing, he plunged it into his left upper arm, and didn't withdraw it. Blood promptly began to flow. His round cheeks grew pale. I pulled out the knife, cut up the sleeve of his overcoat and jacket, tore his shirt sleeve open. Then I ran a little way up and down the road to see if there was anyone who could help. All the branches were almost exaggeratedly visible and motionless. I sucked a little at the deep wound. Then I remembered the gardener's cottage. I ran up the steps leading to the upper lawn on the left side of the house, quickly examined the windows and doors, rang the bell furiously, and stamped my feet, although I knew all the time that the house was uninhabited. Then I looked at the wound which was bleeding in a thin trickle. Having wetted his handkerchief in snow, I tied it clumsily around his arm.

'My dear, dear friend,' said I, 'you've wounded yourself for my sake. You're in such a good position, you're surrounded by well-meaning friends, you can go for a walk in broad daylight when any number of carefully dressed people can be seen far and near among tables or on mountain paths. Just think, in the spring we'll drive into the orchard – no, not we, that's unfortunately true – but you with your Annie will drive out at a happy trot. Oh yes, believe me, I beg you, and the sun will show you off to everyone at your best. Oh, there'll be music, the sound of horses from afar, no need to worry, there'll be shouting and barrel organs will be playing in the avenues.'

'Oh God,' he said, stood up, leaned on me and we went on, 'oh God, that won't help. That won't make me happy. Excuse me. Is it late? Perhaps I ought to do something in the morning. Oh God.'

A lantern was burning close to the wall above; it threw the shadows of the tree trunks across the road and the white snow, while on the slope the shadows of all the branches lay bent, as though broken.

Translated by Tania and James Stern

Wedding Preparations in the Country

I

WHEN Eduard Raban, coming along the passage, walked into the open doorway, he saw that it was raining. It was not raining much.

On the pavement straight in front of him there were many people walking in various rhythms. Every now and again one would step forward and cross the road. A little girl was holding a tired puppy in her outstretched hands. Two gentlemen were exchanging information. The one held his hands palm-upward, raising and lowering them in regular motion, as though he were balancing a load. Then one caught sight of a lady whose hat was heavily laden with ribbons, buckles, and flowers. And hurrying past was a young man with a thin walking stick, his left hand, as though paralyzed, flat on his chest. Now and then there came men who were smoking, bearing small upright elongated clouds along ahead of them. Three gentlemen – two holding lightweight overcoats on their crooked forearms – several times walked forward from the front of the buildings to the edge of the pavement, surveyed what was going on there, and then withdrew again, talking.

Through the gaps between the passers-by one could see the regularly laid stones of the carriageway. There carriages on delicate high wheels were drawn along by horses with arched necks. The people who sat at ease on the upholstered seats gazed silently at the pedestrians, the shops, the balconies, and the sky. If it happened that one carriage overtook another, then the horses would press against each other, and the harness straps hung dangling. The animals tugged at the shafts, the carriage bowled along, swaying as it gathered speed, until the swerve around the carriage ahead was completed and the horses moved apart again, only their narrow quiet heads inclined toward each other.

Some people came quickly toward the front entrance, stopped on the dry mosaic paving, and, turning around slowly, stood gazing out into the rain, which, wedged in by this narrow street, fell confusedly.

Raban felt tired. His lips were as pale as the faded red of his thick tie, which had a Moorish pattern. The lady by the doorsteps over there, who had up to now been contemplating her shoes, which were quite visible under her tightly drawn skirt, now looked at him. She did so indifferently, and she was perhaps, in any case, only looking at the falling rain in front of him or at the small nameplates of firms that were fixed to the door over his head. Raban thought she looked amazed. 'Well,' he thought, 'if I could tell her the whole story, she would cease to be astonished. One works so feverishly at the office that afterwards one is too tired even to enjoy one's holidays properly. But even all that work does not give one a claim to be treated lovingly by everyone; on the contrary, one is alone, a total stranger and only an object of curiosity. And so long as you say "one" instead of "I," there's nothing in it and one can easily tell the story; but as soon as you admit to yourself that it is you yourself, you feel as though transfixed and are horrified.'

He put down the suitcase with the checkered cloth cover, bending his knees in doing so. The rain water was already running along the edge of the carriageway in streaks that almost extended to the lower-lying gutters.

'But if I myself distinguish between "one" and "I," how then dare I complain about the others? Probably they're not unjust, but I'm too tired to take it all in. I'm even too tired to walk all the way to the station without an effort, and it's only a short distance. So why don't I remain in town over these short holidays, in order to recuperate? How unreasonable I'm being! – The journey will make me ill, I know that quite well. My room won't be comfortable enough, it can't be otherwise in the country. And we're hardly in the first half of June, the air in the country is often still very cool. Of course, I've taken precautions in my clothing, but I shall have to join with people who go for walks late in the evening. There are ponds there; one will go for a walk the length of those ponds. That is where I'm sure to catch cold. On the other hand, I shall make but little showing in conversation. I shan't be able to compare the pond with other ponds in some remote country, for I've never traveled, and talking about the moon and feeling bliss and rapturously climbing up on heaps of rubble is, after all, something I'm too old to do without being laughed to scorn.'

People were going past with slightly bent heads, above which they carried their dark umbrellas in a loose grip. A dray also went by; on the driver's seat, which was stuffed with straw, sat a man whose legs were stretched out so negligently that one foot was almost touching the ground, while the other rested safely on straw and rags. It looked as though he were sitting in a field in fine weather. Yet he was holding the reins attentively so that the dray, on which iron bars were clanging against one another, made its way safely through the dense traffic. On the wet surface of the road one could see the reflection of the iron meanderingly and slowly gliding from one row of cobbles to the next. The little boy beside the lady opposite was dressed like an old vintner. His pleated dress formed a great circle at the hem and was only held in, almost under the very armpits, by a leather strap. His hemispherical cap came down to his eyebrows, and a tassel hung down from the top as far as his left ear. He was pleased by the rain. He ran out of the doorway and looked up wide-eyed into the sky in order to catch more of the rain. Often he jumped high into the air so that the water splashed a great deal and passers-by admonished him severely. Then the lady called him and henceforth held him by the hand; yet he did not cry.

Raban started. Had it not grown late? Since he wore his top-coat and jacket open, he quickly pulled out his watch. It was not going. Irritably he asked a neighbor, who was standing a little farther back in the entrance, what the time was. This man was in conversation, and while still laughing together with his companion, said: 'Certainly. Past four o'clock,' and turned away.

Raban quickly put up his umbrella and picked up his suitcase. But when he was about to step into the street, his way was blocked by several women in a hurry and these he therefore let pass first. In doing so he looked down on a little girl's hat, which was made of plaited red straw and had a little green wreath on the wavy brim.

He went on remembering this even when he was in the street, which went slightly uphill in the direction he wished to follow. Then he forgot it, for now he had to exert himself a little; his small suitcase was none too light, and the wind was blowing straight against him, making his coat flutter and bending the front spokes of his umbrella.

He had to breathe more deeply. A clock in a nearby square down below struck a quarter to five; under the umbrella he saw the light short steps of the people coming toward him; carriage wheels squeaked with the brakes on, turning more slowly; the horses stretched their thin forelegs, daring as chamois in the mountains.

Then it seemed to Raban that he would get through the long bad time of the next fortnight, too. For it was only a fortnight, that was to say, a limited period, and even if the annoyances grew ever greater, still, the time during which one had to endure them would be growing shorter and shorter. Thus, undoubtedly courage would increase. 'All the people who try to torment me, and who have now occupied the entire space around me, will quite gradually be thrust back by the beneficent passage of these days, without my having to help them even in the very least. And, as it will come about quite naturally, I can be weak and quiet and let everything happen to me, and yet everything must turn out well, through the sheer fact of the passing of the days.

'And besides, can't I do it the way I always used to as a child in matters that were dangerous? I don't even need to go to the country myself, it isn't necessary. I'll send my clothed body. If it staggers out of the door of my room, the staggering will indicate not fear but its nothingness. Nor is it a sign of excitement if it stumbles on the stairs, if it travels into the country, sobbing as it goes, and there eats its supper in tears. For I myself am meanwhile lying in my bed, smoothly covered over with the yellow-brown blanket, exposed to the breeze that is wafted through that seldom-aired room. The carriages and people in the street move and walk hesitantly on shining ground, for I am still dreaming. Coachmen and pedestrians are shy, and every step they want to advance they ask as a favor from me, by looking at me. I encourage them and encounter no obstacle.

'As I lie in bed I assume the shape of a big beetle, a stag beetle or a cockchafer, I think.'

In front of a shopwindow, in which, behind a wet glass pane, little hats for men were displayed on small pegs, he stopped and looked in, his lips pursed. 'Well, my hat will still do for the holidays,' he thought and walked on, 'and if nobody can stand me because of my hat, then all the better.

'The form of a large beetle, yes. Then I would pretend it was a matter of hibernating, and I would press my little legs to my bulging belly. And I would whisper a few words, instructions to my sad body, which stands close beside me, bent. Soon I shall have done – it bows, it goes swiftly, and it will manage everything efficiently while I rest.'

He came to a domed arch at the top of the steep street, leading onto a small square all around which there were many shops, already lit up. In the middle of the square, somewhat obscured by the light around the edge, was a low monument, the seated meditative figure of a man. The people moved across the lights like narrow shutters, and since the puddles spread all the brilliance far and wide, the square seemed ceaselessly changing.

Raban pressed far on into the square, but jerkily, dodging the drifting carriages, jumping from one dry cobble to further dry cobbles, and holding the open umbrella high in his hand in order to see everything all around. Finally, by a lamppost – a place where the electric tram stopped – which was set up on a small square concrete base, he halted.

'But they're expecting me in the country. Won't they be wondering about me by this time? Still, I haven't written to her all the week she's been in the country, until this morning. So they'll end up by imagining that even my appearance is quite different. They may be thinking that I burst forward when I address a person, yet that isn't my way at all, or that I embrace people when I arrive, and that's something I don't do either. I shall make them angry if I try to pacify them. Oh, if I could only make them thoroughly angry in the attempt to pacify them.'

At that moment an open carriage drove past, not quickly; behind its two lighted lamps two ladies could be seen sitting on dark leather seats. One was leaning back, her face hidden by a veil and the shadow of her hat. But the other lady was sitting bolt upright; her hat was small, it was edged with thin feathers. Everyone could see her. Her lower lip was drawn slightly into her mouth.

As soon as the carriage had passed Raban, some bar blocked the view of the near horse drawing the carriage; then some coachman – wearing a big top hat – on an unusually high box was moved across in front of the ladies – this was now much farther on – then their carriage drove around the corner of a small house that now became strikingly noticeable, and disappeared from sight.

Raban followed it with his gaze, his head lowered, resting the handle of his umbrella on his shoulder in order to see better. He had put his right thumb into his mouth and was rubbing his teeth on it. His suitcase lay beside him, one of its sides on the ground.

Carriages hastened from street to street across the square, the horses' bodies flew along horizontally as though they were being flung through the air, but the nodding of the head and the neck revealed the rhythm and effort of the movement.

Around about, on the edges of the pavements of all the three streets converging here, there were many idlers standing about, tapping the cobbles with little sticks. Among the groups they formed there were little towers in which girls were pouring out lemonade, then heavy street clocks on thin bars, then men wearing before and behind them big placards announcing entertainments in multicolored letters, then messengers . . . [Two pages missing] . . . a little social gathering. Two elegant private carriages, driving diagonally across the square into the street leading downhill, got in the way of some gentlemen from this party, but after the second carriage – even after the first they had timidly tried to do so – these gentlemen formed into a group again with the others, with whom they then stepped onto the pavement in a long cavalcade and pushed their way through the door of a café, overwhelmed by the light of the incandescent lamps hanging over the entrance.

Electric tramcars moved past, huge and very close; others, vaguely visible, stood motionless far away in the streets.

'How bent she is,' Raban thought when he looked at the photograph now. 'She's never really upright and perhaps her back is round. I shall have to pay much attention to this. And her mouth is so wide, and here, beyond doubt, the lower lip protrudes, yes, now I remember that too. And what a dress! Of course, I don't know anything about clothes, but these very tight-sewn sleeves are ugly, I am sure, they look like bandages. And the hat, the brim at every point turned up from the face in a different curve. But her eyes are beautiful, they're brown, if I'm not mistaken. Everyone says her eyes are beautiful.'

Now an electric tramcar stopped in front of Raban and many people around him pushed toward the steps, with slightly open, pointed umbrellas, which they held upright with their hands pressed to their shoulders. Raban, who was holding his suitcase under his arm, was dragged off the pavement and stepped hard into an unseen puddle. Inside the tram a child knelt on a seat, pressing the tips of all its fingers to its lips as though it were saying goodbye to someone going away. Some passengers got out and had to walk a few paces along the tram in order to work their way out of the crowd. Then a lady climbed onto the first step, her long skirt, which she hitched up with both hands, stretched tightly around her legs. A gentleman held on to a brass rod and, with lifted head, recounted something to the lady. All the people who wanted to get in were impatient. The conductor shouted.

Raban, who now stood on the edge of the waiting group, turned around, for someone had called out his name.

'Ah, Lement,' he said slowly and held out to a young man coming toward him the little finger of the hand in which he was holding the umbrella.

'So this is the bridegroom on his way to his bride. He looks frightfully in love,' Lement said and then smiled with his mouth shut.

'Yes, you must forgive my going today,' Raban said. 'I wrote to you this afternoon, anyway. I should, of course, have liked very much to travel with you tomorrow; but tomorrow is Saturday, everything'll be so crowded, it's a long journey.'

'Oh, that doesn't matter. You did promise, but when one's in love. . . . I shall just have to travel alone.' Lement had set one foot on the pavement and the other on the cobbles, supporting his body now on one leg, now on the other. 'You were going to get into the tram. There it goes. Come, we'll walk, I'll go with you. There's still plenty of time.'

'Isn't it rather late, please tell me?'

'It's no wonder you're nervous, but you really have got plenty of time. I'm not so nervous, and that's why I've missed Gillemann now.'

'Gillemann? Won't he be staying out there, too?'

'Yes, with his wife; it's next week they mean to go, and that's just why I promised Gillemann I'd meet him today when he leaves the office. He wanted to give me some instructions regarding the furnishing of their house, that's why I was supposed to meet him. But now somehow I'm late, I had some errands to do. And just as I was wondering whether I shouldn't go to their apartment, I saw you, was at first astonished at the suitcase, and spoke to you. But now the evening's too far gone for paying calls, it's fairly impossible to go to Gillemann now.'

'Of course. And so I shall meet people I know there, after all. Not that I have ever seen Frau Gillemann, though.'

'And very beautiful she is. She's fair, and pale now after her illness. She has the most beautiful eyes I've ever seen.'

'Do please tell me, what do beautiful eyes look like? Is it the glance? I've never found eyes beautiful.'

'All right, perhaps I was exaggerating slightly. Still, she's a pretty woman.'

Through the windowpane of a ground-floor café, close to the window, gentlemen could be seen sitting, reading and eating, around a three-sided table; one had lowered a newspaper to the table, held a little cup raised, and was looking into the street out of the corners of his eyes. Beyond these window tables all the furniture and equipment in the large restaurant were hidden by the customers, who sat side by side in little circles. [Two pages missing] . . . 'As it happens, however, it's not such an unpleasant business, is it? Many people would take on such a burden, I think.'

They came into a fairly dark square, which began on their side of the street, for the opposite side extended farther. On the side of the square along which they were walking, there was an uninterrupted row of houses, from the corners of which two – at first widely distant – rows of houses extended into the indiscernible distance in which they seemed to unite. The pavement was narrow by the houses, which were mostly small; there were no shops to be seen, no carriage passed. An iron post near the end of the street out of which they came had several lamps on it, which were fixed in two rings hanging horizontally, one over the other. The trapeze-shaped flame between conjoined sheets of glass burned in this tower-like wide darkness as in a little room, letting darkness assert itself a few steps farther on.

'But now I am sure it is too late; you have kept it a secret from me, and I shall miss the train. Why?' [Four pages missing]

. . . 'Yes, at most Pirkershofer – well, for what *he's* worth.'

'The name's mentioned, I think, in Betty's letters, he's an assistant railway-clerk, isn't he?'

'Yes, an assistant railway-clerk and an unpleasant person. You'll see I'm right as soon as you've got a glimpse of that small thick nose. I tell you, walking through the dreary fields with that fellow. . . . Anyway, he's been transferred now and he goes away from there, as I believe and hope, next week.'

'Wait, you said just now you advised me to stay here tonight. I've thought it over; it couldn't very well be managed. I've written to say I'm coming this evening; they'll be expecting me.'

'That's quite easy, send a telegram.'

'Yes, that could be done – but it wouldn't be very nice if I didn't go – and I'm tired, yes, I'll go all right. If a telegram came, they'd get a fright, into the bargain. – And what for, where would we go, anyway?'

'Then it's really better for you to go. I was only thinking. . . . Anyway I couldn't go with you today, as I'm sleepy, I forgot to tell you that. And now I shall say goodbye, for I don't want to go through the wet park with you, as I should like to drop in at Gillemann's, after all. It's a quarter to six, so not too late, after all, for paying calls on people you know fairly well. Addio. Well, a good journey, and remember me to everyone!'

Lement turned to the right and held out his right hand to say goodbye, so that for a moment Raban was walking against Lement's outstretched arm.

'Adieu,' Raban said.

From a little distance Lement then called back: 'I say, Eduard, can you hear me? Do shut your umbrella; it stopped raining ages ago. I didn't have a chance to tell you.'

Raban did not answer, shut his umbrella, and the sky closed over him in pallid darkness.

'If at least,' Raban thought, 'I were to get into a wrong train. Then it would at any rate seem to me that the whole enterprise had begun, and if later, after the mistake had been cleared up, I were to arrive in this station again on my way back, then I should certainly feel much better. If the scenery does turn out to be boring, as Lement says, that need not be a disadvantage at all. One will spend more time in the rooms and really never know for certain where all the others are, for if there is a ruin in the district, there will probably be a walk all together to that ruin; it will have been agreed upon some time before. Then, however, one must look forward to it; for that very reason one mustn't miss it. But if there is no such sight to be seen, then there will be no discussion beforehand either, for all will be expected to get together quite easily if suddenly, against all the usual practice, a larger expedition is considered right, for one only has to send the maid into the others' apartments, where they are sitting over a letter or books and are delighted by this news. Well, it is not difficult to protect oneself against such invitations. And yet I don't know whether I shall be able to, for it is not so easy as I imagine it now when I am still alone and can still do everything, can still go back if I want to, for I shall have no one there whom I could pay calls on whenever I like, and no one with whom I could make more strenuous expeditions, no one there who could show me how his crops are doing or show me a quarry he is working there. For one isn't at all sure even of acquaintances of long standing. Wasn't Lement nice to me today? – he explained some things to me, didn't he, and described everything as it will appear to me. He came up and spoke to me and then walked with me, in spite of the fact that there was nothing he wanted to find out from me and that he himself still had something else to do. But now all of a sudden he has gone away, and yet I can't have offended him even with a single word. I did refuse to spend the evening in town, but that was only natural, that can't have offended him, for he is a sensible person.'

The station clock struck, it was a quarter to six. Raban

stopped because he had palpitations, then he walked quickly along the park pool, went along a narrow, badly lighted path between large shrubs, rushed into an open place with many empty benches leaning against little trees, then went more slowly through an opening in the railings into the street, crossed it, leapt through the station entrance, after a while found the booking office, and had to knock for a while on the iron shutter. Then the booking clerk looked out, said it was really high time, took the bank note, and slammed down on the counter the ticket he had been asked for and the change. Now Raban tried to count his change quickly, thinking he ought to be getting more, but a porter who was walking nearby hurried him through a glass door onto the platform. There Raban looked around, while calling out 'Thank you, thank you!' to the porter, and since he found no guard, he climbed up the steps of the nearest coach by himself, each time putting the suitcase on the step above and then following himself, supporting himself on his umbrella with one hand, and on the handle of the suitcase with the other. The coach that he entered was brightly illuminated by the great amount of light from the main hall of the station, in which it was standing; in front of many a windowpane – all were shut right up to the top – a hissing arc lamp hung at about eye level, and the many raindrops on the glass were white, often single ones would move. Raban could hear the noise from the platform even when he had shut the carriage door and sat down on the last little free bit of a light-brown wooden seat. He saw many people's backs, and the backs of their heads, and between them the upturned faces of people on the seat opposite. In some places smoke was curling from pipes and cigars, in one place drifting limply past the face of a girl. Often the passengers would change places, discussing these changes with each other, or they would transfer their luggage, which lay in a narrow blue net over a seat, to another one. If a stick or the metal-covered corner of a suitcase stuck out, then the owner would have his attention drawn to this. He would go over and straighten it.

Raban also bethought himself and pushed his suitcase under his seat.

On his left, at the window, two gentlemen were sitting opposite each other, talking about the price of goods. 'They're commercial travelers,' Raban thought and, breathing regularly, he gazed at them. 'The merchant sends them into the country, they obey, they travel by train, and in every village they go from shop to shop. Sometimes they travel by carriage between the villages. They must not stay long anywhere, for everything must be done fast, and they must always talk only about their goods. With what pleasure, then, one can exert oneself in an occupation that is so agreeable!'

The younger man had jerked a notebook out of the hip pocket of his trousers, rapidly flicked the leaves over with a forefinger moistened on his tongue, and then read through a page, drawing the back of his fingernail down it as he went. He looked at Raban as he glanced up and, indeed, when he now began talking about thread prices, did not turn his face away from Raban, as one gazes steadily at a point in order not to forget anything of what one wants to say. At the same time he drew his brows tightly down over his eyes. He held the half-closed notebook in his left hand, with his thumb on the page he had been reading, in order to be able to refer to it easily if he should need to. And the notebook trembled, for he was not supporting his arm on anything, and the coach, which was now in motion, beat on the rails like a hammer.

The other traveler sat leaning back, listening and nodding at regular intervals. It was evident that he was far from agreeing with everything and later would give his own opinion.

Raban laid his curved hands palm-down on his knees and, leaning forward, between the travelers' heads he saw the window and through the window lights flitting past and others flitting away into the distance. He did not understand anything of what the traveler was talking about, nor would he understand the other's answer. Much preparation would first be required, for here were people who had been concerned with goods since their youth. But if one has held a spool of thread in one's hand so often and handed it to one's customer so often, then one knows the price and can talk about it, while villages come toward us and flash past, while at the same time they turn away into the depths of the country, where for us they must disappear. And yet these villages are inhabited, and there perhaps travelers go from shop to shop.

In a corner at the far end of the coach a tall man stood up, holding playing cards in his hand, and called out:

'I say, Marie, did you pack the zephyr shirts?'

'Of course I did,' said the woman, who was sitting opposite Raban. She had been dozing, and now when the question waked her she answered as though she were talking to herself or to Raban. 'You're going to market at Jungbunzlau, eh?' the vivacious traveler asked her. 'Jungbunzlau, that's right.' 'It's a big market this time, isn't it?' 'A big market, that's right.' She was sleepy, she rested her left elbow on a blue bundle, and her head dropped heavily against her hand, which pressed through the flesh of the cheek to the cheekbone. 'How young she is,' the traveler said.

Raban took the money that he had received from the cashier out of his waistcoat pocket and counted it over. He held up each coin firmly between thumb and forefinger for a long time and also twisted it this way and that on the inner surface of his thumb with the tip of his forefinger. He looked for a long time at the Emperor's image, then he was struck by the laurel wreath and the way it was fastened with knots and bows of ribbon at the back of the head. At last he found the sum was correct and put the money into a big black purse. But now when he was about to say to the traveler: 'They're a married couple, don't you think?' the train stopped. The noise of the journey ceased, guards shouted the name of a place, and Raban said nothing.

The train started again so slowly that one could picture the revolutions of the wheels, but a moment later it was racing down a slope, and all unexpectedly the tall railings of a bridge, outside the windows, were torn apart and pressed together, as it seemed.

Raban was now pleased that the train was going so fast, for he would not have wanted to stay in the last place. 'When it is dark there, when one knows no one there, when it is such a long way home. But then it must be terrible there by day. And is it different at the next station or at the previous ones or at the later ones or at the village I am going to?'

The traveler was suddenly talking more loudly. 'It's a long way yet,' Raban thought. 'Sir, you know just as well as I do, these manufacturers send their travelers around the most godforsaken little villages, they go crawling to the seediest of little shopkeepers, and do you think they offer them prices different from those they offer us big businessmen? Sir, take it from me; exactly the same prices, only yesterday I saw it black on white. I call it villainy. They're squeezing us out of existence; under current conditions it's simply impossible for us to do business.'

Again he looked at Raban; he was not ashamed of the tears in his eyes; he pressed the knuckles of his left hand to his mouth because his lips were quivering. Raban leaned back and tugged faintly at his mustache with his left hand.

The shopwoman opposite woke up and smilingly passed her hands over her forehead. The traveler talked more quietly. Once again the woman shifted as though settling down to sleep, half lying on her bundle, and sighed. The skirt was drawn tight over her right hip.

Behind her sat a gentleman with a traveling cap on his head, reading a large newspaper. The girl opposite him, who was probably a relative of his, urged him – at the same time inclining her head toward her right shoulder – to open the window, because it was so very hot. He said, without looking up, he would do it in a moment, only he must first finish reading an article in the newspaper, and he showed her which article he meant.

The shopwoman could not go to sleep again; she sat upright and looked out of the window; then for a long time she looked at the oil lamp and the flame burning yellow near the ceiling of the carriage. Raban shut his eyes for a little while.

When he glanced up, the shopwoman was just biting into a piece of cake that was spread with brown jam. The bundle next to her was open. The traveler was smoking a cigar in silence and kept on fidgeting as though he were tapping the ash off the end of it. The other was poking about in the works of a pocket watch with the tip of a knife, so that one could hear it scraping.

With his eyes almost shut Raban still had time to see, in a blurred way, the gentleman in the traveling cap pulling at the window strap. There came a gust of cool air, and a straw hat fell from a hook. Raban thought he was waking up and that was why his cheeks were so refreshed, or someone was opening the door and drawing him into the room, or he was in some way mistaken about things, and, breathing deeply, he quickly fell asleep.

II

The steps of the coach were still shaking a little when Raban climbed down them. Into his face, coming out of the air of the carriage, the rain beat, and he shut his eyes. It was raining noisily on the corrugated iron roof of the station building, but out in the open country the rain fell in such a way that it sounded like the uninterrupted blowing of the wind. A barefoot boy came running up – Raban did not see from where – and breathlessly asked Raban to let him carry the suitcase, for it was raining; but Raban said: Yes, it was raining, and he would therefore go by omnibus. He did not need him, he said. Thereupon the boy pulled a face as though he thought it grander to walk in the rain and have one's suitcase carried than to go by bus, and instantly turned around and ran away. When Raban wanted to call him, it was already too late.

There were two lighted lamps, and a station official came out of a door. Without hesitation he walked through the rain to the engine, stood there motionless with his arms folded, and waited until the engine driver leaned over his rail and talked to him. A porter was called, came, and was sent back again. At many of the windows in the train there were passengers standing, and since what they had to look at was an ordinary railway station their gaze was probably dim, the eyelids close together, as though the train were in motion. A girl came hurrying along from the road to the platform under a parasol with a flowered pattern; she set the open parasol on the ground and sat down, pushing her legs apart so that her skirt should dry better, and ran her fingertips over the tight-stretched skirt. There were only two lamps alight; her face was indistinguishable. The porter came past and complained that puddles were forming under the parasol; he held his arms in a semicircle before him in order to demonstrate the size of these puddles, and then moved his hands through the air, one after the other, like fishes sinking into deeper water, in order to make it clear that traffic was also being impeded by this parasol.

The train started, disappeared like a long sliding door, and behind the poplars on the far side of the railway track there was the landscape, so massive that it took away one's breath. Was it a dark view through a gap or was it woods, was it a pool, or a house in which the people were already asleep, was it a church steeple or a ravine between the hills? Nobody must dare to go there, but who could restrain himself?

And when Raban caught sight of the official – he was already at the step up to his office – he ran in front of him and stopped him: 'Excuse me, please, is it far to the village? That's where I want to go.'

'No, a quarter of an hour, but by bus – as it's raining – you'll be there in five minutes.'

'It's raining. It's not a very fine spring,' Raban said.

The official had put his right hand on his hip, and through the triangle formed by the arm and the body Raban saw the girl, who had now shut the parasol, on the seat where she sat.

'If one is going on one's summer holidays now and is going to stay there, one can't but regret it. Actually I thought I should be met.' He glanced around to make it seem plausible.

'You will miss the bus, I'm afraid. It doesn't wait so long. Nothing to thank me for. That's the road, between the hedges.'

The road outside the railway station was not lighted; only from three ground-floor windows in the building there came a misty glimmer, but it did not extend far. Raban walked on tiptoe through the mud and shouted 'Driver!' and 'Hello there!' and 'Omnibus!' and 'Here I am!' many times. But when he landed among scarcely interrupted puddles on the dark side of the road, he had to tramp onwards with his heels down, until suddenly a horse's moist muzzle touched his forehead.

There was the omnibus; he quickly climbed into the empty compartment, sat down by the windowpane behind the driver's box, and hunched his back into the corner, for he had done all that was necessary. For if the driver is asleep, he will wake up toward morning; if he is dead, then a new driver will come, or the innkeeper, and should that not happen either, then passengers will come by the early morning train, people in a hurry, making a noise. In any case one can be quiet, one may even draw the curtains over the windows and wait for the jerk with which the vehicle must start.

'Yes, after all I have already accomplished, it is certain that tomorrow I shall get to Betty and to Mamma; nobody can prevent that. Yet it is true, and was indeed to be foreseen, that my letter will arrive only tomorrow, so that I might very well have remained in town and spent an agreeable night at Elvy's, without having to be afraid of the next day's work, the sort of thing that otherwise ruins every pleasure for me. But look, I've got my feet wet.'

He lit a stub of candle that he had taken out of his waistcoat pocket and set it on the seat opposite. It was bright enough, the darkness outside made it appear as though the omnibus had black distempered walls and no glass in the windows. There was no need to think that there were wheels under the floor and in front the horse between the shafts. Raban rubbed his feet thoroughly on the seat, pulled on clean socks, and sat up straight. Then he heard someone from the station shouting: 'Hi!' if there was anyone in the bus he might say so. 'Yes, yes, and he would like to start now, too,' Raban answered, leaning out of the door, which he had opened, holding on to the doorpost with his right hand, the left hand held open, close to his mouth.

The rain gushed down the back of his neck, inside his collar.

Wrapped in the canvas of two sacks that had been cut up, the driver came over, the reflection of his stable lantern jumping through the puddles at his feet. Irritably he began an explanation: listen here, he said, he had been playing cards with Lebeda and they had just been getting on fine when the train came. It would really have been impossible for him to take a look outside then, still, he did not mean to abuse anyone who did not understand that. Apart from that, this place here was a filthy dump, and no half-measures, and it was hard to see what business a gentleman like this could have here, and he would be getting there soon enough anyway, so that he need not go and complain anywhere. Only just now Herr Pirkershofer – if you please, that's the junior assistant clerk – had come in and had said he thought a small fair man had been wanting to go by the omnibus. Well, so he had at once come and asked, or hadn't he at once come and asked?

The lantern was attached to the end of the shaft; the horse, having been shouted at in a muffled voice, began to pull, and the water on top of the bus, now set stirring, dripped slowly through a crack into the carriage.

The road was perhaps hilly; there was surely mud flying up into the spokes; fans of puddle water formed, with a rushing sound, behind the turning wheels; it was for the most part with loose reins that the driver guided the dripping horse. – Could not all this be used as reproaches against Raban? Many puddles were unexpectedly lit up by the lantern trembling on the shaft, and split up, in ripples, under the wheel. This happened solely because Raban was traveling to his fiancée, to Betty, an oldish pretty girl. And who, if one were going to speak of it at all, would appreciate what merits Raban here had, even if it was only that he bore those reproaches, which admittedly nobody could make openly. Of course he was doing it gladly. Betty was his fiancée, he was fond of her, it would be disgusting if she were to thank him for that as well, but all the same—

Without meaning to, he often bumped his head on the panel against which he was leaning, then for a while he looked up at the ceiling. Once his right hand slipped down from his thigh, where he had been resting it. But his elbow remained in the angle between belly and leg.

The omnibus was now traveling between houses; here and there the inside of the coach had a share of the light from a room; there were some steps – to see the first of them Raban would have had to stand up – built up to a church; outside a park gate there was a lamp with a large flame burning in it, but a statue of a saint stood out in black relief only because of the light from a draper's shop, and Raban saw his candle, which had burnt down, the trickle of wax hanging motionless from the seat.

When the bus stopped outside the inn, and the rain could be heard loudly and – probably there was a window open – so could the voices of the guests, Raban wondered which would be better, to get out at once or to wait until the innkeeper came to the coach. What the custom was in this township he did not know, but it was pretty certain that Betty would have spoken of her fiancé, and according to whether his arrival here was magnificent or feeble, so the esteem in which she was held here would increase or diminish, and with that, again, his own, too. But of course he knew neither what people felt about her nor what she had told them about him, and so everything was all the more disagreeable and difficult. Oh, beautiful city and beautiful the way home! If it rains there, one goes home by tram over wet cobbles; here one goes in a cart through mud to an inn. – 'The city is far from here, and if I were now in danger of dying of homesickness, nobody could get me back there today. – Well, anyway, I shouldn't die – but there I get the meal expected for that evening, set on the table, on the right behind my plate the newspaper, on the left the lamp, here I shall be given some dreadfully fat dish – they don't know that I have a weak stomach, and even if they did know – an unfamiliar newspaper – many people, whom I can already hear, will be there, and one lamp will be lit for all. What sort of light can it provide? Enough to play cards by – but for reading a newspaper?

'The innkeeper isn't coming, he's not interested in guests, he is probably an unfriendly man. Or does he know that I am Betty's fiancé, and does that give him a reason for not coming to fetch me in? It would be in accord with that that the driver kept me waiting so long at the station. Betty has often told me, after all, how much she has been bothered by lecherous men and how she has had to rebuff their insistence; perhaps it is that here too . . . !' [Text breaks off]

[Second Manuscript]

When Eduard Raban, coming along the passage, walked into the open doorway, he could now see how it was raining. It was not raining much.

On the pavement straight in front of him, not higher, not lower, there were, in spite of the rain, many passers-by. Every now and again one would step forward and cross the road.

A little girl was carrying a gray dog on her outstretched arms. Two gentlemen were exchanging information on some subject, at times turning the whole front of their bodies to each other, and then slowly turning aside themselves again; it was like doors ajar in the wind. The one held his hands palm-upward, raising and lowering them in regular motion, as though he were balancing a load, testing the weight of it.

Then one caught sight of a slim lady whose face twitched slightly, like the flickering light of the stars, and whose flat hat was loaded high and to the brim with unrecognizable objects; she appeared to be a stranger to all the passers-by, without intending it, as though by some law. And hurrying past was a young man with a thin walking stick, his left hand, as though paralyzed, lying flat on his chest. Many were out on business; in spite of the fact that they walked fast, one saw them longer than others, now on the pavement, now below; their coats fitted them badly; they did not care how they carried themselves; they let themselves be pushed by the people and they pushed too. Three gentlemen – two holding lightweight overcoats on their crooked forearms – walked from the front of the building to the edge of the pavement, in order to see what was going on in the carriageway and on the farther pavement.

Through the gaps between the passers-by, now fleetingly, then comfortably, one saw the regularly set cobbles in the carriageway, on which carriages, swaying on their wheels, were swiftly drawn by horses with arched necks. The people who sat at ease on the upholstered seats gazed in silence at the pedestrians, the shops, the balconies, and the sky. If it happened that one carriage overtook another, then the horses would press against each other, and the harness straps hung dangling. The animals tugged at the shafts, the carriage bowled along, swaying as it gathered speed, until the swerve around the carriage ahead was completed and the horses moved apart again, still with their narrow heads inclined toward each other.

An elderly gentleman came quickly toward the front entrance, stopped on the dry mosaic paving, turned around. And he then gazed into the rain, which, wedged in by the narrow street, fell confusedly.

Raban put down the suitcase with the black cloth cover, bending his right knee a little in doing so. The rain water was already running along the edge of the carriageway in streaks that almost extended to the lower-lying gutters.

The elderly gentleman stood upright near Raban, who was supporting himself by leaning slightly against the wooden doorpost; from time to time he glanced toward Raban, even though to do so he had to twist his neck sharply. Yet he did this only out of the natural desire, now that he happened to be unoccupied, to observe everything exactly, at least in his vicinity. The result of this aimless glancing hither and thither was that there was a great deal he did not notice. So, for instance, it escaped him that Raban's lips were very pale, not much less so than the very faded red of his tie, which had a once striking Moorish pattern. Now, had he noticed this, he would certainly have made a fuss about it, at least inwardly, which, again, would not have been the right thing, for Raban was always pale, even if, it was a fact, various things might have been making him especially tired just recently.

'What weather!' the gentleman said in a low voice, shaking his head, consciously, it was true, but still in a slightly senile way.

'Yes, indeed, and when one's supposed to be starting on a journey, too,' Raban said, quickly straightening up.

'And it isn't the kind of weather that will improve,' the gentleman said and, in order to make sure of it once more for the last time, bent forward to glance in scrutiny up the street, then down, and then at the sky. 'It may last for days, even for weeks. So far as I recall, nothing better is forecast for June and the beginning of July, either. Well, it's no pleasure to anyone; I for instance shall have to do without my walks, which are extremely important to my health.'

Hereupon he yawned and seemed to become exhausted, since he had now heard Raban's voice and, occupied with this conversation, no longer took any interest in anything, not even in the conversation.

This made quite an impression on Raban, since after all the gentleman had addressed him first, and he therefore tried to show off a little, although it might not even be noticed. 'True,' he said, 'in town one can very easily manage to go without what isn't good for one. If one does not do without it, then one has only oneself to blame for the bad consequences. One will be sorry and in this way come to see for the first time really clearly how to manage the next time. And even if in matters of detail . . . [Two pages missing] . . . 'I don't mean anything by it. I don't mean anything at all,' Raban hastened to say, prepared to excuse the gentleman's absent-mindedness in any way possible, since after all he wanted to show off a little more. 'It's all just out of the book previously mentioned, which I, like other people, happen to have been reading in the evening recently. I have been mostly alone. Owing to family circumstances, you see. But apart from anything else, a good book is what I like best after supper. Always has been. Just recently I read in a prospectus a quotation from some writer or other. "A good book is the best friend there is," and that's really true, it is so, a good book is the best friend there is.'

'Yes, when one is young—' the gentleman said, meaning nothing in particular by this, merely wanting to indicate how it was raining, that the rain was heavier again, and that now it was not going to stop at all; but to Raban it sounded as though at sixty the gentleman still thought of himself as young and energetic and considered Raban's thirty years nothing in comparison, and as though he meant to say besides, insofar as it was permissible, that at the age of thirty he had, of course, been more sensible than Raban. And that he believed even if one had nothing else to do, like himself, for instance, an old man, yet it was really wasting one's time to stand about here in this hall, looking at the rain, but if one spent the time, besides, in chatter, one was wasting it doubly.

Now Raban had believed for some time that nothing other people said about his capabilities or opinions had been able to affect him, on the contrary, that he had positively abandoned the position where he had listened, all submissively, to everything that was said, so that people were now simply wasting their breath whether they happened to be against him or for him. And so he said: 'We are talking about different things, since you did not wait to hear what I was going to say.'

'Please go on, please go on,' the gentleman said.

'Well, it isn't so important,' Raban said. 'I was only going to say books are useful in every sense and quite especially in respects in which one would not expect it. For when one is about to embark on some enterprise, it is precisely the books whose contents have nothing at all in common with the enterprise that are the most useful. For the reader who does after all intend to embark on that enterprise, that is to say, who has somehow become enthusiastic (and even if, as it were, the effect of the book can penetrate only so far as that enthusiasm), will be stimulated by the book to all kinds of thoughts concerning his enterprise. Now, however, since the contents of the book are precisely something of utter indifference, the reader is not at all impeded in those thoughts, and he passes through the midst of the book with them, as once the Jews passed through the Red Sea, that's how I should like to put it.'

For Raban the whole person of the old gentleman now assumed an unpleasant expression. It seemed to him as though he had drawn particularly close to him – but it was merely trifling . . . [Two pages missing] . . . 'The newspaper, too. – But I was about to say, I am only going into the country, that's all, only for a fortnight; I am taking a holiday for the first time for quite a long period, and it's necessary for other reasons too, and yet for instance a book that I was, as I have mentioned, reading recently taught me more about my little journey than you could imagine.'

'I am listening,' the gentleman said.

Raban was silent and, standing there so straight, put his hands into his overcoat pockets, which were rather too high. Only after a while did the old gentleman say: 'This journey seems to be of some special importance to you.'

'Well, you see, you see,' Raban said, once more supporting himself against the doorpost. Only now did he see how the passage had filled up with people. They were standing even around the foot of the staircase, and an official, who had rented a room in the apartment of the same woman as Raban had, when he came down the stairs had to ask the people to make way for him. To Raban, who only pointed at the rain, he called out over several heads, which now all turned to Raban, 'Have a good journey' and reiterated a promise, obviously given earlier, definitely to visit Raban the next Sunday.

[Two pages missing] . . . has a pleasant job, with which he is indeed satisfied and which has always been kept open for him. He has such powers of endurance and is inwardly so gay that he does not need anyone to keep him entertained, but everyone needs him. He has always been healthy. Oh, don't try to tell me.

'I am not going to argue,' the gentleman said.

'You won't argue, but you won't admit your mistake either. Why do you stick to it so? And however sharply you may recollect now, you would, I dare wager, forget everything if you were to talk to him. You would reproach me for not having refuted you more effectively now. If he so much as talks about a book. He's instantly ecstatic about everything beautiful. . . .'

Translated by Ernst Kaiser and Eithne Wilkins

The Student

EVERY EVENING for the past week my neighbor in the adjoining room has come to wrestle with me. He was a stranger to me, even now I haven't yet spoken to him. We merely shout a few exclamations at one another, you can't call that 'speaking.' With a 'well then' the struggle is begun; 'scoundrel!' one of us sometimes groans under the grip of the other; 'there' accompanies a surprise thrust; 'stop!' means the end, yet the struggle always goes on a little while longer. As a rule, even when he is already at the door he leaps back again and gives me a push that sends me to the ground. From his room he then calls good night to me through the wall. If I wanted to give up this acquaintance once and for all I should have to give up my room, for bolting the door is of no avail. Once I had the door bolted because I wanted to read, but my neighbor hacked the door in two with an ax, and, since he can part with something only with the greatest difficulty once he has taken hold of it, I was even in danger of the ax.

I know how to accommodate myself to circumstances. Since he always comes to me at a certain hour, I take up some easy work beforehand which I can interrupt at once, should it be necessary. I straighten out a chest, for example, or copy something, or read some unimportant book. I have to arrange matters in this way – no sooner has he appeared in the door than I must drop everything, slam the chest to at once, drop the penholder, throw the book away, for it is only fighting that he wants, nothing else. If I feel particularly strong I tease him a little by first attempting to elude him. I crawl under the table, throw chairs under his feet, wink at him from the distance, though it is of course in bad taste to joke in this very one-sided way with a stranger. But usually our bodies close in battle at once. Apparently he is a student, studies all day, and wants some hasty exercise in the evening before he goes to bed. Well, in me he has a good opponent; accidents aside, I perhaps am the stronger and more skillful of the two. He, however, has more endurance.

Translated by Martin Greenberg and Hannah Arendt

The Angel

25 JUNE. I paced up and down my room from early morning until twilight. The window was open, it was a warm day. The noises of the narrow street beat in uninterruptedly. By now I knew every trifle in the room from having looked at it in the course of my pacing up and down. My eyes had traveled over every wall. I had pursued the pattern of the

rug to its last convolution, noted every mark of age it bore. My fingers had spanned the table across the middle many times. I had already bared my teeth repeatedly at the picture of the landlady's dead husband.

Toward evening I walked over to the window and sat down on the low sill. Then, for the first time not moving restlessly about, I happened calmly to glance into the interior of the room and at the ceiling. And finally, finally, unless I were mistaken, this room which I had so violently upset began to stir. The tremor began at the edges of the thinly plastered white ceiling. Little pieces of plaster broke off and with a distinct thud fell here and there, as if at random, to the floor. I held out my hand and some plaster fell into it too; in my excitement I threw it over my head into the street without troubling to turn around. The cracks in the ceiling made no pattern yet, but it was already possible somehow to imagine one. But I put these games aside when a bluish violet began to mix with the white; it spread straight out from the center of the ceiling, which itself remained white, even radiantly white, where the shabby electric lamp was stuck. Wave after wave of the color – or was it a light? – spread out toward the now darkening edges. One no longer paid any attention to the plaster that was falling away as if under the pressure of a skillfully applied tool. Yellow and golden-yellow colours now penetrated the violet from the side. But the ceiling did not really take on these different hues; the colors merely made it somewhat transparent; things striving to break through seemed to be hovering above it, already one could almost see the outlines of a movement there, an arm was thrust out, a silver sword swung to and fro. It was meant for me, there was no doubt of that; a vision intended for my liberation was being prepared.

I sprang up on the table to make everything ready, tore out the electric light together with its brass fixture and hurled it to the floor, then jumped down and pushed the table from the middle of the room to the wall. That which was striving to appear could drop down unhindered on the carpet and announce to me whatever it had to announce. I had barely finished when the ceiling did in fact break open. In the dim light, still at a great height, I had judged it badly, an angel in bluish-violet robes girt with gold cords sank slowly down on great white silken-shining wings, the sword in its raised arm thrust out horizontally. 'An angel, then!' I thought; 'it has been flying toward me all the day and in my disbelief I did not know it. Now it will speak to me.' I lowered my eyes. When I raised them again the angel was still there, it is true, hanging rather far off under the ceiling (which had closed again), but it was no living angel, only a painted wooden figurehead off the prow of some ship, one of the kind that hangs from the ceiling in sailors' taverns, nothing more.

The hilt of the sword was made in such a way as to hold candles and catch the dripping tallow. I had pulled the electric light down; I didn't want to remain in the dark, there was still one candle left, so I got up on a chair, stuck the candle into the hilt of the sword, lit it, and then sat late into the night under the angel's faint flame.

Translated by Martin Greenberg and Hannah Arendt

The Village Schoolmaster
[The Giant Mole]

THOSE, and I am one of them, who find even a small ordinary-sized mole disgusting, would probably have died of disgust if they had seen the giant mole that a few years back was observed in the neighborhood of one of our villages, which achieved a certain transitory celebrity on account of the incident. Today it has long since sunk back into oblivion again, and in that only shares the obscurity of the whole incident, which has remained quite inexplicable, but which people, it must be confessed, have also taken no great pains to explain; and as a result of an incomprehensible apathy in those very circles that should have concerned themselves with it, and who in fact have shown enthusiastic interest in far more trifling matters, the affair has been forgotten without ever being adequately investigated. In any case, the fact that the village could not be reached by the railroad was no excuse. Many people came from great distances out of pure curiosity, there were even foreigners among them; it was only those who should have shown something more than curiosity that refrained from coming. In fact, if a few quite simple people, people whose daily work gave them hardly a moment of leisure – if these people had not quite disinterestedly taken up the affair, the rumor of this natural phenomenon would probably have never spread beyond the locality. Indeed, rumor itself, which usually cannot be held within bounds, was actually sluggish in this case; if it had not literally been given a shove it would not have spread. But even that was no valid reason for refusing to inquire into the affair; on the contrary this second phenomenon should have been investigated as well. Instead the old village schoolmaster was left to write the sole account in black and white of the incident, and though he was an excellent man in his own profession, neither his abilities nor his equipment made it possible for him to produce an exhaustive description that could be used as a foundation by others, far less, therefore, an actual explanation of the occurrence. His little pamphlet was printed, and a good many copies were sold to visitors to the village about that time; it also received some public recognition, but the teacher was wise enough to perceive that his fragmentary labors, in which no one supported him, were basically without value. If in spite of that he did not relax in them, and made the question his lifework, though it naturally became more hopeless from year to year, that only shows on the one hand how powerful an effect the appearance of the giant mole was capable of producing, and on the other how much laborious effort and fidelity to his convictions may be found in an old and obscure village schoolmaster. But that he suffered deeply from the cold attitude of the recognized authorities is proved by a brief brochure with which he followed up his pamphlet several years later, by which time hardly anyone could remember what it was all about. In this brochure he complained of the lack of understanding that he had encountered in people where it was least to be expected; complaints that carried conviction less by the skill with which they were expressed than by their honesty. Of such people he said very appositely: 'It is not I, but they, who talk like old village schoolmasters.' And among other things he adduced the pronouncement of a scholar to whom he had gone expressly about his affair. The name of the scholar was not mentioned, but from various circumstances we could guess who it was. After the teacher had managed with great difficulty to secure admittance, he perceived at once from the very way in which he was greeted that the savant had already acquired a rooted prejudice against the matter. The absent-mindedness with which he listened to the long report which the teacher, pamphlet in hand, delivered to him, can be gauged from a remark that he let fall after a pause for ostensible reflection: 'The soil in your neighborhood is particularly black and rich. Consequently it provides the moles with particularly rich nourishment, and so they grow to an unusual size.'

'But not to such a size as that!' exclaimed the teacher, and he measured off two yards on the wall, somewhat exaggerating the length of the mole in exasperation. 'Oh, and why not?' replied the scholar, who obviously looked upon the whole affair as a great joke. With this verdict the teacher had to return to his home. He tells how his wife and six children were waiting for him by the roadside in the snow, and how he had to admit to them the final collapse of his hopes.

When I read of the scholar's attitude toward the old man I was not yet acquainted with the teacher's pamphlet. But I at once resolved myself to collect and correlate all the information I could discover regarding the case. If I could not employ physical force against the scholar, I could at least write a defense of the teacher, or more exactly, of the good intentions of an honest but uninfluential man. I admit that I rued this decision later, for I soon saw that its execution was bound to involve me in a very strange predicament. On the one hand my own influence was far from sufficient to effect a change in learned or even public opinion in the teacher's favor, while on the other the teacher was bound to notice that I was less concerned with his main object, which was to prove that the giant mole had actually been seen, than to defend his honesty, which must naturally be self-evident to him and in need of no defense. Accordingly, what was bound to happen was this: I would be misunderstood by the teacher, though I wanted to collaborate with him, and instead of helping him I myself would probably require support, which was most unlikely to appear. Besides, my decision would impose a great burden of work upon me. If I wanted to convince people I could not invoke the teacher, since he himself had not been able to convince them. To read his pamphlet could only have led me astray, and so I refrained from reading it until I should have finished my own labors. More, I did not even get in touch with the teacher. True, he heard of my inquiries through intermediaries, but he did not know whether I was working for him or against him. In fact he probably assumed the latter, though he denied it later on; for I have proof of the fact that he put various obstacles in my way. It was quite easy for him to do that, for of course I was compelled to undertake anew all the inquiries he had already made, and so he could always steal a march on me. But that was the only objection that could be justly made to my method, an unavoidable reproach, but one that was palliated by the caution and self-abnegation with which I drew my conclusions. But for the rest my pamphlet was quite uninfluenced by the teacher, perhaps on this point, indeed, I showed all too great a scrupulosity; from my words one might have thought nobody had ever inquired into the case before, and I was the first to interrogate those who had seen or heard of the mole, the first to correlate the evidence, the first to draw conclusions. When later I read the schoolmaster's pamphlet – it had a very circumstantial title: 'A mole, larger in size than ever seen before' – I found that we actually did not agree on certain important points, though we both believed we had proved our main point, namely, the existence of the mole. These differences prevented the establishment of the friendly relations with the schoolmaster that I had been looking forward to in spite of everything. On his side there developed a feeling almost of hostility. True, he was always modest and humble in his bearing toward me, but that only made his real feelings the more obvious. In other words, he was of the opinion that I had merely damaged his credit, and that my belief that I had been or could be of assistance to him was simplicity at best, but more likely presumption or artifice. He was particularly fond of saying that all his previous enemies had shown their hostility either not at all, or in private, or at most by word of mouth, while I had considered it necessary to have my censures straightway published. Moreover, the few opponents of his who had really occupied themselves with the subject, if but superficially, had at least listened to his, the schoolmaster's views before they had given expression to their own: while I, on the strength of unsystematically assembled and in part misunderstood evidence, had published conclusions which, even if they were correct as regarded the main point, must evoke incredulity, and among the public no less than the educated. But the faintest hint that the existence of the mole was unworthy of credence was the worst thing that could happen in this case.

To these reproaches, veiled as they were, I could easily have found an answer – for instance, that his own pamphlet achieved the very summit of the incredible – it was less easy, however, to make headway against his continual suspicion, and that was the reason why I was very reserved in my dealings with him. For in his heart he was convinced that I wanted to rob him of the fame of being the first man publicly to vindicate the mole. Now of course he really enjoyed no fame whatever, but only an absurd notoriety that was shrinking more and more, and for which I had certainly no desire to compete. Besides, in the foreword to my pamphlet I had expressly declared that the teacher must stand for all time as the discoverer of the mole – and he was not even that – and that only my sympathy with his unfortunate fate had spurred me on to write. 'It is the aim of this pamphlet' – so I ended up all too melodramatically, but it corresponded with my feelings at that time – 'to help in giving the schoolmaster's book the wide publicity it deserves. If I succeed in that, then may my name, which I regard as only transiently and indirectly associated with this question, be blotted from it at once.' Thus I disclaimed expressly any major participation in the affair; it was almost as if I had foreseen in some manner the teacher's unbelievable reproaches. Nevertheless he found in that very passage a handle against me, and I do not deny that there was a faint show of justice in what he said or rather hinted; indeed I was often struck by the fact that he showed almost a keener penetration where I was concerned than he had done in his pamphlet. For he maintained that my foreword was double-faced. If I was really concerned solely to give publicity to his pamphlet, why had I not occupied myself exclusively with him and his pamphlet, why had I not pointed out its virtues, its irrefutability, why had

I not confined myself to insisting on the significance of the discovery and making that clear, why had I instead tackled the discovery itself, while completely ignoring the pamphlet? Had not the discovery been made already? Was there still anything left to be done in that direction? But if I really thought that it was necessary for me to make the discovery all over again, why had I disassociated myself from the discovery so solemnly in my foreword? One might put that down to false modesty, but it was something worse. I was trying to belittle the discovery, I was drawing attention to it merely for the purpose of depreciating it, while he on the other hand had inquired into and finally established it. Perhaps the affair had sunk somewhat into desuetude; now I had made a noise about it again, but at the same time I had made the schoolmaster's position more difficult than ever. What did he care whether his honesty was vindicated or not? All that he was concerned with was the thing itself, and with that alone. But I was only of disservice to it, for I did not understand it, I did not prize it at its true value, I had no real feeling for it. It was infinitely above my intellectual capacity. He sat before me and looked at me, his old wrinkled face quite composed, and yet this was what he was thinking. Yet it was not true that he was only concerned with the thing itself: actually he was very greedy for fame, and wanted to make money out of the business too, which, however, considering his large family, was very understandable. Nevertheless my interest in the affair seemed so trivial compared with his own, that he felt he could claim to be completely disinterested without deviating very seriously from the truth. And indeed my inner doubts refused to be quite calmed by my telling myself that the man's reproaches were really due to the fact that he clung to his mole, so to speak, with both hands, and was bound to look upon anyone who laid even a finger on it as a traitor. For that was not true; his attitude was not to be explained by greed, or at any rate by greed alone, but rather by the touchiness which his great labors and their complete unsuccess had bred in him.

Yet even his touchiness did not explain everything. Perhaps my interest in the affair was really too trivial. The schoolmaster was used to lack of interest in strangers. He regarded it as a universal evil, but no longer suffered from its individual manifestations. Now a man had appeared who, strangely enough, took up the affair; and even he did not understand it. Attacked from this side I can make no defense. I am no zoologist; yet perhaps I would have thrown myself into the case with my whole heart if I had discovered it; but I had not discovered it. Such a gigantic mole is certainly a prodigy, yet one cannot expect the continuous and undivided attention of the whole world to be accorded it, particularly if its existence is not completely and irrefutably established, and in any case it cannot be produced. And I admit too that even if I had been the discoverer I would probably never have come forward so gladly and voluntarily in defense of the mole as I had in that of the schoolmaster.

Now the misunderstanding between me and the schoolmaster would probably have quickly cleared up if my pamphlet had achieved success. But success was not forthcoming. Perhaps the book was not well enough written, not persuasive enough; I am a businessman, it may be that the composition of such a pamphlet was still further beyond my limited powers than those of the teacher, though in the kind of knowledge required I was greatly superior to him. Besides, my unsuccess may be explicable in other ways; the time at which the pamphlet appeared may have been inauspicious. The discovery of the mole, which had failed to penetrate to a wide public at the time it took place, was not so long past on the one hand as to be completely forgotten, and thus capable of being brought alive again by my pamphlet, while on the other hand enough time had elapsed quite to exhaust the trivial interest that had originally existed. Those who took my pamphlet at all seriously told themselves, in that bored tone which from the first had characterized the debate, that now the old useless labors on this wearisome question were to begin all over again; and some even confused my pamphlet with the schoolmaster's. In a leading agricultural journal appeared the following comment, fortunately at the very end, and in small print: 'The pamphlet on the giant mole has once more been sent to us. Years ago we remember having had a hearty laugh over it. Since then it has not become more intelligible, nor we more hard of understanding. But we simply refuse to laugh at it a second time. Instead, we would ask our teaching associations whether more useful work cannot be found for our village schoolmasters than hunting out giant moles.' An unpardonable confusion of identity. They had read neither the first nor the second pamphlet, and the two perfunctorily scanned expressions, 'giant mole' and 'village schoolmaster,' were sufficient for these gentlemen, as representatives of publicly esteemed interest, to pronounce on the subject. Against this attack measures might have been attempted and with success, but the lack of understanding between the teacher and myself kept me from venturing upon them. I tried instead to keep the review from his knowledge as long as I could. But he very soon discovered it, as I recognized from a sentence in one of his letters, in which he announced his intention of visiting me for the Christmas holidays. He wrote: 'The world is full of malice, and people smooth the path for it,' by which he wished to convey that I was one of the malicious, but, not content with my own innate malice, wished also to make the world's path smooth for it: in other words, was acting in such a way as to arouse the general malice and help it to victory. Well, I summoned the resolution I required, and was able to await him calmly, and calmly greet him when he arrived, this time a shade less polite in his bearing than usual; he carefully drew out the journal from the breast pocket of his old-fashioned padded overcoat, and opening it handed it to me. 'I've seen it,' I replied, handing the journal back unread. 'You've seen it,' he said with a sigh; he had the old teacher's habit of repeating the other person's answers. 'Of course I won't take this lying down!' he went on, tapping the journal excitedly with his finger and glancing up sharply at me, as if I were of a different mind; he certainly had some idea of what I was about to say, for I think I have noticed, not so much from his words as from other indications, that he often has a genuine intuition of my intentions, though he never yields to them but lets himself be diverted. What I said to him I can set down almost word for word, for I made a note of it shortly after our interview. 'Do what you like,' I said, 'our ways part from this moment. I fancy that that is neither unexpected nor unwelcome news to you. The review in this journal is not the real reason for my decision; it has merely finally confirmed it. The real reason is this: originally I thought my intervention might be of some use to you, while now I cannot but recognize that I have damaged you in every direction. Why it has turned out so I cannot say; the causes of success and unsuccess are always ambiguous; but don't look for the sole explanation in my shortcomings. Consider: you too had the best intentions, and yet, if one regards the matter objectively, you failed. I don't intend it as a joke, for it would be a joke against myself, when I say that your connection with me must unfortunately be counted among your failures. It is neither cowardice nor treachery, if I withdraw from the affair now. Actually it involves a certain degree of self-renunciation; my pamphlet itself proves how much I respect you personally, in a certain sense you have become my teacher, and I have almost grown fond of the mole itself. Nevertheless I have decided to step aside; you are the discoverer, and all that I can do is to prevent you from gaining possible fame, while I attract failure and pass it on to you. At least that is your own opinion. Enough of that. The sole expiation that I can make is to beg your forgiveness and, should you require it, to publish openly, that is, in this journal, the admission I have just made to you.'

These were my words; they were not entirely sincere, but what was sincere in them was obvious enough. My explanation had the effect upon him that I had roughly anticipated. Most old people have something deceitful, something mendacious, in their dealings with people younger than themselves; you live at peace with them, imagine you are on the best of terms with them, know their ruling prejudices, receive continual assurances of amity, take the whole thing for granted; and when something decisive happens and those peaceful relations, so long nourished, should come into effective operation, suddenly these old people rise before you like strangers, show that they have deeper and stronger convictions, and now for the first time literally unfurl their banner, and with terror you read upon it the new decree. The reason for this terror lies chiefly in the fact that what the old say now is really far more just and sensible than what they had said before; it is as if even the self-evident had degrees of validity, and their words now were more self-evident than ever. But the final deceit that lies in their words consists in this, that at bottom they have always said what they are saying now. I must have probed deeply into the schoolmaster, seeing that his next words did not entirely take me by surprise. 'Child,' he said, laying his hand on mine and patting it gently, 'how did you ever take it into your head to go into this affair? The very first I heard of it I talked it over with my wife.' He pushed his chair back from the table, got up, spread out his arms, and stared at the floor, as if his tiny little wife were standing there and he were speaking to her. ' "We've struggled on alone," I said to her, "for many years; now, it seems, a noble protector has risen for us in the city, a fine businessman, Mr. So-and-so. We should congratulate ourselves, shouldn't we? A businessman in the city isn't to be sniffed at; when an ignorant peasant believes us and says so it doesn't help us, for what a peasant may say or do is of no account; whether he says the old village schoolmaster is right, or spits to show his contempt, the net result is the same. And if instead of one peasant ten thousand should stand up for us, the result, if possible, would only be still worse. A businessman in the city, on the other hand, that's something else again; a man like that has connections, things he says in passing, as it were, are taken up and repeated, new patrons interest themselves in the question, one of them, it may be, remarks: You can learn even from old village schoolmasters, and next day whole crowds of people are saying it to one another, people you would never imagine saying such things, to look at them. Next, money is found to finance the business, one gentleman goes around collecting for it and the others shower subscriptions on him; they decide that the village schoolmaster must be dragged from his obscurity; they arrive, they don't bother about his external appearance, but take him to their bosoms, and since his wife and children hang onto him, they are taken along too. Have you ever watched city people? They chatter without stopping. When there's a whole lot of them together you can hear their chatter running from right to left and back again, and up and down, this way and that. And so, chattering away, they push us into the coach, so that we've hardly time to bow to everybody. The gentleman on the coachman's seat puts his glasses straight, flourishes his whip, and off we go. They all wave a parting greeting to the village, as if we were still there and not sitting among them. The more impatient city people drive out in carriages to meet us. As we approach they get up from their seats and crane their necks. The gentleman who collected the money arranges everything methodically and in order. When we drive into the city we are a long procession of carriages. We think the public welcome is over; but it really only begins when we reach our hotel. In a city an announcement attracts a great many people. What interests one interests all the rest immediately. They take their views from one another and promptly make those views their own. All the people who haven't managed to drive out and meet us in carriages are waiting in front of the hotel; others could have driven out, but they were too self-conscious. They're waiting too. It's extraordinary, the way that the gentleman who collected the money keeps his eye on everything and directs everything." '

I had listened coolly to him, indeed I had grown cooler and cooler while he went on. On the table I had piled up all the copies of my pamphlet in my possession. Only a few were missing, for during the past week I had sent out a circular demanding the return of all the copies distributed, and had received most of them back. True, from several quarters I had got very polite notes saying that So-and-so could not remember having received such a pamphlet, and that, if it had actually arrived, he was sorry to confess that he must have lost it. Even that was gratifying; in my heart I desired nothing better. Only one reader begged me to let him keep the pamphlet as a curiosity, pledging himself, in accordance with the spirit of my circular, to show it to no one for twenty years. The village teacher had not yet seen my circular. I was glad that his words made it so easy for me to show it to him. I could do that without anxiety in any case, however, as I had drawn it up very circumspectly, keeping his interests in mind the whole time. The crucial passage in the circular ran as follows: 'I do not ask for the return of the pamphlet because I retract in any way the opinions defended there or wish them to be regarded as erroneous or even undemonstrable on any point. My request has purely personal and moreover very urgent grounds; but no conclusion whatever must be drawn from it as regards my attitude to the whole matter. I beg to draw your particular attention to this, and would be glad also if you would make the fact better known.'

For the time being I kept my hand over the circular and said: 'You reproach me in your heart because things have not turned out as you hoped. Why do that? Don't let us embitter our last moments together. And do try to see that, though you've made a discovery, it isn't necessarily greater than every other discovery, and consequently the injustice you suffer under any greater than other injustices. I don't know the ways of learned societies, but I can't believe that in the most favorable circumstances you would have been given a reception even remotely resembling the one you seem to have described to your wife. While I myself still hoped that something might come of my pamphlet, the most I expected was that perhaps the attention of a professor might be drawn to our case, that he might commission some young student to inquire into it, that this student might visit you and check in his own fashion your and my inquiries once more on the spot, and that finally, if the results seemed to him worth consideration – we must not forget that all young students are full of skepticism – he might bring out a pamphlet of his own in which your discoveries would be put on a scientific basis. All the same, even if that hope had been realized nothing very much would have been achieved. The student's pamphlet, supporting such queer opinions, would probably be held up to ridicule. If you take this agricultural journal as a sample, you can see how easily that may happen; and scientific periodicals are still more ruthless in such matters. And that's quite understandable; professors bear a great responsibility toward themselves, toward science, toward posterity; they can't take every new discovery to their bosoms straight away. We others have the advantage of them there. But I'll leave that out of account and assume that the student's pamphlet has found acceptance. What would happen next? You would probably receive honorable mention, and that might perhaps benefit your profession too; people would say: 'Our village schoolmasters have sharp eyes'; and this journal, if journals have a memory or a conscience, would be forced to make you a public apology; also some well-intentioned professor would be found to secure a scholarship for you; it's possible they might even get you to come to the city, find a post for you in some school, and so give you a chance of using the scientific resources of a city so as to improve yourself. But if I am to be quite frank, I think they would content themselves with merely trying to do all this. They would summon you and you would appear, but only as an ordinary petitioner like hundreds of others, and not in solemn state; they would talk to you and praise your honest efforts, but they would see at the same time that you were an old man, that it was hopeless for anyone to begin to study science at such an age, and moreover that you had hit upon your discovery more by chance than by design, and had besides no ambition to extend your labors beyond this one case. For these reasons they would probably send you back to your village again. Your discovery, of course, would be carried further, for it is not so trifling that, once having achieved recognition, it could be forgotten again. But you would not hear much more about it, and what you heard you would scarcely understand. Every new discovery is assumed at once into the sum total of knowledge, and with that ceases in a sense to be a discovery; it dissolves into the whole and disappears, and one must have a trained scientific eye even to recognize it after that. For it is related to fundamental axioms of whose existence we don't even know, and in the debates of science it is raised on these axioms into the very clouds. How can we expect to understand such things? Often as we listen to some learned discussion we may be under the impression that it is about your discovery, when it is about something quite different, and the next time, when we think it is about something else, and not about your discovery at all, it may turn out to be about that and that alone.

'Don't you see that? You would remain in your village, you would be able with the extra money to feed and clothe your family a little better; but your discovery would be taken out of your hands, and without your being able with any show of justice to object; for only in the city could it be given its final seal. And people wouldn't be altogether ungrateful to you, they might build a little museum on the spot where the discovery was made, it would become one of the sights of the village, you would be given the keys to keep, and, so that you shouldn't lack some outward token of honor, they could give you a little medal to wear on the breast of your coat, like those worn by attendants in scientific institutions. All this might have been possible; but was it what you wanted?'

Without stopping to consider his answer he turned on me and said: 'And so that's what you wanted to achieve for me?'

'Probably,' I said, 'I didn't consider what I was doing

carefully enough at the time to be able to answer that clearly now. I wanted to help you, but that was a failure, and the worst failure I have ever had. That's why I want to withdraw now and undo what I've done as far as I'm able.'

'Well and good,' said the teacher, taking out his pipe and beginning to fill it with the tobacco that he carried loose in all his pockets. 'You took up this thankless business of your own free will, and now of your own free will you withdraw. So that's all right.'

'I'm not an obstinate man,' I said. 'Do you find anything to object to in my proposal?'

'No, absolutely nothing,' said the schoolmaster, and his pipe was already going. I could not bear the stink of his tobacco, and so I rose and began to walk up and down the room. From previous encounters I was used to the teacher's extreme taciturnity, and to the fact that in spite of it he never seemed to have any desire to stir from my room once he was in it. That had often disturbed me before. He wants something more, I always thought at such times, and I would offer him money, which indeed he invariably accepted. Yet he never went away before it suited his convenience. Generally his pipe was smoked out by that time, then he would ceremoniously and respectfully push his chair in to the table, make a detour around it, seize his cane standing in the corner, press my hand warmly, and go. But today his silent presence as he sat there was an actual torture to me. When one has bidden a last farewell to someone, as I had done, a farewell accepted in good faith, surely the mutual formalities that remain should be got over as quickly as possible, and one should not burden one's host purposelessly with one's silent presence. As I contemplated the stubborn little old fellow from behind, while he sat at the table, it seemed an impossible idea ever to show him the door.

Translated by Willa and Edwin Muir

Blumfeld, an Elderly Bachelor

ONE EVENING Blumfeld, an elderly bachelor, was climbing up to his apartment – a laborious undertaking, for he lived on the sixth floor. While climbing up he thought, as he had so often recently, how unpleasant this utterly lonely life was: to reach his empty rooms he had to climb these six floors almost in secret, there put on his dressing gown, again almost in secret, light his pipe, read a little of the French magazine to which he had been subscribing for years, at the same time sip at a homemade kirsch, and finally, after half an hour, go to bed, but not before having completely rearranged his bedclothes which the unteachable charwoman would insist on arranging in her own way. Some companion, someone to witness these activities, would have been very welcome to Blumfeld. He had already been wondering whether he shouldn't acquire a little dog. These animals are gay and above all grateful and loyal; one of Blumfeld's colleagues has a dog of this kind; it follows no one but its master and when it hasn't seen him for a few moments it greets him at once with loud barkings, by which it is evidently trying to express its joy at once more finding that extraordinary benefactor, its master. True, a dog also has its drawbacks. However well kept it may be, it is bound to dirty the room. This just cannot be avoided; one cannot give it a hot bath each time before letting it into the room; besides, its health couldn't stand that. Blumfeld, on the other hand, can't stand dirt in his room. To him cleanliness is essential, and several times a week he is obliged to have words with his charwoman, who is unfortunately not very painstaking in this respect. Since she is hard of hearing he usually drags her by the arm to those spots in the room which he finds lacking in cleanliness. By this strict discipline he has achieved in his room a neatness more or less commensurate with his wishes. By acquiring a dog, however, he would be almost deliberately introducing into his room the dirt which hitherto he had been so careful to avoid. Fleas, the dog's constant companions, would appear. And once fleas were there, it would not be long before Blumfeld would be abandoning his comfortable room to the dog and looking for another one. Uncleanliness, however, is but one of the drawbacks of dogs. Dogs also fall ill and no one really understands dogs' diseases. Then the animal sits in a corner or limps about, whimpers, coughs, chokes from some pain; one wraps it in a rug, whistles a little melody, offers it milk – in short, one nurses it in the hope that this, as indeed is possible, is a passing sickness while it may be a serious, disgusting, and contagious disease. And even if the dog remains healthy, one day it will grow old, one won't have the heart to get rid of the faithful animal in time, and then comes the moment when one's own age peers out at one from the dog's oozing eyes. Then one has to cope with the half-blind, weak-lunged animal all but immobile with fat, and in this way pay dearly for the pleasures the dog once had given. Much as Blumfeld would like to have a dog at this moment, he would rather go on climbing the stairs alone for another thirty years than be burdened later on by such an old dog which, sighing louder than he, would drag itself up, step by step.

So Blumfeld will remain alone, after all; he really feels none of the old maid's longing to have around her some submissive living creature that she can protect, lavish her affection upon, and continue to serve – for which purpose a cat, a canary, even a goldfish would suffice – or, if this cannot be, rest content with flowers on the window sill. Blumfeld only wants a companion, an animal to which he doesn't have to pay much attention, which doesn't mind an occasional kick, which even, in an emergency, can spend the night in the street, but which nevertheless, when Blumfeld feels like it, is promptly at his disposal with its barking, jumping, and licking of hands. This is what Blumfeld wants, but since, as he realizes, it cannot be had without serious drawbacks, he renounces it, and yet – in accordance with his thoroughgoing disposition – the idea from time to time, this evening, for instance, occurs to him again.

While taking the key from his pocket outside his room, he is startled by a sound coming from within. A peculiar rattling sound, very lively but very regular. Since Blumfeld has just been thinking of dogs, it reminds him of the sounds produced by paws pattering one after the other over a floor. But paws don't rattle, so it can't be paws. He quickly unlocks the door and switches on the light. He is not prepared for what he sees. For this is magic – two small white celluloid balls with blue stripes jumping up and down side by side on the parquet; when one of them touches the floor the other is in the air, a game they continue ceaselessly to play. At school one day Blumfeld had seen some little pellets jumping about like this during a well-known electrical experiment, but these are comparatively large balls jumping freely about in the room and no electrical experiment is being made. Blumfeld bends down to get a good look at them. They are undoubtedly ordinary balls, they probably contain several smaller balls, and it is these that produce the rattling sound. Blumfeld gropes in the air to find out whether they are hanging from some threads – no, they are moving entirely on their own. A pity Blumfeld isn't a small child, two balls like these would have been a happy surprise for him, whereas now the whole thing gives him rather an unpleasant feeling. It's not quite pointless after all to live in secret as an unnoticed bachelor, now someone, no matter who, has penetrated this secret and sent him these two strange balls.

He tries to catch one but they retreat before him, thus luring him on to follow them through the room. It's really too silly, he thinks, running after balls like this; he stands still and realizes that the moment he abandons the pursuit, they too remain on the same spot. I will try to catch them all the same, he thinks again, and hurries toward them. They immediately run away, but Blumfeld, his legs apart, forces them into a corner of the room, and there, in front of a trunk, he manages to catch one ball. It's a small cool ball, and it turns in his hand, clearly anxious to slip away. And the other ball, too, as though aware of its comrade's distress, jumps higher than before, extending the leaps until it touches Blumfeld's hand. It beats against his hand, beats in ever faster leaps, alters its angle of attack, then, powerless against the hand which encloses the ball so completely, springs even higher and is probably trying to reach Blumfeld's face. Blumfeld could catch this ball too, and lock them both up somewhere, but at the moment it strikes him as too humiliating to take such measures against two little balls. Besides, it's fun owning these balls, and soon enough they'll grow tired, roll under the cupboard, and be quiet. Despite this deliberation, however, Blumfeld, near to anger, flings the ball to the ground, and it is a miracle that in doing so the delicate, all but transparent celluloid cover doesn't break. Without hesitation the two balls resume their former low, well-coordinated jumps.

Blumfeld undresses calmly, arranges his clothes in the wardrobe which he always inspects carefully to make sure the charwoman has left everything in order. Once or twice he glances over his shoulder at the balls, which, unpursued, seem to be pursuing him; they have followed him and are now jumping close behind him. Blumfeld puts on his dressing gown and sets out for the opposite wall to fetch one of the pipes which are hanging in a rack. Before turning around he instinctively kicks his foot out backwards, but the balls know how to get out of its way and remain untouched. As Blumfeld goes off to fetch the pipe the balls at once follow close behind him; he shuffles along in his slippers, taking irregular steps, yet each step is followed almost without pause by the sound of the balls; they are keeping pace with him. To see how the balls manage to do this, Blumfeld turns suddenly around. But hardly has he turned when the balls describe a semicircle and are already behind him again, and this they repeat every time he turns. Like submissive companions, they try to avoid appearing in front of Blumfeld. Up to the present they have evidently dared to do so only in order to introduce themselves; now, however, it seems they have actually entered into his service.

Hitherto, when faced with situations he couldn't master, Blumfeld had always chosen to behave as though he hadn't noticed anything. It had often helped and usually improved the situation. This, then, is what he does now; he takes up a position in front of the pipe rack and, puffing out his lips, chooses a pipe, fills it with particular care from the tobacco pouch close at hand, and allows the balls to continue their jumping behind him. But he hesitates to approach the table, for to hear the sound of the jumps coinciding with that of his own steps almost hurts him. So there he stands, and while taking an unnecessarily long time to fill his pipe he measures the distance separating him from the table. At last, however, he overcomes his faintheartedness and covers the distance with such stamping of feet that he cannot hear the balls. But the moment he is seated he can hear them jumping up and down behind his chair as distinctly as ever.

Above the table, within reach, a shelf is nailed to the wall on which stands the bottle of kirsch surrounded by little glasses. Beside it, in a pile, lie several copies of the French magazine. (This very day the latest issue has arrived and Blumfeld takes it down. He quite forgets the kirsch; he even has the feeling that today he is proceeding with his usual activities only to console himself, for he feels no genuine desire to read. Contrary to his usual habit of carefully turning one page after the other, he opens the magazine at random and there finds a large photograph. He forces himself to examine it in detail. It shows a meeting between the Czar of Russia and the President of France. This takes place on a ship. All about as far as can be seen are many other ships, the smoke from their funnels vanishing in the bright sky. Both Czar and President have rushed toward each other with long strides and are clasping one another by the hand. Behind the Czar as well as behind the President stand two men. By comparison with the gay faces of the Czar and the President, the faces of their attendants are very solemn, the eyes of each group focused on their master. Lower down – the scene evidently takes place on the top deck – stand long lines of saluting sailors cut off by the margin. Gradually Blumfeld contemplates the picture with more interest, then holds it a little further away and looks at it with blinking eyes. He has always had a taste for such imposing scenes. The way the chief personages clasp each other's hand so naturally, so cordially and lightheartedly, this he finds most lifelike. And it's just as appropriate that the attendants – high-ranking gentlemen, of course, with their names printed beneath – express in their bearing the solemnity of the historical moment.)

And instead of helping himself to everything he needs, Blumfeld sits there tense, staring at the bowl of his still unlit pipe. He is lying in wait. Suddenly, quite unexpectedly, his numbness leaves him and with a jerk he turns around in his chair. But the balls, equally alert, or perhaps automatically following the law governing them, also change their position the moment Blumfeld turns, and hide behind his back. Blumfeld now sits with his back to the table, the cold pipe in his hand. And now the balls jump under the table and, since there's a rug there, they are less audible. This is a great advantage: only faint, hollow noises can be heard, one has to pay great attention to catch their sound. Blumfeld, however, does pay great attention, and hears them distinctly. But this is so only for the moment, in a little while he probably won't hear them anymore. The fact that they cannot make themselves more audible on the rug strikes Blumfeld as a great weakness on the part of the balls. What one has to do is lay one or even better two rugs under them and they are all but powerless. Admittedly only for a limited time, and besides, their very existence wields a certain power.

Right now Blumfeld could have made good use of a dog, a wild young animal would soon have dealt with these balls; he imagines this dog trying to catch them with its paws, chasing them from their positions, hunting them all over the room, and finally getting hold of them between its teeth. It's quite possible that before long Blumfeld will acquire a dog.

For the moment, however, the balls have no one to fear but Blumfeld, and he has no desire to destroy them just now, perhaps he lacks the necessary determination. He comes home in the evening tired from work and just when he is in need of some rest he is faced with this surprise. Only now does he realize how tired he really is. No doubt he will destroy the balls, and that in the near future, but not just yet, probably not until tomorrow. If one looks at the whole thing with an unprejudiced eye, the balls behave modestly enough. From time to time, for instance, they could jump into the foreground, show themselves, and then return again to their positions, or they could jump higher so as to beat against the tabletop in order to compensate themselves for the muffling effect of the rug. But this they don't do, they don't want to irritate Blumfeld unduly, they are evidently confining themselves to what is absolutely necessary.

Even this measured necessity, however, is quite sufficient to spoil Blumfeld's rest at the table. He has been sitting there only a few minutes and is already considering going to bed. One of his motives for this is that he can't smoke here, for he has left the matches on his bedside table. Thus he would have to fetch these matches, but once having reached the bedside table he might as well stay there and lie down. For this he has an ulterior motive: he thinks that the balls, with their mania for keeping behind him, will jump onto the bed, and that there, in lying down, on purpose or not, he will squash them. The objection that what would then remain of the balls could still go on jumping, he dismisses. Even the unusual must have its limits. Complete balls jump anyway, even if not incessantly, but fragments of balls never jump, and consequently will not jump in this case, either. 'Up!' he shouts, having grown almost reckless from this reflection and, the balls still behind him, he stamps off to bed. His hope seems to be confirmed, for when he purposely takes up a position quite near the bed, one ball promptly springs onto it. Then, however, the unexpected occurs: the other ball disappears under the bed. The possibility that the balls could jump under the bed as well had not occurred to Blumfeld. He is outraged about the one ball, although he is aware how unjust this is, for by jumping under the bed the ball fulfills its duty perhaps better than the ball on the bed. Now everything depends on which place the balls decide to choose, for Blumfeld does not believe that they can work separately for any length of time. And sure enough a moment later the ball on the floor also jumps onto the bed. Now I've got them, thinks Blumfeld, hot with joy, and tears his dressing gown from his body to throw himself into bed. At that moment, however, the very same ball jumps back under the bed. Overwhelmed with disappointment, Blumfeld almost collapses. Very likely the ball just took a good look around up there and decided it didn't like it. And now the other one has followed, too, and of course remains, for it's better down there. 'Now I'll have these drummers with me all night,' thinks Blumfeld, biting his lips and nodding his head.

He feels gloomy, without actually knowing what harm the balls could do him in the night. He is a good sleeper, he will easily be able to ignore so slight a noise. To make quite sure of this and mindful of his past experience, he lays two rugs on the floor. It's as if he owned a little dog for which he wants to make a soft bed. And as though the balls had also grown tired and sleepy, their jumping has become lower and slower than before. As Blumfeld kneels beside the bed, lamp in hand, he thinks for a moment that the balls might come to rest on the rug – they fall so weakly, roll so slowly along. Then, however, they dutifully rise again. Yet it is quite possible that in the morning when Blumfeld looks under the bed he'll find there two quiet, harmless children's balls.

But it seems that they may not even be able to keep up their jumping until the morning, for as soon as Blumfeld is in bed he doesn't hear them anymore. He strains his ears, leans out of bed to listen – not a sound. The effect of the rugs can't be as strong as that; the only explanation is that the balls are no longer jumping, either because they aren't able to bounce themselves off the rug and have therefore abandoned jumping for the time being or, which is more likely, they will never jump again. Blumfeld could get up and see exactly what's going on, but in his relief at finding peace at last he prefers to remain where he is. He would rather not risk disturbing the pacified balls even with his eyes. Even smoking he happily renounces, turns over on his side, and promptly goes to sleep.

But he does not remain undisturbed; as usual he sleeps without dreaming, but very restlessly. Innumerable times during the night he is startled by the delusion that someone is knocking at his door. He knows quite well that no one is knocking; who would knock at night and at his lonely bachelor's door? Yet although he knows this for certain, he is startled again and again and each time glances in suspense at the door, his mouth open, eyes wide, a strand of hair trembling over his damp forehead. He tries to count how many times he has been woken but, dizzy from the huge numbers he arrives at, he falls back to sleep again. He thinks he knows where the knocking comes from; not from the door, but somewhere quite different; being heavy with sleep, however, he cannot quite remember on what his suspicions are based. All he knows is that innumerable tiny unpleasant sounds accumulate before producing the great strong knocking. He would happily suffer all the unpleasantness of the small sounds if he could be spared the actual knocking, but for some reason it's too late; he cannot interfere, the moment has passed, he can't even speak, his mouth opens but all that comes out is a silent yawn, and furious at this he thrusts his face into the pillows. Thus the night passes.

In the morning he is awakened by the charwoman's knocking; with a sigh of relief he welcomes the gentle tap on the door whose inaudibility has in the past always been one of his sources of complaint. He is about to shout 'Come in!' when he hears another lively, faint, yet all but belligerent knocking. It's the balls under the bed. Have they woken up?

Have they, unlike him, gathered new strength overnight? 'Just a moment,' shouts Blumfeld to the charwoman, jumps out of bed, and, taking great care to keep the balls behind him, throws himself on the floor, his back still toward them; then, twisting his head over his shoulder, he glances at the balls and – nearly lets out a curse. Like children pushing away blankets that annoy them at night, the balls have apparently spent all night pushing the rugs, with tiny twitching movements, so far away from under the bed that they are now once more on the parquet, where they can continue making their noise. 'Back onto the rugs!' says Blumfeld with an angry face, and only when the balls, thanks to the rugs, have become quiet again, does he call in the charwoman. While she – a fat, dull-witted, stiff-backed woman – is laying the breakfast on the table and doing the few necessary chores, Blumfeld stands motionless in his dressing gown by his bed so as to keep the balls in their place. With his eyes he follows the charwoman to see whether she notices anything. This, since she is hard of hearing, is very unlikely, and the fact that Blumfeld thinks he sees the charwoman stopping here and there, holding on to some furniture and listening with raised eyebrows, he puts down to his overwrought condition caused by a bad night's sleep. It would relieve him if he could persuade the charwoman to speed up her work, but if anything she is slower than usual. She loads herself laboriously with Blumfeld's clothes and shuffles out with them into the corridor, stays away a long time, and the din she makes beating the clothes echoes in his ears with slow, monotonous thuds. And during all this time Blumfeld has to remain on the bed, cannot move for fear of drawing the balls behind him, has to let the coffee – which he likes to drink as hot as possible – get cold, and can do nothing but stare at the drawn blinds behind which the day is dimly dawning. At last the charwoman has finished, bids him good morning, and is about to leave; but before she actually goes she hesitates by the door, moves her lips a little, and takes a long look at Blumfeld. Blumfeld is about to remonstrate when she at last departs. Blumfeld longs to fling the door open and shout after her that she is a stupid, idiotic old woman. However, when he reflects on what he actually has against her, he can only think of the paradox of her having clearly noticed nothing and yet trying to give the impression that she has. How confused his thoughts have become! And all on account of a bad night. Some explanation for his poor sleep he finds in the fact that last night he deviated from his usual habits by not smoking or drinking any schnapps. When for once I don't smoke or drink schnapps – and this is the result of his reflections – I sleep badly.

From now on he is going to take better care of his health, and he begins by fetching some cotton wool from his medicine chest which hangs over his bedside table and putting two little wads of it into his ears. Then he stands up and takes a trial step. Although the balls do follow he can hardly hear them; the addition of another wad makes them quite inaudible. Blumfeld takes a few more steps; nothing particularly unpleasant happens. Everyone for himself, Blumfeld as well as the balls, and although they are bound to one another they don't disturb each other. Only once, when Blumfeld turns around rather suddenly and one ball fails to make the countermovement fast enough, does he touch it with his knee. But this is the only incident. Otherwise Blumfeld calmly drinks his coffee; he is as hungry as though, instead of sleeping last night, he had gone for a long walk; he washes in cold, exceedingly refreshing water, and puts on his clothes. He still hasn't pulled up the blinds; rather, as a precaution, he has preferred to remain in semidarkness; he has no wish for the balls to be seen by other eyes. But now that he is ready to go he has somehow to provide for the balls in case they should dare – not that he thinks they will – to follow him into the street. He thinks of a good solution, opens the large wardrobe, and places himself with his back to it. As though divining his intention, the balls steer clear of the wardrobe's interior, taking advantage of every inch of space between Blumfeld and the wardrobe; when there's no other alternative they jump into the wardrobe for a moment, but when faced by the dark out they promptly jump again. Rather than be lured over the edge further into the wardrobe, they neglect their duty and stay by Blumfeld's side. But their little ruses avail them nothing, for now Blumfeld himself climbs backward into the wardrobe and they have to follow him. And with this their fate has been sealed, for on the floor of the wardrobe lie various smallish objects such as boots, boxes, small trunks which, although carefully arranged – Blumfeld now regrets this – nevertheless considerably hamper the balls. And when Blumfeld, having by now pulled the door almost to, jumps out of it with an enormous leap such as he has not made for years, slams the door, and turns the key, the balls are imprisoned. 'Well, that worked,' thinks Blumfeld, wiping the sweat from his face. What a din the balls are making in the wardrobe! It sounds as though they are desperate. Blumfeld, on the other hand, is very contented. He leaves the room and already the deserted corridor has a soothing effect on him. He takes the wool out of his ears and is enchanted by the countless sounds of the waking house. Few people are to be seen, it's still very early.

Downstairs in the hall in front of the low door leading to the charwoman's basement apartment stands that woman's ten-year-old son. The image of his mother, not one feature of the woman has been omitted in this child's face. Bandy-legged, hands in his trouser pockets, he stands there wheezing, for he already has a goiter and can breathe only with difficulty. But whereas Blumfeld, whenever the boy crosses his path, usually quickens his step to spare himself the spectacle, today he almost feels like pausing for a moment. Even if the boy has been brought into the world by this woman and shows every sign of his origin, he is nevertheless a child, the thoughts of a child still dwell in this shapeless head, and if one were to speak to him sensibly and ask him something, he would very likely answer in a bright voice, innocent and reverential, and after some inner struggle one could bring oneself to pat these cheeks. Although this is what

Blumfeld thinks, he nevertheless passes him by. In the street he realizes that the weather is pleasanter than he had suspected from his room. The morning mist has dispersed and patches of blue sky have appeared, brushed by a strong wind. Blumfeld has the balls to thank for his having left his room much earlier than usual; even the paper he has left unread on the table; in any case he has saved a great deal of time and can now afford to walk slowly. It is remarkable how little he worries about the balls now that he is separated from them. So long as they were following him they could have been considered as something belonging to him, something which, in passing judgment on his person, had somehow to be taken into consideration. Now, however, they were mere toys in his wardrobe at home. And it occurs to Blumfeld that the best way of rendering the balls harmless would be to put them to their original use. There in the hall stands the boy; Blumfeld will give him the balls, not lend them, but actually present them to him, which is surely tantamount to ordering their destruction. And even if they were to remain intact they would mean even less in the boy's hands than in the wardrobe, the whole house would watch the boy playing with them, other children would join in, and the general opinion that the balls are things to play with and in no way life companions of Blumfeld would be firmly and irrefutably established. Blumfeld runs back into the house. The boy has just gone down the basement stairs and is about to open the door. So Blumfeld has to call the boy and pronounce his name, a name that to him seems as ludicrous as everything else connected with the child. 'Alfred! Alfred!' he shouts. The boy hesitates for a long time. 'Come here!' shouts Blumfeld, 'I've got something for you.' The janitor's two little girls appear from the door opposite and, full of curiosity, take up positions on either side of Blumfeld. They grasp the situation much more quickly than the boy and cannot understand why he doesn't come at once. Without taking their eyes off Blumfeld they beckon to the boy, but cannot fathom what kind of present is awaiting Alfred.

Tortured with curiosity, they hop from one foot to the other. Blumfeld laughs at them as well as at the boy. The latter seems to have figured it all out and climbs stiffly, clumsily up the steps. Not even in his gait can he manage to belie his mother, who, incidentally, has appeared in the basement doorway. To make sure that the charwoman also understands and in the hope that she will supervise the carrying out of his instructions, should it be necessary, Blumfeld shouts excessively loud. 'Up in my room,' says Blumfeld, 'I have two lovely balls. Would you like to have them?' Not knowing how to behave, the boy simply screws up his mouth, turns around, and looks inquiringly down at his mother. The girls, however, promptly begin to jump around Blumfeld and ask him for the balls. 'You will be allowed to play with them too,' Blumfeld tells them, but waits for the boy's answer. He could of course give the balls to the girls, but they strike him as too unreliable and for the moment he has more confidence in the boy. Meanwhile, the latter, without having exchanged a word, has taken counsel with his mother and nods his assent to Blumfeld's repeated question. 'Then listen,' says Blumfeld, who is quite prepared to receive no thanks for his gift. 'Your mother has the key of my door, you must borrow it from her. But here is the key of my wardrobe, and in the wardrobe you will find the balls. Take good care to lock the wardrobe and the room again. But with the balls you can do what you like and you don't have to bring them back. Have you understood me?' Unfortunately, the boy has not understood. Blumfeld has tried to make everything particularly clear to this hopelessly dense creature, but for this very reason has repeated everything too often, has in turn too often mentioned keys, room, and wardrobe, and as a result the boy stares at him as though he were rather a seducer than his benefactor. The girls, on the other hand, have understood everything immediately, press against Blumfeld, and stretch out their hands for the key. 'Wait a moment,' says Blumfeld, by now annoyed with them all. Time, moreover, is passing, he can't stand about much longer. If only the mother would say that she has understood him and take matters in hand for the boy! Instead of which she still stands down by the door, smiles with the affectation of the bashful deaf, and is probably under the impression that Blumfeld up there has suddenly fallen for the boy and is hearing him his lessons. Blumfeld on the other hand can't very well climb down the basement stairs and shout into the charwoman's ear to make her son for God's sake relieve him of the balls! It had required enough of his self-control as it was to entrust the key of his wardrobe for a whole day to this family. It is certainly not in order to save himself trouble that he is handing the key to the boy rather than himself leading the boy up and there giving him the balls. But he can't very well first give the balls away and then immediately deprive the boy of them by – as would be bound to happen – drawing them after him as his followers. 'So you still don't understand me?' asks Blumfeld almost wistfully after having started a fresh explanation which, however, he immediately interrupts at sight of the boy's vacant stare. So vacant a stare renders one helpless. It could tempt one into saying more than one intends, if only to fill the vacancy with sense. Whereupon 'We'll fetch the balls for him!' shout the girls. They are shrewd and have realized that they can obtain the balls only through using the boy as an intermediary, but that they themselves have to bring about this mediation. From the janitor's room a clock strikes, warning Blumfeld to hurry. 'Well, then, take the key,' says Blumfeld, and the key is more snatched from his hand than given by him. He would have handed it to the boy with infinitely more confidence. 'The key to the room you'll have to get from the woman,' Blumfeld adds. 'And when you return with the balls you must hand both keys to her.' 'Yes, yes!' shout the girls and run down the steps. They know everything, absolutely everything; and as though Blumfeld were infected by the boy's denseness, he is unable to understand how they could have grasped everything so quickly from his explanations.

Now they are already tugging at the charwoman's skirt

but, tempting as it would be, Blumfeld cannot afford to watch them carrying out their task, not only because it's already late, but also because he has no desire to be present at the liberation of the balls. He would in fact far prefer to be several streets away when the girls first open the door of his room. After all, how does he know what else he might have to expect from these balls! And so for the second time this morning he leaves the house. He has one last glimpse of the charwoman defending herself against the girls, and of the boy stirring his bandy legs to come to his mother's assistance. It's beyond Blumfeld's comprehension why a creature like this servant should prosper and propagate in this world.

While on his way to the linen factory, where Blumfeld is employed, thoughts about his work gradually get the upper hand. He quickens his step and, despite the delay caused by the boy, he is the first to arrive in his office. This office is a glass-enclosed room containing a writing desk for Blumfeld and two standing desks for the two assistants subordinate to him. Although these standing desks are so small and narrow as to suggest they are meant for schoolchildren, this office is very crowded and the assistants cannot sit down, for then there would be no place for Blumfeld's chair. As a result they stand all day, pressed against their desks. For them of course this is very uncomfortable, but it also makes it very difficult for Blumfeld to keep an eye on them. They often press eagerly against their desks not so much in order to work as to whisper to one another or even to take forty winks. They give Blumfeld a great deal of trouble; they don't help him sufficiently with the enormous amount of work that is imposed on him. This work involves supervising the whole distribution of fabrics and cash among the women home-workers who are employed by the factory for the manufacture of certain fancy commodities. To appreciate the magnitude of this task an intimate knowledge of the general conditions is necessary. But since Blumfeld's immediate superior has died some years ago, no one any longer possesses this knowledge, which is also why Blumfeld cannot grant anyone the right to pronounce an opinion on his work. The manufacturer, Herr Ottomar, for instance, clearly underestimates Blumfeld's work; no doubt he recognizes that in the course of twenty years Blumfeld has deserved well of the factory, and this he acknowledges not only because he is obliged to, but also because he respects Blumfeld as a loyal, trustworthy person. – He underestimates his work, nevertheless, for he believes it could be conducted by methods more simple and therefore in every respect more profitable than those employed by Blumfeld. It is said, and it is probably not incorrect, that Ottomar shows himself so rarely in Blumfeld's department simply to spare himself the annoyance that the sight of Blumfeld's working methods causes him. To be so unappreciated is undoubtedly sad for Blumfeld, but there is no remedy, for he cannot very well compel Ottomar to spend let us say a whole month on end in Blumfeld's department in order to study the great variety of work being accomplished there, to apply his own allegedly better methods, and to let himself be convinced of Blumfeld's soundness by the collapse of the department – which would be the inevitable result. And so Blumfeld carries on his work undeterred as before, gives a little start whenever Ottomar appears after a long absence, then with the subordinate's sense of duty makes a feeble effort to explain to Ottomar this or that arrangement, whereupon the latter, his eyes lowered and giving a silent nod, passes on. But what worries Blumfeld more than this lack of appreciation is the thought that one day he will be compelled to leave his job, the immediate consequence of which will be pandemonium, a confusion no one will be able to straighten out because so far as he knows there isn't a single soul in the factory capable of replacing him and of carrying on his job in a manner that could be relied upon to prevent months of the most serious interruptions. Needless to say, if the boss underestimates an employee the latter's colleagues try their best to surpass him in this respect. In consequence everyone underestimates Blumfeld's work; no one considers it necessary to spend any time training in Blumfeld's department, and when new employees are hired not one of them is ever assigned to Blumfeld. As a result Blumfeld's department lacks a younger generation to carry on. When Blumfeld, who up to then had been managing the entire department with the help of only one servant, demanded an assistant, weeks of bitter fighting ensued. Almost every day Blumfeld appeared in Ottomar's office and explained to him calmly and in minute detail why an assistant was needed in his department. He was needed not by any means because Blumfeld wished to spare himself, Blumfeld had no intention of sparing himself, he was doing more than his share of work and this he had no desire to change, but would Herr Ottomar please consider how in the course of time the business had grown, how every department had been correspondingly enlarged, with the exception of Blumfeld's department, which was invariably forgotten! And would he consider too how the work had increased just there! When Blumfeld had entered the firm, a time Herr Ottomar probably could not remember, they had employed some ten seamstresses, today the number varied between fifty and sixty. Such a job requires great energy; Blumfeld could guarantee that he was completely wearing himself out in this work, but that he will continue to master it completely he can henceforth no longer guarantee. True, Herr Ottomar had never flatly refused Blumfeld's requests, this was something he could not do to an old employee, but the manner in which he hardly listened, in which he talked to others over Blumfeld's head, made halfhearted promises and had forgotten everything in a few days – this behavior was insulting, to say the least. Not actually to Blumfeld, Blumfeld is no romantic, pleasant as honor and recognition may be, Blumfeld can do without them, in spite of everything he will stick to his desk as long as it is at all possible, in any case he is in the right, and right, even though on occasion it may take a long time, must prevail in the end. True, Blumfeld has at last been given two assistants, but what assistants! One might have thought Ottomar had realized he could express his contempt for the department even better by granting rather than by refusing it these assistants. It was even possible that Ottomar had kept Blumfeld waiting so long because he was looking for two assistants just like these, and – as may be imagined – took a long time to find them. And now of course Blumfeld could no longer complain; if he did, the answer could easily be foreseen: after all, he had asked for one assistant and had been given two, that's how cleverly Ottomar had arranged things. Needless to say, Blumfeld complained just the same, but only because his predicament all but forced him to do so, not because he still hoped for any redress. Nor did he complain emphatically, but only by the way, whenever the occasion arose. Nevertheless, among his spiteful colleagues the rumor soon spread that someone had asked Ottomar if it were really possible that Blumfeld, who after all had been given such unusual aid, was still complaining. To which Ottomar answered that this was correct, Blumfeld was still complaining, and rightly so. He, Ottomar, had at last realized this and he intended gradually to assign to Blumfeld one assistant for each seamstress, in other words some sixty in all. In case this number should prove insufficient, however, he would let him have even more and would not cease until the bedlam, which had been developing for years in Blumfeld's department, was complete. Now it cannot be denied that in this remark Ottomar's manner of speech had been cleverly imitated, but Blumfeld had no doubts whatever that Ottomar would not dream of speaking about him in such a way. The whole thing was a fabrication of the loafers in the offices on the first floor. Blumfeld ignored it – if only he could as calmly have ignored the presence of the assistants! But there they stood, and could not be spirited away. Pale, weak children. According to their credentials they had already passed school age, but in reality this was difficult to believe. In fact their rightful place was so clearly at their mother's knee that one would hardly have dared to entrust them to a teacher. They still couldn't even move properly;

standing up for any length of time tired them inordinately, especially when they first arrived. When left to themselves they promptly doubled up in their weakness, standing hunched and crooked in their corner. Blumfeld tried to point out to them that if they went on giving in to their indolence they would become cripples for life. To ask the assistants to make the slightest move was to take a risk; once when one of them had been ordered to carry something a short distance, he had run so eagerly that he had banged his knee against a desk. The room had been full of seamstresses, the desks covered in merchandise, but Blumfeld had been obliged to neglect everything and take the sobbing assistant into the office and there bandage his wound. Yet even this zeal on the part of the assistant was superficial; like actual children they tried once in a while to excel, but far more often – indeed almost always – they tried to divert their superior's attention and to cheat him. Once, at a time of the most intensive work, Blumfeld had rushed past them, dripping with sweat, and had observed them secretly swapping stamps among the bales of merchandise. He had felt like banging them on the head with his fists, it would have been the only possible punishment for such behavior, but they were after all only children and Blumfeld could not very well knock children down. And so he continued to put up with them. Originally he had imagined that the assistants would help him with the essential chores which at the moment of the distribution of goods required so much effort and vigilance. He had imagined himself standing in the center behind his desk, keeping an eye on everything, and making the entries in the books while the assistants ran to and fro, distributing everything according to his orders. He had imagined that his supervision, which, sharp as it was, could not cope with such a crowd, would be complemented by the assistants' attention; he had hoped that these assistants would gradually acquire experience, cease depending entirely on his orders, and finally learn to discriminate on their own between the seamstresses as to their trustworthiness and requirements. Blumfeld soon realized that all these hopes had been in vain and that he could not afford to let them even talk to the seamstresses. From the beginning they had ignored some of the seamstresses, either from fear or dislike; others to whom they felt partial they would sometimes run to meet at the door. To them the assistants would bring whatever the women wanted, pressing it almost secretly into their hands, although the seamstresses were perfectly entitled to receive it, would collect on a bare shelf for these favorites various cuttings, worthless remnants, but also a few still useful odds and ends, waving them blissfully at the women behind Blumfeld's back and in return having sweets popped into their mouths. Blumfeld of course soon put an end to this mischief and the moment the seamstresses arrived he ordered the assistants back into their glass-enclosed cubicles. But for a long time they considered this to be a grave injustice, they sulked, willfully broke their nibs, and sometimes, although not daring to raise their heads, even knocked loudly against the glass panes in order to attract the seamstresses' attention to the bad treatment that in their opinion they were suffering at Blumfeld's hands.

The wrong they do themselves the assistants cannot see. For instance, they almost always arrive late at the office. Blumfeld, their superior, who from his earliest youth has considered it natural to arrive half an hour before the office opens – not from ambition or an exaggerated sense of duty but simply from a certain feeling of decency – often has to wait more than an hour for his assistants. Chewing his breakfast roll he stands behind his desk, looking through the accounts in the seamstresses' little books. Soon he is immersed in his work and thinking of nothing else when suddenly he receives such a shock that his pen continues to tremble in his hand for some while afterwards. One of the assistants has dashed in, looking as though he is about to collapse; he is holding on to something with one hand while the other is pressed against his heaving chest. All this, however, simply means that he is making excuses for being late, excuses so absurd that Blumfeld purposely ignores them, for if he didn't he would have to give the young man a well-deserved thrashing. As it is, he just glances at him for a moment, points with outstretched hand at the cubicle, and turns back to his work. Now one really might expect the assistant to appreciate his superior's kindness and hurry to his place. No, he doesn't hurry, he dawdles about, he walks on tiptoe, slowly placing one foot in front of the other. Is he trying to ridicule his superior? No. Again it's just that mixture of fear and self-complacency against which one is powerless. How else explain the fact that even today Blumfeld, who has himself arrived unusually late in the office and now after a long wait – he doesn't feel like checking the books – sees, through the clouds of dust raised by the stupid servant with his broom, the two assistants sauntering peacefully along the street? Arm in arm, they appear to be telling one another important things which, however, are sure to have only the remotest and very likely irreverent connections with the office. The nearer they approach the glass door, the slower they walk. One of them seizes the door handle but fails to turn it; they just go on talking, listening, laughing. 'Hurry out and open the door for our gentlemen!' shouts Blumfeld at the servant, throwing up his hands. But when the assistants come in, Blumfeld no longer feels like quarreling, ignores their greetings, and goes to his desk. He starts doing his accounts, but now and again glances up to see what his assistants are up to. One of them seems to be very tired and rubs his eyes. When hanging up his overcoat he takes the opportunity to lean against the wall. On the street he seemed lively enough, but the proximity of work tires him. The other assistant, however, is eager to work, but only work of a certain kind. For a long time it has been his wish to be allowed to sweep. But this is work to which he is not entitled; sweeping is exclusively the servant's job; in itself Blumfeld would have nothing against the assistant sweeping, let the assistant sweep, he can't make a worse job of it than the servant, but if the assistant wants to sweep then he must come earlier, before the servant begins to sweep, and not spend on it time that is reserved exclusively for office work. But since the young man is totally deaf to any sensible argument, at least the servant – that half-blind old buffer whom the boss would certainly not tolerate in any department but Blumfeld's and who is still alive only by the grace of the boss and God – at least the servant might be sensible and hand the broom for a moment to the young man who, being clumsy, would soon lose his interest and run after the servant with the broom in order to persuade him to go on sweeping. It appears, however, that the servant feels especially responsible for the sweeping; one can see how he, the moment the young man approaches him, tries to grasp the broom more firmly with his trembling hands; he even stands still and stops sweeping so as to direct his full attention to the ownership of the broom. The assistant doesn't actually plead in words, for he is afraid of Blumfeld, who is ostensibly doing his accounts; moreover, ordinary speech is useless, since the servant can be made to hear only by excessive shouting. So at first the assistant tugs the servant by the sleeve. The servant knows, of course, what it is about, glowers at the assistant, shakes his head, and pulls the broom nearer, up to his chest. Whereupon the assistant folds his hands and pleads. Actually, he has no hope of achieving anything by pleading, but the pleading amuses him and so he pleads. The other assistant follows the goings-on with low laughter and seems to think, heaven knows why, that Blumfeld can't hear him. The pleading makes not the slightest impression on the servant, who turns around and thinks he can safely use the broom again. The assistant, however, has skipped after him on tiptoe and, rubbing his hands together imploringly, now pleads from another side. This turning of the one and skipping of the other is repeated several times. Finally the servant feels cut off from all sides and realizes – something which, had he been slightly less stupid, he might have realized from the beginning – that he will be tired out long before the assistant. So, looking for help elsewhere, he wags his finger at the assistant and points at Blumfeld, suggesting that he will lodge a complaint if the assistant refuses to desist. The assistant realizes that if he is to get the broom at all he'll have to hurry, so he impudently makes a grab for it. An involuntary scream from the other assistant heralds the imminent decision. The servant saves the broom once more by taking a step back and dragging it after him. But now the assistant is up in arms: with open mouth and flashing eyes he leaps forward, the servant tries to escape, but his old legs wobble rather than run, the assistant tugs at the broom and though he doesn't succeed in getting it he nevertheless causes it to drop and in this way it is lost to the servant. Also apparently to the assistant for, the moment the broom falls, all three, the two assistants and the servant, are paralyzed, for now Blumfeld is bound to discover everything. And sure enough Blumfeld at his peephole glances up as though taking in the situation only now. He stares at each one with a stern and searching eye, even the broom on the floor does not escape his notice. Perhaps the silence has lasted too long or perhaps the assistant can no longer suppress his desire to sweep, in any case he bends down – albeit very carefully, as though about to grab an animal rather than a broom – seizes it, passes it over the floor, but, when Blumfeld jumps up and steps out of his cubicle, promptly casts it aside in alarm. 'Both of you back to work! And not another sound out of you!' shouts Blumfeld, and with an outstretched hand he directs the two assistants back to their desks. They obey at once, but not shamefaced or with lowered heads, rather they squeeze themselves stiffly past Blumfeld, staring him straight in the eye as though trying in this way to stop him from beating them. Yet they might have learned from experience that Blumfeld on principle never beats anyone. But they are overapprehensive, and without any tact keep trying to protect their real or imaginary rights.

Translated by Tania and James Stern

The Hunter Gracchus

TWO BOYS were sitting on the harbor wall playing with dice. A man was reading a newspaper on the steps of the monument, resting in the shadow of a hero who was flourishing his sword on high. A girl was filling her bucket at the fountain. A fruitseller was lying beside his wares, gazing at the lake. Through the vacant window and door openings of a café one could see two men quite at the back drinking their wine. The proprietor was sitting at a table in front and dozing. A bark was silently making for the little harbor, as if borne by invisible means over the water. A man in a blue blouse climbed ashore and drew the rope through a ring. Behind the boatman two other men in dark coats with silver buttons carried a bier, on which, beneath a great flower-patterned fringed silk cloth, a man was apparently lying.

Nobody on the quay troubled about the newcomers; even when they lowered the bier to wait for the boatman, who was still occupied with his rope, nobody went nearer, nobody asked them a question, nobody accorded them an inquisitive glance.

The pilot was still further detained by a woman who, a child at her breast, now appeared with loosened hair on the deck of the boat. Then he advanced and indicated a yellowish two-storeyed house that rose abruptly on the left near the water; the bearers took up their burden and bore it to the low but gracefully pillared door. A little boy opened a window just in time to see the party vanishing into the house, then hastily shut the window again. The door too was now shut; it was of black oak, and very strongly made. A flock of doves which had been flying around the belfry alighted in the street before the house. As if their food were stored within, they assembled in front of the door. One of them flew up to the first storey and pecked at the windowpane. They were bright-hued, well-tended, lively birds. The woman on the boat flung grain to them in a wide sweep; they ate it up and flew across to the woman.

A man in a top hat tied with a band of black crêpe now descended one of the narrow and very steep lanes that led to the harbor. He glanced around vigilantly, everything seemed to distress him, his mouth twisted at the sight of some offal in a corner. Fruit skins were lying on the steps of the monument; he swept them off in passing with his stick. He rapped at the house door, at the same time taking his top hat from his head with his black-gloved hand. The door was opened at once, and some fifty little boys appeared in two rows in the long entry hall, and bowed to him.

The boatman descended the stairs, greeted the gentleman in black, conducted him up to the first storey, led him around the bright and elegant loggia which encircled the courtyard, and both of them entered, while the boys pressed after them at a respectful distance, a cool spacious room looking toward the back, from whose window no habitation, but only a bare, blackish-gray rocky wall was to be seen. The bearers were busied in setting up and lighting several long candles at the head of the bier, yet these did not give light, but only disturbed the shadows which had been immobile till then, and made them flicker over the walls. The cloth covering the bier had been thrown back. Lying on it was a man with wildly matted hair, who looked somewhat like a hunter. He lay without motion and, it seemed, without breathing, his eyes closed; yet only his trappings indicated that this man was probably dead.

The gentleman stepped up to the bier, laid his hand on the brow of the man lying upon it, then kneeled down and prayed. The boatman made a sign to the bearers to leave the room; they went out, drove away the boys who had gathered outside, and shut the door. But even that did not seem to satisfy the gentleman, he glanced at the boatman; the boatman understood, and vanished through a side door into the next room. At once the man on the bier opened his eyes, turned his face painfully toward the gentleman, and said:

'Who are you?' Without any mark of surprise the gentleman rose from his kneeling posture and answered: 'The Burgomaster of Riva.'

The man on the bier nodded, indicated a chair with a feeble movement of his arm, and said, after the Burgomaster had accepted his invitation: 'I knew that, of course, Burgomaster, but in the first moments of returning consciousness I always forget, everything goes around before my eyes, and it is best to ask about anything even if I know. You too probably know that I am the Hunter Gracchus.'

'Certainly,' said the Burgomaster. 'Your arrival was announced to me during the night. We had been asleep for a good while. Then toward midnight my wife cried: "Salvatore" – that's my name – "look at that dove at the window." It was really a dove, but as big as a cock. It flew over me and said in my ear: "Tomorrow the dead Hunter Gracchus is coming; receive him in the name of the city." '

The Hunter nodded and licked his lips with the tip of his tongue: 'Yes, the doves flew here before me. But do you believe, Burgomaster, that I shall remain in Riva?'

'I cannot say that yet,' replied the Burgomaster. 'Are you dead?'

'Yes,' said the Hunter, 'as you see. Many years ago, yes, it must be a great many years ago, I fell from a precipice in the Black Forest – that is in Germany – when I was hunting a chamois. Since then I have been dead.'

'But you are alive too,' said the Burgomaster.

'In a certain sense,' said the Hunter, 'in a certain sense I am alive too. My death ship lost its way; a wrong turn of the wheel, a moment's absence of mind on the pilot's part, the distraction of my lovely native country, I cannot tell what it was; I only know this, that I remained on earth and that ever since my ship has sailed earthly waters. So I, who asked for nothing better than to live among my mountains, travel after my death through all the lands of the earth.'

'And you have no part in the other world?' asked the Burgomaster, knitting his brow.

'I am forever,' replied the Hunter, 'on the great stair that leads up to it. On that infinitely wide and spacious stair I clamber about, sometimes up, sometimes down, sometimes on the right, sometimes on the left, always in motion. The Hunter has been turned into a butterfly. Do not laugh.'

'I am not laughing,' said the Burgomaster in self-defense.

'That is very good of you,' said the Hunter. 'I am always in motion. But when I make a supreme flight and see the gate actually shining before me I awaken presently on my old ship, still stranded forlornly in some earthly sea or other. The fundamental error of my onetime death grins at me as I lie in my cabin. Julia, the wife of the pilot, knocks at the door and brings me on my bier the morning drink of the land whose coasts we chance to be passing. I lie on a wooden pallet, I wear – it cannot be a pleasure to look at me – a filthy winding sheet, my hair and beard, black tinged with gray, have grown together inextricably, my limbs are covered with a great flowered-patterned woman's shawl with long fringes. A sacramental candle stands at my head and lights me. On the wall opposite me is a little picture, evidently of a bushman who is aiming his spear at me and taking cover as best he can behind a beautifully painted shield. On shipboard one often comes across silly pictures, but that is the silliest of them all. Otherwise my wooden cage is quite empty. Through a hole in the side the warm airs of the southern night come in, and I hear the water slapping against the old boat.

'I have lain here ever since the time when, as the Hunter Gracchus living in the Black Forest, I followed a chamois and fell from a precipice. Everything happened in good order. I pursued, I fell, bled to death in a ravine, died, and this ship should have conveyed me to the next world. I can still remember how gladly I stretched myself out on this pallet for the first time. Never did the mountains listen to such songs from me as these shadowy walls did then.

'I had been glad to live and I was glad to die. Before I stepped aboard, I joyfully flung away my wretched load of ammunition, my knapsack, my hunting rifle that I had always been proud to carry, and I slipped into my winding sheet like a girl into her marriage dress. I lay and waited. Then came the mishap.'

'A terrible fate,' said the Burgomaster, raising his hand defensively. 'And you bear no blame for it?'

'None,' said the Hunter. 'I was a hunter; was there any sin in that? I followed my calling as a hunter in the Black Forest, where there were still wolves in those days. I lay in ambush, shot, hit my mark, flayed the skins from my victims: was there any sin in that? My labors were blessed. "The Great Hunter of the Black Forest" was the name I was given. Was there any sin in that?'

'I am not called upon to decide that,' said the Burgomaster, 'but to me also there seems to be no sin in such things. But then, whose is the guilt?'

'The boatman's,' said the Hunter. 'Nobody will read what I say here, no one will come to help me; even if all the people were commanded to help me, every door and window would remain shut, everybody would take to bed and draw the bedclothes over his head, the whole earth would become an inn for the night. And there is sense in that, for nobody knows of me, and if anyone knew he would not know where I could be found, and if he knew where I could be found, he would not know how to deal with me, he would not know how to help me. The thought of helping me is an illness that has to be cured by taking to one's bed.

'I know that, and so I do not shout to summon help, even though at moments – when I lose control over myself, as I have done just now, for instance – I think seriously of it. But to drive out such thoughts I need only look around me and verify where I am, and – I can safely assert – have been for hundreds of years.'

'Extraordinary,' said the Burgomaster, 'extraordinary. And now do you think of staying here in Riva with us?'

'I think not,' said the Hunter with a smile, and, to excuse himself, he laid his hand on the Burgomaster's knee. 'I am here, more than that I do not know, further than that I cannot go. My ship has no rudder, and it is driven by the wind that blows in the undermost regions of death.'

Translated by Willa and Edwin Muir

The Proclamation

IN OUR HOUSE, this vast building on the outskirts of the town, a tenement-house whose fabric is interspersed with indestructible medieval ruins, there were today distributed, on this foggy ice-cold winter morning, copies of the following proclamation:

To all my fellow-tenants.

I possess five toy rifles; they are hanging in my wardrobe, one on each hook. The first belongs to me, the others may be claimed by anyone who wishes; if there are more than four claimants the extra ones must bring their own rifles with them and deposit them in my wardrobe. For uniformity is essential, without uniformity we shall get nowhere. Incidentally, I have only rifles that are quite useless for any other purpose, the mechanism is broken, the corks are torn off, only the cocks still click. So it will not be difficult to obtain more such rifles if required. But in principle even people without rifles will be acceptable to begin with; at the decisive moment those of us who have rifles will rally round those who are unarmed. A tactical method that proved itself with the first American farmers against the Red Indians; why should it not prove successful here as well, since after all the conditions are similar? And so it is even possible to do without rifles permanently. And even the five rifles are not absolutely necessary, and it is only because they just happen to be there that they may as well be used. But should the four others not wish to carry them, then let them do without. In that case I alone, as the leader, will carry one. But we should have no leader, and so I too will break up my rifle or put it away.

That was the first proclamation. Nobody in our house has the time or the wish to read proclamations, let alone to think them over them over. Before long the little sheets of paper were floating in the current of filth that, starting from the attics and fed by all the corridors, pours down the staircase and there struggles with the opposing current that swirls up from below. But after a week there came a second proclamation:

Fellow-tenants!

So far nobody has sent in his name to me. Apart from the hours when I have to earn my living I have been continuously at home, and during the periods of my absence, when the door of my room has always been left open, there has been a sheet of paper on my table where anybody who wished could enter his name. Nobody has done so.

Translated by Malcolm Pasley

The Bridge

I WAS stiff and cold, I was a bridge, I lay over a ravine. My toes on one side, my fingers clutching the other, I had clamped myself fast into the crumbling clay. The tails of my coat fluttered at my sides. Far below brawled the icy trout stream. No tourist strayed to this impassable height, the bridge was not yet traced on any map. So I lay and waited; I could only wait. Without falling, no bridge, once spanned, can cease to be a bridge.

It was toward evening one day – was it the first, was it the thousandth? I cannot tell – my thoughts were always in confusion and perpetually moving in a circle. It was toward evening in summer, the roar of the stream had grown deeper, when I heard the sound of a human step! To me, to me. Straighten yourself, bridge, make ready, railless beams, to hold up the passenger entrusted to you. If his steps are uncertain, steady them unobtrusively, but if he stumbles show what you are made of and like a mountain god hurl him across to land.

He came, he tapped me with the iron point of his stick,

then he lifted my coattails with it and put them in order upon me. He plunged the point of his stick into my bushy hair and let it lie there for a long time, forgetting me no doubt while he wildly gazed around him. But then – I was just following him in thought over mountain and valley – he jumped with both feet on the middle of my body. I shuddered with wild pain, not knowing what was happening. Who was it? A child? A dream? A wayfarer? A suicide? A tempter? A destroyer? And I turned around so as to see him. A bridge to turn around! I had not yet turned quite around when I already began to fall, I fell and in a moment I was torn and transpierced by the sharp rocks which had always gazed up at me so peacefully from the rushing water.

Translated by Willa and Edwin Muir

The Great Wall of China

THE GREAT WALL OF CHINA was finished off at its northernmost corner. From the southeast and the southwest it came up in two sections that finally converged there. This principle of piecemeal construction was also applied on a smaller scale by both of the two great armies of labor, the eastern and the western. It was done in this way: gangs of some twenty workers were formed who had to accomplish a length, say, of five hundred yards of wall, while a similar gang built another stretch of the same length to meet the first. But after the junction had been made the construction of the wall was not carried on from the point, let us say, where this thousand yards ended; instead the two groups of workers were transferred to begin building again in quite different neighborhoods. Naturally in this way many great gaps were left, which were only filled in gradually and bit by bit, some, indeed, not till after the official announcement that the wall was finished. In fact it is said that there are gaps which have never been filled in at all, an assertion, however, that is probably merely one of the many legends to which the building of the wall gave rise, and which cannot be verified, at least by any single man with his own eyes and judgment, on account of the extent of the structure.

Now on first thoughts one might conceive that it would have been more advantageous in every way to build the wall continuously, or at least continuously within the two main divisions. After all, the wall was intended, as was universally proclaimed and known, to be a protection against the peoples of the north. But how can a wall protect if it is not a continuous structure? Not only can such a wall not protect, but what there is of it is in perpetual danger. These blocks of wall left standing in deserted regions could be easily pulled down again and again by the nomads, especially as these tribes, rendered apprehensive by the building operations, kept changing their encampments with incredible rapidity, like locusts, and so perhaps had a better general view of the progress of the wall than we, the builders. Nevertheless the task of construction probably could not have been carried out in any other way. To understand this we must take into account the following: the wall was to be a protection for centuries; accordingly, the most scrupulous care in the building, the application of the architectural wisdom of all known ages and peoples, an unremitting sense of personal responsibility in the builders were indispensable prerequisites for the work. True, for the more purely manual tasks ignorant day laborers from the populace, men, women, and children who offered their services for good money, could be employed; but for the supervision even of every four day laborers an expert versed in the art of building was required, a man who was capable of entering into and feeling with all his heart what was involved. And the higher the task, the greater the responsibility. And such men were actually to be had, if not indeed so abundantly as the work of construction could have absorbed, yet in great numbers.

For the work had not been undertaken without thought. Fifty years before the first stone was laid, the art of architecture, and especially that of masonry, had been proclaimed as the most important branch of knowledge throughout the whole area of a China that was to be walled around, and all other arts gained recognition only insofar as they had reference to it. I can still remember quite well us standing as small children, scarcely sure on our feet, in our teacher's garden, and being ordered to build a sort of wall out of pebbles; and then the teacher, girding up his robe, ran full tilt against the wall, of course knocking it down, and scolded us so terribly for the shoddiness of our work that we ran weeping in all directions to our parents. A trivial incident, but significant of the spirit of the time.

I was lucky inasmuch as the building of the wall was just beginning when, at twenty, I had passed the last examination of the lowest school. I say lucky, for many who before my time had achieved the highest degree of culture available to them could find nothing year after year to do with their knowledge, and drifted uselessly about with the most splendid architectural plans in their heads, and sank by thousands into hopelessness. But those who finally came to be employed in the work as supervisors, even though it might be of the lowest rank, were truly worthy of their task. They were masons who had reflected much, and did not cease to reflect, on the building of the wall, men who with the first stone they sank in the ground felt themselves a part of the wall. Masons of that kind, of course, had not only a desire to perform their work in the most thorough manner, but were also impatient to see the wall finished in its complete perfection. Day laborers have not this impatience, for they look only to their wages, and the higher supervisors, indeed even the supervisors of middle rank, could see enough of the manifold growth of the construction to keep their spirits confident and high. But to encourage the subordinate supervisors, intellectually so vastly superior to their apparently petty tasks, other measures must be taken. One could not, for instance, expect them to lay one stone on another for months or even years on end, in an uninhabited mountainous region, hundreds of miles from their homes; the hopelessness of such hard toil, which yet could not reach completion even in the longest lifetime, would have cast them into despair and above all made them less capable for the work. It was for this reason that the system of piecemeal building was decided on. Five hundred yards could be accomplished in about five years; by that time, however, the supervisors were as a rule quite exhausted and had lost all faith in themselves, in the wall, in the world. Accordingly, while they were still exalted by the jubilant celebrations marking the completion of the thousand yards of wall, they were sent far, far away, saw on their journey finished sections of the wall rising here and there, came past the quarters of the high command and were presented with badges of honor, heard the rejoicings of new armies of labor streaming past from the depths of the land, saw forests being cut down to become supports for the wall, saw mountains being hewn into stones for the wall, heard at the holy shrines hymns rising in which the pious prayed for the completion of the wall. All this assuaged their impatience. The quiet life of their homes, where they rested some time, strengthened them; the humble credulity with which their reports were listened to, the confidence with which the simple and peaceful burgher believed in the eventual completion of the wall, all this filled their hearts with a new buoyancy. Like eternally hopeful children they then said farewell to their homes; the desire once more to labor on the wall of the nation became irresistible. They set off earlier than they needed; half the village accompanied them for long distances. Groups of people with banners and streamers waving were on all the roads; never before had they seen how great and rich and beautiful and worthy of love their country was. Every fellow countryman was a brother for whom one was building a wall of protection, and who would return lifelong thanks for it with all he had and did. Unity! Unity! Shoulder to shoulder, a ring of brothers, a current of blood no longer confined within the narrow circulation of one body, but sweetly rolling and yet ever returning throughout the endless leagues of China.

Thus, then, the system of piecemeal construction becomes comprehensible; but there were still other reasons for it as well. Nor is there anything odd in my pausing over this question for so long; it is one of the crucial problems in the whole building of the wall, unimportant as it may appear at first glance. If I am to convey and make understandable the ideas and feelings of that time I cannot go deeply enough into this very question.

First, then, it must be said that in those days things were achieved scarcely inferior to the construction of the Tower of Babel, although as regards divine approval, at least according to human reckoning, strongly at variance with that work. I say this because during the early days of building a scholar wrote a book in which he drew the comparison in the most exhaustive way. In it he tried to prove that the Tower of Babel failed to reach its goal, not because of the reasons universally advanced, or at least that among those recognized reasons the most important of all was not to be found. His proofs were drawn not merely from written documents and reports; he also claimed to have made inquiries on the spot, and to have discovered that the tower failed and was bound to fail because of the weakness of the foundation. In this respect at any rate our age was vastly superior to that ancient one. Almost every educated man of our time was a mason by profession and infallible in the matter of laying foundations. That, however, was not what our scholar was concerned to prove; for he maintained that the Great Wall alone would provide for the first time in the history of mankind a secure foundation for a new Tower of Babel. First the wall, therefore, and then the tower. His book was in everybody's hands at that time, but I admit that even today I cannot quite make out how he conceived this tower. How could the wall, which did not form even a circle, but only a sort of quarter- or half-circle, provide the foundation for a tower? That could obviously be meant only in a spiritual sense. But in that case why build the actual wall, which after all was something concrete, the result of the lifelong labor of multitudes of people? And why were there in the book plans, somewhat nebulous plans, it must be admitted, of the tower, and proposals worked out in detail for mobilizing the people's energies for the stupendous new work?

There were many wild ideas in people's heads at that time – this scholar's book is only one example – perhaps simply because so many were trying to join forces as far as they could for the achievement of a single aim. Human nature, essentially changeable, unstable as the dust, can endure no restraint; if it binds itself it soon begins to tear madly at its bonds, until it rends everything asunder, the wall, the bonds, and its very self.

It is possible that these very considerations, which militated against the building of the wall at all, were not left out of account by the high command when the system of piecemeal construction was decided on. We – and here I speak in the name of many people – did not really know ourselves until we had carefully scrutinized the decrees of the high command, when we discovered that without the high command neither our book learning nor our human understanding would have sufficed for the humble tasks which we performed in the great whole. In the office of the command – where it was and who sat there no one whom I have asked knew then or knows now – in that office one may be certain that all human thoughts and desires revolved in a circle, and all human aims and fulfillments in a countercircle. And through the window the reflected splendors of divine worlds fell on the hands of the leaders as they traced their plans.

And for that reason the incorruptible observer must hold that the command, if it had seriously desired it, could also have overcome those difficulties that prevented a system of continuous construction. There remains, therefore, nothing but the conclusion that the command deliberately chose the system of piecemeal construction. But the piecemeal construction was only a makeshift and therefore inexpedient. Remains the conclusion that the command willed something inexpedient. Strange conclusion! True, and yet in one respect it has much to be said for it. One can perhaps safely discuss it now. In those days many people, and among them the best, had a secret maxim which ran: Try with all your might to comprehend the decrees of the high command, but only up to a certain point; then avoid further meditation. A very wise maxim, which moreover was elaborated in a parable that was later often quoted: Avoid further meditation, but not because it might be harmful; it is not at all certain that it would be harmful. What is harmful or not harmful has nothing to do with the question. Consider rather the river in spring. It rises until it grows mightier and nourishes more richly the soil on the long stretch of its banks, still maintaining its own course until it reaches the sea, where it is all the more welcome because it is a worthier ally. Thus far may you urge your meditations on the decrees of the high command. But after that the river overflows its banks, loses outline and shape, slows down the speed of its current, tries to ignore its destiny by forming little seas in the interior of the land, damages the fields, and yet cannot maintain itself for long in its new expanse, but must run back between its banks again, must even dry up wretchedly in the hot season that presently follows. Thus far may you not urge your meditations on the decrees of the high command.

Now though this parable may have had extraordinary point and force during the building of the wall, it has at most only a restricted relevance for my present essay. My inquiry is purely historical; no lightning flashes any longer from the long since vanished thunderclouds, and so I may venture to seek for an explanation of the system of piecemeal construction which goes farther than the one that contented people then. The limits that my capacity for thought imposes upon me are narrow enough, but the province to be traversed here is infinite.

Against whom was the Great Wall to serve as a protection? Against the people of the north. Now, I come from the southeast of China. No northern people can menace us there. We read of them in the books of the ancients; the cruelties they commit in accordance with their nature make us sigh in our peaceful arbors. The faithful representations of the artist show us these faces of the damned, their gaping mouths, their jaws furnished with great pointed teeth, their half-shut eyes that already seem to be seeking out the victim which their jaws will rend and devour. When our children are unruly we show them these pictures, and at once they fly weeping into our arms. But nothing more than that do we know about these northerners. We have not seen them, and if we remain in our villages we shall never see them, even if on their wild horses they should ride as hard as they can straight toward us – the land is too vast and would not let them reach us, they would end their course in the empty air.

Why, then, since that is so, did we leave our homes, the stream with its bridges, our mothers and fathers, our weeping wives, our children who needed our care, and depart for the distant city to be trained there, while our thoughts journeyed still farther away to the wall in the north? Why? A question for the high command. Our leaders know us. They, absorbed in gigantic anxieties, know of us, know our petty pursuits, see us sitting together in our humble huts, and approve or disapprove the evening prayer which the father of the house recites in the midst of his family. And if I may be allowed to express such ideas about the high command, then I must say that in my opinion the high command has existed from old time, and was not assembled, say, like a gathering of mandarins summoned hastily to discuss somebody's fine dream in a conference as hastily terminated, so that that very evening the people are drummed out of their beds to carry out what has been decided, even if it should be nothing but an illumination in honor of a god who may have shown great favor to their masters the day before, only to drive them into some dark corner with cudgel blows tomorrow, almost before the illuminations have died down. Far rather do I believe that the high command has existed from all eternity, and the decision to build the wall likewise. Unwitting peoples of the north, who imagined they were the cause of it! Honest, unwitting Emperor, who imagined he decreed it! We builders of the wall know that it was not so and hold our tongues.

During the building of the wall and ever since to this very day I have occupied myself almost exclusively with the comparative history of races – there are certain questions that one can probe to the marrow, as it were, only by this method – and I have discovered that we Chinese possess certain folk and political institutions that are unique in their clarity, others again unique in their obscurity. The desire to trace the cause of these phenomena, especially the latter, has always intrigued me and intrigues me still, and the building of the wall is itself essentially involved with these problems.

Now one of the most obscure of our institutions is that

of the empire itself. In Peking, naturally, at the imperial court, there is some clarity to be found on this subject, though even that is more illusive than real. Also the teachers of political law and history in the schools of higher learning claim to be exactly informed on these matters, and to be capable of passing on their knowledge to their students. The farther one descends among the lower schools the more, naturally enough, does one find teachers' and pupils' doubts of their own knowledge vanishing, and superficial culture mounting sky-high around a few precepts that have been drilled into people's minds for centuries, precepts which, though they have lost nothing of their eternal truth, remain eternally invisible in this fog of confusion.

But it is precisely this question of the empire which in my opinion the common people should be asked to answer, since after all they are the empire's final support. Here, I must confess, I can only speak once more for my native place. Except for the nature gods, and their ritual which fills the whole year in such beautiful and rich alternation, we think only about the Emperor. But not about the present one; or rather we would think about the present one if we knew who he was or knew anything definite about him. True – and it is the sole curiosity that fills us – we are always trying to get information on this subject, but, strange as it may sound, it is almost impossible to discover anything, either from pilgrims, though they have wandered through much of our land, or from near or distant villages, or from sailors, though they have navigated not only our little stream, but also the sacred rivers. One hears a great many things, true, but can gather nothing definite.

So vast is our land that no fable could do justice to its vastness, the heavens can scarcely span it – and Peking is only a dot in it, and the imperial palace less than a dot. The Emperor as such, on the other hand, is mighty throughout all the hierarchies of the world: admitted. But the existent Emperor, a man like us, lies much like us on a couch which is of generous proportions, perhaps, and yet very possibly may be quite narrow and short. Like us he sometimes stretches himself and when he is very tired yawns with his delicately cut mouth. But how should we know anything about that – thousands of miles away in the south – almost on the borders of the Tibetan Highlands? And besides, any tidings, even if they did reach us, would arrive far too late, would have become obsolete long before they reached us. The Emperor is always surrounded by a brilliant and yet ambiguous throng of nobles and courtiers – malice and enmity in the guise of servants and friends – who form a counterweight to the imperial power and perpetually labor to unseat the ruler from his place with poisoned arrows. The Empire is immortal, but the Emperor himself totters and falls from his throne, yes, whole dynasties sink in the end and breathe their last in one death rattle. Of these struggles and sufferings the people will never know; like tardy arrivals, like strangers in a city, they stand at the end of some densely thronged side street peacefully munching the food they have brought with them, while far away in front, in the Market Square at the heart of the city, the execution of their ruler is proceeding.

There is a parable that describes this situation very well: The Emperor, so it runs, has sent a message to you, the humble subject, the insignificant shadow cowering in the remotest distance before the imperial sun; the Emperor from his deathbed has sent a message to you alone. He has commanded the messenger to kneel down by the bed, and has whispered the message to him; so much store did he lay on it that he ordered the messenger to whisper it back into his ear again. Then by a nod of the head he has confirmed that it is right. Yes, before the assembled spectators of his death – all the obstructing walls have been broken down, and on the spacious and loftily mounting open staircases stand in a ring the great princes of the Empire – before all these he has delivered his message. The messenger immediately sets out on his journey; a powerful, an indefatigable man; now pushing with his right arm, now with his left, he cleaves a way for himself through the throng; if he encounters resistance he points to his breast, where the symbol of the sun glitters; the way is made easier for him than it would be for any other man. But the multitudes are so vast; their numbers have no end. If he could reach the open fields how fast he would fly, and soon doubtless you would hear the welcome hammering of his fists on your door. But instead how vainly does he wear out his strength; still he is only making his way through the chambers of the innermost palace; never will he get to the end of them; and if he succeeded in that nothing would be gained; he must next fight his way down the stair; and if he succeeded in that nothing would be gained; the courts would still have to be crossed; and after the courts the second outer palace; and once more stairs and courts; and once more another palace; and so on for thousands of years; and if at last he should burst through the outermost gate – but never, never can that happen – the imperial capital would lie before him, the center of the world, crammed to bursting with its own sediment. Nobody could fight his way through here even with a message from a dead man. But you sit at your window when evening falls and dream it to yourself.

Just so, as hopelessly and as hopefully, do our people regard the Emperor. They do not know what Emperor is reigning, and there exist doubts regarding even the name of the dynasty. In school a great deal is taught about the dynasties with the dates of succession, but the universal uncertainty in this matter is so great that even the best scholars are drawn into it. Long-dead emperors are set on the throne in our villages, and one that only lives on in song recently had a proclamation of his read out by the priest before the altar. Battles that are old history are new to us, and one's neighbor rushes in with a jubilant face to tell the news. The wives of the emperors, pampered and overweening, seduced from noble custom by wily courtiers, swelling with ambition, vehement in their greed, uncontrollable in their lust, practice their abominations ever anew. The more deeply they are buried in time the more glaring are the colors in which their deeds are painted, and with a loud cry of woe our village eventually hears how an Empress drank her husband's blood in long draughts thousands of years ago.

Thus, then, do our people deal with departed emperors, but the living ruler they confuse among the dead. If once, only once in a man's lifetime, an imperial official on his tour of the provinces should arrive by chance at our village, make certain announcements in the name of the government, scrutinize the tax lists, examine the school children, inquire of the priest regarding our doings and affairs, and then, before he steps into his sedan chair, should sum up his impressions in verbose admonitions to the assembled commune – then a smile flits over every face, people throw surreptitious glances at each other, and bend over their children so as not to be observed by the official. Why, they think to themselves, he's speaking of a dead man as if he were alive, this Emperor of his died long ago, the dynasty is blotted out, the good official is having his joke with us, but we will behave as if we did not notice it, so as not to offend him. But we shall obey in earnest no one but our present ruler, for not to do so would be a crime. And behind the departing sedan chair of the official there rises in might as ruler of the village some figure fortuitously exalted from an urn already crumbled to dust.

Similarly our people are but little affected by revolutions in the state or contemporary wars. I recall an incident in my youth. A revolt had broken out in a neighboring, but yet quite distant, province. What caused it I can no longer remember, nor is it of any importance now; occasions for revolt can be found there any day, the people are an excitable people. Well, one day a leaflet published by the rebels was brought to my father's house by a beggar who had crossed that province. It happened to be a feast day, our rooms were filled with guests, the priest sat in the center and studied the sheet. Suddenly everybody started to laugh, in the confusion the sheet was torn, the beggar, who however had already received abundant alms, was driven out of the room with blows, the guests dispersed to enjoy the beautiful day. Why? The dialect of this neighboring province differs in some essential respects from ours, and this difference occurs also in certain turns of the written word, which for us have an archaic character. Hardly had the priest read two pages before we had come to our decision. Ancient history told long ago, old sorrows long since healed. And though – so it seems to me in recollection – the gruesomeness of the living present was irrefutably conveyed by the beggar's words, we laughed and shook our heads and refused to listen any longer. So eager are our people to obliterate the present.

If from such appearances anyone should draw the conclusion that in reality we have no Emperor, he would not be far from the truth. Over and over again it must be repeated: There is perhaps no people more faithful to the Emperor than ours in the south, but the Emperor derives no advantage from our fidelity. True, the sacred dragon stands on the little column at the end of our village, and ever since the beginning of human memory it has breathed out its fiery breath in the direction of Peking in token of homage – but Peking itself is far stranger to the people in our village than the next world. Can there really be a village where the houses stand side by side, covering all the fields for a greater distance than one can see from our hills, and can there be dense crowds of people packed between these houses day and night? We find it more difficult to picture such a city than to believe that Peking and its Emperor are one, a cloud, say, peacefully voyaging beneath the sun in the course of the ages.

Now the result of holding such opinions is a life on the whole free and unconstrained. By no means immoral, however; hardly ever have I found in my travels such pure morals as in my native village. But yet a life that is subject to no contemporary law, and attends only to the exhortations and warnings that come to us from olden times.

I guard against generalizations, and do not assert that in all the ten thousand villages in my province it is so, far less in all the five hundred provinces of China. Yet perhaps I may venture to assert on the basis of the many writings on this subject which I have read, as well as from my own observation – the building of the wall in particular, with its abundance of human material, provided a man of sensibility with the opportunity of traversing the souls of almost all the provinces – on the basis of all this, then, perhaps I may venture to assert that the prevailing attitude to the Emperor shows persistently and universally something fundamentally in common with that of our village. Now I have no wish whatever to represent this attitude as a virtue; on the contrary. True, the essential responsibility for it lies with the government, which in the most ancient empire in the world has not yet succeeded in developing, or has neglected to develop, the institution of the empire to such precision that its workings extend directly and unceasingly to the farthest frontiers of the land. On the other hand, however, there is also involved a certain feebleness of faith and imaginative power on the part of the people, that prevents them from raising the empire out of its stagnation in Peking and clasping it in all its palpable living reality to their own breasts, which yet desire nothing better than but once to feel that touch and then to die.

This attitude then is certainly no virtue. All the more remarkable is it that this very weakness should seem to be one of the greatest unifying influences among our people; indeed, if one may dare to use the expression, the very ground on which we live. To set about establishing a fundamental defect here would mean undermining not only our consciences, but, what is far worse, our feet. And for that reason I shall not proceed any further at this stage with my inquiry into these questions.

Translated by Willa and Edwin Muir

The Knock at the Manor Gate

IT WAS SUMMER, a hot day. With my sister I was passing the gate of a great house on our way home. I cannot tell now whether she knocked on the gate out of mischief or out of absence of mind, or merely threatened it with her fist and did not knock at all. A hundred paces further on along the road, which here turned to the left, began the village. We did not know it very well, but no sooner had we passed the first house when people appeared and made friendly or warning signs to us; they were themselves apparently terrified, bowed down with terror. They pointed toward the manor house that we had passed and reminded us of the knock on the gate. The proprietor of the manor would charge us with it, the interrogation would begin immediately. I remained quite calm and also tried to calm my sister's fears. Probably she had not struck the door at all, and if she had, nowhere in the world would that be a reason for prosecution. I tried to make this clear to the people around us; they listened to me but refrained from passing any opinion. Later they told me that not only my sister, but I too, as her brother, would be charged. I nodded and smiled. We all gazed back at the manor, as one watches a distant smoke cloud and waits for the flames to appear. And right enough we presently saw horsemen riding in through the wide-open gate. Dust rose, concealing everything, only the tops of the tall spears glittered. And hardly had the troop vanished into the manor courtyard before they seemed to have turned their horses again, for they were already on their way to us. I urged my sister to leave me, I myself would set everything right. She refused to leave me. I told her that she should at least change, so as to appear in better clothes before these gentlemen. At last she obeyed and set out on the long road to our home. Already the horsemen were beside us, and even before dismounting they inquired after my sister. She wasn't here at the moment, was the apprehensive reply, but she would come later. The answer was received almost with indifference; the important thing seemed their having found me. The chief members of the party appeared to be a young lively fellow, who was a judge, and his silent assistant, who was called Assmann. I was asked to enter the farmhouse. Shaking my head and hitching up my trousers, I slowly began to move, while the sharp eyes of the party scrutinized me. I still half believed that a word would be enough to free me, a city man, and with honor too, from this peasant folk. But when I had stepped over the threshold of the parlor the judge, who had hastened in front and was already awaiting me, said: 'I'm really sorry for this man.' And it was beyond all possibility of doubt that by this he did not mean my present state, but something that was to happen to me. The room looked more like a prison cell than the parlor of a farmhouse. Great stone flags on the floor, dark, quite bare walls, into one of which an iron ring was fixed, in the middle something that looked half a pallet, half an operating table.

Could I still endure any other air than prison air? That is the great question, or rather it would be if I still had any prospect of release.

Translated by Willa and Edwin Muir

An Ancient Sword

I HAD AGREED to go picknicking on Sunday with two friends, but quite unexpectedly slept past the hour when we were to meet. My friends, who knew how punctual I ordinarily am, were surprised, came to the house where I lived, waited outside awhile, then came upstairs and knocked on my door. I was very startled, jumped out of bed, and thought only of getting ready as soon as I could. When I emerged fully dressed from my room, my friends fell back in manifest alarm. 'What's that behind your head?' they cried. Since my awakening I had felt something preventing me from bending back my head, and I now groped for it with my hand. My friends, who had grown somewhat calmer, had just shouted 'Be careful, don't hurt yourself!' when my hand closed behind my head on the hilt of a sword. My friends came closer, examined me, led me back to the mirror in my room, and stripped me to the waist. A large, ancient knight's sword with a cross-shaped handle was buried to the hilt in my back, but the blade had been driven with such incredible precision between my skin and flesh that it had caused no injury. Nor was there a wound at the spot on my neck where the sword had penetrated; my friends assured me that there was an opening large enough to admit the blade, but dry and showing no trace of blood. And when my friends now stood on chairs and slowly, inch by inch, drew out the sword, I did not bleed, and the opening on my neck closed until no mark was left save a scarcely discernible slit. 'Here is your sword,' laughed my friends, and gave it to me. I hefted it in my two hands; it was a splendid weapon, Crusaders might have used it.

Who tolerates this gadding about of ancient knights in dreams, irresponsibly brandishing their swords, stabbing innocent sleepers who are saved from serious injury only because the weapons in all likelihood glance off living bodies, and also because there are faithful friends knocking at the door, prepared to come to their assistance?

Translated by Martin Greenberg and Hannah Arendt

New Lamps

YESTERDAY I was in the directors' offices for the first time. Our night shift has chosen me as their spokesman, and since the construction and fueling of our lamps is inadequate I was to go along there and press for these defects to be remedied. The appropriate office was pointed out to me; I knocked and went in. A delicate young man, very pale, smiled at me from behind his large desk. He nodded his head a great deal, a great deal too much. I did not know whether I ought to sit down; although there was a chair available I thought perhaps I had better not sit down straightaway on my first visit, and so I told my story standing. But obviously I caused the young man some trouble by this very modesty of mine, for he was obliged to turn his face round and up at me, unless he was prepared to turn his chair round, and that he wasn't prepared to do. On the other hand, in spite of all his willingness, he could not screw his neck round quite far enough, and so with it halfway round he gazed up askew at the ceiling during my story, and I could not help doing the same. When I had finished he got up slowly, patted me on the back, said: 'Well, well – well, well,' and pushed me into the adjoining room, where a gentleman with a great wild growth of beard had evidently been waiting for us, for on his desk there was no trace of any sort of work to be seen, on the contrary, an open glass door led out into a little garden full of flowers and shrubs. A short briefing, consisting of a few words whispered to him by the young man, sufficed for the gentleman to grasp our manifold complaints. He stood up at once and said: 'Well now, my good –,' here he paused; I thought he wanted to know my name and so I was just opening my mouth to introduce myself again when he caught me up short: 'Yes, yes, all right, all right, I know all about you – well now, your request, or that of your workmates and yourself, is certainly justifiable, I myself and the other gentlemen on the board of directors are certainly the last not to recognize that. Believe me, the welfare of our men is something that we have more at heart than the welfare of the concern. And why not? The concern can always be built up all over again, it only costs money, hang the money, but if a human being is destroyed, there you have it, a human being is destroyed and we're left with the widow, the children. Ah dear me, yes! And so that is why every suggestion for the introduction of new safeguards, new reliefs, new comforts and luxuries, is most welcome to us. Anyone who comes along with such a suggestion is the man for us. So you just leave your proposals here with us, we shall examine them closely, and if it should turn out that any kind of brilliant little novelty can be appended, we shall certainly not suppress it, and as soon as everything is finished you men will get the new lamps. But tell this to your workmates below: we will not rest here until we have turned your shaft into a drawing-room, and we'll see to it that you meet your end down there in patent-leather shoes, or not at all. And so a very good day to you!'

Translated by Malcolm Pasley

My Neighbor

MY BUSINESS rests entirely on my own shoulders. Two girl clerks with typewriters and ledgers in the anteroom, my own room with writing desk, safe, consulting table, easy chair, and telephone: such is my entire working apparatus. So simple to control, so easy to direct. I'm quite young, and lots of business comes my way. I don't complain, I don't complain.

At the beginning of the year a young man snapped up the empty premises next to mine, which very foolishly I had hesitated to rent until it was too late. They also consist of a room and an anteroom, with a kitchen, however, thrown in – the room and anteroom, I would certainly have found some use for, my two girl clerks feel somewhat overdriven as it is – but what use would a kitchen have been to me? This petty consideration was solely responsible for my allowing the premises to be snatched from under my nose. Now that young man sits there. Harras, his name is. What he actually does there I have no idea. On the door is a sign: 'Harras Bureau.' I have made inquiries and I am told it is a business similar to mine. One can't exactly warn people against extending the fellow credit, for after all he is a young and pushing man who probably has a future; yet one can't go so far as to advise it, for by all appearances he has no assets yet. The usual thing said by people who don't know.

Sometimes I meet Harras on the stairs; he seems always to be in an extraordinary hurry, for he literally shoots past me. I have never got a good look at him yet, for his office key is always in his hand when he passes me. In a trice he has the door open. Like the tail of a rat he has slipped through and I'm left standing again before the sign 'Harras Bureau,' which I have read already far oftener than it deserves.

The wretchedly thin walls betray the honorable and capable man, but shield the dishonest. My telephone is fixed to the wall that separates me from my neighbor. But I single that out merely as a particularly ironical circumstance. For even if it hung on the opposite wall, everything could be heard in the next room. I have accustomed myself to refrain from naming the names of my customers when speaking on the telephone to them. But of course it does not need much skill to guess the names from characteristic but unavoidable turns of the conversation. Sometimes I absolutely dance with apprehension around the telephone, the receiver at my ear, and yet can't help divulging secrets.

Because of all this my business decisions have naturally become unsure, my voice nervous. What is Harras doing while I am telephoning? If I wanted to exaggerate – and one must often do that so as to make things clear in one's mind – I might assert that Harras does not require a telephone, he uses mine, he pushes his sofa against the wall and listens; while I at the other side must fly to the telephone, listen to all the requests of my customers, come to difficult and grave decisions, carry out long calculations – but worst of all, during all this time, involuntarily give Harras valuable information through the wall.

Perhaps he doesn't wait even for the end of the conversation, but gets up at the point where the matter has become clear to him, flies through the town with his usual haste, and, before I have hung up the receiver, is already at his goal working against me.

Translated by Willa and Edwin Muir

A Crossbreed
[A Sport]

I HAVE a curious animal, half kitten, half lamb. It is a legacy from my father. But it only developed in my time; formerly it was far more lamb than kitten. Now it is both in about equal parts. From the cat it takes its head and claws, from the lamb its size and shape; from both its eyes, which are wild and flickering, its hair, which is soft, lying close to its body, its movements, which partake both of skipping and slinking. Lying on the window sill in the sun it curls up in a ball and purrs; out in the meadow it rushes about like mad and is scarcely to be caught. It flees from cats and makes to attack lambs. On moonlight nights its favorite promenade is along the eaves. It cannot mew and it loathes rats. Beside the hen coop it can lie for hours in ambush, but it has never yet seized an opportunity for murder.

I feed it on milk; that seems to suit it best. In long draughts it sucks the milk in through its fanglike teeth. Naturally it is a great source of entertainment for children. Sunday morning is the visiting hour. I sit with the little beast on my knees, and the children of the whole neighborhood stand around me.

Then the strangest questions are asked, which no human being could answer: Why there is only one such animal, why I rather than anybody else should own it, whether there was ever an animal like it before and what would happen if it died, whether it feels lonely, why it has no children, what it is called, etc.

I never trouble to answer, but confine myself without further explanation to exhibiting my possession. Sometimes the children bring cats with them; once they actually brought two lambs. But against all their hopes there was no scene of recognition. The animals gazed calmly at each other with their animal eyes, and obviously accepted their reciprocal existence as a divine fact.

Sitting on my knees, the beast knows neither fear nor lust of pursuit. Pressed against me it is happiest. It remains faithful to the family that brought it up. In that there is certainly no extraordinary mark of fidelity, but merely the true instinct of an animal which, though it has countless step-relations in the world, has perhaps not a single blood relation, and to which consequently the protection it has found with us is sacred.

Sometimes I cannot help laughing when it sniffs around me and winds itself between my legs and simply will not be parted from me. Not content with being lamb and cat, it almost insists on being a dog as well. Once when, as may happen to anyone, I could see no way out of my business problems and all that they involved, and was ready to let everything go, and in this mood was lying in my rocking chair in my room, the beast on my knees, I happened to glance down and saw tears dropping from its huge whiskers. Were they mine, or were they the animal's? Had this cat, along with the soul of a lamb, the ambitions of a human being? I did not inherit much from my father, but this legacy is quite remarkable.

It has the restlessness of both beasts, that of the cat and that of the lamb, diverse as they are. For that reason its skin feels too tight for it. Sometimes it jumps up on the armchair beside me, plants its front legs on my shoulder, and put its muzzle to my ear. It is as if it were saying something to me, and as a matter of fact it turns its head afterwards and gazes in my face to see the impression its communication has made. And to oblige it I behave as if I had understood, and nod. Then it jumps to the floor and dances about with joy.

Perhaps the knife of the butcher would be a release for this animal; but as it is a legacy I must deny it that. So it must wait until the breath voluntarily leaves its body, even though it sometimes gazes at me with a look of human understanding, challenging me to do the thing of which both of us are thinking.

Translated by Willa and Edwin Muir

A Splendid Beast

I LAY on the ground by a wall, writhing in pain, trying to burrow into the damp earth. The huntsman stood beside me and lightly pressed one foot into the small of my back. 'A splendid beast,' he said to the beater, who was cutting open my collar and coat in order to feel my flesh. Already tired of me and eager for fresh action, the hounds were running senselessly against the wall. The coach came, and, bound hand and foot, I was flung in beside the gentleman, over the back seat, so that my head and arms hung down outside the carriage. The journey passed swiftly and smoothly; perishing of thirst, with open mouth, I breathed in the high-whirling dust, and now and then felt the gentleman's delighted touch on my calves.

Translated by Eithne Wilkins and Ernst Kaiser

The Watchman

I RAN past the first watchman. Then I was horrified, ran back again and said to the watchman: 'I ran through here while you were looking the other way.' The watchman gazed ahead of him and said nothing. 'I suppose I really oughtn't to have done it,' I said. The watchman still said nothing. 'Does your silence indicate permission to pass?'

Translated by Eithne Wilkins and Ernst Kaiser

A Common Confusion

A COMMON EXPERIENCE, resulting in a common confusion. A. has to transact important business with B. in H. He goes to H. for a preliminary interview, accomplishes the journey there in ten minutes, and the journey back in the same time, and on returning boasts to his family of his expedition. Next day he goes again to H., this time to settle his business finally. As that by all appearances will require several hours, A. leaves very early in the morning. But although all the surrounding circumstances, at least in A.'s estimation, are exactly the same as the day before, this time it takes him ten hours to reach H. When he arrives there quite exhausted in the evening he is informed that B., annoyed at his absence, had left half an hour before to go to A.'s village, and that they must have passed each other on the road. A. is advised to wait. But in his anxiety about his business he sets off at once and hurries home.

This time he covers the distance, without paying any particular attention to the fact, practically in an instant. At home he learns that B. had arrived quite early, immediately after A.'s departure, indeed that he had met A. on the threshold and reminded him of his business; but A. had replied that he had no time to spare, he must go at once.

In spite of this incomprehensible behavior of A., however, B. had stayed on to wait for A.'s return. It is true, he had asked several times whether A. was not back yet, but he was still sitting up in A.'s room. Overjoyed at the opportunity of seeing B. at once and explaining everything to him, A. rushes upstairs. He is almost at the top, when he stumbles, twists a sinew, and almost fainting with the pain, incapable even of uttering a cry, only able to moan faintly in the darkness, he hears B. – impossible to tell whether at a great distance or quite near him – stamping down the stairs in a violent rage and vanishing for good.

Translated by Willa and Edwin Muir

The Truth About Sancho Panza

WITHOUT making any boast of it Sancho Panza succeeded in the course of years, by feeding him a great number of romances of chivalry and adventure in the evening and night hours, in so diverting from himself his demon, whom he later called Don Quixote, that this demon thereupon set out, uninhibited, on the maddest exploits, which, however, for the lack of a preordained object, which should have been Sancho Panza himself, harmed nobody. A free man, Sancho Panza philosophically followed Don Quixote on his crusades, perhaps out of a sense of responsibility, and had of them a great and edifying entertainment to the end of his days.

Translated by Willa and Edwin Muir

The Silence of the Sirens

PROOF that inadequate, even childish measures may serve to rescue one from peril:

To protect himself from the Sirens Ulysses stopped his ears with wax and had himself bound to the mast of his ship. Naturally any and every traveler before him could have done the same, except those whom the Sirens allured even from a great distance; but it was known to all the world that such things were of no help whatever. The song of the Sirens could pierce through everything, and the longing of those they seduced would have broken far stronger bonds than chains and masts. But Ulysses did not think of that, although he had probably heard of it. He trusted absolutely to his handful of wax and his fathom of chain, and in innocent elation over his little stratagem sailed out to meet the Sirens.

Now the Sirens have a still more fatal weapon than their song, namely their silence. And though admittedly such a thing has never happened, still it is conceivable that someone might possibly have escaped from their singing; but from their silence certainly never. Against the feeling of having triumphed over them by one's own strength, and the consequent exaltation that bears down everything before it, no earthly powers can resist.

And when Ulysses approached them the potent songstresses actually did not sing, whether because they thought that this enemy could be vanquished only by their silence, or because the look of bliss on the face of Ulysses, who was thinking of nothing but his wax and his chains, made them forget their singing.

But Ulysses, if one may so express it, did not hear their silence; he thought they were singing and that he alone did not hear them. For a fleeting moment he saw their throats rising and falling, their breasts lifting, their eyes filled with tears, their lips half-parted, but believed that these were accompaniments to the airs which died unheard around him. Soon, however, all this faded from his sight as he fixed his gaze on the distance, the Sirens literally vanished before his resolution, and at the very moment when they were nearest to him he knew of them no longer.

But they – lovelier than ever – stretched their necks and turned, let their awesome hair flutter free in the wind, and freely stretched their claws on the rocks. They no longer had any desire to allure; all that they wanted was to hold as long as they could the radiance that fell from Ulysses' great eyes.

If the Sirens has possessed consciousness they would have been annihilated at that moment. But they remained as they had been; all that had happened was that Ulysses had escaped them.

A codicil to the foregoing has also been handed down. Ulysses, it is said, was so full of guile, was such a fox, that not even the goddess of fate could pierce his armor. Perhaps he had really noticed, although here the human understanding is beyond its depths, that the Sirens were silent, and held up to them and to the gods the aforementioned pretense merely as a sort of shield.

Translated by Willa and Edwin Muir

Prometheus

THERE ARE four legends concerning Prometheus:

According to the first he was clamped to a rock in the Caucasus for betraying the secrets of the gods to men, and the gods sent eagles to feed on his liver, which was perpetually renewed.

According to the second Prometheus, goaded by the pain of the tearing beaks, pressed himself deeper and deeper into the rock until he became one with it.

According to the third his treachery was forgotten in the

course of thousands of years, forgotten by the gods, the eagles, forgotten by himself.

According to the fourth everyone grew weary of the meaningless affair. The gods grew weary, the eagles grew weary, the wound closed wearily.

There remained the inexplicable mass of rock. The legend tried to explain the inexplicable. As it came out of a substratum of truth it had in turn to end in the inexplicable.

Translated by Willa and Edwin Muir

The City Coat of Arms

AT FIRST all the arrangements for building the Tower of Babel were characterized by fairly good order; indeed the order was perhaps too perfect, too much thought was given to guides, interpreters, accommodations for the workmen, and roads of communication, as if there were centuries before one to do the work in. In fact, the general opinion at that time was that one simply could not build too slowly; a very little insistence on this would have sufficed to make one hesitate to lay the foundations at all. People argued in this way: The essential thing in the whole business is the idea of building a tower that will reach to heaven. In comparison with that idea everything else is secondary. The idea, once seized in its magnitude, can never vanish again; so long as there are men on the earth there will be also the irresistible desire to complete the building. That being so, however, one need have no anxiety about the future; on the contrary, human knowledge is increasing, the art of building has made progress and will make further progress, a piece of work which takes us a year may perhaps be done in half the time in another hundred years, and better done, too, more enduringly. So why exert oneself to the extreme limit of one's present powers? There would be some sense in doing that only if it were likely that the tower could be completed in one generation. But that is beyond all hope. It is far more likely that the next generation with their perfected knowledge will find the work of their predecessors bad, and tear down what has been built so as to begin anew. Such thoughts paralyzed people's powers, and so they troubled less about the tower than the construction of a city for the workmen. Every nationality wanted the finest quarter for itself, and this gave rise to disputes, which developed into bloody conflicts. These conflicts never came to an end; to the leaders they were a new proof that, in the absence of the necessary unity, the building of the tower must be done very slowly, or indeed preferably postponed until universal peace was declared. But the time was spent not only in conflict; the town was embellished in the intervals, and this unfortunately enough evoked fresh envy and fresh conflict. In this fashion the age of the first generation went past, but none of the succeeding ones showed any difference; except that technical skill increased and with it occasion for conflict. To this must be added that the second or third generation had already recognized the senselessness of building a heaven-reaching tower; but by that time everybody was too deeply involved to leave the city.

All the legends and songs that came to birth in that city are filled with longing for a prophesied day when the city would be destroyed by five successive blows from a gigantic fist. It is for that reason too that the city has a closed fist on its coat of arms.

Translated by Willa and Edwin Muir

Poseidon

POSEIDON sat at his desk, going over the accounts. The administration of all the waters gave him endless work. He could have had as many assistants as he wanted, and indeed he had quite a number, but since he took his job very seriously he insisted on going through all the accounts again himself, and so his assistants were of little help to him. It cannot be said that he enjoyed the work; he carried it out simply because it was assigned to him; indeed he had frequently applied for what he called more cheerful work, but whenever various suggestions were put to him it turned out that nothing suited him so well as his present employment. Needless to say, it was very difficult to find him another job. After all, he could not possibly be put in charge of one particular ocean. Quite apart from the fact that in this case the work involved would not be less, only more petty, the great Poseidon could hold only a superior position. And when he was offered a post unrelated to the waters, the very idea made him feel sick, his divine breath came short and his brazen chest began to heave. As a matter of fact, no one took his troubles very seriously; when a mighty man complains one must pretend to yield, however hopeless the case may seem. No one ever really considered relieving Poseidon of his position; he had been destined to be God of the Seas since time immemorial, and that was how it had to remain.

What annoyed him most – and this was the chief cause of discontent with his job – was to learn of the rumors that were circulating about him; for instance, that he was constantly cruising through the waves with his trident. Instead of which here he was sitting in the depths of the world's ocean endlessly going over the accounts, an occasional journey to Jupiter being the only interruption of the monotony, a journey moreover from which he invariably returned in a furious temper. As a result he had hardly seen the oceans, save fleetingly during his hasty ascent to Olympus, and had never really sailed upon them. He used to say that he was postponing this until the end of the world, for then there might come a quiet moment when, just before the end and having gone through the last account, he could still make a quick little tour.

Translated by Tania and James Stern

Fellowship

WE ARE five friends, one day we came out of a house one after the other, first one came and placed himself beside the gate, then the second came, or rather he glided through the gate like a little ball of quicksilver, and placed himself near the first one, then came the third, then the fourth, then the fifth. Finally we all stood in a row. People began to notice us, they pointed at us and said: Those five just came out of that house. Since then we have been living together; it would be a peaceful life if it weren't for a sixth one continually trying to interfere. He doesn't do us any harm, but he annoys us, and that is harm enough; why does he intrude where he is not wanted? We don't know him and don't want him to join us. There was a time, of course, when the five of us did not know one another, either; and it could be said that we still don't know one another, but what is possible and can be tolerated by the five of us is not possible and cannot be tolerated with this sixth one. In any case, we are five and don't want to be six. And what is the point of this continual being together anyhow? It is also pointless for the five of us, but here we are together and will remain together; a new combination, however, we do not want, just because of our experiences. But how is one to make all this clear to the sixth one? Long explanations would almost amount to accepting him in our circle, so we prefer not to explain and not to accept him. No matter how he pouts his lips we push him away with our elbows, but however much we push him away, back he comes.

Translated by Tania and James Stern

At Night

DEEPLY LOST in the night. Just as one sometimes lowers one's head to reflect, thus to be utterly lost in the night. All around people are asleep. It's just play acting, an innocent self-deception, that they sleep in houses, in safe beds, under a safe roof, stretched out or curled up on mattresses, in sheets, under blankets; in reality they have flocked together as they had once upon a time and again later in a deserted region, a camp in the open, a countless number of men, an army, a people, under a cold sky on cold earth, collapsed where once they had stood, forehead pressed on the arm, face to the ground, breathing quietly. And you are watching, are one of the watchmen, you find the next one by brandishing a burning stick from the brushwood pile beside you. Why are you watching? Someone must watch, it is said. Someone must be there.

Translated by Tania and James Stern

The Problem of Our Laws

OUR LAWS are not generally known; they are kept secret by the small group of nobles who rule us. We are convinced that these ancient laws are scrupulously administered; nevertheless it is an extremely painful thing to be ruled by laws that one does not know. I am not thinking of possible discrepancies that may arise in the interpretation of the laws, or of the disadvantages involved when only a few and not the whole people are allowed to have a say in their interpretation. These disadvantages are perhaps of no great importance. For the laws are very ancient; their interpretation has been the work of centuries, and has itself doubtless acquired the status of law; and though there is still a possible freedom of interpretation left, it has now become very restricted. Moreover the nobles have obviously no cause to be influenced in their interpretation by personal interests inimical to us, for the laws were made to the advantage of the nobles from the very beginning, they themselves stand above the laws, and that seems to be why the laws were entrusted exclusively into their hands. Of course, there is wisdom in that – who doubts the wisdom of the ancient laws? – but also hardship for us; probably that is unavoidable.

The very existence of these laws, however, is at most a matter of presumption. There is a tradition that they exist and that they are a mystery confided to the nobility, but it is not and cannot be more than a mere tradition sanctioned by age, for the essence of a secret code is that it should remain a mystery. Some of us among the people have attentively scrutinized the doings of the nobility since the earliest times and possess records made by our forefathers – records which we have conscientiously continued – and claim to recognize amid the countless number of facts certain main tendencies which permit of this or that historical formulation; but when in accordance with these scrupulously tested and logically ordered conclusions we seek to adjust ourselves somewhat for the present or the future, everything becomes uncertain, and our work seems only an intellectual game, for perhaps these laws that we are trying to unravel do not exist at all. There is a small party who are actually of this opinion and who try to show that, if any law exists, it can only be this: The Law is whatever the nobles do. This party see everywhere only the arbitrary acts of the nobility, and reject the popular tradition, which according to them possesses only certain trifling and incidental advantages that do not offset its heavy drawbacks, for it gives the people a false, deceptive, and overconfident security in confronting coming events. This cannot be gainsaid, but the overwhelming majority of our people account for it by the fact that the tradition is far from complete and must be more fully inquired into, that the material available, prodigious as it looks, is still too meager, and that several centuries will have to pass before it becomes really adequate. This view, so comfortless as far as the present is concerned, is lightened only by the belief that a time will eventually come when the tradition and our research into it will jointly reach their conclusion, and as it were gain a breathing space, when everything will have become clear, the law will belong to the people, and the nobility will vanish. This is not maintained in any spirit of hatred against the nobility; not at all, and by no one. We are more inclined to hate ourselves, because we have not yet shown ourselves worthy of being entrusted with the laws. And that is the real reason why the party who believe that there is no law have remained so few – although their doctrine is in certain ways so attractive, for it unequivocally recognizes the nobility and its right to go on existing.

Actually one can express the problem only in a sort of paradox: Any party that would repudiate not only all belief in the laws, but the nobility as well, would have the whole people behind it; yet no such party can come into existence, for nobody would dare to repudiate the nobility. We live on this razor's edge. A writer once summed the matter up in this way: The sole visible and indubitable law that is imposed upon us is the nobility, and must we ourselves deprive ourselves of that one law?

Translated by Willa and Edwin Muir

The Conscription of Troops

THE conscription of troops, often necessary on account of the never-ending frontier wars, takes place in the following manner:

The order goes out that on a certain day in a certain part of town all inhabitants – men, women, and children without exception – have to remain indoors. Usually at about noon the young nobleman in charge of the conscription appears at the entrance of that part of town where a detachment of soldiers, both infantry and cavalry, has been waiting since dawn. He is a young man, slender, not tall, weak, carelessly dressed, with tired eyes, waves of restlessness continually passing through him like the shivers of a fever. Without looking at anyone he makes a sign with a whip, his sole equipment, whereupon several soldiers join him and he enters the first house. A soldier, who knows personally all the inhabitants in this part of town, reads out the list of the inmates. As a rule they are all present, lined up in the room, their eyes fixed on the nobleman, as though they were soldiers already. It can happen, however, that here and there someone, it's invariably a man, is missing. In this case no one will dare to utter an excuse, let alone a lie, everyone is silent, all eyes are lowered, the pressure of the command which someone in this house has evaded is almost unbearable, but the silent presence of the nobleman keeps everyone nevertheless in his place. The nobleman makes a sign, it's not even a nod, it can be read only in his eyes, and two soldiers begin the search for the missing man. This is not difficult. He is never out of the house, never really intends to evade military service, it's only fear that has prevented him from turning up, yet it's not fear of the service itself that keeps him away, it's the general reluctance to show himself, for him the command is almost too great, so frighteningly great that he cannot appear of his own accord. This is why he does not flee, he simply goes into hiding, and on learning that the nobleman is in the house he even leaves his hiding place and creeps to the door of the room where he is promptly caught by the soldiers in search of him. He is brought before the nobleman who seizes the whip with both hands – he is so weak he can't do it with one hand – and gives the man a thrashing. Having inflicted no great pain, he drops the whip, half from exhaustion, half from disgust, whereupon the beaten man has to pick it up and hand it to him. Only then may he join the line with the others; incidentally, it is almost certain that he will not be recruited. But it also happens, and this is more frequent, that a greater number of people appear than are listed. There, for instance, stands an unknown girl, staring at the nobleman; she is from out of town, from the provinces perhaps, the conscription has lured her here. There are many women who cannot resist the temptation of a conscription in another town, conscriptions at home meaning something quite different. And, strangely enough, it is not considered disgraceful for a woman to surrender to this temptation; on the contrary, in the opinion of many, this is something women have to go through, a debt which they pay to their sex. Moreover, it invariably takes the same course. The girl or the woman learns that somewhere, perhaps very far away, at the home of relatives or friends, a conscription is going to take place; she asks her family for permission to undertake the journey, which is granted – it cannot very well be refused – she puts on her best clothes, is gayer than usual, at the same time calm and friendly, no matter what she may be like at other times; and yet behind all the calm and friendliness she is inaccessible, like an utter stranger who is on her way home and can think of nothing else. In the family where the conscription is going to take place she is received quite differently from an ordinary guest; everyone flatters her, she is invited to walk through all the rooms in the house, lean out of all the windows, and if she puts her hand on someone's head it means more than a father's blessing. When the family is preparing for the conscription she is given the best place, which is near the door where she has the best chance of being seen by the nobleman and can best see him. She is honored in this way, however, only until the nobleman enters; thereafter she begins to fade. He looks at her as little as at the others, and even when his eye rests on someone, that person is not aware of being looked at. This is something she has not expected or rather she certainly has, for it cannot be otherwise, yet it wasn't the expectation of the opposite that had driven her here, it was just something that had now definitely come to an end. She feels shame to a degree which our women possibly feel at no other time; only now is she fully aware of having forced her way into a foreign conscription, and when the soldier has read out the list and her name is not on it and there comes a moment of silence, she flees stooped and trembling out of the door, receiving in addition a blow in the back from a soldier's fist.

Should the person not on the list be a man, his only desire is to be conscripted with the others although he does not belong to this house. But this too is utterly out of the question, an outsider of this kind has never been conscripted and nothing of the sort will ever happen.

Translated by Tania and James Stern

The Test

I AM a servant, but there is no work for me. I am timid and don't push myself to the fore, indeed I don't even push myself into line with the others, but that is only one reason for my nonemployment, it's even possible that it has nothing to do with my nonemployment, in any case the main thing is that I am not called upon to serve, others have been called yet they have not tried harder than I, indeed perhaps they have not even felt the desire to be called, whereas I, at least sometimes, have felt it very strongly.

So I lie on the pallet in the servants' hall, stare at the beams in the ceiling, fall asleep, wake up, and promptly fall asleep again. Occasionally I walk over to the tavern where they sell a sour beer, occasionally I have even poured away a glass in disgust, but at other times I drink it. I like sitting there because from behind the closed little window, without the possibility of being discovered, I can see across to the windows of our house. Not that one sees very much there, to my knowledge only the windows of the corridors look out on the street, and moreover not even those of the corridors leading to my employers' apartments. But it is also possible that I am mistaken; someone, without my having asked him, once said so, and the general impression of this house front confirms this. Only rarely are the windows opened, and when this does occur it is done by a servant who may lean against the balustrade to look down for a while. It follows therefore that these are corridors where he cannot be taken by surprise. As a matter of fact I am not personally acquainted with these servants; those who are permanently employed upstairs sleep elsewhere, not in my room.

Once when I arrived at the tavern, a guest was sitting at my observation post. I did not dare look at him closely and was about to turn around in the door and leave. The guest, however, called me over, and it turned out that he too was a servant whom I had once seen somewhere before, but without having spoken to him.

'Why do you want to run away? Sit down and have a drink! I'll pay.' So I sat down. He asked me several things, but I couldn't answer, indeed I didn't even understand his questions. So I said: 'Perhaps you are sorry now that you invited me, so I'd better go,' and I was about to get up. But he stretched his hand out over the table and pressed me down. 'Stay,' he said, 'that was only a test. He who does not answer the questions has passed the test.'

Translated by Tania and James Stern

The Vulture

A VULTURE was hacking at my feet. It had already torn my boots and stockings to shreds, now it was hacking at the feet themselves. Again and again it struck at them, then circled several times restlessly around me, then returned to continue its work. A gentleman passed by, looked on for a while, then asked me why I suffered the vulture. 'I'm helpless,' I said. 'When it came and began to attack me, I of course tried to drive it away, even to strangle it, but these animals are very strong, it was about to spring at my face, but I preferred to sacrifice my feet. Now they are almost torn to bits.' 'Fancy letting yourself be tortured like this!' said the gentleman.

'One shot and that's the end of the vulture.' 'Really?' I said. 'And would you do that?' 'With pleasure,' said the gentleman, 'I've only got to go home and get my gun. Could you wait another half-hour?' 'I'm not sure about that,' said I, and stood for a moment rigid with pain. Then I said: 'Do try it in any case, please.' 'Very well,' said the gentleman, 'I'll be as quick as I can.' During this conversation the vulture had been calmly listening, letting its eye rove between me and the gentleman. Now I realized that it had understood everything; it took wing, leaned far back to gain impetus, and then, like a javelin thrower, thrust its beak through my mouth, deep into me. Falling back, I was relieved to feel him drowning irretrievably in my blood, which was filling every depth, flooding every shore.

Translated by Tania and James Stern

The Helmsman

'AM I NOT the helmsman here?' I called out. 'You?' asked a tall, dark man and passed his hands over his eyes as though to banish a dream. I had been standing at the helm in the dark night, a feeble lantern burning over my head, and now this man had come and tried to push me aside. And as I would not yield, he put his foot on my chest and slowly crushed me while I still clung to the hub of the helm, wrenching it around in falling. But the man seized it, pulled it back in place, and pushed me away. I soon collected myself, however, ran to the hatchway which gave on to the mess quarters, and cried out: 'Men! Comrades! Come here, quick! A stranger has driven me away from the helm!' Slowly they came up, climbing the companion ladder, tired, swaying, powerful figures. 'Am I the helmsman?' I asked. They nodded, but they had eyes only for the stranger, stood around him in a semicircle, and when, in a commanding voice, he said: 'Don't disturb me!' they gathered together, nodded at me, and withdrew down the companion ladder. What kind of people are these? Do they ever think, or do they only shuffle pointlessly over the earth?

Translated by Tania and James Stern

The Top

A CERTAIN PHILOSOPHER used to hang about wherever children were at play. And whenever he saw a boy with a top, he would lie in wait. As soon as the top began to spin the philosopher went in pursuit and tried to catch it. He was not perturbed when the children noisily protested and tried to keep him away from their toy; so long as he could catch the top while it was still spinning, he was happy, but only for a moment; then he threw it to the ground and walked away. For he believed that the understanding of any detail, that of a spinning top, for instance, was sufficient for the understanding of all things. For this reason he did not busy himself with great problems, it seemed to him uneconomical. Once the smallest detail was understood, then everything was understood, which was why he busied himself only with the spinning top. And whenever preparations were being made for the spinning of the top, he hoped that this time it would succeed: as soon as the top began to spin and he was running breathlessly after it, the hope would turn to certainty, but when he held the silly piece of wood in his hand, he felt nauseated. The screaming of the children, which hitherto he had not heard and which now suddenly pierced his ears, chased him away, and he tottered like a top under a clumsy whip.

Translated by Tania and James Stern

Hands

MY TWO HANDS began a fight. They slammed the book I had been reading and thrust it aside so that it should not be in the way. Me they saluted, and appointed me referee. And an instant later they had locked fingers with each other and were already rushing away over the edge of the table, now to the right, now to the left, according to which of them was bringing most pressure to bear on the other. I never turned my gaze from them. If they are my hands, I must referee fairly, otherwise I shall bring down on myself the agonies of a wrong decision. But my function is not easy, in the darkness between the palms of the hands various holds are brought into play that I must not let pass unnoticed, and so I press my chin on the table and now nothing escapes me. All my life long I have made a favorite of the right, without meaning the left any harm. If the left had ever said anything, indulgent and just as I am, I should at once have put a stop to the abuse. But it never grumbled, it hung down from me, and while, say, the right was raising my hat in the street, the left was timidly fumbling down my thigh. That was a bad way of preparing for the struggle that is now going on. How in the long run, left wrist, will you resist the pressure of this powerful right hand? How maintain your girlish finger's stand in the grip of the five others? This seems to me to be no longer a fight, but the natural end of the left hand. Even now it has been pushed to the extreme left rim of the table, and the right is pounding regularly up and down on it like the piston of an engine. If, confronted with this misery, I had not got the saving idea that these are my own hands and that with a slight jerk I can pull them away from each other and so put an end to the fight and the misery – if I had not got this idea, the left hand would have been broken out of the wrist, would have been flung from the table, and then the right, in the wild recklessness of knowing itself the victor, might have leapt, like five-headed Cerberus, straight into my attentive face. Instead, the two now lie one on top of the other, the right stroking the back of the left, and I, dishonest referee, nod in approval.

Translated by Eithne Wilkins and Ernst Kaiser

A Little Fable

'ALAS,' said the mouse, 'the world is growing smaller every day. At the beginning it was so big that I was afraid, I kept running and running, and I was glad when at last I saw walls far away to the right and left, but these long walls have narrowed so quickly that I am in the last chamber already, and there in the corner stands the trap that I must run into.' 'You only need to change your direction,' said the cat, and ate it up.

Translated by Willa and Edwin Muir

Isabella

IT IS ISABELLA, the dapple-gray, the old horse, I should never have recognized her in the crowd, she has become a lady, we met only recently in a garden, at a charity fête. There is a little copse there, standing somewhat apart and enclosing a cool, shaded lawn, which is crossed this way and that by several narrow paths, and at times it is a very pleasant place to be. I used to know the garden in the old days, and when I was tired of the fête, I turned aside into this copse. Scarcely had I stepped among the trees when I saw a tall lady coming toward me from the other side; I was almost dismayed at her tallness, there was nobody else nearby whom I could have compared her with, but I was sure I knew no woman whom this one would not have overtopped by several heads – in my first amazement I even thought by innumerable heads. But as I drew nearer, I was quickly reassured. My old friend Isabella! 'Well, and how did you get out of your stable?' 'Oh, that wasn't difficult, the fact is I am really kept on only for old times' sake, my day is over. When I explain to my master that instead of standing in the stable, being no use to anyone, I want to see a little of the world now too, while I can, as long as I have the strength for it –

when I explain this to my master, he understands me, he looks out some of the late mistress's clothes, helps me to dress and then sends me off out with his best wishes.' 'How beautiful you are!' I said, not quite sincerely, but also not altogether dishonestly.

Translated by Eithne Wilkins and Ernst Kaiser

Home-coming

I HAVE RETURNED, I have passed under the arch and am looking around. It's my father's old yard. The puddle in the middle. Old, useless tools, jumbled together, block the way to the attic stairs. The cat lurks on the banister. A torn piece of cloth, once wound around a stick in a game, flutters in the breeze. I have arrived. Who is going to receive me? Who is waiting behind the kitchen door? Smoke is rising from the chimney, coffee is being made for supper. Do you feel you belong, do you feel at home? I don't know, I feel most uncertain. My father's house it is, but each object stands cold beside the next, as though preoccupied with its own affairs, which I have partly forgotten, partly never known. What use can I be to them, what do I mean to them, even though I am the son of my father, the old farmer? And I don't dare knock at the kitchen door, I only listen from a distance, I only listen from a distance, standing up, in such a way that I cannot be taken by surprise as an eavesdropper. And since I am listening from a distance, I hear nothing but a faint striking of the clock passing over from childhood days, but perhaps I only think I hear it. Whatever else is going on in the kitchen is the secret of those sitting there, a secret they are keeping from me. The longer one hesitates before the door, the more estranged one becomes. What would happen if someone were to open the door now and ask me a question? Would not I myself then behave like one who wants to keep his secret?

Translated by Tania and James Stern

A Chinese Puzzle

ONCE THERE WAS a Chinese puzzle, a cheap simple toy, not much bigger than a pocket-watch and without any sort of surprising contrivances. Cut into the flat wood, which was painted reddish-brown, there were some blue labyrinthine paths, which all led into a little hole. The ball, which was also blue, had to be got into one of the paths by means of tilting and shaking the box, and then into the hole. Once the ball was in the hole, the game was over, and if one wanted to start all over again, one had first to shake the ball out of the hole. The whole thing was covered over with a strong, convex glass, one could put the puzzle in one's pocket and carry it about with one, and wherever one was, one could take it out and play with it.

If the ball was unemployed, it spent most of the time strolling to and fro, its hands clasped behind its back, on the plateau, avoiding the paths. It held the view that it was quite enough bothered with the paths during the game and that it had every right to recuperate on the open plain when no game was going on. Sometimes it would look up at the vaulted glass, but merely out of habit and quite without any intention of trying to make out anything up there. It had a rather straddling gait and maintained that it was not made for those narrow paths. That was partly true, for indeed the paths could hardly contain it, but it was also untrue, for the fact was that it was very carefully made to fit the width of the paths exactly, but the paths were certainly not meant to be comfortable for it, or else it would not have been a puzzle at all.

Translated by Eithne Wilkins and Ernst Kaiser

The Departure

I ORDERED my horse to be brought from the stables. The servant did not understand my orders. So I went to the stables myself, saddled my horse, and mounted. In the distance I heard the sound of a trumpet, and I asked the servant what it meant. He knew nothing and had heard nothing. At the gate he stopped me and asked: 'Where is the master going?' 'I don't know,' I said, 'just out of here, just out of here. Out of here, nothing else, it's the only way I can reach my goal.' 'So you know your goal?' he asked. 'Yes,' I replied, 'I've just told you. Out of here – that's my goal.'

Translated by Tania and James Stern

Advocates

I WAS not at all certain whether I had any advocates, I could not find out anything definite about it, every face was unfriendly, most people who came toward me and whom I kept meeting in the corridors looked like fat old women; they had huge blue-and-white striped aprons covering their entire bodies, kept stroking their stomachs and swaying awkwardly to and fro. I could not even find out whether we were in a law court. Some facts spoke for it, others against. What reminded me of a law court more than all the details was a droning noise which could be heard incessantly in the distance; one could not tell from which direction it came, it filled every room to such an extent that one had to assume it came from everywhere, or, what seemed more likely, that just the place where one happened to be standing was the very place where the droning originated, but this was probably an illusion, for it came from a distance. These corridors, narrow and austerely vaulted, turning in gradual curves with high, sparsely decorated doors, seemed to have been created specially for profound silence; they were the corridors of a museum or a library. Yet if it were not a law court, why was I searching for an advocate here? Because I was searching for an advocate everywhere; he is needed everywhere, if anything less in court than elsewhere, for a court, one assumes, passes judgment according to the law. If one were to assume that this was being done unfairly or frivolously, then life would not be possible; one must have confidence that the court allows the majesty of the law its full scope, for this is its sole duty. Within the law all is accusation, advocacy, and verdict; any interference by an individual here would be a crime. It is different, however, in the case of the verdict itself; this is based on inquiries being made here and there, from relatives and strangers, from friends and enemies, in the family and public life, in town and village – in short, everywhere. Here it is most necessary to have advocates, advocates galore, the best possible advocates, one next to the other, a living wall, for advocates are by nature hard to set in motion; the plaintiffs, however, those sly foxes, those slinking weasels, those little mice, they slip through the tiniest gaps, scuttle through the legs of the advocates. So look out! That's why I am here, I'm collecting advocates. But I have not found any as yet, only those old women keep on coming and going; if I were not on my search it would put me to sleep. I'm not in the right place – alas, I cannot rid myself of the feeling that I'm not in the right place. I ought to be in a place where all kinds of people meet, from various parts of the country, from every class, every profession, of all ages; I ought to have an opportunity of choosing carefully out of a crowd those who are kind, those who are able, and those who have an eye for me. Perhaps the most suitable place for this would be a huge fairground; instead of which I am hanging about in these corridors where only these old women are to be seen, and not even many of them, and always the same ones, and even those few will not let themselves be cornered, despite their slowness; they slip away from me, float about like rain clouds, and are completely absorbed by unknown activities. Why is it then that I run headlong into a house without reading the sign over the door, promptly find myself in these corridors, and settle here with such obstinacy that I cannot even remember ever having been in front of the house, ever having run up the stairs! But back I cannot go, this waste of time, this admission of having been on the wrong track would be unbearable for me. What? Run downstairs in this brief, hurried life accompanied as it is by that impatient droning? Impossible. The time allotted to you is so short that if you lose one second you have already lost your whole life, for it is no longer, it is always just as long as the time you lose. So if you have started out on a walk, continue it whatever happens; you can only gain, you run no risk, in the end you may fall over a precipice perhaps, but had you turned back after the first steps and run downstairs you would have fallen at once – and not perhaps, but for certain. So if you find nothing in the corridors open the doors, if you find nothing behind these doors there are more floors, and if you find nothing up there, don't worry, just leap up another flight of stairs. As long as you don't stop climbing, the stairs won't end, under your climbing feet they will go on growing upwards.

Translated by Tania and James Stern

Investigations of a Dog

HOW MUCH my life has changed, and yet how unchanged it has remained at bottom! When I think back and recall the time when I was still a member of the canine community, sharing in all its preoccupations, a dog among dogs, I find on closer examination that from the very beginning I sensed some discrepancy, some little maladjustment, causing a slight feeling of discomfort which not even the most decorous public functions could eliminate; more, that sometimes, no, not sometimes, but very often, the mere look of some fellow dog of my own circle that I was fond of, the mere look of him, as if I had just caught it for the first time, would fill me with helpless embarrassment and fear, even with despair. I tried to quiet my apprehensions as best I could; friends, to whom I divulged them, helped me; more peaceful times came – times, it is true, in which these sudden surprises were not lacking, but in which they were accepted with more philosophy, fitted into my life with more philosophy, inducing a certain melancholy and lethargy, it may be, but nevertheless allowing me to carry on as a somewhat cold, reserved, shy, and calculating, but all things considered normal enough dog. How, indeed, without these breathing spells, could I have reached the age that I enjoy at present; how could I have fought my way through to the serenity with which I contemplate the terrors of youth and endure the terrors of age; how could I have come to the point where I am able to draw the consequences of my admittedly unhappy, or, to put it more moderately, not very happy disposition, and live almost entirely in accordance with them? Solitary and withdrawn, with nothing to occupy me save my hopeless but, as far as I am concerned, indispensable little investigations, that is how I live; yet in my distant isolation I have not lost sight of my people, news often penetrates to me, and now and then I even let news of myself reach them. The others treat me with respect but do not understand my way of life; yet they bear me no grudge, and even young dogs whom I sometimes see passing in the distance, a new generation of whose childhood I have only a vague memory, do not deny me a reverential greeting.

For it must not be assumed that, for all my peculiarities, which lie open to the day, I am so very different from the rest of my species. Indeed when I reflect on it – and I have time and disposition and capacity enough for that – I see that dogdom is in every way a marvelous institution. Apart from us dogs there are all sorts of creatures in the world, wretched, limited, dumb creatures who have no language but mechanical cries; many of us dogs study them, have given them names, try to help them, educate them, uplift them, and so on. For my part I am quite indifferent to them except when they try to disturb me, I confuse them with one another, I ignore them. But one thing is too obvious to have escaped me; namely how little inclined they are, compared with us dogs, to stick together, how silently and unfamiliarly and with what a curious hostility they pass each other by, how only the basest of interests can bind them together for a little in ostensible union, and how often these very interests give rise to hatred and conflict. Consider us dogs, on the other hand! One can safely say that we all live together in a literal heap, all of us, different as we are from one another on account of numberless and profound modifications which have arisen in the course of time. All in one heap! We are drawn to each other and nothing can prevent us from satisfying that communal impulse; all our laws and institutions, the few that I still know and the many that I have forgotten, go back to this longing for the greatest bliss we are capable of, the warm comfort of being together. But now consider the other side of the picture. No creatures to my knowledge live in such wide dispersion as we dogs, none have so many distinctions of class, of kind, of occupation, distinctions too numerous to review at a glance; we, whose one desire is to stick together – and again and again we succeed at transcendent moments in spite of everything – we above all others live so widely separated from one another, engaged in strange vocations that are often incomprehensible even to our canine neighbors, holding firmly to laws that are not those of the dog world, but are actually directed against it. How baffling these questions are, questions on which one would prefer not to touch – I understand that standpoint too, even better than my own – and yet questions to which I have completely capitulated. Why do I not do as the others: live in harmony with my people and accept in silence whatever disturbs the harmony, ignoring it as a small error in the great account, always keeping in mind the things that bind us happily together, not those that drive us again and again, as though by sheer force, out of our social circle?

I can recall an incident in my youth; I was at the time in one of those inexplicable blissful states of exaltation which everyone must have experienced as a child; I was still quite a puppy, everything pleased me, everything was my concern. I believed that great things were going on around me of which I was the leader and to which I must lend my voice, things which must be wretchedly thrown aside if I did not run for them and wag my tail for them – childish fantasies that faded with riper years. But at the time their power was very great, I was completely under their spell, and presently something actually did happen, something so extraordinary that it seemed to justify my wild expectations. In itself it was nothing very extraordinary, for I have seen many such things, and more remarkable things too, often enough since, but at the time it struck me with all the force of a first impression, one of those impressions which can never be erased and influence much of one's later conduct. I encountered, in short, a little company of dogs, or rather I did not encounter them, they appeared before me. Before that I had been running along in darkness for some time, filled with a premonition of great things – a premonition that may well have been delusive, for I always had it. I had run in darkness for a long time, up and down, blind and deaf to everything, led on by nothing but a vague desire, and now I suddenly came to a stop with the feeling that I was in the right place, and looking up saw that it was bright day, only a little hazy, and everywhere a blending and confusion of the most intoxicating smells; I greeted the morning with an uncertain barking, when – as if I had conjured them up – out of some place of darkness, to the accompaniment of terrible sounds such as I had never heard before, seven dogs stepped into the light. Had I not distinctly seen that they were dogs and that they themselves brought the sound with them – though I could not recognize how they produced it – I would have run away at once; but as it was I stayed. At that time I still knew hardly anything of the creative gift for music with which the canine race alone is endowed, it had naturally enough escaped my but slowly developing powers of observation; for though music had surrounded me as a perfectly natural and indispensable element of existence ever since I was a suckling, an element which nothing impelled me to distinguish from the rest of existence, my elders had drawn my attention to it only by such hints as were suitable for a childish understanding; all the more astonishing, then, indeed devastating, were these seven great musical artists to me. They did not speak, they did not sing, they remained generally silent, almost determinedly silent; but from the empty air they conjured music. Everything was music, the lifting and setting down of their feet, certain turns of the head, their running and their standing still, the positions they took up in relation to one another, the symmetrical patterns which they produced by one dog setting his front paws on the back of another and the rest following suit until the first bore the weight of the other six, or by all lying flat on the ground and going through complicated concerted evolutions; and none made a false move, not even the last dog, though he was a little unsure, did not always establish contact at once with the others, sometimes hesitated, as it were, on the stroke of the beat, but yet was unsure only by comparison with the superb sureness of the others, and even if he had been much more unsure, indeed quite unsure, would not have been able to do any harm, the others, great masters all of them, keeping the rhythm so unshakably. But it is too much to say that I even saw them, that I actually even saw them. They appeared from somewhere, I inwardly greeted them as dogs, and although I was profoundly confused by the sounds that accompanied them, yet they were dogs nevertheless, dogs like you and me; I regarded them by force of habit simply as dogs I had happened to meet on my road, and felt a wish to approach them and exchange greetings; they were quite near too, dogs much older than me, certainly, and not of my woolly, long-haired kind, but yet not so very alien in size and shape, indeed quite familiar to me, for I had already seen many such or similar dogs; but while I was still involved in these reflections the music gradually got the upper hand, literally knocked the breath out of me and swept me far away from those actual little dogs, and quite against my will, while I howled as if some pain were being inflicted upon me, my mind could attend to nothing but this blast of music which seemed to come from all sides, from the heights, from the deeps, from everywhere, surrounding the listener, overwhelming him, crushing him, and over his swooning body still blowing fanfares so near that they seemed far away and almost inaudible. And then a respite came, for one was already too exhausted, too annulled, too feeble to listen any longer; a respite came and I beheld again the seven little dogs carrying out their evolutions, making their leaps; I longed to shout to them in spite of their aloofness, to beg them to enlighten me, to ask them what they were doing – I was a child and believed I could ask anybody about anything – but hardly had I begun, hardly did I feel on good and familiar doggish terms with the seven, when the music started again, robbed me of my wits, whirled me around in its circles as if I myself were one of the musicians instead of being only their victim, cast me hither and thither, no matter how much I begged for mercy, and rescued me finally from its own violence by driving me into a labyrinth of wooden bars which rose around that place, though I had not noticed it before, but which now firmly caught me, kept my head pressed to the ground, and though the music still resounded in the open space behind me, gave me a little time to get my breath back. I must admit that I was less surprised by the artistry of the seven dogs – it was incomprehensible to me, and also quite definitely beyond my capacities – than by their courage in facing so openly the music of their own making, and their power to endure it calmly without collapsing. But now from my hiding hole I saw, on looking more closely, that it was not so much coolness as the most extreme tension that characterized their performance; these limbs apparently so sure in their movements quivered at every step with a perpetual apprehensive twitching; as if rigid with despair the dogs kept their eyes fixed on one another, and their tongues, whenever the tension weakened for a moment, hung wearily from their jowls. It could not be fear of failure that agitated them so deeply; dogs that could dare and achieve such things had no need to fear that. Then why were they afraid? Who then forced them to do what they were doing? And I could no longer restrain myself, particularly as they now seemed in some incomprehensible way in need of help, and so through all the din of the music I shouted out my questions loudly and challengingly. But they – incredible! incredible! – they never replied, behaved as if I were not there. Dogs who make no reply to the greeting of other dogs are guilty of an offense against good manners which the humblest dog would never pardon any more than the greatest. Perhaps they were not dogs at all? But how should they not be dogs? Could I not actually hear on listening more closely the subdued cries with which they encouraged each other, drew each other's attention to difficulties, warned each other against errors; could I not see the last and youngest dog, to whom most of those cries were addressed, often stealing a glance at me as if he would have dearly wished to reply, but refrained because it was not allowed? But why should it not be allowed, why should the very thing which our laws unconditionally command not be allowed in this one case? I became indignant at the thought and almost forgot the music. Those dogs were violating the law. Great magicians they might be, but the law was valid for them too, I knew that quite well though I was a child. And having recognized that, I now noticed something else. They had good grounds for remaining silent, that is, assuming that they remained silent from a sense of shame. For how were they conducting themselves? Because of all the music I had not noticed it before, but they had flung away all shame, the wretched creatures were doing the very thing which is both most ridiculous and indecent in our eyes; they were walking on their hind legs. Fie on them! They were uncovering their nakedness, blatantly making a show of their nakedness: they were doing that as though it were a meritorious act, and when, obeying their better instincts for a moment, they happened to let their front paws fall, they were literally appalled as if at an error, as if Nature were an error, hastily raised their legs again, and their eyes seemed to be begging for forgiveness for having been forced to cease momentarily from their abomination. Was the world standing on its head? Where could I be? What could have happened? If only for my own sake I dared not hesitate any longer now, I dislodged myself from the tangle of bars, took one leap into the open and made toward the dogs – I, the young pupil, must be the teacher now, must make them understand what they were doing, must keep them from committing further sin. 'And old dogs too! And old dogs too!' I kept on saying to myself. But scarcely was I free and only a leap or two away from the dogs, when the music again had me in its power. Perhaps in my eagerness I might even have managed to withstand it, for I knew it better now, if in the midst of all its majestic amplitude, which was terrifying, but still not inconquerable, a clear, piercing, continuous note which came without variation literally from the remotest distance – perhaps the real melody in the midst of the music – had not now rung out, forcing me to my knees. Oh, the music these dogs made almost drove me out of my senses! I could not move a step farther, I no longer wanted to instruct them; they could go on raising their front legs, committing sin and seducing others to the sin of silently regarding them; I was such a young dog – who could demand such a difficult task from me? I made myself still more insignificant than I was, I whimpered, and if the dogs had asked me now what I thought of their performance, probably I would have had not a word to say against it. Besides, it was not long before the dogs vanished with all their music and their radiance into the darkness from which they had emerged.

As I have already said, this whole episode contains nothing of much note; in the course of a long life one encounters all sorts of things which, taken from their context and seen through the eyes of a child, might well seem far more astonishing. Besides, one may, of course – in the pungent popular phrase – have 'got it all wrong,' as well as everything connected with it; then it could be demonstrated that this was simply a case where seven musicians had assembled to practice their art in the morning stillness, that a very young dog had strayed to the place, a burdensome intruder whom they had tried to drive away by particularly terrifying or lofty music, unfortunately without success. He pestered them with his questions: Were they, already disturbed enough by the mere presence of the stranger, to be expected to attend to his distracting interruptions as well and make them worse by responding to them? Even if the law commands us to reply to everybody, was such a tiny stray dog in truth a somebody worthy of the name? And perhaps they did not even understand him, for he likely enough barked his questions very indistinctly. Or perhaps they did understand him and with great self-control answered his questions, but he, a mere puppy unaccustomed to music, could not distinguish the answer from the music. And as for walking on their hind legs, perhaps, unlike other dogs, they actually used only these for walking; if it was a sin, well, it was a sin. But they were alone, seven friends together, an intimate gathering within their own four walls so to speak, quite private so to speak; for one's friends, after all, are not the public, and where the public is not present an inquisitive little street dog is certainly not capable of constituting it; but, granting this, is it not as if nothing at all had happened? It is not quite so, but very nearly so, and parents should not let their children run about so freely, and had much better teach them to hold their tongues and respect the aged.

If all this is admitted, then it disposes of the whole case. But many things that are disposed of in the minds of grown-ups are not yet settled in the minds of the young. I rushed about, told my story, asked questions, made accusations and investigations, tried to drag others to the place where all this had happened, and burned to show everybody where I had stood and where the seven had stood, and where and how they had danced and made their music; and if anyone had come with me, instead of shaking me off and laughing at me, I would probably have sacrificed my innocence and tried myself to stand on my hind legs so as to reconstruct the scene clearly. Now children are blamed for all they do, but also in the last resort forgiven for all they do. And I have preserved my childlike qualities, and in spite of that have grown to be an old dog. Well, just as at that time I kept on unceasingly discussing the foregoing incident – which today I must confess I lay far less importance upon – analyzing it into constituent parts, arguing it with my listeners without regard to the company I found myself in, devoting my whole time to the problem, which I found as wearisome as everybody else, but which – that was the difference – for that very reason I was resolved to pursue indefatigably until I solved it, so that I might be left free again to regard the ordinary, calm, happy life of every day. Just so have I, though with less childish means – yet the difference is not so very great – labored in the years since and go on laboring today.

But it began with that concert. I do not blame the concert; it is my innate disposition that has driven me on, and it would certainly have found some other opportunity of coming into action had the concert never taken place. Yet the fact that it happened so soon used to make me feel sorry for myself; it robbed me of a great part of my childhood; the blissful life of the young dog, which many can spin out for years, in my case lasted for only a few short months. So be it. There are more important things than childhood. And perhaps I have the prospect of far more childlike happiness, earned by a life of hard work, in my old age than any actual child would have the strength to bear, but which then I shall possess.

I began my inquiries with the simplest things; there was no lack of material; it is the actual superabundance, unfortunately, that casts me into despair in my darker hours. I began to inquire into the question what the canine race nourished itself upon. Now that is, if you like, by no means a simple question, of course; it has occupied us since the dawn of time, it is the chief object of all our meditation, countless observations and essays and views on this subject have been published, it has grown into a province of knowledge which in its prodigious compass is not only beyond the comprehension of any single scholar, but of all our scholars collectively, a burden which cannot be borne except by the whole of the dog community, and even then with difficulty and not quite in its totality; for it ever and again crumbles away like a neglected ancestral inheritance and must laboriously be rehabilitated anew – not to speak at all of the difficulties and almost unfulfillable conditions of my investigation. No one need point all this out to me, I know it all as well as any average dog; I have no ambition to meddle with real scientific matters, I have all the respect for knowledge that it deserves, but to increase knowledge I lack the equipment, the diligence, the leisure, and – not least, and particularly during the past few years – the desire as well. I swallow down my food, but the slightest preliminary methodical politico-economical observation of it does not seem to me worth while. In this connection the essence of all knowledge is enough for me, the simple rule with which the mother weans her young ones from her teats and sends them out into the world: 'Water the ground as much as you can.' And in this sentence is not almost everything contained? What has scientific inquiry, ever since our first fathers inaugurated it, of decisive importance to add to this? Mere details, mere details, and how uncertain they are: but this rule will remain as long as we are dogs. It concerns our main staple of food: true, we have also other resources, but only at a pinch, and if the year is not too bad we could live on this main staple of our food; this food we find on the earth, but the earth needs our water to nourish it and only at that price provides us with our food, the emergence of which, however, and this should not be forgotten, can also be hastened by certain spells, songs, and ritual movements. But in my opinion that is all; there is nothing else that is fundamental to be said on the question. In this opinion, moreover, I am at one with the vast majority of the dog community, and must firmly dissociate myself from all heretical views on this point. Quite honestly I have no ambition to be peculiar, or to pose as being in the right against the majority; I am only too happy when I can agree with my comrades, as I do in this case. My own inquiries, however, are in another direction. My personal observation tells me that the earth, when it is watered and scratched according to the rules of science, extrudes nourishment, and moreover in such quality, in such abundance, in such ways, in such places, at such hours as the laws partially or completely established by science demand. I accept all this; my question, however, is the following: 'Whence does the earth procure this food?' A question which people in general pretend not to understand, and to which the best answer they can give is: 'If you haven't enough to eat, we'll give you some of ours.' Now consider this answer. I know that it is not one of the virtues of dogdom to share with others food that one has once gained possession of. Life is hard, the earth stubborn, science rich in knowledge but poor in practical results: anyone who has food keeps it to himself; that is not selfishness, but the opposite, dog law, the unanimous decision of the people, the outcome of their victory over egoism, for the possessors are always in a minority. And for that reason this answer: 'If you haven't enough to eat, we'll give you some of ours' is merely a way of speaking, a jest, a form of raillery. I have not forgotten that. But all the more significant did it seem to me, when I was rushing about everywhere with my questions during those days, that they put mockery aside as far as I was concerned; true, they did not actually give me anything to eat – where could they have found it at a moment's notice? – and even if anyone chanced to have some food, naturally he forgot everything else in the fury of his hunger; yet they all seriously meant what they said when they made the offer, and here and there, right enough, I was presently allowed some slight trifle if I was only smart enough to snatch it quickly. How came it that people treated me so strangely, pampered me, favored me? Because I was a lean dog, badly fed and neglectful of my needs? But there were countless badly fed dogs running about, and the others snatched even the wretchedest scrap from under their noses whenever they could, and often not from greed, but rather on principle. No, they treated me with special favor; I cannot give much detailed proof of this, but I have a firm conviction that it was so. Was it my questions, then, that pleased them, and that they regarded as so clever? No, my questions did not please them and were generally looked on as stupid. And yet it could only have been my questions that won me their attention. It was as if they would rather do the impossible, that is, stop my mouth with food – they did not do it, but they would have liked to do it – than endure my questions. But in that case they would have done better to drive me away and refuse to listen to my questions. No, they did not want to do that; they did not indeed want to listen to my questions, but it was because I asked these questions that they did not want to drive me away. That was the time – much as I was ridiculed and treated as a silly puppy, and pushed here and pushed there – the time when I actually enjoyed most public esteem; never again was I to enjoy anything like it; I had free entry everywhere, no obstacle was put in my way, I was actually flattered, though the flattery was disguised as rudeness. And all really because of my questions, my impatience, my thirst for knowledge. Did they want to lull me to sleep, to divert me, without violence, almost lovingly, from a false path, yet a path whose falseness was not so completely beyond all doubt that violence was permissible? Also a certain respect and fear kept them from employing violence. I divined even in those days something of this; today I know it quite well, far better than those who actually practiced it at the time: what they wanted to do was really to divert me from my path. They did not succeed; they achieved the opposite; my vigilance was sharpened. More, it became clear to me that it was I who was trying to seduce the others, and that I was actually successful up to a certain point. Only with the assistance of the whole dog world could I begin to understand my own questions. For instance when I asked: 'Whence does the earth procure this food?' was I troubled, as appearances might quite well indicate, about the earth; was I troubled about the labors of the earth? Not in the least; that, as I very soon recognized, was far from my mind; all that I cared for was the race of dogs, that and nothing else. For what is there actually except our own species? To whom but it can one appeal in the wide and empty world? All knowledge, the totality of all questions and all answers, is contained in the dog. If one could but realize this knowledge, if one could but bring it into the light of day, if we dogs would but own that we know infinitely more than we admit to ourselves! Even the most loquacious dog is more secretive of his knowledge than the places where good food can be found. Trembling with desire, whipping yourself with your own tail, you steal cautiously upon your fellow dog, you ask, you beg, you howl, you bite, and achieve – and achieve what you could have achieved just as well without any effort: amiable attention, friendly contiguity, honest acceptance, ardent embraces, barks that mingle as one: everything is directed toward achieving an ecstasy, a forgetting and finding again; but the one thing that you long to win above all, the admission of knowledge, remains denied to you. To such prayers, whether silent or loud, the only answers you get, even after you have employed your powers of seduction to the utmost, are vacant stares, averted glances, troubled and veiled eyes. It is much the same as it was when, a mere puppy, I shouted to the dog musicians and they remained silent.

Now one might say: 'You complain about your fellow dogs, about their silence on crucial questions; you assert that they know more than they admit, more than they will allow to be valid, and that this silence, the mysterious reason for which is also, of course, tacitly concealed, poisons existence and makes it unendurable for you, so that you must either alter it or have done with it; that may be; but you are yourself a dog, you have also the dog knowledge; well, bring it out, not merely in the form of a question, but as an answer. If you utter it, who will think of opposing you? The great choir of dogdom will join in as if it had been waiting for you. Then you will have clarity, truth, avowal, as much of them as you desire. The roof of this wretched life, of which you say so many hard things, will burst open, and all of us, shoulder to shoulder, will ascend into the lofty realm of freedom. And if we should not achieve that final consummation, if things should become worse than before, if the whole truth should be more insupportable than the half-truth, if it should be proved that the silent are in the right as the guardians of existence, if the faint hope that we still possess should give way to complete hopelessness, the attempt is still worth the trial, since you do not desire to live as you are compelled to live. Well, then, why do you make it a reproach against the others that they are silent, and remain silent yourself?' Easy to answer: Because I am a dog; in essentials just as locked in silence as the others, stubbornly resisting my own questions, dour out of fear. To be precise, is it in the hope that they might answer me that I have questioned my fellow dogs, at least since my adult years? Have I any such foolish hope? Can I contemplate the foundations of our existence, divine their profundity, watch the labor of their construction, that dark labor, and expect all this to be forsaken, neglected, undone, simply because I ask a question? No, that I truly expect no longer. I understand my fellow dogs, am flesh of their flesh, of their miserable, ever-renewed, ever-desirous flesh. But it is not merely flesh and blood that we have in common, but knowledge also, and not only knowledge, but the key to it as well. I do not possess that key except in common with all the others; I cannot grasp it without their help. The hardest bones, containing the richest marrow, can be conquered only by a united crunching of all the teeth of all dogs. That of course is only a figure of speech and exaggerated; if all teeth were but ready they would not need even to bite, the bones would crack themselves and the marrow would be freely accessible to the feeblest of dogs. If I remain faithful to this metaphor, then the goal of my aims, my questions, my inquiries, appears monstrous, it is true. For I want to compel all dogs thus to assemble together, I want the bones to crack open under the pressure of their collective preparedness, and then I want to dismiss them to the ordinary life that they love, while all by myself, quite alone, I lap up the marrow. That sounds monstrous, almost as if I wanted to feed on the marrow, not merely of a bone, but of the whole canine race itself. But it is only a metaphor. The marrow that I am discussing here is no food; on the contrary, it is a poison.

My questions only serve as a goad to myself; I only want to be stimulated by the silence which rises up around me as the ultimate answer. 'How long will you be able to endure the fact that the world of dogs, as your researches make more and more evident, is pledged to silence and always will be? How long will you be able to endure it?' That is the real great question of my life, before which all smaller ones sink into insignificance; it is put to myself alone and concerns no one else. Unfortunately I can answer it more easily than the smaller, specific questions: I shall probably hold out till my natural end; the calm of old age will put up a greater and greater resistance to all disturbing questions. I shall very likely die in silence and surrounded by silence, indeed almost peacefully, and I look forward to that with composure. An admirably strong heart, lungs that it is impossible to use up before their time, have been given to us dogs as if in malice; we survive all questions, even our own, bulwarks of silence that we are.

Recently I have taken more and more to casting up my life, looking for the decisive, the fundamental, error that I must surely have made; and I cannot find it. And yet I must have made it, for if I had not made it and yet were unable by the diligent labor of a long life to achieve my desire, that would prove that my desire is impossible, and complete hopelessness must follow. Behold, then, the work of a lifetime. First of all my inquiries into the question: Whence does the earth procure the food it gives us? A young dog, at bottom naturally greedy for life, I renounced all enjoyments, apprehensively avoided all pleasures, buried my head between my front paws when I was confronted by temptation, and addressed myself to my task. I was no scholar, neither in the information I acquired, nor in method, nor in intention. That was probably a defect, but it could not have been a decisive one. I had had little schooling, for I left my mother's care at an early age, soon got used to independence, led a free life; and premature independence is inimical to systematic learning. But I have seen much, listened to much, spoken with dogs of all sorts and conditions, understood everything, I believe, fairly intelligently, and correlated my particular observations fairly intelligently; that has compensated somewhat for my lack of scholarship, not to mention that independence, if it is a disadvantage in learning things, is an actual advantage when one is making one's own inquiries. In my case it was all the more necessary as I was not able to employ the real method of science, to avail myself, that is, of the labors of my predecessors, and establish contact with contemporary investigators. I was entirely cast on my own resources, began at the very beginning, and with the consciousness, inspiriting to youth, but utterly crushing to age, that the fortuitous point to which I carried my labors must also be the final one. Was I really so alone in my inquiries, at the beginning and up to now? Yes and no. It is inconceivable that there must not always have been and that there are not today individual dogs in the same case as myself. I cannot be so accursed as that. I do not deviate from the dog nature by a hairbreadth. Every dog has like me the impulse to question, and I have like every dog the impulse not to answer. Everyone has the impulse to question. How otherwise could my questions have affected my hearers in the slightest – and they were often affected, to my ecstatic delight, an exaggerated delight, I must confess – and how otherwise could I have done? And that I have the compulsion to remain silent needs unfortunately no particular proof. I am at bottom, then, no different from any other dog; everybody, no matter how he may differ in opinion from me and reject my views, will gladly admit that, and I in turn will admit as much of any other dog. Only the mixture of the elements is different, a difference very important for the individual, insignificant for the race. And now can one credit that the composition of these available elements has never chanced through all the past and present to result in a mixture similar to mine, one, moreover, if mine be regarded as unfortunate, more unfortunate still? To think so would be contrary to all experience. We dogs are all engaged in the strangest occupations, occupations in which one would refuse to believe if one had not the most reliable information concerning them. The best example that I can quote is that of the soaring dog. The first time I heard of one I laughed and simply refused to believe it. What? One was asked to believe that there was a very tiny species of dog, not much bigger than my head even when it was full grown, and this dog, who must of course be a feeble creature, an artificial, weedy, brushed and curled fop by all accounts, incapable of making an honest jump, this dog was supposed, according to people's stories, to remain for the most part high up in the air, apparently doing nothing at all but simply resting there? No, to try to make me swallow such things was exploiting the simplicity of a young dog too outrageously, I told myself. But shortly afterwards I heard from another source an account of another soaring dog. Could there be a conspiracy to fool me? But after that I saw the dog musicians with my own eyes, and from that day I considered everything possible, no prejudices fettered my powers of apprehension, I investigated the most senseless rumors, following them as far as they could take me, and the most senseless seemed to me in this senseless world more probable than the sensible, and moreover particularly fertile for investigation. So it was too with the soaring dogs. I discovered a great many things about them; true, I have succeeded to this day in seeing none of them, but of their existence I have been firmly convinced for a long time, and they occupy an important place in my picture of the world. As usual, it is not, of course, their technique that chiefly gives me to think. It is wonderful – who can gainsay it? – that these dogs should be able to float in the air: in my amazed admiration for that I am at one with my fellow dogs. But far more strange to my mind is the senselessness, the dumb senselessness of these existences. They have no relation whatever to the general life of the community, they hover in the air, and that is all, and life goes on its usual way; someone now and then refers to art and artists, but there it ends. But why, my good dogs, why on earth do these dogs float in the air? What sense is there in their occupation? Why can one get no word of explanation regarding them? Why do they hover up there, letting their legs, the pride of dogs, fall into desuetude, preserving a detachment from the nourishing earth, reaping without having sowed? being particularly well provided for, as I hear, and at the cost of the dog community too. I can flatter myself that my inquiries into these matters made some stir. People began to investigate after a fashion, to collect data; they made a beginning, at least, although they are never likely to go farther. But after all that is something. And though the truth will not be discovered by such means – never can that stage be reached – yet they throw light on some of the profounder ramifications of falsehood. For all the senseless phenomena of our existence, and the most senseless most of all, are susceptible to investigation. Not completely, of course – that is the diabolical jest – but sufficiently to spare one painful questions. Take the soaring dogs once more as an example; they are not haughty as one might imagine at first, but rather particularly dependent upon their fellow dogs; if one tries to put oneself in their place one will see that. For they must do what they can to obtain pardon, and not openly – that would be a violation of the obligation to keep silence – they must do what they can to obtain pardon for their way of life, or else divert attention from it so that it may be forgotten – and they do this, I have been told, by means of an almost unendurable volubility. They are perpetually talking, partly of their philosophical reflections, with which, seeing that they have completely renounced bodily exertion, they can continuously occupy themselves, partly of the observations which they have made from their exalted stations; and although, as is very understandable considering their lazy existence, they are not much distinguished for intellectual power, and their philosophy is as worthless as their observations, and science can make hardly any use of their utterances, and besides is not reduced to draw assistance from such wretched sources, nevertheless if one asks what the soaring dogs are really doing one will invariably receive the reply that they contribute a great deal to knowledge. 'That is true,' remarks someone, 'but their contributions are worthless and wearisome.' The reply to that is a shrug, or a change of the subject, or annoyance, or laughter, and in a little while, when you ask again, you learn once more that they contribute to knowledge, and finally when you are asked the question you yourself will reply – if you are not careful – to the same effect. And perhaps indeed it is well not to be too obstinate, but to yield to public sentiment, to accept the extant soaring dogs, and without recognizing their right to existence, which cannot be done, yet to tolerate them. But more than this must not be required; that would be going too far, and yet the demand is made. We are perpetually being asked to put up with new soaring dogs who are always appearing. One does not even know where they come from. Do these dogs multiply by propagation? Have they actually the strength for that? – for they are nothing much more than a beautiful coat of hair, and what is there in that to propagate? But even if that improbable contingency were possible, when could it take place? For they are invariably seen alone, self-complacently floating high up in the air, and if once in a while they descend to take a run, it lasts only for a minute or two, a few mincing struts and also always in strict solitude, absorbed in what is supposed to be profound thought, from which, even when they exert themselves to the utmost, they cannot tear themselves free, or at least so they say. But if they do not propagate their kind, is it credible that there can be dogs who voluntarily give up life on the solid ground, voluntarily become soaring dogs, and merely for the sake of the comfort and a certain technical accomplishment choose that empty life on cushions up there? It is unthinkable; neither propagation nor voluntary transition is thinkable. The facts, however, show that there are always new soaring dogs in evidence; from which one must conclude that, in spite of obstacles which appear insurmountable to our understanding, no dog species, however curious, ever dies out, once it exists, or, at least, not without a tough struggle, not without being capable of putting up a successful defense for a long time.

But if that is valid for such an out-of-the-way, externally odd, inefficient species as the soaring dog, must I not also accept it as valid for mine? Besides, I am not in the least queer outwardly; an ordinary middle-class dog such as is very prevalent, in this neighborhood, at least, I am neither particularly exceptional in any way, nor particularly repellent in any way; and in my youth and to some extent also in maturity, so long as I attended to my appearance and had lots of exercise, I was actually considered a very handsome dog. My front view was particularly admired, my slim legs, the fine set of my head; but my silvery white and yellow coat, which curled only at the hair tips, was very pleasing too; in all that there was nothing strange; the only strange thing about me is my nature, yet even that, as I am always careful to remember, has its foundation in universal dog nature. Now if not even the soaring dogs live in isolation, but invariably manage to encounter their fellows somewhere or other in the great dog world, and even to conjure new generations of themselves out of nothingness, then I too can live in the confidence that I am not quite forlorn. Certainly the fate of types like mine must be a strange one, and the existence of my colleagues can never be of visible help to me, if for no other reason than that I should scarcely ever be able to recognize them. We are the dogs who are crushed by the silence, who long to break through it, literally to get a breath of fresh air; the others seem to thrive on silence: true, that is only so in appearance, as in the case of the musical dogs, who ostensibly were quite calm when they played, but in reality were in a state of intense excitement; nevertheless the illusion is very strong, one tries to make a breach in it, but it mocks every attempt. What help, then, do my colleagues find? What kind of attempts do they make to manage to go on living in spite of everything? These attempts may be of various kinds. My own bout of questioning while I was young was one. So I thought that perhaps if I associated with those who asked many questions I might find my real comrades. Well, I did so for some time, with great self-control, a self-control made necessary by the annoyance I felt when I was interrupted by perpetual questions that I mostly could not answer myself: for the only thing that concerns me is to obtain answers. Moreover, who but is eager to ask questions when he is young, and how, when so many questions are going about, are you to pick out the right questions? One question sounds like another; it is the intention that counts, but that is often hidden even from the questioner. And besides, it is a peculiarity of dogs to be always asking questions, they ask them confusedly all together; it is as if in doing that they were trying to obliterate every trace of the genuine questions. No, my real colleagues are not to be found among the youthful questioners, and just as little among the old and silent, to whom I now belong. But what good are all these questions, for they have failed me completely; apparently my colleagues are cleverer dogs than I, and have recourse to other excellent methods that enable them to bear this life, methods which, nevertheless, as I can tell from my own experience, though they may perhaps help at a pinch, though they may calm, lull to rest, distract, are yet on the whole as impotent as my own, for, no matter where I look, I can see no sign of their success. I am afraid that the last thing by which I can hope to recognize my real colleagues is their success. But where, then, are my real colleagues? Yes, that is the burden of my complaint; that is the kernel of it. Where are they? Everywhere and nowhere. Perhaps my next-door neighbor, only three jumps away, is one of them; we often bark across to each other, he calls on me sometimes too, though I do not call on him. Is he my real colleague? I do not know, I certainly see no sign of it in him, but it is possible. It is possible, but all the same nothing is more improbable. When he is away I can amuse myself, drawing on my fancy, by discovering in him many things that have a suspicious resemblance to myself; but once he stands before me all my fancies become ridiculous. An old dog, a little smaller even than myself – and I am hardly medium size – brown, short-haired, with a tired hang of the head and a shuffling gait; on top of all this he trails his left hind leg behind him a little because of some disease. For a long time now I have been more intimate with him than with anybody else; I am glad to say that I can still get on tolerably well with him, and when he goes away I shout the most friendly greetings after him, though not out of affection, but in anger at myself; for if I follow him I find him just as disgusting again, slinking along there with his trailing leg and his much too low hindquarters. Sometimes it seems to me as if I were trying to humiliate myself by thinking of him as my colleague. Nor in our talks does he betray any trace of similarity of thought; true, he is clever and cultured enough as these things go here, and I could learn much from him; but is it for cleverness and culture that I am looking? We converse usually about local questions, and I am astonished – my isolation has made me more clear-sighted in such matters – how much intelligence is needed even by an ordinary dog, even in average and not unfavorable circumstances, if he is to live out his life and defend himself against the greater of life's customary dangers. True, knowledge provides the rules one must follow, but even to grasp them imperfectly and in rough outline is by no means easy, and when one has actually grasped them the real difficulty still remains, namely to apply them to local conditions – here almost nobody can help, almost every hour brings new tasks, and every new patch of earth its specific problems; no one can maintain that he has settled everything for good and that henceforth his life will go on, so to speak, of itself, not even I myself, though my needs shrink literally from day to day. And all this ceaseless labor – to what end? Merely to entomb oneself deeper and deeper in silence, it seems, so deep that one can never be dragged out of it again by anybody.

People often praise the universal progress made by the dog community throughout the ages, and probably mean by that more particularly the progress in knowledge. Certainly knowledge is progressing, its advance is irresistible, it actually progresses at an accelerating speed, always faster, but what is there to praise in that? It is as if one were to praise someone because with the years he grows older, and in consequence comes nearer and nearer to death with increasing speed. That is a natural and moreover an ugly process, in which I find nothing to praise. I can only see decline everywhere, in saying which, however, I do not mean that earlier generations were essentially better than ours, but only younger; that was their great advantage, their memory was not so overburdened as ours today, it was easier to get them to speak out, and even if nobody actually succeeded in doing that, the possibility of it was greater, and it is indeed this greater sense of possibility that moves us so deeply when we listen to those old and strangely simple stories. Here and there we catch a curiously significant phrase and we would almost like to leap to our feet, if we did not feel the weight of centuries upon us. No, whatever objection I may have to my age, former generations were not better, indeed in a sense they were far worse, far weaker. Even in those days wonders did not openly walk the streets for anyone to seize; but all the same, dogs – I cannot put it in any other way – had not yet become so doggish as today, the edifice of dogdom was still loosely put together, the true Word could still have intervened, planning or replanning the structure, changing it at will, transforming it into its opposite; and the Word was there, was very near at least, on the tip of everybody's tongue, anyone might have hit upon it. And what has become of it today? Today one may pluck out one's very heart and not find it. Our generation is lost, it may be, but it is more blameless than those earlier ones. I can understand the hesitation of my generation, indeed it is no longer mere hesitation; it is the thousandth forgetting of a dream dreamt a thousand times and forgotten a thousand times; and who can damn us merely for forgetting for the thousandth time? But I fancy I understand the hesitation of our forefathers too, we would probably have acted just as they did; indeed I could almost say: well for us that it was not we who had to take the guilt upon us, that instead we can hasten in almost guiltless silence toward death in a world darkened by others. When our first fathers strayed they had doubtless scarcely any notion that their aberration was to be an endless one, they could still literally see the crossroads, it seemed an easy matter to turn back whenever they pleased, and if they hesitated to turn back it was merely because they wanted to enjoy a dog's life for a little while longer; it was not yet a genuine dog's life, and already it seemed intoxicatingly beautiful to them, so what must it become in a little while, a very little while, and so they strayed farther. They did not know what we can now guess at, contemplating the course of history: that change begins in the soul before it appears in ordinary existence, and that, when they began to enjoy a dog's life, they must already have possessed real old dogs' souls, and were by no means so near their starting point as they thought, or as their eyes feasting on all doggish joys tried to persuade them. But who can still speak of youth today? These were the really young dogs, but their sole ambition unfortunately was to become old dogs, truly a thing which they could not fail to achieve, as all succeeding generations show, and ours, the last, most clearly of all.

Naturally I do not talk to my neighbor of these things, but often I cannot but think of them when I am sitting opposite him – that typical old dog – or bury my nose in his coat, which already has a whiff of the smell of cast-off hides. To talk to him, or even to any of the others, about such things would be pointless. I know what course the conversation would take. He would urge a slight objection now and then, but finally he would agree – agreement is the best weapon of defense – and the matter would be buried: why indeed trouble to exhume it at all? And in spite of this there is a profounder understanding between my neighbor and me, going deeper than mere words. I shall never cease to maintain that, though I have no proof of it and perhaps am merely suffering from an ordinary delusion, caused by the fact that for a long time this dog has been the only one with whom I have held any communication, and so I am bound to cling to him. 'Are you after all my colleague in your own fashion? And ashamed because everything has miscarried with you? Look, the same fate has been mine. When I am alone I weep over it; come, it is sweeter to weep in company.' I often have such thoughts as these and then I give him a prolonged look. He does not lower his glance, but neither can one read anything from it; he gazes at me dully, wondering why I am silent and why I have broken off the conversation. But perhaps that very glance is his way of questioning me, and I disappoint him just as he disappoints me. In my youth, if other problems had not been more important to me then, and I had not been perfectly satisfied with my own company, I would probably have asked him straight out and received an answer flatly agreeing with me, and that would have been worse even than today's silence. But is not everybody silent exactly in the same way? What is there to prevent me from believing that everyone is my colleague, instead of thinking that I have only one or two fellow inquirers – lost and forgotten along with their petty achievements, so that I can never reach them by any road through the darkness of ages or the confused throng of the present: why not believe that all dogs from the beginning of time have been my colleagues, all diligent in their own way, all unsuccessful in their own way, all silent or falsely garrulous in their own way, as hopeless research is apt to make one? But in that case I need not have severed myself from my fellows at all, I could have remained quietly among the others, I had no need to fight my way out like a stubborn child through the closed ranks of the grownups, who indeed wanted as much as I to find a way out, and who seemed incomprehensible to me simply because of their knowledge, which told them that nobody could ever escape and that it was stupid to use force.

Such ideas, however, are definitely due to the influence of my neighbor; he confuses me, he fills me with dejection; and yet in himself he is happy enough, at least when he is in his own quarters I often hear him shouting and singing; it is really unbearable. It would be a good thing to renounce this last tie also, to cease giving way to the vague dreams which all contact with dogs unavoidably provokes, no matter how hardened one may consider oneself, and to employ the short time that still remains for me exclusively in prosecuting my researches. The next time he comes I shall slip away, or pretend I am asleep, and keep up the pretense until he stops visiting me.

Also my researches have fallen into desuetude, I relax, I grow weary, I trot mechanically where once I raced enthusiastically. I think of the time when I began to inquire into the question: 'Whence does the earth procure this food?' Then indeed I really lived among the people, I pushed my way where the crowd was thickest, wanted everybody to know my work and be my audience, and my audience was even more essential to me than my work; I still expected to produce some effect or other, and that naturally gave me a great impetus, which now that I am solitary is gone. But in those days I was so full of strength that I achieved something unprecedented, something at variance with all our principles, and that every contemporary eyewitness assuredly recalls now as an uncanny feat. Our scientific knowledge, which generally makes for an extreme specialization, is remarkably simple in one province. I mean where it teaches that the earth engenders our food, and then, after having laid down this hypothesis, gives the methods by which the different foods may be achieved in their best kinds and greatest abundance. Now it is of course true that the earth brings forth all food, of that there can be no doubt; but as simple as people generally imagine it to be the matter is not; and their belief that it is simple prevents further inquiry. Take an ordinary occurrence that happens every day. If we were to be quite inactive, as I am almost completely now, and after a perfunctory scratching and watering of the soil lay down and waited for what was to come, then we should find the food on the ground, assuming, that is, that a result of some kind is inevitable. Nevertheless that is not what usually happens. Those who have preserved even a little freedom of judgment on scientific matters – and their numbers are truly small, for science draws a wider and wider circle around itself – will easily see, without having to make any specific experiment, that the main part of the food that is discovered on the ground in such cases comes from above; indeed customarily we snap up most of our food, according to our dexterity and greed, before it has reached the ground at all. In saying that, however, I am saying nothing against science; the earth, of course, brings forth this kind of food too. Whether the earth draws one kind of food out of itself and calls down another kind from the skies perhaps makes no essential difference, and science, which has established that in both cases it is necessary to prepare the ground, need not perhaps concern itself with such distinctions, for does it not say: 'If you have food in your jaws you have solved all questions for the time being.' But it seems to me that science nevertheless takes a veiled interest, at least to some extent, in these matters, inasmuch as it recognizes two chief methods of procuring food; namely the actual preparation of the ground, and secondly the auxiliary perfecting processes of incantation, dance, and song. I find here a distinction in accordance with the one I have myself made; not a definitive distinction, perhaps, but yet clear enough. The scratching and watering of the ground, in my opinion, serves to produce both kinds of food, and remains indispensable; incantation, dance, and song, however, are concerned less with the ground food in the narrower sense, and serve principally to attract the food from above. Tradition fortifies me in this interpretation. The ordinary dogs themselves set science right here without knowing it, and without science being able to venture a word in reply. If, as science claims, these ceremonies minister only to the soil, giving it the potency, let us say, to attract food from the air, then logically they should be directed exclusively to the soil; it is the soil that the incantations must be whispered to, the soil that must be danced to. And to the best of my knowledge science ordains nothing else than this. But now comes the remarkable thing; the people in all their ceremonies gaze upwards. This is no insult to science, since science does not forbid it, but leaves the husbandman complete freedom in this respect; in its teaching it takes only the soil into account, and if the husbandman carries out its instructions concerning the preparation of the ground it is content; yet, in my opinion, it should really demand more than this if it is logical. And, though I have never been deeply initiated into science, I simply cannot conceive how the learned can bear to let our people, unruly and passionate as they are, chant their incantations with their faces turned upwards, wail our ancient folk songs into the air, and spring high in their dances as though, forgetting the ground, they wished to take flight from it forever. I took this contradiction as my starting point, and whenever, according to the teachings of science, the harvest time was approaching, I restricted my attention to the ground, it was the ground that I scratched in the dance, and I almost gave myself a crick in the neck keeping my head as close to the ground as I could. Later I dug a hole for my nose, and sang and declaimed into it so that only the ground might hear, and nobody else beside or above me.

The results of my experiment were meager. Sometimes the food did not appear, and I was already preparing to rejoice at this proof, but then the food would appear; it was exactly as if my strange performance had caused some confusion at first, but had shown itself later to possess advantages, so that in my case the usual barking and leaping could be dispensed with. Often, indeed, the food appeared in greater abundance than formerly, but then again it would stay away altogether. With a diligence hitherto unknown in a young dog I drew up exact reports of all my experiments, fancied that here and there I was on a scent that might lead me further, but then it lost itself again in obscurity. My inadequate grounding in science also undoubtedly held me up here. What guarantee had I, for instance, that the absence of the food was not caused by unscientific preparation of the ground rather than by my experiments, and if that should be so, then all my conclusions were invalid. In certain circumstances I might have been able to achieve an almost scrupulously exact experiment; namely, if I had succeeded only once in bringing down food by an upward incantation without preparing the ground at all, and then had failed to extract food by an incantation directed exclusively to the ground. I attempted indeed something of this kind, but without any real belief in it and without the conditions being quite perfect; for it is my fixed opinion that a certain amount of ground-preparation is always necessary, and even if the heretics who deny this are right, their theory can never be proved in any case, seeing that the watering of the ground is done under a kind of compulsion, and within certain limits simply cannot be avoided. Another and somewhat tangential experiment succeeded better and aroused some public attention. Arguing from the customary method of snatching food while still in the air, I decided to allow the food to fall to the ground, but to make no effort to snatch it. Accordingly I always made a small jump in the air when the food appeared, but timed it so that it might always fail of its object; in the majority of instances the food fell dully and indifferently to the ground in spite of this, and I flung myself furiously upon it, with the fury both of hunger and of disappointment. But in isolated cases something else happened, something really strange; the food did not fall but followed me through the air; the food pursued the hungry. That never went on for long, always for only a short stretch, then the food fell after all, or vanished completely, or – the most common case – my greed put a premature end to the experiment and I swallowed down the tempting food. All the same I was happy at that time, a stir of curiosity ran through my neighborhood, I attracted uneasy attention, I found my acquaintances more accessible to my questions, I could see in their eyes a gleam that seemed like an appeal for help; and even if it was only the reflection of my own glance I asked for nothing more. I was satisfied. Until at last I discovered – and the others discovered it simultaneously – that this experiment of mine was a commonplace of science, had already succeeded with others far more brilliantly than with me, and though it had not been attempted for a long time on account of the extreme self-control it required, had also no need to be repeated, for scientifically it had no value at all. It only proved what was already known, that the ground not only attracts food vertically from above, but also at a slant, indeed sometimes in spirals. So there I was left with my experiment, but I was not discouraged, I was too young for that; on the contrary, this disappointment braced me to attempt perhaps the greatest achievement of my life. I did not believe the scientists' depreciations of my experiment, yet belief was of no avail here, but only proof, and I resolved to set about establishing that and thus raise my experiment from its original irrelevance and set it in the very center of the field of research. I wished to prove that when I retreated before the food it was not the ground that attracted it at a slant, but I who drew it after me. This first experiment, it is true, I could not carry any farther; to see the food before one and experiment in a scientific spirit at the same time – one cannot keep that up indefinitely. But I decided to do something else; I resolved to fast completely as long as I could stand it, and at the same time avoid all sight of food, all temptation. If I were to withdraw myself in this manner, remain lying day and night with closed eyes, trouble myself neither to snatch food from the air nor to lift it from the ground, and if, as I dared not expect, yet faintly hoped, without taking any of the customary measures, and merely in response to the unavoidable irrational watering of the ground and the quiet recitation of the incantations and songs (the dance I wished to omit, so as not to weaken my powers) the food were to come of itself from above, and without going near the ground were to knock at my teeth for admittance – if that were to happen, then, even if science was not confuted, for it has enough elasticity to admit exceptions and isolated cases – I asked myself what would the other dogs say, who fortunately do not possess such extreme elasticity? For this would be no exceptional case like those handed down by history, such as the incident, let us say, of the dog who refuses, because of bodily illness or trouble of mind, to prepare the ground, to track down and seize his food, upon which the whole dog community recite magical formulae and by this means succeed in making the food deviate from its customary route into the jaws of the invalid. I, on the contrary, was perfectly sound and at the height of my powers, my appetite so splendid that it prevented me all day from thinking of anything but itself; I submitted, moreover, whether it be credited or not, voluntarily to my period of fasting, was myself quite able to conjure down my own supply of food and wished also to do so, and so I asked no assistance from the dog community, and indeed rejected it in the most determined manner.

I sought a suitable place for myself in an outlying clump of bushes, where I would have to listen to no talk of food, no sound of munching jaws and bones being gnawed; I ate my fill for the last time and laid me down. As far as possible I wanted to pass my whole time with closed eyes; until the food came it would be perpetual night for me, even though my vigil might last for days or weeks. During that time, however, I dared not sleep much, better indeed if I did not sleep at all – and that made everything much harder – for I must not only conjure the food down from the air, but also be on my guard lest I should be asleep when it arrived; yet on the other hand sleep would be very welcome to me, for I would manage to fast much longer asleep than awake. For those reasons I decided to arrange my time prudently and sleep a great deal, but always in short snatches. I achieved this by always resting my head while I slept on some frail twig, which soon snapped and so awoke me. So there I lay, sleeping or keeping watch, dreaming or singing quietly to myself. My first vigils passed uneventfully; perhaps in the place whence the food came no one had yet noticed that I was lying there in resistance to the normal course of things, and so there was no sign. I was a little disturbed in my concentration by the fear that the other dogs might miss me, presently find me, and attempt something or other against me. A second fear was that at the mere wetting of the ground, though it was unfruitful ground according to the findings of science, some chance nourishment might appear and seduce me by its smell. But for a time nothing of that kind happened and I could go on fasting. Apart from such fears I was more calm during this first stage than I could remember ever having been before. Although in reality I was laboring to annul the findings of science, I felt within me a deep reassurance, indeed almost the proverbial serenity of the scientific worker. In my thoughts I begged forgiveness of science; there must be room in it for my researches too; consolingly in my ears rang the assurance that no matter how great the effect of my inquiries might be, and indeed the greater the better, I would not be lost to ordinary dog life; science regarded my attempts with benevolence, it itself would undertake the interpretation of my discoveries, and that promise already meant fulfillment; while until now I had felt outlawed in my innermost heart and had run my head against the traditional walls of my species like a savage, I would now be accepted with great honor, the long- yearned-for warmth of assembled canine bodies would lap around me, I would ride uplifted high on the shoulders of my fellows. Remarkable effects of my first hunger. My achievement seemed so great to me that I began to weep with emotion and self-pity there among the quiet bushes, which it must be confessed was not very understandable, for when I was looking forward to my well-earned reward why should I weep? Probably out of pure happiness. It is always when I am happy, and that is seldom enough, that I weep. After that, however, these feelings soon passed. My beautiful fancies fled one by one before the increasing urgency of my hunger; a little longer and I was, after an abrupt farewell to all my imaginations and my sublime feelings, totally alone with the hunger burning in my entrails. 'That is my hunger,' I told myself countless times during this stage, as if I wanted to convince myself that my hunger and I were still two things and I could shake it off like a burdensome lover; but in reality we were very painfully one, and when I explained to myself: 'That is my hunger,' it was really my hunger that was speaking and having its joke at my expense. A bad, bad time! I still shudder to think of it, and not merely on account of the suffering I endured then, but mainly because I was unable to finish it then and consequently shall have to live through that suffering once more if I am ever to achieve anything; for today I still hold fasting to be the final and most potent means of my research. The way goes through fasting; the highest, if it is attainable, is attainable only by the highest effort, and the highest effort among us is voluntary fasting. So when I think of those times – and I would gladly pass my life in brooding over them – I cannot help thinking also of the time that still threatens me. It seems to me that it takes almost a lifetime to recuperate from such an attempt; my whole life as an adult lies between me and that fast, and I have not recovered yet. When I begin upon my next fast I shall perhaps have more resolution than the first time, because of my greater experience and deeper insight into the need for the attempt, but my powers are still enfeebled by that first essay, and so I shall probably begin to fail at the mere approach of these familiar horrors. My weaker appetite will not help me; it will only reduce the value of the attempt a little, and will, indeed, probably force me to fast longer than would have been necessary the first time. I think I am clear on these and many other matters, the long interval has not been wanting in trial attempts, often enough I have literally got my teeth into hunger; but I was still not strong enough for the ultimate effort, and now the unspoiled ardor of youth is of course gone forever. It vanished in the great privations of that first fast. All sorts of thoughts tormented me. Our forefathers appeared threateningly before me. True, I held them responsible for everything, even if I dared not say so openly; it was they who involved our dog life in guilt, and so I could easily have responded to their menaces with countermenaces; but I bow before their knowledge, it came from sources of which we know no longer, and for that reason, much as I may feel compelled to oppose them, I shall never actually overstep their laws, but content myself with wriggling out through the gaps, for which I have a particularly good nose. On the question of fasting I appealed to the well-known dialogue in the course of which one of our sages once expressed the intention of forbidding fasting, but was dissuaded by a second with the words: 'But who would ever think of fasting?'

whereupon the first sage allowed himself to be persuaded and withdrew the prohibition. But now arises the question: 'Is not fasting really forbidden after all?' The great majority of commentators deny this and regard fasting as freely permitted, and holding as they think with the second sage do not worry in the least about the evil consequences that may result from erroneous interpretations. I had naturally assured myself on this point before I began my fast. But now that I was twisted with the pangs of hunger, and in my distress of mind sought relief in my own hind legs, despairingly licking and gnawing at them up to the very buttocks, the universal interpretation of this dialogue seemed to me entirely and completely false, I cursed the commentators' science, I cursed myself for having been led astray by it; for the dialogue contained, as any child could see, more than merely one prohibition of fasting; the first sage wished to forbid fasting; what a sage wishes is already done, so fasting was forbidden; as for the second sage, he not only agreed with the first, but actually considered fasting impossible, piled therefore on the first prohibition a second, that of dog nature itself; the first sage saw this and thereupon withdrew the explicit prohibition, that was to say, he imposed upon all dogs, the matter being now settled, the obligation to know themselves and to make their own prohibitions regarding fasting. So here was a threefold prohibition instead of merely one, and I had violated it. Now I could at least have obeyed at this point, though tardily, but in the midst of my pain I felt a longing to go on fasting, and I followed it as greedily as if it were a strange dog. I could not stop; perhaps too I was already too weak to get up and seek safety for myself in familiar scenes. I tossed about on the fallen forest leaves, I could no longer sleep, I heard noises on every side; the world, which had been asleep during my life hitherto, seemed to have been awakened by my fasting, I was tortured by the fancy that I would never be able to eat again, and I must eat so as to reduce to silence this world rioting so noisily around me, and I would never be able to do so; but the greatest noise of all came from my own belly, I often laid my ear against it with startled eyes, for I could hardly believe what I heard. And now that things were becoming unendurable my very nature seemed to be seized by the general frenzy, and made senseless attempts to save itself; the smell of food began to assail me, delicious dainties that I had long since forgotten, delights of my childhood; yes, I could smell the very fragrance of my mother's teats; I forgot my resolution to resist all smells, or rather I did not forget it; I dragged myself to and fro, never for more than a few yards, and sniffed as if that were in accordance with my resolution, as if I were looking for food simply to be on my guard against it. The fact that I found nothing did not disappoint me; the food must be there, only it was always a few steps away, my legs failed me before I could reach it. But simultaneously I knew that nothing was there, and that I made those feeble movements simply out of fear lest I might collapse in this place and never be able to leave it. My last hopes, my last dreams vanished; I would perish here miserably; of what use were my researches? – childish attempts undertaken in childish and far happier days; here and now was the hour of deadly earnest, here my inquiries should have shown their value, but where had they vanished? Only a dog lay here helplessly snapping at the empty air, a dog who, though he still watered the ground with convulsive haste at short intervals and without being aware of it, could not remember even the shortest of the countless incantations stored in his memory, not even the little rhyme which the newly born puppy says when it snuggles under its mother. It seemed to me as if I were separated from all my fellows, not by a quite short stretch, but by an infinite distance, and as if I would die less of hunger than of neglect. For it was clear that nobody troubled about me, nobody beneath the earth, on it, or above it; I was dying of their indifference; they said indifferently: 'He is dying,' and it would actually come to pass. And did I not myself assent? Did I not say the same thing? Had I not wanted to be forsaken like this? Yes, brothers, but not so as to perish in that place, but to achieve truth and escape from this world of falsehood, where there is no one from whom you can learn the truth, not even from me, born as I am a citizen of falsehood. Perhaps the truth was not so very far off, and I not so forsaken, therefore, as I thought; or I may have been forsaken less by my fellows than by myself, in yielding and consenting to die.

But one does not die so easily as a nervous dog imagines. I merely fainted, and when I came to and raised my eyes a strange hound was standing before me. I did not feel hungry, but rather filled with strength, and my limbs, it seemed to me, were light and agile, though I made no attempt to prove this by getting to my feet. My visual faculties in themselves were no keener than usual; a beautiful but not at all extraordinary hound stood before me; I could see that, and that was all, and yet it seemed to me that I saw something more in him. There was blood under me, at first I took it for food; but I recognized it immediately as blood that I had vomited. I turned my eyes from it to the strange hound. He was lean, long-legged, brown with a patch of white here and there, and had a fine, strong, piercing glance. 'What are you doing here?' he asked. 'You must leave this place.' 'I can't leave it just now,' I said, without trying to explain, for how could I explain everything to him; besides, he seemed to be in a hurry. 'Please go away,' he said, impatiently lifting his feet and setting them down again. 'Let me be,' I said, 'leave me to myself and don't worry about me; the others don't.' 'I ask you to go for your own sake,' he said. 'You can ask for any reason you like,' I replied. 'I can't go even if I wanted to.' 'You need have no fear of that,' he said, smiling. 'You can go all right. It's because you seem to be feeble that I ask you to go now, and you can go slowly if you like; if you linger now you'll have to race off later on.' 'That's my affair,' I replied. 'It's mine too,' he said, saddened by my stubbornness, yet obviously resolved to let me lie for the time being, but at the same time to seize the opportunity of paying court to me. At any other time I would gladly have submitted to the blandishments of such a beautiful creature, but at that moment, why, I cannot tell, the thought filled me with terror. 'Get out!' I screamed, and all the louder as I had no other means of protecting myself. 'All right, I'll leave you then,' he said, slowly retreating. 'You're wonderful. Don't I please you?' 'You'll please me by going away and leaving me in peace,' I said, but I was no longer so sure of myself as I tried to make him think. My senses, sharpened by fasting, suddenly seemed to see or hear something about him; it was just beginning, it was growing, it came nearer, and I knew that this hound had the power to drive me away, even if I could not imagine to myself at the moment how I was ever to get to my feet. And I gazed at him – he had merely shaken his head sadly at my rough answer – with ever mounting desire. 'Who are you?' I asked. 'I'm a hunter,' he replied. 'And why won't you let me lie here?' I asked. 'You disturb me,' he said. 'I can't hunt while you're here.' 'Try,' I said, 'perhaps you'll be able to hunt after all.' 'No,' he said, 'I'm sorry, but you must go.' 'Don't hunt for this one day!' I implored him. 'No,' he said, 'I must hunt.' 'I must go; you must hunt,' I said, 'nothing but musts. Can you explain to me why we must?' 'No,' he replied, 'but there's nothing that needs to be explained, these are natural, self-evident things.' 'Not quite so self-evident as all that,' I said, 'you're sorry that you must drive me away, and yet you do it.' 'That's so,' he replied. 'That's so,' I echoed him crossly, 'that isn't an answer. Which sacrifice would you rather make: to give up your hunting, or give up driving me away?' 'To give up my hunting,' he said without hesitation. 'There!' said I, 'don't you see that you're contradicting yourself?' 'How am I contradicting myself?' he replied. 'My dear little dog, can it be that you really don't understand that I must? Don't you understand the most self-evident fact?' I made no answer, for I noticed – and new life ran through me, life such as terror gives – I noticed from almost invisible indications, which perhaps nobody but myself could have noticed, that in the depths of his chest the hound was preparing to upraise a song. 'You're going to sing,' I said. 'Yes,' he replied gravely,

'I'm going to sing, soon, but not yet.' 'You're beginning already,' I said. 'No,' he said, 'not yet. But be prepared.' 'I can hear it already, though you deny it,' I said, trembling. He was silent, and then I thought I saw something such as no dog before me had ever seen, at least there is no slightest hint of it in our tradition, and I hastily bowed my head in infinite fear and shame in the pool of blood lying before me. I thought I saw that the hound was already singing without knowing it, nay, more, that the melody, separated from him, was floating on the air in accordance with its own laws, and as though he had no part in it, was moving toward me, toward me alone. Today, of course, I deny the validity of all such perceptions and ascribe them to my overexcitation at that time, but even if it was an error it had nevertheless a sort of grandeur, and is the sole, even if delusive, reality that I have carried over into this world from my period of fasting, and shows at least how far we can go when we are beyond ourselves. And I was actually quite beyond myself. In ordinary circumstances I would have been very ill, incapable of moving; but the melody, which the hound soon seemed to acknowledge as his, was quite irresistible. It grew stronger and stronger; its waxing power seemed to have no limits, and already almost burst my eardrums. But the worst was that it seemed to exist solely for my sake, this voice before whose sublimity the woods fell silent, to exist solely for my sake; who was I, that I could dare to remain here, lying brazenly before it in my pool of blood and filth. I tottered to my feet and looked down at myself; this wretched body can never run, I still had time to think, but already, spurred on by the melody, I was careering from the spot in splendid style. I said nothing to my friends; probably I could have told them all when I first arrived, but I was too feeble, and later it seemed to me that such things could not be told. Hints which I could not refrain from occasionally dropping were quite lost in the general conversation. For the rest I recovered physically in a few hours, but spiritually I still suffer from the effects of that experiment.

Nevertheless, I next carried my researches into music. True, science had not been idle in this sphere either; the science of music, if I am correctly informed, is perhaps still more comprehensive than that of nurture, and in any case established on a firmer basis. That may be explained by the fact that this province admits of more objective inquiry than the other, and its knowledge is more a matter of pure observation and systematization, while in the province of food the main object is to achieve practical results. That is the reason why the science of music is accorded greater esteem than that of nurture, but also why the former has never penetrated so deeply into the life of the people. I myself felt less attracted to the science of music than to any other until I heard that voice in the forest. My experience with the musical dogs had indeed drawn my attention to music, but I was still too young at that time. Nor is it by any means easy even to come to grips with that science; it is regarded as very esoteric and politely excludes the crowd. Besides, although what struck me most deeply at first about these dogs was their music, their silence seemed to me still more significant; as for their affrighting music, probably it was quite unique, so that I could leave it out of account; but thenceforth their silence confronted me everywhere and in all the dogs I met. So for penetrating into real dog nature, research into food seemed to me the best method, calculated to lead me to my goal by the straightest path. Perhaps I was mistaken. A border region between these two sciences, however, had already attracted my attention. I mean the theory of incantation, by which food is called down. Here again it is very much against me that I have never seriously tackled the science of music and in this sphere cannot even count myself among the half-educated, the class on whom science looks down most of all. This fact I cannot get away from. I could not – I have proof of that, unfortunately – I could not pass even the most elementary scientific examination set by an authority on the subject. Of course, quite apart from the circumstances already mentioned, the reason for that can be found in my incapacity for scientific investigation, my limited powers of thought, my bad memory, but above all in my inability to keep my scientific aim continuously before my eyes. All this I frankly admit, even with a certain degree of pleasure. For the more profound cause of my scientific incapacity seems to me to be an instinct, and indeed by no means a bad one. If I wanted to brag I might say that it was this very instinct that invalidated my scientific capacities, for it would surely be a very extraordinary thing if one who shows a tolerable degree of intelligence in dealing with the ordinary daily business of life, which certainly cannot be called simple, and moreover one whose findings have been checked and verified, where that was possible, by individual scientists if not by science itself, should *a priori* be incapable of planting his paw even on the first rung of the ladder of science. It was this instinct that made me – and perhaps for the sake of science itself, but a different science from that of today, an ultimate science – prize freedom higher than everything else. Freedom! Certainly such freedom as is possible today is a wretched business. But nevertheless freedom, nevertheless a possession.

Translated by Willa and Edwin Muir

The Married Couple

BUSINESS in general is so bad that sometimes, when my work in the office leaves me a little time, I myself pick up the case of samples and call on my customers personally. Long since I had intended to visit sometime, among others, N., with whom once I had constant business relations, which, however, during the last year have almost completely lapsed for some reason unknown to me. Besides, there need not always be real reasons for such disruptions; in the present unstable state of affairs often a mere nothing, a mood, will turn the scale, and in the same way a mere nothing, a word, can put things right again. To gain admittance to N., however, is a somewhat ticklish business; he is an old man, grown somewhat infirm too of late, and though he still insists on attending to business matters himself, he is hardly ever to be seen in his office; if you want to speak to him you have to go to his house, and one likes to put off a business call of that kind.

Last evening after six I nevertheless set out for his house; it was really no time for paying calls, but my visit after all was a business, not a social, one, and might be regarded accordingly. I was in luck. N. was in; he had just come back with his wife from a walk, the servant told me, and was now in the bedroom of his son, who was unwell and confined to his bed. I was requested to go there; at first I hesitated, but then the desire to get my disagreeable visit over as quickly as possible turned the scale, and I allowed myself to be conducted as I was, in my overcoat and hat, with my case of samples, through a dark room into a faintly lit one, where a small company was gathered.

My first glance fell, probably by instinct, on an agent only too well known to me, a trade rival of myself in some respects. So he had stolen a march on me, it seemed. He was sitting comfortably by the bed of the sick man, just as if he were a doctor; he sat there brazenly in his beautiful ample overcoat, which was unbuttoned; the sick man too probably had his own thoughts as he lay there with his cheeks faintly flushed with fever, now and then glancing at his visitor. He was no longer young either, N.'s son, a man of about my own age with a short beard, somewhat unkempt on account of his illness. Old N., a tall, broad-shouldered man, but to my astonishment grown very thin because of some creeping malady, bent and infirm, was still wearing the fur coat in which he had entered, and mumbling something to his son. His wife, small and frail, but immensely vivacious, yet only when she spoke to him – us others she scarcely noticed – was occupied in helping him to take off his overcoat, which, considering the great difference in their height, was a matter of some difficulty, but at last was achieved. Perhaps, indeed, the real difficulty was caused by N.'s impatience, for with restless hands he kept on feeling for the easy chair, which his wife, after the overcoat was off, quickly pushed forward for him. She herself then took up the fur coat, beneath which she almost vanished, and carried it out.

Now at last, it seemed to me, my moment had come, or rather it had not come and probably would never come; yet if I was to attempt anything it must be done at once, for I felt that here the conditions for a business interview could only become increasingly unfavorable; and to plant myself down here for all time, as the agent apparently intended, was not my way: besides, I did not want to take the slightest notice of him. So I began without ceremony to state my business, although I saw that N. would have liked at that moment to have a chat with his son. Unfortunately I have a habit when I have worked myself up – and that takes a very short time, and on this occasion took a shorter time than usual – of getting up and walking about while I am talking. Though a very good arrangement in one's own office, in a strange house it may be somewhat burdensome. But I could not restrain myself, particularly as I was feeling the lack of my usual cigarette. Well, every man has his bad habits, yet I can congratulate myself on mine when I think of the agent's. For what is to be said of his behavior, of the fact, for instance, that every now and then he would suddenly and quite unexpectedly clap his hat on his head; he had been holding it on his knee until then, slowly pushing it up and down there. True, he took it off again immediately, as if he had made a blunder, but he had had it on his head nevertheless for a second or two, and besides he repeated this performance again and again every few minutes. Surely such conduct must be called unpardonable. It did not disturb me, however, I walked up and down, completely absorbed in my own proposals, and ignored him; but there are people whom that trick with the hat might have put off completely. However, when I am thoroughly worked up I disregard not only such annoyances as these, but everything. I see, it is true, all that is going on, but do not admit it, so to speak, to my consciousness until I am finished, or until some objection is raised. Thus I noticed quite well, for instance, that N. was by no means in a receptive state; holding on to the arms of his chair, he twisted about uncomfortably, never even glanced up at me, but gazed blankly, as if searching for something, into vacancy, and his face was so impassive that one might have thought no syllable of what I was saying, indeed no awareness of my presence, had penetrated to him. Yes, his whole bearing, the bearing of a sick man, in itself inauspicious for me, I took in quite well; nevertheless I talked on as if I had still some prospect of putting everything right again by my talk, by the advantageous offers I made – I was myself alarmed by the concessions I granted, concessions that had not even been asked for. It gave me a certain satisfaction also to notice that the agent, as I verified by a fleeting glance, had at last left his hat in peace and folded his arms across his chest; my performance, which was partly, I must confess, intended for him, seemed to have given a severe blow to his designs. And in the elation produced by this result I might perhaps have gone on talking for a long time still, if the son, whom until now I had regarded as a secondary factor in my plans, had not suddenly raised himself in his bed and pulled me up by shaking his fist. Obviously he wanted to say something, to point out something, but he had not strength enough. At first I thought that his mind was wandering, but when I involuntarily glanced at old N. I understood better.

N. sat with wide-open, glassy, bulging eyes, which seemed on the point of failing; he was trembling and his body was bent forward as if someone were holding him down or striking him on the shoulders; his lower lip, indeed the lower jaw itself with the exposed gums, hung down helplessly; his whole face seemed out of joint; he still breathed, though with difficulty; but then, as if released, he fell back against the back of his chair, closed his eyes, the mark of some great strain passed over his face and vanished, and all was over. I sprang to him and seized his lifeless hand, which was so cold that it sent a chill through me; no pulse beat there now. So it was all over. Still, he was a very old man. We would be fortunate if we all had such an easy death. But how much there was to be done! And what should one do first? I looked around for help; but the son had drawn the bedclothes over his head, and I could hear his wild sobbing; the agent, cold as a fish, sat immovably on his chair, two steps from N., and was obviously resolved to do nothing, to wait for what time would bring; so I, only I was left to do something, and the hardest thing that anyone could be asked to do, that was to tell the news to his wife in some bearable form, in a form that did not exist, in other words. And already I could hear her eager shuffling steps in the next room.

Still wearing her outdoor clothes – she had not found time to change – she brought in a nightshirt that she had warmed before the fire for her husband to put on. 'He's fallen asleep,' she said, smiling and shaking her head, when she found us sitting so still. And with the infinite trustfulness of the innocent she took up the same hand that I had held a moment before with such fear and repugnance, kissed it playfully, and – how could we three others have borne the sight? – N. moved, yawned loudly, allowed his nightshirt to be put on, endured with a mixture of annoyance and irony his wife's tender reproaches for having overstrained himself by taking such a long walk, and strangely enough said in reply, to provide no doubt a different explanation for his having fallen asleep, something about feeling bored. Then, so as not to catch cold by going through the draughty passage into a different room, he lay down for the time being in his son's bed; his head was bedded down beside his son's feet on two cushions hastily brought by his wife. After all that had gone before I found nothing particularly odd in that. Then he asked for the evening paper, opened it without paying any attention to his guests, but did not read it, only glancing through it here and there, and made several very unpleasant observations on our offers, observations which showed astonishing shrewdness, while he waved his free hand disdainfully, and by clicking his tongue indicated that our business methods had left a bad taste in his mouth. The agent could not refrain from making one or two untimely remarks, no doubt he felt in his insensitive way that some compensation was due to him after what had happened, but his way of securing it was the worst he could have chosen. I said goodbye as soon as I could, I felt almost grateful to the agent; if he had not been there I would not have had the resolution to leave so soon.

In the lobby I met Frau N. again. At the sight of that pathetic figure I said impulsively that she reminded me a little of my mother. And as she remained silent I added: 'Whatever people say, she could do wonders. Things that we destroyed she could make whole again. I lost her when I was still a child.' I had spoken with deliberate slowness and distinctness, for I assumed the old lady was hard of hearing. But she must have been quite deaf, for she asked without transition: 'And how does my husband look to you?' From a few parting words I noticed, moreover, that she confused me with the agent; I like to think that otherwise she would have been more forthcoming.

Then I descended the stairs: The descent was more tiring than the ascent had been, and not even that had been easy. Oh, how many business calls come to nothing, and yet one must keep going.

Translated by Willa and Edwin Muir

Give It Up!

IT WAS very early in the morning, the streets clean and deserted, I was on my way to the station. As I compared the tower clock with my watch I realized it was much later than I had thought and that I had to hurry; the shock of this discovery made me feel uncertain of the way, I wasn't very well acquainted with the town as yet; fortunately, there was a policeman at hand, I ran to him and breathlessly asked him the way. He smiled and said: 'You asking me the way?' 'Yes,' I said, 'since I can't find it myself.' 'Give it up! Give it up!' said he, and turned with a sudden jerk, like someone who wants to be alone with his laughter.

Translated by Tania and James Stern

On Parables

MANY complain that the words of the wise are always merely parables and of no use in daily life, which is the only life we have. When the sage says: 'Go over,' he does not mean that we should cross to some actual place, which we could do anyhow if the labor were worth it; he means some fabulous yonder, something unknown to us, something that he cannot designate more precisely either, and therefore cannot help us here in the very least. All these parables set out to say merely that the incomprehensible is incomprehensible, and we know that already. But the cares we have to struggle with every day: that is a different matter.

Concerning this a man once said: Why such reluctance? If you only followed the parables you yourselves would become parables and with that rid of all your daily cares.

Another said: I bet that is also a parable.

The first said: You have won.

The second said: But unfortunately only in parable.

The first said: No, in reality: in parable you have lost.

Translated by Willa and Edwin Muir

The Burrow

I HAVE COMPLETED the construction of my burrow and it seems to be successful. All that can be seen from outside is a big hole; that, however, really leads nowhere; if you take a few steps you strike against natural firm rock. I can make no boast of having contrived this ruse intentionally; it is simply the remains of one of my many abortive building attempts, but finally it seemed to me advisable to leave this one hole without filling it in. True, some ruses are so subtle that they defeat themselves, I know that better than anyone, and it is certainly a risk to draw attention by this hole to the fact that there may be something in the vicinity worth inquiring into. But you do not know me if you think I am afraid, or that I built my burrow simply out of fear. At a distance of some thousand paces from this hole lies, covered by a movable layer of moss, the real entrance to the burrow; it is secured as safely as anything in this world can be secured; yet someone could step on the moss or break through it, and then my burrow would lie open, and anybody who liked – please note, however, that quite uncommon abilities would also be required – could make his way in and destroy everything for good. I know that very well, and even now, at the zenith of my life, I can scarcely pass an hour in complete tranquility; at that one point in the dark moss I am vulnerable, and in my dreams I often see a greedy muzzle sniffing around it persistently. It will be objected that I could quite well have filled in the entrance too, with a thin layer of hard earth on top and with loose soil further down, so that it would not cost me much trouble to dig my way out again whenever I liked. But that plan is impossible; prudence itself demands that I should have a way of leaving at a moment's notice if necessary, prudence itself demands, as alas! so often, to risk one's life. All this involves very laborious calculation, and the sheer pleasure of the mind in its own keenness is often the sole reason why one keeps it up. I must have a way of leaving at a moment's notice, for, despite all my vigilance, may I not be attacked from some quite unexpected quarter? I live in peace in the inmost chamber of my house, and meanwhile the enemy may be burrowing his way slowly and stealthily straight toward me. I do not say that he has a better scent than I; probably he knows as little about me as I of him. But there are insatiable robbers who burrow blindly through the ground, and to whom the very size of my house gives the hope of hitting by chance on some of its far-flung passages. I certainly have the advantage of being in my own house and knowing all the passages and how they run. A robber may very easily become my victim and a succulent one too. But I am growing old; I am not as strong as many others, and my enemies are countless; it could well happen that in flying from one enemy I might run into the jaws of another. Anything might happen! In any case I must have the confident knowledge that somewhere there is an exit easy to reach and quite free, where I have to do nothing whatever to get out, so that I might never – Heaven shield us! – suddenly feel the teeth of the pursuer in my flank while I am desperately burrowing away, even if it is at loose easy soil. And it is not only by external enemies that I am threatened. There are also enemies in the bowels of the earth. I have never seen them, but legend tells of them and I firmly believe in them. They are creatures of the inner earth; not even legend can describe them. Their very victims can scarcely have seen them; they come, you hear the scratching of their claws just under you in the ground, which is their element, and already you are lost. Here it is of no avail to console yourself with the thought that you are in your own house; far rather are you in theirs. Not even my exit could save me from them; indeed in all probability it would not save me in any case, but rather betray me; yet it is a hope, and I cannot live without it. Apart from this main exit I am also connected with the outer world by quite narrow, tolerably safe passages which provide me with good fresh air to breathe. They are the work of the field mice. I have made judicious use of them, transforming them into an organic part of my burrow. They also give me the possibility of scenting things from afar, and thus serve as a protection. All sorts of small fry, too, come running through them, and I devour these; so I can have a certain amount of subterranean hunting, sufficient for a modest way of life, without leaving my burrow at all; and that is naturally a great advantage.

But the most beautiful thing about my burrow is the stillness. Of course, that is deceptive. At any moment it may be shattered and then all will be over. For the time being, however, the silence is still with me. For hours I can stroll through my passages and hear nothing except the rustling of some little creature, which I immediately reduce to silence between my jaws, or the pattering of soil, which draws my attention to the need for repair; otherwise all is still. The fragrance of the woods floats in; the place feels both warm and cool. Sometimes I lie down and roll about in the passage with pure joy. When autumn sets in, to possess a burrow like mine, and a roof over your head, is great good fortune for anyone getting on in years. Every hundred yards I have widened the passages into little round cells; there I can curl myself up in comfort and lie warm. There I sleep the sweet sleep of tranquility, of satisfied desire, of achieved ambition; for I possess a house. I do not know whether it is a habit that still persists from former days, or whether the perils even of this house of mine are great enough to awaken me; but invariably every now and then I start up out of profound sleep and listen, listen into the stillness which reigns here unchanged day and night, smile contentedly, and then sink with loosened limbs into still profounder sleep. Poor homeless wanderers in the roads and woods, creeping for warmth into a heap of leaves or a herd of their comrades, delivered to all the perils of heaven and earth! I lie here in a room secured on every side – there are more than fifty such rooms in my burrow – and pass as much of my time as I choose between dozing and unconscious sleep.

Not quite in the center of the burrow, carefully chosen to serve as a refuge in case of extreme danger from siege if not from immediate pursuit, lies the chief cell. While all the rest of the burrow is the outcome rather of intense intellectual than of physical labor, this Castle Keep was fashioned by the most arduous labor of my whole body. Several times, in the despair brought on by physical exhaustion, I was on the point of giving up the whole business, flung myself down panting and cursed the burrow, dragged myself outside and left the place lying open to all the world. I could afford to do that, for I had no longer any wish to return to it, until at last, after four hours or days, back I went repentantly, and when I saw that the burrow was unharmed I could almost have raised a hymn of thanksgiving, and in sincere gladness of heart started on the work anew. My labors on the Castle Keep were also made harder, and unnecessarily so (unnecessarily in that the burrow derived no real benefit from those labors), by the fact that just at the place where, according to my calculations, the Castle Keep should be, the soil was very loose and sandy and had literally to be hammered and pounded into a firm state to serve as a wall for the beautifully vaulted chamber. But for such tasks the only tool I possess is my forehead. So I had to run with my forehead thousands and thousands of times, for whole days and nights, against the ground, and I was glad when the blood came, for that was a proof that the walls were beginning to harden; and in that way, as everybody must admit, I richly paid for my Castle Keep.

In the Castle Keep I assemble my stores; everything over and above my daily wants that I capture inside the burrow, and everything I bring back with me from my hunting expeditions outside, I pile up here. The place is so spacious that food for half a year scarcely fills it. Consequently I can divide up my stores, walk about among them, play with them, enjoy their plenty and their various smells, and reckon up exactly how much they represent. That done, I can always arrange accordingly, and make my calculations and hunting plans for the future, taking into account the season of the year. There are times when I am so well provided for that in my indifference to food I never even touch the smaller fry that scuttle about the burrow, which, however, is probably imprudent of me. My constant preoccupation with defensive measures involves a frequent alteration or modification, though within narrow limits, of my views on how the building can best be organized for that end. Then it sometimes seems risky to make the Castle Keep the basis of defense; the ramifications of the burrow present me with manifold possibilities, and it seems more in accordance with prudence to divide up my stores somewhat, and put part of them in certain of the smaller rooms; thereupon I mark off every third room, let us say, as a reserve storeroom, or every fourth room as a main and every second as an auxiliary storeroom, and so forth. Or I ignore certain passages altogether and store no food in them, so as to throw any enemy off the scent, or I choose quite at random a very few rooms according to their distance from the main exit. Each of these new plans involves of course heavy work; I have to make my calculations and then carry my stores to their new places. True, I can do that at my leisure and without any hurry, and it is not at all unpleasant to carry such good food in your jaws, to lie down and rest whenever you like, and to nibble an occasional tasty tidbit. But it is not so pleasant when, as sometimes happens, you suddenly fancy, starting up from your sleep, that the present distribution of your stores is completely and totally wrong, might lead to great dangers, and must be set right at once, no matter how tired or sleepy you may be; then I rush, then I fly, then I have no time for calculation; and although I was about to execute a perfectly new, perfectly exact plan, I now seize whatever my teeth hit upon and drag it or carry it away, sighing, groaning, stumbling, and even the most haphazard change in the present situation, which seems so terribly dangerous, can satisfy me. Until little by little full wakefulness sobers me, and I can hardly understand my panic haste, breathe in deeply the tranquility of my house, which I myself have disturbed, return to my resting place, fall asleep at once in a new-won exhaustion, and on awakening find hanging from my jaws, say, a rat, as indubitable proof of night labors which already seem almost unreal. Then again there are times when the storing of all my food in one place seems the best plan of all. Of what use to me could my stores in the smaller rooms be, how much could I store there in any case? And whatever I put there would block the passage, and be a greater hindrance than help to me if I were pursued and had to fly. Besides, it is stupid but true that one's self-conceit suffers if one cannot see all one's stores together, and so at one glance know how much one possesses. And in dividing up my food in those various ways might not a great deal get lost? I can't be always scouring through all my passages and cross-passages so as to make sure that everything is in order. The idea of dividing up my stores is of course a good one, but only if one had several rooms similar to my Castle Keep. Several such rooms! Indeed! And who is to build them? In any case, they could not be worked into the general plan of my burrow at this late stage. But I will admit that that is a fault in my burrow; it is always a fault to have only one piece of anything. And I confess too that during the whole time I was constructing the burrow a vague idea that I should have more such cells stirred in my mind, vaguely, yet clearly enough if I had only welcomed it; I did not yield to it, I felt too feeble for the enormous labor it would involve, more, I felt too feeble even to admit to myself the necessity for that labor, and comforted myself as best I could with the vague hope that a building which in any other case would clearly be inadequate, would in my own unique, exceptional, favored case suffice, presumably because providence was interested in the preservation of my forehead, that unique instrument. So I have only one Castle Keep, but my dark premonitions that one would not suffice have faded. However that may be, I must content myself with the one big chamber, the smaller ones are simply no substitute for it, and so, when this conviction has grown on me, I begin once more to haul all my stores back from them to the Castle Keep. For some time afterwards I find a certain comfort in having all the passages and rooms free, in seeing my stores growing in the Castle Keep and emitting their variegated and mingled smells, each of which delights me in its own fashion, and every one of which I can distinguish even at a distance, as far as the very remotest passages. Then I usually enjoy periods of particular tranquility, in which I change my sleeping place by stages, always working in toward the center of the burrow, always steeping myself more profoundly in the mingled smells, until at last I can no longer restrain myself and one night rush into the Castle Keep, mightily fling myself upon my stores, and glut myself with the best that I can seize until I am completely gorged. Happy but dangerous hours; anyone who knew how to exploit them could destroy me with ease and without any risk. Here too the absence of a second or third large storeroom works to my detriment; for it is the single huge accumulated mass of food that seduces me. I try to guard myself in various ways against this danger; the distribution of my stores in the smaller rooms is really one of these expedients; but unfortunately, like other such expedients, it leads through renunciation to still greater greed, which, overruling my intelligence, makes me arbitrarily alter my plans of defense to suit its ends.

To regain my composure after such lapses I make a practice of reviewing the burrow, and after the necessary improvements have been carried out, frequently leave it, though only for a short spell. Even at such moments the hardship of being without it for a long time seems too punitive to me, yet I recognize clearly the need for occasional short excursions. It is always with a certain solemnity that I approach the exit again. During my spells of home life I avoid it, steer clear even of the outer windings of the corridor that leads to it; besides, it is no easy job to wander about out there, for I have contrived there a whole little maze of passages; it was there that I began my burrow, at a time when I had no hope of ever completing it according to my plans; I began, half in play, at that corner, and so my first joy in labor found riotous satisfaction there in a labyrinthine burrow which at the time seemed to me the crown of all burrows, but which I judge today, perhaps with more justice, to be too much of an idle *tour de force*, not really worthy of the rest of the burrow, and though perhaps theoretically brilliant – here is my main entrance, I said in those days, ironically addressing my invisible enemies and seeing them all already caught and stifled in the outer labyrinth – is in reality a flimsy piece of jugglery that would hardly withstand a serious attack or the struggles of an enemy fighting for his life. Should I reconstruct this part of my burrow? I keep on postponing the decision, and the labyrinth will probably remain as it is. Apart from the sheer hard work that I should have to face, the task would also be the most dangerous imaginable. When I began the burrow I could work away at it in comparative peace of mind, the risk wasn't much greater than any other risk; but to attempt that today would be to draw the whole world's attention, and gratuitously, to my burrow; today the whole thing is impossible. I am almost glad of that, for I still have a certain sentiment about this first achievement of mine. And if a serious attack were attempted, what pattern of entrance at all would be likely to save me? An entrance can deceive, can lead astray, can give the attacker no end of worry, and the present one too can do that at a pinch. But a really serious attack has to be met by an instantaneous mobilization of all the resources in the burrow and all the forces of my body and soul – that is self-evident. So this entrance can very well remain where it is. The burrow has so many unavoidable defects imposed by natural causes that it can surely stand this one defect for which I am responsible, and which I recognize as a defect, even if only after the event. In spite of that, however, I do not deny that this fault worries me from time to time, indeed always. If on my customary rounds I avoid this part of the burrow, the fundamental reason is that the sight of it is painful to me, because I don't want to be perpetually reminded of a defect in my house, even if that defect is only too disturbingly present in my mind. Let it continue to exist ineradicably at the entrance; I can at least refuse to look at it as long as that is possible. If I merely walk in the direction of the entrance, even though I may be separated from it by several passages and rooms, I find myself sensing an atmosphere of great danger, actually as if my hair were growing thin and in a moment might fly off and leave me bare and shivering, exposed to the howls of my enemies. Yes, the mere thought of the door itself, the end of the domestic protection, brings such feelings with it, yet it is the labyrinth leading up to it that torments me most of all. Sometimes I dream that I have reconstructed it, transformed it completely, quickly, in a night, with a giant's strength, nobody having noticed, and now it is impregnable; the nights in which such dreams come to me are the sweetest I know, tears of joy and deliverance still glisten on my beard when I awaken.

So I must thread the tormenting complications of this labyrinth physically as well as mentally whenever I go out, and I am both exasperated and touched when, as sometimes happens, I lose myself for a moment in my own maze, and the work of my hands seems to be still doing its best to prove its sufficiency to me, its maker, whose final judgment has long since been passed on it. But then I find myself beneath the mossy covering, which has been left untouched for so long – for I stay for long spells in my house – that it has grown fast to the soil around it, and now only a little push with my head is needed and I am in the upper world. For a long time I do not dare to make that little movement, and if it were not that I would have to traverse the labyrinth once more, I would certainly leave the matter for the time being and turn back again. Just think. Your house is protected and self-sufficient. You live in peace, warm, well nourished, master, sole master of all your manifold passages and rooms, and all this you are prepared – not to give up, of course – but to risk it, so to speak; you nurse the confident hope, certainly, that you will regain it; yet is it not a dangerous, a far too dangerous stake that you are playing for? Can there be any reasonable grounds for such a step? No, for such acts as these there can be no reasonable grounds. But all the same, I then cautiously raise the trap door and slip outside, let it softly fall back again, and fly as fast as I can from the treacherous spot.

Yet I am not really free. True, I am no longer confined by narrow passages, but hunt through the open woods, and feel new powers awakening in my body for which there was no room, as it were, in the burrow, not even in the Castle Keep, though it had been ten times as big. The food too is better up here; though hunting is more difficult, success more rare, the results are more valuable from every point of view; I do not deny all this; I appreciate it and take advantage of it at least as fully as anyone else, and probably more fully, for I do not hunt like a vagrant out of mere idleness or desperation, but calmly and methodically. Also I am not permanently doomed to this free life, for I know that my term is measured, that I do not have to hunt here forever, and that, whenever I am weary of this life and wish to leave it, Someone, whose invitation I shall not be able to withstand, will, so to speak, summon me to him. And so I can pass my time here quite without care and in complete enjoyment, or rather I could, and yet I cannot. My burrow takes up too much of my thoughts. I fled from the entrance fast enough, but soon I am back at it again. I seek out a good hiding place and keep watch on the entrance of my house – this time from outside – for whole days and nights. Call it foolish if you like; it gives me infinite pleasure and reassures me. At such times it is as if I were not so much looking at my house as at myself sleeping, and had the joy of being in a profound slumber and simultaneously of keeping vigilant guard over myself. I am privileged, as it were, not only to dream about the specters of the night in all the helplessness and blind trust of sleep, but also at the same time to confront them in actuality with the calm judgment of the fully awake. And strangely enough I discover that my situation is not so bad as I had often thought, and will probably think again when I return to my house. In this connection – it may be in others too, but in this one especially – these excursions of mine are truly indispensable. Carefully as I have chosen an out-of-the-way place for my door, the traffic that passes it is nevertheless, if one takes a week's observation, very great; but so it is, no doubt, in all inhabited regions, and probably it is actually better to hazard the risks of dense traffic, whose very impetus carries it past, than to be delivered in complete solitude to the first persistently searching intruder. Here enemies are numerous and their allies and accomplices still more numerous, but they fight one another, and while thus employed rush past my burrow without noticing it. In all my time I have never seen anyone investigating the actual door of my house, which is fortunate both for me and for him, for I would certainly have launched myself at his throat, forgetting everything else in my anxiety for the burrow. True, creatures come, in whose vicinity I dare not remain, and from whom I have to fly as soon as I scent them in the distance; on their attitude to the burrow I really can't pronounce with certainty, but it is at least a reassurance that when I presently return I never find any of them there, and the entrance is undamaged. There have been happy periods in which I could almost assure myself that the enmity of the world toward me had ceased or been assuaged, or that the strength of the burrow had raised me above the destructive struggle of former times. The burrow has probably protected me in more ways than I thought or dared think while I was inside it. This fancy used to have such a hold over me that sometimes I have been seized by the childish desire never to return to the burrow again, but to settle down somewhere close to the entrance, to pass my life watching the entrance, and gloat perpetually upon the reflection – and in that find my happiness – how steadfast a protection my burrow would be if I were inside it. Well, one is soon roughly awakened from childish dreams. What does this protection which I am looking at here from the outside amount to after all? Dare I estimate the danger which I run inside the burrow from observations which I make when outside? Can my enemies, to begin with, have any proper awareness of me if I am not in my burrow? A certain awareness of me they certainly have, but not full awareness. And is not that full awareness the real definition of a state of danger? So the experiments I attempt here are only half-experiments or even less, calculated merely to reassure my fears and by giving me false reassurance to lay me open to great perils. No, I do not watch over my own sleep, as I imagined; rather it is I who sleep, while the destroyer watches. Perhaps he is one of those who pass the entrance without seeming to notice it, concerned merely to ascertain, just like myself, that the door is still untouched and waits for their attack, and only pass because they know that the master of the house is out, or because they are quite aware that he is guilelessly lying on the watch in the bushes close by. And I leave my post of observation and find I have had enough of this outside life; I feel that there is nothing more that I can learn here, either now or at any time. And I long to say a last goodbye to everything up here, to go down into my burrow never to return again, let things take their course, and not try to retard them with my profitless vigils. But spoiled by seeing for such a long time everything that happened around the entrance, I find great difficulty in summoning the resolution to carry out the actual descent, which might easily draw anyone's attention, and without knowing what is happening behind my back and behind the door after it is fastened. I take advantage of stormy nights to get over the necessary preliminaries, and quickly bundle in my spoil; that seems to have come off, but whether it has really come off will only be known when I myself have made the descent; it will be known, but not by me, or by me, but too late. So I give up the attempt and do not make the descent. I dig an experimental burrow, naturally at a good distance from the real entrance, a burrow just as long as myself, and seal it also with a covering of moss. I creep into my hole, close it after me, wait patiently, keep vigil for long or short spells, and at various hours of the day, then fling off the moss, issue from my hole, and summarize my observations. These are extremely heterogeneous, and both good and bad; but I have never been able to discover a universal principle or an infallible method of descent. In consequence of all this I have not yet summoned the resolution to make my actual descent, and am thrown into despair at the necessity of doing it soon. I almost screw myself to the point of deciding to emigrate to distant parts and take up my old comfortless life again, which had no security whatever, but was one indiscriminate succession of perils, yet in consequence prevented one from perceiving and fearing particular perils, as I am constantly reminded by comparing my secure burrow with ordinary life. Certainly such a decision would be an arrant piece of folly, produced simply by living too long in senseless freedom; the burrow is still mine, I have only to take a single step and I am safe. And I tear myself free from all my doubts and by broad daylight rush to the door, quite resolved to raise it now; but I cannot, I rush past it and fling myself into a thorn bush, deliberately, as a punishment, a punishment for some sin I do not know of. Then, at the last moment, I am forced to admit to myself that I was right after all, and that it was really impossible to go down into the burrow without exposing the thing I love best, for a little while at least, to all my enemies, on the ground, in the trees, in the air. And the danger is by no means a fanciful one, but very real. It need not be any particular enemy that is provoked to pursue me, it may very well be some chance innocent little creature, some disgusting little beast which follows me out of curiosity, and thus, without knowing it, becomes the leader of all the world against me; nor need it be even that, it may be – and that would be just as bad, indeed in some respects worse – it may be someone of my own kind, a connoisseur and prizer of burrows, a hermit, a lover of peace, but all the same a filthy scoundrel who wishes to be housed where he has not built. If he were actually to arrive now, if in his obscene lust he were to discover the entrance and set about working at it, lifting the moss; if he were actually to succeed, if he were actually to wriggle his way in in my stead, until only his hindquarters still showed; if all this were actually to happen, so that at last, casting all prudence to the winds, I might in my blind rage leap on him, maul him, tear the flesh from his bones, destroy him, drink his blood, and fling his corpse among the rest of my spoil, but above all – that is the main thing – were at last back in my burrow once more, I would have it in my heart to greet the labyrinth itself with rapture; but first I would draw the moss covering over me, and I would want to rest, it seems to me, for all the remainder of my life. But nobody comes and I am left to my own resources. Perpetually obsessed by the sheer difficulty of the attempt, I lose much of my timidity, I no longer attempt even to appear to avoid the entrance, but make a hobby of prowling around it; by now it is almost as if I were the enemy spying out a suitable opportunity for successfully breaking in. If I only had some-one I could trust to keep watch at my post of observation; then of course I could descend in perfect peace of mind. I would make an agreement with this trusty confederate of mine that he would keep a careful note of the state of things during my descent and for quite a long time afterwards, and if he saw any sign of danger knock on the moss covering, and if he saw nothing do nothing. With that a clean sweep would be made of all my fears, no residue would be left, or at most my confidant. For would he not demand some counterservice from me; would he not at least want to see the burrow? That in itself, to let anyone freely into my burrow, would be exquisitely painful to me. I built it for myself, not for visitors, and I think I would refuse to admit him, not even though he alone made it possible for me to get into the burrow would I let him in. But I simply could not admit him, for either I must let him go in first by himself, which is simply unimaginable, or we must both descend at the same time, in which case the advantage I am supposed to derive from him, that of being kept watch over, would be lost. And what trust can I really put in him? Can I trust one whom I have had under my eyes just as fully when I can't see him, and the moss covering separates us? It is comparatively easy to trust anyone if you are supervising him or at least can supervise him; perhaps it is possible even to trust someone at a distance; but completely to trust someone outside the burrow when you are inside the burrow, that is, in a different world, that, it seems to me, is impossible. But such considerations are not in the least necessary; the mere reflection is enough that during or after my descent one of the countless accidents of existence might prevent my confidant from fulfilling his duty, and what incalculable results might not the smallest accident of that kind have for me? No, if one takes it by and large, I have no right to complain that I am alone and have nobody that I can trust. I certainly lose nothing by that and probably spare myself trouble. I can only trust myself and my burrow. I should have thought of that before and taken measures to meet the difficulty that worries me so much now. When I began the burrow it would at least have been partly possible. I should have so constructed the first passage that it had two entrances at a moderate distance from each other, so that after descending through the one entrance with that slowness which is unavoidable, I might rush at once through the passage to the second entrance, slightly raise the moss covering, which would be so arranged as to make that easy, and from there keep watch on the position for several days and nights. That would have been the only right way of doing it. True, the two entrances would double the risk, but that consideration need not delay me, for one of the entrances, serving merely as a post of observation, could be quite narrow. And with that I lose myself in a maze of technical speculations, I begin once more to dream my dream of a completely perfect burrow, and that somewhat calms me; with closed eyes I behold with delight perfect or almost perfect structural devices for enabling me to slip out and in unobserved. While I lie there thinking such things I admire these devices very greatly, but only as technical achievements, not as real advantages; for this freedom to slip out and in at will, what does it amount to? It is the mark of a restless nature, of inner uncertainty, disreputable desires, evil propensities that seem still worse when one thinks of the burrow, which is there at one's hand and can flood one with peace if one only remains quite open and receptive to it. For the present, however, I am outside it seeking some possibility of returning, and for that the necessary technical devices would be very desirable. But perhaps not so very desirable after all. Is it not a very grave injustice to the burrow to regard it in moments of nervous panic as a mere hole into which one can creep and be safe? Certainly it is a hole among other things, and a safe one, or should be, and when I picture myself in the midst of danger, then I insist with clenched teeth and all my will that the burrow should be nothing but a hole set apart to save me, and that it should fulfill that clearly defined function with the greatest possible efficiency, and I am ready to absolve it from every other duty. Now the truth of the matter – and one has no eye for that in times of great peril, and only by a great effort even in times when danger is threatening – is that in reality the burrow does provide a considerable degree of security, but by no means enough, for is one ever free from anxieties inside it? These anxieties are different from ordinary ones, prouder, richer in content, often long repressed, but in their destructive effects they are perhaps much the same as the anxieties that existence in the outer world gives rise to. Had I constructed the burrow exclusively to assure my safety I would not have been disappointed, it is true; nevertheless the relation between the enormous labor involved and the actual security it would provide, at least insofar as I could feel it and profit by it, would not have been in my favor. It is extremely painful to have to admit such things to oneself, but one is forced to do it, confronted by that entrance over there which now literally locks and bars itself against me, the builder and possessor. Yet the burrow is not a mere hole for taking refuge in. When I stand in the Castle Keep surrounded by my piled-up stores, surveying the ten passages which begin there, raised and sunken passages, vertical and rounded passages, wide and narrow passages, as the general plan dictates, and all alike still and empty, ready by their various routes to conduct me to all the other rooms, which are also still and empty – then all thought of mere safety is far from my mind, then I know that here is my castle, which I have wrested from the refractory soil with tooth and claw, with pounding and hammering blows, my castle which can never belong to anyone else, and is so essentially mine that I can calmly accept in it even my enemy's mortal stroke at the final hour, for my blood will ebb away here in my own soil and not be lost. And what but that is the meaning of the blissful hours which I pass, now peacefully slumbering, now happily keeping watch, in these passages, these passages which suit me so well, where one can stretch oneself out in comfort, roll about in childish delight, lie and dream, or sink into blissful sleep. And the smaller rooms, each familiar to me, so familiar that in spite of their complete similarity I can clearly distinguish one from the other with my eyes shut by the mere feel of the wall: they enclose me more peacefully and warmly than a bird is enclosed in its nest. And all, all still and empty.

But if that is the case, why do I hang back? Why do I dread the thought of the intruding enemy more than the possibility of never seeing my burrow again? Well, the latter alternative is fortunately an impossibility; there is no need for me even to take thought to know what the burrow means to me; I and the burrow belong so indissolubly together that in spite of all my fears I could make myself quite comfortable out here, and not even need to overcome my repugnance and open the door; I could be quite content to wait here passively, for nothing can part us for long, and somehow or other I shall quite certainly find myself in my burrow again. But on the other hand how much time may pass before then, and how many things may happen in that time, up here no less than down there? And it lies with me solely to curtail that interval and to do what is necessary at once.

And then, too exhausted to be any longer capable of thought, my head hanging, my legs trembling with fatigue, half asleep, feeling my way rather than walking, I approach the entrance, slowly raise the moss covering, slowly descend, leaving the door open in my distraction for a needlessly long time, and presently remember my omission, and get out again to make it good – but what need was there to get out for that? All that was needed was to draw to the moss covering; right; so I creep in again and now at last draw to the moss covering. Only in this state, and in this state alone, can I achieve my descent. So at last I lie down beneath the moss on the top of my bloodstained spoil and can now enjoy my longed-for sleep. Nothing disturbs me, no one has tracked me down, above the moss everything seems to be quiet thus far at least, but even if all were not quiet I question whether I could stop to keep watch now; I have changed my place, I have left the upper world and am in my burrow, and I feel its effect at once. It is a new world, endowing me with new powers, and what I felt as fatigue up there is no longer that here. I have returned from a journey dog-tired with my wanderings, but the sight of the old house, the thought of all the things that are waiting to be done, the necessity at least to cast a glance at all the rooms, but above all to make my way immediately to the Castle Keep; all this transforms my fatigue into ardent zeal; it is as though at the moment when I set foot in the burrow I had wakened from a long and profound sleep. My first task is a very laborious one and requires all my attention; I mean getting my spoil through the narrow and thin-walled passages of the labyrinth. I shove with all my might, and the work gets done too, but far too slowly for me; to hasten it I drag part of my flesh supply back again and push my way over it and through it; now I have only a portion of my spoil before me and it is easier to make progress; but my road is so blocked by all this flesh in these narrow passages, through which it is not always easy for me to make my way even when I am alone, that I could quite easily smother among my own stores; sometimes I can only rescue myself from their pressure by eating and drinking a clear space for myself. But the work of transport is successful, I finish it in quite a reasonable time, the labyrinth is behind me, I reach an ordinary passage and breathe freely, push my spoil through a communication passage into a main passage expressly designed for the purpose, a passage sloping down steeply to the Castle Keep. What is left to be done is not really work at all; my whole load rolls and flows down the passage almost of itself. The Castle Keep at last! At last I can dare to rest. Everything is unchanged, no great mishap seems to have occurred, the few little defects that I note at a first glance can soon be repaired; first, however, I must go my long round of all the passages, but that is no hardship, that is merely to commune again with friends, as I often did in the old days or – I am not so very old yet, but my memory of many things is already quite confused – as I often did, or as I have often heard that it was done. Now I begin with the second passage, purposefully slow, now that I have seen the Castle Keep I have endless time – inside the burrow I always have endless time – for everything I do there is good and important and satisfies me somehow. I begin with the second passage, but break off in the middle and turn into the third passage and let it take me back again to the Castle Keep, and now of course I have to begin at the second passage once more, and so I play with my task and lengthen it out and smile to myself and enjoy myself and become quite dazed with all the work in front of me, but never think of turning aside from it. It is for your sake, ye passages and rooms, and you, Castle Keep, above all, that I have come back, counting my own life as nothing in the balance, after stupidly trembling for it for so long, and postponing my return to you. What do I care for danger now that I am with you? you belong to me, I to you, we are united; what can harm us? What if my foes should be assembling even now up above there and their muzzles be preparing to break through the moss? And with its silence and emptiness the burrow answers me, confirming my words. But now a feeling of lassitude overcomes me and in some favorite room I curl myself up tentatively, I have not yet surveyed everything by a long way, though still resolved to examine everything to the very end; I have no intention of sleeping here, I have merely yielded to the temptation of making myself comfortable and pretending I want to sleep, I merely wish to find out if this is as good a place for sleeping as it used to be. It is, but it is a better place for sleep than for waking, and I remain lying where I am in deep slumber.

I must have slept for a long time. I was only wakened when I had reached the last light sleep which dissolves of itself, and it must have been very light, for it was an almost inaudible whistling noise that wakened me. I recognized what it was immediately; the small fry, whom I had allowed far too much latitude, had burrowed a new channel somewhere during my absence, this channel must have chanced to intersect an older one, the air was caught there, and that produced the whistling noise. What an indefatigably busy lot these small fry are, and what a nuisance their diligence can be! First I shall have to listen at the walls of my passages and locate the place of disturbance by experimental excavations, and only then will I be able to get rid of the noise. However, this new channel may be quite welcome as a further means of ventilation, if it can be fitted into the plan of the burrow. But after this I shall keep a much sharper eye on the small fry than I used to; I shall spare none of them.

As I have a good deal of experience in investigations of this kind the work probably will not take me long and I can start upon it at once; there are other jobs awaiting me, it is true, but this is the most urgent. I must have silence in my passages. This noise, however, is a comparatively innocent one; I did not hear it at all when I first arrived, although it must certainly have been there; I must first feel quite at home before I could hear it; it is, so to speak, audible only to the ear of the householder. And it is not even constant, as such noises usually are; there are long pauses, obviously caused by stoppages of the current of air. I start on my investigations, but I can't find the right place to begin at, and though I cut a few trenches I do it at random; naturally that has no effect, and the hard work of digging and the still harder work of filling the trenches up again and beating the earth firm is so much labor lost. I don't seem to be getting any nearer to the place where the noise is, it goes on always on the same thin note, with regular pauses, now a sort of whistling, but again like a kind of piping. Now I could leave it to itself for the time being; it is very disturbing, certainly, but there can hardly be any doubt that its origin is what I took it to be at first; so it can scarcely become louder, on the contrary, such noises may quite well – though until now I have never had to wait so long for that to happen – may quite well vanish of themselves in the course of time through the continued labors of these little burrowers; and apart from that, often chance itself puts one on the track of the disturbance, where systematic investigation has failed for a long time. In such ways I comfort myself, and resolve simply to continue my tour of the passages, and visit the rooms, many of which I have not even seen yet since my return, and enjoy myself contemplating the Castle Keep now and then between times; but my anxiety will not let me, and I must go on with my search. These little creatures take up much, far too much, time that could be better employed. In such cases as the present it is usually the technical problem that attracts me; for example, from the noise, which my ear can distinguish in all its finest shades, so that it has a perfectly clear outline to me, I deduce its cause, and now I am on fire to discover whether my conclusion is valid. And with good reason, for as long as that is not established I cannot feel safe, even if it were merely a matter of discovering where a grain of sand that had fallen from one of the walls had rolled to. And a noise such as this is by no means a trifling matter, regarded from that angle. But whether trifling or important, I can find nothing, no matter how hard I search, or it may be that I find too much. This had to happen just in my favorite room, I think to myself, and I walk a fair distance away from it, almost halfway along the passage leading to the next room; I do this more as a joke, pretending to myself that my favorite room is not alone to blame, but that there are disturbances elsewhere as well, and with a smile on my face I begin to listen; but soon I stop smiling, for, right enough, the same whistling meets me here too. It is really nothing to worry about; sometimes I think that nobody but myself would hear it; it is true, I hear it now more and more distinctly, for my ear has grown keener through practice; though in reality it is exactly the same noise wherever I may hear it, as I have convinced myself by comparing my impressions. Nor is it growing louder; I recognize this when I listen in the middle of the passage instead of pressing my ear against the wall. Then it is only with an effort, indeed with great intentness, that I can more guess at than hear the merest trace of a noise now and then. But it is this very uniformity of the noise everywhere that disturbs me most, for it cannot be made to agree with my original assumption. Had I rightly divined the cause of the noise, then it must have issued with greatest force from some given place, which it would be my task to discover, and after that have grown fainter and fainter. But if my hypothesis does not meet the case, what can the explanation be? There still remains the possibility that there are two noises, that up to now I have been listening at a good distance from the two centers, and that while its noise increases, when I draw near to one of them, the total result remains approximately the same for the ear in consequence of the lessening volume of sound from the other center. Already I have almost fancied sometimes, when I have listened carefully, that I could distinguish, if very indistinctly, differences of tone which support this new assumption. In any case I must extend my sphere of investigation much farther than I have done. Accordingly I descend the passage to the Castle Keep and begin to listen there. Strange, the same noise there too. Now it is a noise produced by the burrowing of some species of small fry who have infamously exploited my absence; in any case they have no intention of doing me harm, they are simply busied with their own work, and so long as no obstacle comes in their way they will keep on in the direction they have taken: I know all this, yet that they should have dared to approach the very Castle Keep itself is incomprehensible to me and fills me with agitation, and confuses the faculties which I need so urgently for the work before me. Here I have no wish to discover whether it is the unusual depth at which the Castle Keep lies, or its great extent and correspondingly powerful air suction, calculated to scare burrowing creatures away, or the mere fact that it is the Castle Keep, that by some channel or other has penetrated to their dull minds. In any case, I have never noticed any sign of burrowing in the walls of the Castle Keep until now. Crowds of little beasts have come here, it is true, attracted by the powerful smells; here I have had a constant hunting ground, but my quarry has always burrowed a way through in the upper passages, and come running down here, somewhat fearfully, but unable to withstand such a temptation. But now, it seems, they are burrowing in all the passages. If I had only carried out the best of the grand plans I thought out in my youth and early manhood, or rather, if I had only had the strength to carry them out, for there would have been no lack of will. One of these favorite plans of mine was to isolate the Castle Keep from its surroundings, that is to say, to restrict the thickness of its walls to about my own height, and leave a free space of about the same width all around the Castle Keep, except for a narrow foundation, which unfortunately would have to be left to bear up the whole. I had always pictured this free space, and not without reason, as the loveliest imaginable haunt. What a joy to lie pressed against the rounded outer wall, pull oneself up, let oneself slide down again, miss one's footing and find oneself on firm earth, and play all those games literally upon the Castle Keep and not inside it; to avoid the Castle Keep, to rest one's eyes from it whenever one wanted, to postpone the joy of seeing it until later and yet not have to do without it, but literally hold it safe between one's claws, a thing that is impossible if you have only an ordinary open entrance to it; but above all to be able to stand guard over it, and in that way to be so completely compensated for renouncing the actual sight of it that, if one had to choose between staying all one's life in the Castle Keep or in the free space outside it, one would choose the latter, content to wander up and down there all one's days and keep guard over the Castle Keep. Then there would be no noises in the walls, no insolent burrowing up to the very Keep itself; then peace would be assured there and I would be its guardian; then I would not have to listen with loathing to the burrowing of the small fry, but with delight to something that I cannot hear now at all: the murmurous silence of the Castle Keep.

But that beautiful dream is past and I must set to work, almost glad that now my work has a direct connection with the Castle Keep, for that wings it. Certainly, as I can see more and more clearly, I need all my energies for this task, which at first seemed quite a trifling one. I listen now at the walls of the Castle Keep, and wherever I listen, high or low, at the roof or the floor, at the entrance or in the corners, everywhere, everywhere, I hear the same noise. And how much time, how much care must be wasted in listening to that noise, with its regular pauses. One can, if one wishes, find a tiny deceitful comfort in the fact that here in the Castle Keep, because of its vastness, one hears nothing at all, as distinguished from the passages, when one stands back from the walls. Simply as a rest and a means to regain my composure I often make this experiment, listen intently and am overjoyed when I hear nothing. But the question still remains, what can have happened? Confronted with this phenomenon my original explanation completely falls to the ground. But I must also reject other explanations which present themselves to me. One could assume, for instance, that the noise I hear is simply that of the small fry themselves at their work. But all my experience contradicts this; I cannot suddenly begin to hear now a thing that I have never heard before though it was always there. My sensitiveness to disturbances in the burrow has perhaps become greater with the years, yet my hearing has by no means grown keener. It is of the very nature of small fry not to be heard. Would I have tolerated them otherwise? Even at the risk of starvation I would have exterminated them. But perhaps – this idea now insinuates itself – I am concerned here with some animal unknown to me. That is possible. True, I have observed the life down here long and carefully enough, but the world is full of diversity and is never wanting in painful surprises. Yet it cannot be a single animal, it must be a whole swarm that has suddenly fallen upon my domain, a huge swarm of little creatures, which, as they are audible, must certainly be bigger than the small fry, but yet cannot be very much bigger, for the sound of their labors is itself very faint. It may be, then, a swarm of unknown creatures on their wanderings, who happen to be passing by my way, who disturb me, but will presently cease to do so. So I could really wait for them to pass, and need not put myself to the trouble of work that will be needless in the end. Yet if these creatures are strangers, why is it that I never see any of them? I have already dug a host of trenches, hoping to catch one of them, but I can find not a single one. Then it occurs to me that they may be quite tiny creatures, far tinier than any I am acquainted with, and that it is only the noise they make that is greater. Accordingly I investigate the soil I have dug up, I cast the lumps into the air so that they break into quite small particles, but the noisemakers are not among them. Slowly I come to realize that by digging such small fortuitous trenches I achieve nothing; in doing that I merely disfigure the walls of my burrow, scratching hastily here and there without taking time to fill up the holes again; at many places already there are heaps of earth which block my way and my view. Still, that is only a secondary worry; for now I can neither wander about my house, nor review it, nor rest; often already I have fallen asleep at my work in some hole or other, with one paw clutching the soil above me, from which in a semistupor I have been trying to tear a lump. I intend now to alter my methods. I shall dig a wide and carefully constructed trench in the direction of the noise and not cease from digging until, independent of all theories, I find the real cause of the noise. Then I shall eradicate it, if that is within my power, and if it is not, at least I shall know the truth. That truth will bring me either peace or despair, but whether the one or the other, it will be beyond doubt or question. This decision strengthens me. All that I have done till now seems to me far too hasty; in the excitement of my return, while I had not yet shaken myself free from the cares of the upper world, and was not yet completely penetrated by the peace of the burrow, but rather hypersensitive at having had to renounce it for such a long time, I was thrown into complete confusion of mind by an unfamiliar noise. And what was it? A faint whistling, audible only at long intervals, a mere nothing to which I don't say that one could actually get used, for no one could get used to it, but which one could, without actually doing anything about it at once, observe for a while; that is, listen every few hours, let us say, and patiently register the results, instead of, as I had done, keeping one's ear fixed to the wall and at every hint of noise tearing out a lump of earth, not really hoping to find anything, but simply so as to do something to give expression to one's inward agitation. All that will be changed now, I hope. And then, with furious shut eyes, I have to admit to myself that I hope nothing of the kind, for I am still trembling with agitation just as I was hours ago, and if my reason did not restrain me I would probably like nothing better than to start stubbornly and defiantly digging, simply for the sake of digging, at some place or other, whether I heard anything there or not; almost like the small fry, who burrow either without any object at all or simply because they eat the soil. My new and reasonable plan both tempts me and leaves me cold. There is nothing in it to object to, I at least know of no objection; it is bound, so far as I can see, to achieve my aim. And yet at bottom I do not believe in it; I believe in it so little that I do not even fear the terrors which its success may well bring, I do not believe even in a dreadful denouement; indeed it seems to me that I have been thinking ever since the first appearance of the noise of such a methodical trench, and have not begun upon it until now simply because I put no trust in it. In spite of that I shall of course start on the trench; I have no other alternative; but I shall not start at once, I shall postpone the task for a little while. If reason is to be reinstated on the throne, it must be completely reinstated; I shall not rush blindly into my task. In any case I shall first repair the damage that I have done to the burrow with my wild digging; that will take a good long time, but it is necessary; if the new trench is really to reach its goal it will probably be long, and if it should lead to nothing at all it will be endless; in any case this task means a longish absence from the burrow, though an absence by no means so painful as an absence in the upper world, for I can interrupt my work whenever I like and pay a visit to my house; and even if I should not do that the air of Castle Keep will be wafted to me and surround me while I work; nevertheless it means leaving the burrow and surrendering myself to an uncertain fate, and consequently I want to leave the burrow in good order behind me; it shall not be said that I, who am fighting for its peace, have myself destroyed that peace without reinstating it at once. So I begin by shoveling the soil back into the holes from which it was taken, a kind of work I am familiar with, that I have done countless times almost without regarding it as work, and at which, particularly as regards the final pressing and smoothing down – and this is no empty boast, but the simple truth – I am unbeatable. But this time everything seems difficult, I am too distracted, every now and then, in the middle of my work, I press my ear to the wall and listen, and without taking any notice let the soil that I have just lifted trickle back into the passage again. The final embellishments, which demand a stricter attention, I can hardly achieve at all. Hideous protuberances, disturbing cracks remain, not to speak of the fact that the old buoyancy simply cannot be restored again to a wall patched up in such a way. I try to comfort myself with the reflection that my present work is only temporary. When I return after peace has been restored I shall repair everything properly: work will be mere play to me then. Oh yes, work is mere play in fairy tales, and this comfort of mine belongs to the realm of fairy tales too. It would be far better to do the work thoroughly now, at once, far more reasonable than perpetually to interrupt it and wander off through the passages to discover new sources of noise, which is easy enough, all that is needed being to stop at any point one likes and listen. And that is not the end of my useless discoveries. Sometimes I fancy that the noise has stopped, for it makes long pauses; sometimes such a faint whistling escapes one, one's own blood is pounding all too loudly in one's ears; then two pauses come one after another, and for a while one thinks that the whistling has stopped forever. I listen no longer, I jump up, all life is transfigured; it is as if the fountains from which flows the silence of the burrow were unsealed. I refrain from verifying my discovery at once, I want first to find someone to whom in all good faith I can confide it, so I rush to the Castle Keep, I remember, for I and everything in me has awakened to new life, that I have eaten nothing for a long time, I snatch something or other from among my store of food half-buried under the debris and hurriedly begin to swallow it while I hurry back to the place where I made my incredible discovery, I only want to assure myself about it incidentally, perfunctorily, while I am eating; I listen, but the most perfunctory listening shows at once that I was shamefully deceived: away there in the distance the whistling still remains unshaken. And I spit out my food, and would like to trample it underfoot, and go back to my task, not caring which I take up; anyplace where it seems to be needed, and there are enough places like that, I mechanically start on something or other, just as if the overseer had appeared and I must make a pretense of working for his benefit. But hardly have I begun to work in this fashion when it may happen that I make a new discovery. The noise seems to have become louder, not much louder, of course – here it is always a matter of the subtlest shades – but all the same sufficiently louder for the ear to recognize it clearly. And this growing-louder is like a coming-nearer; still more distinctly than you hear the increasing loudness of the noise, you can literally see the step that brings it closer to you. You leap back from the wall, you try to grasp at once all the possible consequences that this discovery will bring with it. You feel as if you had never really organized the burrow for defense against attack; you had intended to do so, but despite all your experience of life the danger of an attack, and consequently the need to organize the place for defense, seemed remote – or rather not remote (how could it possibly be!) – but infinitely less important than the need to put it in a state where one could live peacefully; and so that consideration was given priority in everything relating to the burrow. Many things in this direction might have been done without affecting the plan of the whole; most incomprehensibly they have been neglected. I have had a great deal of luck all those years, luck has spoiled me; I have had anxieties, but anxiety leads to nothing when you have luck to back you.

The thing to do, really to do now, would be to go carefully over the burrow and consider every possible means of defending it, work out a plan of defense and a corresponding plan of construction, and then start on the work at once with the vigor of youth. That is the work that would really be needed, for which, I may add, it is now far too late in the day; yet that is what would really be needed, and not the digging of a grand experimental trench, whose only real result would be to deliver me hand and foot to the search for danger, out of the foolish fear that it will not arrive quickly enough of itself. Suddenly I cannot comprehend my former plan. I can find no slightest trace of reason in what had seemed so reasonable; once more I lay aside my work and even my listening; I have no wish to discover any further signs that the noise is growing louder; I have had enough of discoveries; I let everything slide; I would be quite content if I could only still the conflict going on within me. Once more I let my passages lead me where they will, I come to more and more remote ones that I have not yet seen since my return, and that are quite unsullied by my scratching paws, and whose silence rises up to meet me and sinks into me. I do not surrender to it, I hurry on, I do not know what I want, probably simply to put off the hour. I stray so far that I find myself at the labyrinth; the idea of listening beneath the moss covering tempts me; such distant things, distant for the moment, chain my interest. I push my way up and listen. Deep stillness; how lovely it is here, outside there nobody troubles about my burrow, everybody has his own affairs, which have no connection with me; how have I managed to achieve this? Here under the moss covering is perhaps the only place in my burrow now where I can listen for hours and hear nothing. A complete reversal of things in the burrow; what was once the place of danger has become a place of tranquility, while the Castle Keep has been plunged into the melee of the world and all its perils. Still worse, even here there is no peace in reality, here nothing has changed; silent or vociferous, danger lies in ambush as before above the moss, but I have grown insensitive to it, my mind is far too much taken up with the whistling in my walls. Is my mind really taken up with it? It grows louder, it comes nearer, but I wriggle my way through the labyrinth and make a couch for myself up here under the moss; it is almost as if I were already leaving the house to the whistler, content if I can only have a little peace up here. To the whistler? Have I come, then, to a new conclusion concerning the cause of the noise? But surely the noise is caused by the channels bored by the small fry? Is not that my considered opinion? It seems to me that I have not retreated from it thus far. And if the noise is not caused directly by these channels, it is indirectly. And even if it should have no connection with them whatever, one is not at liberty to make *a priori* assumptions, but must wait until one finds the cause, or it reveals itself. One could play with hypotheses, of course, even at this stage; for instance, it is possible that there has been a water burst at some distance away, and what seems a piping or whistling to me is in reality a gurgling. But apart from the fact that I have no experience in that sphere – the groundwater that I found at the start I drained away at once, and in this sandy soil it has never returned – apart from this fact the noise is undeniably a whistling and simply not to be translated into a gurgling. But what avail all exhortations to be calm; my imagination will not rest, and I have actually come to believe – it is useless to deny it to myself – that the whistling is made by some beast, and moreover not by a great many small ones, but by a single big one. Many signs contradict this. The noise can be heard everywhere and always at the same strength, and moreover uniformly, both by day and night. At first, therefore, one cannot but incline to the hypothesis of a great number of little animals; but as I must have found some of them during my digging and I have found nothing, it only remains for me to assume the existence of a great beast, especially as the things that seem to contradict the hypothesis are merely things which make the beast, not so much impossible, as merely dangerous beyond all one's powers of conception. For that reason alone have I resisted this hypothesis. I shall cease from this self-deception. For a long time already I have played with the idea that the beast can be heard at such a great distance because it works so furiously; it burrows as fast through the ground as another can walk on the open road; the ground still trembles at its burrowing when it has ceased; this reverberation and the noise of the boring itself unite into one sound at such a great distance, and I, as I hear only the last dying ebb of that sound, hear it always at the same uniform strength. It follows from this also that the beast is not making for me, seeing that the noise never changes; more likely it has a plan in view whose purpose I cannot decipher; I merely assume that the beast – and I make no claim whatever that it knows of my existence – is encircling me; it has probably made several circles around my burrow already since I began to observe it. The nature of the noise, the piping or whistling, gives me much food for thought. When I scratch and scrape in the soil in my own fashion the sound is quite different. I can explain the whistling only in this way: that the beast's chief means of burrowing is not its claws, which it probably employs merely as a secondary resource, but its snout or its muzzle, which, of course, apart from its enormous strength, must also be fairly sharp at the point. It probably bores its snout into the earth with one mighty push and tears out a great lump; while it is doing that I hear nothing; that is the pause; but then it draws in the air for a new push. This indrawal of its breath, which must be an earthshaking noise, not only because of the beast's strength, but of its haste, its furious lust for work as well: this noise I hear then as a faint whistling. But quite incomprehensible remains the beast's capacity to work without stopping; perhaps the short pauses provide also the opportunity of snatching a moment's rest; but apparently the beast has never yet allowed itself a really long rest, day and night it goes on burrowing, always with the same freshness and vigor, always thinking of its object, which must be achieved with the utmost expedition, and which it has the ability to achieve with ease. Now I could not have foreseen such an opponent. But apart altogether from the beast's peculiar characteristics, what is happening now is only something which I should really have feared all the time, something against which I should have been constantly prepared: the fact that someone would come. By what chance can everything have flowed on so quietly and happily for such a long time? Who can have diverted my enemies from their path, and forced them to make a wide detour around my property? Why have I been spared for so long, only to be delivered to such terrors now? Compared with this, what are all the petty dangers in brooding over which I have spent my life! Had I hoped, as owner of the burrow, to be in a stronger position than any enemy who might chance to appear? But simply by virtue of being owner of this great vulnerable edifice I am obviously defenseless against any serious attack. The joy of possessing it has spoiled me, the vulnerability of the burrow has made me vulnerable; any wound to it hurts me as if I myself were hit. It is precisely this that I should have foreseen; instead of thinking only of my own defense – and how perfunctorily and vainly I have done even that – I should have thought of the defense of the burrow. Above all, provision should have been made for cutting off sections of the burrow, and as many as possible of them, from the endangered sections when they are attacked; this should have been done by means of improvised landslides, calculated to operate at a moment's notice; moreover these should have been so thick, and have provided such an effectual barrier, that the attacker would not even guess that the real burrow only began at the other side. More, these landslides should have been so devised that they not only concealed the burrow, but also entombed the attacker. Not the slightest attempt have I made to carry out such a plan, nothing at all has been done in this direction, I have been as thoughtless as a child, I have passed my manhood's years in childish games, I have done nothing but play even with the thought of danger, I have shirked really taking thought for actual danger. And there has been no lack of warning.

Nothing, of course, approaching the present situation has happened before; nevertheless there was an incident not unlike it when the burrow was only beginning. The main difference between that time and this is simply that the burrow was only beginning then. . . . In those days I was literally nothing more than a humble apprentice, the labyrinth was only sketched out in rough outline, I had already dug a little room, but the proportions and the execution of the walls were sadly bungled; in short, everything was so tentative that it could only be regarded as an experiment, as something which, if one lost patience some day, one could leave behind without much regret. Then one day as I lay on a heap of earth resting from my labors – I have rested far too often from my labors all my life – suddenly I heard a noise in the distance. Being young at the time, I was less frightened than curious. I left my work to look after itself and set myself to listen; I listened and listened, and had no wish to fly up to my moss covering and stretch myself out there so that I might not have to hear. I did listen, at least. I could clearly recognize that the noise came from some kind of burrowing similar to my own; it was somewhat fainter, of course, but how much of that might be put down to the distance one could not tell. I was intensely interested, but otherwise calm and cool. Perhaps I am in somebody else's burrow, I thought to myself, and now the owner is boring his way toward me. If that assumption had proved to be correct I would have gone away, for I have never had any desire for conquest or bloodshed, and begun building somewhere else. But after all I was still young and still without a burrow, so I could remain quite cool. Besides, the further course of the noise brought no real cause for apprehension, except that it was not easy to explain. If whoever was boring there was really making for me, because he had heard me boring, then if he changed his direction, as now actually happened, it could not be told whether he did this because my pause for rest had deprived him of any definite point to make toward, or because – which was more plausible – he had himself changed his plans. But perhaps I had been deceived altogether, and he had never been actually making in my direction; at any rate the noise grew louder for a while as if he were drawing nearer, and being young at that time I probably would not have been displeased to see the burrower suddenly rising from the ground; but nothing of that kind happened, at a certain point the sound of boring began to weaken, it grew fainter and fainter, as if the burrower were gradually diverging from his first route, and suddenly it broke off altogether, as if he had decided now to take the diametrically opposite direction and were making straight away from me into the distance. For a long time I still went on listening for him in the silence, before I returned once more to my work. Now that warning was definite enough, but I soon forgot it, and it scarcely influenced my building plans.

Between that day and this lie my years of maturity, but is it not as if there were no interval at all between them? I still take long rests from my labors and listen at the wall, and the burrower has changed his intention anew, he has turned back, he is returning from his journey, thinking he has given me ample time in the interval to prepare for his reception. But on my side everything is worse prepared for than it was then; the great burrow stands defenseless, and I am no longer a young apprentice, but an old architect, and the powers I still have fail me when the decisive hour comes; yet old as I am it seems to me that I would gladly be still older, so old that I should never be able to rise again from my resting place under the moss. For to be honest I cannot endure the place, I rise up and rush, as if I had filled myself up there with new anxieties instead of peace, down into the house again. What was the state of things the last time I was here? Had the whistling grown fainter? No, it had grown louder. I listen at ten places chosen at random and clearly notice the deception; the whistling is just the same as ever, nothing has altered. Over there, there are no changes, there one is calm and not worried about time; but here every instant frets and gnaws at the listener. I go once more the long road to the Castle Keep, all my surroundings seem filled with agitation, seem to be looking at me, and then look away again so as not to disturb me, yet cannot refrain the very next moment from trying to read the saving solution from my expression. I shake my head, I have not yet found any solution. Nor do I go to the Castle Keep in pursuance of any plan. I pass the spot where I had intended to begin the experimental trench, I look it over once more, it would have been an admirable place to begin at, the trench's course would have been in the direction where lay the majority of the tiny ventilation holes, which would have greatly lightened my labors; perhaps I should not have had to dig very far, should not even have had to dig to the source of the noise; perhaps if I had listened at the ventilation holes it would have been enough. But no consideration is potent enough to animate me to this labor of digging. This trench will bring me certainty, you say? I have reached the stage where I no longer wish to have certainty. In the Castle Keep I choose a lovely piece of flayed red flesh and creep with it into one of the heaps of earth; there I shall have silence at least, such silence, at any rate, as still can be said to exist here. I munch and nibble at the flesh, think of the strange beast going its own road in the distance, and then again that I should enjoy my store of food as fully as possible, while I still have the chance. This last is probably the sole plan I have left that I can carry out. For the rest I try to unriddle the beast's plans. Is it on its wanderings, or is it working on its own burrow? If it is on its wanderings then perhaps an understanding with it might be possible. If it should really break through to the burrow I shall give it some of my stores and it will go on its way again. It will go its way again, a fine story! Lying in my heap of earth I can naturally dream of all sorts of things, even of an understanding with the beast, though I know well enough that no such thing can happen, and that at the instant when we see each other, more, at the moment when we merely guess at each other's presence, we shall both blindly bare our claws and teeth, neither of us a second before or after the other, both of us filled with a new and different hunger, even if we should already be gorged to bursting. And with entire justice, for who, even if he were merely on his wanderings, would not change his itinerary and his plans for the future on catching sight of the burrow? But perhaps the beast is digging in its own burrow, in which case I cannot even dream of an understanding. Even if it should be such a peculiar beast that its burrow could tolerate a neighbor, my burrow could not tolerate a neighbor, at least not a clearly audible one. Now actually the beast seems to be a great distance away; if it would only withdraw a little farther the noise too would probably disappear; perhaps in that case everything would be peaceful again as in the old days; all this would then become a painful but salutary lesson, spurring me on to make the most diverse improvements on the burrow; if I have peace, and danger does not immediately threaten me, I am still quite fit for all sorts of hard work; perhaps, considering the enormous possibilities which its powers of work open before it, the beast has given up the idea of extending its burrow in my direction, and is compensating itself for that in some other one. That consummation also cannot, of course, be brought about by negotiation, but only by the beast itself, or by some compulsion exercised from my side. In both cases the decisive factor will be whether the beast knows about me, and if so what it knows. The more I reflect upon it the more improbable does it seem to me that the beast has even heard me; it is possible, though I can't imagine it, that it can have received news of me in some other way, but it has certainly never heard me. So long as I still knew nothing about it, it simply cannot have heard me, for at that time I kept very quiet, nothing could be more quiet than my return to the burrow; afterwards, when I dug the experimental trenches, perhaps it could have heard me, though my style of digging makes very little noise; but if it had heard me I must have noticed some sign of it, the beast must at least have stopped its work every now and then to listen. But all remained unchanged.

Translated by Willa and Edwin Muir

TITLES IN EVERYMAN'S LIBRARY

CHINUA ACHEBE
Things Fall Apart

AESCHYLUS
The Oresteia

ISABEL ALLENDE
The House of the Spirits

THE ARABIAN NIGHTS
(in 2 vols, tr. Husain Haddawy)

MARGARET ATWOOD
The Handmaid's Tale

JOHN JAMES AUDUBON
The Audubon Reader

AUGUSTINE
The Confessions

JANE AUSTEN
Emma
Mansfield Park
Northanger Abbey
Persuasion
Pride and Prejudice
Sanditon and Other Stories
Sense and Sensibility

HONORÉ DE BALZAC
Cousin Bette
Eugénie Grandet
Old Goriot

GIORGIO BASSANI
The Garden of the Finzi-Continis

SIMONE DE BEAUVOIR
The Second Sex

SAMUEL BECKETT
Molloy, Malone Dies,
The Unnamable
(US only)

SAUL BELLOW
The Adventures of Augie March

HECTOR BERLIOZ
The Memoirs of Hector Berlioz

WILLIAM BLAKE
Poems and Prophecies

JORGE LUIS BORGES
Ficciones

JAMES BOSWELL
The Life of Samuel Johnson
The Journal of a Tour to
the Hebrides

CHARLOTTE BRONTË
Jane Eyre
Villette

EMILY BRONTË
Wuthering Heights

MIKHAIL BULGAKOV
The Master and Margarita

SAMUEL BUTLER
The Way of all Flesh

JAMES M. CAIN
The Postman Always Rings Twice
Double Indemnity
Mildred Pierce
Selected Stories
(in 1 vol. US only)

ITALO CALVINO
If on a winter's night a traveler

ALBERT CAMUS
The Outsider (UK)
The Stranger (US)
The Plague, The Fall,
Exile and the Kingdom,
and Selected Essays
(in 1 vol.)

GIACOMO CASANOVA
History of My Life

WILLA CATHER
Death Comes for the Archbishop
My Ántonia

MIGUEL DE CERVANTES
Don Quixote

RAYMOND CHANDLER
The novels (in 2 vols)
Collected Stories

GEOFFREY CHAUCER
Canterbury Tales

ANTON CHEKHOV
The Complete Short Novels
My Life and Other Stories
The Steppe and Other Stories

KATE CHOPIN
The Awakening

CARL VON CLAUSEWITZ
On War

S. T. COLERIDGE
Poems

WILKIE COLLINS
The Moonstone
The Woman in White

CONFUCIUS
The Analects

JOSEPH CONRAD
Heart of Darkness
Lord Jim
Nostromo
The Secret Agent
Typhoon and Other Stories
Under Western Eyes
Victory

THOMAS CRANMER
The Book of Common Prayer
(UK only)

ROALD DAHL
Collected Stories

DANTE ALIGHIERI
The Divine Comedy

CHARLES DARWIN
The Origin of Species
The Voyage of the Beagle
(in 1 vol.)

DANIEL DEFOE
Moll Flanders
Robinson Crusoe

CHARLES DICKENS
Barnaby Rudge
Bleak House
David Copperfield
Dombey and Son
Great Expectations
Hard Times
Little Dorrit
Martin Chuzzlewit
The Mystery of Edwin Drood
Nicholas Nickleby
The Old Curiosity Shop
Oliver Twist
Our Mutual Friend
The Pickwick Papers
A Tale of Two Cities

DENIS DIDEROT
Memoirs of a Nun

JOAN DIDION
We Tell Ourselves Stories in Order
to Live (US only)

JOHN DONNE
The Complete English Poems

FYODOR DOSTOEVSKY
The Adolescent
The Brothers Karamazov
Crime and Punishment
Demons
The Double and The Gambler
The Idiot
Notes from Underground

W. E. B. DU BOIS
The Souls of Black Folk
(US only)

UMBERTO ECO
The Name of the Rose

GEORGE ELIOT
Adam Bede
Daniel Deronda
Middlemarch
The Mill on the Floss
Silas Marner

JOHN EVELYN
The Diary of John Evelyn
(UK only)

WILLIAM FAULKNER
The Sound and the Fury
(UK only)

HENRY FIELDING
Joseph Andrews and Shamela
(UK only)
Tom Jones

F. SCOTT FITZGERALD
The Great Gatsby
This Side of Paradise
(UK only)

PENELOPE FITZGERALD
The Bookshop
The Gate of Angels
The Blue Flower
(in 1 vol.)
Offshore
Human Voices
The Beginning of Spring
(in 1 vol.)

GUSTAVE FLAUBERT
Madame Bovary

FORD MADOX FORD
The Good Soldier
Parade's End

E. M. FORSTER
Howards End
A Passage to India

ELIZABETH GASKELL
Mary Barton

EDWARD GIBBON
The Decline and Fall of the Roman Empire
Vols 1 to 3: The Western Empire
Vols 4 to 6: The Eastern Empire

J. W. VON GOETHE
Selected Works

NIKOLAI GOGOL
Dead Souls

IVAN GONCHAROV
Oblomov

GÜNTER GRASS
The Tin Drum

GRAHAM GREENE
Brighton Rock
The Human Factor

DASHIELL HAMMETT
The Maltese Falcon
The Thin Man
Red Harvest
(in 1 vol.)

THOMAS HARDY
Far From the Madding Crowd
Jude the Obscure
The Mayor of Casterbridge
The Return of the Native
Tess of the d'Urbervilles
The Woodlanders

JAROSLAV HAŠEK
The Good Soldier Švejk

NATHANIEL HAWTHORNE
The Scarlet Letter

JOSEPH HELLER
Catch-22

ERNEST HEMINGWAY
A Farewell to Arms
The Collected Stories
(UK only)

GEORGE HERBERT
The Complete English Works

HERODOTUS
The Histories

PATRICIA HIGHSMITH
The Talented Mr. Ripley
Ripley Under Ground
Ripley's Game
(in 1 vol.)

HINDU SCRIPTURES
(tr. R. C. Zaehner)

JAMES HOGG
Confessions of a Justified Sinner

HOMER
The Iliad
The Odyssey

VICTOR HUGO
Les Misérables

HENRY JAMES
The Awkward Age
The Bostonians
The Golden Bowl
The Portrait of a Lady
The Princess Casamassima
The Wings of the Dove
Collected Stories (in 2 vols)

SAMUEL JOHNSON
A Journey to the Western Islands of Scotland

JAMES JOYCE
Dubliners
A Portrait of the Artist as a Young Man
Ulysses

FRANZ KAFKA
Collected Stories
The Castle
The Trial

JOHN KEATS
The Poems

SØREN KIERKEGAARD
Fear and Trembling and The Book on Adler

MAXINE HONG KINGSTON
The Woman Warrior and China Men
(US only)

RUDYARD KIPLING
Collected Stories
Kim

THE KORAN
(tr. Marmaduke Pickthall)

CHODERLOS DE LACLOS
Les Liaisons dangereuses

GIUSEPPE TOMASI DI LAMPEDUSA
The Leopard

WILLIAM LANGLAND
Piers Plowman
with (anon.) Sir Gawain and the Green Knight, Pearl, Sir Orfeo (UK only)

D. H. LAWRENCE
Collected Stories
The Rainbow
Sons and Lovers
Women in Love

MIKHAIL LERMONTOV
A Hero of Our Time

PRIMO LEVI
If This is a Man and The Truce (UK only)
The Periodic Table

THE MABINOGION

NICCOLÒ MACHIAVELLI
The Prince

NAGUIB MAHFOUZ
The Cairo Trilogy
Three Novels of Ancient Egypt

THOMAS MANN
Buddenbrooks
Collected Stories (UK only)
Death in Venice and Other Stories (US only)
Doctor Faustus
Joseph and His Brothers
The Magic Mountain

KATHERINE MANSFIELD
The Garden Party and Other Stories

MARCUS AURELIUS
Meditations

GABRIEL GARCÍA MÁRQUEZ
The General in His Labyrinth
Love in the Time of Cholera
One Hundred Years of Solitude

ANDREW MARVELL
The Complete Poems

W. SOMERSET MAUGHAM
Collected Stories

CORMAC McCARTHY
The Border Trilogy (US only)

HERMAN MELVILLE
The Complete Shorter Fiction
Moby-Dick

JOHN STUART MILL
On Liberty and Utilitarianism

JOHN MILTON
The Complete English Poems

YUKIO MISHIMA
The Temple of the Golden Pavilion

MARY WORTLEY MONTAGU
Letters

MICHEL DE MONTAIGNE
The Complete Works

THOMAS MORE
Utopia

TONI MORRISON
Beloved
Song of Solomon

ALICE MUNRO
Carried Away and Other Stories (US only)

MURASAKI SHIKIBU
The Tale of Genji

VLADIMIR NABOKOV
Lolita
Pale Fire
Pnin
Speak, Memory

V. S. NAIPAUL
A House for Mr Biswas

R. K. NARAYAN
Swami and Friends
The Bachelor of Arts
The Dark Room
The English Teacher
(in 1 vol.)
Mr Sampath – The Printer of Malgudi
The Financial Expert
Waiting for the Mahatma
(in 1 vol.)

THE NEW TESTAMENT
(King James Version)

THE OLD TESTAMENT
(King James Version)

GEORGE ORWELL
Animal Farm
Nineteen Eighty-Four
Essays

THOMAS PAINE
Rights of Man
and Common Sense

BORIS PASTERNAK
Doctor Zhivago

SYLVIA PLATH
The Bell Jar (US only)

PLATO
The Republic
Symposium and Phaedrus

EDGAR ALLAN POE
The Complete Stories

MARCEL PROUST
In Search of Lost Time
(in 4 vols, UK only)

ALEXANDER PUSHKIN
The Collected Stories

FRANÇOIS RABELAIS
Gargantua and Pantagruel

JOSEPH ROTH
The Radetzky March

JEAN-JACQUES
ROUSSEAU
Confessions
The Social Contract and
the Discourses

SALMAN RUSHDIE
Midnight's Children

JOHN RUSKIN
Praeterita and Dilecta

WALTER SCOTT
Rob Roy

WILLIAM SHAKESPEARE
Comedies Vols 1 and 2
Histories Vols 1 and 2
Romances
Sonnets and Narrative Poems
Tragedies Vols 1 and 2

MARY SHELLEY
Frankenstein

ADAM SMITH
The Wealth of Nations

ALEXANDER SOLZHENITSYN
One Day in the Life of
Ivan Denisovich

SOPHOCLES
The Theban Plays

MURIEL SPARK
The Prime of Miss Jean Brodie,
The Girls of Slender Means, The
Driver's Seat, The Only Problem
(in 1 vol.)

CHRISTINA STEAD
The Man Who Loved Children

JOHN STEINBECK
The Grapes of Wrath

STENDHAL
The Charterhouse of Parma
Scarlet and Black

LAURENCE STERNE
Tristram Shandy

ROBERT LOUIS STEVENSON
The Master of Ballantrae and
Weir of Hermiston
Dr Jekyll and Mr Hyde
and Other Stories

HARRIET BEECHER STOWE
Uncle Tom's Cabin

ITALO SVEVO
Zeno's Conscience

JONATHAN SWIFT
Gulliver's Travels

JUNICHIRŌ TANIZAKI
The Makioka Sisters

W. M. THACKERAY
Vanity Fair

HENRY DAVID THOREAU
Walden

ALEXIS DE TOCQUEVILLE
Democracy in America

LEO TOLSTOY
Collected Shorter Fiction (in 2 vols)
Anna Karenina
Childhood, Boyhood and Youth
The Cossacks
War and Peace

ANTHONY TROLLOPE
Barchester Towers
Can You Forgive Her?
Doctor Thorne
The Eustace Diamonds
Framley Parsonage
The Last Chronicle of Barset
Phineas Finn
The Small House at Allington
The Warden

IVAN TURGENEV
Fathers and Children
First Love and Other Stories
A Sportsman's Notebook

MARK TWAIN
Tom Sawyer
and Huckleberry Finn

JOHN UPDIKE
The Complete Henry Bech
Rabbit Angstrom

GIORGIO VASARI
Lives of the Painters, Sculptors and Architects (in 2 vols)

VIRGIL
The Aeneid

VOLTAIRE
Candide and Other Stories

EVELYN WAUGH
The Complete Short Stories
Black Mischief, Scoop, The Loved One, The Ordeal of Gilbert Pinfold (in 1 vol.)
Brideshead Revisited
Decline and Fall (US)
Decline and Fall, Vile Bodies, Put Out More Flags (UK)
A Handful of Dust
The Sword of Honour Trilogy
Waugh Abroad: Collected Travel Writing

EDITH WHARTON
The Age of Innocence
The Custom of the Country
The House of Mirth
The Reef

OSCAR WILDE
Plays, Prose Writings and Poems

MARY WOLLSTONECRAFT
A Vindication of the Rights of Woman

VIRGINIA WOOLF
To the Lighthouse
Mrs Dalloway

WILLIAM WORDSWORTH
Selected Poems (UK only)

W. B. YEATS
The Poems (UK only)

ÉMILE ZOLA
Germinal

This book is set in EHRHARDT. The precise origin of the typeface is unclear. Most of the founts were probably cut by the Hungarian punch-cutter Nicholas Kis for the Ehrhardt foundry in Leipzig, where they were left for sale in 1689. In 1938 the Monotype foundry produced the modern version.